CW00833388

Part 24, Including Title and Contents to Vol. II.   [To be completed in about 36 Parts.]   Price 8½d.

OLD AND NEW EDINBURGH. ILLUSTRATED.

CASSELL, PETTER, GALPIN & CO.:

LONDON, PARIS & NEW YORK.

Part 24, Including Title and Contents to Vol. II. [To be completed in about 36 Parts.] Price 8¼d.

OLD AND NEW EDINBURGH. ILLUSTRATED.

CASSELL, PETTER, GALPIN & CO.:

LONDON, PARIS & NEW YORK.

18

MEETING OF THE GENERAL ASSEMBLY OF THE KIRK OF SCOTLAND IN THE OLD KIRK, ST. GILES'S CATHEDRAL, 1787.
(*After a Drawing by David Allan, in the British Museum*).

CASSELL'S

OLD AND NEW EDINBURGH:

Its History, its People, and its Places.

BY

JAMES GRANT,

AUTHOR OF "MEMORIALS OF THE CASTLE OF EDINBURGH," "BRITISH BATTLES ON LAND AND SEA," ETC.

Illustrated by numerous Engravings.

VOL. II.

CASSELL, PETTER, GALPIN & CO.:

LONDON, PARIS & NEW YORK.

1882.

CONTENTS.

————◦◦◦————

CHAPTER I.

THE CANONGATE.

PAGE

Its Origin—Songs concerning it—Records—Market Cross—St. John s and the Girth Crosses—Early History—The Town of Herbergare—Canongate Paved—The Governing Body—Raising the Devil—Purchase of the Earl of Roxburgh's "Superiority"—The Foreign Settlement—George Heriot the Elder—Huntly's House—Sir Walter Scott's Story of a Fire—The Morocco Land—Houses of Oliphant of Newland, Lord David Hay, and Earl of Angus—Jack's Land—Shoemaker's Lands—Marquis of Huntly's House—Nisbet of Dirleton's Mansion—Golfers' Land—John and Nicol Paterson—The Porch and Gatehouse of the Abbey—Lucky Spence 1

CHAPTER II.

THE CANONGATE (*continued*).

Execution of the Marquis of Montrose—The First Dromedary in Scotland—The Streets Cleansed—Roxburgh House—London Stages of 1712 and 1754—Religious Intolerance—Declension of the Burgh 13

CHAPTER III.

THE CANONGATE (*continued*).

Closes and Alleys on the North Side—Flesh-market and Coull's Closes—Canongate High School—Rae's Close—Kinloch's Lodging—New Street and its Residents—Hall of the Shoemakers—Sir Thos. Dalyell—The Canongate Workhouse—Panmure House—Hannah Robertson—The White Horse Hostel—The Water Gate 17

CHAPTER IV.

THE CANONGATE (*continued*).

Closes and Alleys on the South Side—Chessel's Court—The Canongate Theatre—Riots Therein—"Douglas" Performed—Mr. Digges and Mrs. Bellamy—St. John's Close—St. John's Street and its Residents—The Hammerman's Close—Horse Wynd, Abbey—House of Lord Napier 22

CHAPTER V.

THE CANONGATE (*continued*).

Separate or Detached Edifices therein—Sir Walter Scott in the Canongate—The Parish Church—How it came to be built—Its Official Position—Its Burying Ground—The Grave of Fergusson—Monument to Soldiers interred there—Eccentric Henry Prentice—The Tolbooth—Testimony as to its Age—Its later uses—Magdalene Asylum—Linen Hall—Moray House—Its Historical Associations—The Winton House—Whiteford House—The Dark Story of Queensberry House 27

CHAPTER VI.

THE CANONGATE (*concluded*).

Lothian Hut—Lord Palmerston—St. Thomas's Hospital—The Tennis Court and its Theatre—Queen Mary's Bath—The Houses of Croft-an-Righ and Clock-mill 38

CHAPTER VII.

HOLYROOD ABBEY.

Foundation of the Abbey—Text of King David's Charter—Original Extent of the Abbey Church—The so-called Miraculous Cross—The Patronages of the Canons—Its Thirty-one Abbots—Its Relics and Revenues 42

CHAPTER VIII.

HOLYROOD ABBEY (*concluded*).

PAGE

Charter of William I.—Trial of the Scottish Templars—Prendergast's Revenge—Charters by Robert II. and III.—The Lord of the Isles
—Coronation of James II.—Marriages of James II. and III.—Church, &c., burned by the English—Plundered by them—Its
Restoration by James VII.—The Royal Vault—Description of the Chapel Royal – Plundered at the Revolution—Ruined in 1768—The
West Front—The Belhaven Monument—The Churchyard—Extent of Present Ruin—The Sanctuary—The Abbey Bells 50

CHAPTER IX.

HOLYROOD PALACE.

First Notice of its History—Marriage of James IV.- The Scots of the Days of Flodden—A Brawl in the Palace—James V.'s Tower—The
Gudeman of Ballengeich—His Marriage Death of Queen Magdalene—The Council of November, 1542—A Standing Army Proposed—
The Muscovite Ambassadors Entertained by the Queen Regent 60

CHAPTER X.

HOLYROOD PALACE (*continued*).

Queen Mary's Apartments—Her Arrival in Edinburgh—Riot in the Chapel Royal—"The Queen's Maries "—Interview with Knox—
Mary's Marriage with Darnley—The Position of Rizzio—The Murder of Rizzio—Burial of Darnley—Marriage of Mary and Bothwell—
Mary's Last Visit to Holyrood—James VI. and the " Mad " Earl of Bothwell—Baptism of the Queen of Bohemia and Charles I.—
Taylor the Water-poet at Holyrood—Charles I.'s Imprisonment—Palace Burned and Re-built—The Palace before 1650—The Present
Palace—The Quadrangle—The Gallery of the Kings - The Tapestry—The Audience-Chamber 66

CHAPTER XI.

HOLYROOD PALACE (*concluded*).

The King's Birthday in 1665—James Duke of Albany—The Duchess of Albany and General Dalzell—Funeral of the Duke of Rothes—
A Gladiatorial Exhibition—Departure of the Scottish Household Troops—The Hunters' Company's Balls—First and Second
Visits of the Royal Family of France—Recent Improvements –St. Anne's Yard removed—The Ornamental Fountain built .   .   . 74

CHAPTER XII.

THE MOUND.

The North Loch used for Sousings and Duckings—The Boats, Swans, Ducks, and Eels—Accidents in the Loch—Last Appearance of the
Loch - Formation of the Mound—"Geordie Boyd's Mud Brig"—The Rotunda—Royal Institution—Board of Manufactures—History of
the Board—The Equivalent Money—Sir J. Shaw Lefevre's Report—School of Design—Gallery of Sculpture—Royal Society of
Edinburgh—Museum of Antiquities 80

CHAPTER XIII.

THE MOUND (*concluded*).

The Art Galleries—The National Gallery—The Various Collections—The Royal Scottish Academy—Early Scottish Artists—The Institution—The First Exhibition in Edinburgh—Foundation of the Academy—Presidents : G. Watson, Sir William Allan, Sir J. W.
Gordon, Sir George Harvey, Sir Daniel Macnee—The Spalding Fund 88

CHAPTER XIV.

THE HEAD OF THE MOUND.

The Bank of Scotland—Its Charter—Rivalry of the Royal Bank Notes for £5 and for 5s.—The New Bank of Scotland—Its Present Aspect
—The Projects of Mr. Trotter and Sir Thomas Dick Lauder—The National Security Savings Bank of Edinburgh—The Free
Church College and Assembly Hall—Their Foundation—Constitution—Library—Museum—Bursaries—Missionary and Theological
Societies—The Dining Hall, &c.—The West Princes Street Gardens—The Proposed Canal and Seaport—The East Princes Street
Gardens—Railway Terminus—Waverley Bridge and Market 93

CHAPTER XV.

THE CALTON HILL.

PAGE

Origin of the Name—Gibbet and Battery thereon—The Quarry Holes—The Monastery of Greenside Built—The Leper Hospital—The Tournament Ground and Playfield—Church of Greenside—Burgh of Calton—Rev. Rowland Hill—Regent Bridge Built—Observatory and Astronomical Institution—Bridewell Built—Hume's Tomb—The Political Martyrs' Monument—The Jews' Place of Burial—Monument of Nelson—National Monument, and those of Stewart, Playfair, and Burns—The High School—Foundation Laid—Architecture and Extent—The Opening—Instruction—Rectors of the New School—Lintel of the Old School—Lord Brougham's Opinion of the Institution 100

CHAPTER XVI.

THE NEW TOWN.

The Site before the Streets—The Lang Dykes—Wood's Farm—Drumsheugh House—Bearford's Parks—The Houses of Easter and Wester Coates—Gabriel's Road—Craig's Plan of the New Town—John Young builds the First House Therein—Extension of the Town Westward 114

CHAPTER XVII.

PRINCES STREET.

A Glance at Society—Change of Manners, &c.—The Irish Giants—Poole's Coffee-house—Shop of Constable & Co.—Weir's Museum, 1794—The Grand Duke Nicholas—North British Insurance Life Association—Old Tax Office and New Club—Craig of Riccarton—" The White Rose of Scotland "—St. John's Chapel—Its Tower and Vaults, &c.—The Scott Monument and its Museum—The Statues of Professor Wilson, Allan Ramsay, Adam Black, Sir James Simpson, and Dr. Livingstone—The General Improvements in Princes Street 119

CHAPTER XVIII.

THE CHURCH OF ST. CUTHBERT.

History and Antiquity—Old Views of it Described—First Protestant Incumbents—The Old Manse—Old Communion Cups—Pillaged by Cromwell—Ruined by the Siege of 1689, and again in 1745—Deaths of Messrs. McVicar and Pitcairn—Early Body-snatchers—Demolition of the Old Church—Erection of the New—Case of Heart-burial—Old Tombs and Vaults—The Nisbets of Dean—The Old Poor House—Kirkbraehead Road—Lothian Road—Dr. Candlish's Church—Military Academy—New Caledonian Railway Station . . . 131

CHAPTER XIX.

GEORGE STREET.

Major Andrew Fraser—The Father of Miss Ferrier—Grant of Kilgraston—William Blackwood and his Magazine—The Mother of Sir Walter Scott—Sir John Hay, Banker—Colquhoun of Killermont—Mrs. Murray of Henderland—The Houses of Sir J. W. Gordon, Sir James Hall, and Sir John Sinclair of Ulbster—St. Andrew's Church—Scene of the Disruption—Physicians' Hall—Glance at the History of the College of Physicians—Sold and Removed—The Commercial Bank—Its Constitution—Assembly Rooms—Rules of 1789—Banquet to Black Watch—" The Author of ' Waverley ' "—The Music Hall—The New Union Bank—Its Formation, &c.—The Masonic Hall—Watson's Picture of Burns—Statues of George IV., Pitt, and Chalmers 139

CHAPTER XX.

QUEEN STREET.

The Philosophical Institution—House of Baron Orde—New Physicians' Hall—Sir James V. Simpson, M.D.—The House of Professor Wilson—Sir John Leslie—Lord Rockville—Sir James Grant of Grant—The Hopetoun Rooms—Edinburgh Educational Institution for Ladies 151

CHAPTER XXI.

THE STREETS CROSSING GEORGE STREET, AND THOSE PARALLEL WITH IT.

Rose Street—Miss Burns and Baillie Creech—Sir Egerton Leigh—Robert Pollok—Thistle Street—The Dispensary—Hill Street—Count d'Albany—St. Andrew Street—Hugo Arnot—David, Earl of Buchan—St. David Street—David Hume—Sir Walter Scott and Basil Hall—Hanover Street—Sir J. Graham Dalyell—Offices of Association for the Improvement of the Poor—Frederick Street—Grant of Corrimony—Castle Street—A Dinner with Sir Walter Scott—Skene of Rubislaw—Macvey Napier—Castle Street and Charlotte Street . 158

CHAPTER XXII.

ST. ANDREW SQUARE.

PAGE

St. Andrew Square—List of Early Residents—Count Borowlaski—Miss Gordon of Cluny—Scottish Widows' Fund—Dr. A. K. Johnston—Scottish Provident Institution—House in which Lord Brougham was Born—Scottish Equitable Society—Charteris of Amisfield—Douglas's Hotel—Sir Philip Ainslie—British Linen Company—National Bank—Royal Bank—The Melville and Hopetoun Monuments—Ambrose's Tavern 166

CHAPTER XXIII.

CHARLOTTE SQUARE.

Charlotte Square—Its Early Occupants—Sir John Sinclair, Bart.—Lamond of that Ilk—Sir William Fettes—Lord Chief Commissioner Adam—Alexander Dirom—St. George's Church—The Rev. Andrew Thomson—Prince Consort's Memorial—The Parallelogram of the first New Town 172

CHAPTER XXIV.

ELDER STREET—LEITH STREET—BROUGHTON STREET.

Elder Street—Leith Street—The old "Black Bull"—Margarot—The Theatre Royal—Its Predecessors on the same Site—The Circus—Corri's Rooms—The Pantheon—Caledonian Theatre—Adelphi Theatre—Queen's Theatre and Opera House—Burned and Rebuilt—St. Mary's Chapel—Bishop Cameron 176

CHAPTER XXV.

THE VILLAGE AND BARONY OF BROUGHTON.

Broughton—The Village and Barony—The Loan—Broughton first mentioned—Feudal Superiors—Witches Burned—Leslie's Head-quarters—Gordon of Ellon's Children Murdered—Taken *Red Hand*—The Tolbooth of the Burgh—The Minute Books—Free Burgesses—Modern Churches erected in the Bounds of the Barony 180

CHAPTER XXVI.

THE NORTHERN NEW TOWN.

Picardy Place—Lords Eldin and Craig—Sir David Milne—John Abercrombie—Lord Newton—Commissioner Osborne—St. Paul's Church—St. George's Chapel—William Douglas, Artist—Professor Playfair—General Scott of Bellevue—Drummond Place—C. K. Sharpe of Hoddam—Lord Robertson—Abercrombie Place and Heriot Row—Miss Ferrier—House in which H. McKenzie died—Rev. A. Alison—Great King Street—Sir R. Christison—Sir William Hamilton—Sir William Allan—Lord Colonsay, &c. 185

CHAPTER XXVII.

THE NORTHERN NEW TOWN (*concluded*).

Admiral Fairfax—Bishop Terrot—Brigadier Hope—Sir T. M. Brisbane—Lord Meadowbank—Ewbank the R.S.A.—Death of Professor Wilson—Moray Place and its District—Lord President Hope—The Last Abode of Jeffrey—Baron Hume and Lord Moncrieff—Forres Street—Thomas Chalmers, D.D.—St. Colme Street—Captain Basil Hall—Ainslie Place—Dugald Stewart—Dean Ramsay—Great Stuart Street—Professor Aytoun—Miss Graham of Duntroon—Lord Jerviswoode 198

CHAPTER XXVIII.

THE WESTERN NEW TOWN—HAYMARKET—DALRY—FOUNTAINBRIDGE.

Maitland Street and Shandwick Place—The Albert Institute—Last Residence of Sir Walter Scott in Edinburgh—Lieutenant-General Dundas—Melville Street—Patrick F. Tytler—Manor Place—St. Mary's Cathedral—The Foundation Laid—Its Size and Aspect—Opened for Service—The Copestone and Cross placed on the Spire—Haymarket Station—Winter Garden—Donaldson's Hospital—Castle Terrace—Its Churches—Castle Barns—The U. P. Theological Hall—Union Canal—First Boat Launched—Dalry—The Chiealies—The Caledonian Distillery—Fountainbridge—Earl Grey Street—Professor G. J. Bell—The Slaughter-houses—Bain Whyt of Bainfield—North British India Rubber Works—Scottish Vulcanite Company—Adam Ritchie 209

CHAPTER XXIX.

WEST PORT.

PAGE

The West Port—Its Boundaries—Malefactors' Heads—The City Gates—Royal Entrances—Mary of Guise—Anne of Denmark—Charles I. General Assembly Expelled—A Witch—Jesuit Church—The Lawsons of the Highriggs—Lady Lawson's Wynd—The Tilting Ground —King's Stables—The Vennel—Tanner's Close—Burke and Hare—Their Native Country—Their " Den," Log's Lodgings—Their Murders—The Mode of them · Trial and Sentence—Execution and Dismemberment 221

CHAPTER XXX.

THE GRASSMARKET.

The Grassmarket—The Mart of 1477—Margaret Tudor—Noted Executions—" Half Hangit Maggie Dickson "—Italian Mountebanks—Grey Friary Founded by James I.—Henry VI. of England a Fugitive—The Grey Friars Port—New Corn Exchange—The White Horse Inn—Carriers—The Castle Wynd—First Gaelic Chapel there—Currie's Close—The Cockpit—Story of Watt and Downie " The Friends of the People "—Their Trial and Sentence—Execution of Watt 230

CHAPTER XXXI.

THE COWGATE.

The Cowgate—Origin and General History of the Thoroughfare—First Houses built there—The Vernour's Tenement—Alexander Alesse— Division of the City in 1512—" Dichting the Calsay " in 1518—The Cowgate Port—Beggars in 1616—Gilbert Blakhal—Names of the most Ancient Closes—the North Side of the Street—MacLellan's Land—Mrs. Syme—John Nimmo—Dr. Graham—The House of Sir Thomas Hope and Lady Mar—The Old Back Stairs—Tragic Story of Captain Cayley—Old Meal Market—Riots in 1763—The Episcopal Chapel, now St. Patrick's Roman Catholic Church—Trial of the Rev. Mr. Fitzsimmons 238

CHAPTER XXXII.

COWGATE (concluded).

The South Side of the Street—The High School Wynd—" Claudero "—Robertson's Close—House of the Bishops of Dunkeld—Tomb of Gavin Douglas—Kirk-of-Field and College Wynd—House of the Earls of Queensberry—Robert Monteith—Oliver Goldsmith—Dr. Joseph Black—House in which Sir Walter Scott was born—St. Peter's Pend—House of Andro Symson, the Printer, 1697—The Horse Wynd—Galloway House—Guthrie Street—Tailors' Hall—French Ambassador's Chapel and John Dickison's House—Tam o' the Cowgate and James VI.—The Hammermen's Land and Hall—Magdalene Chapel—John Craig—A Glance at the Ancient Corporations —The Hammermen—Their Charter—Seal and Progress—The Cordiners—First Strike in the Trade—Skinners and Furriers—Websters —Hat and Bonnet makers—Fleshers—Coopers—Tailors—Candle-makers—Baxters—Barbers—Chirurgeons 250

CHAPTER XXXIII.

THE SOCIETY.

The Candlemaker Row—The " Cunzie Nook "—Time of Charles I.—The Candlemakers' Hall—The Affair of Dr. Symons—The Society, 1598 —Brown Square—Proposed Statue to George III., 1764—Distinguished Inhabitants—Sir Islay Campbell—Lord Glenlee—Haig of Bemerside—Sir John Leslie—Miss Jeannie Elliot—Argyle Square—Origin of it—Dr. Hugh Blair—The Sutties of that Ilk—Trades Maiden Hospital—Minto House and the Elliots—New Medical School—Baptist Church—Chambers Street—Industrial Museum of Science and Art—Its Great Hall and adjoining Halls—Aim of the Architect—Contents and Models briefly glanced at—New Watt Institution and School of Arts—Phrenological Museum—New Free Tron Church—New Training College of the Church of Scotland —The Dental Hospital—The Theatre of Varieties 267

CHAPTER XXXIV.

THE LORD PROVOSTS OF EDINBURGH.

The First Magistrate of Edinburgh—Some noted Provosts—William de Dederyk, Alderman—John Wigmer and the Ransom of David II. —John of Quhitness, First Provost—William Bertraham—The Golden Charter—City Pipers—Archibald Bell-the-cat—Lord Home —Arran and Kilspindie—Lord Maxwell—" Greysteel's " Penance—James VI., and the Council—Lord Fyvie—Provost Tod and Gordon's Map—The First Lord Provost—George Drummond—Freedom of the City given to Benjamin Franklin—Sir Lawrence Dundas and the Parliamentary Contest—Sir James Hunter Blair—Riots of 1792—Provost Coulter's Funeral—Lord Lynedoch— Recent Provosts—The First Englishman who was Lord Provost of Edinburgh 277

CHAPTER XXXV.

INFIRMARY STREET AND THE OLD HIGH SCHOOL.

PAGE

Blackfriars Monastery—Its Foundation—Destroyed by Fire—John Black the Dominican—The Friary Gardens—Lady Yester: her
Church and Tomb—The Burying Ground—The Old High School—The Ancient Grammar School—David Vocat—School
Founded—Hercules Rollock—Early Classes—The House Destroyed by the English—The Bleis-Silver—David Malloch—The Old
High School—Thomas Ruddiman, Rector—Barclay's Class—Henry Mackenzie's Reminiscences—Dr. Adam, Rector: his Grammar—
New Edifice Proposed and Erected—The School-boy Days of Sir Walter Scott—Allan Masterton—The School in 1803—Death
of Rector Adam—James Pillans, M.A., and A. R. Carson, Rectors—The New School Projected—The Old one Abandoned   .   .   . 284

CHAPTER XXXVI.

THE OLD ROYAL INFIRMARY—SURGEON SQUARE.

The Old Royal Infirmary—Projected in time of George I.—The First Hospital Opened—The Royal Charter—Second Hospital Built—
Opened 1741—Size and Constitution—Benefactors' Patients—Struck by Lightning—Chaplain's Duties—Cases in the Present Day—
The Keith Fund—Notabilities of Surgeon Square—The House of Curriehill—The Hall of the Royal and Medical Society—Its
Foundation—Bell's Surgical Theatre   297

CHAPTER XXXVII.

ARTHUR'S SEAT AND ITS VICINITY.

The Sanctuary—Geology of the Hill—Origin of its Name, and that of the Craigs—The Park Walls, 1554—A Banquet al fresco—The
Pestilence—A Duel—"The Guttit Haddie"—Mutiny of the Old 78th Regiment—Proposed House on the Summit—Muschat and
his Cairn—Radical Road Formed—May Day—Skeletons found at the Wells o' Wearie—Park Improvements—The Hunter's Bog
—Legend of the Hangman's Craig—Duddingston—The Church—Rev. J. Thomson—Robert Monteith—The Loch—Its Swans—Skaters
—The Duddingston Thorn—The Argyle and Abercorn Families—The Earl of Moira—Lady Flora Hastings—Cauvin's Hospital—
Parson's Green—St. Anthony's Chapel and Well—The Volunteer Review before the Queen.   303

CHAPTER XXXVIII.

BRISTO AND THE POTTERROW.

Bristo Street—The Darien House—The Earl of Rosebery—Old Charity Workhouse—A Strike in 1764—Old George Inn—U. P. Church
—Dr. Peddie—Sir Walter Scott's First School—The General's Entry and the Dalrymples of Stair—Burns and Clarinda—Crichton
Street—Alison Rutherford of Fairnielee—The Eastern Portsburgh—The Duke of Lennox Men—The Plague—The Covenanters' Gun
Foundry—A Witch—A Contumacious Barber—Tailors' Hall—Story of Jean Brown—Duke of Douglas's House—Thomas Campbell
the Poet—Earl of Murray's House—Charles Street and Field   323

CHAPTER XXXIX.

NICOLSON STREET AND SQUARE.

Lady Nicolson—Her Pillar—Royal Riding School—M. Angelo—New Surgeons' Hall—The Earl of Leven—Dr. Borthwick Gilchrist—The
Blind Asylum—John Maclaren—Sir David Wilkie—Roxburgh Parish—Lady Glenorchy's Chapel   334

CHAPTER XL.

GEORGE SQUARE AND THE VICINITY.

Ross House—The last Lord Ross—Earlier Residents in the Square—House of Walter Scott, W.S.—Sir Walter's Boyhood—Bickers—Green
Breeks—The Edinburgh Light Horse—The Scots Brigade—Admiral Duncan—Lord Advocate Dundas—The Grants of Kilgraston—
Baron Dundas—Sedan Chairs—Campbells of Succoth—Music Class Room—The Eight Southern Districts—Chapel of Ease—Windmill
Street—Buccleuch Place—Jeffrey's First House there—The Burgh Loch—Society of Improvers—The Meadows   338

CHAPTER XLI.

HOPE PARK END.

"The Douglas Cause," or Story of Lady Jane Douglas-Stewart—Hugh Lord Semple—"The Chevalier"—The Archers' Hall—Royal
Company of Archers formed—Their Jacobitism—Their Colours—Early Parades—Constitution and Admission—Their Hall built—
Messrs. Nelsons' Establishment—Thomas Nelson 349

CHAPTER XLII.

LAURISTON.

The New University Buildings—The Estimates and Accommodation—George Watson's Hospital—Founded—Opened and Sold—The New Royal Infirmary—Its Capabilities for Accommodation—Simpson Memorial Hospital—Sick Children's Hospital—Merchant Maiden Hospital—Watson's Schools—Lauriston United Presbyterian Church—St. Catharine's Convent 355

CHAPTER XLIII.

GEORGE HERIOT'S HOSPITAL AND THE GREYFRIARS CHURCH.

Notice of George Heriot—Dies Childless—His Will—The Hospital founded—Its Progress—The Master Masons—Opened—Number of Scholars—Dr. Balcanquall—Alterations—The Edifice—The Architecture of it—Heriot's Day and Infant Schools in the City—Lunardi's Balloon Ascent—Royal Edinburgh Volunteers—The Heriot Brewery—Old Greyfriars Church—The Covenant—The Cromwellians—The Covenanting Prisoners—The Martyr's Tomb—New Greyfriars—Dr. Wallace—Dr. Robertson—Dr. Erskine—Old Tombs in the Church —Grant by Queen Mary—Morton Interred—State of the Ground in 1779—The Graves of Buchanan and others—Bones from St. Giles's Church 363

ERRATA.

Page 135, col 1, lines 3, 4, from foot, for "he preached on the death of Dr ," &c., read "preached at his death by Dr ," &c.

Page 142, col. 2, delete lines 14 to 25 from top.

Page 144, col. 1, delete lines 3 to 6 from top.

Page 156, col. 2, line 10 from foot, for "20" read "99."

Page 158, col. 2, line 13 from top, for "1876" read "1871."

Page 168, col. 1, line 22 from top, for "was till 1879" read "is."

Page 168, col. 2, line 31 from top, for "now" read "was till 1879."

Page 170, col. 2, line 4 from top, for "Provident Institution," read "Scottish Union and National Insurance Company;" and for "6" read "47, George Street, and 22, St. Andrew Square, these two companies having been amalgamated in 1879."

Page 171, col. 1, line 10 from top, for "west" read "east."

Page 171, col. 1, line 12 from top, for "Provident Institution" read "Scottish Union and National Insurance Company."

Page 172. The engraving represents the "Scottish Union and National Insurance Company" and not the "Scottish Provident Institution."

NOTE.—Mr. Hugh James Rollo, W.S., factor for the Walker trustees, writes:—"At page 211 it is represented that a capital of £400,000 was bequeathed by the Misses Walker for the erection of St. Mary's Cathedral, whereas the amount of personal estate left was about £80,000, besides heritage very valuable for feuing purposes, which at the death of Miss Mary Walker yielded an income of about £4,000 a year. The income at present is about £6,500, the first charge on which is a sum of £1,400 for stipends to clergy of the cathedral, bursaries to students, and allowance to the poor of the cathedral. Then there is a sum of £1,150 to be annually set aside for thirty years to repay part of the cost of the cathedral, and the interest on this diminishing loan. The surplus income is at the disposal of the trustees for behoof of the Episcopal Church in Scotland, the City of Edinburgh having always a preference. The ultimate income will be about £8,000 a year."

LIST OF ILLUSTRATIONS.

MEETING OF THE GENERAL ASSEMBLY OF THE KIRK OF SCOTLAND IN THE OLD KIRK, ST. GILES'S CATHEDRAL, 1787 (*after David Allan*). — *Frontispiece.*

	PAGE
The Canongate Tolbooth	1
The Burgh Seal of the Canongate	3
The Market Cross, Canongate	3
Haddington's Entry	4
East End of High Street, Nether Bow, and West End of Canongate	5
Effigy of the Moor, Morocco Land	7
The Marquis of Huntly's House, from the Canongate .	8
The Marquis of Huntly's House, from Bakehouse Close	9
Nisbet of Dirleton's House	12
The Golfers' Land	13
The Canongate—Continuation Eastward of Plan on page 5	16
Tolbooth Wynd	20
Lintel of John Hunter's House, Panmure Close .	21
The Water Gate	24
Chessel's Buildings	25
Lintel above the Door of Sir A. Acheson's House	27
Smollett's House, St. John Street	28
The Canongate Church	29
Fergusson's Grave	30
The Stocks, from the Canongate Tolbooth . .	31
Levee Room in Moray House ; Summer House in the Garden of Moray House ; Arbour in the Garden of Moray House ; Portion of a Ceiling in Moray House	32
Moray House	33
East End of the Canongate	36
The Canongate, looking West	37
The Palace Gate	40
Queen Mary's Bath	41
Croft-an-righ House	44
Holyrood Palace and Abbey	45
Seal of Holyrood Abbey	46
The Abbey Church	48

	PAGE
Interior of the Chapel Royal of Holyrood House, 1687	49
Ground Plan of the Chapel Royal of Holyrood House	52
West Front of Holyrood Abbey Church . . .	53
Interior of Holyrood Church, looking East . .	56
North Entrance to the Nave of Holyrood Abbey Church	57
The Belhaven Monument, Holyrood Church . .	60
Isometric Projection of the Royal Palace of Holyrood House	61
The Abbey Port	64
The Queen Mary Apartments, Holyrood Palace *To face page*	66
Holyrood Palace, the Regent Moray's House, the Royal Gardens, and Ancient Horologe . .	68
The Palace of Holyrood House, the South and North Gardens, the Abbey Kirk, and the Kirkyard .	69
Holyrood Palace as it was before the Fire of 1650 .	72
Holyrood Palace and Abbey Church, from the South-East	73
The Royal Apartments, Holyrood Palace *To face page*	74
The Quadrangle, Holyrood Palace	76
The Gallery of the Kings, Holyrood Palace . .	77
Holyrood Palace, West Front	80
The Holyrood Fountain	81
The Royal Institution as it was in 1829 . . .	84
The Royal Institution	85
The National Gallery	88
Interior of the National Gallery	89
The Bank of Scotland, from Princes Street Gardens .	96
Head of the Mound, prior to the erection of the Free Church College, 1844 . . *To face page*	97
Library of the Free Church College	97
West Princes Street Gardens, 1875	101
Nelson's Monument, Calton Hill, from Princes Street .	104
The Calton Hill, Calton Gaol, Burying-ground, and Monuments	105

	PAGE
The Calton Burying-ground : Hume's Grave . .	108
The National Monument, Calton Hill . . .	109
Dugald Stewart's Monument	111
Burns's Monument, Calton Hill	112
The High School	113
The Mansion of Easter Coates	116
Craig's Plan of the New Streets and Squares intended	
for the City of Edinburgh	117
The Old Town, from Princes Street, 1814 *To face page*	120
Archibald Constable	121
Princes Street, looking East from Scott's Monument .	124
The Castle, Ramsay Gardens, Bank of Scotland, and	
Earthen Mound, from Princes Street, 1814	
To face page	125
Princes Street, looking West	125
Dean Ramsay	128
The Scott Monument, Princes Street . . .	129
Professor Wilson's Statue	130
Allan Ramsay's Statue	130
St. Cuthbert's Church	133
Old West Kirk, and Walls of the Little Kirk, 1772 .	136
St. Cuthbert's Church	137
Kirkbraehead House	140
George Street . . . . *To face page*	141
The Saloon in Messrs. Blackwoods' Establishment .	141
St. Andrew's Church	145
Interior of St. Andrew's Church	148
Old Physicians' Hall, George Street, 1829 . .	149
The Music Hall, George Street	152
Sir James Young Simpson	156
Queen Street	160
Lord Kames and Hugo Arnot	161
Sir Walter Scott's House, Castle Street . .	164
St. Andrew Square	169
The Royal Bank of Scotland ; the British Linen Com-	
pany's Bank ; the Scottish Union and National	
Insurance Company's Office ; the Scottish Widows'	
Fund Office	172
Charlotte Square, showing St. George's Church . .	173
Adam's Design for St. George's Church, Charlotte Square	176
The Albert Memorial, Charlotte Square . .	177
Remains of the Village of Old Broughton, 1852 .	180
The Broughton Tolbooth	181
Broughton Burn, 1850	184
Picardy Village and Gayfield House . . .	185
The New Town, Edinburgh, 1804 . . .	189
The Excise Office, Drummond Place . . .	192
The Right Hon. Charles Hope, commanding the	
Edinburgh Volunteers	197

	PAGE
Heriot Row ; Royal Circus ; India Place ; Ainslie	
Place ; Moray Place	201
Francis, Lord Jeffrey	204
Dr. Chalmers in 1821	205
William Edmonstoune Aytoun	208
St. Mary's Cathedral, Exterior View . . .	212
St. Mary's Cathedral, Interior View . . .	213
Donaldson's Hospital . . . *To face page*	214
Edinburgh Castle from Port Hopetoun, 1825 . .	216
Dalry Manor House	217
The Suburbs of the West Port, 1646 . . .	220
Portsburgh Court House	221
Highriggs House, 1854	222
Old Houses in the West Port, near the haunts of Burke	
and Hare	224
The Grassmarket, from the West Port, 1825 . .	225
The Grassmarket in 1646	228
Ballantyne's Close, Grassmarket, 1850 . .	229
The Temple Lands, Grassmarket . . .	232
East End of the Grassmarket, showing the West Bow,	
the Gallows, and Old Corn Market . . .	233
The Corn Exchange, Grassmarket	236
Head of Cowgate, from Grassmarket, 1825 ; Grass-	
market from Cowgate ; the Vennel ; South Side	
of Grassmarket, 1820 ; Grassmarket looking West	
To face page	237
The White Hart Inn, Grassmarket	237
Old Houses in the Cowgate, near the South Bridge,	
1850	240
The Cowgate, from the Port to College Wynd, 1646 .	241
Old Houses in the Cowgate	244
East End of the Cowgate, looking towards the South	
Back of Canongate	245
The Meal Market, Cowgate	248
The Episcopal Chapel, Cowgate	249
Tailors' Hall, Cowgate	252
High School Wynd	253
Sir Walter Scott	254
Sir Walter Scott's Arms	254
College Wynd	256
Symson the Printer's House	257
The French Ambassador's Chapel	260
The Cowgate, from the College Wynd to the Grass-	
market	261
The Chapel and Hospital of St. Mary Magdalene .	264
Interior of the Chapel of St. Mary Magdalene .	265
Tablet on the Chapel of St. Mary Magdalene .	268
The Cunzie House, Candlemaker Row, 1850 .	269
Old Houses, Society	272

	PAGE
The First Trades Maiden Hospital, 1830 . . .	273
The Industrial Museum . . . *To face page*	275
Old Minto House	276
Chambers Street	277
Sir James Falshaw, Bart., and H.M. Lieutenant of	
Edinburgh	285
Lady Yester's Church, 1820	288
Carved Stone which was over the Main Entrance to	
the High School from 1578 to 1777 . . .	289
The High School erected in 1578	292
The Second High School, 1820	296
Dr. Adam	297
The Old Royal Infirmary	300
The Old Royal Infirmary, 1820	301
Plan of Arthur's Seat (the Sanctuary of Holyrood) .	304
The Holyrood Dairy	305
Clockmill House, 1780	308
Duddingston Village, from the Queen's Drive . .	309
St. Margaret's Well	311
Duddingston Church (Exterior)	312
Duddingston Church (Interior)	313
Gateway of Duddingston Church, showing the Jougs	
and Louping-on-Stone	314
Duddingston Loch	316
Prince Charlie's House, Duddingston	317
Ruins of St. Anthony's Chapel, looking towards Leith	320
The Volunteer Review in the Queen's Park, 1860	
To face page	321
St. Anthony's Chapel in 1544 and 1854 . . .	321
St. Anthony's Well	322
The Charity Workhouse, 1820	324
Darien House, 1750	325
The Merchant Maiden's Hospital, Bristo, 1820 .	328
Bristo Port, 1820	329
Clarinda's House, General's Entry . . .	332

	PAGE
Room in Clarinda's House, General's Entry . .	333
The Mahogany Land, Potterrow, 1821 . . .	336
Surgeon's Hall	337
The Blind Asylum (formerly the house of Dr. Joseph	
Black), Nicolson Street, 1820	340
George Square, showing house (second on the left) of	
Sir Walter Scott's father	341
Park Place, showing Campbell of Succoth's House .	344
The Organ in the Music-class Room	345
The Meadows, about 1810	348
The Burgh Loch	349
The Archers' Hall	352
Archers' Hall: the Dining Hall	353
Thomas Nelson	356
The Edinburgh University Medical School, Lauriston .	357
George Watson's Hospital	360
Bird's-eye View of the New Royal Infirmary, from the	
North-East, 1878	361
Reduced Facsimile of a View of Heriot's Hospital by	
Gordon of Rothiemay	364
George Heriot	365
Reduced Facsimile of an Old Engraving of Heriot's	
Hospital	368
Heriot's Hospital, from the South-west *To face page*	369
The Chapel, Heriot's Hospital	369
Heriot's Hospital: the Council Room . . .	372
The North Gateway of Heriot's Hospital . . .	373
Heriot's Hospital, 1779; Porter's Lodge; Dining	
Hall; Quadrangle, looking North; Quadrangle,	
looking South	376
A Royal Edinburgh Volunteer	377
The Repentance Stool, from Old Greyfriars Church .	379
Greyfriars Church	380
Tombs in Greyfriars Churchyard, Edinburgh . .	381
Monogram of George Heriot's Name	384

THE CANONGATE TOLBOOTH.

OLD AND NEW EDINBURGH.

CHAPTER I.

THE CANONGATE.

Its Origin—Songs concerning it—Records—Market Cross—St. John's and the Girth Crosses—Early History—The Town of Herbergare—Canongate Paved—The Governing Body—Raising the Devil—Purchase of the Earl of Roxburgh's "Superiority"—The Foreign Settlement—George Heriot the Elder—Huntly's House—Sir Walter Scott's Story of a Fire—The Morocco Land—Houses of Oliphant of Newland, Lord David Hay, and Earl of Angus—Jack's Land—Shoemakers' Lands—Marquis of Huntly's House—Nisbet of Dirleton's Mansion—Golfer's Land—John and Nicol Paterson—The Porch and Gatehouse of the Abbey—Lucky Spence.

THE Canongate—of old the Court-end of Edinburgh—takes its name from the Augustine monks of Holyrood, who were permitted to build it by the charter of David I. in 1128, and to rule it as a burgh of regality. "The canons," says Chalmers, "were empowered to settle here a village, and from them the street of this settlement was called the Canongate, from the Saxon *gaet*, a way or street,

according to the practice of the twelfth and thirteenth centuries in Scotland and England. The immunities which the canons and their villagers enjoyed from David's grant, soon raised up a town, which extended from the Abbey to the Nether Port of Edinburgh, and the townsmen performed their usual devotions in the church of the Abbey till the Reformation," after which it continued to

49

retain its distinct dignity as a burgh of regality. In its arms it bears the white hart's head, with the cross-crosslet of the miraculous legend between the horns, and the significant motto, "SIC ITUR AD ASTRA."

As the main avenue from the palace to the city, so a later writer tells us, it has borne upon its pavement the burden of all that was beautiful and gallant, and all that has become historically interesting in Scotland for the last seven hundred years; and though many of its houses have been modernised, it still preserves its aspect of great quaintness and vast antiquity.

It sprang up independent of the capital, adhering naturally to the monastery, whose vassals and dependents were its earliest builders, and retaining to the last legible marks of a different parentage from the city. Its magistrates claimed a feudal lordship over the property of the regality as the successors of its spiritual superiors; hence many of the title-deeds therein ran thus:—"To be holden of the Magistrates of the Canongate, as come in place of the Monastery of the Holy Cross."

The Canongate seems to have been a favourite with the muse of the olden time, and is repeatedly alluded to in familiar lyrics and in the more polished episodes of the courtly poets of the sixteenth and seventeenth centuries. A Jacobite song has it :—

> "As I cam doun the Canongate,
> The Canongate, the Canongate,
> As I cam doun the Canongate,
> I heard a lassie sing,
> 'Merry may the keel rowe.
> That my true love is in,'" &c.

The "Satire on Court Ladies" tells us,

> "The lasses o' the Canongate,
> Oh they are wondrous nice ;
> They winna gie a single kiss
> But for a *double* price."

And an old song concerning a now-forgotten belle says :—

> "A' doun alang the Canongate
> Were beaux o' ilk degree ;
> And mony ane turned round to look
> At bonny Mally Lee.
> And we're a' gaun east and west,
> We're a' gaun agee,
> We're a' gaun east and west,
> Courtin' Mally Lee !"

The earliest of the register-books preserved in the archives of this little burgh commences in 1561 —about a hundred years before Cromwell's invasion; but the volume, which comes down to 1588, had been long in private hands, and was only restored at a recent date, though much of it is printed in the "Maitland Miscellany" for 1840.

Unlike Edinburgh, the Canongate had no walls for defence—its gates and enclosures being for civic purposes only. If it relied on the sanctity of its monastic superiors as a protection, it did so in vain, when, in 1380, Richard II. of England gave it to the flames, and the Earl of Hertford in 1544; and in the civil wars during the time of Charles I., the *Journal of Antiquities* tells us that "the Canongate suffered severely from the barbarity of the English—so much so that scarcely a house was left standing."

In 1450, when the first wall of the city was built, its eastern extremity was the Nether Bow Port. Open fields, in all probability, lay outside the latter, and though the increasing suburb was then building, the city claimed jurisdiction within it as far as the Cross of St. John, and the houses crept gradually westward up the slope, till they formed the present unbroken street from the Nether Bow to the palace porch; but it seems strange that even in the disastrous year 1513, when the Cowgate was enclosed by a wall, no attempt was made to secure the Canongate, though it had gates which were shut at night, and it had boundary walls, but not of a defensive character.

Of old, three crosses stood in the main street: that of St. John, near the head of the present St. John Street, at which Charles I. knighted the Provost on his entering the city in 1633; the ancient Market Cross, which formerly stood opposite the present Tolbooth, and is represented in Gordon's Map as mounted on a stone gallery, like that of the City Cross, and the shaft of which, a very elegant design, still exists, attached to the southeast corner of the just-named edifice. Its chief use in later times was a pillory, and the iron staple yet remains to which culprits were attached by the iron collar named the *jougs*. The third, or Girth Cross, stood at the foot of the Canongate, 100 feet westward from the Abbey-strand. "It consisted," says Kincaid, "of three steps as a base and a pillar upon the top, and was called the Girth Cross from its being the western limit of the Sanctuary ; but in paving the street it was removed, and its place is now known by a circle of stones upon the west side of the well within the Water Gate."

In the earlier ages of its history the canons to whom the burgh belonged had liberty to buy and sell in open market. It has been supposed by several writers that a village of some kind had existed on the site prior to the erection of the Abbey, as the king says in more than one version of the foundation charter of the latter, " I likewise grant to the said canons the town of *Herbergare*, lying betwixt the said church, and my town (of Edinburgh), and that the burgesses thereof have the liberty of buying and selling goods and merchandise in open market as freely, and without molestation and reproach, as any of my own burgesses." According to Sir Walter Scott, in his " Provincial Antiquities," the Canongate was formerly denominated the Herbergérie (or Hospitium) of the monastery. But in time it came to be called Canongate, from its proprietors. Be this as it may, many privileges were conferred upon it by Robert, Abbot of Holyrood, and these were confirmed and extended by David II., Robert III., James II., and James III., who "granted to the bailies, council, and community of the burgh of the Canongate the several annuities payable at the Exchequer by the said burgh, the common muir lying between the lands of Broughton on the west, those of Pilrig on the east, and the way leading from Edinburgh to Leith on the south, with all the rights and customs thereunto belonging, together with all the liberties, commodities, privileges, and immunities appertaining to a burgh of regality."

The Canongate would appear to have been paved about the same time as the High Street, and in 1535 James V. granted to the Abbot of Holyrood a duty of one penny upon every loaded cart, and of a halfpenny upon every empty one, to repair and maintain the causeway.

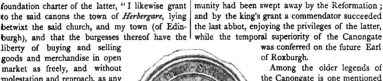

THE BURGH SEAL OF THE CANONGATE.

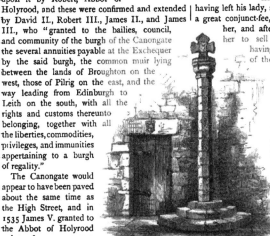

THE MARKET CROSS, CANONGATE.

According to the record books of the Canongate, it was governed in 1561 by four old bailies, three deacons, two treasurers, and four councillors, "chosen and elected;" and, as enacted in 1567, the council met every eighth day, on *fuirsdaye*. The Tolbooth was then, as till a late period, the council-room, court-house, and place of punishment.

By 1561 the monastic superiority over the community had been swept away by the Reformation; and by the king's grant a commendator succeeded the last abbot, enjoying the privileges of the latter, while the temporal superiority of the Canongate was conferred on the future Earl of Roxburgh.

Among the older legends of the Canongate is one mentioned by Sir John Scott of Scotstarvit, who tells us that Sir Lewis Bellenden, a Lord of Session, Council, and Exchequer, about the year 1591, "dealt with a warlock, called Richard Graham, to raise the devil," which he did in the back-yard of his own house in the Canongate, "and he was thereby so terrified that he took sickness, and thereof died. And having left his lady, sister to the Lord Livingstone, a great conjunct-fee, the Earl of Orkney married her, and after some years, having moved her to sell her conjunct-fee-lands, and having disposed of all the monies of the same, sent her back to the Canongate, where she lived divers years very miserably, and there died in extreme poverty."

In 1636 the superiority acquired by the Earl of Roxburgh was purchased by the magistrates of Edinburgh. This included the Canongate, North Leith, part of Broughton, and the village of the Pleasance — a purchase which was confirmed by Charles I., and cost 42,100 merks Scots. By this the Canongate became subordinate to Edinburgh, and was governed by a "baron and bailiff" appointed by the council of the latter; but the real glory of the Canongate may be said to have departed with the court when James VI. succeeded to the throne of England in 1603, though, as we shall show, it long continued to be a fashionable quarter of the metropolis even after the time of the Union.

In pursuing the general history of the suburbs, we find that in 1609, under favour of James VI., when a number of foreigners were introduced into the kingdom to teach the making of cloths of various kinds, a colony of them settled in the Canongate, under John Sutherland, and a Fleming named Jacob Van Headen, where they "daily exercised in their art of making, dressing, and litting of stuffs," giving great "light and knowledge

Among the inhabitants of the Canongate was a George Heriot, who died in the following year, 1610, aged seventy. He was the father of the founder of that famous and magnificent hospital, which is perhaps the greatest ornament of either Old or New Edinburgh.

HADDINGTON'S ENTRY.

of their calling to the country people." Notwithstanding that these industrious and inoffensive men had royal letters investing them with special privileges, they were—as too often happens in those cases where the enterprise of foreigners appears to clash with the interests of natives—much molested and harassed by the magistrates of the Canongate, with a view of forcing them to become burgesses and free men in the regular way; but an appeal to the Privy Council affirmed their exemption.

In 1639, we learn from Spalding that George, second Marquis of Huntly, who in his youth had commanded the Scottish Guard of Louis XIII. was residing at his old family mansion in the Canongate, wherein, about the month of November, two of his daughters were married "with great solemnities"—the Lady Anne, who was "ane precise Puritan," to the Lord Drummond; and Lady Henrietta, who was a Roman Catholic, to Lord Seton, son of the Earl of Winton. These ladies had each 40,000 merks Scots as a fortune, their uncle, the Earl of Argyle, being cautioner for the payment, "for relief whereof he got the wadset of Lochaber and Badenoch." Lady Jean, a third daughter, was also married in the ensuing January, with a fortune of 30,000 merks, to Thomas, Earl of Haddington, who perished in the following year,

possessed in Edinburgh, were sometimes the scenes of strange and mysterious transactions, a divine of singular sanctity was called up at midnight to pray with a person at the point of death. This was no unusual summons ; but what followed was alarming. He was put into a sedan-chair, and after he had been transported to a remote part of the town the

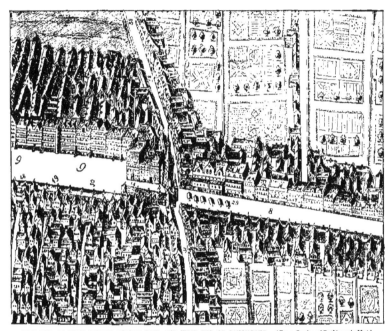

EAST END OF HIGH STREET, NETHER BOW, AND WEST END OF CANONGATE. *(From Gordon of Rothiemay's Map.)*

48, Blackfriars Wynd ; 49, Todrig's Wynd ; 50, Gray's Wynd ; 51, St. Mary's Wynd ; 38, Leith Wynd ; 8, Suburbs of the Canongate ; 9, High Street ; 14, The Nether Bow ; A, The Nether-bow Port ; 28, The Flesh Stocks in the Canongate.

when the Castle of Dunglass was blown up by gunpowder.

An old house at the head of the Canongate, on the north side, somewhere in the vicinity of Coull's Close, but now removed, was always indicated as being the scene of that wild story which Scott relates in his notes to the fifth canto of "Rokeby," and in his language we prefer to give it here.

He tells us that "about the beginning of the eighteenth century, when the large castles of the Scottish nobles, and even the secluded hotels, like those of the French noblesse, which they

bearers insisted upon his being blindfolded. The request was enforced by a cocked pistol, and submitted to ; but in the course of the discussion he conjectured, from the phrases employed by the chairmen, and from some parts of their dress not completely concealed by their cloaks, that they were greatly above the menial station they had assumed. After many turnings and windings the chair was carried up-stairs into a lodging, where his eyes were uncovered, and he was introduced into a bed-room, where he found a lady newly delivered of an infant, and he was commanded by his attendants to say such prayers by her bedside as were fitting for a person not expected to survive a mortal disorder.

"He ventured to remonstrate, and observed that her safe delivery warranted better hopes; but he was sternly commanded to obey the orders first given, and with difficulty recollected himself sufficiently to acquit himself of the task imposed on him. He was then again hurried into the chair; but as they conducted him down-stairs he heard the report of a pistol! He was safely conducted home, and a purse of gold was forced upon him; but he was warned at the same time that the least allusion to this dark transaction would cost him his life. He betook himself to rest, and after long and broken musing, fell into a deep sleep. From this he was awakened with the dismal news that a fire of uncommon fury had broken out in the house of ——, near the head of the Canongate, and that it was totally consumed, with the shocking addition that the daughter of the proprietor, a young lady eminent for beauty and accomplishments, had perished in the flames. The clergyman had his suspicions; but to have made them public would have availed nothing. He was timid; the family was of the first distinction; above all, the deed was done, and could not be amended.

"Time wore away, and with it his terrors; but he became unhappy at being the solitary depositary of this fearful mystery, and mentioned it to some of his brethren, through whom the anecdote acquired a sort of publicity. The divine had long been dead when a fire broke out on the same spot where the house of —— had formerly stood, and which was now occupied by buildings of an inferior description. When the flames were at their height, the tumult that usually attends such a scene was suddenly suspended by an unexpected apparition. A beautiful female in a nightdress, extremely rich, but at least half a century old, appeared in the very midst of the fire, and uttered these tremendous words in her vernacular idiom:—'*Anes* burned— *twice* burned—the *third* time I'll scare you all!' The belief in this story was so strong, that on a fire breaking out, and seeming to approach the fatal spot, there was a good deal of anxiety testified lest the apparition should make good her denunciation."

According to a statement in *Notes and Queries*, this story was current in Edinburgh before the childhood of Scott, and the murder part of it was generally credited. He mentions a person acquainted with the city in 1743 who used to tell the tale and point out the site of the house. It is remarkable that a great fire did happen there in the seventeenth century, and the lofty buildings on the spot date from that time.

Of the plague, which in 1645 nearly depopulated the Canongate as well as the rest of Edinburgh, a singular memorial still remains, a little lower down the street, on the north side, in the form of a huge square tenement, called the Morocco Land, from the effigy of a turbaned Moor, which projects from a recess above the second floor, and having an alley passing under it, inscribed with the following legend:—

"MISERERE MEI, DOMINE : A PECCATO, PROBRO, DEBITO, ET MORTE SUBITA. LIBERA ME. I.6.18."

Of the origin of this edifice various romantic stories are told : one by Chambers, to the effect that a young woman belonging to Edinburgh, having been taken upon the sea by an African rover, was sold to the harem of the Emperor of Morocco, whose favourite wife she became, and enabled her brother to raise a fortune by merchandise, and that in building this stately edifice he erected the black nude figure, with turban and necklace of beads, as a memorial of his royal brother-in-law; but the most complete and consistent outline of its history is that given by Wilson in his "Memorials," from which it would appear that during one of the tumults which occurred in the city after the accession of Charles I., the house of the Provost, who had rendered himself obnoxious to the rioters, was assaulted and set on fire. Among those arrested as a ringleader was Andrew Gray, a younger son of the Master of Gray, whose descendants inherit the ancient honours of Kinfauns, and who, notwithstanding the influence of his family, was tried, and sentenced to be executed on the second day thereafter.

On the very night that the scaffold was being erected at the Cross he effected his escape from the City Tolbooth by means of a rope conveyed to him by a friend, who had previously given some drugged liquor to the sentinel at the Puir-folks-purses, and provided a boat for him, by which he crossed the North Loch and fled beyond pursuit.

Time passed on, and the days of the great civil war came. "Gloom and terror now pervaded the streets of the capital. It was the terrible year 1645—the last visitation of the pestilence to Edinburgh—when, as tradition tells us," says Wilson, "grass grew thickly about the Cross, once as crowded a centre of thoroughfare as Europe could boast of."

The Parliament was compelled to sit at Stirling, and the Town Council, on the 10th of April, agreed with Joannes Paulitius, M.D., that he should visit the infected at a salary of £80 Scot per month. A number of the ailing were hutted in the King's Park, a few were kept at home, and aid for all was invoked from the pulpits. The Session of the Canongate ordained, on the 27th of June, that, "to avoid contention in this fearful time," all those who died in the park should be buried therein ; for it would seem that those who perished by the plague were buried in places apart from churchyards, lest the infection might burst forth anew if ever the graves were reopened.*

Maitland records that such was the terror prevailing at this period that the prisoners in the Tolbooth were all set at liberty, and all who were not free men were compelled, under severe penalties, to quit the city, until at length, " by the unparalleled ravages committed by the plague, it was spoiled of its inhabitants to such a degree that there were scarcely *sixty* men left capable of assisting in the defence of the town in case of an attack."

At this crisis a large armed vessel of peculiar rig and aspect entered the Firth of Forth, and came to anchor in Leith Roads. By experienced seamen she was at once pronounced to be an Algerine rover, and dismay spread over all the city. This soon reached a culminating point when a strong band landed from her, and, entering the Canongate by the Water Gate, advanced to the Netherbow Port and required admittance. The magistrates parleyed with their leader, who demanded an exorbitant ransom, and scoffed at the risk to be run in a plague-stricken city.

The Provost at this time was Sir John Smith, of Groat Hall, a small mansion-house near Craigleith, and he, together with his brother-in-law, Sir William Gray, Bart., of Pittendrum, a staunch Cavalier, and one of the wealthiest among the citizens, to whom we have referred in our account of Lady Stair's Close, agreed to ransom the city for a large sum, while at the same time his eldest son was demanded by the pirates as a hostage. " It seems, however," says Wilson, "that the Provost's only child was a daughter, who then lay stricken of the plague, of which her cousin, Egidia Gray, had recently died. This information seemed to work an immediate change on the leader of the

EFFIGY OF THE MOOR, MOROCCO LAND.

Moors. After some conference with his men he intimated his possession of an elixir of wondrous potency, and demanded that the Provost's daughter should be entrusted to his skill, engaging that if he did not cure her immediately to embark with his men, and free the city without ransom. After considerable parley the Provost proposed that the leader should enter the city and take up an abode in his house."

This was rejected, together with higher offers of ransom, till Sir John Smith yielded to the exhortations of his friends, and the proposal of the Moor was accepted, and the fair sufferer was borne to a house at the head of the Canongate, wherein the corsair had taken up his residence, and from thence she went forth quickly restored and in health.

The most singular part of this story is its denouement, from which it would appear that the corsair and physician proved to be no other than the condemned fugitive Andrew Gray, who had risen high in the favour and service of the Emperor of Morocco. "He had returned to Scotland," says Wilson, "bent on revenging his own early wrongs on the magistrates of Edinburgh, when, to his surprise, he found in the destined object of his special vengeance a relation of his own. He married the Provost's daughter, and settled down a wealthy citizen in the burgh of Canongate. The house to which his fair patient was borne, and whither he afterwards brought her as his bride, is still adorned with an effigy of his royal patron, the Emperor of Morocco, and the tenement has ever since borne the name of the Morocco Land. . . . . We have had the curiosity to obtain a sight of the title-deeds of the property, which prove to be of recent date. The earliest, a disposition of 1731, so far confirms the tale that the proprietor at that date is John Gray, merchant, a descendant, it may be, of the Algerine rover and the Provost's daughter. The figure of the Moor has ever been a subject of popular admiration and wonder, and a variety of legends are told to account for its existence. Most of them, though differing in almost every other point, seem to agree in connecting it with the last visitation of the plague."

Near this tenement, a little to the eastward, was the mansion of John Oliphant of Newland, second

---

* "Dom. Ann.," Vol. II.

son of Laurence, fourth Lord Oliphant, and father of the sixth lord who bore that title. His elder brother, the master, was one of the Ruthven conspirators in 1582, and perished at sea when fleeing from Scotland.

Beside it, a building of the same age was the residence of Lord David Hay, of Belton, son of only a portion of the walls of which were standing in 1847. It is supposed to have been the abode of Archibald, ninth Earl of Angus, who, as nephew and ward of the Regent Morton, was involved in his ruin, and fled the realm to England, where he became, as Godscroft tells us, the favourite " of that worthie Queen Elizabeth, partly in memorie of

THE MARQUIS OF HUNTLY'S HOUSE, FROM THE CANONGATE.

John, second Earl of Tweeddale (who was among the first to join the royal standard at Nottingham in 1642), and who granted that barony to the former in 1687, at a time when he, the earl, was oppressed by debts which compelled him to sell his whole estate of Tweeddale to the Duke of Queensberry.

Northward of this edifice, and partly on the site now occupied by the Chapel of Ease in New Street, was the ancient residence of the Earl of Angus, his uncle, but no lesse for his own sake." Moreover, he adds that he became the friend of Dudley, Walsingham, and Sir Philip Sidney, who was then writing his " Arcadia," which " hee delighted much to impart to Angus, and Angus took as much pleasure to be partaker thereof."

Returning to Scotland, he became involved in many troubles, and died in 1588—the victim, it was alleged, of sorcery, by the spells, says Godscroft, of Barbara Napier, in Edinburgh, "wife to Archibald

Douglas, of Carshogle, who was apprehended on suspition," but set at liberty. "Anna Simson, a famous witch, is reported to have confessed at her death that a picture of waxe was brought to her having A. D. written on it, which, as they said to

On the same side of the street, opposite to the archway leading into St. John Street, Jack's Land, a lofty stone tenement, formed, in her latter years, the residence of the beautiful Susannah, Countess of Eglinton, and there she was frequently visited

THE MARQUIS OF HUNTLY'S HOUSE, FROM BAKEHOUSE CLOSE.

her, did signifie Archibald Davidson, and she (not thinking of the Earl of Angus, whose name was Archibald Douglas, and might have been Davidson, because his father was David) did consecrate or execrate it after her forms, which, she said, she would not have done for all the world. . . . . His body was buried at Abernethy and his heart in Douglas, by his oune direction. He was the last Earle of the race of George, Master of Angus, who was slain at Flowden."

by the famous Lady Jane Douglas during the vexed progress of "the Douglas cause;" and in another flat thereof resided David Hume, who came thither from Riddel's Land in 1753, while engaged on his "History of England."

"The Shoemakers' Lands, which stand to the east of Jack's Land," says Wilson, writing in 1847, "are equally lofty and more picturesque buildings. One of them especially, opposite to Moray House, is a very singular and striking object in the stately range of substantial stone tenements that extend from New Street to the Canongate Tolbooth. A highly-adorned tablet surmounts the main entrance, enriched with angels' heads and a border of Elizabethan ornament enclosing the shoemakers' arms, with the date 1677. An open book is inscribed with the first verse of the Scottish metre version of the one hundred and thirty-third Psalm—a motto which appears to have been of special repute towards the close of the seventeenth century among the suburban corporations, being also inscribed over the Tailors' Hall of Eastern Portsburgh and the Shoemakers' Land in the West Port. The turnpike stair, the entrance to which is graced by this motto and the further inscription, in smaller letters, 'IT IS AN HONOUR FOR MAN TO CEASE FROM STRIFE,' rises above the roof of the building, and is crowned by an ogee roof of singular character, flanked on either side by picturesque gables to the street. The first of the two tenements to the west of this, at the head of Shoemakers' Close, has an open panel on its front, from which the inscription appears to have been removed; but the other, which bears the date 1725, is still adorned with the same arms, and the following moral aphorism :—

"'BLESSED IS HE THAT WISELY DO
TH THE POOR MAN'S CASE CONSIDER.'"

We have referred to the mansion of the Marquis of Huntly, in the Canongate, and the marriage of his daughters therein. This singularly picturesque and antique edifice stands on the southern side of the street, opposite the old Tolbooth, and is erroneously said to have been at one time the Royal Mint.

Here George, sixth Earl and first Marquis of Huntly, is said to have resided—the same noble who was suspected of corresponding and conspiring with Spain. In his "History of the Troubles," Spalding tells us that this peer, in June, 1636, was borne from his lodging in the Canongate, in the desire of reaching his northern house in Badenoch, but got no farther than Dundee, where he died, in his seventy-fourth year.

Here, too, abode his son, the second marquis, who was forfeited in 1645 by the Covenanting Parliament for his steady adherence to the king, and after being deprived of his stately castles of Gicht and Strathbogie, lost his head on the block at the Market Cross in 1649, ten years after the marriage festivities referred to.

When Maitland wrote, in 1753, this house was the residence of the Dowager of Cosmo George, third Duke of Gordon, who had been Lady Catharine Gordon, of the Aberdeen family.

It still presents a picturesque row of timber-fronted gables to the street, resting on a row of carved corbels and a cornice projecting from the basement, and a series of sculptured tablets adorn it, filled with certain pious phrases peculiar to the sixteenth century. One of these is—"*Vt tu lingvæ tuæ, sic e,o mear; avrium Dominvs svm;*" another is—"*Constanti pectori res mortalivm vmbra.*"

Lower down the street, on the same side, at the head of Reid's Close, a square projecting turret, corbelled well out over the pavement, with a huge gable, indicates the town mansion of the Nisbets of Dirleton, an old baronial family in East Lothian, erected in the year 1624. In accordance with the general style of all Scottish houses in those days, the basement storey is arched with stone; and the first of the family who resided there seems to have been Sir John Nisbet of Dirleton, who was raised to the bench in 1664, "a man of great learning, both in law and many other things, chiefly in Greek," according to Burnet, who adds that "he was a person of great integrity, and always stood firm to the law." He was the son of Patrick Nisbet, Lord Eastbank in 1636, and was appointed King's Advocate, and was author of an old legal work, well known as "Dirleton's Doubts." He died in 1678. He was a tool of the bishops, and rendered himself unpopular by his zeal in prosecuting the unfortunate Covenanters. Of this Wodrow relates an instance. One named Robert Gray having been brought before the Privy Council, and examined as to his knowledge of their hiding-places without success, Sir John Nisbet artfully and cruelly took a ring from his finger, and sent it to Mrs. Gray, with a message that her husband had revealed *all* he knew of the Whigs. Deceived by this, she told all that *she* knew of their lurking-places, and thus many were arrested, which so affected her husband that he sickened, and died a few days after.

Nearly opposite Queensberry House, and on the north side of the street, a narrow, old-fashioned edifice is known as John Paterson's House, or "The Golfers' Land," concerning which there is recorded a romantic episode connected with James VII., when, as Duke of Albany, he held his court at Holyrood. Conspicuously placed high upon the wall is a coat-armorial, and a slab above the entrance door contains the two following inscriptions :—

"CUM VICTOR LUDO, SCOTIS QUI PROPRIUS, ESSET,
TER TRES VICTORES POST REMEDITOS AVOS,
PATERSONUS, HUMO TUNC EDUCEBAT IN ALTUM
HANC, QUÆ VICTORES TOT TULET UNA, DOMUM."
"I HATE NO PERSON."

The latter is an anagram on the name of "John Paterson," while the quatrain was the production of Dr. Pitcairn, and is referred to in the first volume of Gilbert Stuart's *Edinburgh Magazine and Review* for 1774, and may be rendered thus: —"In the year when Paterson won the prize in golfing, a game peculiar to the Scots (in which his ancestors had nine times won the same honour), he then raised this mansion, a victory more honourable than all the rest."

According to tradition, two English nobles at Holyrood had a discussion with the said duke as to the native country of golf, which he was frequently in the habit of playing on the Links of Leith with the Duke of Lauderdale and others, and which the two strangers insisted to be an English game as well. No evidence of this being forthcoming, while many Scottish Parliamentary edicts, some as old as the days of James II., in 1457, could be quoted concerning the said game, the Englishmen, who both vaunted their expertness, offered to test the legitimacy of their pretensions on the result of a match to be played by them against His Royal Highness and any other Scotsman he chose to select. After careful inquiry he chose a man named John Paterson, a poor shoe-maker in the Canongate, but the worthy descendant of a long line of illustrious golfers, and the association will by no means surprise, even in the present age, those who practise the game in the true old Scottish spirit. The strangers were ignominiously beaten, and the heir to the throne had the best of this practical argument, while Paterson's merits were rewarded by the stake played for, and he built the house now standing in the Canongate. On its summit he placed the Paterson arms—three pelicans *vulned;* on a chief three mullets; crest, a dexter-hand grasping a golf club, with the well-known motto—FAR AND SURE. Concerning this old and well-known tradition, Chambers says, "it must be admitted there is some uncertainty. The house, the arms, and the inscriptions only indicate that Paterson built the house after being victor at golf, and that Pitcairn had a hand in decorating it."

In this doubt Wilson goes further, and believes that the Golfers' Land was *lost*, not won, by the gambling propensities of its owner. It was acquired by Nicol Paterson in 1609, a maltman in Leith, and from him it passed, in 1632, to his son John (and Agnes Lyel, his spouse), who died 23rd April, 1663, as appears by the epitaph upon his tomb in the churchyard of Holyrood, which was extant in Maitland's time, and the strange epitaph on which is given at length by Monteith. He would appear to have been many times Bailie of the Canongate.

Both Nicol and John, it may be inferred from the inscriptions on the ancient edifice, were able and successful golfers. The style of the building, says Wilson, confirms the idea that it had been rebuilt by him "with the spoils, as we are bound to presume, which he won on Leith Links, from 'our auld enemies of England.' The title-deeds, however, render it probable that other stakes had been played for with less success. In 1691 he grants a bond over the property for £400 Scots. This is followed by letters of caption and horning, and other direful symptoms of legal assault, which pursue the poor golfer to his grave, and remain behind as his sole legacy to his heirs."

The whole tradition, however, is too serious to be entirely overlooked, but may be taken by the reader for what it seems worth.

Bailie Paterson's successor in the old mansion was John, second Lord Bellenden of Broughton and Auchnoule, Heritable Usher of the Exchequer, who married Mary, Countess Dowager of Dalhousie, and daughter of the Earl of Drogheda. Therein he died in 1704, and was buried in the Abbey Church; and as the Union speedily followed, like other tenements so long occupied by the old courtiers in this quarter, the Golfers' Land became, as we find it now, the abode of plebeians.

Immediately adjoining the Abbey Court-house was an old, dilapidated, and gable-ended mansion of no great height, but of considerable extent, which was long indicated by oral tradition as the abode of David Rizzio. It has now given place to buildings connected with the Free Church of Scotland. Opposite these still remain some of the older tenements of this once patrician burgh, distinguishable by their lofty windows filled in with small square panes of glass; and on the south side of the street, at its very eastern end, a series of pointed arches along the walls of the Sanctuary Court-house, alone remain to indicate the venerable Gothic porch and gate-house of the once famous Abbey of Holyrood, beneath which all that was great and good, and much that was ignoble and bad have passed and repassed in the days that are no more.

This edifice, of which views from the east and west are still preserved, is supposed to have been the work of "the good Abbot Ballantyne," who rebuilt the north side of the church in 1490, and to whom we shall have occasion to refer elsewhere. His own mansion, or lodging, stood here on the north side of the street, and the remains of it, together with the porch, were recklessly destroyed and removed by the Hereditary Keeper of the Palace in 1753.

A little gable-ended house now occupies the site of the former, and was long known as the dwelling of a very different personage, a Lucky Spence, of unenviable notoriety, whose "Last dow on the ground floor, a cavity was found in the solid wall, containing the skeleton of a child, with some remains of fine linen cloth in which it had been wrapped. Our authority," says Wilson,

NISBET OF DIRLETON'S HOUSE.

Advice" figures somewhat coarsely in the poems of Allan Ramsay.

About 1833 a discovery was made, during some alterations in this house, which was deemed illustrative of the desperate character of its seventeenth-century occupant. "In breaking out a new win-"a worthy shoemaker, who had occupied the house for forty-eight years, was present when the discovery was made, and described very graphically the amazement and horror of the workman, who threw away his crowbar, and was with difficulty persuaded to resume his operations."

THE GOLFERS' LAND.

CHAPTER II.

THE CANONGATE (*continued*).

Execution of the Marquis of Montrose—The First Dromedary in Scotland—The Streets Cleansed—Roxburgh House—London Stages of 1712 and 1754—Religious Intolerance—Declension of the Burgh.

OF all the wonderful and startling spectacles witnessed amid the lapse of ages from the windows of the Canongate, none was perhaps more startling and pitiful than the humiliating procession which conducted the great Marquis of Montrose to his terrible doom.

On the 18th of May, 1650, he was brought across the Forth to Leith, after his defeat and capture by the Covenanters at the battle of Invercarron, where he had displayed the royal standard; and it is impossible now to convey an adequate idea of the sensation excited in the city, when the people became aware that the Graham, the victor in so many battles, and the slayer of so many thousands of the best troops of the Covenant, was almost at their gates.

Placed on a cart-horse, he was brought in by the eastern barrier of the city, as it was resolved, by the influence of his rival and enemy, Argyle, to protract the spectacle of his humiliation as long as possible, by compelling him to traverse the entire length of the excited and tumultuous metropolis, by the Canongate and High Street, "overlooked by the loftiest houses in Europe, with their forestairs, balconies, bartizans, and outshots, that afforded every facility for beholding the spectacle. On this day the whole length of that vast thoroughfare was one living mass of human beings; but for one who had come to pity, there were more than a hundred whose hearts were filled with a tiger-like ferocity, which the clergy had inspired to a dangerous degree, and for the most ungenerous purpose."

The women of the kail-market and the "saints of the Bowhead" were all there, their tongues trembling with abuse, and their hands full of stones or mud to launch at the head of the fallen Cavalier, who passed through the Water Gate at four in the afternoon, greeted by a storm of yells. Seated on a lofty hurdle, he was bound with cords so tightly that he was unable to raise his hands to save his face; preceded by the magistrates in their robes, he was bareheaded, his hat having been torn from him. Though in the prime of manhood and perfection of manly beauty, we are told that he "looked pale, worn, and hollow-eyed, for many of the wounds he had received at Invercarron were yet green and smarting. A single horse drew the hurdle, and thereon sat the executioner of the city, clad in his ghastly and sable livery, and wearing his bonnet as a mark of disrespect." He was escorted by the city guard, under the notorious Major Weir—Weir the wizard, whose terrible fate has been recorded elsewhere.

In front marched a number of Cavalier prisoners, bareheaded and bound with cords. Many of the people now shed tears on witnessing this spectacle; but, says Kincaid, they were publicly rebuked by the clergy, "who declaimed against this movement of rebel nature, and reproached them with their profane tenderness;" while the "Wigton Papers" state that how even the widows and the mothers of those who had fallen in his wars wept for Montrose, who looked around him with the profoundest serenity as he proceeded up the Canongate, even when he came to Moray House—

" Then, as the Graham looked upward, he met the ugly
    smile
Of him who sold his king for gold, the master-fiend
    Argyle ! "

On the broad stone balcony which there projects into the street was Argyle, with a gay bridal party in their brave dresses. His son, Lord Lorne, had just been wedded to the Earl of Moray's daughter,

Lady Mary Stuart, and the young couple were there, with the Marchioness, the Countess of Haddington, Sir Archibald Johnston of Warriston, and others, to exult over the fallen Royalist. "Their malice was not confined to that," says Monteith of Salmonet; "they caused the cart to be stopped for some time before the Earl of Moray's house, where, by an unparalleled baseness, Argyle, with the chief men of his cabal, who never durst look Montrose in the face while he had his sword in his hand, appeared in the balcony in order to feed merrily their sight with a spectacle which struck horror into all good men. But Montrose astonished them with his looks, and his resolution confounded them."

Then with broad vulgarity the marchioness spat full in his face! Argyle shrank back at this, and an English Cavalier who stood among the crowd below reviled him sharply, while Lorne and his bride continued to toy and smile in the face of the people. ("Wigton Papers.")

So protracted was this melancholy spectacle that seven o'clock had struck before the hurdle reached the gate of the Tolbooth, where Montrose, when unbound, gave the executioner a gold coin, saying —" This is your reward, my man, for driving the cart."

On the following day, Sunday, the ministers in their pulpits, according to Wishart, rebuked the people for not having stoned him. One declared that "he was a faggot of hell, and that he already saw him burning," while he was constantly taunted by Major Weir as "a dog, atheist, and murderer."

The story of Montrose's execution on the 21st of May, when he was hanged at the Cross on a gibbet thirty feet high, with the record of his battles suspended from his neck, how he died with glorious magnanimity and was barbarously quartered, belongs to the general annals of the nation; but the City Treasurer's account contains some curious items connected with that great legal tragedy :—

		£	s.	d.
1650. Ffebruar.	To making a scaffold at ye Cross for burning ye Earl of Montrose's papers	2	8	0
May 13.	For making a seat on a cart to carry him from ye Water Gate to ye Tolbooth	12	16	0
„	For making a high new gallows and double leather, and setting up a galbert	12	8	4
„	Pd. 6 workmen for carrying ye trunk of his body and burying it in ye Burrow-muir	2	0	0
„	Pd. the Lockman for making sd. grave deeper and covering it again	1	16	0
„	Pd. for sharping the axe for striking away the head, legs, and arms from the body	0	12	0

As a set-off against these items, we have the following, in 1660-1, when Argyle's fate came :—

To Alexander Davidson for a new axe to ye
  Maiden, and is to maintain it all ye days of his
  life 70 12 0
To 4 Drummers when *Argyle* and *Swinton* were
  brought from Leith 14 8 0
To 17 extra Drummers, 2 days, when Montrose
  was buried and Argyle executed   .   .   . 21 12 0

The marquis was interred amid great pomp in the Church of St. Giles at the Restoration; but when a search was made for his remains in the Chepman aisle, in April, 1879, no trace of them whatever could be found there.

Amid the gloom and horror of scenes such as these executions, and the general events of the wars of the Covenant, all traces of gaiety, and especially of theatrical entertainments, disappeared in Edinburgh, as forbidden displays; but in January, 1659, the citizens were regaled with the sight of a travelling dromedary, the first that had ever been in Scotland. Nicoll describes it as "ane heigh great beast, callit ane dummodary, quhilk being keepit clos in the Canongate, none had a sight of it, without three pence the person. . . . . It was very big, and of great height, cloven futted like unto a kow, and on the bak ane saitt, as it were a sadill to sit on. Thair was brocht in with it ane lytill baboun, faced lyke unto an aip."

In 1686 the public attendance at mass by some of the officers of state excited a tumult in the city, and many persons of rank were insulted on returning therefrom by the rioters. One of these, a journeyman baker, was, by order of the Privy Council, whipped through the Canongate, and ultimately the Foot Guards had to fire on the mob that assembled.

In that year an Act of Parliament empowered the magistrates to impose a tax of £500 sterling yearly, for three years, to cleanse the town and Canongate, and free both from beggars; and in 1687 the whole members of the College of Justice voluntarily offered to bear their full share of this tax, and appointed two of their body to be present when it was levied.

In 1692 we find an instance in the Canongate of one of the many troubles which in those days arose from corporation privileges, by which the poor and industrious tradesman was made the victim of monopoly.

In the open ground which now surrounds Milton House, there stood in those days the mansion of the Earls of Roxburgh, surrounded by a beautiful garden. In October, 1692, William Somerville, a wright-burgess of the city, was engaged on some repairs in this house, when Thomas Kinloch, Deacon of the Wrights in the Canongate, came with others, and violently carried off all the tools of Somerville and his workmen, on the plea that they were not freemen of the burgh; and when the tools were demanded formally, two days after, they were withheld.

Robert, Earl of Roxburgh (who afterwards died on his travels abroad), was then a minor, but his curators resented the proceedings of Kinloch, and sued him for riot and oppression. Apparently, if the Roxburgh mansion had been subject to the jurisdiction of the Canongate, the Privy Council would have given no redress; but when the earl's ancestor, in 1636, had given up the superiority of the Canongate, as he reserved his house to be holden of the Crown, it was found that the local corporation had no right to interfere with his workmen, and Somerville's tools were restored to him by order of the Council.

Earl Robert was succeeded in this house by his brother John, fifth Earl and first Duke of Roxburgh, K.G., who sold his Union vote for £500, became Secretary of State for Scotland in 1716, and died in 1741.

Long ere that time the effect of the Union had done its worst upon the old court burgh. Maitland, writing in 1753, says :—"This place has suffered more by the union of the kingdoms than all the other parts of Scotland : for having, before that period, been the residence of the chief of the Scottish nobility, it was then in a flourishing condition ; but being deserted by them, many of their houses are fallen down, and others in a ruinous condition ; it is in a piteous case !"

Five years after the Union we find a London coach announced as starting from the Canongate, the advertisement for which, with regard to expedition, comfort, and economy, presents a curious contrast to the announcements of to-day, and is worth giving at length, as we find it in the *Newcastle Courant* of October, 1712.

"Edinburgh, Berwick, Newcastle, Durham, and London Stage-coach begins on Monday, 13th October, 1712. All that desire to pass from Edinbro' to London, or from London to Edinbro', or any place on that road, let them repair to Mr. John Baillie's, at the *Coach and Horses* at the head of the Canongate, every Saturday, or the *Black Swan* in Holborn, every other Monday, at both of which places they may be received in a stage-coach which performs the whole journey in thirteen days, without any stoppage (if God permit), having eighty able horses to perform the whole stage. Each passenger paying £4 10s. for the whole journey, alowing each 20 lbs. weight, and all above to pay 6d. per lb. The coach sets off at six in the morning. Performed by Henry Harrison, Nich. Speighl, Rob. Garbe, Rich. Croft."

When we consider the cost of food on a thirteen days' journey, the fees to successive guards and drivers, the small allowance of luggage, and the

Canongate, every other Tuesday. "In the winter to set out from London and Edinburgh every other Monday morning, and to go to Burrowbridge on Saturday night; and to set out from thence on Monday morning, and to get to London and Edinburgh on Saturday night. Passengers to pay as usual. Performed (if God permits) by your dutiful

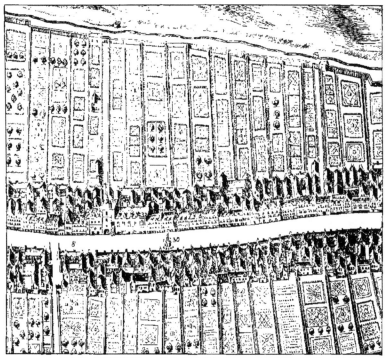

THE CANONGATE—CONTINUATION EASTWARD OF PLAN ON PAGE 5. (*From Gordon of Rothiemay's Map.*)
8, Moray House; 30, Canongate Cross; 32, Canongate Tolbooth.

overcharge, the contrast of travelling in the days of Anne and Victoria seems great indeed.

In July, 1754, the *Edinburgh Courant* advertises the stage-coach, drawn by six horses, with a postillion on one of the leaders, as "a new, genteel, two-end glass machine, hung on steel springs; exceeding light and easy, to go in ten days in summer and twelve in winter," setting out from Hosea Eastgate's, at the *Coach and Horses*, Dean Street, Soho, and from John Somerville's, in the

servant, HOSEA EASTGATE. Care is taken of small parcels, *according to their value.*"

A few years before this move in the way of progress, the Canongate had been the scene of a little religious persecution; thus we find that on a Sunday in the April of 1722 the Duchess Dowager of Gordon, Elizabeth Howard, daughter of the Duke of Norfolk, venturing to have mass celebrated at her house in the Canongate for herself and some fifty other Roman Catholics, Bailie Hawthorn, magistrate of the burgh, broke open the doors at the head of an armed party, and seized the whole. The ladies he permitted to depart on bail, but John Wallace, the priest, he cast into prison ; this he did all the more zealously that some thirty-five years before the latter had been—according to Wodrow —a Protestant clergyman.   Thomas Kennedy, the Lord Advocate, refused bail for him, though five persons of rank offered it.   It was at length taken to the extent of 5,000 merks, and failing to stand his trial under the statute of 1700, according to Arnot's "Criminal Trials," he was outlawed.

Notwithstanding the gloom, ruin, and desertion of which Maitland wrote in 1753, many persons of rank and note continued to linger in the Canongate, and a curious list of them is given by Robert Chambers, as taken down by "the late Mr. Chal-

mers Izett, whose memory extended back to 1769." It includes two dukes, sixteen earls, two dowager countesses, seven lords, and seven lords of session, thirteen baronets, four commanders of the forces in Scotland, and five eminent men— Adam Smith, Drs. Young, Dugald Stewart, Gardner, and Gregory ; and he adds that the last blow was given to the locality by the opening of the road along the Calton Hill in 1817, which rendered it no longer the avenue of approach to the city from the east.

Among the last of the old *noblesse* who resided in it was the Lady Janet Sinclair, daughter of William, Lord Strathnaver (who died in July, 1720). She was the relict of George Sinclair of Ulbster, and mother of Sir John Sinclair, the famous agriculturist. She died in her seventy-eighth year, in June, 1795.

CHAPTER III.

THE CANONGATE—(*continued*).

Closes and Alleys on the North Side—Flesh-market and Coull's Closes—Canongate High School—Rae's Close—Kinloch's Lodging—New Street and its Residents—Hall of the Shoemakers—Sir Thos. Dalyell—The Canongate Washhouse—Panmure House—Hannah Robertson—The White Horse Hostel—The Water Gate.

AMONG the earliest breaches made in the Old Town by the City Improvement Trustees were those at the head of the Canongate, where several closes were swept away, especially on the north side, where we now find the entrances to Jeffrey and Cranston Streets.

The first of these was the old Fleshmarket Close (which adjoined Leith Wynd on the east), once a thickly-peopled locality, but a *cul-de-sac*, the bottom of which was blocked up by ancient buildings. On the west side of this squalid and filthy alley there stood a mansion, the interior of which presented undoubted evidence of its magnificence in the sixteenth century, as it had among its many carved details a beautifully canopied, cusped, and ornate Gothic niche, with two shields, of which a drawing has been preserved, and which, in details, is identical with those found in the palace of Mary of Guise.   Traditionally it was named "the *old* Parliament House," wherein it is supposed the Regent Lennox, with Morton, Mar, Glencairn, and others, held their meetings in the troublesome time subsequent to the enforced abdication of Queen Mary.   At the foot of the close there was once an opening to the old Flesh-market of the Canongate—hence its name—an area shown in Edgar's map as entered by a gate, and measuring about 100 feet by 60.

Coull's Close lay next, with a very narrow en-

trance, and latterly it opened into Macdowal Street, and long exhibited—ere it absolutely tumbled into ruins—many a sculptured doorway, and many an inscription dictated by the piety or pride of its former inhabitants, of whom not even the name can now be traced.

The High School Close adjoined it, so named as leading to a large and handsome edifice which stood in an open court at its foot, and was long occupied as the burgh High School.   In the central pediment, which bore a sundial, was the date 1704, and Dutch-looking dormer windows studded its roof, but the school had a date far beyond the days of Queen Anne ; it appears to have been founded by the monks of Holyrood, and is referred to in a charter granted by James V. in 1529; therein mention is made of Henryson, clerk and orator of the monastery, having taught with success in the grammar school of the Canongate, and many notices of this old educational establishment occur in the Register of the Burgh, printed in the "Maitland Club Miscellany."

Under date 5th of April, 1580, Gilbert Tailyour, schoolmaster, renounced his gift of the school, given him for his lifetime by Adam Bothwell, Bishop of Orkney, in favour of the bailies and Council, who therefore restored it to him.

Of Midcommon Close, a narrow, blocked-up, and tortuous alley, little more is known than the name;

but there once stood on its eastern side a stately old tenement, bearing the date 1614, with this pious legend: I. TAKE. THE. LORD. JESUS. AS. MY. ONLY. ALL. SUFFICIENT. PORTION. TO. CONTENT. ME. This was cut in massive Roman letters, and the house was adorned by handsome dormer windows and moulded stringcourses; but of the person who dwelt therein no memory remains. And the same must be said of the edifices in the closes called Morocco and Logan's, and several others.

Between these two lies Rae's Close, very dark and narrow, leading only to a house with a back green, beyond which can be seen the Calton Hill. In the sixteenth century this alley was the only open thoroughfare to the north between Leith Wynd and the Water Gate. In 1568 the foot of it was closed by a stone wall for security, and there was ordered to be "cast ane stank at the slope yatt comis fra the Justice Clark landis to the Abbaye, on the south side of this burghe." In 1574 a gate with a secure lock was placed upon it for the same purpose. In 1647 only three open thoroughfares are shown to the north—one the Tolbooth Wynd—and all are closed by arched gates in a wall bounding the Canongate on the north, and lying parallel with a long watercourse flowing away towards Craigentinnie, and still extant.

Kinloch's Close, described in 1856 as "short, dark, and horrible," took its name from Henry Kinloch, a wealthy burgess of the Canongate in the days of Queen Mary, who committed to his hospitality, in 1565, when she is said to have acceded to the League of Bayonne, the French ambassadors M. de Rambouillet and Clernau, who came on a mission from the Court of France. Their ostensible visit, however, was more probably to invest Darnley with the order of St. Michael. They had come through England with a train of thirty-six mounted gentlemen. After presenting themselves before the king and queen at Holyrood, according to the "Diurnal of Occurrents," they "there after depairtit to Heny Kynloches lugeing in the Cannogait besyid Edinburgh."

A few days after Darnley was solemnly invested with the collar of St. Michael in the abbey church; and on the 11th of February the ambassadors were banqueted, and a masked ball was given, when "the Queenis Grace and all her Maries and ladies were cled in men's apparell," and each of them presented a sword, "brawlie and maist artificiallie made and embroiderit with gold, to the said ambassatour and his gentlemen." Next day they were banqueted in the castle by the Earl of Mar, and on the next ensuing they took their departure for France via England.

Kinloch's mansion and that which adjoined it—the abode of the Earls of Angus—were pulled down about 1760, when New Street was built, "a curious sample of fashionable modern improvement, prior to the bold scheme of the New Town," and first called Young Street, according to Kincaid. Though sorely faded and decayed, it still presents a series of semi-aristocratic, detached, and not indigent mansions of the plain form peculiar to the time. Among its inhabitants were Lords Kames and Hailes, Sir Philip Ainslie, the Lady Betty Anstruther, Christian Ramsay daughter of the poet, Dr. Young the eminent physician, and others.

Henry Home, Lord Kames, who was raised to the bench in 1752, occupied a self-contained house at the head of the street facing the Canongate on the east side, and then deemed one of the best in the city; thus strangers were taken by their friends to see it as one of the local sights, with its front of grooved ashlar-work. Born in 1695, he early exhibited great talent with profound legal knowledge, and the mere enumeration of his works on law and history would fill a large page. He was of a playful disposition, and fond of practical jokes; but during the latter part of his life he entertained a nervous dread that he would outlive his noble faculties, and was pleased to find that by the rapid decay of his frame he would escape that dire calamity; and he died, after a brief illness, in 1782, in the eighty-seventh year of his age. The great Dr. Hunter, of the Tron church, afterwards lived and died in this house.

Lord Hailes, to whom we have referred elsewhere, resided during his latter years in New Street; but prior to his promotion to the bench he generally lived at New Hailes. His house, No. 23, was latterly possessed by Mr. Ruthven, the ingenious improver of the Ruthven printing-press.

Christian Ramsay, the daughter of "honest Allan," and so named from her mother, Christian Ross, lived for many years in New Street. She was an amiable and kind-hearted woman, and possessed something of her father's gift of verse. In her seventy-fourth year she was thrown down by a hackney-coach and had her leg broken; yet she recovered, and lived to be eighty-eight. Leading a solitary life, she took a great fancy to cats, and besides supporting many in her house, cosily disposed of in bandboxes, she laid out food for others around her house. "Not a word of obloquy would she listen to against the species," says the author of "Traditions of Edinburgh," "alleging, when any wickedness of a cat was spoken of, that the animal must have acted under provocation, for by nature, she asserted, they were harmless.

Often did her maid go with morning messages to her friends, inquiring, with her compliments, after their pet cats. Good Miss Ramsay was also a friend to horses, and indeed to all creatures. When she observed a carter ill-treating his horse she would march up to him, tax him with cruelty, and by the very earnestness of her remonstrances arrest the barbarian's hand. So, also, when she saw one labouring in the street with the appearance of defective diet, she would send rolls to its master, entreating him to feed the animal. These peculiarities, though a little eccentric, are not unpleasing; and I cannot be sorry to record those of the daughter of one whose head and heart were an honour to his country."

The hideous chapel of ease built in New Street in 1794 occupied the site of the houses of Henry Kinloch and the Earls of Angus, the latter of which formed during the eighteenth century the banking office of the unfortunate firm of Douglas, Heron, and Co., whose failure spread ruin and dismay far and wide in Scotland.

Little Jack's Close, a narrow alley leading by a bend into New Street, and Big Jack's Close, which led to an open court, adjoin the thoroughfare of 1760, and both are doubtless named from some forgotten citizen or speculative builder of other days.

In the former stood the hall of the once wealthy corporation of the Cordiners or Shoemakers of the Canongate, on the west side, adorned with all the insignia of the craft, and furnished for their convivialia with huge tables and chairs of oak, in addition to a carved throne, surmounted by a crowned paring-knife, and dated 1682, for the solemn inauguration of King Crispin on St. Crispin's Day, the 25th of October.

This corporation can be traced back to the 10th of June, 1574, when William Quhite was elected Deacon of the Cordiners in the Canongate, in place of the late Andrew Purvis.

It was of old their yearly custom to elect a king, who held his court in this Corporation Hall, from whence, after coronation, he was borne in procession through the streets, attended by his subject souters clad in fantastic habiliments. Latterly he was conducted abroad on a finely-caparisoned horse, and clad in ermined robes, attended by mock officers of state and preceded by a champion in armour; and in fooleries such as these the funds of the corporation became, in time, utterly exhausted before the close of the last century.

The Shoemakers' Close was, at the end of the last century, the abode of a curious dwarf, known

as Geordie Cranstoun, who figures twice in Kay's remarkable portraits.

In Big Jack's Close there was extant, until within a few years ago, the town mansion of General Sir Thomas Dalyell of Binns, commander-in-chief of the Scottish forces, whose beard remained uncut after the death of Charles I., and who raised the Scots Greys on the 25th of November, 1681, and clad them first in grey uniform, and at their head served as a merciless persecutor of the outlawed Covenanters, with a zest born of his service in Russia. The chief apartment in this house has been described as a large hall, with an arched or coach roof, adorned, says Wilson, with a painting of the sun in the centre, surrounded by gilded rays on an azure dome. Sky, clouds, and silver stars filled up the remaining space. The large windows were partially closed with oak shutters in the old Scottish fashion. " The kitchen also was worthy of notice, for a fireplace formed of a plain circular arch, of such unusual dimensions that popular credulity might have assigned it for the perpetration of those rites it had ascribed to him of spitting and roasting his miserable captives ! . . . . . A chapel formerly stood on the site of the open court, but all traces of it were removed in 1779. It is not at all inconsistent with the character of the fierce old Cavalier that he should have erected a private chapel for his own use."

It was to this house in Big Jack's Close that the Rev. John Blackadder was brought a prisoner in 1681, guarded by soldiers under Johnstone, the town major, and accompanied by his son Thomas, who died a merchant in New England, and where that interview took place which is related in "Blackadder's Memories," by D. A. Crichton :—

"I have brought you a prisoner," said Major Johnstone.

"Take him to the guard," said Dalyell, who was about to walk forth.

On this, the poor divine, whose emotions must have been far from enviable in such a terrible presence, said, timidly, " May I speak with you a little, sir ? "

"You have already spoken too much, sir," replied Dalyell, whose blood always boiled at the sight of a Covenanter, "and I should hang you with my own hands over that outshot ! "

On this, Major Johnstone, dreading what might ensue, took hastily away his prisoner, who, by order of the Privy Council, was sent to the Bass Rock, escorted by a party of the Life Guards, and there he died, a captive, in his seventieth year.

In the Tolbooth Wynd, on the east side thereof and near the foot, was built the old Charity Workhouse of the burgh. It was established by subscription, and opened for the reception of the poor in 1761, the expense being defrayed by collections at the church doors and voluntary contributions, without any assessment whatever ; and in those days the managers were chosen annually from the public at the foot of Monroe's Close, and bore, till within the last few years, the appearance of those partly quadrangular manor-houses so common in Scotland during the seventeenth century. It became greatly altered after being brought into juxtaposition with the prosaic details of the Panmure Iron

TOLBOOTH WYND.

societies of the Canongate. The city plan of 1647 shows but seven houses within the gate, on the west side of the Wynd, and open gardens on the other, eastward nearly to the Water Gate.

Panmure Close, the third alley to the eastward— one with a good entrance, and generally more pleasant than most of those narrow old streets—is so named from its having been the access to Panmure House, an ancient mansion, which still remains Foundry, but it formed the town residence of the Earls of Panmure, the fourth of whom, James, who distinguished himself as a volunteer at the siege of Luxemburg, and was Privy Councillor to James VII., a bitter opponent of the Union, lost his title and estates after the battle of Sheriffmuir, and died, an exile, in Paris. His nephew, William Maule, who served in the Scots Guards at Dettingen and Fontenoy, obtained an Irish peerage in 1743 as Earl

Panmure of Forth, and was the last who possessed this house, in which he was resident in the middle of the last century, and was succeeded in it by the Countess of Aberdeen.

From 1778 till his death, in 1790, it formed the residence of Adam Smith, author of "The Wealth of Nations," after he came to Edinburgh as Commissioner of the Customs, an appointment obtained by the friendship of the Duke of Buccleuch. A few days before his death, at Panmure House, he gave orders to destroy all his manuscripts except some detached essays, which were afterwards published by his executors, Drs. Joseph Black and James Hutton, and his library, a valuable one, he left to his nephew, Lord Reston. From that old mansion the philosopher was borne to his grave in an obscure nook of the Canongate churchyard. During the last years of his blameless life his bachelor household had been managed by a female cousin, Miss Jeanie Douglas, who acquired a great control over him.

At the end of Panmure Close was the mansion of John Hunter, a wealthy burgess, who was Treasurer of the Canongate in 1568, and who built it in 1565, when Mary was on the throne. Wilson refers to it as the earliest private edifice in the burgh, and says "it consists, like other buildings of the period, of a lower erection of stone with a forestair leading to the first floor, and an ornamental turnpike within, affording access to the upper chambers. At the top of a very steep wooden stair, constructed alongside of the latter, a very rich specimen of carved oak panelling remains in good preservation, adorned with the Scottish lion, displayed within a broad wreath and surrounded by a variety of ornaments. The doorway of the inner turnpike bears on the sculptured lintel the initials I. H., a shield charged with a chevron, and a hunting horn in base, and the date 1565." It bore also a comb with six teeth. It was demolished in August, 1853.

A little lower down are Big and Little Lochend Closes, which join each other near the bottom and run into the north back of the Canongate. In the former are some good houses, but of no great antiquity. One of these was occupied by Mr. Gordon of Carlton in 1784; and in the other, during the close of the last and first years of the present century, there resided a remarkable old lady, named Mrs. Hannah Robertson, who was well known in her time as a reputed grand-daughter of Charles II.

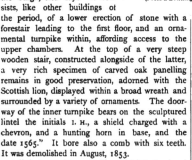

LINTEL OF JOHN HUNTER'S HOUSE, PANMURE CLOSE.
(From a Drawing by the Author.)

From her published memoir—which, after its first appearance in 1792, reached a tenth edition in 1806, and was printed by James Tod in Forrester's Wynd—and from other sources, we learn that she was the widow of Robert Robertson, a merchant in Perth, and was the daughter of a burgess named George Swan, son of Charles II. and Dorothea Helena, daughter of John Kirkhoven, Dutch baron of Ruppa, the beautiful Countess of Derby, who had an intrigue with the king during the protracted absence of her husband in Holland, Charles, eighth earl, who died in 1672 without heirs.

According to her narrative, the child was given to nurse to the wife of Swan, a gunner at Windsor, a woman whose brother, Bartholomew Gibson, was the king's farrier at Edinburgh; and it would further appear that the latter obtained on trust for George Swan, from Charles II. or his brother the Duke of York, a grant of lands in New Jersey, where Gibson's son died about 1750, as would appear from a notice in the London Chronicle for 1771.

Be all this as it may, the old lady referred to was a great favourite with all those of Jacobite proclivities, and at the dinners of the Jacobite Club always sat on the right hand of the president, till her death, which occurred in Little Lochend Close in 1808, when she had attained her eighty-fourth year, and a vast concourse attended her funeral, which took place in the Friends' burial-place at the Pleasance. Unusually tall in stature, and beautiful even in old age, her figure, with black velvet capuchin and cane, was long familiar in the streets of Edinburgh.

From a passage in the "Edinburgh Historical Register" for 1791–2, she would appear to have been a futile applicant for a pension to the Lords of the Treasury, though she had many powerful friends, including the Duchess of Gordon and the Countess of Northesk, to whom she dedicated a book named "The Lady's School of Arts."

One of the most picturesque and interesting houses in the Canongate is one situated in what was called Davidson's Close, the old "White Horse Hostel," on a dormer window of which is the date 1603. It was known as the "White Horse" a century and more before the accession of the House of Hanover, and is traditionally said to have taken its name from a favourite white palfrey when the range of stables that form its basement had been occupied as the royal mews. The adjacent Water Gate took its name from a great horse-pond which was, no doubt, an appendage of this establishment. In 1639, when Charles I. had made his first peace with the Covenanters, and came temporarily to Berwick, he sent messages to the chief nobles of the National Church party to have a conference with him.

In obedience to this, with their various retinues, they were all mounting their horses in the yard of this inn, to which a kind of arched *porte-cochère* gives access from the main street, when a mob, taught wisely by the clergy to distrust a monarch who was under English influences, compelled them to desist and abandon their intended journey. The Earl of Montrose alone broke through all restraint; he went to the king, and from thenceforward was lost to the cause of the Covenant for ever.

The invariable mode of a gentleman setting out for London in those days was to come to the White Horse with his saddle-bags, boots, and gambadoes, and there engage a suitable roadster to convey him the whole way. In more recent times it was associated with the Cavalier officers and Highland gentleman of Charles Edward's picturesque court, and the quarters of Scott's hero, Captain Waverley. According to a passage in the *Gentleman's Magazine* for 1786, there were then set apart, "in the inns at Edinburgh, Glasgow, &c., English rooms, where English travellers could eat and converse together."

When the White Horse ceased to be an inn is unknown, but the vicinity is connected with the memory of more than one Episcopal dignitary. A tenement which serves to complete the courtyard is pointed out as the residence of John Paterson, Bishop of Edinburgh in 1679, a special object of hate to the Covenanters, as he had been chaplain to the cruel and brutal Duke of Lauderdale.

After his translation to Glasgow in 1687, he was succeeded by Bishop Alexander Rose, who was ejected in the following year by the Revolution party—the last survivor of established Episcopacy in Edinburgh. He has been described by Bishop Keith as a man of sweet disposition and most venerable aspect. He died on the 20th of March, 1720, in his sister's house in the Canongate. "Tradition," says Chambers, "points to the floor, immediately above the *porte-cochère* (of the White Horse), by which the stable-yard is entered, as the humble mansion in which the bishop breathed his last. I know at least one person who never goes past the place without an emotion of respect, remembering the self-abandoning devotion of the Scottish prelates to their engagements at the Revolution."

A barrier called the Water Gate, existing now only in name, closed the lower end of the street on the north side. It was by this avenue that the English entered Edinburgh in 1544, and advanced to their futile attack on the Castle. It was its principal entrance from the east, not only to the Canongate, but to the whole city prior to the North Bridge; nearly all public entrances were made by it, and many state prisoners, on their way to execution, have passed through it; but the Water Gate, and the "Post and yet passand in to the Abbaye Knok," have long been numbered with the past. A single rib, or arch of wood, surmounted by a ball, indicated the locality latterly, till it was blown down in 1822.

According to the "City Records," the Council granted to the Baron Bailie, of the Canongate, as a gift of escheat, all the goods and chattels of witches found therein; accordingly that official, in 1661, was not long in discovering a certain Barbara Mylne, who Janet Allen, burnt for witchcraft, once saw enter by the Water Gate in the "likeness of a catt, and did change her garment under her owin staire, and went into her house."

Canongate dues were long levied at the site of the gate after it had ceased to exist; but on the fall of the ornamental structure referred to, the fishwomen of Musselburgh and Newhaven stoutly refused payment of all burghal customs on the contents of their creels, till the magistrates again restored—but for a time only—the arch of wood across the street.

CHAPTER IV.

THE CANONGATE (*continued*).

Closes and Alleys on the South Side—Chessel's Court The Canongate Theatre—Riots Therein ."Douglas" Performed—Mr. Digges and Mrs. Bellamy—St. John's Close—St. John's Street and its Residents—The Hammerman's Close Horse Wynd, Abbey—House of Lord Napier.

LIKE most burghs in former ages, the Canongate had a piper, of whom repeated notices occur in the treasurer's accounts, with reference at times to his "claise and pasements thereto." This official was superseded in 1587 by a drummer, whose duty it was to beat through the streets at "ffour houres in the morning;" and of the sanitary state of the community in those days some idea may be gathered from the fact that swine ran loose in the Canongate till 1583, when an attempt was made to put down the nuisance. In the city this was done earlier, as we find that in 1490 the magistrates ordain "the lokman, quhairwer he fyndis ony swyne betwix the Castell and the Netherbow upon the Gaitt," to seize them, with a fine of fourpence upon each sow taken.

Again, in 1506, swine found in the streets or kennels are to be slaughtered by the "lokman" and escheated; and in 1513 swine were again forbidden to wander, under pain of the owners being banished, and each sow to be escheat. At the same time fruit was forbidden to be sold on the streets, or in crames, "holden thairupon, under the pain of escheitt"—that is, of forfeit.

In 1562 no flesh was to be eaten or even cooked on Friday or Saturday, under a penalty of ten pounds; and in 1563 all markets were forbidden in the streets upon Sunday.

Among the first operations of the Improvement Trust were the demolitions at the head of St. Mary's Wynd, including with them the removal of the Closes of Hume and Boyd, the first alleys at the head of the street on the south side, and the erection on their site of lofty and airy tenements in a species of Scottish style.

Four alleys to the eastward, Bell's, Gillon's, Gibbs' and Pirie's Closes, all narrow, dark, and filthy, have been without history or record; but Chessel's Court, numbered as 240, exhibits a very superior style of architecture, and in 1788 was the scene of that daring robbery of the Excise Office which brought to the gallows the famous Deacon Brodie and his assistant, thus closing a long career of secret villainy, his ingenuity as a mechanic giving him every facility in the pursuits to which he addicted himself. "It was then customary for the shopkeepers of Edinburgh to hang their keys upon a nail at the back of their doors, or at least to take no pains in concealing them during the day. Brodie used to take impressions of them in putty or clay, a piece of which he used to carry in the palm of his hand. He kept a blacksmith in his pay, who forged exact copies of the keys he wanted, and with these it was his custom to open the shops of his fellow-tradesmen during the night."

In a house of Chessel's Court there died, in 1854, an aged maiden lady of a very ancient Scottish stock—Elizabeth Wardlaw, daughter of Sir William Wardlaw, Bart., of the line of Balmule and Pitreavie in Fifeshire.

In the Playhouse Close, a *cul-de-sac*, and its neighbour the Old Playhouse Close, a narrow and gloomy alley, we find the cradle of the legitimate drama in Edinburgh.

In the former, in 1747, a theatre was opened, on such a scale as was deemed fitting for the Scottish capital, where the drama had skulked in holes and corners since the viceregal court had departed from Holyrood, in the days of the Duke of Albany and York. From 1727 till after 1753 itinerant companies, despite the anathemas of the clergy, used with some success the Tailors' Hall in the Cowgate, which held, in professional phraseology, from £40 to £45 nightly. In the first-named year a Mr. Tony Alston endeavoured to start a theatre, in the same house which saw the failure of poor Allan Ramsay's attempt, but the Society of High Constables endeavoured to suppress his "abominable stage plays;" and when the clergy joined issue with the Court of Session against him, his performances had to cease. But, according to Wodrow, there had been some talk of building another theatre as early as 1728.

In 1746 the foundation of the theatre within a back area (near St. John's Cross), now called the Playhouse Close, was laid by Mr. John Ryan, a London actor of considerable repute in his day, who had to contend with the usual opposition of the ignorant or illiberal, and that lack of prudence and thrift incidental to his profession generally. The house was capable of holding £70; the box seats were half-a-crown, the pit one-and-sixpence; and for several years it was the scene of good acting under Lee, Digges, Mrs. Bellamy, and Mrs. Ward.

After the affair of 1745 the audiences were apt to display a spirit of political dissension. On the anniversary of the battle of Culloden, 1749, some English officers who were in the theatre commanded the orchestra, in an insolent and unruly manner, to strike up an obnoxious air known as *Culloden;* but in a spirit of opposition, and to please the people, the musicians played "You're welcome, Charlie Stuart." The military at once drew their swords and attacked the defenceless musicians and players, but were assailed by the audience with torn-up benches and every missile that could be procured. The officers now attempted to storm the galleries; but the doors were secured. They were then vigorously attacked in the rear by the Highland chairmen with their poles, disarmed, and most ignominiously drubbed and expelled; but in consequence of this and similar disturbances, bills were put up notifying that no music would be played but such as the management selected.

Another disturbance ensued soon after, occasioned by the performance of Garrick's farce, "High

Life below Stairs," which the fraternity of footmen bitterly resented, and resolved to stop. On the second night of its being announced, Mr. Love, one of the management, came upon the stage and read a letter containing the most bitter denunciations of vengeance upon all concerned if the piece should be performed. It was, nevertheless, proceeded with, and the gentlemen who were in the theatre having provided accommodation for their servants in the gallery, the moment the farce began "a prodigious noise was heard from that quarter."

The liverymen were ordered to be silent, but without success. Their masters, assisted by some others of the audience, endeavoured to quiet them by force; swords and sticks were freely resorted to, but it was not until after a tough battle that the gentlemen of the cloth were fairly expelled; "and servants from this time were deprived of the freedom of the theatre."

About 1752 Mr. Lee purchased the Canongate Theatre from the original proprietors for £648 and £100 per annum during the lives of the lessees; but he failed in his engagement, and James Callender, a merchant of the city, undertook to conduct the business, with Mr. Digges as stage manager. Callender soon after resigned his charge to Mr. David Beatt, another citizen, who had ventured in the past time to read Prince Charles's proclamations at the Cross. Mr. Love also withdrew from the charge, and was succeeded by Mr. John Dawson of Newcastle; but dissensions arose among the performers themselves. Two parties were formed in the theatre, which, during a performance of "Hamlet," they utterly wrecked and demolished, and set on fire in a riot, to the supreme delight of all opponents of the drama.

Legal actions and counter-actions ensued; the house was again fitted up, and nothing of interest

THE WATER GATE. (*After a Drawing by Storer, published in 1820.*)

occurred till the night of the 14th December, 1756, when, to the dismay of all Scotland, there was brought out the tragedy of "Douglas," written by the pen of a minister of the kirk!

The original cast was thus:—Douglas, Mr. Digges; Lord Randolph, Mr. Younger; Glenalvon, Mr. Love; Norval, Mr. Hayman; Lady Randolph, Mrs. Ward; Anna, Mrs. Hopkins.

With redoubled zeal the clergy returned to the assault, and though they could no more crush the players, they compelled John Home, the author of the obnoxious tragedy, to "renounce the orders that had been tarnished by a composition so unwonted and unclerical." Ultimately he became captain in the Buccleuch Fencibles, and lived long enough to see the prejudices of many of his countrymen pass away; but he was long viewed with obloquy. "To account for this extraordinary phenomenon," says Dr. Carlisle, "so far down in the eighteenth century, it is to be observed that not a few well-meaning people and all the zealots of the time were seriously offended with a clergyman for writing a tragedy, even with a virtuous tendency, and with his brethren for giving him countenance. They were joined by others out of mere *envy*."

The Presbytery of Edinburgh suspended all clergymen who had witnessed the representation of "Douglas," and at the same time "emitted an admonition and exhortation, levelled against *all* who frequented what they supposed to be the Temple of the *Father of Lies*, and ordered it to be read in all the churches within their bounds."

The personal elegance of Digges and the rare beauty of Mrs. Bellamy were traditionally remembered in the beginning of the present century, and made them even objects of interest to those by whom their scandalous life was regarded with just reprehension. They lived in a small country house at Bonnington, near Leith. It is remembered that Mrs. Bellamy was extremely fond of singing birds, and when visiting Glasgow was wont to have them carried by a porter all the way, lest they might suffer by the jolting of a carriage, and people wondered to hear of ten guineas being expended for such a purpose. "Persons under the social ban for their irregular lives often win the love of individuals by their benevolence and sweetness of disposition—qualities, it is to be remarked,

front land, through which an arch gives access to the old Playhouse Close, is a fine specimen of the Scottish street architecture in the time of Charles I. It has a row of dormer windows, with another of storm-windows on a steep roof, that reminds one of those in Bruges and Antwerp. Over a doorway within the close is an ornamental tablet, the inscription on which has become defaced, and the old theatre itself has long since given place to private dwellings. In one of these lived, in 1784,

CHESSEL'S BUILDINGS. (*From a Drawing by Storer, published in 1820.*)

not unlikely to have been concerned in their first trespasses. This was the case with Mrs. Bellamy. Her waiting-maid, Anne Waterstone, who is mentioned in her 'Memoirs,' lived many years after in Edinburgh, and continued to the last to adore the memory of her mistress. Nay, she was, from this cause, a zealous friend of all players, and would never allow a slighting remark upon them to pass unreproved. It was curious to find in a poor old Scotchwoman of the humbler class such a sympathy with the follies and eccentricities of the children of Thespis."

The erection of the New Theatre Royal in the extended royalty eclipsed its predecessor in the Canongate, which was deserted in 1767. The

a man named Wilson Gavin, whose name appears in "Peter Williamson's Directory" as an "Excellent Shoemaker and Leather Tormentor."

The adjoining alley, St. John's Close, is open towards St. John's Street. Narrow and ancient, it shows over a door-lintel on its west side the legend, within a sunk panel, THE LORD IS ONLY MY SUPORT. The doorway is but three feet wide.

Near this a spacious elliptical archway gives access to St. John's Street, so named with reference to St. John's Cross, a broad, airy, and handsome thoroughfare, "one of the heralds of the New Town," and associated with the names of many of the Scottish aristocracy who lingered in the old city, with judges and country gentlemen. By a date over a doorway in it, this street had been in progress in 1768.

At the head of the street, with its front windows overlooking the Canongate, is the house on the first floor of which was the residence of Mrs. Telfer of Scotstown, the sister of Tobias Smollett, who was her guest in 1766, on his second and last visit to his native country, and where, though in feeble health, he mixed with the best society of the capital, the men and manners of which he so graphically portrays in his last novel, "Humphrey Clinker," a work in which fact and fiction are curiously blended, and in which he mentions that he owed an introduction into the literary circles to Dr. Carlyle, the well-known incumbent of Inveresk.

Mrs. Telfer, though then a widow with moderate means, moved in good society. She has been described as a tall, sharp-visaged lady, with a hooked nose and a great partiality for whist. Her brother had then returned from that protracted Continental tour, the experiences of which are given in his "Travels through France and Italy," in two volumes. The novelist has been described as a tall and handsome man, somewhat prone to satirical innuendo, but with a genuine vein of humour, polished manners, and great urbanity. On the latter Dr. Carlyle particularly dwells, and refers to an occasion when Smollett supped in a tavern with himself, Hepburn of Keith, Home the author of "Douglas," Commissioner Cardonel, and others. The beautiful "Miss R——n," with whom Jerry Milford is described as dancing at the hunters' ball, was the grand-daughter of Susannah Countess of Eglinton, whose daughter Lady Susan became the wife of Renton of Lamerton in the Merse. The wife of the novelist, Anne Lascelles, the Narcissa of "Roderick Random," was a pretty Creole lady, of a somewhat dark complexion, whom he left at his death nearly destitute in a foreign land, and for whom a benefit was procured at the old Theatre Royal in March, 1784. A sister of Miss Renton's was married to Smollett's eldest nephew, Telfer, who inherited the family estate and assumed the name of Smollett. She afterwards became the wife of Sharpe of Hoddam, and, "strange to say, the lady whose bright eyes had flamed upon poor Smollett's soul in the middle of the last century was living so lately as 1836."

The house in which Smollett resided with his sister in 1766 was also the residence, prior to 1788, of James Earl of Hopetoun, who in early life had served in the Scots Guards and fought at Minden, and of whom it was said that he "maintained the dignity and noble bearing of a Scottish baron with the humility of a Christian, esteeming the religious character of his family to be its highest distinction. He was an indulgent landlord, a munificent benefactor to the poor, and a friend to all."

No. 1 St. John Street was the house of Sir Charles Preston, Bart., of Valleyfield, renowned for his gallant defence of Fort St. John against the American general Montgomery, when major of the Cameronians. No. 3 was occupied by Lord Blantyre; No. 5 by George Earl of Dalhousie, who was Commissioner to the General Assembly from 1777 to 1782; No. 8 was the house of Andrew Carmichael the last Earl of Hyndford.

In No. 10 resided James Ballantyne, the friend, partner, and confidant of Sir Walter Scott—when the Great Unknown—and it was the scene of those assemblies of select and favoured guests to whom "the hospitable printer read snatches of the forthcoming novel, and whetted, while he seemed to gratify, their curiosity by many a shrewd wink and mysterious hint of confidential insight into the literary riddle of the age." No. 10 must have been the scene of many a secret council connected with the publication of the Waverley Novels. Scott himself, Lockhart who so graphically describes these scenes, Erskine, Terry, Sir William Allan, George Hogarth, W.S. (Mrs. Ballantyne's brother), and others, were frequent guests here. In this house Mrs. Ballantyne died in 1829, and Ballantyne's brother John died there on the 16th of June, 1821. The house is now a Day Home for Destitute Children.

In No. 13 dwelt Lord Monboddo and his beautiful daughter, who died prematurely of consumption at Braid on the 17th of June, 1790, and whom Burns—her father's frequent guest there—describes so glowingly in his "Address to Edinburgh:"—

> "Fair Burnet strikes the adoring eye,
>   Heaven's beauties on my fancy shine ;
> I see the sire of Love on high,
>   And own his work indeed divine !"

The fair girl's early death he touchingly commemorates in a special ode. She was the ornament of the elegant society in which she moved; she was her old father's pride and the comfort of his domestic life. Dr. Gregory, whom she is said to have refused, also lived in St. John Street, as did Lady Suttie, Sinclair of Barrock, Sir David Rae, and Lord Eskgrove, one of the judges who tried the Reformers of 1793, a man of high ability and integrity. He removed thither from the old Assembly Close, and lived in St. John Street till his death in 1804.

Among the residents there in 1784 were Sir John Dalrymple and Sir John Stewart of Allanbank, and afterwards the Earl of Aboyne. The first house on the west side of the street was the meeting place of the old Canongate Kilwinning lodge, where Burns was affiliated and crowned as poet laureate, in presence of Lord Napier and many other masonic worthies of the day. A house a little to the south of this, having a gable to the street and a garden on the south, was, in 1780, the residence of the Earl of Wemyss, whose brother, Lord Elcho, was attainted after the battle of Culloden. A Lady Betty Charteris of this ancient family occupied the farthest house to the south on the same side. She had a romantic and melancholy history; being thwarted in an affair of the heart, she lay in bed for six-and-twenty years, till removed by death.

No. 18 is the Royal Maternity Hospital, which was founded in 1835, an institution the benefits of which are cordially extended to all who come to it, though many patients are attended at their own homes.

Eastward of St. John's Street is the Bakehouse Close, on the east side of which stands the mansion built and occupied by Sir Archibald Acheson, Bart., of Glencairnie, who was one of Charles I.'s Secretaries of State for Scotland. An archway, ornamented, and having a pendent keystone, gives access to the picturesque little quadrangle, three sides of which are formed by his house, which is all built of polished ashlar, with sculptured dormer windows, fine stringcourses, and other architectural details of the period. The heavily moulded doorway, which measures only three feet by six, is surmounted by the date 1633, and a huge monogram including the initials of himself and his wife Dame Margaret Hamilton. Over all is a cock on a trumpet and scroll, with the motto *Vigilantibus.* He had been a puisne judge in Ireland, and was first knighted by Charles I., for suggesting the measure of issuing out a commission under the great seal for the surrender of tithes. He was the friend of Drummond

of Hawthornden and of Sir William Alexander Earl of Stirling.

A succession of narrow and obscure alleys follows till we come to the Horse Wynd, on the

LINTEL ABOVE THE DOOR OF SIR A. ACHESON'S HOUSE.

east side of which lay the royal stables at the time of Darnley's murder. In this street, on the site of a school-house, &c., built by the Duchess of Gordon for the inhabitants of the Sanctuary, stood an old tenement, in one of the rooms on the first floor of which the first rehearsal of Home's "Douglas" took place, and in which the reverend author was assisted by several eminent lay and clerical friends, among whom were Robertson and Hume the historians, Dr. Carlyle of Inveresk and the author taking the leading male parts in the cast, while the ladies were represented by the Rev. Dr. Blair and Professor Fergusson. A dinner followed in the Erskine Club at the Abbey, when they were joined by the Lords Elibank, Kames, Milton, and Monboddo. To the south of this house was the town mansion of Francis Scott Lord Napier, who inherited that barony at the demise of his grandmother, Lady Napier, in 1706, and assumed the name of Napier, and died at a great old age in 1773.

At its southern end the wynd was closed by an arched gate in the long wall, which ran from the Cowgate Port to the south side of the Abbey Close.

CHAPTER V.

THE CANONGATE (*continued*).

Separate or Detached Edifices therein—Sir Walter Scott in the Canongate—The Parish Church—How it came to be built—Its Official Position —Its Burying Ground—The Grave of Fergusson—Monument to Soldiers interred there—Eccentric Henry Prentice—The Tolbooth— Testimony as to its Age—Its later uses—Magdalene Asylum—Linen Hall—Moray House—Its Historical Associations—The Winton House —Whiteford House—The Dark Story of Queensberry House.

THE advancing exigencies of the age and the necessity for increased space and modern sanitary improvements have made strange havoc among the old alleys and mansions of the great central street of the court suburb, but there still remain some to which belong many historical and literary associations of an interesting nature. Scott was never weary of lingering among them, and recalling the days that were no more. " No funeral hearse," says Lockhart, " crept more leisurely than did his landau up the Canongate ; and not a queer, tottering gable but recalled to him some long-buried memory of splendour or bloodshed, which, by a few

Most Noble Order of the Thistle, which he had now [re]erected, could not meet in St. Andrews church (*i.e.*, the cathedral in Fife), being demolished in the Rebellion; and so it was necessary for them to have this church, and the Provost of Edinburgh

SMOLLETT'S HOUSE, ST. JOHN'S STREET.

words, he set before the hearer in the reality of life." The Canongate church, a most unpicturesque-looking edifice, of nameless style, with a species of Doric porch, was built in 1688.   The Abbey church of Holyrood had hitherto been the parish church of the Canongate, but in July, 1687, King James VII. wrote to the Privy Council, that the church of the Abbey " was the chapel belonging to his palace of Holyrood, and that the knights of the

was ordained to see the keys of it given to them. After a long silence," says Fountainhall, " the Archbishop of Glasgow told that it was a mansal and patrimonial church of the bishopric of Edinburgh, and though the see was vacant, yet it belonged not to the Provost to deliver the keys."

Yet the congregation were ordered to seek accommodation in Lady Yester's church till other could be found for them, and the Canongate church was accordingly built for them, at the expense, says Arnot, of £2,400 sterling. A portion of this consisted of 20,000 merks, left, in 1649, by Thomas Moodie, a citizen, called by some Sir Thomas Moodie of Sauchtonhall, to re-build the church partially erected on the Castle Hill, and demolished by the English during the siege of 1650.

Two ministers were appointed to the Canongate church. The well-known Dr. Hugh Blair and the splendid scabbard. This life is full of contrasts; so when the magistrates, in ermine and gold, took their seats behind this sword of state in the front gallery, on the right of the minister, and in the gallery, too, were to be seen congregated the humble paupers from the Canongate poorhouse, now divested of its inmates and turned into a hospital. Our dear old Canongate, too, had its Baron Bailie and Resident Bailies before the

THE CANONGATE CHURCH.

late Principal Lee have been among the incumbents. It is of a cruciform plan, and has the summit of its ogee gable ornamented with the crest of the burgh—the stag's head and cross of King David's legendary adventure—and the arms of Thomas Moodie form a prominent ornament in front of it. "In our young days," says a recent writer in a local paper, "the Incorporated Trades, eight in number, occupied pews in the body of the church, these having the names of the occupiers painted on them; and in mid-summer, when the Town Council visited it, as is still their wont, the tradesmen placed large bouquets of flowers on their pews, and as our sittings were near this display, we used to glance with admiration from the flowers up to the great sword standing erect in the front gallery in its

Reform Bill in 1832 ruthlessly swept them away. Halberdiers, or Lochaber-axe-men, who turned out on all public occasions to grace the officials, were the civic body-guard, together with a body in plain clothes, whose office is on the ground flat under the debtors' jail."

But there still exists the convenery of the Canongate, including weavers, dyers, and cloth-dressers, &c., as incorporated by royal charter in 1630, under Charles I.

In the burying-ground adjacent to the church, and which was surrounded by trees in 1765, lie the remains of Dugald Stewart, the great philosopher, of Adam Smith, who wrote the "Wealth of Nations;" Dr. Adam Fergusson, the historian of the Roman Republic; Dr. Burney, author of the

" History of Music ; " Dr. Gregory ; David Allan ; Lord Cromarty ; and many others who have left their " footprints on the sands of time."

There, too, is the grave of the ill-fated Fergusson the poet, above which is the tombstone placed at the order of Robert Burns by Gowans, a marble-cutter in the Abbey Hill, " to remain for ever sacred to the memory of him whose name it bears," with the inscription Burns penned :—

> " HERE LIES ROBERT FERGUSSON.
> Born Sept. 5th, 1751. Died October 16th, 1774.
> No sculptured marble here, nor pompous lay,
> No storied urn nor animated bust ;
> This simple stone directs pale Scotia's way
> To pour her sorrows o'er her poet's dust."

Here, on the 16th of June, 1821, Sir Walter Scott attended the funeral of John Ballantyne, and displayed considerable emotion. " He cast his eyes along the overhanging line of the Calton Hill, with its gleaming walls and towers, and then turning to the grave again, 'I feel,' he whispered in Lockhart's ear, 'I feel as if there would be less sunshine for me from this day forth.' "

In May 1880 there was erected here a monument of rose-coloured granite, twenty-six feet high, by Mr. Ford of the Holyrood Glass Works, " In memory of the soldiers who died in Edinburgh Castle, situated in the Parish of Canongate, interred here from the year 1692 to 1880." It is very ornate, has on its base sculptured trophies, and was inaugurated in presence of General Hope, his staff, and the 71st Highlanders. Prior to its erection the spot where so many soldiers have found their last home was only a large square patch covered by grass.

In the " Domestic Annals " we find recorded the death, in 1788, of Henry Prentice, by whom the field culture of the potato was first introduced into the county of Edinburgh, in 1746. He had made a little money as a travelling merchant, was an eccentric character, and in 1784 sunk £140 with the managers of the Canongate poorhouse for a weekly subsistence. He had his coffin made, with the date of his birth thereon, 1703, and long had his gravestone conspicuously placed in the burgh churchyard, inscribed thus :—

FERGUSSON'S GRAVE.

> " Henry Prentice. Died . . . .
> Be not curious to know how I lived ;
> But rather how yourself should die."

He was, however, eventually interred at Restalrig.

At least three tenements of three storeys each would seem to have occupied the site of the church.

One of the picturesque relics of the past in Edinburgh is the old Canongate Tolbooth, with its sombre tower and spire, Scoto-French corbelled turrets, huge projecting clock, dark-mouthed archway, its moulded windows, and many sculptured stones. Above the arch is the inscription—

> S. L. B.
> PATRIÆ ET POSTERIS 1591 ;

and in a niche are the usual insignia of the burgh, the stag's head and cross, with the motto SIC ITUR AD ASTRA, while the appropriate motto ESTO FIDUS surmounts the inner doorway to the courthouse. At the south-east corner is the old shaft of the cross and pillory, near the entrance to the police-station.

Altogether it is a fine example of the polished edifices of the reign of James VI. In the tower are two bells, one inscribed SOLI DEO HONOR ET GLORIA, 1608, and a larger one, cast in 1796. Between the stately windows of the Council Hall is a pediment surmounted by a great thistle and the legend :—

> J. R. 6. JUSTITIA ET PIETAS VALIDE SUNT PRINCIPIS ARCES.

Herein the magistrates who came as successors of the abbots of Holyrood as over-lords of the burgh, held weekly courts for the punishment of offenders, the adjustment of small debts, and the affairs of the little municipality. That the building is older than any of the dates upon it, or that it had a *predecessor*, the following extracts from the " Burgh Records " attest :—

> " Vndecimo decembris, an : 1567.
> " The quhilk day it was concludit, be the Baillies and Counsall, to pursew quhatsomever person that is known and brutit wt the breking of the Tolbooth of this burcht, the tyme of the furth letting of Janet Robertsoun, being werdit within the samyn, &c."

In 1572 the following item occurs :—

> " To sax pynonis (pioneers ?) att the Baillies command for taking doun of the lintel-stone of the *Auld* Tolbooth window—iij-s vi-d."

In 1654 several Scottish prisoners of war, confined here under a guard of Cromwell's soldiers, effected their escape by rending their blankets and sheets into strips.   In January, 1675, the captain of the Edinburgh Tolbooth complained to the Lords of Council that his brother official in the Canongate used to set debtors at liberty at his own free will, or by consent of the creditor by whom they were imprisoned without permission accorded.

After the erection of the Calton gaol this edifice was used for the incarceration of debtors alone; and the number therein in October, 1834, was only seventeen, so little had it come to be wanted for that purpose.

Within a court adjoining the Tolbooth was the old Magdalene Asylum, instituted in 1797 for the reception of about sixty females; but the foundation-stone of a new one was laid in October, 1805, by the Provost, Sir William Fettes, Bart., in presence of the clergy and a great concourse of citizens. "In the stone was deposited a sealed bottle, containing various papers relating to the rise, progress, and present state of the

THE STOCKS, FROM THE CANONGATE TOLBOOTH.
(*Now in the Scottish Antiquarian Museum*)

asylum."   This institution was afterwards transferred to Dalry.

A little below St. John Street, within a court, stood the old British Linen Hall, opened in 1766 by the Board of Manufactures for the Sale and Custody of Scottish Linens—an institution to be treated of at greater length when we come to its new home on the Earthen Mound.   Among the curious booth-holders therein was "old John Guthrie, latterly of the firm of Guthrie and Tait, Nicholson Street," who figures in "Kay's Portraits," and whose bookstall in the hall—after he ceased being a travelling chapman—was the resort of all the curious book collectors of the time, till he removed to the Nether Bow.

A little below the Canongate Church there was still standing a house, occupied in 1761 by Sir James Livingstone of Glentenan, which possessed stables, hay-lofts, and a spacious flower-garden.

By far the most important private edifice still remaining in this region of ancient grandeur and modern squalor is that which is usually styled Moray House, being a portion of the entailed property of that noble family, in whose possession it remained exactly 200 years, having become the property of Margaret Countess of Moray in 1645

by an arrangement with her younger sister, Anne Home, then Countess of Lauderdale, by whom the mansion was built.   "It is old and it is magnificent, but its age and magnificence are both different from those of the lofty piled-up houses of the Scottish aristocracy of the Stuart dynasty."

Devoid of the narrow, suspicious apertures, barred and loopholed, which connect old Scottish houses with the external air, the entrances and proportions of this house are noble, spacious, and pleasing, though the exterior has little ornament save the balcony, on enormous trusses, projecting into the street, with ornate entablatures over their great windows and the stone spires of its gateway.   There are two fine rooms within, both of them dome-roofed and covered with designs in bas-relief.

The initials of its builder, M. H., surmounted by a coronet, are sculptured on the south window, and over another on the north are the lions of Home and Dudley impaled in a lozenge, for she was the daughter of Lord Dudley Viscount Lyle, and then the widow of Alexander first Earl of Home, who accompanied James VI. into England.   She erected the house some years before the coronation of Charles I. at Edinburgh in 1633; and she contributed largely to the enemies of his crown, as appears by a repayment to her by the English Parliament of £70,000 advanced by her in aid of the Covenanters; and hence, no doubt, it was, that when Cromwell gained his victory over the Duke of Hamilton in the north of England, we are told, when the (then) Marquis of Argyle conducted Cromwell and Lambert, with their army, to Edinburgh, they kept their quarters at the Lady Home's house in the Canongate, according to Guthrie, and there, adds Sir James Turner, they came to the terrible conclusion "*that there was a necessitie to take away the king's life;*" so that if these old walls had a tongue they might reveal dark conferences connected with the most dreadful events of that sorrowful time.   In conclave with Cromwell and Argyle were the Earls of Loudon and Lothian, the Lords Arbuthnot, Elcho, and Burleigh, with Blair, Dixon, Guthrie, and other Puritans.   Here, two years subsequently, occurred, on the balcony, the cruel and ungenerous episode connected with the fallen Montrose, amid the joyous banquetings and revelry on the occasion of

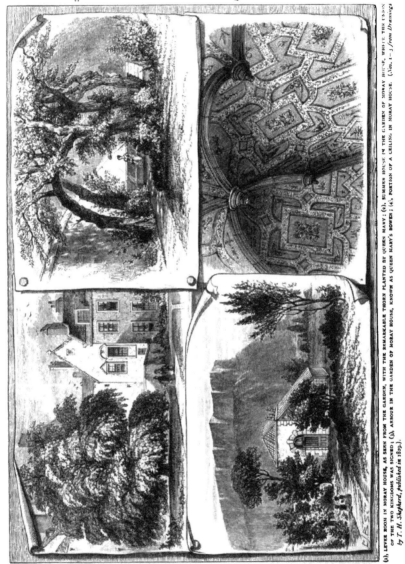

(1), LEVEE ROOM IN MORAY HOUSE, AS SEEN FROM THE GARDEN, WITH THE REMARKABLE THORN PLANTED BY QUEEN MARY; (2), SUMMER HOUSE IN THE GARDEN OF MORAY HOUSE, WHERE THE UNION OF THE TWO KINGDOMS WAS SIGNED; (3), ARBOUR IN THE GARDEN OF MORAY HOUSE, KNOWN AS QUEEN MARY'S BOWER; (4), PORTION OF A CEILING IN MORAY HOUSE. (Nos. 1-3 from Drawings by T. H. Shepherd, published in 1829).

Lord Lorne's marriage—that Lorne better known as the luckless Earl of Argyle—with Lady Mary Stuart, of the House of Moray.

In the highest terrace of the old garden an ancient thorn-tree was pointed out as having been planted by Queen Mary—a popular delusion, born of the story that the house had belonged to her brother, the subtle Regent; but there long remained the old stone summer-house, surmounted by two

in the very centre of what was then the most aristocratic quarter of the city, was admirably suited for his courtly receptions, all the more so that about that period the spacious gardens on the south were, like those of Heriot's Hospital, a kind of public promenade or lounging place, as would appear chiefly from a play called "The Assembly," written by the witty Dr. Pitcairn in 1692.

The union of the kingdoms is the next historical

MORAY HOUSE. (*From a Drawing by Shepherd, published in 1829.*)

greyhounds—the Moray supporters—wherein, after a flight from "the Union cellar," many of the signatures were affixed to the Act of Union, while the cries of the exasperated mob rang in the streets without the barred gates.

When James VII. so rashly urged those measures in 1686 which were believed to be a prelude to the re-establishment of the Catholic hierarchy, under the guise of toleration, a new Scottish ministry was formed, but chiefly consisting of members of the king's own faith. Among these was the proprietor of this old house, Alexander Earl of Moray, a recent convert from Protestantism, then Lord High Commissioner to the Parliament, and as such the representative of royalty in festive hall as well as the Senate; and his mansion, being

event connected with Moray House; and that much of the intrigue and discussion, and of the foul and degrading bribery connected with that event took place within its walls, may safely be inferred from the fact that it was the residence of the Earl of Seafield, then Lord High Chancellor, and one of the commissioners for the negotiation of the treaty, by which he pocketed £490, paid by the Earl of Godolphin; and he it was who, on giving the royal assent by touching the Act of Union with the sceptre, said, with a brutal laugh, "There's an end of an auld sang."

From those days Moray House ceased, like many others, to be the scene of state pageantries. For a time it became the office of the British Linen Company's Bank. Then the entail was broken by a clause in one of the Acts of the North British Railway; and since 1847 it has fortunately become the property of the Free Church of Scotland, by whom it is now used as a training college or normal school, managed by a rector and very efficient staff.

On the same side, but to the eastward, is Milton House, a large and handsome mansion, though heavy and sombre in style, built in what had been originally the garden of Lord Roxburghe's house, or a portion thereof, during the eighteenth century, by Andrew Fletcher of Milton, raised to the bench in 1724 in succession to the famous Lord Fountainhall, and who remained a senator of the Court of Session till his death. He was the nephew of the noble and patriotic Fletcher of Salton, and was an able coadjutor with his friend Archibald the great Duke of Argyle, during whose administration he exercised a wise control over the usually-abused Government patronage in Scotland. He sternly discouraged all informers, and was greatly esteemed for the mild and gentle manner in which he used his authority when Lord Justice Clerk after the battle of Culloden.

From the drawing-room windows on the south a spacious garden extended to the back of the Canongate, and beyond could be seen the hill of St. Leonard and the stupendous craigs. Its walls are still decorated with designs and landscapes, having rich floral borders painted in distemper, and rich stucco ceilings are among the decorations, and "interspersed amid the ornamental borders there are various grotesque figures, which have the appearance," says Wilson, "of being copies from an illuminated missal of the fourteenth century. They represent a cardinal, a monk, a priest, and other churchmen, painted with great humour and drollery of attitude and expression. They so entirely differ from the general character of the composition, that their insertion may be conjectured to have originated in a whim of Lord Milton's, which the artist has contrived to execute without sacrificing the harmony of his design."

Lord Milton was the guardian of the family of Susannah Countess of Eglinton for many years, and took a warm and fatherly interest in her beautiful girls after the death of the earl in 1729; and the terms of affectionate intimacy in which he stood with them are amusingly shown in "The petition of the six vestal virgins of Eglinton," signed by them all, and addressed "To the Honourable Lord Milton, at his lodgings, Edinburgh," in 1735—a curious and witty production, printed in the "Eglinton Memorials."

Lord Milton died at his house of Brunstane,

near Musselburgh, on the 13th of December, 1766, aged seventy-four. Four years after that event the *Scots Magazine* for 1770 gives us a curious account of a remarkable mendicant that had long haunted his gates:—"Edinburgh, Sept. 29th. A gentleman, struck with the uncommon good appearance of an elderly man who generally sits bareheaded under a dead wall in the Canongate, opposite to Lord Milton's house, requesting alms of those who pass, had the curiosity to inquire into his history, and learned the following melancholy account of him. He is an attainted baronet, named Sir John Mitchell of Pitreavie, and had formerly a very affluent estate. In the early part of his life he was a captain in the Scots Greys, but was broke for sending a challenge to the Duke of Marlborough, in consequence of some illiberal reflections thrown out by his Grace against the Scottish nation. Queen Anne took so personal a part in his prosecution that he was condemned to transportation for the offence; and this part of his sentence was, with difficulty, remitted at the particular instance of John Duke of Argyle. Exposed, in the hundredth year of his age, to the inclemencies of the weather, it is hoped the humane and charitable of this city will attend to his distresses, and relieve him from a situation which appears too severe a punishment for what, at worst, can be termed his spirited imprudence. A subscription for his annual support is opened at Balfour's coffee-house, where those who are disposed to contribute towards it will receive every satisfaction concerning the disposal of their charity and the truth of the foregoing relation."

The aged mendicant referred to may have been a knight, but the name of Mitchell is not to be found in the old list of Scottish baronets, and Pitreavie belonged to the Wardlaws.

In later years Milton House was occupied as a Catholic school, under the care of the Sisters of Charity, who, with their pupils, attracted considerable attention in 1842, on the occasion of the first visit of Queen Victoria to Holyrood, from whence they strewed flowers before her up the ancient street. It was next a school for deaf and dumb, anon a temporary maternity hospital, and then the property of an engineering firm.

Where Whiteford House stands now, in Edgar's map for 1765 there are shown two blocks of buildings (with a narrow passage between, and a garden 150 feet long) marked, "Ruins of the Earl of Winton's house," a stately edifice, which, no doubt, had fallen into a state of dilapidation from its extreme antiquity and abandonment after the attainder of George, fourth Earl of Winton, who was taken prisoner in the fight at Preston in 1715, but who, after being sentenced to death, escaped to Rome, where he died in 1749, without issue, according to Sir Robert Douglas; and, of course, is the same house that has been mentioned in history as the Lord Seton's lodging "in the Cannogait," wherein on his arrival from England, "Henrie Lord Dernlie, eldest son of Matho, erle of Lennox," resided when, prior to his marriage, he came to Edinburgh on the 13th of February, 1565, as stated in the "Diurnal of Occurrents."

In the same house was lodged, in 1582, according to Moyse, Mons. De Menainville, who came as an extra ambassador from France, with instructions to join La Motte Fenelon. He landed at Burntisland on the 18th of January, and came to Edinburgh, where he had an audience with James VI. on the 23rd, to the great alarm of the clergy, who dreaded this double attempt to revive French influence in Scottish affairs. One Mr. James Lawson "pointed out the French ambassaye" as the mission of the King of Babylon, and characterised Menainville as the counterpart of the blaspheming Rabshakeh.

Upon the 10th February, says Moyse, "La Motte having received a satisfying answer to his commission, with a great banquet at Archibald Stewart's lodgings in Edinburgh, took his journey homeward, and called at Seaton by the way. The said Monsieur Manzeville remained still here, and lodging at my Lord Seaton's house in the Canongate, had daily access to the king's majesty, to whom he imparted his negotiations at all times."

In this house died, of hectic fever, in December, 1638, Jane, Countess of Sutherland, grand-daughter of the first Earl of Winton. She "was interred at the collegiat churche of Setton, without any funerall ceremoney, by night."

In front of this once noble mansion, in which Scott lays some of the scenes of the "Abbot," there sprang up a kind of humble tavern, built chiefly of lath and plaster, known as "Jenny Ha's," from Mrs. Hall, its landlady, famous for her claret. Herein Gay, the poet, is said to "have boosed during his short stay in Edinburgh;" and to this tavern it was customary for gentlemen to adjourn after dinner parties, to indulge in claret from the butt.

On the site of the Seton mansion, and surrounded by its fine old gardens, was raised the present edifice known as Whiteford House, the residence of Sir John Whiteford, Bart., of that ilk and Ballochmyle, a locality in Ayrshire, on which the muse of Burns has conferred celebrity, and whose father is said to have been the prototype of Sir Arthur Wardour in the "Antiquary." Sir John was one of the early patrons of Burns, who had been introduced to him by Dr. Mackenzie, and the grateful bard never forgot the kindness he accorded to him. The failure of Douglas, Heron, & Co., in whose bank he had a fatal interest, compelled him to dispose of beautiful Ballochmyle, after which he resided permanently in Whiteford House, where he died in 1803. To the last he retained a military bearing, having served in the army, and been a major in 1762.

Latterly, and for many years, Whiteford House was best known as the residence of Sir William Macleod Bannatyne, who was raised to the bench on the death of Lord Swinton, in 1799, and was long remembered as a most pleasing example of the old gentleman of Edinburgh. "before its antique mansions and manners had fallen under the ban of modern fashion."

One of the last survivors of the Mirror Club, in private life his benevolent and amiable qualities of head and heart, with his rich stores of literary and historical anecdote, endeared him to a numerous and highly distinguished circle of friends. Robert Chambers speaks of breakfasting with him in Whiteford House so late as 1832, "on which occasion the venerable old gentleman talked as familiarly of the levees of the *sous-ministre* for Lord Bute in the old villa at the Abbey Hill as I could have talked of the Canning administration, and even recalled, as a fresh picture of his memory, his father drawing on his boots to go to make interest in London on behalf of some men in trouble for the '45, particularly his own brother-in-law, the Clanranald of that day." He died at Whiteford House on the 30th of November, 1833, in the ninety-first year of his age. His mansion was latterly used as a type-foundry.

On the south side of the street, nearly opposite the site of the Seton lodging, the residence of the Dukes of Queensberry still towers up, a huge, dark, gloomy, and quadrangular mass, the scene of much stately life, of low corrupt intrigue, and in one instance of a horrible tragedy.

It was built by Lord Halton on land belonging to the Lauderdale family; and by a passage in Lord Fountainhall's folios would seem to have been sold by him, in June, 1686, to William first Duke of Queensberry and Marquis of Dumfries-shire, Lord High Treasurer and President of the Council, a noted money-lender and land-acquirer, who built the castle of Drumlanrig, and at the exact hour of whose death, in 1695, it is said, a Scottish skipper, being in Sicily, saw one day a coach and six driving to flaming Mount Etna, while a diabolical voice was heard to exclaim, "Way for the

Duke of Drumlanrig!" He died in Queensberry House.

His daughter, Anne Countess of Wemyss, died a miserable death on the 16th of February, 1700. She set fire accidentally to her apron, "nightrail, and steinkirk. Her nose was burnt off and her eyes burnt out. Opening her mouth to call,

he fled from Edinburgh, but was elected as one of the peers to represent Scotland. On his return to London he was met by a cavalcade of noblemen and gentlemen, and was preceded to his house at Kensington by forty coaches and four hundred horsemen. Next day he was presented to the queen, who, to reward his services and servility,

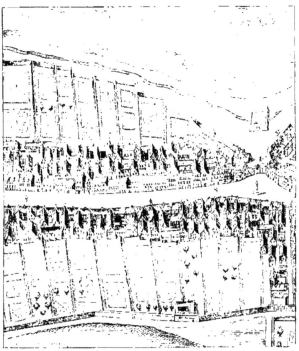

EAST END OF THE CANONGATE. (*From Gordon of Rothiemay's Map.*)
8, the Canongate: 31, the Tennis Court: *k*, the Water Port

the flame went in and burnt her tongue and throat."

His son James, the second duke, resigned all his many appointments under James VII., including the command of the Scots Horse Guards, and was received by William of Orange with great cordiality. He made him a captain in his Dutch Guards, and Lord of the Bedchamber and Treasury. He was one of the commissioners for the Treaty of Union, to achieve which the sum of £12,325 was paid him by the Earl of Godolphin, and then

created him Duke of Dover, Marquis of Beverley, and Baron Ripon.

Connected with his residence in Queensberry House, against which the whole fury and maledictions of the mobs were directed at the time of the Union, there is a tale of awful mystery and horror. His eldest son, James Earl of Drumlanrig, is simply stated in the old peerages "to have died young." It is now proved, however, that he was an idiot of the most wretched kind, rabid and gluttonous as a wild animal, and grew to an enormous stature, as his leaden and un-ornamented coffin in the family vault at Durisdeer attests at this day. This monstrous and unfortunate creature was always confined in a ground-floor room of the western wing of Queensberry House; and "till within these few years the boards still remained by which the windows of the dreadful receptacle were darkened to prevent the idiot from looking out or being seen."

stripped and spitted him, and he was found devouring the half-roasted body when the duke returned with his train from his political triumph, to find dire horror awaiting him. "The common people, among whom the dreadful tale soon spread, in spite of the duke's endeavours to suppress it, said that it was a judgment upon him for his odious share in the Union. The story runs that the duke, who had previously regarded his dreadful offspring

THE CANONGATE, LOOKING WEST; SHOWING, ON THE IMMEDIATE RIGHT, THE HOUSE IN WHICH GAY RESIDED, AND ON THE LEFT THE GATE OF MILTON HOUSE. (*From a Drawing by Shephe d, published in 1829.*)

On the day the Treaty of Union was passed all Edinburgh crowded to the vicinity of the Parliament House to await the issue of the final debate, and the whole household of the duke—the High Commissioner—went thither *en masse* for that purpose, and perhaps to prevent him from being torn to pieces by the exasperated people, and among them went the valet whose duty it was to watch and attend the Earl of Drumlanrig.

Hearing all unusually still in the vast house, the latter contrived to break out of his den, and roamed wildly from room to room, till certain savoury odours drew him into the great kitchen, where a little turnspit sat quietly on a stool by the fire. He seized the boy, took the meat from the fire,

with no eye of affection, immediately ordered the creature to be smothered. But this is a mistake; the idiot is known to have died in England, and to have survived his father many years, though he did not succeed him upon his death in 1711, when the titles devolved upon Charles, a younger brother."

The latter, who was born in Queensberry House, had been created Earl of Solway in 1706, says Douglas, "when very young, his elder brother being then alive." He married Catharine Hyde, the second daughter of Henry Earl of Clarendon and Rochester, and they frequently resided in the old Canongate mansion. The duchess was altogether an extraordinary woman, whose eccentricity bordered on madness, and, indeed, prior to her marriage she had been confined in a strait-waist-coat. Her beauty has been celebrated coarsely by Pope, and her irrepressible temper by Prior:—

> " Thus Kitty, beautiful and young,
>   And wild as colt untamed,
> Bespoke the fair from whom she sprung,
>   By little rage inflamed:
> Inflamed with rage at sad restraint,
>   Which wise mamma ordained ;
> And sorely vexed to play the saint
>   Whilst wit and beauty reigned."

After the duke and duchess had embroiled themselves with the Court in 1729, in consequence of patronising the poet Gay, they came to Queensberry House, and brought him with them. Tradition used to indicate an attic in an old mansion opposite, as the place where—appropriate abode of a poet—Gay wrote the " Beggar's Opera "—" an entirely gratuitous assumption," says Mr. Chambers. " In the history of his writings nothing of consequence occurs at this time. He had finished the second part of the opera some time before, and after his return to the south he is found engaged in new writing a damned play, which he wrote several years before, called " The Wife of Bath," a task which he accomplished while living with the Duke of Queensberry in Oxfordshire, during the ensuing months of August, September, and October."

The Duchess Catharine disliked the Scots and their manners, particularly the use of a knife in lieu of a fork, on which she would scream out and beseech them not to cut their throats. "To the lady I live with," wrote Gay to Swift in 1729, " I owe my life and fortune. Think of her with respect, value and esteem her as I do, and never more despise a fork with three prongs." When in Scotland she always dressed herself as a peasant-girl, to ridicule the stately dresses and demeanour of the Scottish dames who visited Queensberry House or Drumlanrig, and this freak of costume led to her being roughly repelled at a review. Her eldest

son, the Earl of Drumlanrig, was altogether mad, and contracted himself to one lady while he married another, a daughter of the Earl of Hopetoun. He served two campaigns under the Earl of Stair, and commanded two battalions of Scots in the Dutch service. But in 1754 the family malady proved so strong for him, that during a journey to London he rode on before the coach in which the duchess travelled, and shot himself with one of his pistols. It was given out that it had gone off by accident. His brother Charles, after narrowly escaping the earthquake at Lisbon in 1755, died in the following year.

On the death of their father, in 1778, the title and estates devolved on his cousin, the Earl of March, an old debauchee, better known as " Old Q." In his time, and before it, Queensberry House had other occupants than the Douglases.

In 1747 the famous Marshal Earl of Stair died there ; and in 1784 it was the residence of the Right Hon. James Montgomery of Stanhop, Lord Chief Baron of Exchequer—the first Scotsman who held that office after the establishment of the Court at the Union. Prior to his removal to Queensberry House (of which the duke gave him gratuitous use) he had occupied the third flat of the Bishop's Land, formerly occupied by the Lord President Dundas.

In 1801 the *blasé* " Old Q. " ordered Queensberry House to be stripped of its decorations, and sold. With fifty-eight fire rooms, and a noble gallery seventy feet long, besides a spacious garden, it was offered at the singularly low upset price of £900, and was bought by Government as a barrack. It is now, and has been since 1853, a House of Refuge for the Destitute, in which upwards of 12,000 persons are relieved every year, or an average of thirty-three nightly for the twelvemonth, while during the same period nearly 40,000 meals of broth and bread are issued from the soup kitchen. A very handsome building, in baronial style, called Queensberry Lodge, adjoins it, for the reception and treatment of inebriates—but ladies only.

CHAPTER VI.

THE CANONGATE (*concluded*).

Lothian Hut—Lord Palmerston—St. Thomas's Hospital—The Tennis Court and its Theatre—Queen Mary's Bath—The Houses of Croft an-Righ and Clockmill.

In the map of the city engraved in 1787 for the quarto edition of " Arnot's History " there is shown, on the west side of the Horse Wynd, adjoining the Abbey Close, an edifice called Lothian Hut, sur-

rounded by trees. This was the small but magnificently finished town mansion of the Lothian family, and was built by William, the third Marquis, about the year 1750, when Lord Clerk Register of

Scotland, and who for some years had been Commissioner to the General Assembly. In this house he died, 28th July, 1767, as recorded in the *Scots Magazine*, and was succeeded by his son, Major-General the Earl of Ancrum, Colonel of the 11th Light Dragoons (now Hussars). His second son, Lord Robert, had been killed at Culloden.

His marchioness, Margaret, the daughter of Sir Thomas Nicholson, Bart., of Kempnay, who survived him twenty years, resided in Lothian Hut till her death. It was afterwards occupied by the dowager of the fourth Marquis, Lady Caroline D'Arcy, who was only daughter of Robert Earl of Holderness, and great-grand-daughter of Charles Louis, the Elector Palatine, a lady whose character is remembered traditionally to have been both grand and amiable. Latterly the Hut was the residence of Professor Dugald Stewart, who, about the end of the last century, entertained there many English pupils of high rank. Among them, perhaps the most eminent was Henry Temple, afterwards Lord Palmerston, whose education, commenced at Harrow, was continued at the University of Edinburgh. When he re-visited the latter city in 1865, during his stay he was made aware that an aged woman, named Peggie Forbes, who had been a servant with Dugald Stewart at Lothian Hut, was still alive, and residing at No. 1, Rankeillor Street. There the great statesman visited her, and expressed the pleasure he felt at renewing the acquaintance of the old domestic.

Lothian Hut, the scene of Dugald Stewart's most important literary labours, was pulled down in 1825, to make room for a brewery ; but a house of the same period, at the south-west corner of the Horse Wynd, bears still the name of Lothian Vale.

A little to the eastward of the present White Horse hostel, and immediately adjoining the Water Gate, stood the Hospital of St. Thomas, founded in 1541 by George Crichton, Bishop of Dunkeld, "dedicated to God, the Blessed Virgin Mary, and all the saints." It consisted of an almshouse and chapel, the bedesmen of which were "to celebrate the founder's anniversary *obit.* by solemnly singing in the choir of Holyrood church yearly, on the day of his death, 'the *Placebo* and *Dirige* for the repose of his soul" and the soul of the King of Scotland. "Special care," says Arnot, "was taken in allotting money for providing candles to be lighted during the anniversary mass of requiem, and the number and size of the tapers were fixed with a precision which shows the importance in which these circumstances were held by the founder. The number of masses, paternosters, ave-marias,

and credos, to be said by the chaplain and bedesmen is distinctly ascertained."

The patronage of the institution was vested by the founder in himself and a certain series of representatives named by him.

In 1617, with the consent of David Crichton of Lugton, the patron, who had retained possession of the endowments, the magistrates of the Canongate purchased the chapel and almshouse from the chaplains and bedesmen, and converted the institution into a hospital for the poor of the burgh. Over the entrance they placed the Canongate arms, supported by a pair of cripples, an old man and woman, with the inscription—

HELP HERE THE POORE, AS ZE WALD GOD DID ZOV.
JUNE 19, 1617.

The magistrates of the Canongate sold the patronage of the institution in 1634 to the Kirk Session, by whom its revenues "were entirely embezzled ;" by 1747 the buildings were turned into coach-houses, and in 1787 were pulled down, and replaced by modern houses of hideous aspect.

On the opposite side of the Water Gate was the Royal Tennis Court, the buildings of which are very distinctly shown in Gordon's map of 1647. Maitland says it was anciently called the Catchpel, from Cache, a game now called *Fives*, a favourite amusement in Scotland as early as the reign of James IV. The house, a long, narrow building, with a court, after being a weavers' workhouse, was burned down in 1771, and rebuilt in the tasteless fashion of that period ; but the locality is full of interest, as being connected not only with the game of tennis, as played there by the Duke of Albany, Law the great financial schemer, and others, but the early and obscure history of the stage in Scotland.

In 1554 there was a "litill farsche and play maid be William Lauder," and acted before the Queen Regent, Mary of Guise, for which he was rewarded by two silver cups. Where it was acted is not stated. Neither are we told where was performed another play, "made by Robert Simple" at Edinburgh, before the grim Lord Regent and others of the nobility in 1567, and for which the author was paid £66 13s. 4d.

The next record of a post-Reformation theatre is in the time of James VI. when several companies came from London for the amusement of the court, including one of which Shakspere was a member, though his appearance cannot be substantiated. In 1599 the company of English comedians was interdicted by the clergy and Kirk Session, though their performances, says Spottiswoode in his "Church History," were licensed by the king! This interdict was annulled by proclamation at the Market Cross. In 1601 an English company, headed by Laurence Fletcher, "comedian to his Majestie," was again in Scotland; and Mr. Charles Knight, in his "Life of Shakspere," concludes that the illustrious dramatist must have been in Scotland with Fletcher, and thus sketched out the plan of his great Scottish tragedy. According to the same testimony, the name of Shakspere has been invariably associated with the Tennis Court Theatre; but from the departure of

missioner, at his court at Holyrood, and soon after the theatre in the Tennis Court was in the zenith of its brief prosperity, in defiance of the city pulpits. There, on the 15th November, 1681, "being the Queen of Brittain's birthday," as Fountainhall records, while bonfires blazed in the city and salutes were fired by cannon, there was performed, "before their Royall Hynesses," a comedy, called "Mithridates, King of Pontus," wherein the future Queen Anne and the ladies of honour were the only actresses.

The drama vanished from Scotland at the Revo-

THE PALACE GATE. (*After an Etching by James Skene, of Rubislaw.*)

James VI. to England, in 1603, till the arrival of his grandson the Duke of Albany and York, in 1680, there are doubts if anything like a play was performed in the Edinburgh of that gloomy period; though Sir George Mackenzie mentions that in June, 1669, "Thomas Sydserf, having pursued Mungo Murray for invading him in his *Playhouse,* &c., that invasion was not punished as hamesucken, but with imprisonment;" and a "Playhouse," kept at Edinburgh in the same month, when a thousand prisoners, after Bothwell Bridge, were confined in the Greyfriars Churchyard, is referred to in the Acts of Council in 1679.

Some kind of a drama, called "Marciano, or The Discovery," was produced on the festival of St. John by Sir Thomas Sydserff (the same referred to), before His Grace the Earl of Rothes, High Com-

lution; and though a concert was given in 1705 in the Tennis Court, under the patronage of the Duke of Argyle, and "The Spanish Friar" is said to have been performed there before the members of the Union Parliament, no more is heard of it till 1714, when "Macbeth" was played at the Tennis Court, in presence of a brilliant array of Scottish nobles and noblesse, after an archery meeting. On this occasion many present called for the song, "The king shall enjoy his own again," while others opposed the demand; whereupon swords were resorted to, and—as an anticipation of the battle of Dunblane—a regular *mêlée* ensued.

A little to the north-eastward of the Tennis Court stands the singularly picturesque, but squat little corbelled tower called Queen Mary's Bath, in what was of old the open garden ground attached to the palace. The tradition of its having been the Queen's bath is of considerable antiquity. Pennant records an absurd story to the effect that she was wont to use a bath of white wine ; but the spring of limpid water that now wells under the earthen floor attests that she resorted to no other expedient than *aqua pura* to exalt or shield her charms. And the story is also referred to in a poem called " Craigmillar," published about 1770.

"That chamber where the
    queen, whose charms divine
Made wond'ring nations own
    the power of love,
Oft bathed her snowy limbs in
    sparkling wine,
Now proves a lonely refuge
    for the dove."

In 1789, when a house was built adjoining this edifice, a turret staircase that led to the roof was demolished, and in the sarking thereof was found a richly-inlaid dagger of ancient workmanship, which was, not without much reason, supposed to have belonged to one of Rizzio's murderers, some of whom made their escape through the royal gardens in that quarter. This house was entirely removed when the bath was completely repaired in 1852, and its ancient surroundings in some degree restored.

The old-fashioned suburb at the Abbey Hill that rose around the northern skirts of the palace, lies beyond what was of old the Artillery Park and this little tower, and possesses still some mansions that formed the residence of Scottish courtiers in the days of other years. The most remarkable of these is the ancient house of *Croft-an-Righ*, or the Field of the King. Corbelled turrets adorn its southern gable, and dormer windows its northern front, while many of the ceilings exhibit elaborate stucco details, including several royal insignia. Traditionally this house, which, in 1647, was approached from the Abbey burying-ground by an arched gate between two lodges, has been erroneously associated with Mary of Guise ; but is supposed to be the mansion that was purchased by

QUEEN MARY'S BATH.

William Graham, the last Earl of Airth, who died in 1694, from the Earl of Linlithgow. By him it is described as being situated at the back of Holyrood, and having before belonged to Lord Elphinstone.

The " History of Holyrood," published in 1821, states that the old house of Croft-an-Righ, an edifice of the sixteenth century, had been the residence of the Regent Moray, and with its garden was " gifted, along with several of the adjoining properties, by James VI. to a favourite servant of the name of French."

For repairing the house and making it suitable for the keeper of the royal gardens, Government paid £420 in 1859. At the same time £840 was paid for the re-purchase of Queen Mary's Bath, with the tenement thereunto adjoining and now removed.

Eastward of Croft-an-Righ House, there stood, until it was removed as unsightly, another old mansion, gloomy, dark, and quadrangular, named the Clockmill House, surrounded by ancient trees.[*] Long anterior to its existence the locality is referred to in a process before the Supreme Court, 7th May, 1569, concerning the privilege of sanctuary, "fra the Girth Corse doun to the Clokisrwne Mylne." Before that tribunal (as quoted from the *Acta Dom. Concilii et Sessionis*), it is stated that "our Soverane Lordis predecessouris, Kingis of Scotland, for the tyme, has of auld, at the foundation of the said Abbey of Halirudhouse, grantit the privilige of the Girth (protection and sanctuary) to the hail boundis of the said Abbey, and to that part of the burghe of the Cannogait, fra the Girth Corse (cross) down to the Clokisrwne Mylne, quhilk privilige has bene inviolablie observit to all manner of personis cumond wytin the boundes aforsaid, not committand the crymes expresslie exceptit for all maner of girth, and that in all tymes bigane past memorie of man."

---

[*] An engraving of the Clockmill House will be found on p. 308.

CHAPTER VII.

HOLYROOD ABBEY.

Foundation of the Abbey—Text of King David's Charter—Original Extent of the Abbey Church—The so-called Miraculous Cross—The Patronages of the Canons—its Thirty-one Abbots—Its Relics and Revenues.

WE now enter on the precincts of time-hallowed Holyrood, the scene of many brilliant gatherings, many a solemn and sad event. There the actors of long-departed historical dramas seem to rise to the mind's eye, from the days of David to those of Charles Edward, and to glide past like Banquo's shadowy line. Could these old Gothic walls speak, what secrets might they not reveal! There generations have assembled in devotion ere they went down to darkness and to "dusty death;" there have mitred prelates preached and blessed, while kings knelt and listened, ere they rode forth to fight for Scotland, and in more than one instance to die, with a faith, valour, and patriotism unsurpassed by any regal race in Europe.

"There sleeps the sovereign in his shroud, the warrior in
    his mail,
    The saint to holy vigils vowed, the faithful and the frail!
    There, though the weeds have warped the shrine, the Rose
        of Gueldres prayed;
    There, daughter of St. Louis' line, thy bridal couch was
        made!"

In our history of the Castle we have already related the pious old legend of the white hart in the wood of Drumsheugh—the alleged miracle which led to the foundation of Holyrood Abbey by David I. The charter granted by this monarch to the abbey is without date. The original is in the archives of the city, but is only known, from the names of those by whom it is witnessed, to have been granted between the years 1143 and 1147. It is beautifully written on vellum, and runs thus:—

"In the name of our Lord Jesus Christ, and in honour of the Holy Rood, of St. Mary the Virgin, and of all the saints, I, David, by the grace of God, King of Scots, of my royal authority, with the assent of Henry, my son, and the bishops of my kingdom, with the confirmation and testimony of the earls and barons, the clergy and people also assenting, of divine prompting, grant all the things under written to the church of the Holy Rood of Edinburgh, and in perpetual peace confirm them. These are what we grant to the aforesaid church and to the canons serving God therein in free and perpetual alms.

"To wit, the church of the Castle, with all its appendages and rights, and the trial of battle, water, and hot iron, as far as belongs to ecclesiastical dignity; and with Saughton by its right marches, and the church of St. Cuthbert, with the parish and all things that pertain to that church; and with Kyrchetun by its right marches, and with the land in which that church is situate, and with the other land that lies under the Castle: to wit, from the spring that rises near the corner of my garden, by the road that leads to the church of St. Cuthbert, and, on the other side, under the castle until you come to a crag which is under the same castle towards the east; and with the two chapels which pertain to the same church of St. Cuthbert: to wit, Corstorphine, with two oxgates and six acres of land; and that chapel of Liberton, with two oxgates of land, and all tithes and the rights, as well of the living as of the dead, which Macbeth gave to that church, and which I have granted; and the church of Hereth [Airth?], with the land that belongs to that church, and with all the land that I have given to it, as my servants and good men walked its bounds, and give it over to Alwin the Abbot, with one salt work in Hereth and twenty-six acres of land.

"Which church and land aforenamed I will that the canons of the Holy Cross hold and possess for ever, freely and quietly; and I strictly forbid that any one unjustly oppress or trouble the canons or their men who live in that land, or unjustly exact from them any works or aids or secular customs. I will, moreover, that the same canons have liberty of making a mill in that land, and that they have in Hereth all those customs, and rights, and easements, to wit, in waters, fishings, meadows, pastures, and in all other necessary things, as they best held them on the day in which I had it in my domain; and Broughton, with its right marches; and that Inverleith which is nearest the harbour, with its right marches, and with that harbour, with the half of the fishing, and with a whole tythe of all the fishing which belongs to the church of St. Cuthbert; and Pittendreich, Hamar, and Ford, with their right marches; and the hospital, with one plough of land, and forty shillings from my Burgh of Edinburgh yearly; and a rent of a hundred shillings yearly to the clothing of the canons from my cane [kind?] of Perth, and this from the first ships that come to Perth for the sake of trade; and if it happen that they do not come, I grant the aforesaid church from my rent of Edinburgh forty shillings, from Stirling twenty shillings, and from Perth forty shillings; and one toft in Stirling, and the draught of one net for fishing; and one toft in my Burgh of Edinburgh, free and quit of all custom and exaction; and one toft in Berwick, and the draught of two nets in Scypwell; one toft in Renfrew of five perches, the draught of one net for salmon, and to fish there for herrings freely; and I forbid any one to exact from you or your men any customs therefor.

"I moreover grant to the aforesaid canons from my exchequer yearly ten pounds for the lights of the church, for the works of that church, and repairing these works for ever. I charge, moreover, all my servants and foresters of Stirlingshire and Clackmannan, that the abbot and convent have free power in all my woods and forests, of taking as much timber as they please for the building of their church and of their houses, and for any purpose of theirs; and I enjoin that their men who take timber for their use in the said woods have my firm peace, and so that ye do not permit them to be disturbed in any way; and the swine, the property of the aforesaid church, I grant in all my woods to be quit of pannage [food].

"I grant, moreover, to the aforesaid canons the half of the fat, tallow, and hides of the slaughter of Edinburgh; and a tithe of all the whales and sea-beasts which fall to me from Avon to Coldbrandspath; and a tithe of all my pleas and gains from Avon to Coldbrandspath; and the half of my tithe of cane, and of my pleas and gains of Cantyre and Argyll; and all the skins of rams, ewes, and lambs of the castle and of Linlithgow which die of my flock; and eight chalders of malt and eight of meal, with thirty cart-loads of bush from Liberton; and one of my mills of Dean; and a tithe of the mill of Liberton, and of Dean, and of the new mill of Edinburgh, and of Craggenemarf, as much as I have for the same in my domain, and as much as Vuieth the White gave them of alms of the same Crag.

"I grant likewise to them leave to establish a burgh between that church and my burgh.* And I grant that the burgesses have common right of selling their wares and of buying in my market, freely and quit of claim and custom, in like manner as my own burgesses; and I forbid that any one take in this burgh, bread, ale, or cloth, or any ware by force, or without consent of the burgesses. I grant, moreover, that the canons be quit of toll

and of all custom in all my burghs and throughout all my land: to wit, all things that they buy and sell.

"And I forbid any one to take pledge on the land of the Holy Rood, unless the abbot of that place shall have refused to do right and justice. I will, moreover, that they hold all that is above written as freely and quietly as I hold my own lands; and I will that the abbot hold his court as freely, fully, and honourably as the Bishop of St. Andrews and the Abbots of Dunfermline and Kelso hold their courts.

"Witnesses:—Robert Bishop of St. Andrews, John Bishop of Glasgow, Henry my son, William my grandson, Edward the Chancellor, Herbert the Chamberlain, Gillemichael the Earl, Gospatrick the brother of Dolphin, Robert of Montague, Robert of Burneville, Peter of Brus, Norman the Sheriff, Oggu, Leising, Gillise, William of Graham, Turston of Crechtune, Blein the Archdeacon, Aelfric the Chaplain, Walerain the Chaplain."†

This document is interesting from its simplicity, and curious as mentioning many places still known under the same names.

The canons regular of the order of St. Augustine were brought there from St. Andrews in Fifeshire. The order was first established in Scotland by Alexander I. in 1114, and ere long possessed twenty-eight monasteries or foundations in the kingdom.

So, in process of time, "in the hollow between two hills" where King David was saved from the white hart, there rose the great abbey house, with its stately cruciform church, having three towers, of which but a fragment now remains— a melancholy ruin. Till its completion the canons were housed in the Castle, where they resided till about 1176, occupying an edifice which had previously been a nunnery.

The southern aisle of the nave is the only part of the church on which a roof remains, and of the whole range of beautifully clustered pillars on the north side but two fragments alone survive. The entire ruin retains numerous traces of the original work of the twelfth century, though enriched by the additions of subsequent ages. With reference to the view of it in the old print which has been copied in these pages,‡ it has been observed that therein "the abbey church appears with a second square tower, uniform with the one still standing at the north of the great doorway. The transepts are about the usual proportions, but the choir is much shorter than it is proved from other

---

* Here there is no mention of the town of *Herbergare*, alleged to have occupied the site of the Canongate.

† "Charters relating to City of Edinburgh," A.D. 1143-1540. 4to. 1871.
‡ See *ante*, vol. i., p. 5.

evidence to have originally been, the greater part of it having perhaps been reduced to ruins before the view was taken. During the levelling of the ground around the palace, and digging a foundation for the substantial railing with which it was recently enclosed, the workmen came upon the bases of two pillars in a direct line with the nave, proving that the ancient choir had been of unusual length. A mound of earth which extends still farther to the east no doubt marks the foundation

The railing referred to was replaced in 1857 by the present rampart wall, when near the same site two stone coffins of the twelfth century, now in the nave, were found. Each is six feet four inches in length, inside measurement.

In the abbey was preserved, enshrined in silver, the alleged miraculous cross which was placed in King David's hand when his horse fell before the stag. It remained on the high altar till the fatal battle of Durham in 1346, whither it was taken by

CROFT-AN-RIGH HOUSE.

of other early buildings [perhaps the abbey house?], and from their being in the direct line of the building it is not improbable that a Lady chapel or other addition to the abbey church may have stood to the east of the choir. . . . A curious relic of the ancient tenants of the monastery was found by the workmen, consisting of a skull, which had no doubt formed the solitary companion of one of the monks. It had a hole in the top of the cranium, which served, most probably, for securing a crucifix, and over the brow was traced in antique characters, *Memento mori.* This solitary relic of the furniture of the abbey was procured by the late Sir Patrick Walker, and is still in possession of his family."

David II., and where all virtue seemed to have deserted it (*mirabile dictu!*) as it fell into the hands of the enemy, by whom it was long preserved with zealous veneration in the great cathedral near the field. The texture of this remarkable cross was said to have been of such a nature that no mortal artificer could tell whether it was of wood, horn, or metal.

Besides the provisions and privileges contained in the charter of David I., the abbey was liberally endowed by many other persons from time to time, till it became so opulent as to excite both admiration and envy. In the canons were vested the patronages of several churches in different parts of the realm, and eventually the following were among

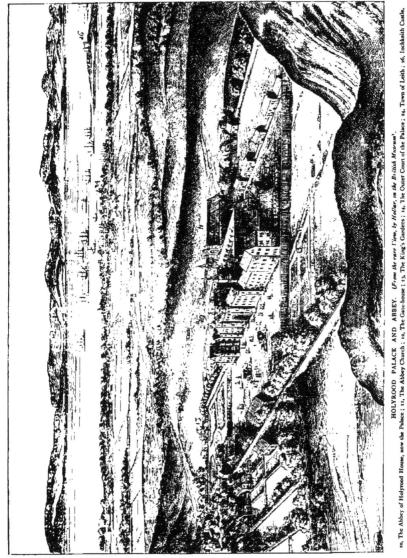

HOLYROOD PALACE AND ABBEY. (From the rare View, by Hollar, in the British Museum).

10, The Abbey of Holyrood House, now the Palace; 11, The Abbey Church; 12, The Gate-house; 13, The King's Gardens; 14, The Outer Court of the Palace; 24, Town of Leith; 26, Inchkeith Castle.

these ecclesiastical foundations :—The Priory of St. Mary's Isle, in Galloway, gifted by Fergus, Lord of Galloway, who died a monk of Holyrood in 1161 ; the Priory of Blantyre, secluded on a rock above the Clyde ; Rowadill, in Herries, gifted by Mac-Leod of Herries ; Oransay and Colonsay—in the former still stands their priory, built by a Lord of the Isles, one of the finest relics of religious antiquity in the Hebrides ; the church of Melgynch, granted to them by Matthew, Abbot of Dunkeld, in 1289 ; the church of Dalgarnock, granted to them by John, Bishop of Glasgow, in 1322 ; and the church and vicarage of Kirkcudbright, by Henry, Bishop of Galloway, in 1334, &c.

Before narrating some of the events of which the abbey and its church were the scenes, we shall give the following list of the abbots, so far as they can be traced in history :—

I. ALWIN was the first abbot ; he resigned the office in 1150, and is said to have died in 1155. He was the confessor of King David, and author of a "Book of Homilies and Epistles."

II. OSBERT died on the 15th of December, 1150. He wrote the "Acts of King David I.," and was buried with great pomp before the high altar. He built some part of the monastery, and "gave an image of God the Father, of solid silver."

SEAL OF HOLYROOD ABBEY.

III. WILLIAM I. succeeded in 1152. He witnessed several charters of Malcolm IV. and William the Lion ; and when he became aged and infirm, he vowed to God that he would say his psalter every day. He enclosed the abbey with a strong wall.

IV. ROBERT is said to have been abbot about the time of William the Lion. "He granted to the inhabitants of the newly-projected burgh of the Canongate various privileges, which were confirmed, with additional benefactions, by David II., Robert III., and James III. These kings granted to the bailies and community the annuities payable by the burgh, and also the common muir between the lands of Broughton on the west and the lands of Pilrig on the east, on the north side of the road from Edinburgh to Leith."

V. JOHN, abbot in 1173, witnessed a charter of Richard Bishop of St. Andrews (chaplain to Malcolm IV.), granting to his canons the church

of Haddington, *cum terra de Clerkynton, per rectas divisas.* In 1177 the monastery was still in the Castle of Edinburgh. In 1180 Alexius, a sub-deacon, held a council of the Holy Cross near Edinburgh, with reference to the long-disputed consecration of John Scott, Bishop of St. Andrews, when a double election had taken place.

VI. WILLIAM II., abbot in 1206. During his time, John Bishop of Candida Casa resigned his mitre, became a canon of Holyrood, and was buried in the chapter-house, where a stone long marked his grave.

VII. WALTER, Prior of Inchcolm, abbot in 1209, died on the 2nd of January, 1217. He was renowned for learning and piety.

VIII. WILLIAM III., of whom nothing is known but the name, and that he was ejected from his office.

IX. WILLIAM IV., the son of Owen, resigned his office in 1227, when old and infirm, and became a hermit on Inchkeith, but returning, died a monk of Holyrood. His name occurs in a crown charter of Alexander III., confirming the lands of Newbattle, 24th June, 1224.

X. ELIAS I., the son of Nicholas. According to Father Hay, he drained the marshes around the abbey, built the back wall of the cemetery, and at his death was buried behind the high altar in the chapel of St. Mary.

XI. HENRY, the next abbot, was named Bishop of Galloway in 1253 ; consecrated in 1255 by the Archbishop of York.

XII. RADULPH, abbot, is mentioned in a gift of lands at Pittendreich to the monks of St. Marie de Newbattle.

XIII. ADAM, a traitor, and adherent of England, who did homage to Edward I. in 1292, and for whom he examined the records in the Castle of Edinburgh. He is called Alexander by Dempster.

XIV. ELIAS II. is mentioned as abbot at the time of the Scots Templar Trials in 1309, and in a deed of William Lamberton, Bishop of St. Andrews, in 1316. In his time, Holyrood, like Melrose and Dryburgh, was ravaged by the baffled army of Edward II. in 1322.

XV. SYMON OF WEDALE, abbot at the vigil of St. Barnabas, 1326, when Robert I. held a Parliament in Holyrood, at which was ratified a concord

, between Randolph the famous Earl of Moray and Sir William Oliphant, in connection with the forfeited estate of William of Monte Alto. Another species of Parliament was held at Holyrood on the 10th of February, in the year 1333-4, when Edward III. received the enforced homage of his creature Baliol.

XVI. JOHN II., abbot, appears as a witness to three charters in 1338, granted to William of Livingston, William of Creighton, and Henry of Brade (Braid ?).

XVII. BARTHOLOMEW, abbot in 1342.

XVIII. THOMAS, abbot, witnessed a charter to William Douglas of that ilk, Sir James of Sandilands, and the Lady Elenora Bruce, relict of Alexander Earl of Carrick, nephew of Robert I., of the lands of the West Calder. On the 8th of May, 1366, a council was held at Holyrood, at which the Scottish nobles treated with ridicule and contempt the pretensions of the kings of England, and sanctioned an assessment for the ransom of David II., taken prisoner at the battle of Durham. That monarch was buried before the high altar in 1371, and Edward III. granted a safe conduct to certain persons proceeding to Flanders to provide for the tomb in which he was placed.

XIX. JOHN III., abbot on the 11th of January, 1372. During his term of office, John of Gaunt Duke of Lancaster, fourth son of Edward III., was hospitably entertained at Holyrood, when compelled to take flight from his enemies in England.

XX. DAVID, abbot on the 18th of January, in the thirteenth year of Robert II. The abbey was burned by the army of Richard II. whose army encamped at Restalrig; but it was soon after repaired. David is mentioned in a charter dated at Perth, 1384-5.

XXI. JOHN (formerly Dean of Leith) was abbot on the 8th of May, 1386. His name occurs in several charters and other documents, and for the last time in the indenture or lease of the Canonmills to the city of Edinburgh, 12th September, 1423. In his time Henry IV. spared the monastery in gratitude for the kindness of the monks to his exiled father John of Gaunt.

XXII. PATRICK, abbot 5th September, 1435. In his term of office James II., who had been born in the abbey, was crowned there in his sixth year, on the 25th March, 1436-7; and another high ceremony was performed in the same church when Mary of Gueldres was crowned as Queen Consort in July, 1449. In the preceding year, John Bishop of Galloway elect became an inmate of the abbey, and was buried in the cloisters.

XXIII. JAMES, abbot 26th April, 1450.

XXIV. ARCHIBALD CRAWFORD, abbot in 1457. He was son of Sir William Crawford of Hairing, and had previously been Prior of Holyrood. In 1450 he was one of the commissioners who treated with the English at Coventry concerning a truce; and again in 1474, concerning a marriage between James Duke of Rothesay and the Princess Cecile, second daughter of Edward IV. of England. He was Lord High Treasurer of Scotland in 1480. He died in 1483. On the abbey church (according to Crawford) his arms were carved more than thirty times. "He added the buttresses on the walls of the north and south aisles, and probably built the rich doorway which opens into the north aisle." Many finely executed coats armorial are found over the niches, among them Abbot Crawford's frequently—a fesse ermine, with a star of five points, in chief, surmounted by an abbot's mitre resting on a pastoral staff.

XXV. ROBERT BELLENDEN, abbot in 1486, when commissioner concerning a truce with England. He was still abbot in 1498, and his virtues are celebrated by his namesake, the archdean of Moray, canon of Ross, and translator of Boëce, who says "he left the abbey, and died ane Chartour-monk." In 1507 the Papal legate presented James IV., in the name of Pope Julius II., in the church, amid a brilliant crowd of nobles, with a purple crown adorned by golden lilies, and a sword of state studded with gems, which is still preserved in the Castle of Edinburgh. He also brought a bull, bestowing upon James the title of Defender of the Faith. Abbot Bellenden, in 1493, founded a chapel in North Leith, dedicated to St. Ninian, latterly degraded into a victual granary The causes moving the abbot to build this chapel, independent of the spiritual wants of the people, were manifold, as set forth in the charter of erection. The bridge connecting North and South Leith, over which he levied toll, was erected at the same time. The piers still remain.

XXVI. GEORGE CRICHTOUN, abbot in 1515, and Lord Privy Seal, was promoted to the see of Dunkeld in 1528. As we have recorded elsewhere, he was the founder of the Hospital of St. Thomas, near the Water Gate. An interesting relic of his abbacy exists at present in England.

About the year 1750, when a grave was being dug in the chancel of St. Stephen's church, St. Albans, in Hertfordshire, there was found buried in the soil an ancient lectern bearing his name, and which is supposed to have been concealed there at some time during the Civil Wars. It is of cast brass, and handsome in design, consisting of an eagle with expanded wings, supported by a shaft decorated with several mouldings, partly circular and partly hexagonal. The eagle stands upon a globe, and the shaft has been originally supported on three feet, which are now gone. The lectern at present is five feet seven inches in height, and is inscribed:—"GEORGIUS CREICHTOUN, EPISCOPUS DUNKENENSIS."

He died on January 24th, 1543, and the probability is that the lectern had been presented to Holyrood on his elevation to Dunkeld as a farewell

1528. He had been previously provost of the collegiate church of Corstorphine, and was twice High Treasurer, in 1529 and 1537. In 1538 he was elected Bishop of Ross, and held that office, together with the Abbacy of Ferne, till his death, 31st November, 1545.

XXIX. ROBERT STUART, of Strathdon, a son of James V. by Eupham Elphinstone, had a grant of the abbacy when only seven years of age, and in manhood he joined the Reformation party, in 1559.

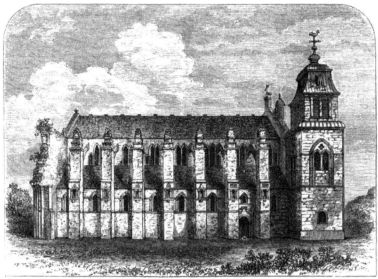

THE ABBEY CHURCH.   (From an Engraving in Maitland's "History of Edinburgh.")

gift, and that it had been stolen from the abbey by Sir Richard Lea of Sopwell, who accompanied the Earl of Hertford in the invasion of 1544, and who carried off the famous brazen font from Holyrood, and presented it to the parish church of St. Albans, with a magniloquent inscription. "This font, which was abstracted from Holyrood, is no longer known to exist, and there seems no reason to doubt that the lectern, which was saved by being buried during the Civil Wars, was abstracted at the same time, and given to the church of St. Albans by the donor of the font."

XXVII. WILLIAM DOUGLAS, Prior of Coldingham, was the next abbot. He died in 1528.

XXVIII. ROBERT CAIRNCROSS, abbot September

He married in 1561, and received from his sister, Queen Mary, a gift of some Crown lands in Orkney and Shetland in 1565, with a large grant out of the queen's third of Holyrood in the following year. In 1569 he exchanged his abbacy with Adam Bishop of Orkney for the temporalities of that see, and his lands in Orkney and Shetland were erected into an earldom in his favour 28th October, 1581.

XXX. ADAM BOTHWELL, who acquired the abbacy in commendam by this strange and lawless compact, did not find his position a very quiet one, and several articles against him were presented in the General Assembly in 1570. The fifth of these stated that all the twenty-seven churches of the abbey wherein divine service had been performed "are decayit, and made some sheep-folds, and some sa ruinous that none dare enter into thame for fear of falling, especially Halyrud Hous, althocht the Bishop of Sanct Androw's, in time of Papistry,

the necessary repairs. He resigned his so-called abbacy in favour of his son before 1583, and died in 1593. He was interred near the third pillar from the south-east corner, on the south side of the church.

INTERIOR OF THE CHAPEL ROYAL OF HOLYROOD HOUSE, 1687. *(After Wyck and P. Maxell.)*

sequestrat the haill rentis of the said abbacy, because only the glassen windows wer not holden up and repairt." To this Bothwell answered that the churches referred to had been pillaged and ruined before his time, especially Holyrood Church, "quhilk hath been thir twintie yeris bygane ruinous through decay of twa principal pillars, sa that none wer assurit under it," and that two thousand pounds would not be sufficient for

XXXI. JOHN BOTHWELL, his eldest son, held the abbey *in commendam* under the great seal, 24th February, 1581, and was a Lord of Session in 1593. In 1607 part of the abbey property, together with the monastery itself, was converted into a temporal peerage for him and his heirs, by the title of Lord Holyroodhouse. John Lord Bothwell died without direct heirs male, and though the title should have descended to his brother

William, who had property in Broughton, after his death, none bore even nominally the title of abbot. A part of the lands fell to the Earl of Roxburghe, from whom the superiority passed, as narrated elsewhere.

The "Chronicon Sanctæ Crucis" was commenced by the canons of Holyrood, but the portion that has been preserved comes down only to 1163, and breaks off at the time of their third abbot. "Even the Indices Sanctorum and the 'two Calendars of Benefactors and Brethren, begun from the earliest times, and continued by the care of numerous monks,' may—when allowance is made for the magniloquent style of the recorder—mean nothing more than the united calendar, martyrology, and ritual book, which is fortunately still preserved. It is a large folio volume of 132 leaves of thick vellum, in oak boards covered with stamped leather, which resembles the binding of the sixteenth century."

The extent of the ancient possessions of this great abbey may be gathered from the charters and gifts in the valuable *Munimenta Ecclesiæ Sanctæ Crucis de Edwinesburg* and the series of *Stent Rolls.* To enumerate the vestments, ornaments, jewels, relics, and altar vessels of gold and silver set with precious stones, would far exceed our limits, but they are to be found at length in the second volume of the "Bannatyne Miscellany." When the monastery was dissolved at the Reformation its revenues were great, and according to the two first historians of Edinburgh its annual income then was stated as follows :

By Maitland : In wheat. 27 chalders, 10 bolls.
,, In bear... 40 ,, 9 ,,
,, In oats .. 34 ,, 15 ,, 3½ pecks.
501 capons, 24 hens, 24 salmon, 12 loads of salt, and an unknown number of swine. In money, £2,926 8s. 6d. Scots.

By Arnot : In wheat ....442 bolls.
,, In bear ....640 ,,
,, In oats ....560 ,,
with the same amount in other kind, and £250 sterling.

CHAPTER VIII.

HOLYROOD ABBEY *(concluded).*

Charter of William I.—Trial of the Scottish Templars—Prendergast's Revenge—Charters by Robert II. and III.—The Lord of the Isles—Coronation of James II.—Marriages of James II. and III.—Church, &c. Burned by the English—Plundered by them—Its Restoration by James VII.—The Royal Vault—Description of the Chapel Royal - Plundered at the Revolution—Ruined in 1768—The West Front—The Belhaven Monument—The Churchyard—Extent of Present Ruin—The Sanctuary—The Abbey Bells.

KING WILLIAM THE LION, in a charter under his great seal, granted between the years 1171 and 1177, addressed to "all the good men of his whole kingdom, French, English, Scots, and Galwegians," confirmed the monks of Holyrood in all that had been given them by his grandfather, King David, together with many other gifts, including the pasture of a thousand sheep in Rumanach (Romanno ?), a document witnessed in the castle, "*apud Edensebvrch.*"

In 1309, when Elias II. was abbot, there occurred an interesting event at Holyrood, of which no notice has yet been taken in any history of Scotland—the trial of the Scottish Knights of the Temple on the usual charges made against the order, after the terrible murmurs that rose against it in Paris, London, and elsewhere, in consequence of its alleged secret infidelity, sorcery, and other vices.

According to the *Processus factus contra Templarios in Scotia,* in Wilkins' "Concilia," a work of great price and rarity, it was in the month of December, 1309—when the south of Scotland was overrun by the English, Irish, Welsh, and Norman troops of Edward II., and John of Bretagne, Earl of Richmond, was arrogantly called lieutenant of the kingdom, though Robert Bruce, succeeding to the power and popularity of Wallace, was in arms in the north—that Master John de Soleure, otherwise styled of Solerio, "chaplain to our lord the Pope," together with William Lamberton, Bishop of St. Andrews, met at the Abbey of Holyrood "for the trial of the Templars, and two brethren of that order undernamed, the only persons of the order present in the kingdom of Scotland, by command of our most holy lord Clement V." Some curious light is thrown upon the inner life of the order by this trial, which it is impossible to give at full length.

In the first place appeared Brother Walter of Clifton, who, being sworn on the Gospels, replied that he had belonged to the military order of the Temple for ten years, since the last feast of All Saints, and had been received into it at Temple Bruer, at Lincoln, in England, by Brother William de la More (whom Raynouard, in his work on the order, calls a Scotsman), and that the Scottish brother knights received the statutes and observances of the order from the Master of England, who received them from the Grand Master at Jerusalem and the Master at Cyprus. He had then to detail the mode of his reception into the order, begging admission with clasped hands and bended knees, affirming that he had no debts and was not affianced to any woman, and that he "vowed to be a perpetual servant to the master and the brotherhood, and to defend the Eastern land; to be for ever chaste and obedient, and to live without his own will and property." A white mantle had then been put upon his shoulder (to be worn over his chain armour, but looped up to leave the sword-arm free); a linen coif and the kiss of fraternity were then given him. On his knees he then vowed "never to dwell in a house where a woman was in labour, nor be present at the marriage or purification of one; that from thence forward he would sleep in his shirt and drawers, with a cord girt over the former."

The inquisitors, who were perhaps impatient to hear of the four-legged idol, the cat, and the devil, concerning all of which such curious confessions had been made by the Florentine Templars, now asked him if he had ever heard of scandals against the order during his residence at Temple in Lothian, or of knights that had fled from their preceptories; and he answered:—

"Yes; Brother Thomas Tocci and Brother John de Husflete, who for two years had been preceptor before him at Balantradoch (Temple), and also two other knights who were natives of England."

Being closely interrogated upon all the foolish accusations in the papal bull of Clement, he boldly replied to each item in the negative. Two of the charges were that their chaplains celebrated mass without the words of consecration, and that the knights believed their preceptors could absolve sins. He explained that such powers could be delegated, and that he himself "had received it a considerable time ago."

Sir William de Middleton, clad in the military order of the Temple, was next sworn and interrogated in the same manner. He was admitted into the order, he said, by Sir Brian le Jay, then Master of England, who was slain by Wallace at the battle of Falkirk, and had resided at Temple in Lothian and other preceptories of the order, and gave the same denials to the clauses in the bull that had been given by Clifton, with the addition that he "was prohibited from receiving any service from women, not even water to wash his hands."

After this he was led from the court, and forty-one witnesses, summoned to Holyrood, were examined. These were chiefly abbots, priests, and even

serving-men of the order, but nothing of a criminal nature against it was elicited; though during similar examinations at Lincoln, Brother Thomas Tocci de Thoroldby, a Templar, declared that he had heard the late Brian le Jay (Master of Scotland and afterwards of England) say a hundred times over, "that Christ was not the true God, but a mere man, and that the smallest hair out of the beard of a Saracen was worth any Christian's whole body;" and that once, when he was standing in Sir Brian's presence, certain beggars sought alms "for the love of God and our Blessed Lady," on which he threw a halfpenny in the mud, and made them hunt for it, though in midwinter, saying, "Go to your lady and be hanged!" Another Templar, Stephen de Stapelbrvgge, declared that Sir Brian ordered him at his admission to spit upon the cross, but he spat beside it.

The first witness examined at Holyrood was Hugh Abbot of Dunfermline, who stated that he had ever viewed with suspicion the midnight chapters and "clandestine admission of brethren." Elias Lord Abbot of Holyrood, and Gervase Lord Abbot of Newbattle, were then examined, together with Master Robert of Kydlawe, and Patrick Prior of the Dominicans in the fields near Edinburgh, and they agreed in all things with the Abbot of Dunfermline.

The eighth witness, Adam of Wedale (now called Stow), a Cistercian, accused the Templars of selfishness and oppression of their neighbours, and John of Byres, a monk of Newbattle, John of Mumphat and Gilbert of Haddington, two monks of Holyrood, entirely agreed with him; while the rector of Ratho maintained that the Scottish Templars were not free from the crimes imputed to the order, adding "that he had never known when any Templar was buried or heard of one dying a natural death, and that the whole order was generally against the Holy Church." The former points had evident reference to the rumour that the order burned their dead and drank the ashes in wine!

Henry de Leith Rector of Restalrig, Nicholas Vicar of Lasswade, John Chaplain of St. Leonard's, and others, agreed in all things with the Abbot of Dunfermline, as did nine Scottish barons of rank who added that "the knights were ungracious to the poor, practising hospitality alone to the great and wealthy, and then only under the impulse of fear; and moreover, that had the Templars been good Christians they would never have lost the Holy Land."

The forty-first and last witness, John Thyng, who for seventeen years had been a serving brother of the order in Scotland, coincided with the others, adding, "that many brethren of the Temple, being common people, indifferently absolve excommunicated persons, saying that they derived power from their lord the Supreme Pontiff;" and also, "that the chapters were held so secretly that none save a Templar ever had access to them."

So ended the inquisition at Holyrood, "which could not be made more solemn on account of the

to a rich booty near Calder Muir by a soldier named Robert Prendergast, an adherent of Baliol, who served under the English banner. Upon returning to the castle, instead of being rewarded, as he expected, the Scottish traitor, at dinner in the hall, was placed among the serving-men and below the salt.

Filled with rage and mortification, he remained

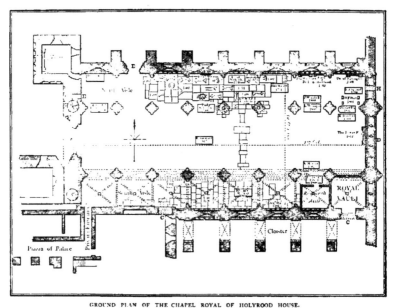

GROUND PLAN OF THE CHAPEL ROYAL OF HOLYROOD HOUSE.
(From an Engraving in the History of the Abbey, published in 1821.)

A, Great West Entrance ; B, North Door ; C C, Doors from South Aisle to Cloisters, now walled up ; D, Great East Window ; E, Stair to Rood loft ; F, Door to the Palace, shut up ; G, Remaining Pillars, north side ; H, Screen-work in Stone.

daily incursions of *the enemy*"—*i.e.*, the Scottish patriots under Bruce.

We may conclude that on the departure of John of Solerio, the preceptor and his companion were set at liberty ; but on the suppression of the order throughout Scotland, their vast possessions were given to their rivals, the Knights of St. John at Torphichen.

In 1337, about the time that John II. was abbot, sanctuary was given in Holyrood church to a remarkable fugitive from the Castle of Edinburgh, which at that time was held by an English garrison under Thomas Knyton. In one of the forays made by him in search of supplies, he had been guided

silent, and declined to eat. Thomas Knyton observing this, asked the reason in a jesting tone, and on receiving a haughty and sullen reply, passionately struck Prendergast on the head with a weapon that lay near, and so severe was the blow that his blood bespattered the floor. He affected to bear with this new outrage, and nursing his wrath, quitted the fortress ; but next day, when Thomas Knyton rode through the gate into the city with a few attendants, Prendergast rushed from a place of concealment—probably a Close head—and passing a long sword through his heart, dashed him a corpse on the causeway.

He then leaped on Knyton's horse, and spurring

down the street, reached Holyrood, where he sought sanctuary in the chapel of St. Augustine; there his English pursuers found him on his knees before the altar.

As they dared not, under pain of excommunica-

ever intent on revenge, joined Sir William Douglas, the Black Knight of Liddesdale, whose forces lay in the fastnesses of Pentland Muir.

From there one night he led the Liddesdale men, and being well acquainted with all the avenues to

WEST FRONT OF HOLYROOD ABBEY CHURCH.

tion, violate the sanctuary, they set a guard upon the church, resolving to starve him into surrender; but fortunately for Robert Prendergast, the monks of Holyrood were loyal to their king, and thinking probably an Englishman less in the world mattered little from a Scottish point of view, they conveyed to him provisions every night unseen by the guard. For twelve days and nights he lurked by the altar of St. Augustine, until, disguised in a monk's cowl and gown, he effected an escape; and more than

the then open and unwalled city, attacked the English, and left 400 of them dead in the streets. Sir William Douglas re-captured the fortress in the following year.

In 1370 David II. was interred with every solemnity before the high altar, the site of which is now in the Palace Garden. It was inscribed, "*Hic Rex sub lapide David inclitus est tumulatus*," as given by Fordun.

On the 18th of January, 1384-5, Robert II.,

under his great seal, granted to David, Abbot of Holyrood, a piece of land within the Castle of Edinburgh whereon to erect a house, to which the monks, their servants and families, might repair in time of peace and war. This piece of ground was eighty feet in length and eighty in breadth, wherever the abbot might choose, "beyond the site of our manor" (the royal lodging?); "the said abbot and his successors paying therefor to us and to our heirs a silver penny at the said castle on Whitsunday yearly, if asked only, so that the foresaid abbot and his successors and their servants shall be bound to take the oath of fidelity for the due security of the said castle to the keeper thereof, who may be for the time, have free ish and entry to the said castle at accustomed and proper hours."

On the 5th April, 1391, King Robert III., under his great seal, granted a charter to the Abbey of Holyrood, confirming the charter of David II. to the abbey, dated 30th December, 1343. It is dated at Edinburgh. When the abbey became a species of palace has never been distinctly ascertained, but Robert III. appears sometimes to have made Holyrood his residence. James I. occasionally kept his court there; and in the abbey his queen was delivered of twin princes, on the 16th October, 1416—Alexander, who died, and James, afterwards second of that name.

In 1428 a remarkable episode occurred in the abbey church. Alexander, Lord of the Isles, who had been in rebellion against James I., but had been utterly defeated by the royal troops in Lochaber, sent messengers to the king to sue for mercy. But the latter, justly incensed, refused to enter into any negotiations with an outlawed fugitive. Alexander, driven to despair, and compelled to fly from place to place, was compelled at last to trust to the royal clemency. Travelling secretly to Edinburgh, he suddenly presented himself, upon a solemn festival, before the high altar of Holyrood, and holding his drawn sword by the point, he presented the hilt to the astonished king, in token of his unconditional submission, and falling on his knees, in presence of Queen Jane and the whole court, implored the royal mercy. The ill-fated James granted him his life, at the tender intercession of his royal consort, but sent him a prisoner to the sequestered castle of Tantallon, on its sea-beat rock, under the charge of his nephew, the Earl of Angus. The island chief eventually received a free pardon, was restored to all his honours, castles, and estates, and stood as sponsor for the twin princes, Alexander and James, at the font.

In 1437 the Parliament met at Edinburgh, on the 25th March, after the murder of James I., and adopted immediate measures for the government of the country. Their first act was the coronation of the young prince, in his sixth year, on whose head at Holyrood, as James II., the crown was solemnly placed by James Kennedy, Bishop of St. Andrews, in presence of a great concourse of the nobles, clergy, and representatives of towns, amid the usual testimonies of devotion and loyalty.

On March 27th, 1439, Patrick Abbot of Holyrood and his convent granted a charter to Sir Robert Logan of Restalrig, and his heirs, of the office of bailie over their lands of St. Leonard's, in the town of Leith, "from the end of the great volut of William Logane, on the east part of the common gate that passes to the ford over the water of Leith, beside the waste land near the house of John of Turyng on the west part, and common Venale called St. Leonard's Wynd, as it extended of old on the south part, and the water of the port of Leith on the north, and . . . . in the ninth year of the pontificate of our most holy father and lord, Eugenius IV., by Divine Providence Pope."

Chronologically, the next event connected with the abbey was the arrival of Mary of Gueldres in 1449. In company with John Railston, Bishop of Dunkeld, and Nicholas Otterburn, official of Lothian, the Lord Chancellor Crichton went to France to seek among the princesses of that friendly court a suitable bride for young James II.; but no match being suitable, by the advice of Charles VII. these ambassadors proceeded to Burgundy, and, with the cordial concurrence of Duke Philip the Good, made proposals to his kinswoman, Mary, the only daughter and heiress of Arnold, Duke of Gueldres, and in 1449 the engagement was formally concluded. Philip promised to pay £60,000 in gold as a dowry, while James, on the other hand, settled 10,000 crowns upon her, secured on land in Strathearn, Athole, Methven, and East Lothian, while relinquishing all claim to the Duchy of Gueldres, in the event of an heir male being born to Duke Arnold ; and the Parliament met at Stirling, resolved that the royal nuptials should be conducted on a scale of splendour suited to the occasion.

The fleet containing the bride anchored in June in the Forth. She was "young, beautiful, and of a masculine constitution," says Hawthornden, and came attended by a splendid train of knights and nobles from France and Burgundy, including the Archduke Sigismund of Austria, the Duke of Brittany, and the Lord of Campvere (the three brothers-in-law of the King of Scotland), together with the Dukes of Savoy and Burgundy. She landed at Leith amid a vast concourse of all classes of the people, and, escorted by a body-guard of 300 men-at-arms, all *cap-à-pie*, with the citizens also in their armour, under Patrick Cockburn of Newbigging, Provost of Edinburgh and Governor of the Castle, was escorted to the monastery of the Greyfriars, where she was warmly welcomed by her future husband, then in his twentieth year, and was visited by the queen-mother on the following day.

The week which intervened between her arrival and her marriage was spent in a series of magnificent entertainments, during which, from her great beauty and charms of manner, she won the devoted affection of the loyal nobles and people.

A contemporary chronicler has given a minute account of one of the many chivalrous tournaments that took place, in which three Burgundian nobles, two of them brothers named Lalain, and the third Hervé Meriadet, challenged any three Scottish knights to joust with lance, battle-axe, sword, and dagger, a defiance at once accepted by Sir James Douglas, James Douglas of Lochleven, and Sir John Ross of Halkhead, Constable of Renfrew. Lances were shivered and sword and axe resorted to with nearly equal fortune, till the king threw down his truncheon and ended the combat.

The royal marriage, which took place in the church at Holyrood amid universal joy, concluded these stirring scenes. At the bridal feast the first dish was in the form of a boar's head, painted and stuck full of tufts of coarse flax, served up on an enormous platter, with thirty-two banners, bearing the arms of the king and principal nobles; and the flax was set aflame, amid the acclamations of the numerous assembly that filled the banquet-hall.

Ten years after Holyrood beheld a sorrowful scene, when, in 1460, James, who had been slain by the bursting of a cannon at the siege of Roxburgh on the 3rd August, in his thirtieth year, was laid in the royal vault, "with the teares of his people and his haill army," says Balfour.

In 1467 there came from Rome, dated 22nd February, the bull of Pope Paul II., granting, on the petition of the provost, bailies, and community of the city, a commission to the Bishop of Galloway, "*et dilecto filio Abbati Monasterii Sanctæ Crucis extra muros de Edynburgh*," to erect the Church of St. Giles into a collegiate institution.

Two years afterwards Holyrood was again the scene of nuptial festivities, when the Parliament met, and Margaret of Norway, Denmark, and Sweden, escorted by the Earl of Arran and a gallant train of Scottish and Danish nobles, landed

at Leith in July, 1469. She was in her sixteenth year, and had as her dowry the isles of Orkney and Shetland, over which her ancestors had hitherto claimed feudal superiority. James III., her husband, had barely completed his eighteenth year when they were married in the abbey church, where she was crowned queen-consort. "The marriage and coronation gave occasion to prolonged festivities in the metropolis and plentiful congratulations throughout the kingdom. Nor was the flattering welcome undeserved by the queen; in the bloom of youth and beauty, amiable and virtuous, educated in all the feminine accomplishments of the age, and so richly endowed, she brought as valuable an accession of lustre to the court as of territory to the kingdom."

In 1477 there arrived "heir in grate pompe," says Balfour, "Husman, the legate of Pope Xystus the Fourth," to enforce the sentence of deprivation and imprisonment pronounced by His Holiness upon Patrick Graham, Archbishop of St. Andrews, an eminent and unfortunate dignitary of the Church of Scotland. He was the first who bore that rank, and on making a journey to Rome, returned as legate, and thus gained the displeasure of the king and of the clergy, who dreaded his power. He was shut up in the monastery of Inchcolm, and finally in the castle of Lochleven. Meanwhile, in the following year, William Schivez, a great courtier and favourite of the king, was solemnly consecrated in Holyrood Church by the papal legate, from whose hands he received a pall, the ensign of archiepiscopal dignity, and with great solemnity was proclaimed " Primate and Legate of the realm of Scotland." His luckless rival died of a broken heart, and was buried in St. Serf's Isle, where his remains were recently discovered, buried in a peculiar posture, with the knees drawn up and the hands down by the side.

In 1531, when Robert Cairncross was abbot, there occurred an event, known as "the miracle of John Scott," which made some noise in its time. This man, a citizen of Edinburgh, having taken shelter from his creditors in the sanctuary of Holyrood, subsisted there, it is alleged, for forty days without food of any kind.

Impressed by this circumstance, of which some exaggerated account had perhaps been given to him, James V. ordered his apparel to be changed and strictly searched. He ordered also that he should be conveyed from Holyrood to a vaulted room in David's Tower in the castle, where he was barred from access by all and closely guarded. Daily a small allowance of bread and water were placed before him, but he abstained from both for thirty-two days. He was then brought forth, nude, in presence of a multitude, who regarded him with fear and wonder, and to whom he affirmed "that by the aid of the Blessed Virgin, he could fast as long as he pleased."

" As there appeared to be more simplicity than guile in his behaviour, he was released, and afterwards went to Rome, where he fasted long enough to convince Pope Gregory of the miracle. From

Holyrudhous;" but the days of its declension and destruction were at hand.

The English army which invaded Scotland under the Earl of Hertford, in 1543-4, barbarously burned down the temporal edifices of the abbey; and among other plunder there were carried off the brass lectern which has been already described, and a famous brass font of curious workmanship, by Sir Richard Lea, knight, captain of English

INTERIOR OF HOLYROOD CHURCH, LOOKING EAST.

Rome he went to Venice, where he received fifty ducats of gold to convey him to Jerusalem, in performance of a vow he had made. He returned to Scotland in the garb of a pilgrim, wearing palm-leaves, and bearing a bag filled with large stones, which he said were taken out of the pillar to which the Saviour was bound when he was scourged. He became a preacher, and in an obscure suburb of the city performed mass before an altar, on which his daughter, a girl of beauty, stood with wax tapers around her to represent the Virgin—a double impiety, which soon brought him under the ridicule and contempt he deserved."

In 1532, the " Diurnal of Occurrents " records, there "was made ane great abjuration of the favouraris of Martene Lutar in the abbey of

Pioneers, who presented it to the Church of St. Albans, in Hertfordshire, with the following absurd inscription, which is given in Latin in Camden's " Britannia":—

"When Leith, a town of good account in Scotland, and Edinburgh, the principal city of that nation, were on fire, Sir Richard Lea, knyght, saved me out of the flames, and brought me to England. In gratitude for his kindness, I, who heretofore served only at the baptism of kings, do now most willingly render the same service even to the meanest of the English nation. Lea the conqueror hath so commanded! Adieu. The year of man's salvation, 1543-4, in the thirty-sixth year of King Henry VIII."

Father Hay records that among other things

brought to the abbey by Abbot Bellenden were " the gret bellis and the gret brasin fownt."

During the civil wars in the time of Charles I. this relic was converted into money by the Puritans, and in all probability was utterly destroyed.

After the battle of Pinkie, in 1547, the English

sioners, making first theyr visitacion there, they found the moonkes all gone, but the church and mooch parts of the house well covered with leade. Soon after thei pluct of the leade and had down the bels, which wear but two, and, according to the statute, did somewhat hearby disgrace the hous.

NORTH ENTRANCE TO THE NAVE OF HOLYROOD ABBEY CHURCH.

troops returned to complete the destruction of the abbey, which in the interval had been completely repaired, and their proceedings are thus recorded by one of themselves, Patten, in his account of the expedition into Scotland :—" Thear stood to the westward, about a quarter of a mile from our campe, a monasterie; they call it Hollyroode Abbey. Sir Walter Bonham and Edward Chamberlayne got license to suppress it; whereupon these commis-

As touching the moonkes, becaus they wear gone, they put them to their pencions at large."

These repeated destructions at the hands of a wanton enemy, rather than any outrages by the Reformers, were the chief cause that now we find nothing remaining of the church but the fragment of one tower and the shattered nave; though much of the choir and transepts were in existence for many years later, and might have been so still had proper exertions been made for their repair and preservation, particularly by the Bishop of Orkney, and ere it shrank to the proportions of a chapel. But even when the Reformation was in full progress the following entry appears in the accounts of the Lord High Treasurer, under date the 8th February, 1557-8 :—£36 " to David Melville, indweller in Leith, for ane pair of organs to the chapel in the palace of Holyroodhouse."

The remains of George Earl of Huntly, who was slain at the battle of Corrichie, when he was in rebellion against the Crown, were brought by sea to Edinburgh in 1562, and kept all winter unburied in the Abbey of Holyrood—most probably in the church. Then an indictment for high treason was exhibited against him in the month of May following, " eftir that he was deid and departit frae this mortal lyfe," and the corpse was laid before Parliament : in this instance showing the rancour of party and the absurdity of old feudal laws.

It was somewhere about this time that the new royal vault was constructed in the south aisle of the nave, and the remains of the kings and queens were removed from their ancient resting-place near the high altar. It is built against the ancient Norman doorway of the cloisters, which still remains externally, with its slender shafts and beautiful zigzag mouldings of the days of David I. "The cloisters," says Wilson, " appear to have enclosed a large court, formed in the angle of the nave and transept. The remains of the north are clearly traceable still, and the site of the west side is occupied by palace buildings. Here was the ambulatory for the old monks, when the magnificent foundation of St. David retained its pristine splendour, and remained probably till the burning of the abbey after the death of James V.," who was buried there beside his first queen in December 1542, and his second son, Arthur Duke of Albany, a child eight days old, who died at Stirling.

In the royal vault also lie the remains of David II. ; Prince Arthur, third son of James IV., who died in the castle, July 15th, 1510, aged nine months ; Henry, Lord Darnley, murdered 1567 ; and Jane, Countess of Argyle, who was at supper with her sister, the queen, on the night of Rizzio's assassination. " Dying without issue, she was enclosed in one of the richest coffins ever seen in Scotland, the compartments and inscriptions being all of solid gold." In the same vault were deposited the remains of the Duchess de Grammont, who died an exile at Holyrood in 1803 ; and, in the days of Queen Victoria, the remains of Mary of Gueldres, queen of James II.

Among the altars in the church were two dedicated to St. Andrew and St. Catharine, a third dedicated to St. Anne by the tailors of Edinburgh, and a fourth by the Cordiners to St. Crispin, whose statutes were placed upon it.

On the 18th of June, 1567, two days after the imprisonment of Queen Mary, the Earl of Glencairn and others, " with a savage malignity, laid waste this beautiful chapel," broke in pieces its most valuable furniture, and laid its statues and other ornaments in ruins.

On the 18th of June, 1633, Charles I. was crowned with great pomp in the abbey church and amid the greatest demonstrations of loyalty, when the silver keys of the city were delivered to him by the Provost, after which they were never again presented to a monarch until the time of George IV. ; but afterwards the religious services were performed at Holyrood with great splendour, according to the imposing ritual of the English Church—" an innovation which the Presbyterians beheld with indignation, as an insolent violation of the laws of the land."

In 1687 the congregation of the Canongate were removed from the church by order of James VII., and the abbey church—now named a chapel— was richly decorated, and twelve stalls were placed therein for the Knights of the Thistle. An old view of the interior by Wyck and Mazell, taken prior to the fall of the roof, represents it entire, with all its groining and beautiful imperial crowns and coronets on the drooping pendants of the interlaced arches. They show the clerestory entire, and within the nave the stalls of the knights, six on each side. Each of these stalls had five steps, and on each side a Corinthian column supported an entablature of the same order, each surmounted by two great banners and three trophies, each composed of helmets and breastplates, making in all twenty-four banners and thirty-six trophies over the stalls. At the eastern end was the throne, surmounted by an imperial crown. On each side were two panels, having the crown, sword, and sceptre within a wreath of laurel, and below, other two panels, with the royal cypher, J.R., and the crown. Wyck and Mazell show the throne placed upon a lofty dais of seven steps, on six of which were a unicorn and lion, making six of the former on the right, and six of the latter on the left, all crowned. Behind this rose a Corinthian canopy, entablature, and garlands, all of carved oak, and over all the royal arms as borne in Scotland ; the crest of Scotland, the lion sejant ; on the right the ensign of St. Andrew; *In defence* on the left the ensign of St. George. Amid a star of spears, swords, and cannon were two ship's masts, fully rigged, one on the right bearing the Scottish flag, another on the left bearing the English. "Above all these rose the beautiful eastern window, shedding a flood of light along the nave, eclipsing the fourteen windows of the clerestory. The floor was laid with ornamental tiles, some portions of which are yet preserved."

In the royal yacht there came to Leith from London an altar, vestments, and images, to complete the restoration of the church to its ancient uses. As if to hasten on the destruction of his house, James VII., not content with securing to his Catholic subjects within the precincts of Holyrood that degree of religious toleration now enjoyed by every British subject, had mass celebrated there, and established a college of priests, whose rules were published on the 22nd of March, 1688, inviting people to send their children there, to be educated gratis, as Fountainhall records. He also appointed a Catholic printer, named Watson (who availed himself of the protection afforded by the sanctuary) to be "King's printer in Holyrood;" and obtained a right from the Privy Council to print all the "prognostications at Edinburgh," an interesting fact which accounts for the number of old books bearing Holyrood on their title-pages. Prior to all this, on St. Andrew's Day, 30th November, the whole church was sprinkled with holy water, re-consecrated, and a sermon was preached in it by a priest named Widerington.

Tidings of the landing of William of Orange roused the Presbyterian mobs to take summary vengeance, and on being joined by the students of the University, they assailed the palace and chapel royal. The guard, 100 strong—" the brats of Belial "—under Captain Wallace, opened a fire upon them, killing twelve and wounding many more, but they were ultimately compelled to give way, and the chapel doors were burst open. The whole interior was instantly gutted and destroyed, and the magnificent throne, stalls, and organ, were ruthlessly torn down, conveyed to the Cross, and there consigned to the flames, amid the frantic shrieks and yells of thousands. Not content with all this, in a spirit of mad sacrilege, the mob, now grown lawless, burst into the royal vault, tore some of the leaden coffins asunder, and, according to Arnot, carried off the lids.

By the middle of the eighteenth century the roof, which had become ruinous, was restored with flagstones in a manner too ponderous for the ancient arches, which gave way beneath the superincumbent weight on the 2nd of December, 1768; and again

the people of Edinburgh became seized by a spirit of the foullest desecration, and from thenceforward, until a comparatively recent period, the ruined church remained open to all, and was appropriated to the vilest uses. Grose thus describes what he saw when the rubbish had been partly cleared away :—" When we lately visited it we saw in the middle of the chapel the columns which had been borne down by the weight of the roof. Upon looking into the vaults which were open, we found that what had escaped the fury of the mob at the Revolution became a prey to the mob who ransacked it after it fell. In A.D. 1776 we had seen the body of James V. and others in their leaden coffins; the coffins are now stolen. The head of Queen Margaret (Magdalene ?), which was then entire, and even beautiful, and the skull of Darnley, were also stolen, and were last traced to the collection of a statuary in Edinburgh."

In 1795 the great east window was blown out in a violent storm, but in 1816 was restored from its own remains, which lay scattered about on the ground. In the latter year the north-west tower, latterly used as a vestry, was still covered by an ogee leaden roof. Ultimately this also fell.

The west front of what remains, though the work perhaps of different periods, is in the most beautiful style of Early English, and the boldly-cut heads in its sculptured arcade and rich variety of ornament in the doorway are universally admired. The windows above it were additions made so lately as the time of Charles I., and the inscriptions which that unfortunate king had carved on the ornamental tablet between them is a striking illustration of the vanity of human hopes. One runs :—

" *Basilicam hanc, Carolus Rex, Optimus instauravit*, 1633."

The other :—

" HE SHALL ESTABLISH ANE HOUSE FOR MY NAME, AND I WILL ESTABLISH THE THRONE OF HIS KINGDOM FOR EVER."

In the north-west tower is a marble monument to Robert, Viscount Belhaven, who was interred there in January, 1639. His nephews, Sir Archibald and Sir Robert Douglas, placed there that splendid memorial to perpetuate his virtues as a man and steadiness as a patriot. A row of tombs of Scottish nobility and others lie in the north aisle. The Roxburgh aisle adjoins the royal vault in the south aisle, and in front of it lies the tomb of the Countess of Errol, who died in 1808. Close by it is that of the Bishop of Orkney, already referred to. "A flattering inscription enumerates the bishop's titles, and represents this worldly hypocrite and intriguing apostate as one of the greatest and best men of his time."

In the churchyard, now all turned into flower beds and garden ground, there long remained a few plain grave-stones, the inscriptions on some of which are preserved by Menteith in his "Theatre of Mortality," and by Maitland in his "History." One alone remains now, that of Mylne (the builder of the palace), which was removed from its old site (the north-east angle of the ancient choir) in 1857, and placed against the eastern wall of the church.

The extent of the ruin as it now remains is 127 feet in length by 39 feet in breadth, within the walls; and there still exist nominally six deans and seven chaplains of the Chapel Royal, all, of course, clergymen of the Church of Scotland.

The whole ruin has an air of intense gloom and damp desolation; the breeze waves the grass and rank weeds between the lettered grave-stones, the ivy rustles on the wall, and by night the owl hoots in the royal vault and the roofless tower where stands the altar-tomb of Belhaven.

For a considerable space around the church and palace of Holyrood—embracing a circuit of four miles and a quarter—the open ground has been, since the days of David I., a sanctuary, and is so now, from arrest on civil process. This spacious

THE BELHAVEN MONUMENT, HOLYROOD CHURCH.

range "is of a very singular nature to be in the vicinity of a populous city, being little else than an assemblage of hills, rocks, precipices, morasses, and lakes." It includes Arthur's Seat and Salisbury Craigs, and, of course, as a refuge, originated in the old ecclesiastical privilege of sanctuary, with the exemptions of those attached to a monarch's court. When the law of debtor and creditor was more stringent than it is now, this peculiarity brought many far from respectable visitors to a cluster of houses round the palace—a cluster nearly entirely swept away about 1857—as varied in their appearance as the chequered fortunes of their bankrupt inmates; and it is believed to have been in a great measure owing to some private claims, likely to press heavily upon him, that Charles X. in his second exile sought a residence in deserted Holyrood.

The House of Inchmurry, formerly called Kirkland, in the parish of St. Martin's, was a country residence of the abbots of Holyrood.

One of the bells that hung in the remaining tower was placed in the Tron church steeple, another in St. Cuthbert's chapel of ease, and the third in St. Paul's, York Place, the congregation of which had it in their former church in the Canongate, which was built 1771-4. This last is small, and poor in sound.

CHAPTER IX.

HOLYROOD PALACE.

First Notice of its History—Marriage of James IV.—The Scots of the Days of Flodden—A Brawl in the Palace—James V.'s Tower—The Gudeman of Ballengeich—His Marriage—Death of Queen Magdalene—The Council of November, 1542—A Standing Army Proposed—The Muscovite Ambassadors Entertained by the Queen Regent.

THE occasional residence of so many of his kingly ancestors at the abbey of Holyrood, and its then sequestered and rural locality, doubtless suggested to James IV. the expediency of having a royal dwelling near it; thus, we find from the Records of the Privy Seal the earliest mention of a palace at Holyrood occurs on the 10th of September, 1504, when "to Maister Leonard Logy, for his gude and

thankful service, done and to be done, to the kingis hieness, and speciallie for his diligent and grete laboure made be him in the building of the palace beside the Abbey of the Holy Croce," of "the soume of forty pounds." This is the first genuine notice of the grand old Palace of Holyrood.

In 1503 the then new edifice witnessed the marriage festival of James IV. and Margaret Tudor, whose contract is still preserved in the city archives. A minute account of her reception at Edinburgh has been preserved by one of her attendants, John Young, the Somerset Herald, who records in a pleasing light the wealth, refinement, and chivalry of the court of Scotland. The king met his fair bride, who was then in her fourteenth year, at Dalkeith, where she was entertained by John Earl of Morton. She had scarcely taken possession of her chamber when the tramp of horses was heard in the quadrangle, and among the English using a stirrup, and spurred on at full gallop, leaving who might to follow; but hearing that the Earl of Surrey—his future foe—and other nobles were behind, he returned and saluted them bareheaded. At their next meeting Margaret played also on the lute and clavichord, while the monarch listened with bended knee and head uncovered. Who, then, could have foreseen the disastrous day of Flodden!

When she left Newbattle to proceed to the capital, James, attired in a splendid costume, met her on

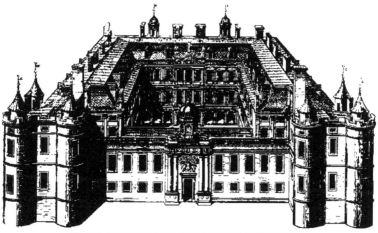

ISOMETRIC PROJECTION OF THE ROYAL PALACE OF HOLYROOD HOUSE.
(From an Engraving in Maitland's "History of Edinburgh.")

attendants the cry rang through the castle, "The king! The King of Scotland has arrived!"

The whole interview between the royal pair, as described by the Somerset Herald, presents a curious picture of the times. "James was dressed simply in a velvet jacket, with his hawking lure flung over his shoulder; his hair and beard curled naturally, and were rather long. . . . . . He took her hand and kissed her, and saluted all her ladies by kissing them. Then the king took the queen aside, and they communed together for a long space." He then returned to Holyrood. Next night he visited her at Newbattle, when he found her playing cards; and James, who is said to have composed the air of "Here's a health to my true love," entertained her by a performance on the clavichord and lute; and on taking leave he sprang on his horse, "a right fair courser," without a bay horse trapped with gold. Before him rode Bothwell, bearing the sword of state, with the leading nobles. He took the queen from "her litre," and placing her behind him on a pillion, they rode onward to the city. On the way they were entertained by a scene of chivalry—a knight errant in full armour rescuing a distressed lady from a rival. The royal pair were met at their entrance by the Grey Friars, whose monastery they had to pass, bearing, in solemn procession, banner and cross and their most valued relics, which were presented to receive the kiss of Margaret and James; and thereafter they had to tarry at an embattled barrier, at the windows of which were "angells syning joyously," one of whom presented to her the keys of the city.

Descending the crowded streets, they were met by the whole Chapter of St. Giles's in their richest vestments, bearing the arm-bone of the saint; then they passed the Cross, the fountain of which flowed with wine, "whereof all might drink," says Leland. Personages representing the angel Gabriel, the Virgin, Justice treading Nero under foot, Force bearing a pillar, Temperance holding a horse's bit, and Prudence triumphing over Sardanapalus, met them at the Nether Bow; and from there, preceded by music, they proceeded to Holyrood, where a glittering crowd of ecclesiastics, abbots, and friars, headed by the Archbishop of St. Andrews, conveyed them to the high altar, and after *Te Deum* was sung, they passed through the cloisters into the new palace. Fresh ceremonies took place in a great chamber thereof, the arras of which represented Troy, and the coloured windows of which were filled with the arms of Scotland and England, the Bishop of Moray acting as master of the ceremonies, which seems to have included much "kyssing" all round.

On the 8th of August the marriage took place, and all the courtiers wore their richest apparel. James sat in a chair of crimson velvet, "the pannels of that sam gylte under hys cloth of estat, of blue velvet figured with gold." On his right hand was the Archbishop of York, on his left the Earl of Surrey, while the Scottish prelates and nobles led in the girl-queen, crowned "with a vary riche crowne of gold, garnished with perles," to the high altar, where, amid the blare of trumpets, the Archbishop of Glasgow solemnised the marriage. The banquet followed in a chamber hung with red and blue, where the royal pair sat under a canopy of cloth of gold; and Margaret was served at the first course with a slice from "a wyld borres hed gylt, within a fayr platter." Lord Grey held the ewer and Lord Huntly the towel.

The then famous minstrels of Aberdeen came to Holyrood to sing on this occasion, and were all provided with silver badges, on which the arms of the granite city were engraved.

Masques and tournaments followed. James, skilled in all the warlike exercises of the time, appeared often in the lists as the savage knight, attended by followers dressed as Pans and satyrs. The festivities which accompanied this marriage indicate an advancement in refinement and splendour, chiefly due to the princely nature kindness, and munificence of James IV.

"The King of Scotland," wrote the Spanish ambassador Don Pedro de Ayala, "is of middle height; his features are handsome; he never cuts his hair or beard, and it becomes him well. He expressed himself gracefully in Latin, French, German, Flemish, Italian, and Spanish. His pronuncia-

tion of Spanish was clearer than that of other foreigners. In addition to his own, he speaks the language of the savages (or Celts) who live among the distant mountains and islands. The books which King James reads most are the Bible and those of devotion and prayer. He also studies old Latin and French chronicles. . . . . . He never ate meat on Wednesday, Friday, or Saturday. He would not for any consideration mount horseback on Sunday, not even to go to mass. Before transacting any business he heard two masses. In the smallest matters, and even when indulging in a joke, he always spoke the truth. . . . . . The Scots," continues De Ayala, "are often considered in Spain to be handsomer than the English. The women of quality were free in their manners and courteous to strangers. The Scottish ladies reign absolute mistresses in their own houses, and the men in all domestic matters yield a chivalrous obedience to them. The people live well, having plenty of beef, mutton, fowl, and fish. The humbler classes—the women especially—are of a very religious turn of mind. Altogether, I found the Scots to be a very agreeable and, I must add, an amiable people."

Such, says the author of the "Tudor Dynasty," was the Scotland of the sixteenth century, a period described by modern writers as one of barbarism, ignorance, and superstition; but thus it was the Spanish ambassador painted the king and his Scots of the days of Flodden.

"In the year 1507," says Hawthornden, "James, Prince of Scotland and the Isles, was born at Holyrood House the 21st of January," and the queen being brought nigh unto death, "the king, overcome by affection and religious vows," went on a pilgrimage to St. Ninian's in Galloway, and "at his return findeth the queen recovered."

In 1517 we read in Holyrood, when James Wardlaw, for striking Robert Roger to the effusion of blood within "my Lord Governor's chalmer and palace of pece," was conveyed to the Tron, had his hand stricken through, and was banished for life, under pain of death.

The governor was the Regent Albany, who took office after Flodden, and during his residence at Holyrood seems to have proceeded immediately with the works at the palace which the fatal battle had interrupted, and which James IV. had continued till his death. The accounts of the treasurer show that building was in progress then, throughout the years 1515 and 1516; and after Albany quitted the kingdom for the last time, James V. came to Holyrood, where he was crowned in 1524, and remained there, as Pitscottie tells, for "the space of one year, with great triumph and merriness." He diligently continued the works begun by his gallant father, and erected the north-west towers, which have survived more than one conflagration, and on the most northern of which could be traced, till about 1820, his name, IACOBVS REX SCOTORVM, in large gilt Roman letters.

In 1528 blood was again shed in Holyrood during a great review of Douglases and Hamiltons held there prior to a march against the English borders. A groom of the Earl of Lennox perceiving among those present Sir James Hamilton of Finnart, who slew that noble at Linlithgow, intent on vengeance, tracked him into the palace "by a dark staircase which led to a narrow gallery," and there attacked him, sword in hand. Sir James endeavoured to defend himself by the aid of his velvet mantle, but fell, pierced by six wounds, none of which, however, were mortal. The gates were closed, and while a general mêlée was on the point of ensuing between the Douglases and Hamiltons, the would-be assassin was discovered with his bloody weapon, put to the torture, and then his right hand was cut off, on which "he observed, with a sarcastic smile, that it was punished less than it deserved for having failed to revenge the murder of his beloved master."

James V. was still in the palace in 1530, as we find in the treasurer's accounts for that year : "Item, to the Egiptianis that dansit before the king in Holyrud House, 40s." He was a monarch whose pure benevolence of intention often rendered his romantic freaks venial, if not respectable, since from his anxiety to learn the wants and wishes of his humbler subjects he was wont, like *Il Bondocani*, or Haroun Alráschid, to traverse the vicinity of his palaces in the plainest of disguises ; and two comic songs, composed by himself, entitled "We'll gang nae mair a-roving," and "The Gaberlunzie Man," are said to have been founded on his adventures while masked as a beggar; and one of these, which nearly cost him his life at Cramond, some five miles from Holyrood, is given in Scott's "Tales of a Grandfather."

While visiting a pretty peasant girl in Cramond village he was beset by four or five persons, against whom he made a stand with his sword upon the high and narrow bridge that spans the Almond, in a wooded hollow. Here, when well-nigh beaten, and covered with blood, he was succoured and rescued by a peasant armed with a flail, who conducted him into a barn, where he bathed his wounds; and in the course of conversation James discovered that the summit of his deliverer's earthly wishes was to be proprietor of the little farm of Braehead,

on which he was then a labourer. Aware that it was Crown property, James said, "Come to Holyrood, and inquire for the gudeman of Ballengeich," referring to a part of Stirling Castle which he was wont to adopt as a cognomen.

The peasant came as appointed, and was met by the king in his disguise, who conducted him through the palace, and asked him if he wished to see the king. John Howison—for such was his name—expressed the joy it would give him, "provided he gave no offence. But how shall I know him?" he added.

"Easily," replied James. "All others will be bareheaded, the king alone will wear his bonnet."

Scared by his surroundings and the uncovered crowd in the great hall, John Howison looked around him, and then said, naïvely, "The king must be either you or me, for all but us are bareheaded." James and his courtiers laughed ; but he bestowed upon Howison the lands of Braehead, "on condition that he and his successors should be ready to present an ewer and basin for the king to wash his hands when His Majesty should come to Holyrood or pass the bridge of Cramond. Accordingly, in the year 1822, when George IV. came to Scotland, a descendant of John Howison, whose family still possess the estate, appeared at a solemn festival, and offered His Majesty water from a silver ewer, that he might perform the service by which he held his land."

Such pranks as these were ended by the king's marriage in 1537 to the Princess Magdalene, the beautiful daughter of Francis I., with unwonted splendour in the cathedral of Notre Dame, in presence of the Parliament of Paris, of Francis, the Queens of France and Navarre, the Dauphin, Duke of Orleans, and all the leading peers of Scotland and of France. On the 27th of May the royal pair landed at Leith, amid every display of welcome, and remained a few days at Holyrood, till the enthusiastic citizens prepared to receive them in state with a procession of magnificence.

Magdalene, over whose rare beauty consumption seemed to spread a veil more tender and alluring, was affectionate and loving in nature. On landing, in the excess of her love for James, she knelt down, and, kissing the soil, prayed God to bless the land of her adoption—Scotland, and its people.

The "Burgh Records" bear witness how anxious the Provost and citizens were to do honour to the bride of "the good King James. All beggars were warned off the streets : "ane honest man of ilk close or two," were to see this order enforced ; the rubbish near John Makgill's house and "the litster treyes beneath the Over Bow to be removit ;" the meal market, &c., to be removed from the High Street to foot of James Aikman's Close, and the grass market to the kirkyard foot ; twelve chief citizens were to be arrayed in velvet gowns ; the craftsmen to be arrayed in French cloth, with doublets of velvet, satin, and damask ; thirty-seven citizens to be mounted with velvet foot-mantles and velvet gowns, and all the town officers to be richly arrayed, with the town arms on their sleeves.

Mary of Guise, the widow of the Duke de Longueville, who landed at Balcomie, escorted by an admiral of France, and the nuptials were celebrated with pomp at St. Andrews ; and on St. Margaret's Day in the same year, this new queen—destined to enact so important a part in the future history of the realm—made her public entry into Edinburgh by the West Port, and rode to Holyrood Palace, while great sports and gaiety were in progress " throw all the pairts of the town,'

THE ABBEY PORT. (From a Drawing by J. Brown, 1768.)

To the inexpressible grief of James and the whole nation, Magdalene, then only in her seventeenth year, died of her insidious disease on the 10th of July. She was interred with great pomp in the royal vault, near the coffin of James II., and her untimely death was the occasion of the first general mourning ever worn in the kingdom. In the treasurer's accounts are many entries of the "Scots claith, French blak, Holland claith, and corsses upon the velvet." On her coffin was inscribed in Saxon characters, " *Magdalena Francisci Regis Franciæ, Primo-genita Regina Scotiæ Sponsa Jacobi V. Regis, A.D.* 1537, *obiit.*"

James, however, was not long a widower, and in June, 1538, he brought to Scotland a new bride,

says Pitscottie. Curious plays were made for her entertainment, and gold, spices, and wines were lavished upon her by the magistrates, who well-nigh exhausted the finances of the city.

Amid the State turmoils and horrors that culminated in the rout of Solway, James V. held a council at Holyrood on the 3rd of November, 1542, when, according to Knox, a scroll was presented to him by Cardinal Beaton, containing the names of more than one hundred of the principal nobles and gentry, including the Earl of Arran, then, by deaths in the royal family, next heir to the throne, who were undoubtedly in the pay of England, tainted with heresy, or in league with the then outlawed clan of Douglas.

Appended to this scroll was a minute of their possessions, with a hint of the pecuniary advantages to result from forfeiture. This dangerous policy James repelled by exclaiming, "Pack you, javels! (knaves). Get you to your religious charges; reform your lives, and be not instruments of discord between me and my nobles, or else I shall reform you, not as the King of Denmark does, by imprisonment, nor yet as the King of England does by hanging and heading, but by sharp swords, if I hear of such motion of you again!"

From this speech it has been supposed that James contemplated some reform in the then dissolute Church. But the rout at Solway followed; his heart was broken, and on learning the birth of his daughter Mary, he died in despair at Falkland, yet, says Pitscottie, holding up his hands to God, as he yielded his spirit. He was interred in the royal vault, in December, 1542, at Holyrood, where, according to a MS. in the Advocates' Library, his body was seen by the Earl of Forfar, the Lord Strathnaver, and others, who examined that vault in 1683. "We viewed the body of James V. It lyeth within ane wodden coffin, and is coverit with ane lead coffin. There seemed to be hair upon the head still. The body was two lengths of my staff with twa inches more, which is twae inches and more above twae Scots elms, for I measured the staff with an ellwand afterward. The body was coloured black with ye balsam that preserved it, and which was lyke melted pitch. The Earl of Forfar took the measure with his staf lykewayes."· On the coffin was the inscription, *Illustris Scotorum, Rex Jacobus, ejus Nominis V.*, with the dates of his age and death.

The first regent after that event was James, second Earl of Arran (afterwards Duke of Chatelherault, who had been godfather to James, the little Duke of Rothesay, next heir to the crown, failing the issue of the infant Queen Mary), and in 1545 this high official was solemnly invested at Holyrood, together with the Earls of Angus, Huntly, and Argyle, with the collar and robes of St. Michael, sent by the King of France, and at the hands of the Lyon King of Arms.

We have related how the Church suffered at the hands of English pillagers after Pinkie, in 1547. The Palace did not escape. Seacombe, in his "History of the House of Stanley," mentions that Norris, of Speke Hall, Lancashire, an English commander at that battle, plundered from Holyrood all or most of the princely library of the deceased King of Scots, James V., "particularly four large folios, said to contain the Records and Laws of Scotland at that time." He also describes a grand piece of wainscot, now in Speke Hall, as having been brought from the palace, but this is considered, from its style, doubtful.

During the turmoils and troubles that ensued after Mary of Guise assumed the regency, her proposal, on the suggestion of the French Court, to form a Scottish standing army like that of France, so exasperated the nobles and barons, that three hundred of them assembled at Holyrood in 1555, and after denouncing the measure in strong terms, deputed the Laird of Wemyss and Sir James Sandilands of Calder to remonstrate with her on the unconstitutional step she was meditating, urging that Scotland had never wanted brave defenders to fight her battles in time of peril, and that they would never submit to this innovation on their ancient customs. This spirited remonstrance from Holyrood had the desired effect, as the regent abandoned her project. She came, after an absence, to the palace in the November of the following year, when the magistrates presented her with a quantity of new wine, and dismissed McCalzean, an assessor of the city, who spoke to her insultingly in the palace on the affairs of Edinburgh; and in the following February she received and entertained the ambassador of the Duke of Muscovy, who had been shipwrecked on his way to England, whither she sent him, escorted by 500 lances, under the Lord Home.

After the death of Mary of Guise and the arrival of her daughter to assume the crown of her ancestors, the most stirring scenes in the history of the palace pass in review.

CHAPTER X.

HOLYROOD PALACE (continued).

Queen Mary's Apartments—Her Arrival in Edinburgh—Riot in the Chapel Royal—"The Queen's Maries"—Interview with Knox—Mary's Marriage with Darnley—The Position of Rizzio—The Murder of Rizzio—Burial of Darnley—Marriage of Mary and Bothwell—Mary's Last Visit to Holyrood—James VI. and the "Mad" Earl of Bothwell—Baptism of the Queen of Bohemia and Charles I.—Taylor the Water-poet at Holyrood—Charles I.'s Imprisonment—Palace Burned and Re-built—The Palace before 1650—The Present Palace—The Quadrangle—The Gallery of the Kings—The Tapestry—The Audience-Chamber.

A WINDING stair in the Tower of James V. gives access to the oldest portion of the palace, known as "Queen Mary's Apartments," on the third floor, and forming the most interesting portion of the whole edifice. To the visitor, in Mary's bed-chamber there seems a solemn gloom which even the summer sunshine cannot brighten, ruddy though the glare may be which streams through that tall window, where we can see the imperial crown upon its octagon turret. The light seems only to lay too bare the fibres of the old oak floor and all the mouldering finery ; a sense of the pathetic, with something of horror and much of sadness, mingles in the thoughtful mind; and much of this was felt even by Dr. Johnson, when he stood there with Boswell on the 15th of August, 1773.

With canopy and counterpane, dark and in shadow, there stands the old pillared bed, with its crimson silk and satin faded into orange, wherein slept, and doubtless too often wept, the fair young Queen of Scotland—she who spent her happy teens at the Bourbon court, her passionate youth so sorrowfully in grim grey Scotland, and who gave up her soul to God at Fotheringay, in premature old age, and with a calm grandeur that never saint surpassed.

On the wall there hangs the arras wrought with the fall of Phaeton, now green and amber-tinted, revealing the gloomy little door through which pale Ruthven and stern Darnley burst with their daring associates, and close by is the supper-room from whence the shrieking Rizzio was dragged, and done to death with many a mortal wound. To the imaginative Scottish mind the whole place conjures up scenes and events that can never die.

The day on which the queen arrived at Leith, after a thirteen years' absence from her native land, was, as Knox tells us, the most dull and gloomy in the memory of man. She had come ten days before she was expected, and such preparations as the now impoverished people made—impoverished by foreign and domestic strife since Pinkie had been lost—were far from complete. The ship containing her horses and favourite palfrey had been lawlessly captured by an English admiral; but her brother, Lord James Stuart, supplied steeds ;

and Mary, who was accompanied by her uncles, the Dukes d'Aumale, Guise, Nemours, the Cardinal of Lorraine, the Grand Prior, the Marquis d'Elbœuf, and others, could not restrain her tears of mortification at the gloom and general poverty that appeared on every hand.

She made her public entry into the city on the 1st of September, and her reception, though homely, was sincere and cordial, for the Scots of old had a devotion to their native monarchs that bordered on the sublime ; and now the youth and beauty of Mary, and the whole peculiarity of her position, were calculated to engage the interest and affection of her people.

The twelve citizens who bore a canopy over her head were apparelled in black velvet gowns and doublets of crimson satin, with velvet bonnets and hose. All citizens in the procession had black silk gowns faced with velvet and satin doublets, while the young craftsmen, who marched in front, wore taffeta. The Upper and Salt Trons, Tolbooth, and Netherbow were all decorated with banners and garlands as she proceeded to Holyrood.

The apartments she first occupied were on the ground floor, and Brantôme gives an amusing account of the manner in which the citizens endeavoured to provide for her amusement for several nights, to the grievous annoyance of her refined French attendants. "There came under her windows," says he, "five or six hundred citizens, who gave her a concert of the vilest fiddles and little rebecs, which are as bad as they can be in that country, and accompanied them with singing psalms, but so wretchedly out of tune and concord that nothing could be worse. Ah ! what melody it was ! what a lullaby for the night !" "They were a company of honest men," according to Knox, "who with instruments of music gave her their salutations at her chamber window." Mary, with policy, expressed her thanks, but removed to a part of the palace beyond the reach of this terrible minstrelsy.

She was only nineteen, with few advisers and none on whom she could rely, and was ignorant of the people over whom she had been called to govern. Protestantism was now the only legal

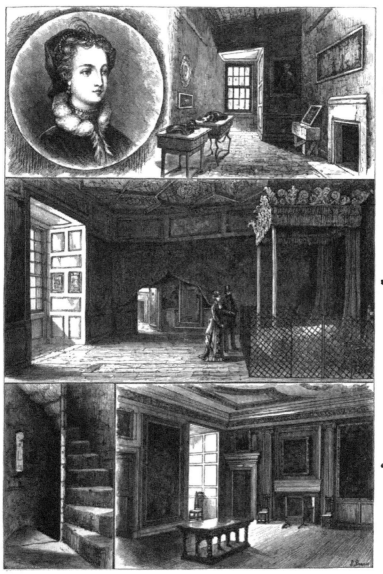

THE QUEEN MARY APARTMENTS, HOLYROOD PALACE.

1, Queen Mary; 2, Supper-room; 3, Bed-room; 4, Lord Darnley's Room; 5, Private Staircase.

religion of the land, yet on the first Sunday subsequent to her return she ordered mass to be said in the chapel royal. Tidings of this caused a dreadful excitement in the city, and the Master of Lindsay, with other gentlemen, burst into the palace, shouting, "The idolatrous priest shall die the death!" for death was by law the penalty of celebrating mass; and the multitude, pouring towards the chapel, strove to lay violent hands on the priest. Lord James—afterwards Regent—Moray succeeded in preventing their entrance by main strength, and thus gave great offence to the people, though he alleged, as an excuse, he wished to prevent "any Scot from witnessing a service so idolatrous." After the function was over, the priest was committed to the protection of Lord Robert Stuart, Commendator of Holyrood, and Lord John of Coldingham, who conducted him in safety to his residence. "But the godly departed in great grief of heart, and that afternoon repaired to the Abbey in great companies, and gave plain signification that they could not abide that the land which God had, by His power, purged from idolatry should be polluted again." The noise and uproar of these "companies" must have made Mary painfully aware that she was without a regular guard or armed protection; but she had been barely a week in Holyrood when she held her first famous interview with the great Reformer, which is too well known to be recapitulated here, but which—according to himself—he concluded by these remarkable words :—" I pray God, madam, that ye may be as blessed within the commonwealth of Scotland, if it be the pleasure of God, as ever Deborah was in the commonwealth of Israel."

The Queen's Maries, so celebrated in tradition, in history, and in song, who accompanied her to France—namely, Mary, daughter of Lord Livingston, Mary, daughter of Lord Fleming, Mary, daughter of Lord Seton, and Mary Beaton of Balfour, were all married in succession; but doubtless, so long as she resided at Holyrood she had her maids of honour, and the name of "Queen's Maries" became a general designation for her chosen attendants; hence the old ballad :—

> "Now bear a hand, my Maries a'
> And busk me braw and fine."

Her four Maries, who received precisely the same education as herself, and were taught by the same masters, returned with her to Scotland with their acknowledged beauty refined by all the graces the Court of France could impart; and in a Latin masque, composed by Buchanan, entitled the "Pomp of the Gods," acted at Holyrood in July, 1567, before her marriage with Darnley,

Diana speaks to Jupiter of her *five* Maries—the fifth being the queen herself; and well known is the pathetic old ballad which says :—

> "Yest'reen the Queen had four Maries,
>   This night she'll have but three;
>   There was Marie Beaton and Marie Seaton,
>   And Mary Carmichael and me."

In a sermon delivered to the nobles previous to the dissolution of Mary's first Parliament, Knox spoke with fury on the rumours then current concerning the intended marriage of the Queen to a Papist, which "would banish Christ Jesus from the realm and bring God's vengeance on the country." He tells that his own words and his manner of speaking them were deemed intolerable, and that Protestants and Catholics were equally offended. And then followed his second interview with Mary, who summoned him to Holyrood, where he was introduced into her presence by Erskine of Dun, and where she complained of his daring answers and ingratitude to herself, who had courted his favour; but grown undaunted again, he stood before her in a cloth cap, Geneva cloak, and falling bands, and with "iron eyes beheld her weep in vain."

"Knox," says Tytler, "affirmed that when in the pulpit he was not master of himself, but must obey His commands who bade him speak plain, and flatter no flesh. As to the favours which had been offered to him, his vocation, he said, was neither to wait in the courts of princes nor in the chambers of ladies, but to preach the Gospel. 'I grant it so,' reiterated the queen ; 'but what have you to do with my marriage, and what are you within the commonwealth?' 'A subject born within the same ; and albeit, madam, neither baron, lord nor belted earl, yet hath God made me, however abject soever in your eyes, a useful and profitable member. As such, it is my duty to forewarn the people of danger ; and, therefore, what I have said in public I repeat to your own face ! Whenever the nobility of this realm so far forget themselves that you shall be subject to an unlawful husband, they do as much as in them lieth to renounce Christ, to banish the truth, betray the freedom of the realm, and perchance be but cold friends to yourself!' This new attack brought on a still more passionate burst of tears, and Mary commanded Knox to quit the apartment."

Then it was, as he was passing forth, "observing a circle of the ladies of the queen's household sitting near in their gorgeous apparel, he could not depart without a word of admonition. 'Ah, fair ladies,' said he, 'how pleasant were this life of yours if it should ever abide, and then in the end we might pass to Heaven with all this gear! But fie on the knave Death!—that will come whether ye will or not; and when he hath laid on the arrest, then foul worms will be busy with this flesh, be it ever so fair and tender, and the silly soul, I fear, shall be feeble, that it can neither carry with it gold, garnishing, targating, pearl, nor precious stone.' In the midst of these speeches the Laird of Dun came out of the queen's

created Duke of Albany, but he looked forward to wearing the crown. His headstrong, dissolute, foolish, and in many instances brutal disposition, soon weakened the affections of the queen, and her imprudent love for him, which had at one time been so violent and generous, was—especially after the murder of Rizzio—converted into abhorrence. The appointment of the latter—said by Rymer to be a pensioner of the Pope—to the important and

HOLYROOD PALACE, THE REGENT MORAY'S HOUSE (ADJOINING THE PALACE, ON THE NORTH), THE ROYAL GARDENS, AND ANCIENT HOROLOGE. (*From a Drawing by Blore, published in 1826.*)

cabinet, and requested him to go home; nor does it appear that Mary took any further notice of his officious and uncalled-for interference with her marriage."

Soon after, another mob broke into the chapel royal during mass, but was driven out by the Provost, the Laird of Pitarrow, and others, an event which led to a futile trial of Knox before the Privy Council.

Great events now followed each other fast, and on the 29th of July, 1565, Mary was married to her wretched and dissipated cousin, the handsome Darnley, at Stirling Castle, in which an apartment had been fitted up as a Roman Catholic chapel by David Rizzio.

Three days before this Darnley had been

confidential office of secretary to the queen had given great offence to the haughty nobles of Scotland; and such was his influence over her, that it has been more than once supposed that he was her confessor in disguise, which, could it be proved, would throw a new light on his history and that of Mary, by accounting for his influence over her, and her horror of his murderers. A footnote to *Acta Regia*, vol. iv., says that "he was an old, crabbed, and deformed fellow, and that 'twas his loyalty and sagacity which made him so dear to the queen." *Thuanus* too, says that notwithstanding his mean origin she made him sit at table with her every day. He certainly fitted up the chapel for her marriage, and is known to have had a brother, Joseph, said to be in holy

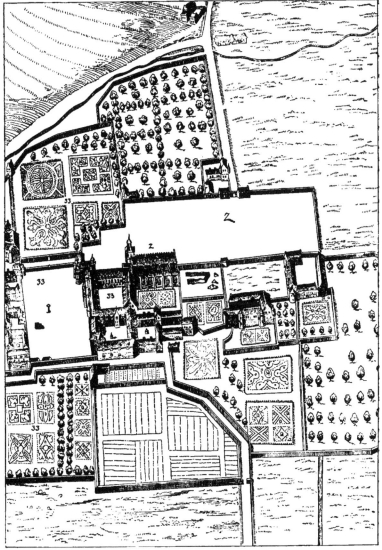

THE PALACE OF HOLYROOD HOUSE (33), THE SOUTH AND NORTH GARDENS (33), THE ABBEY KIRK (2)
AND THE KIRKYARD (2). (*After Gordon of Rothiemay's Plan.*)

orders, who was on his way to Scotland at the time of the murder. Darnley's unsuccessful attempt to obtain the crown-matrimonial roused all the vengeance of himself and his father, who now determined to put Rizzio to death and deprive Mary of the throne.

How and why the conspiracy spread belongs to history; suffice it that it was on the evening of Saturday, the 9th of March, 1566, the conspirators determined to strike the blow, in terms of their "Articles" with "the noble and mighty Prince Henry, King of Scotland, husband to our sovereign Lady," signed 1st March, 1566; and they seem to have entered the palace unnoticed by the sentinels, for Mary had, since 1562, a garde-du-corps of seventy archers, under Sir Arthur Erskine of Scotscraig.

In the dusk of the spring evening the Earl of Morton arrived with 500 of his personal retainers, and on being joined by the other lords, his accomplices, assembled secretly in the vicinity of the palace, into which they had passed, Morton, ordering the gates to be locked, took possession of the keys, while Darnley, George Douglas, known as the Postulate (i.e., a candidate for some office), the Lords Lindsay and Ruthven, were waiting to proceed to the queen's apartments in the Tower of James V., where they expected to find their victim. It had been originally intended to murder Rizzio in his own apartment, a plan abandoned for the double reason that they might have failed to find him, as he frequently slept in the room of his brother Joseph, and that to slay him under Mary's eyes would malign and terrify her more.

At this time she, altogether unsuspicious, was at supper in the closet with her sister the Countess of Argyle, her brother Robert, Commendator of Holyrood, her Master of the Household, the Captain of the Archers, and Rizzio, while two servants of the Privy Chamber were waiting by a side-table, at which, Camden states, Rizzio was seated. Ascending the private staircase, Darnley entered alone, and kissing the queen, seated himself by her side; but a minute scarcely elapsed when Ruthven drew aside the tapestry, entered, and without ceremony threw himself into a chair. He was in full armour, with his sword drawn, and looked pale, wan, and ghastly, having been long a-bed with an incurable disease. Mary, now far advanced in pregnancy, repressed her terror, and said, "My lord, hearing you were still ill, I was about to visit you, and now you enter our presence in armour. What does it mean?" "I have been ill indeed," replied the savage noble, sternly; "but am well enough to come here for your good."

"You come not in the fashion of one who meaneth well," said Mary. "There is no harm intended to your grace, nor any one but yonder poltroon, David." "What hath he done?" "Ask the king, your husband, madam." Mary now assumed an air of authority, and demanding an explanation of Darnley, commanded Ruthven to begone. On this, the Master of the Household and the captain of the archers attempted to expel him by force, but he brandished his sword, exclaiming, "Lay no hands on me—for I will not be so handled!"

Another conspirator, Kerr of Faudonside, now burst in with a horse-petronel cocked, and the private stair beyond was seen crowded by others. "Do you seek my life?" exclaimed Mary, on finding the weapon levelled at her breast. "No," replied Ruthven; "but we will have out yonder villain, Davie." He now tried to drag forth the hapless Italian, who had retreated into the recess of a window, a dagger in one hand, and with the other clinging to the skirt of the interposing queen. "If my secretary has been guilty of any misdemeanour," said she, "he shall be dealt with according to the forms of justice." "Here is justice, madam!" cried one, producing a rope, from which we learn by Knox and the work of Prince Lebanoff, that the first intention had been to hang Rizzio. "Fear not," said the queen to him; "the king will not suffer you to be slain in my presence, nor will he forget your faithful services."

"A Douglas!—a Douglas!" was now resounding through the palace, as Morton and his vassals rushed up the great staircase and burst into the presence-chamber, the light of their glaring torches and flashing of their weapons adding to the terror of the little group in the closet. The supper-table, which had hitherto interposed between Rizzio and his murderers, was now overturned before the queen, and had not the Countess of Argyle caught one of the falling candles, the room would have been involved in darkness. Rizzio, who on this fatal night was dressed in black figured damask, trimmed with fur, a satin doublet, russet velvet hose, and wore at his neck a magnificent jewel — never seen after that night — now clung in despair to the weeping queen, crying, "*Giustizia! Giustizia! Sauve ma vie, madame, —sauve ma vie!*"

But he was stabbed over her shoulder by George Douglas with the king's own dagger, and other daggers and swords followed fast. By force the usually half-drunken Darnley tore the queen's skirt from the clutch of the poor bleeding creature, who, amid ferocious shouts and hideous oaths, was dragged through the bed-room to the door of the presence-chamber, where the conspirators gathered about him and completed the bloody outrage. So eager were all to take part in the murder that they frequently wounded each other, eliciting greater curses and yells; and the body of Rizzio, gashed by fifty-six wounds, was left in a pool of blood, with the king's dagger driven to the hilt in it, in token that he had sanctioned the murder. After a time the corpse was flung down-stairs, stripped naked, dragged to the porter's lodge, and treated with every indignity.

Darnley and the queen were meanwhile alone together in the cabinet, into which a lady rushed to announce that Rizzio was dead, as she had seen the body. "Is it so?" said the weeping queen; "then I will study revenge!" Then she swooned, but was roused by the entrance of Ruthven, who, reeking with blood, staggered into a chair and called for wine. After receiving much coarse and unseemly insolence, the queen exclaimed, "I trust that God, who beholdeth all this from the high heavens, will avenge my wrongs, and move that which shall be born of me to root out you and your treacherous posterity!" —a denunciation terribly fulfilled by the total destruction of the house of Ruthven in the reign of her son, James VI.

In the middle of a passage leading from the quadrangle to the chapel is shown a flat square stone, which is said to mark the grave of Rizzio; but it is older than his day, and has probably served for the tomb of some one else.

The floor at the outer door of Mary's apartments presents to this day a dark irregular stain, called Rizzio's blood, thus exciting the ridicule of those who do not consider the matter. The floor is of great antiquity here—manifestly older than that of the adjacent gallery, laid in the time of Charles I. "We know," says Robert Chambers, in his "Book of Days," "that the stain has been shown there since a time long antecedent to that extreme modern curiosity regarding historical matters which might have induced an imposture, for it is alluded to by the son of Evelyn as being shown in 1722."

Joseph Rizzio, who arrived in Scotland soon after his brother's murder, was promoted to his vacant office by the queen, and was publicly named as one of the abettors of Morton and Bothwell in the murder of Darnley—in which, with true Italian instinct, he might readily have had a hand. After the tragedy at the Kirk of Field in 1567, the body of Darnley was brought to Holyrood, where Michael Picauet, the queen's apothecary, embalmed it, by her order; the treasurer's accounts, dated Feb. 12th, contain entries for "drogges, spices—colis, tabbis, hardis, barrelis," and other matters necessary "for bowalling of King's Grace," who was interred in the chapel royal at night, in presence of only the Lord Justice Clerk Bellenden, Sir James Tracquair, and others.

After Bothwell's seizure of Mary's person, at the head of 1,000 horse, and his production of the famous bond, signed by the most powerful nobles in Scotland, recommending him as the most fitting husband for her—a transaction in which her enemies affirm she was a willing actor—their marriage ceremony took place in the great hall of the palace on the 15th of May, 1567, at four o'clock in the morning, a singular hour, for which it is difficult to account, unless it be, that Mary had yielded in despair at last. There it was performed by the reformed prelate Adam Bothwell, Bishop of Orkney, together with Knox's coadjutor, Craig, according to the Protestant form, and on the same day, in private, according to the Catholic ritual. To the latter, perhaps, Birrel refers when he says they were married in the chapel royal. Only five of the nobles were present, and there were no rejoicings in Edinburgh, where the people looked on with grief and gloom; and on the following morning there was found affixed to the palace gate the ominous line from Ovid's *Fasti*, book v. : "*Mense malas Maio nubere vulgus ait.*"

The revolt of the nobles, the flight of Bothwell, and the surrender of Mary at Carberry to avoid bloodshed, quickly followed, and the last visit she paid to her palace of Holyrood was when, under a strong guard, she was brought thither a prisoner from the Black Turnpike, on the 18th of June and ere the citizens could rescue her; as a preliminary step to still more violent proceedings, she was secretly taken from Holyrood at ten at night, without having even a change of raiment, mounted on a miserable hack, and compelled to ride at thirty miles an hour, escorted by the murderers Ruthven and Lindsay, who consigned her a prisoner to the lonely castle of Lochleven, where she signed the enforced abdication which placed her son upon the throne.

Holyrood was one of the favourite residences of the latter, and the scene of many a treaty and council during his reign in Scotland.

In the great hall there, on Sunday, the 23rd of October, he created a great number of earls with much splendour of ceremony, with a corresponding number of knights.

Another Earl of Bothwell, the horror of James VI., now figures in history, eldest son of the

Commendator of Coldingham. He was created, in right of his mother (who was the only sister of the notorious peer), Earl of Bothwell and Lord High Admiral of Scotland in 1587. He became an avowed enemy of the king, and Holyrood was the scene of more than one frantic attempt made by him upon the life of James. One of these, in 1591, reads like a daring frolic, as related by Sir James Melville, when the earl attacked the palace at the head of his followers. " I was

at the Girth Cross. On the 24th July, 1593, Bothwell, who had been outlawed, again burst into the palace with his retainers, and reached the royal apartments. Then the king, incapable of resisting him, desired Bothwell, to "consummate his treasons by piercing his sovereign's heart;" but Bothwell fell on his knees and implored pardon, which the good-natured king at once granted, though a minute before he had, as Birrel records, been seeking flight by the back stair, "with his breeks in his hand."

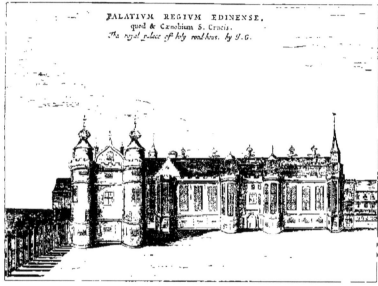

PALATIVM REGIVM EDINENSE.
quod & Cænobium S. Crucis.
The royal palace of holy roodhous. by J. G.

HOLYROOD PALACE AS IT WAS BEFORE THE FIRE OF 1650. *(Facsimile, after Gordon of Rothiemay.)*

at supper with my Lord Duke of Lennox, who took his sword and pressed forth; but he had no company and the place was full of enemies. We were compelled to fortify the doors and stairs with tables, forms, and stools, and be spectators of that strange hurlyburly for the space of an hour, beholding with torchlight, forth of the duke's gallery, their reeling and rumbling with halberts, the clacking of the culverins and pistols, the dunting of mells and hammers, and crying for justice." The earl and his followers ultimately drew off, but left the master stabler and another lying dead, and the king was compelled to go into the city; but eight of Bothwell's accomplices were taken and hanged

In 1596 the future Queen of Bohemia was baptised in Holyrood, held in the arms of the English ambassador, while the Lyon King proclaimed her from the windows as "the Lady Elizabeth, first daughter of Scotland;" and on the 23rd December, 1600, the palace was the scene of the baptism of her brother, the future Charles I., with unusual splendour in the chapel royal, in presence of the nobles, heralds, and officers of state. " The bairn was borne by the Marquis de Rohan, and the Lord Lyon proclaimed him out of the west window of the chapel as 'Lord Charles of Scotland, Duke of Albany, Marquis of Ormond, Earl of Ross, and Lord Ardmannoch. Largesse ! Largesse ! Largesse !'" Then the castle fired a salute, while silver was scattered to the multitude. Three years afterwards the king and court had departed, and Holyrood was consigned to silence and gloom.

On James VI. re-visiting Scotland in 1617, the palace was fitted up for him with considerable splendour, but his project of putting up statues of the apostles in the chapel caused great excitement in the city. Taylor, the Water-poet, who was at Holyrood in the following year, states that he

the gardens known as Queen Mary's sun-dial, although the cyphers of Charles, his queen, and eldest son appear upon it. Cromwell quartered a body of his infantry in the palace, and by accident they set it on fire, on the 13th November, 1650, when it was destroyed, all save the Tower of James V., with its furniture and decorations.

Of this palace a drawing by Gordon of Rothiemay has been preserved, which shows the main entrance to have been where we find it

HOLYROOD PALACE AND ABBEY CHURCH, FROM THE SOUTH-EAST.

saw this legend over the royal arms at the gate : "'Nobis hæc invicta miserunt 106 proavi.' I inquired what the English of it was. It was told me as followeth, which I thought worthy to be recorded : —'106 forefathers have left this to us unconquered.'"

When Charles I. visited Edinburgh, in 1633, the magistrates employed the famous Jameson to paint portraits of the Scottish monarchs, and, imitative of his master Rubens, he wore his hat when Charles I. sat to him ; but it is probable that after the latter's last visit, in 1641, the palace must have become somewhat dilapidated, otherwise Cromwell would have taken up his residence there. The improvements effected by Charles were considerable, and among other memorials of his residence still remaining, is the beautiful dial in

now. Round embattled towers flank it, with bow windows in them, and above the grand gate are the royal arms of Scotland. On either side is a large range of buildings having great windows ; and the now empty panels in the Tower of James V. appear to have been filled in with armorial bearings, doubtless destroyed by Cromwell. In his map of 1657 the same artist shows a louping-on-stone in the centre of the palace yard.

The palace was rebuilt to a certain extent, by order of Cromwell, in 1658, but the whole of his work, at the Restoration, was pulled down by royal warrant two years after, as the work " built by the usurper, and doth darken the court."

Engrafted on the part that survived the conflagration, and designed, it is said, after the noble

53

château of Chantilly, from plans by the royal architect, Sir William Bruce of Balcaskie and Kinross, the palace as we find it now was built by Charles II. and James VII., with a zeal that has been supposed to imply forethought of having a fit retreat in their ancient capital if driven from that of England. The inscription in large Roman letters—

FVN . BE . RO . MYLNE . MM . IVL . 1671—

marks the site of the foundation of the modern additions; it is in a pier of the north-west piazza.

Before the Antiquarian Society in 1858 was read a statement of the "Accounts of Sir William Bruce of Balcaskie, General Surveyor of H.M. Works, 1674–9." The reckoning between these years was £160,000 Scots, of which sum four-fifths were spent on Holyrood, the new works on which had been begun, in 1671, and so vigorously carried on, that by January, 1674, the mason-work had been nearly completed. The Dutch artist, Jacob de Urt, was employed to paint "One piece of historia in the king's bed-chamber" for £120 Scots. The coats-of-arms which are above the great entrance and in the quadrangle were cut from his designs.

Holyrood Palace is an imposing quadrangular edifice, enclosing a piazza-bounded Palladian court, ninety-four feet square. Its front faces the west, and consists of battlemented double towers on each flank. In the centre is the grand entrance, having double Doric columns, above which are the royal arms of Scotland, and over them an octagonal clock-tower, terminating in an imperial crown.

The Gallery of the Kings, the largest apartment in the palace, is 150 feet long by 27 feet broad, and is decorated by a hundred fanciful portraits of the Scottish kings, from Fergus I. to James VII., by Jacob de Urt, and there is an interesting portrait of Mary and of the latter monarch, and at the end of the gallery are four remarkable paintings, taken from Scotland by James VI., and sent back from Hampton Court in 1857. They represent James III. and his queen Margaret of Denmark (about 1484), at devotion; on the reverses are Sir Edward Boncle, Provost of Trinity College; the figure of St. Cecilia at the organ represents Mary of Gueldres, and the whole, which are by an artist of the delicate Van Eck school, are supposed to have formed a portion of the altar-piece of the old Trinity College Church. In this gallery the elections of the Scottish peers take place. Beyond it are Lord Darnley's rooms; among the portraits there are those of Darnley and his brother, and from thence a stair leads to Queen Mary's apartments above. The Tapestry Room contains two large pieces of arras, and among several valuable portraits one of James Duke of Hamilton, beheaded in 1649.

The Audience Chamber—the scene of Mary's stormy interviews with Knox—is panelled and embellished with various royal initials and coats-armorial; the furniture is richly embroidered, and includes a venerable state-bed, used by Charles I., by Prince Charles Edward, and by Cumberland on the night of the 30th January, 1746. Mary's bed-chamber measures only 22 feet by 18 feet, and at its south-west corner is her dressing-room. The ancient furniture, the faded embroideries and tapestries, and general aspect of this wing, which is consigned peculiarly to memories of the past are all in unison with the place; but the royal nursery, with its blue-starred dome, the Secretary of State's room, with the royal private apartments generally now in use, are all in the south and eastern sides of the palace, and are reached by a grand staircase from the south-east angle of the court.

CHAPTER XI.

HOLYROOD PALACE (concluded).

The King's Birthday in 1665—James Duke of Albany—The Duchess of York and General Dalzell—Funeral of the Duke of Rothes — A Gladiatorial Exhibition—Departure of the Scottish Household Troops—The Hunters' Company's Balls—First and Second Visits of the Royal Family of France—Recent Improvements—St. Anne's Yard removed—The Ornamental Fountain built.

IN the *Intelligence* for the 1st of June, 1665, we have a description of the exuberant loyalty that followed the downfall of the Commonwealth. "Edinburgh, May 29, being His Majesty's birthday, was most solemnly kept by all ranks in this city. My Lord Commissioner, in his state, with his life-guard on horseback, and Sir Andrew Ramsay, Lord Provost, Bailies, and Council in their robes, accompanied by all the Trained Bands in arms, went to church and heard the Bishop of Edinburgh upon a text well applied for the work of the day. Thereafter thirty-five aged men in

THE ROYAL APARTMENTS, HOLYROOD PALACE.

1, The Throne Room; 2, The Breakfast Parlour; 3, Evening Drawing-room; 4, Grand Staircase; 5, Morning Drawing-room.

blew gowns, each having got thirty-five shillings in a purse, came up from the abbey to the great church, praying all along for His Majesty. Sermon being ended, His Grace entertained all the nobles and gentlemen with a magnificent feast and open table. After dinner the Lord Provost and Council went to the Cross, where was a green arbour loaded with oranges and lemons, wine running liberally for divers hours at eight conduits, to the great solace of the indigent commons there. Having drunk all the royal healths, which were seconded by great guns from the castle, sound of trumpets and drums, volleys from the Trained Bands, and joyful acclamations from the people, they plentifully entertained the multitude. After which, my Lord Commissioner, Provost, and Bailies went to the castle, where they were entertained with all sorts of wine and sweatmeats; and returning, the Provost countenancing all neighbours that had put up bonfires by appearing at their fires, which jovialness continued, with ringing of bells and shooting of great guns, till 12 o'clock at night."

In October, 1679, the Duke of Albany and York, with his family, including the future queens, Mary and Anne, took up his residence at Holyrood, where the gaiety and brilliance of his court gave great satisfaction. The princesses were easy and affable, and the duke left little undone to win the love of the people, but the time was an unpropitious one, for they were at issue with him on matters of faith; yet it is clearly admitted by Fountainhall that his birthday was observed more cordially than that of the king. The duke golfed frequently at Leith. "I remember in my youth," wrote Mr. William Tytler, "to have conversed with an old man named Andrew Dickson, a golf-club maker, who said that when a boy he used to carry the duke's golf-clubs, and run before him to announce where the balls fell."

The sixteen companies of the Trained Bands attended the duke's arrival in the city, and sixty selected men from each company were ordered "to attend their royal highnesses, apparelled in the best manner," and the latter were banqueted in the Parliament House, at the cost of £1,231 13s. sterling. The brilliance of the little court was long remembered after the royal race were in hopeless exile. One of the most celebrated beauties of its circle was the wife of Preston of Denbrae, who survived till the middle of the last century. In the Cupar burial register this entry occurs concerning her:—" Buried 21st December, 1757, Lady Denbrae, aged 107 years."

The duke and duchess are said to have been early warned of the haughty punctilio of the Scottish noblesse by a speech of General Dalzell of Binns, whom the former had invited to dine at the palace, when Mary d'Este, as a daughter of the ducal-prince of Modena, declined to take her place at table with a subject. "Madam," said the grim veteran, "I have dined at a table, where your father must have stood at my back!" In this instance it is supposed that he alluded to the table of the Emperor of Germany, whom the Duke of Modena, if summoned, must have attended as an officer of the household.

The same commander having ordered a guardsman who had been found asleep on his post at the palace to be shot, he was forgiven by order of the duke.

In August, 1681, one of the grandest funerals ever seen in Scotland left Holyrood—that of the High Chancellor, the Duke of Rothes, who died there on the 26th July. The account of the procession fills six quarto pages of Arnot's "History," and enumerates among the troops present the Scots Foot Guards, a train of Artillery, the Scots Fusiliers, and Horse Guards of the Scottish army.

In April, 1705, John, the great Duke of Argyle, took up his residence at the palace as Commissioner to the Parliament, on which occasion he was received by a double salvo from the castle batteries, by the great guns in the Artillery Park, "and from all the men-of-war, both Dutch and Scottish, then lying in the road of Leith."

In 1711 the Scottish Household troops, viz., the Life and Horse Guards, Horse Grenadier Guards, and the two battalions of the Foot Guards, ceased to do duty at Holyrood, being all removed permanently to London, though a detachment of the last named corps garrisoned the Bass Rock till the middle of the last century.

A strange gladiatorial exhibition is recorded as taking place on a stage at the back of the palace on the 23rd of June, 1726, when one of those public combats then so popular at the Bear Garden in London, ensued between a powerful young Irishman named Andrew Bryan (who had sent a drum through the city defying all men) and a veteran of Killiecrankie, named Donald Bane, then in his sixty-second year.

They fought with various weapons, in presence of many noblemen, gentlemen, and military officers, for several hours, and Bryan was totally vanquished, after receiving some severe wounds from his unscathed antagonist.

The annual ball of the Honourable Company of Hunters at Holyrood, begins to be regularly chronicled in the Edinburgh papers about this

period, and in 1736 one of unusual brilliance
was given in January, the Hon. Charles Hope
(afterwards Muster Master-General for Scotland)
being king, and the Hon. Lady Helen Hope
queen. In the Gallery of the Kings a table was
covered with 300 dishes *en ambigu*, at which sat
150 ladies at a time . . . . illuminated with 400
wax candles. "The plan laid out by the council
of the Company was exactly followed with the
their dark days had found refuge at St. Germains.
He entered Holyrood under a salute from the
castle, while the approaches were lined by the
Hopetoun Fencibles and Windsor Foresters. He
held a levée next day at the palace, where he was
soon after joined by his son, the Duc d'Angoulême.
The royal family remained several years at Holyrood, when they endeared themselves to all in
Edinburgh, where their presence was deemed but

THE QUADRANGLE, HOLYROOD PALACE. (*From a Drawing by Shepherd, published in 1829.*)

greatest order and decency, and concluded without
the least air of disturbance."

Yet brawls were apt to occur then and for long
after, as swords were worn in Edinburgh till a
later period than in England ; and an advertisement in the *Courant* for June, 1761, refers to a
silver-mounted sword having been taken in mistake at an election of peers in that year at
Holyrood.

The ancient palace had once more royal inmates when, on the 6th of June, 1796, there
landed at Leith, under a salute from the fort,
H.R.H. the Comte d'Artois, Charles Philippe, the
brother of Louis XVI., in exile, seeking a home
under the roof of the royal race that had so
often intermarried with his family, and which in
a natural link of the old alliance that used to exist
between Scotland and France.

The count, with his sons the Duc d'Angoulême
and the Duc de Berri, was a constant attender at the
drills of the Edinburgh Volunteers, in the meadows
or elsewhere, though he never got over a horror of
the uniform they wore then—blue, faced with red—
which reminded him too sadly of the ferocious
National Guard of France. He always attended in
his old French uniform, with the order of St.
Ampoule on his left breast, just as we may see him
in Kay's Portraits. He was present at St. Anne's
Yard when, in 1797, the Shropshire Militia, under
Lord Clive—the *first* English regiment of militia
that ever entered Scotland—was reviewed by Lord
Adam Gordon, the commander-in-chief.

THE GALLERY OF THE KINGS, HOLYROOD PALACE.

The *Edinburgh Herald* of April, 1797, mentions the departure from Holyrood of the Duc d'Angoulême for Hamburg, to join the army of the Prince of Condé, and remarks, "We wish His Highness a prosperous voyage, and we may add (the valediction of his ancestor, Louis XIV., to the unfortunate James VII.), may we never see his face again on the same errand!"

The Comte d'Artois visited Sweden in 1804, but was in Britain again in 1806. His levées and balls "tended in some degree to excite in the minds of the inhabitants a faint idea of the days of other years, when the presence of its monarchs communicated splendour and animation to this ancient metropolis, inspiring it with a proud consciousness of the remote antiquity and hereditary independence of the Scottish throne."

His farewell address to the magistrates and people, dated from the palace 5th August, 1799, is preserved among the records of the city.

Among those who pressed forward to meet him was a Newhaven fishwife, who seized his hand as he was about to enter his carriage, and shook it heartily, exclaiming, " My name 's Kinty Ramsay, sir. I am happy to see you again among decent folk ! "

When the events of the Three Days compelled Charles X. to abdicate the throne of France, he waived his rights in favour of his nephew, the young Duc de Bordeaux, and quitting his throne, contemplated at once returning to Holyrood, where he had experienced some years of comparative happiness, and still remembered with gratitude the kindness of the citizens. This he evinced by his peculiar favour to all Scotsmen, and his munificence to the sufferers by the great fire in the Parliament Square. He and his suite—consisting of 100 exiles, including the Duc de Bordeaux, Duc de Polignac, Duchesse de Berri, Baron de Damas, Marquis de Brabançois, and the Abbé de Moligny—landed at Newhaven on the 20th October, 1830, amid an enthusiastic crowd, which pressed forward on all sides with outstretched hands, welcoming him back to Scotland, and escorted him to Holyrood. Next morning many gentlemen dined in Johnston's tavern at the abbey in honour of the event, sang "Auld lang syne" under his windows, and gave three ringing cheers "for the King of France."

The Duc and Duchesse d'Angoulême, after residing during the winter at 21, Regent Terrace, joined the king at Holyrood when their apartments were ready. To the poor of the Canongate and the city generally, the exiled family were royally liberal, and also to the poor Irish, and their whole bearing was unobtrusive, religious, and exemplary. Charles was always thoughtful and melancholy. "He walked frequently in Queen Mary's garden, being probably pleased by its seclusion and proximity to the palace. Here, book in hand, he used to pass whole hours in retirement, sometimes engaged in the perusal of the volume, and anon stopping short, apparently absorbed in deep reflection. Charles sometimes indulged in a walk through the city, but the crowds that usually followed him, anxious to gratify their curiosity, in some measure detracted from the pleasure of these perambulations. . . . . . Arthur's Seat and the King's Park afforded many a solitary walk to the exiled party, and they seemed much delighted with their residence. It was evident from the first that Charles, when he sought the shores of Scotland, intended to make Holyrood his home; and it may be imagined how keenly he felt, when, after a residence of nearly two years, he was under the necessity of removing to another country. Full of the recollection of former days, which time had not effaced from his memory, he said he had anticipated spending the remainder of his life in the Scottish capital, and laying his bones among the dust of our ancient kings in the chapel of Holyrood." (Kay, vol. ii.)

In consequence of a remonstrance from Louis Philippe, a polite but imperative order compelled the royal family to prepare to quit Holyrood, and the most repulsive reception given to the Duc de Blacas in London, was deemed the forerunner of harsher measures if Charles hesitated to comply ; but when it became known that he was to depart, a profound sensation of regret was manifested in Edinburgh. The 18th September, 1832, was named as the day of embarkation. Early on that morning a deputation, consisting of the Lord Provost Learmonth of Dean, Colonel G. Macdonell, Menzies of Pitfoddels (the last of an ancient line), Sir Charles Gordon of Drimnin, James Browne, LL.D., Advocate, the historian of the Highlands, and other gentlemen, bearers of an address drawn up by, and to be read by the last-named, appeared before the king at Holyrood. One part of this address contained an allusion to the little Duc de Bordeaux so touching that the poor king was overwhelmed with emotion, and clasped the document to his heart. "I am unable to express myself," he exclaimed, "but this I will conserve among the most precious possessions of my family."

After service in the private chapel, many gentlemen and ladies appeared before Charles, the Duc d'Angoulême, and Duc de Bordeaux, when they bade them farewell in the Gallery of the Kings, while a vast concourse assembled outside, all wearing the white cockade. Another multitude was collected at Newhaven, where the Fishermen's Society formed a kind of body-guard to cover the embarkation.

"A few gentlemen," says the editor of "Kay's Portraits," "among whom were Colonel Macdonel, the Rev. Mr. (afterwards Bishop) Gillis, John Robinson, Esq., and Dr. Browne, accompanied His Majesty on board the steamer, which they did not leave till she was under weigh. The distress of the king, and particularly of the dauphin, at being obliged to quit a country to which they were so warmly attached was in the highest degree affecting. The Duc de Bordeaux wept bitterly, and the Duc d'Angoulême, embracing Mr. Gillis à la Française, gave unrestrained scope to his emotion. The act of parting with one so beloved, whom he had known and distinguished in the salons of the Tuileries and St. Cloud, long before his family had sought an asylum in the tenantless halls of Holyrood, quite overcame his fortitude, and excited feelings too powerful to be repressed. When this ill-fated family bade adieu to our shores they carried with them the grateful benedictions of the poor, and the respect of all men of all parties who honour misfortune when ennobled by virtue."

In Edinburgh it is well known that had H.R.H. the late Prince Consort—whose love of the picturesque and historic led him to appreciate its natural beauties—survived a few years longer, many improvements would have taken place at Holyrood; and to him it is said those are owing which have already been effected.

Southward of the palace, the unsightly old tenements and enclosed gardens at St. Anne's Yard were swept away, including a quaint-looking dairy belonging to the Duke of Hamilton, and by 1857-8-9 the royal garden was extended south some 500 feet from the wall of the south wing, and a new approach was made from the Abbey Hill, a handsome new guard-house was built, and the carved door of the old garden replaced in the wall between it and the fragment of the old abbey porch; and it was during the residence of H.R.H. the Prince of Wales at Holyrood that the beautiful fountain in the Palace Yard was completed, on the model of the ancient one that stands in ruin now, in the quadrangle of Linlithgow, and which is referred to by Defoe in his "Tour in Great Britain."

The fountain rises from a basin twenty-four feet in diameter to the height of twenty-eight feet, divided into three stages, and by flying buttresses has the effect of a triple crown. From the upper of these the water flows through twenty ornate gurgoils into three successive basins. The basement is of a massive character, divided by buttresses into eight spaces, each containing a lion's head gurgoil. This is surmounted by eight panels having rich cusping, and between these rise pedestals and pinnacles. The former support heraldic figures with shields. These consist of the unicorn bearing the Scottish shield, a lion bearing a shield charged with the arms of James IV. and his queen, Margaret of England; a deer supports two shields, with the arms of the queens of James V., Magdalene of France, and Mary of Guise; and the griffin holds the shields of James IV. and his queen, Margaret of Denmark. The pinnacles are highly floriated, and enriched with flowers and medallions.

It is in every way a marvellous piece of stone carving. The flying buttresses connecting the stages are deeply cusped. On the second stage are eight figures typical of the sixteenth century, representing soldiers, courtiers, musicians, and a lady-falconer, each two feet six inches in height. On the upper stage are four archers of the Scottish Guard, supporting the imperial crown. It occupies the site whereon for some years stood a statue of Queen Victoria, which has now disappeared.

Still, as of old, since the union of the crowns, for a fortnight in each year the Lord High Commissioner to the General Assembly of the Church of Scotland holds semi-royal state in Holyrood, gives banquets in its halls, and holds his levées in the Gallery of the Kings.

HOLYROOD PALACE, WEST FRONT.

CHAPTER XII.

THE MOUND.

The North Loch used for Sousings and Duckings—The Boats, Swans, Ducks, and Eels—Accidents in the Loch—Last Appearance of the Loch
—Formation of the Mound—"Geordie Boyd's Mud Brig"—The Rotunda—Royal Institution—Board of Manufactures—History of the Board
—The Equivalent Money—Sir J. Shaw Lefevre's Report—School of Design—Gallery of Sculpture—Royal Society of Edinburgh—Museum
of Antiquities.

THE garden wherein St. David budded trees and cultivated such fruits and flowers as were then known in Britain is a place of flowers and shrubs again, save where it is intersected by the prosaic railway or the transverse Earthen Mound; but those who see the valley now may find it difficult to realise, that for 300 years it was an impassable lake, formed for the defence of the city on the north, when the wall of 1450 was built; but the well that fed it is flowing still, as when David referred to it in his Holyrood charter. Fed by it and other springs, the loch was retained by a dam and sluice at the foot of Halkerston's Wynd—the dam being a passable footway from the city to the northern fields.

In the royal gardens a tournament was held in 1396, by order of Annabel Drummond, queen of Robert III., at which, according to Bower, the continuator of Fordun, her eldest son, David, Duke of Rothesay, the same prince who perished so miserably at Falkland, presided when in his twentieth year.

In 1538, prior to committing the effigy of St. Giles to the flames, the Reformers ducked it in the loch—it being the legal place for sousing all offenders against the seventh commandment.

In 1562 the Town Council enacted that all persons of loose life should be ducked in a certain part of the loch, wherein a pillar and basin were formed for the purpose; but this not having the desired effect, all such persons were ordered to be committed, without distinction, to the iron room of the Tolbooth, to be kept therein for a month on bread and water, and to be then whipped out of the city at a cart's tail. The deacon of the fleshers having fallen under this law, the crafts, deeming it an indignity to their order, assembled in arms, broke open the prison, and released him.

For the sake ot ornament the magistrates kept swans and wild ducks on the loch, and various entries for their preservation occur in their accounts; and one passed in Council between 1589-94 ordained a boll of oats to be procured for feeding them. A man was outlawed for shooting a swan in the said loch, and obliged to find another

rash act. Hearing the tumult, the father of the late Lord Henderland threw up his window in James's Court, and leaning out, cried down the brae to the people: 'What's all the noise about? Can't ye e'en let the man gang to the deil his ain gate?' Whereupon the honest man quietly walked out of the loch, to the no small amusement of the

THE HOLYROOD FOUNTAIN.

in its place. "The loch," says Chambers, "seems to have been a favourite place for boating. Various houses in the neighbourhood had servitudes of the use of a boat upon it, and these, in later times, used to be employed to no little purpose in smuggling whisky into the town. . . . . It was also the frequent scene of suicide, and on this point one or two droll anecdotes are related. A man was proceeding deliberately to drown himself, when a crowd of the townspeople rushed down to the water-side, venting cries of horror and alarm at the spectacle, yet without actually venturing into the water to prevent him from accomplishing the

lately appalled neighbours." There a lady was saved from suicide by her hoop-petticoat.

The loch must have abounded in some kind of fish, as the Council Register refers to an eel-ark set therein, at ten merks yearly, for the benefit of the Trinity Hospital; and in February, 1655, Nicoll records that in consequence of the excessively stormy weather, some thousands of dead eels were cast .pon its banks, "to the admiration of many."

On the 11th February, 1682, three men were drowned in the loch by the ice giving way. "We have a proverb," says Lord Fountainhall, under whose windows perhaps the accident occurred, "that the fox will not set his foot on the ice after Candlemas, especially in the heat of the sun, as this was, at two o'clock; and at any time the fox is so sagacious as to lay his ear on the ice to see if it be frozen to the bottom, or if he hear the murmuring and current of the water."

In 1715, when the magistrates took measures for the defence of the city, the sluice of the loch was completely dammed up to let the water rise, a precaution omitted by their successors in 1745. In Edgar's plan, twenty years later, the bed of the loch is shown as "now devised," measuring 1,700 feet in length, from the foot of Ramsay Garden to the foot of Halkerston's Wynd, and 400 feet broad at the foot of the gardens below the Advocate's Close. From the upper point to the West Church the bed is shown as "bog or marsh."

"Yet many in common with myself," says Chambers, "must remember the by no means distant time when the remains of this sheet of water, consisting of a few pools, served as an excellent sliding and skating ground in winter, while their neglected, grass-grown precincts too frequently formed an arena whereon the high and mighty quarrels of the Old and New Town *cowlies* were brought to lapidarian arbitration;" and until a very recent period woodcocks, snipe, and water-ducks used to frequent the lower part of the West Princes Street Gardens, attracted by the damp of the locality.

"The site of the North Loch," says a writer in the *Edinburgh Magazine* for 1790, "is disgusting below as well as above the bridge, and the balustrades of the east side ought to be filled up like those of the west, as they are only meant to show a beautiful stream, not slaughter-houses."

The statute for the improvement of the valley westward of the mound was not passed until 1816; but Lord Cockburn describes it as being then an impassable fetid marsh, "open on all sides, the receptacle of many sewers, and seemingly of all the worried cats, drowned dogs, and blackguardism of the city. Its abomination made it so solitary that the volunteers used to practise ball-firing across it. The men stood on its north side, and the targets were set up along the lower edge of the castle hill, or rock. The only difficulty was in getting across the swamp to place and examine the targets, which could only be done in very dry weather and at one or two places."

In the maps of 1798 a "new mound" would seem to have been projected across it, at an angle, from South Castle Street to the Ferry Road, by the western base of the castle rock—a design, for-tunately, never carried out. One of the greatest mistakes committed as a matter of taste was the erection of the Earthen Mound across the beautiful valley of the loch, from the end of Hanover Street to a point at the west end of Bank Street. It is simply an elongated hill, like a huge railway embankment, a clumsy, enormous, and unremovable substitute for a bridge which should have been there, and its creation has been deplored by every topographical writer on Edinburgh.

Huge as the mass is, it originated in a very accidental operation. When the bed of the loch was in a state of marsh, a shopkeeper, Mr. George Boyd, clothier, at Gosford's Close, in the old town, was frequently led from business or curiosity to visit the rising buildings of the new, and accommodated himself with "steps" across this marsh, and he was followed in the construction of this path by other persons similarly situated, who contributed their quota of stone or plank to fill up, widen, and heighten what, in rude compliment to the founder, was becoming known as "Geordie Boyd's Mud Brig." The inconvenience arising from the want of a direct communication between the old town and the new began to be seriously felt about 1781, when the latter had been built as far west as Hanover Street.

Hence a number of residents, chiefly near the Lawnmarket, held a meeting in a small public-house, kept by a man called Robert Dunn, and called in burlesque, "Dunn's Hotel," after a fashionable hotel of that name in Princes Street, and subscriptions were opened to effect a communication of some kind; but few were required, as Provost Grieve, who resided at the corner of Hanover Street, in order to fill up a quarry before his house, obtained leave to have the rubbish from the foundations of the various new streets laid down there. From that time the progress of the Mound proceeded with rapidity, and from 1781 till 1830 augmentations to its breadth and height were continually made, till it became the mighty mass it is. By the latter date the Mound had become levelled and macadamised, its sides sown with grass, and in various ways embellished so as to assume the appearance of being completed. It is upwards of 800 feet in length, on the north upwards of 60 feet in height, and on the south about 100 feet. Its breadth is proportionally much greater than its height, averaging about 300 feet. It is computed to contain more than 2,000,000 of cartloads of travelled earth, and on the moderate supposition that each load, if paid for, was worth 6d., must have cost the large sum of £50,000.

It was first enclosed by rough stone walls, and

was almost a permanent place for caravans and wild beast shows. A row of miserable temporary workshops, and at one time a little theatre, disfigured its western side. Among other edifices that were there until about 1850 was the huge wooden peristrophic Rotunda, which was first opened in 1823 to exhibit some great pictures of the battles of Trafalgar and Waterloo.

In the same year was laid the foundation of the Royal Institution, after the protracted and laborious process of driving about 2,000 piles into the site, to make firm the travelled earth at its southern end. Though founded in 1823, it was not finally completed until 1836, after designs by W. H. Playfair, at a cost of £40,000. As shown in the view on the next page, it was at first without enrichment in the pediments, and was finished above the cornice, by a plain parapet all round, with a base and moulding ; and had eight large pedestals, intended for statues, against the walls, between the flat Grecian pilasters. The building was, however, subsequently largely altered and improved. It is in the pure Doric style of Pericles, and forms an oblong, nearly akin in character to that of a peripteral temple, with fluted columns all rising from a uniform base of steps, and surmounted by a pure Greek entablature. There projects from its north front a triple octostyle portico, and from its south front a double octostyle portico, and the pediments of both are filled with beautifully-carved Greek scroll-work and honeysuckle. From the flanks of these, at both ends, there projects a distyle portico. Behind the apex of the northern portico, facing Hanover Street, is a colossal statue of Queen Victoria, seated, with crown, sceptre, and robes of state, sculptured by Steel. Eight sphinxes adorn the four angles of this stately edifice, which, like all others in the New Town, is built of pure white freestone, and contains a school of design, a gallery of sculpture, the antiquarian museum, the apartments of the Royal Society, and those of the Board of Trustees for Manufactures in Scotland. We shall treat of the last first.

By the fifteenth article of the Treaty of Union with England, among other provisions for giving Scotland some equivalent for the increase of duties of Customs and Excise, it was agreed that for some years £2,000 per annum should be applied by the new Imperial Parliament towards the encouragement and formation of manufactures in the coarse wool of those counties that produced it, and afterwards to be wholly employed towards "encouraging and promoting the fisheries and such other manufactures and improvements in Scotland as

may conduce to the general good of the United Kingdom."

In 1718 this £2,000 was made payable for ever out of the Customs and Excise in Scotland. In 1725 an addition was made to this sum by an Act which provided that when the produce of threepence per bushel to be laid on malt should exceed £20,000 per annum, such surplus should be added to it and applied to the same purposes. In 1726 the Crown was empowered to appoint twenty-one trustees, who were named in 1727 by letters patent, which prescribed their duties and the plan for expending the funds at their disposal in the encouragement of the woollen, linen, and hempen manufactures and the Scottish fisheries, which had always been fostered by the Stuart kings, as numerous laws, enacted by the Third, Fourth, Fifth, and Sixth Jameses, attest.

But in regarding a Scottish institution which now occupies a place so conspicuous in the eye of the public, it is curious to trace the difficulties it had to contend with, in consequence of the lack of local government and the monetary vacuum caused by a conflict between the banks. On the 26th of June, 1728, Duncan Forbes, then Lord Advocate, wrote to the Duke of Newcastle :—" The trustees appointed by His Majesty for taking care of the manufactures proceed with great zeal and industry ; but at present credit is run so low, by a struggle between the bank lately erected by His Majesty and the old bank, that money can scarcely be found to go to market with."

Matters, however, improved, and the activity and use of the Board were shown in the promotion of the linen manufacture, which, under the stimulus given by premiums, rose from an export sale of 2,183,978 yards in 1727 to 4,666,011 yards in 1738, 7,358,098 yards in 1748, and 12,823,048 yards in 1764.

In 1766 the trustees opened a hall in Edinburgh (The British Linen Hall) for the custody and sale of Scottish linens, which the owners thereof might sell, either personally or by their factors. " For whatever period the goods should remain in the hall unsold," says Arnot, " their respective owners pay nothing to the proprietors of the hall ; but upon their being sold, 5 per cent. upon the value of the linens sold is demanded by way of rent. As the opening of this hall was found to be attended with good consequences to the linen manufactures, so in 1776 the trustees extended it upon the same terms to the woollen manufactures of Scotland."

Under these trustees and their successors the business of the Board was carried on until 1828 with little change of system, save that in 1809 their number was increased from twenty-one to twenty-eight, and out of that number the Crown was empowered to appoint seven to be Commissioners for the Herring Fishery; and from that time the Fishery Board and the Board of Manufactures have virtually been separate bodies.

Regarding the Royal Institution, in which it now has chambers, Lord Cockburn says :—"Strictly, it ought to have been named after the old historical mental art, and also in taste and design in manufacture. In the same year Sir John Shaw Lefevre was sent down by Government to report on the constitution and management of the Board and the erection of the Galleries of Art in Edinburgh.

Since the Board began to give premiums for the encouragement of the linen trade, that branch of business has made giant strides in Scotland. "It takes about six months," says David Bremner, "from the purchase of the raw material before the

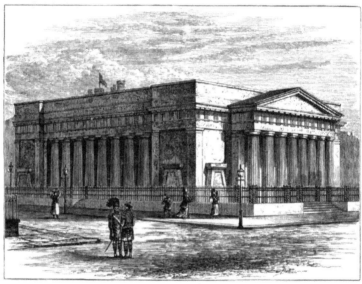

THE ROYAL INSTITUTION AS IT WAS IN 1829. (*From a Drawing by Shepherd.*)

board of trustees, because it was by their money and for their accommodation chiefly it was made, and 'the Trustees' Hall' had been the title ever since the Union, of the place in the old town where they had met."

In 1828 new letters patent were issued, giving to the trustees a wider discretion, and empowering them to apply their funds to the encouragement not only of manufactures, but also of such other undertakings in Scotland as should most conduce to the general welfare of the United Kingdom.

In 1847 an Act was passed by which the Treasury was enabled to direct the appropriation of their funds towards the purposes of education in the fine arts generally, in decorative and orna- goods can be manufactured and the proceeds drawn, so that the stock-in-trade of manufacturers and merchants will amount to £5,000,000. It would thus appear that a capital of £12,000,000 is required for carrying on the linen trade of Scotland."

It was under this Board of Manufactures that the quality of Scottish linen was improved. One of their earliest acts was to propose to Nicholas d'Assaville, a cambric weaver of St. Quintin, in France, to bring over ten experienced weavers in cambric, with their families, to settle in Scotland and teach their art to others. The proposal was accepted, and the trustees purchased from the governors of Heriot's Hospital five acres of ground eastward of Broughton Loan, whereon were built houses for the French weavers, who, in memory of their native land, named the colony Little Picardy, and thereon now stands Picardy Place. This was in 1729. The men taught weaving, their wives and daughters the art of spinning cambric yarn; and by the trustees a man well skilled in all the branches of the linen trade was at the same time brought from Ireland, and appointed to travel the country and instruct the weavers and others in the best modes of making cloth.

"Secondly, to indemnify for any losses they might sustain by *reducing* the coin of Scotland to the standard and value of England; and thirdly, in *bribing* a majority of the Scottish Parliament when matters came to the *last push*.

"Of the whole equivalent, therefore, *only* £40,000 was left for national purposes; and so lost to public spirit and to all sense of honour were the representatives of Scotland, three or four noblemen alone excepted, that this balance was supposed to

THE ROYAL INSTITUTION.

Before proceeding further, we shall here quote the comprehensive statement concerning the Board of Trustees which appears in Knox's "View of the British Empire," London, 1785 :—

"By the Treaty of Union it was stipulated that £398,085 should be paid to the Scots as an equivalent for the customs, taxes, and excises to be levied upon that kingdom in consequence of the English debt, £20,000,000, though estimated at £17,000,000. This equivalent, if it may be so called, was applied in the following manner :—

"Firstly, to pay off the capital of the Scottish India Company, which was to be abolished in favour of the English Company trading to the East Indies.

be useless in the English Treasury till the year 1727, when the royal burghs began to wake from their stupor, and to apply the interest of the £40,000 towards raising a little fund for improving the manufactures and fisheries of the country."

"An Act of Parliament" (the Act quoted before) "now directed the application of the funds to the several purposes for which they were designed, and appointed twenty-one commissioners, who were entrusted with the management of the same and other matters relative thereto."

In Lefevre's Report of July 20th, 1850, it is stated that "having regard to the origin of this Board as connected with the existence of Scotland as a separate kingdom, and to the unbroken series of distinguished trustees of whom it has been composed since its formation; considering also that the power of appointing persons to be members of the Board offers the means of conferring distinction on eminent individuals belonging to Scotland, I entertain a strong conviction that this Board should be kept up to its present number, and that its vacancies should be supplied as they occur. I am disposed to think also that it would be desirable to give this Board a corporate character by a charter or Act of Incorporation."

Under the fostering care of the Board of Manufactures first sprang up the Scottish School of Design, which had its origin in 1760. On the 27th of June in that year, in pursuance of previous deliberations of the Board, as its records show, "a scheme or scroll of an advertisement anent the drawing school was read, and it was referred to Lord Kames to take evidence of the capacity and genius for drawing of persons applying for instruction before they were presented to the drawing school, and to report when the salary of Mr. Délacour, painter, who had been appointed to teach the school, should commence."

This was the first School of Design established in the three kingdoms at the public expense. "It is," said the late Sir W. Stirling-Maxwell, in an address to the institution in 1870, "a matter of no small pride to us as Scotsmen to find a Scottish judge in 1760 and two Scottish painters in 1837 taking the lead in a movement which in each case became national."

The latter were Mr. William Dyce and Mr. Charles Heath Wilson, who, in a letter to Lord Meadowbank on "the best means of ameliorating arts and manufactures in point of taste," had all the chief principles which they urged brought into active operation by the present Science and Art Department; and when the Royal Scottish Academy was in a position to open its doors to art pupils, the life school was transferred from the Board to the Academy. Of the success of these schools it is only necessary to say that almost every Scotsman who has risen to distinction in art has owed something of that distinction to the training received here. There are annual examinations and competitions for prizes. The latter though small in actual and intrinsic value, possess a very high value to minds of the better order. "They are," said Sir W. Stirling-Maxwell, "tokens of the sympathy with which the State regards the exertions of its students. They are rewards which those who now sit or have sat in high places of a noble profession—the Harveys, the Patons, the Faeds, the Robertses, and the Wilkies—have been proud to win, and whose success in these early competitions was the beginning of a long series of triumphs." In the same edifice is the gallery of sculpture, a good collection of casts from the best ancient works, such as the Elgin marbles and celebrated statues of antiquity, of the well-known Ghiberti gates of Florence, and a valuable series of antique Greek and Roman busts known as the Albacini collection, from which family they were purchased for the Gallery.

In the western portion of the Royal Institution are the apartments of the Royal Society of Edinburgh, which was instituted in 1783, under the presidency of Henry Duke of Buccleuch, K.G. and K.T., with Professor John Robinson, LL.D., as secretary, and twelve councillors whose names are nearly all known to fame, and are as follows :—

Mr. Baron Gordon.	Dr. Munro.
Lord Elliock.	Dr. Hope.
Major-Gen. Fletcher Campbell.	Dr. Black.
Adam Smith, Esq.	Dr. Hutton.
Mr. John McLaurin.	Prof. Dugald Stewart.
Dr. Adam Ferguson.	Mr. John Playfair.

The central portion of the Royal Institution is occupied by the apartments and museum of the Society of Antiquaries of Scotland, which was founded in 1780 by a body of noblemen and gentlemen, who were anxious to secure a more accurate and extended knowledge of the historic and national antiquities of their native country than single individual zeal or skill could hope to achieve. "For this purpose, a building and an area formerly occupied as the post office, situated in the Cowgate, then one of the chief thoroughfares of Edinburgh, were purchased for £1,000. Towards this, the Earl of Buchan, founder of the Society, the Dukes of Montrose and Argyle, the Earls of Fife, Bute, and Kintore, Sir Laurence Dundas, Sir John Dalrymple, Sir Alexander Dick, Macdonnel of Glengarry, Mr. Fergusson of Raith, Mr. Ross of Cromarty, and other noblemen and gentlemen, liberally contributed. Many valuable objects of antiquity and original MSS. and books were in like manner presented to the Society."

After being long in a small room in 24, George Street, latterly the studio of the well-known Samuel Bough, R.S.A., the museum was removed to the Institution, on the erection of the new exhibition rooms for the Scottish Academy in the art galleries. Among the earliest contributions towards the foundation of this interesting museum were the extensive and valuable collection of bronze weapons referred to in an early chapter as being dredged from Duddingstone Loch, presented by Sir Alexander Dick, Bart., of Prestonfield, in 1781, and a selection of upwards of one hundred Scottish gold, silver, and copper coins, presented in the same year by Dr. William Hunter, the celebrated founder of the Hunterian Museum, which, together with a donation of the same date by Lord MacDonald of Slate, formed the nucleus of the noble numismatic collection now possessed by the Society, a body which has attained both numbers and influence.

The first difficulty it experienced arose in consequence of the application for a royal charter, in which the members were, singular to say, opposed by various learned and literary bodies, as rivals; but fortunately the advisers of the Crown were guided by more liberal views, and the charter passed the great seal on the 5th of May, 1783.

The success of the Society, according to the third volume of its "Transactions," "during the first ten years of its existence was owing to the patriotic zeal and personal exertions of its founder, the Earl of Buchan. Under this nobleman's protection nothing was wanting to ensure the prosperity of the institution, except some addition to its funds with the view of establishing a permanent museum."

During the earlier years of the Society's existence objects of natural history formed a prominent feature in its collection, under the auspices of Mr. William Smellie, author of "The Philosophy of Natural History," who was secretary in 1793. These have ceased to be included among the pursuits of the Society, whose "Transactions" furnish gratifying evidence that, notwithstanding the many vicissitudes it has undergone, scarcely a single article of any value is missing of all the objects of archæological interest presented to the museum since its foundation.

In the year 1829, by an arrangement with the Royal Society, all the objects of natural history collected by Mr. Smellie and others were transferred to the museum of that body, the Antiquaries receiving in return such objects as more properly came within the compass of their pursuits, including bricks impressed with cuneiform inscriptions from Babylon, and several large Indian idols.

The museum is visited by thousands of visitors annually; and every year the collection receives considerable additions by purchase and donation; and the value of such depository is proved, not only by the preservation for study and popular education of so large a collection of antiquities, which must otherwise have been scattered or lost; but also by the fact that the domestic implements and personal ornaments which in its earlier years were only beginning to fall into disuse, have now, after the lapse of nearly a century, become curious illustrations of Scottish manners and a state of society almost obsolete.

Through Mr. Robert Hay, Under Secretary of State, the Government presented the Society, in 1830, with a magnificent collection of Cyrenaic antiquities; and the Barons of the Scottish Exchequer have given valuable contributions from time to time.

Many interesting Northern antiquities were presented by his Danish Majesty, Christian IX., in 1844, and some Roman and mediæval remains from London, by the Marquis of Breadalbane, in 1846; but one of the most valuable gifts bestowed on the Society was the bequest in the same year by Mr. E. W. A. Drummond Hay (H.M. Consul-General to the Barbary States) of his whole private collection, including 603 Roman gold and silver coins, upwards of 2,000 Roman brass, a large collection of Scottish, English, and foreign coins, besides bronzes, medallions, and other objects of antiquity.

Among the multifarious contents of this most valuable museum may be briefly enumerated a splendid collection of Egyptian antiquities; sculptures and works in terra-cotta from various countries; ancient British implements, warlike and domestic; examples of Roman-British pottery and glass; old Scottish wood carvings; ancient cannon and armour, and various Scottish instruments of punishment and torture, including that famous old guillotine, the Maiden, by which the Regent Morton was beheaded in 1581, Sir John Gordon of Haddo in 1644, President Spottiswood in 1642; the two Argyles, and a multitude of others; the repentance stool of the old Greyfriars' church; the pulpit of Knox; the alleged "creepie" of Jenny Geddes; a banner borne by the Covenanters at Bothwell Bridge; a portrait of Cardinal Innes, advanced to the purple by Pope John XXIII.—the first Scotsman who ever attained that rank; the blue ribbon worn by Prince Charles as Knight of the Garter, and his ring, the farewell gift of Flora Macdonald; Rob Roy's purse; the witches' iron branks; copies of the national covenant, signed by Montrose and all the Scottish nobles and notables of the period; autograph letters of Mary, James VI., Charles I. Cromwell, and a vast collection of objects of antiquity generally.

THE NATIONAL GALLERY.

CHAPTER XIII.

THE MOUND (concluded).

The Art Galleries—The National Gallery The Various Collections—The Royal Scottish Academy—Early Scottish Artists—The Institution—
The First Exhibition in Edinburgh—Foundation of the Academy—Presidents: G. Watson, Sir William Allan, Sir J. W. Gordon,
Sir George Harvey, Sir Daniel Macnee—The Spalding Fund.

THEIR objects being akin, the Royal Institution and Art Galleries stand in convenient proximity to each other. The formation of the latter was one of the results of the Report, referred to, by Sir John Shaw Lefevre on the constitution of the Board of Manufactures; and subsequent negotiations with the Treasury led to the erection of the Galleries, the foundation stone of which was laid by the Prince Consort on the 30th of August, 1850, and they were opened in 1859. The Treasury furnished £30,000, the Board £20,000, and the city a portion of the site at a nominal rate. By these arrangements the Scottish people have a noble National Gallery of great and increasing value, and the Royal Scottish Academy has also been provided with saloons for its annual exhibitions.

Designed by W. H. Playfair, the Galleries are so situated that a railway tunnel crosses beneath their foundation and a lofty green bank overlooks the south end. They form a cruciform edifice, the main length of which lies north and south, with a broad and high transept intersecting the centre; at the south and north ends, or fronts, are beautiful Ionic porticoes, and on each face of the transept

is a handsome hexastyle Ionic portico. The eastern range is occupied by the Royal Scottish Academy's Exhibition from February till May in each year, and the western range is permanently used as the National Gallery, containing a collection of paintings by old masters and modern artists and a few works of sculpture, among which, terminating the long vista of the saloons, is Flaxman's fine statue of Robert Burns. The first of these contains specimens of the Flemish, Dutch, and French schools of the sixteenth and seventeenth centuries; the central or second saloon specimens of the Italian, Venetian, Genoese, Florentine, Flemish, and other schools of the same period; while the third room is devoted to examples of the Scottish school.

The collections generally include some fine specimens of Vandyke, Titian, Tintoretto, Velasquez, Paul Veronese, Spagnoletto, Rembrandt, and others. There is also a noble series of portraits by Sir Thomas Lawrence, Sir Henry Raeburn, George Watson (first President of the Academy), Sir John Watson Gordon, and Graham Gilbert. In one of the rooms set apart for modern works may be seen Sir Noel Paton's two wonderful pictures of Oberon and Titania; others by Erskine Nicol, Herdman, Faed, W. Fettes, Douglas, James Drummond, Sir George Harvey, Horatio Macculloch, R. S. Lauder, Roberts, Dyce, and Etty, from whose brush there are those colossal paintings of "Judith with the Head of Holofernes" and "The Woman Interceding for the Vanquished."

Among the many fine paintings bequeathed to this Scottish Gallery is Gainsborough's celebrated portrait of Mrs. Graham, depicting a proud and

are outlined; and the great and accurately detailed picture of the battle of Bannockburn.

There is a small full-length picture of Burns, painted by Nasmyth, as a memento of the poet, and another by the same artist, presented by the poet's son, Colonel W. Nicol Burns, and a fine portrait of Sir John Moore, the property of the officers of the Black Watch.

The choice collection of water colours embraces some of the best works of "Grecian" Williams; a series of drawings bequeathed to the Gallery

INTERIOR OF THE NATIONAL GALLERY.

beautiful girl, grief for whose death in early life caused her husband, the future Lord Lynedoch, "the hero of Barossa," to have it covered up that he might never look upon it again. There are also some beautiful and delicate works by Greuze, the gift of Lady Murray; and one by Thomson of Duddingstone, presented by Lady Stuart of Allanbank; and Landseer's "Rent Day in the Wilderness," a Jacobite subject, bequeathed by the late Sir Roderick Murchison, Bart.

Not the least interesting works here are a few that were among the last touched by deceased artists, and left unfinished on their easels, such as Wilkie's "John Knox Dispensing the Sacrament at Calder House," of which a few of the faces alone

by Mr. Scott, including examples of Robert Cattermole, Collins, Cox, Girtin, Prout, Nash, and Cristall; and a set of studies of the most striking peculiarities of the Dutch, Spanish, Venetian, and Flemish schools. Of great interest, too, are the waxen models by Michael Angelo.

The Gallery also contains a collection of marbles and bronzes, bequeathed by Sir James Erskine of Torrie, and a cabinet of medallion portraits and casts from gems, by James and William Tassie, the celebrated modellers, who, though born of obscure parents in Renfrewshire, acquired such fame and reputation that the first cabinets in Europe were open to their use.

The Royal Scottish Academy of Painting and

Sculpture had its origin early in the present century, though in past times the Scottish School of Painters ranked among its number several celebrities. Of these the most noted was George Jameson, born at Aberdeen in 1586; he studied under Rubens, and won himself the name of the Scottish Vandyke. Charles I. sat to him for his portrait, as did many other great Scotsmen of the period. He was succeeded by the elder Scougal, a painter of many works; Scougal the younger; De Witte; Nicolas Hude, a French Protestant refugee; John Baptisto Medina, a native of Brussels, whose son John was a "Limner" in Hyndford's Close in 1784; Aikman; Wait; Allan Ramsay (son of the poet); Norrie, the landscape painter; the Runcimans, Brown, and latterly David Allan, Graham, Wilkie, Gibson, Thomson, Raeburn, and the Watsons.

The first movement towards fostering native art was, undoubtedly, the appointment by the Board of Trustees, in 1760, of a permanent master for the instruction of the youth of both sexes in drawing, thus laying the foundation of a School of Design. The second important organisation was that named the "Institution for the Encouragement of the Fine Arts," founded on the 1st of February, 1819, on the model of the British Institution of London, for the annual exhibition of pictures by old masters, and subsequently those of living artists. It consisted chiefly of gentlemen, who, on the payment of £50, became shareholders or life-members. The first exhibition by the Institution was in York Place, in March, 1819, but owing to certain complications between it and artists generally, they were, even if members, not permitted to exercise the slightest control over the funds.

Prior to this time the leading artists resident in Edinburgh had associated together for the purpose of having an annual exhibition of their works, which was also held in York Place. The first of these occurred in 1808, and Lord Cockburn refers to it as the most gratifying occurrence of the period, and as one that "proclaimed the dawn of modern Scottish art."

Among the pictures shown on that auspicious occasion the catalogue records three by George Watson, including the portrait of the celebrated Bishop Hay; three by A. Nasmyth; two by Douglas, one being a portrait of Mrs. Boswell of Auchinleck; three fancy pictures by Carse; "The Earl of Buchan crowning Master Gattie," by W. Lizars; a black chalk landscape by Thomson; and in the succeeding year, 1809, the catalogue mentions, briefly noted, five by Raeburn, including

his Walter Scott; three by Gorge Watson, one being the "Portrait of an Old Scots Jacobite;" three by Thomson of Duddingston; a fancy picture of Queen Mary, by John Watson, afterwards Sir J. W. Gordon.

Carse, called the Teniers of Scotland, died early; but "this exhibition did incalculable good. It drew such artists as we had out of their obscurity; it showed them their strength and their weakness: it excited public attention: it gave them importance."

During five exhibitions, between 1809 and 1813, the members thus associated saved £1,888, but not being sufficiently restricted by their laws from dissolving at any time, the sum amassed proved a temptation, and it was divided among the exhibitors. The Society then broke up and dispersed, and it was while they were in this state of disorganisation that the Directors of the Institution, finding the old masters not sufficiently attractive to the public, made overtures to the artists for an exhibition of modern pictures and sculpture under their auspices, and to set the proceeds aside for the benefit of the said artists and their families.

Thus the first exhibition of the works of living artists under the direction of the Institution took place in 1821, and it proved such a success that it was repeated yearly till 1829.

The Institution had in 1826, besides one hundred and thirty-one ordinary members, thirteen honorary, five of whom were artists, under the title of Associate Members, and the exhibitions were held in the Galleries of the Royal Institution, for which an annual rent of £380 was paid; but as great discontent was expressed by artists who were Associate Members, because they were denied all consideration in the management in the year mentioned, they resolved to found a Scottish Academy.

It was in the summer of 1826 that the document by which this important movement was inaugurated went round for signature in the hands of Mr. William Nicholson. When published, twenty-four names appeared to it: those of thirteen Academicians, nine Associates, and two Associate Engravers.

The first general meeting of "The Scottish Academy of Painting, Sculpture, and Architecture," was held on the 27th of May, 1826, Mr. Patrick Syme in the chair, and the following gentlemen were elected as office-bearers for the year:—George Watson, *President;* William Nicholson, *Secretary;* Thomas Hamilton, *Treasurer.* The Council consisted of four.

Mr. George Watson, who has been justly deemed the founder of the Academy, was the son of John Watson of Overmains, in Berwickshire, his mother being Frances Veitch, of the Elliock family. He was a cousin of Sir Walter Scott's, and was born in 1767. He studied art under Nasmyth and Sir Joshua Reynolds, and before the time of his election had won a high reputation as a portrait painter. From 1808 to 1812 he was President of the Associated Artists of Scotland. His brother, Captain Watson, R.N., was the father of Sir John Watson-Gordon, also a president of the Academy; and his nephew, William Stewart Watson, was an artist of some repute, whose chief work is the "Inauguration of Burns as Poet Laureate or Grand Bard," now in the Masonic Hall, George Street, and, as a collection of portraits, is historically curious. George Watson's son, W. Smellie Watson, was also R.S.A., and died in No. 10 Forth Street in 1874, the same house in which his father had held some early exhibitions about the close of the last century or beginning of the present.

The President and Council resolved that the first exhibition of their infant Academy should take place early in February, 1827, in two large galleries which they rented, in 24 Waterloo Place, for three months at eighty guineas, and subsequently at one hundred and thirty pounds per annum. Opposed by those who should have aided it, the Academy had a hard struggle for a time in the first years of its existence. Application was made to the Home Secretary, the future Sir Robert Peel, for a charter of incorporation, and it was favourably viewed by those in office, and submitted to the Lord Advocate. But though the application was generously and warmly seconded by Sir Thomas Lawrence, then President of the Royal Academy of London, it was put off for two years, "and ultimately refused," says Sir George Harvey "on grounds which the Academy could never learn; and though they applied for permission to do so, they were never allowed to peruse the document which induced his lordship to decide against their claim. . . . Curiously enough, although the request of the Academy for a charter of incorporation was at this time denied, the Institution had that distinction conferred upon it, and henceforth came to be designated the Royal Institution."

The first general exhibition of the Scottish Academy being advertised for February, 1827, "the Royal Institution, *under the immediate patronage of His Majesty*," was, in a spirit of genuine opposition, advertised to open at the same time; but by the time of the third Exhibition, "the Royal Institution," says Sir George, "was fairly driven out of the field ;" and among the contributors were the future Sir Francis Grant, John Linnell, and

John Martin, and one of Etty's magnificent works, now the property of the Academy, was for the first time hung upon its walls, while many Scottish artists in London or elsewhere, watched with patriotic interest the progress of art in their native land, and the Institution rapidly began to take a subordinate position; and by a minute of the 10th July, 1829, twenty-four of its artists, weary of its rule, were admitted as members of the Scottish Academy, thus raising the numerical force of the latter to thirty-nine. Eventually the number of Academicians became forty-two. In the rank of Associate Engravers was the well-known William Lizars, for as the law stood then he could not be elected an Academician, engravers being then limited to the position of Associate, but after a time they were rendered eligible to occupy any rank in the Academy.

George Watson, the first President of the Scottish Academy, died on the 24th of August, 1837, at No. 10 Forth Street, in his seventieth year. For a long time previously his occupation of the chair had been nominal, his age and declining health precluding his attendance at council meetings. A white marble slab in the west wall of the West Kirkyard marks his grave and that of "Rebecca Smellie, his spouse, who died 5th May, 1839, aged 74 years."

In the subsequent November William Allan, R.A. (afterwards knighted), was elected president, and during his term of office the long-desired object was accomplished, and the Academy came to be designated at last "The Royal Scottish Academy," incorporated by royal charter on the 13th of August, 1838, consisting now of thirty Academicians and twenty Associates—a consummation of their wishes for which they were greatly indebted to the warm and earnest interest of Lord Cockburn.

By its charter the Academy is to consist of artists by profession, being men of fair moral character and of high repute in art, settled and resident in Scotland at the dates of their elections. It ordains that there shall be an annual exhibition of paintings, sculptures, and designs, in which all artists of distinguished merit may be permitted to exhibit their works, to continue open six weeks or longer. It likewise ordains that so soon as the funds of the Academy will allow it, there shall be in the Royal Scottish Academy professors of painting, sculpture, architecture, perspective, and anatomy, elected according to the laws framed for the Royal Academy of London; and that there shall be schools to provide the means of studying the human form with respect both to anatomical knowledge and taste of design, which shall consist of two departments : the one appropriated to the remains of ancient sculpture, and the other to the study of living models.

From that time matters went on peacefully and pleasantly till 1844, when a dispute about entrance to their galleries ensued with the subordinates of the Board of Manufactures, in whose building they were—a dispute ultimately smoothed over. In 1847 another ensued between the directors of the Royal Institution and the Academy, which led to some acrimonious correspondence ; but all piques and jealousies between the Academy and the Royal Institution were ended by the erection of the Art Galleries, founded in 1850.

Six months before that event Sir William Allan, the second president, died on the 22nd of February, after occupying the presidential chair for thirteen years with much ability. It is to be regretted that no such good example of his genius as his "Death of Rizzio" finds a place in the Scottish National Gallery, his principal work there being his large unfinished picture of the "Battle of Bannockburn," a patriotic labour of love, showing few of the best qualities of his master-hand, as it was painted literally when he was dying. "To those who were with Sir William in his latter days it was sadly interesting to see him wrapped up in blankets, cowering by his easel, with this great canvas stretched out before him, labouring on it assiduously, it may be truly said, till the day on which he died," writes a brother artist, who has since followed him. "The constant and only companion of his studio, a long-haired, glossy Skye terrier, on his master's death, refused to be comforted, to eat, or to live."

His successor was Sir John Watson, who added the name of Gordon to his own. He was the son of Captain James Watson, R.N., who served in Admiral Digby's squadron during the first American war. Among his earlier works were the "Shipwrecked Sailor," "Queen Margaret and the Robber," "A Boy with a Rabbit," "The Sleeping Boy and Watching Girl" (his own brother and sister); but it was as a painter of portraits strictly that he made his high reputation ; though it is said that the veteran, his father, when looking at the "Venus and Adonis" of Paul Veronese, declared it "hard as flints," adding, "I wouldn't give my Johnny's ' Shipwrecked Sailor' for a shipload of such."

In early life he lived with his father in 27 Anne Street, which he left regularly every morning at nine o'clock, "and walking down the beautiful and picturesque footpath that skirted the bank of the Water of Leith, he passed St. Bernard's, where almost invariably he was joined by the portly figure of Sir Henry Raeburn. Engaged in conversation, no doubt beneficial to the younger but rising artist, they proceeded to Edinburgh—Raeburn to his gallery and painting-room, No. 32 York Place, and John Watson to his apartments in the first flat of No. 19 South St. David Street, or, latterly, 24 South Frederick Street."

During his presidency the Art Galleries were completed and opened. By the Act 13 and 14 Vict., cap. 86, the entire building and property were vested in the Board of Manufactures, as well as the appropriation of the buildings when completed, subject to the approbation of the Treasury, without the sanction of which no fee for admittance was to be charged on any occasion, except to the annual exhibition of the Royal Scottish Academy. "The general custody and maintenance of the whole building shall be vested in the Board of Manufactures," says the Government minute of 28th February, 1858 ; "but the Royal Scottish Academy shall have the entire charge of the council-room and library and of the exhibition galleries during their annual exhibitions."

After continuing in the exercise of his profession until within a few weeks of his death, Sir John Watson died at his house in George Street, 1st June, 1864, in his seventy-sixth year, having been born in 1788.

He was succeeded as president and trustee by Sir George Harvey, born in Stirlingshire in 1805, and well known as a painter successfully of historical subjects and *tableaux de genre*, many of them connected with the stirring events of the Covenant. He became a Scottish Academician in 1829, since when his popularity spread far and wide by the dissemination of numerous engravings from his works. He was president only twelve years, and died at Edinburgh on the 22nd of January, 1876, in his seventy-first year.

He was succeeded by Sir Daniel Macnee, R.S.A., who was also born in Stirlingshire in 1806, and began early to study at the Trustees' Academy with Duncan, Lauder, Scott, and other artists of native repute. He rapidly became a favourite portrait painter in both countries, and his famous portrait of the Rev. Dr. Wardlaw won a gold medal at the Paris International Exhibition of 1855. He has painted many of the most prominent men of the time, among them Lord Brougham for the College of Justice at Edinburgh.

In connection with Scottish art we may here refer to the Spalding Fund, of which the directors of the Royal Institution were constituted trustees by the will of Peter Spalding, who died in 1826, leaving property, "the interest or annual proceeds whereof are to be applied for ever for the support of decayed and superannuated artists." This property consisted mainly of ancient houses, situated in the old town, the free proceeds of which were only £220. It was sold, and the whole value of it, amounting to £5,420 10s., invested in Bank of Scotland and British Linen Company Stock, and has been so carefully husbanded that the directors now possess stock to the value of more than £6,618. "It was originally given in annuities varying from £50 to £100 a year; but the directors some years ago thought it advisable to restrict the amount of these, so as to extend the benefit of the fund over a larger number of annuitants, and they now do not give annuities to a larger amount than £35, and they require that the applications for these shall in all cases be accompanied by a recommendation from two members of the Royal Scottish Academy who know the circumstances of the applicant."

CHAPTER XIV.

THE HEAD OF THE EARTHEN MOUND.

The Bank of Scotland--Its Charter--Rivalry of the Royal Bank Notes for £5 and for 5s.--The New Bank of Scotland--Its Present Aspect-- The Projects of Mr. Trotter and Sir Thomas Dick Lauder--The National Security Savings Bank of Edinburgh--The Free Church College and Assembly Hall--Their Foundation--Constitution--Library--Museum--Bursaries--Missionary and Theological Societies--The Dining Hall, &c.--The West Princes Street Gardens--The Proposed Canal and Seaport--The East Princes Street Gardens--Railway Terminus--Waverley Bridge and Market.

"How well the ridge of the old town was set off by a bank of elms that ran along the front of James's Court, and stretched eastward over the ground now partly occupied by the Bank of Scotland," says Cockburn, in his "Memorials;" but looking at the locality now, it is difficult to realise the idea that such a thing had been; yet Edgar shows us a pathway running along the slope, between the foot of the closes and a row of gardens that bordered the loch.

Bank Street, which was formed in 1798 a few yards westward of Dunbar's Close, occasioning in its formation the destruction of some buildings of great antiquity, looks at first sight like a broad cul-de-sac blocked up by the front of the Bank of Scotland, but in reality forms the carriage-way downward from the head of the Mound to Princes Street.

While as yet the bank was in the old narrow alley that so long bore its name, we read in the Edinburgh Herald and Chronicle of March, 1800, "that the directors of the Bank of Scotland have purchased from the city an area at the south end of the Earthen Mound, on which they intend to erect an elegant building, with commodious apartments for carrying on their business."

Elsewhere we have briefly referred to the early progress of this bank, the oldest of the then old "chartered banks" which was projected by John Holland, a retired London merchant, according to the scheme devised by William Paterson, a native of Dumfries, who founded the Bank of England.

The Act of the Scottish Parliament for starting the Bank of Scotland, July, 1695, recites, by way of exordium, that "our sovereign lord, considering how useful a public bank may be in this kingdom, according to the custom of other kingdoms and states, and that the same can only be best set up and managed by persons in company with a joint stock, sufficiently endowed with those powers, authorities, and liberties necessary and usual in such cases, hath therefore allowed, with the advice and consent of the Estates of Parliament, a joint stock of £1,200,000 money (Scots) to be raised by the company hereby established for the carrying on and managing a public bank."

After an enumeration of the names of those who were chosen to form the nucleus of the company, including those of five Edinburgh merchants, the charter proceeds to state that they have full powers to receive in a book the subscriptions of either native Scots or foreigners, "who shall be willing to subscribe and pay into the said joint stock, which subscriptions the aforesaid persons, or their quorum, are hereby authorised to receive in the foresaid book, which shall lie open every Tuesday or Friday, from nine to twelve in the forenoon, and from three to six in the afternoon, between the first day of November next and the first day of January next following, in the public hall or chamber appointed in the city of Edinburgh; and therein all persons shall have liberty to subscribe for such sums of money as they shall think fit to adventure in the said joint stock, £1,000 Scots being lowest sum and £20,000 Scots the highest, and the two-third parts of the said stocks belonging always to persons residing in Scotland. Likewise, each and every person, at the time of his subscribing, shall pay into the hands of the forenamed persons, or any three of them, ten of the hundred of the sums set down in their respective subscriptions towards carrying on the bank, and all and every the persons subscribing and paying to the said stock as aforesaid shall be, and hereby are declared to be, one body corporate and politic, by the name and company of THE BANK OF SCOTLAND," etc.

The charter, while detailing minutely all that the bank may do in the way of lending money and giving laws for its internal government, fails to define in any way the liability of the shareholders to each other or to the public. For the space of twenty-one years it was to be free from all public burdens, and during that time all other persons in the realm of Scotland are prohibited from setting up any rival company.

To preclude the breaking of the bank contrary to the object in view, it is declared that the sums of the present subscriptions and shares may only be conveyed and transmitted by the owners to others who shall become partners in their place, or by adjudication or other legal means. It is also provided by the charter that all foreigners on acquiring the bank stock must become "naturalised Scotsmen, to all intents and purposes whatsoever," a privilege that became abused, and was abolished in 1822. The charter further ordains that no member of the said company shall, upon any "pretence whatever, directly or indirectly, use, exercise, or follow any other traffic or trade with the said joint stock to be employed in the said bank, or any part thereof, or profits arising therefrom, excepting the trade of lending and borrowing money upon interest, and negotiating bills of exchange, allenarly [*i.e.*, these things only], and no other."

By various subsequent statutes the capital of this bank was increased till it stood nominally at £1,500,000, a third of which has not been called; and by the Act 36 and 37 Victoria, cap. 99, further powers to raise capital were granted, without the Act being taken advantage of. The additional amount authorised is £3,000,000, which would give a total capital of £4,500,000 sterling.

The monopoly conferred on the bank by the Parliament of Scotland was not renewed at the expiry of the first twenty-one years; and on its being found that banking business was on the increase, another establishment, the Royal Bank of Scotland, was chartered in 1727, and immediately became the rival of its predecessor.

"It purchased up," says Arnot, "all the notes of the Bank of Scotland that they (the directors) could lay hands on, and caused such a run upon this bank as reduced them to considerable difficulties. To avoid such distresses for the future,

the Bank of Scotland, on the 29th of November, 1730, began to issue £5 notes, payable on demand, or £5 2s. 6d. six months after their being presented for payment, in the option of the bank. On the 12th of December, 1732, they began to issue £1 notes with a similar clause."

The other banking companies in Scotland found it convenient to follow the example, and universally framed their notes with these optional clauses. They were issued for the most petty sums, and were currently accepted in payment, insomuch that notes for five shillings were perfectly common, and silver was, in a manner, banished from Scotland. To remedy these banking abuses, an Act of the British Parliament was passed in 1765, prohibiting all promissory notes payable to the bearer under £1 sterling, and also prohibiting and declaring void all the optional clauses.

In the year 1774, when the Bank of Scotland obtained an Act to enlarge their capital to £2,400,000 Scots, or £200,000 sterling, a clause provided that no individual should possess in whole, or more than, £40,000 in stock, and the qualification for the offices of governor and directors was doubled.

The present offices of the Bank of Scotland were completed from the original design in 1806 by Mr. Richard Crichton, and the institution was moved thither in that year from the old, narrow, and gloomy close where it had transacted business for one hundred and eleven years.

In digging the foundation of this edifice, the same obstacle came in the way that eventually occasioned the fall of the North Bridge. After excavating to a great depth, no proper foundation could be found—all being travelled earth. The quantity of this carted away was such that the foundations of some of the houses in the nearest closes were shaken and their walls rent, so that the occupants had to remove. A solid foundation was at last found, and the vast structure was reared at the cost of £75,000. "The quantity of stone and mortar which is buried below the present surface is immense, and perhaps as much of the building is below the ground as above it," says Stark in 1820. "The dead wall on the north of the edifice, where the declivity is greatest, is covered by a stone curtain, ornamented with a balustrade. The south front is elegant. A small dome rises from the centre, and in the front are four projections. A range of Corinthian pilasters decorates the second floor, and over the door in the recess is a Venetian window, ornamented with two columns of the Corinthian order, surmounted by the arms of the bank."

Much of all this was altered when the bank was enlarged, restored, and most effectively re-decorated by David Bryce, R.S.A., in 1868—70. It now presents a lofty, broad, and arch-based rear front of colossal proportions to Princes Street, from whence, and every other point of view, it forms a conspicuous mass, standing boldly from among the many others that form the varied outline of the Old Town, and consists of the great old centre with new wings, surmounted by a fine dome, crowned by a gilded figure of Fame, seven feet high. In length the façade measures 175 feet, and 112 in height from the pavement in Bank Street to the summit, and is embellished all round with much force and variety, in details of a Grecian style. The height of the campanile towers is ninety feet.

The bank has above seventy branches; the subscribed capital in 1878 was £1,875,000; the paid-up capital £1,250,000. There are a governor (the Earl of Stair, K.T.), a deputy, twelve ordinary and twelve extra-ordinary directors.

The Bank of Scotland issues drafts on other places in Scotland besides those in which it has branches, and also on the chief towns in England and Ireland, and it has correspondents throughout the whole continent of Europe, as well as in British America, the States, India, China, Australia, New Zealand, South Africa, and elsewhere—a ramification of business beyond the wildest dreams of John Holland and the original projectors of the establishment in the old Bank Close in 1695.

Concerning the Earthen Mound, the late Alexander Trotter of Dreghorn had a scheme for joining the Old Town to the New, and yet avoiding Bank Street, by sinking the upper end of the mound to the level of Princes Street, and carrying the Bank Street end of it eastward along the north of the Bank of Scotland, in the form of a handsome terrace, and thence south into the High Street by an opening right upon St. Giles's Church. The next project was one by the late Sir Thomas Dick Lauder. He also proposed to bring down the south end of the mound "to the level of Princes Street, and then to cut a Roman arch through the Lawnmarket and under the houses, so as to pass on a level to George Square. This," says Cockburn, "was both practical and easy, but it was not expounded till too late."

Not far from the Bank of Scotland, in 16 North Bank Street, ensconced among the mighty mass of buildings that overlook the mound, are the offices of the National Security Savings Bank of Edinburgh, established under statute in 1836, and certified in terms of the Act 26 and 27 Victoria, cap. 87, managed by a chairman and committee

of management, the Bank of Scotland being treasurer.

Of this most useful institution for the benefit of the thrifty poorer classes, suffice it to say, as a sample of its working, that on striking the yearly accounts on the 20th of November, 1880, "the balance due to depositors was on that date £1,305,279 14s. 7d., and that the assets at the same date were £1,309,392 8s., invested with the Commissioners for the Reduction of the National Debt, and £3,104 3s. 9d., at the credit of the bank's account in the Bank of Scotland, making the total assets £1,312,496 11s. 9d., which, after deduction of the above sum of £1,305,279 14s. 7d., leaves a clear surplus of £7,216 17s. 2d. at the credit of the trustees."

The managers are, ex officio, the Lord Provost, the Lord Advocate, the senior Bailie of the city, the Members of Parliament for the city, county, and Leith, the Provost of Leith, the Solicitor-General, the Convener of the Trades, the Lord Dean of Guild, and the Master of the Merchant Company.

In the same block of buildings are the offices of the Free Church of Scotland, occupying the site of the demolished half of James's Court. They were erected in 1851—61, and are in a somewhat florid variety of the Scottish baronial style, from designs by the late David Cousin.

In striking contrast to the terraced beauty of the New Town, the south side of the vale of the old loch, from the North Bridge to the esplanade of the Castle, is overhung by the dark and lofty gables and abutments of those towering edifices which terminate the northern alleys of the High Street, and the general grouping of which presents an aspect of equal romance and sublimity. From amid these sombre masses, standing out in the white purity of new freestone, are the towers and façade of the Free Church College and Assembly Hall, at the head of the Mound.

Into the history of the crises which called these edifices into existence we need not enter here, but true it is, as Macaulay says, that for the sake of religious opinion the Scots have made sacrifices for which there is no parallel in the annals of England; and when, at the Disruption, so many clergymen of the Scottish Church cast their bread upon the waters, in that spirit of independence and self-reliance so characteristic of the race, they could scarcely have foreseen the great success of their movement.

This new college was the first of those instituted in connection with the Free Church. The idea was originally entertained of making provision for arts classes as well as those for theology; and accordingly Mr. Patrick C. Macdougal was appointed, in 1844, Professor of Moral Philosophy, the Rev. John Millar was appointed Classical Tutor, and in 1845 the Rev. Alexander C. Fraser was appointed Professor of Logic. To give effect to the view long cherished by the revered Dr. Chalmers, that logic and ethics should follow the mathematical and physical sciences in the order of study, the usual order thereof was practically altered, though not imperatively so.

procured in George Street, and there the business of the college was conducted until 1850.

These class-rooms were near the house of Mr. Nasmyth, an eminent dentist, and as the students were in the habit of noisily applauding Dr. Chalmers, their clamour often startled the patients under the care of Mr. Nasmyth, who by letter requested the reverend principal to make the students moderate their applause, or express it some other way than beating on the floor with their feet. On this, Dr. Chalmers promptly informed

THE ROYAL BANK OF SCOTLAND, FROM PRINCES STREET GARDENS.

The provision thus made for arts classes was greatly due to the circumstance that at that time the tests imposed upon professors in the established universities were of such a nature and mode of application as to exclude from the professorial chairs all members of the Free Church.

When these tests were abolished, and Professors Fraser and Macdougal were elected to corresponding chairs in the University of Edinburgh, in 1853 and 1857, this extended platform was renounced, and the efforts of the Free Church of Scotland were concentrated exclusively upon training in theology.

Premises—however, inadequate for the full development of the intended system—were at once

them of the dentist's complaint, and begged that they would comply with his request. "I would be sorry indeed if we were to give offence to any neighbour," said the principal; adding, with a touch of that dry humour which was peculiar to him, "but more especially Mr. Nasmyth, a gentleman so very much in the *mouths* of the public."

Immediately after the Disruption, Dr. Chalmers had taken active steps to secure for the Free Church a proper system of theological training, in full accordance with the principles he had advocated so long, and subscription lists were at once opened to procure a building suited to the object. Each contributor gave £2,000, and Dr. Welsh succeeded in obtaining from twenty-

HEAD OF THE MOUND, PRIOR TO THE ERECTION OF THE FREE CHURCH COLLEGE, 1841.

(From the Roof of the Royal Institution.)

one persons £1,000 each, a sum which more than suffiked to purchase the site of the college—the old Guise Palace, with its adjacent closes—and to erect the edifice, while others were built at Glasgow and Aberdeen.

Plans by W. H. Playfair, architect, were prepared and adopted, after a public competition had been resorted to, and the new buildings were at once proceeded with. The foundation stone was laid on the 4th of June, 1846, by Dr. Chalmers,

The stairs on the south side of the quadrangle lead to the Free Assembly Hall, on the exact site of the Guise Palace. It was erected from designs by David Bryce, at a cost of £7,000, which was collected by ladies alone belonging to the Free Church throughout Scotland.

The structure was four years in completion, and was opened on the 6th of November, 1850, under the sanction of the Commission of the Free General Assembly, by their moderator, Dr. N. Paterson,

LIBRARY OF THE FREE CHURCH COLLEGE. (*From a Photograph by G. W. Wilson and Co.*)

exactly one year previous to the day which saw his remains consigned to the tomb. The ultimate cost was £46,506 8s. 10d., including the price of the ground, £10,000.

The buildings are in the English collegiate style, combining the common Tudor with some of the later Gothic. They form an open quadrangle (entered by a handsome groined archway), 165 feet from east to west and 177 from south to north, including on the east the Free High Church. The edifice has two square towers (having each four crocketed pinnacles), 121 feet in height, buttressed at the corners from base to summit. There is a third tower, 95 feet in height. The college contains seven great class-rooms, a senate hall, a students' hall, and a library, the latter adorned with a statue of Dr. Chalmers as Principal, by Steel.

who delivered a sermon and also a special address to the professors and students. Subsequently, this inaugural sermon and the introductory lectures delivered on the same occasion to their several classes by Professors Cunningham, Buchanan, Bannerman, Duncan, Black, Macdougal, Fraser, and Fleming, were published in a volume, as a record of that event.

The constitution of this college is the same as that of the Free Church colleges elsewhere. The Acts of Assembly provide for vesting college property and funds, for the election of professors, and for the general management and superintendence of college business. The college buildings are vested in trustees appointed by the Church. A select committee is also appointed by the General Assembly, consisting of "eleven ministers and ten elders, of whom five shall retire by rotation from year to year, two only of whom may be re-elected, and reserving the rights competent to all parties under the laws of the Church; with authority to undertake the general administration of college property and finances, to give advice in cases of difficulty; to originate and prosecute before the Church Court processes against any of the professors for heresy or immorality, and to make necessary inquiries for that purpose; to originate also, and prepare for the decision of the General Assembly, proposals for the retirement of professors disabled by age or infirmity, and for fixing the retiring allowance they are to receive." The convener is named by the Assembly, and his committees meet as often as may be necessary. They submit to the Assembly an annual report of their proceedings, with a summary of the attendance during the session.

The election of professors is vested in the General Assembly; but they are inducted into their respective offices by the Presbytery. There is a *Senatus Academicus*, composed of the Principal and professors.

The library of this college originated with Dr. Welsh, who in 1843 brought the subject before the Assembly. He obtained large and valuable donations in money and books from friends and from Scottish publishers in this country and America. Among the benefactors were the Earl of Dalhousie, Lords Effingham and Rutherford, General McDowall of Stranraer, Buchan of Kelloe, and others. The endowment now amounts to about £139 per annum. The library is extensive and valuably, numbering about 35,000 volumes. It is peculiarly rich in patristic theology, ecclesiastical history, systematic theology, and works belonging to the epoch of the Reformation.

The museum was begun by Dr. Fleming, but was mainly indebted to the efforts of the late Mrs. Macfie of Longhouse, who, at its commencement, enriched it with a large number of valuable specimens, and led many of her friends to take an interest in its development. The geological department, which is on the same floor with the class-room, contains a large number of fossils, many of which are very curious. In the upper museum is the varied and valuable collection of minerals, given by the late Dr. Johnston of Durham. In the same room are numerous specimens of comparative anatomy. The herbarium is chiefly composed of British plants.

The endowment fund now amounts to above £44,000, exclusive of £10,000 bequeathed for the endowment of a chair for natural science.

The whole scheme of scholarships in the Free Church College originated with Mr. James Hog of Newliston, who, in 1845, by personal exertions, raised about £700 for this object, and continued to do so for eight years subsequently. Legacies and donations at length accumulated such a fund as to render subscriptions no longer necessary.

A dining hall, wherein the professors preside by turn, is attached to the New College, to which all matriculated students, *i.e.*, those paying the common fee, or securing as foreigners a free ticket, are entitled to dine on payment of a moderate sum.

The common hall of the college is converted into a reading-room during the session. All students may become members on the payment of a trifling fee, and the arrangements are conducted by a committee of themselves. Since 1867 a large gymnasium has been fitted up for the use of the students, under the management of eight of their number, the almost nominal subscription of sixpence from each being found sufficient to defray the current expenses.

Westward of the Earthen Mound, the once fetid morass that formed the bed of the loch, and which had been styled "a pest-bed for all the city," is now a beautiful garden, so formed under the powers of a special statute in 1816-20, by which the ground there belonging originally to the citizens became the private property of a few proprietors of keys—the improvements being in the first instance urged by Skene, the friend of Sir Walter Scott.

In his "Journal," under date of January, 1826, Sir Walter says:—"Wrote till twelve a.m., finishing half of what I call a good day's work, ten pages of print, or rather twelve. Then walked in the Princes Street pleasure grounds with the Good Samaritan James Skene, the only one among my numerous friends who can properly be termed *amicus curarum mearum*, others being too busy or too gay. The walks have been conducted on the whole with much taste, though Skene has undergone much criticism, the usual reward of public exertions, on account of his plans. It is singular to walk close beneath the grim old castle and think what scenes it must have seen, and how many generations of three-score and ten have risen and passed away. It is a place to cure one of too much sensation over earthly subjects of imitation."

He refers here to James Skene of Rubislaw, a cornet of the Light Horse Volunteers, the corps of which he himself was quartermaster, and to whom he dedicated the fourth canto of "Marmion," and refers thus :—

"And such a lot, my Skene, was thine,
　When thou of late wert doomed to twine—
　Just when thy bridal hour was by—
　The cypress with the myrtle tie.
　Just on thy bride her sire had smiled,
　And blessed the union of his child,
　When love must change its joyous cheer,
　And wipe affection's filial tear."

In the subsequent March Scott had left his beloved house in Castle Street for ever.

Among the memorials of the Pictish race, illustrated so ably in Dr. Stuart's "Sculptured Stones of Scotland," is one with the peculiar emblems of the crescent and sceptre, which was found under the Castle rock and near the west churchyard.

The line of railway which intersects the garden, and passes by a tunnel under the new portion of St. Cuthbert's churchyard, fails to mar its beauty, as it is almost entirely hidden by trees and shrubbery, especially about the base of the rock, from which the castle "looks down upon the city as if out of another world: stern with all its peacefulness, its garniture of trees, its slopes of grass. The rock is dingy enough in colour, but after a shower its lichens laugh out greenly in the returning sun, while the rainbow is brightening on the lowering sky beyond. How deep the shadow which the castle throws at noon on the gardens at its feet, where the children play! How grand when giant bulk and towery crown blacken against the sunset!"

In the extreme western portion of the gardens lie some great fragments of masonry, which have fallen down in past sieges from some of the older walls in the vicinity of the sallyport, while the foundations of these are to be traced from point to point, some feet on the outside of the present fortifications, and lower down the rock.

In the western hollow is an ornamental fountain of considerable beauty, and formed of iron, named after its donor, Mr. Ross, who spent £3,000 on its erection. In 1876 the gardens were acquired by the citizens, and were then much improved. They are used in summer for musical promenades, and in contour and embellishment, though much more extensive, have a certain resemblance to the gardens on the east side of the Earthen Mound.

For long years after the loch had passed away the latter was but a reedy, marshy hollow, intersected by what was called the Little Mound, that led from near South St. Andrew Street to the foot of Mary King's Close. The ground was partially drained when the North Bridge was built, but more effectually about 1821, when it was let as a nursery.

When the Union canal was projected, towards the close of the last century, the plans for it, not unlike those of the Earl of Mar in 1728, included the continuation of it through the bed of the North Loch, past where a street was built, and actually called Canal Street. "From thence it was proposed to conduct it to Greenside, in the area of which was an immense harbour; and this, again, being connected by a broad canal with the sea, it was expected that by such means the New Town would be converted into a seaport, and the unhappy traders of Leith compelled either to abandon their traffic or remove within the precincts of their jealous rivals. Chimerical as this project may now appear, designs were furnished by experienced engineers, a map of the whole plan was engraved on a large scale, and no doubt our civic reformers rejoiced in the anticipation of surmounting the disadvantages of an inland position, and seeing the shipping of the chief ports of Europe crowding into the heart of their new capital!"

The operations for forming the canal were delayed in 1776 by a dispute between the magistrates and the feuars of the extended royalty relative to Canal Street, that ended in the Court of Session, which sustained "the defences pled by the magistrates of Edinburgh, and assoilie from the conclusion of the declarator; but with respect to the challenge brought with regard to particular houses being built contrary to the Act of Parliament, 1698, remit to the Lord Ordinary to hear parties to do as he shall see cause." The Lord President, the Lord Justice Clerk, and Lord Covington, were of a different opinion from the rest of the court, and condemned the conduct of the magistrates in very severe terms.

The Act of 1698, referred to, was one restricting the height of houses within the city, and to the effect that none should be above five storeys, with a front wall of three feet in thickness at the base. In March, 1776, the dispute was adjusted, and a print of the time tells us that the public "will now be gratified with a pleasure-ground upon the south side of Princes Street, to a considerable extent; and the loch will in time be formed into a canal, which will not only be ornamental, but of great benefit to the citizens."

This Utopian affair was actually commenced, for in the *Edinburgh Weekly Magazine* of the 28th March, 1776, we are told that on the 25th instant twenty labourers "began to work at the banks of the intended canal between the old and new town;" but how far the work proceeded we have no means of knowing.

The site of the projected canal is now occupied

by the railway terminus and Waverley Bridge. The former extends eastward under the North Bridge, and occupies a great space, including the sites on which stood old streets, two churches, and two hospitals, which we have already described, a public market, and superseding the original termini, but retaining some of the works pertaining to the Edinburgh and Glasgow, the North British, and the Edinburgh, Perth, and Dundee Railways. Between 1869 and 1873 it underwent extensive reconstruction and much enlargement. It has a pedestrian access, about twelve feet wide, from the north-east corner of the Green Market, and a spacious carriage-way round the western side of that market and from the Old Town by the Waverley Bridge, and serves for the entire North British system, with pleasant and sheltered accommodation for the arrival and departure of trains.

The site of the Little Mound we have referred to is now occupied by the Waverley Bridge, which, after striking rectangularly from Princes Street, about 270 yards westward of the new post office, crosses the vale of the old loch, southward to the foot of Cockburn Street. The bridge was originally a stone railway structure, consisting of several arches that spanned the Edinburgh and Glasgow lines, and afforded carriage access to all the three original termini. Proving unsuitable for the increased requirements of the station, it was in 1870–3 replaced by a handsome iron skew bridge, in three reaches, that are respectively 310, 293, and 276 feet in length, with 48 feet of a carriage-way and 22 feet of footpaths.

The Green Market, which lies immediately westward of the block of houses at the west side of the North Bridge, occupies, or rather covers, the original terminus of the Edinburgh, Perth, and Dundee Railway, and was formed and opened on the 6th March, 1868, in lieu of the previous market at the eastern end of the valley, removed by the North British Railway. It stands on a basement of lofty arches, constructed of strength sufficient to bear the weight of such a peculiar edifice. It was covered by an ornamental terraced roof, laid out in tastefully-arranged gardens, level with Princes Street, and having well lights and a gallery; changes, however, were effected in 1877, when it was to suffer encroachment on its roof by the street improvements, and when it received a further ornamentation of the former, and acquired at its north-west corner a handsome staircase. In the spacious area of this edifice, promenade concerts, cattle and flower shows, are held.

The East Princes Street Gardens, which extend from the Waverley Bridge to the east side of the Mound, after being, as we have said, a nursery, were first laid out in 1830, and after suffering mutilation and curtailment by the formation of the Edinburgh and Glasgow Railway, were re-formed and ornamented anew in 1849-50, at the expense of about £4,500.

The high graduated banks with terraced walks descend to a deep central hollow, and comprise within their somewhat limited space a pleasant variety of promenade and garden ground.

CHAPTER XVI.

THE CALTON HILL.

Origin of the Name—Gibbet and Battery thereon—The Quarry Holes—The Monastery of Greenside Built—The Leper Hospital—The Tournament Ground and Playfield—Church of Greenside—Burgh of Calton—Rev. Rowland Hill—Regent Bridge Built—Observatory and Astronomical Institution—Bridewell Built—Hume's Tomb—The Political Martyrs' Monument—The Jews' Place of Burial—Monument of Nelson—National Monument, and those of Stewart, Playfair, and Burns—The High School—Foundation Laid—Architecture and Extent—The Opening—Instruction—Rectors of the New School—Lintel of the Old School—Lord Brougham's Opinion of the Institution.

THE Calton Hill, till the erection of the Regent Bridge, was isolated from the line of Princes Street, and rises to the altitude of 355 feet above the level of the sea, presenting an abrupt and rocky face to the south-west, and descending in other directions by rapid but not untraversable declivities. "Calton, or Caldoun, is admitted to be a hill covered with bushes," according to Dalrymple's "Annals"; but with reference to the forest of Drumsheugh, by which it was once surrounded, it is more likely to be Choille-dun.

In the oldest views we possess of it, the hill is always represented bare, and denuded of all trees and bushes, and one lofty knoll on the south was long known as the Miller's Knowe. In some of the earlier notices of this hill, it is called the Dow Craig. The Gaelic *Dhu*, or Black Craig, is very appropriate for this lofty mass of trap rock, and it is rendered by Gordon of Rothiemay in his view, in 1647, by its Latin equivalent, *Nigelli Rupes.* "In a title-deed of the eighteenth century," says Wilson, "the tenement of land in Calton, called the Sclate Land, is described as bounded on the east by McNeill's Craigs, possibly a travesty of Gordon's *Nigelli Rupes.*"

Concerning an execution there in September, 1554, we have the following items in the City Accounts :—

midnight on the bare and desolate scalp of the Calton Hill.

The Lords Balmerino were superiors of the hill, until the Common Council purchased the superiority from the last lord of that loyal and noble family, who presented the old Calton burying-ground to his vassals as a place of sepulchre, and it is said, offered them the whole hill for £40.

At the extreme eastern end of the hill were the Quarry Holes, some places where stone had been

WEST PRINCES STREET GARDENS, 1875.

"Item, the . . day of . . . 1554, for taking of ane gret gibet furth of the Nether Tolbooth, and beiring it to the hecht of the Dow Craig to. haif hangit hommill [beardless] Jok on, and bringing it again to Sanct Paullis Wark, xijd."

"Item, for cords to bynd and hang him with, viijd."

Again, in the Diurnal of Occurrents, under date 1571, we read of a battery erected on "the Dow Craig above Trinitie College, to ding and siege the north-east quarter of the burgh" during the contest against the Queen's-men.

Among many old superstitions peculiar to Leith was one of the Fairy Boy, who acted as drummer to certain elves that held a weekly rendezvous at

excavated. This lonely spot was famous as a rendezvous for those who fought duels and private rencontres, and there it was, that during the wars of the Reformation, in 1557, a solemn interview took place between the Earls of Arran and Huntly and certain leaders of the Congregation, including the Earls of Argyll and Glencairn, and the Lord James Stewart, with reference to the proceedings of the Queen Regent.

At the western side of the hill stood the Carmelite monastery of Greenside, the name of which is still preserved in a street there, and which must have been derived from the verdant and turfy slope that overhung the path to Leith. Though these White Friars were introduced into Scotland in the thirteenth century, it was not until 1518, when the Provost James, Earl of Arran, and the Bailies of the city, conveyed by charter, under date 13th April, to John Malcolme, Provincial of the Carmelites, and his successors, their lands of Greenside, and the chapel or kirk of the Holy Cross there. The latter had been an edifice built at some remote period, of which no record now remains, but it served as the nucleus of this Carmelite monastery, nearly the last of the religious foundations in Scotland prior to the Reformation.

In December, 1520, the Provost (Robert Logan of Coatfield), the Bailies and Council, again conferred the ground and place of "the Greensyde to the Freris Carmelitis, now beand in the Ferry, for their reparation and bigging to be maid," and Sir Thomas Cannye was constituted chaplain thereof. From this it would appear that the friary had been in progress, and that till ready for their reception the priests were located at the Queensferry, most probably in the Carmelite monastery built there in 1380 by Sir George Dundas of that ilk. In October, 1525, Sir Thomas, chaplain of the place and kirk of the Rood of Greenside, got seisin "thairof be the guid town," and delivered the keys into the hands of the magistrates in favour of Friar John Malcolmson, "*pro marerall* (*sic*) of the ordour."

In 1534, two persons, named David Straiton and Norman Gourlay, the latter a priest, were tried for heresy and sentenced to be burned at the stake. On the 27th of August they were carried to the Rood of Greenside, and there suffered that terrible death. After the suppression of the order, the buildings must have been tenantless until 1591, when they were converted into a hospital for lepers, founded by John Robertson, a benevolent merchant of the city, "pursuant to a vow on his receiving a signal mercy from God." "At the institution of this hospital," says Arnot, "seven lepers, all of them inhabitants of Edinburgh, were admitted in one day. The severity of the regulations which the magistrates appointed to be observed by those admitted, segregating them from the rest of mankind, and commanding them to remain within its walls day and night, demonstrate the loathsome and infectious nature of the distemper." A gallows whereon to hang those who violated the rules was erected at one end of the hospital, and even to open its gate between sunset and sunrise ensured the penalty of death.

It is a curious circumstance that, though not a stone remains of the once sequestered Carmelite monastery, there is still perpetuated, as in the case of the abbots of Westminster, in the convent of the Carmelites at Rome, an official who bears the title of *Il Padre Priore di Greenside*. ("Lectures on the Antiquities of Edin.," 1845.)

In the low valley which skirts the north-eastern base of the hill, now occupied by workshops and busy manufactories, was the place for holding tournaments, open-air plays, and revels.

In 1456 King James II. granted under his great seal, in favour of the magistrates and community of the city and their successors for ever, the valley and low ground lying betwixt the rock called Cragingalt on the east, and the common way and passage on the west (now known as Greenside) for performing thereon tournaments, sports, and other warlike deeds, at the pleasure of the king and his successors. This grant was dated at Edinburgh, 13th of August, in presence of the Bishops of St. Andrews and Brechin, the Lords Erskine, Montgomery, Darnley, Lyle, and others.

This place witnessed the earliest efforts of the dramatic muse in Scotland, for many of those pieces in the Scottish language by Sir David Lindesay, such as his "Pleasant Satyre of the Three Estaits," were acted in the play field there, "when weather served," between 1539 and 1544; but in consequence of the tendency of these representations to expose the lives of the Scottish clergy, by a council of the Church, held at the Black Friary in March, 1558, Sir David's books were ordered to be burned by the public executioner.

"The Pleasant Satyre" was played at Greenside, in 1544, in presence of the Queen Regent, "as is mentioned," says Wilson, "by Henry Charteris, the bookseller, who sat patiently nine hours on the bank to witness the play. It so far surpasses any effort of contemporary English dramatists, that it renders the barrenness of the Scottish muse in this department afterwards the more apparent."

Ten years subsequent a new place would seem to have been required, as we find in the "Burgh Records" in 1554, the magistrates ordaining their treasurer, Robert Grahame, to pay "the Maister of Werke the soume of xlij *li* xiij *s* iiij *d*, makand in hale the soume of 100 merks, and that to complete the play field, now bigging in the Greensid."

This place continued to be used as the scene of feats of arms until the reign of Mary, and there, Pennant relates, Bothwell first attracted her attention, by leaping his horse into the ring, after galloping "down the dangerous steeps of the the adjacent hill"—a very apocryphal story. Until the middle of the last century this place was all unchanged. "In my walk this evening," he writes in 1769, "I passed by a deep and wide hollow beneath the Caltoun Hill, the place where those imaginary criminals, witches, and sorcerers in less enlightened times were burned; and where at festive seasons the gay and gallant held their tilts and tournaments."

On the north-western shoulder of the hill stands the modern Established Church of Greenside, at the end of the Royal Terrace, a conspicuous and attractive feature among the few architectural decorations of that district. Its tower rises 100 feet above the porch, is twenty feet square, and contains a bell of 10 cwt.

The main street of the old barony of the Calton was named, from the ancient chapel which stood there, St. Ninian's Row, and a place so called still exists; and the date and name ST. NINIAN'S Row, 1752, yet remains on the ancient well. Of old, the street named the High Calton, was known as the Craig End.

In those days a body existed known as the High Constables of the Calton, but the new Municipality Act having extinguished the ancient boundaries of the city, the constabulary, in 1857, adopted the following resolution, which is written on vellum, to the Society of Antiquaries of Scotland:—

"The district of Calton, or Caldton, formed at one time part of the estate of the Elphinstone family, one of whom—Sir James, third son of the third Lord Elphinstone—was created Lord Balmerino in 1603-4. In 1631 the then Lord Balmerino granted a charter to the trades of Calton, constituting them a society or corporation; and in 1669 a royal charter was obtained from Charles II., erecting the district into a burgh of barony. A court was held by a bailie appointed by the lord of the manor, and there was founded in connection therewith, the Society of High Constables of Calton, who have been elected by, and have continued to act under, the orders of succeeding Baron Bailies. Although no mention is made of our various constabulary bodies in the 'Municipality Extension Act, 1856,' the venerable office of Baron Bailie has thereby become extinct, and the ancient burghs of Canongate, Calton, Eastern and Western Portsburgh, are now annexed to the city. Under these circumstances the constabulary of Calton held an extraordinary meeting on the 17th of March, 1857, at which, *inter alia*, the following motion was carried with acclamation, viz.: 'That the burgh having ceased to exist, the constabulary, in order that some of the relics and other insignia belonging to this body should be preserved for the inspection of future generations, unanimously resolve to present as a free gift to the Royal Society of Antiquaries of Scotland the following, viz :—Constabulary bâton, 1747, moderator's official bâton, marble bowl, moderator's state staff, silver-mounted horn with fourteen medals, members' small bâton; report on the origin and standing of the High Constables of Calton, 1855, and the laws of the society, 1847.'"

These relics of the defunct little burgh are consequently now preserved at the museum in the Royal Institution.

A kind of round tower, or the basement thereof, is shown above the south-west angle of the Calton cliffs in Gordon's view in 1647; but of any such edifice no record remains; and in the hollow where Nottingham Place lies now, a group of five isolated houses, called "Mud Island," appears in the maps of 1787 and 1798. In 1796, and at many other times, the magistrates ordained that "All-hallow fair be held on the lands of Calton Hill," as an open and unenclosed place, certainly a perilous one, for tipsy drovers and obstinate cattle. An agriculturist named Smith farmed the hill and lands adjacent, now covered by great masses of building, for several years, till about the close of the 18th century; and his son, Dr. John Smith, who was born in 1798, died only in February, 1879, after being fifty years physician to the old charity workhouse in Forrest Road.

In 1798, when the Rev. Rowland Hill (the famous son of Sir Rowland Hill, of Shropshire) visited Edinburgh for the first time, he preached in some of the churches every other day, but the crowds became so immense, that at last he was induced to hold forth from a platform erected on the Calton Hill, where his audience was reckoned at not less than 10,000, and the interest excited by his eloquence is said to have been beyond all precedent. On his return from the West, he preached on the hill again to several audiences, and on the last of these occasions, when a collection was made for the charity workhouse, fully 20,000 were present. Long years after, when speaking to a friend of the multitude whom he had addressed there, he said, pleasantly, "Well do I remember the spot; but I understand that it has now been converted into a den of thieves," referring to the gaol now built on the ground where his platform stood.

The first great change in the aspect of the hill was effected by the formation of the Regent Road, which was cut through the old burying-ground, the soil of which avenue was decently carted away, covered with white palls, and full of remnants of humanity, to the new Calton burying-ground on the southern slope; and the second was the opening of the Regent Bridge, the foundation stone of which was laid in 1815, forming a magnificent entrance to the New Town from the east. The arch is fifty feet wide, and about the same in height, having on the top of the side ledges, arches, and ornamental pillars, connected with the houses in Waterloo Place. The whole was finished in 1819, and formally opened on the visit of Prince Leopold, afterwards King of Belgium ; but the bridge must have been open for traffic two years before, as it was crossed by the 88th Connaught Rangers, in 1817,

mass of rock, fully fifty tons in weight, fell from under Nelson's monument with a great crash from a height of twenty-five feet, and carrying all before it, rolled on the roadway below.

On the 15th September, 1834, there occurred the only local event of interest since the visit of George IV.—the Grey banquet. A great portion of the citizens had signalised themselves in their zeal for the Reform Bill, the passing of which, in August, 1832, they celebrated by a grand procession of the trades, amounting to more than

NELSON'S MONUMENT, CALTON HILL, FROM PRINCES STREET. (*From a Drawing by A. Nasmyth, published in 1806.*)

on their return from the Army of Occupation in France, under Colonel Wallace.

One of the last feasts of St. Crispin was held in the Calton Convening Rooms, in 1820, when six hundred of the ancient Corporation of Cordiners, bearing St. Crispin with regal pomp, marched from Holyrood. "On reaching the Cross," says the *Weekly Journal* for that year, " it was found impossible to proceed farther, from the mass of people collected ; the procession therefore filed off into the Royal Exchange, until a guard of the 13th Foot arrived from the Castle ; then it proceeded along the mound to the New Town." It is added that forty-four years had elapsed since the last procession of the kind.

The same paper, in 1828, records that a mighty

15,000 men, and about the date above mentioned, Earl Grey entered the city amid a vast concourse of admirers. He was presented with the freedom of the city in a gold box, and was afterwards entertained at a public banquet, in a pavilion erected for the occasion, 113 feet long by 101 broad. in the eastern compartment of the High School on the south side of the Calton Hill. Archibald, Earl of Rosebery, K.T., in absence of the Duke of Hamilton, occupied the chair.

On the north-west shoulder of the hill is the old observatory, a rough, round-buttressed tower, three storeys in height. The scheme for the erection of a building of this kind was first projected in 1736, but the local commotions occasioned by the Porteous mob caused it to be relinquished till 1741, when it was again revived, and the patriotic Earl of Morton gave a sum for the purpose, leaving the management thereof to Colin Maclaurin, Professor of Mathematics, and others of the Senatus Academicus. Maclaurin, with his characteristic liberality, added to the earl's gift by the profits arising from a course of lectures on experimental philosophy; but his death, in 1746, put a stop a second time to the execution of the project.

and proposed to give Mr. Short the funds at their disposal for the purpose of building an observatory, and to allow him to draw the whole emoluments arising from the use of his apparatus for a certain number of years; "but," says Arnot, "on condition that the students should, in the meantime, have access to the observatory for a small gratuity, and that the building, with all the instruments, should be vested in the Town Council for ever, as trustees for the public, and become their absolute property

THE CALTON HILL, CALTON GAOL, BURYING-GROUND, AND MONUMENTS.

In 1776 there came to Edinburgh Mr. Short, brother and executor to Mr. James Short, F.R.S., formerly an optician in Leith, and who brought with him all his brother's optical apparatus, particularly a large reflecting telescope that magnified 1,200 times, "and is," says the *Weekly Magazine* for that year, "superior to any in Europe, but one in possession of the King of Spain." Mr. Short intended to erect an observatory, which was to be his own private property, and from which he expected to draw considerable emoluments; but Dr. Alexander Monro, Professor of Anatomy, one of Lord Morton's trustees, showed that an observatory unconnected with the Council and University would conduce but little to the progress of science,

after a certain period. Mr. Short readily agreed, and the Council were applied to for their concurrence and patronage."

It appears from their Register that in the summer of 1776 the Council granted to Mr. Short, his sons and grandsons, a life-rent lease of half an acre on the Calton Hill. A plan of the intended building was made by James Craig, architect, and the foundation-stone was laid by Provost James Stodart, in presence of the Senatus, 25th July, 1776; and upon the suggestion of Adam, the famous architect, in consequence of the high and abrupt nature of the site, the whole edifice was constructed to have the aspect of a fortification. In the partial execution of this faulty design, the money appropriated for the work was totally exhausted, and the luckless observatory was once more left to its fate, and when thus abandoned, was the scene of a singular disturbance in 1788. It was assailed by ten armed persons, who severely wounded a gentleman who endeavoured to oppose them in capturing the place, which was next literally stormed by the City Guard, "without any killed or wounded," says Kincaid, "but in the hurry of conducting their prisoners to the guard-house, they omitted to take a list of the stores and ammunition found there." On the 26th February, 1789, there were arraigned by the Procurator Fiscal these ten persons, among whom were Jacobina, relict of Thomas Short, optician in Edinburgh, John McFadzean, medical student, for forcibly entering, on the 7th November, "the observatory formerly possessed by Thomas Short, optician, in order to dispossess therefrom James Douglas, grandson of the said Thomas Short, with pistols, naked swords, cutlasses, and other lethal weapons, attacking and wounding Robert Maclean, accountant of Excise," &c. For this, eight were dismissed from the bar, and two were imprisoned and fined 500 merks each. (*Edin. Advert.*, 1789.)

In 1792 the observatory was completed by the magistrates, but in a style far inferior to what the utility of such an institution deserved; and being without proper instruments, or a fund for procuring them, it remained in this condition till 1812, when a more fortunate attempt was made to establish an observatory on a proper footing by the formation in Edinburgh of an Astronomical Institution, and the old edifice is now used for a self-registering anemometer, or rain-gauge, in connection with the new edifice.

The latter had its origin in a few public-spirited individuals, who, in 1812, formed themselves into the Astronomical Institution, and circulated an address, written by their President, Professor Playfair, urging the necessity for its existence and progress. "He used to state," says Lord Cockburn, "in order to show its necessity, that a foreign vessel had been lately compelled to take refuge in Leith, and that before setting sail again, the master wished to adjust his timepiece, but found that he had come to a large and learned metropolis, where nobody could tell him what o'clock it was."

A little to the east of the old institution, the new observatory was founded on the 25th April, 1818, by Sir George Mackenzie, Vice-President, from a Grecian design by W. H. Playfair, after the model of the Temple of the Winds, and consists of a central cross of sixty-two feet, with four projecting pediments supported by six columns fronting the four points of the compass. The central dome, thirteen feet in diameter, contains a solid cone or pillar nineteen feet high, for the astronomical circle. To the east are piers for the transit instrument and astronomical clock; in the west end are others for the mural circle and clock.

"The original Lancastrian School," says Lord Cockburn, "was a long wood and brick erection, stretched on the very top of the Calton Hill, where it was then the fashion to stow away anything that was too abominable to be tolerated elsewhere."

The great prison buildings of the city occupy the summit of the Dow Craig, to which we have referred more than once.

The first of these, the "Bridewell," was founded 30th November, 1791, by the Earl of Morton, Grand Master of Scotland, heading a procession which must have ascended the hill by the tortuous old street at the back of the present Convening Rooms. The usual coins and papers were enclosed in two bottles blown at the glass-house in Leith, and deposited in the stone, with a copper plate containing a long Latin inscription. The architect was Robert Adam.

Prior to this the city had an institution of a similar kind, named the House of Correction, for the reception of strolling poor and loose characters. It had been projected as far back as 1632, and the buildings therefor had been situated near Paul's Work. Afterwards a building near the Charity Workhouse was used for the purpose, but being found too small, after a proposal to establish a new one at the foot of Forrester's Wynd, the idea was abandoned, the present new one projected and carried out. It was finished in 1796, at the expense of the city and county, aided by a petty grant from Government. In front of it, shielded by a high wall and ponderous gate, on the street line, is the house for the governor. Semicircular in form, the main edifice has five floors, the highest being for stores and the hospital. All round on each floor, at the middle of the breadth, is a corridor, with cells on each side, lighted respectively from the interior and exterior of the curvature. Those on the inner are chiefly used as workshops, and can all be surveyed from a dark apartment in the house of the governor without the observer being visible. On the low floor is a treadmill, originally constructed for the manufacture of corks, but now mounted and moved only in cure of idleness or the punishment of delinquency.

The area within the circle is a small court, glazed overhead. The house is under good regulations, and is made as much as possible the scene rather of the reclamation and the comfortable industry of its unhappy inmates than of the punishment of their offences.

At one time a number of French prisoners of war were confined here.

At the east end of Waterloo Place, and adjoining Bridewell, is the town and county gaol. It was founded in 1815 and finished in 1817, when the old "Heart of Midlothian" was taken down. In a Saxon style of architecture, it is an extensive building, and somewhat castellated—in short, the whole masses of these buildings, with their towers and turrets overhanging the steep rocks, resemble a feudal fortress of romance, and present a striking and interesting aspect. Along the street line are apartments for the turnkeys. Behind these, with an area intervening, is the gaol, 194 feet long by 40 wide, four storeys high, with small grated windows. In the centre is a chapel, with long, ungrated windows. Along the interior run corridors, opening into forty-eight cells, each 8 feet by 6, besides other apartments of larger dimensions.

From the lower flat behind a number of small airing yards, separated by high walls, radiate to a point, where they are all overlooked and commanded by a lofty octagonal watch-tower, occupied by the deputy governor.   Farther back, and perched on the sheer verge of the precipice which overhangs the railway, is the castellated tower, occupied by the governor.   The whole gaol is classified into wards, is clean and well managed, and possesses facilities for the practice of approved prison discipline, but is seriously damaged in some of its capacities by being a gaol for both criminals and debtors, thus lacking the proper accommodation for each alike.

From the Calton Hill the view is so vast, so grand, and replete with everything that in either city, sea, or landscape can thrill or delight, that it has been said he is a bold artist who attempts to depict it with either pen or pencil ; for far around the city, old and new, there stretches a panorama which combines in its magnificent expanse the richest elements of the sublime and beautiful, while the city itself is opulent, beyond all parallel, in the attractions of the picturesque.

Prior to the erection of the Regent Bridge, Princes Street, says Lord Cockburn, was closed at its east end " by a mean line of houses running north and south. All to the east of these was a burial-ground, of which the southern portion still remains ; and the way of reaching the Calton Hill was to go by Leith Street to its base (as may yet be done), and then up a narrow, steep street, which still remains, and was then the only approach. Scarcely any sacrifice could be too great that removed the houses from the end of Princes Street and made a level to the hill, or, in other words, produced the Waterloo Bridge."

On the south side of the narrow street referred to is the old entrance to the burying-ground, which Lord Balmerino gifted to his vassals, and through which the remains of David Hume must have been borne to their last resting-place, in what is now the southern portion of the cemetery, and in the round tower of Roman design at the south-eastern corner thereof. Near it is the great obelisk, called the Martyrs' Monument, erected to the memory of those who were tried and banished from Scotland in 1793 for advocating parliamentary reform. It is inscribed, in large Roman letters :—" TO THE MEMORY OF THOMAS MUIR, THOMAS FYSSHE PALMER, WILLIAM SKIRVING, MAURICE MARGAROT AND JOSEPH GERALD. ERECTED BY THE FRIENDS OF PARLIAMENTARY REFORM IN SCOTLAND AND ENGLAND, 1844."

In this burying-ground lie the remains of Professor George Wilson · and many other eminent citizens.

On the northern slope of the hill is a species of cavern or arched vault in the rock, closed by a gate, and known as the Jews' burial-place. It is the property of the small Jewish community, but when or how acquired, the Rabbi and other officials, from their migratory nature, are quite unable to state, and only know that two individuals, a man and his wife, lie in that solitary spot. Concerning this place, a rare work by Viscount D'Arlincourt, a French writer, has the following anecdote, which may be taken for what it is worth. " A Jew, named Jacob Isaac, many years ago asked leave to lay his bones in a little corner of this rock. As it was at that time bare of monuments, he thought that in such a place his remains ran no risk of being disturbed by the neighbourhood of Christian graves. His request was granted for the sum of 700 guineas. Jacob paid the money without hesitation, and has long been at rest in a corner of the Calton. But, alas ! he is now surrounded on all sides by the tombs of the Nazarenes."

Though not correct at its close, this paragraph evidently points to the cave in the rock where one Jew lies.

On the very apex of the hill stands the monument to Lord Viscount Nelson, an edifice in such doubtful taste that its demolition has been more than once advocated. Begun shortly after the battle of Trafalgar, it was not finished till 1816. A conspicuous object from every point of view, by sea or land, with all its defects it makes a magnificent termination to the vista along Princes Street from the west. The base is a battlemented edifice, divided into small apartments and occupied as a restaurant. Above its entrance is the crest of Nelson, with a sculpture representing the stern of the *San Joseph*, and underneath an inscription,

of which the monument rises possesses an outline which, by a curious coincidence, presents a profile of Nelson, when viewed from Holyrood.

The time-ball, which is in electric communication with the time-gun at the Castle, falls every day at one o'clock simultaneously with the discharge of

THE CALTON BURYING-GROUND : HUME'S GRAVE.

recording that the grateful citizens of Edinburgh "have erected this monument, not to express their unavailing sorrow for his death, nor yet to celebrate the matchless glories of his life, but by his noble example to teach their sons to emulate what they admire, and like him, when duty requires it, to die for their country."

From this pentangular base rises, to the height of more than 100 feet, a circular tower, battlemented at the top, surmounted by the time-ball and a flag-staff, where a standard is always hoisted on the anniversary of Trafalgar, and used also to be run up on the 1st of August in memory of the battle of Aboukir. Around the edifice are a garden and plots of shrubbery, from amid which, peeping grimly forth, are three Russian trophies—two cannon from Sebastopol and one from Bomarsund, placed there in 1857. The precipice from the edge

the gun which is fired from Greenwich. A common joke of the High School boys is that the Duke of Wellington gets off his horse in front of the Register House *when* he hears the gun, lunches, and re-mounts his statuesque steed at two o'clock !

A little to the north of it, on a flat portion of the hill, stand twelve magnificent Grecian Doric columns, the fragment of the projected national monument to the memory of all Scottish soldiers and sailors who fell by land and sea in the long war with France ; and, with a splendour of design corresponding to the grandeur of the object, it was meant to be a literal restoration of the Parthenon at Athens. The contributors were incorporated by Act of Parliament.

The foundation stone was laid on the 27th August, 1822, the day on which George IV. visited Melville Castle. Under the Duke of Hamilton,

Grand Master of Scotland, the various lodges proceeded in procession from the Parliament Square, accompanied by the commissioners for the King, and a brilliant concourse. The foundation-stone of the edifice (which was to be 228 feet long, by 102 broad) weighed six tons, and amid salutes of cannon from the Castle, Salisbury Craigs, Leith

Majesty, the patron of the undertaking. The celebrated Parthenon of Athens being model of the edifice." The Scots Greys and 3rd Dragoons formed the escorts. Notwithstanding the enthusiasm displayed when the undertaking was originated, and though a vast amount of money was subscribed, the former subsided, and the western peristyle alone

THE NATIONAL MONUMENT, CALTON HILL.

Fort, and the royal squadron in the roads, the inscription plates were deposited therein. One is inscribed thus, and somewhat fulsomely :—

"To the glory of God, in honour of the King, for the good of the people, this monument, the tribute of a grateful country to her gallant and illustrious sons, as a memorial of the past and incentive to the future heroism of the men of Scotland, was founded on the 27th day of August in the year of our Lord 1822, and in the third year of the glorious reign of George IV., under his immediate auspices, and in commemoration of his most gracious and welcome visit to his ancient capital, and the palace of his royal ancestors; John Duke of Atholl, James Duke of Montrose, Archibald Earl of Rosebery, John Earl of Hopetoun, Robert Viscount Melville, and Thomas Lord Lynedoch, officiating as commissioners, by the special appointment of his august

was partially erected. In consequence of this remarkable end to an enterprise that was begun under the most favourable auspices, the national monument is often referred to as "Scotland's pride and poverty." The pillars are of gigantic proportions, formed of beautiful Craigleith stone ; each block weighed from ten to fifteen tons, and each column as it stands, with the base and frieze, cost upwards of £1,000. As a ruin it gives a classic aspect to the whole city. According to the original idea, part of the edifice was to be used as a Scottish Valhalla.

On the face of the hill overlooking Waterloo Place is the monument of one of Scotland's greatest philosophers. It is simply inscribed :—

DUGALD STEWART.
BORN NOVEMBER 22ND, 1753;
DIED JUNE 11TH, 1828.

It was finished in 1832, and is a beautiful restoration, with some variations, of the choragic monument of Lysicrates, from a design by W. H. Playfair.

The chaste Greek monument of Professor Playfair, at the south-east angle of the new observatory serves also to enhance the classic aspect of the hill, and was designed by his nephew. This memorial to the great mathematician and eminent natural philosopher is inscribed thus, in large Roman characters :—

JOANNI PLAYFAIR
AMICORUM PIETAS
DESIDERIIS ICTA FIDELIBUS
QUO IPSE LOCO TEMPLUM URANAE SUAE
OLIM DICAVERIT
POSUIT.
NAT. VI. IDUS. MART. MDCCXLVIII.
OBIIT. XIV. KAL. SEXTIL. MDCCCXIX.

Passing the eastern gate of the new prison, and Jacob's Ladder, a footway which, in two mutually diverging lines, each by a series of steep traverses and flights of steps, descends the sloping face of the hill, to the north back of the Canongate, we find Burns's monument, perched over the line of the tunnel, built in 1830, after a design by Thomas Hamilton, in the style of a Greek peripteral temple, its cupola being a literal copy from the monument of Lysicrates at Athens. The original object of this edifice was to serve as a shrine for Flaxman's beautiful statue of Burns, now removed to the National Gallery, and replaced by an excellent bust of the poet, by William Brodie, R.S.A., one of the best of Scottish sculptors. This round temple contains many interesting relics of Burns.

The entire length of the upper portion of the hill is now enclosed by a stately terrace, more than 1,000 yards in length, with Grecian pillared doorways, continuous iron balconies, and massive cornices, commanding much of the magnificent panorama seen from the higher elevations; but, by far the most important, interesting, and beautiful edifice on this remarkable hill is the new High School of Edinburgh, on its southern slope, adjoining the Regent Terrace.

The new High School is unquestionably one of the most chaste and classical edifices in Edinburgh. It is a reproduction of the purest Greek, and in every way quite worthy of its magnificent site, which commands one of the richest of town and country landscapes in the city and its environs, and is in itself one of the most striking features of the beautiful scenery with which it is grouped.

When the necessity for having a new High School in place of the old, within the city wall—the old which had so many striking memories and traditions (and to which we shall refer elsewhere)—came to pass, several situations were suggested as a site for it, such as the ground opposite to Princes Street, and the then Excise Office (now the Royal Bank), in St. Andrew Square; but eventually the magistrates fixed on the green slope of the Calton Hill, to the eastward of the Miller's Knowe. In digging the foundations copper ore in some quantities was dug out, together with some fragments of native copper.

The ceremony of laying the foundation stone took place amid great pomp and display on the 28th of July, 1825. All the public bodies in the city were present, with the then scholars from the Old School, the senators, academicians, clergy, rector, and masters, and, at the request of Lord Provost Henderson, the Rev. Dr. Brunton implored the Divine blessing on the undertaking. The stone was laid by Viscount Glenorchy, Grand Master of Scotland, and the building was proceeded with rapidly. It is of pure white stone, designed by Thomas Hamilton, and has a front of 400 feet, including the temples, or wings, which contain the writing and mathematical class-rooms. The central portico is a hexastyle, and, having a double range of twelve columns, projects considerably in front of the general façade. The whole edifice is of the purest Grecian Doric, and, even to its most minute details, is a copy of the celebrated Athenian Temple of Theseus. A spacious flight of steps leading up to it from the closing wall in front, and a fine playground behind, is overlooked by the entrances to the various class-rooms. The interior is distributed into a large hall, seventy-three feet by forty-three feet; a rector's class-room, thirty-eight feet by thirty-four feet; four class-rooms for masters, each thirty-eight feet by twenty-eight feet; a library; and two small rooms attached to each of the class-rooms. On the margin of the roadway, on a lower site than the main building, are two handsome lodges, each two storeys in height, one occupied by the janitor, and the other containing class-rooms. The area of the school and playground is two acres, and is formed by cutting deep into the face of the hill. The building cost when finished, according to the City Chamberlain's books, £34,199 11s. 6d. There are a rector, and ten teachers of classics and languages, in addition to seven lecturers on science.

The school, the most important in Scotland, and intimately connected with the literature and progress of the kingdom, although at first only a classical seminary, now furnishes systematic instruction in all departments of a commercial as well as liberal education. Every branch of literature, including reading, orthography, recitation, grammar, and composition, together with British history, forms the prominent parts of the system; while the entire curriculum of study—which occupies six years—embraces the Latin, Greek, French, and German languages, history, geography, physiology, chemistry, natural philosophy, zoology, botany, algebra, geometry, drawing, fencing, gymnastics, and military drill. In the library are seven thousand volumes.

The building was completed in 1829, and the pupils proceeded thither on the 23rd of June from the time-honoured old school, in a procession arranged by Sir Patrick Walker of Coates, preceded by the band of the 17th Lancers, each class marching with a master at its head, followed by the High Constables, the magistrates, professors of the university, and all "those noblemen and gentlemen who had attended the High School, in fours."

A long and elaborate Latin inscription on the front of the buildings commemorates the founding of the edifice, with a reference to the Old School, founded 300 years before; but two statues, which formed a part of Hamilton's design, and were to have been in front of the portico, have never been placed there, and in all likelihood never will be.

DUGALD STEWART'S MONUMENT.

In the long roll of its scholars are the names of the most distinguished men of all professions, and in every branch of science and literature, many of whom have helped to form and consolidate British India. It also includes three natives of Edinburgh, "High School callants," who have been Lord Chancellors of Great Britain—Wedderburn, Erskine, and Brougham.

The annual examinations always take place in presence of the Lord Provost and magistrates, a number of the city clergy and gentlemen connected with the other numerous educational establishments in the city. There is also a large concourse of the parents and friends of the pupils. The citizens have ever rejoiced in this ancient school, and are justly proud of it, not only for the prominent position it occupies, but from the peculiarity of its constitu-

tion, as its classes embrace all sects and grades of society—the peer and peasant sit together in the same form, each possessing no advantage over his schoolfellow. "Edinburgh has reason to be proud of this noble institution," said Lord Provost Black at the examination in 1845, "as one which has conferred a lustre upon our city, and which has given a tone to the manners and intellect of its inhabitants. Whether they remain in Edinburgh or betake themselves to other lands, and whatever be the walk of life in which they are led, I believe the students of this seminary will be found everywhere, and at all times, ably sustaining the character of the city, and the institution in which they spent their youthful years."

In 1834 a French master— M. Senebier—was first appointed to teach the French language; and in 1845 Dr. Carl E. Aue became the first teacher of German. In 1849 Mr. William Rhind was elected Lecturer on Natural History, and Dr. John Murray on Chemistry.

The first Rector in the present or New School was Aglionby-Ross Carson, M.A., LL.D., a native of Dumfries-shire, who obtained a mastership in the Old School in 1806, and was made Rector in 1820, when his predecessor, James Pillans, M.A. (the "paltry Pillans" of Byron's savage "English Bards and Scotch Reviewers"), became Professor of Humanity. Dr. Carson held the office till October, 1845, when feeble health compelled him to resign, and he was succeeded by Dr. Leonhard Schmitz (as twenty-sixth Rector, from D. Vocat, Rector in 1519), the first foreigner who ever held a classical mastership in the High School. He was a graduate of the University of Bonn, and a native of Eupen, in Rhenish Prussia. He was the author of a continuation of Niebuhr's "History of Rome," in three volumes, and many other works, and in 1844 obtained from his native monarch the gold medal for literature, awarded "as a mark of his Majesty's sense of the honour thereby conferred on the memory of Niebuhr, one of the greatest scholars of Germany." In 1859 he was selected by her Majesty the Queen to give a course of historical study to H.R.H. the Prince of Wales, and during the winter of 1862-3, he gave a similar course to the Duke of Edinburgh, when both were resident in the city.

On his removal to London in 1866 he was succeeded as Rector by James Donaldson, LL.D., one of the ablest preceptors that Scotland has produced. Dr. Donaldson was born at Aberdeen on the 26th of April, 1831, and was educated at the Grammar School and Marischal College and University of his native city, and the University of Berlin. In 1852 he was appointed Greek tutor in

ship and liberal views. Particularly has he distinguished himself by his exhaustive study of the early Christian Fathers, and his "Critical History of Christian Literature and Doctrine from the Death of the Apostles to the Nicene Council" (3 vols.), is a standard work on the important subject with which it deals ; while the "Ante-Nicene Christian Library," of which he is joint-editor, affords further proof of the great and permanent interest which Dr. Donaldson has manifested in this

BURNS'S MONUMENT, CALTON HILL.

Edinburgh University, Rector of the High School of Stirling in 1854, classical master in the High School of Edinburgh in 1856, and Rector of the same school in 1866, in succession, as has been seen, to Dr. Leonhard Schmitz. During his rectorship the High School conspicuously sustained the world-wide reputation which it has always enjoyed for the all-round excellence of its education. Though Dr. Donaldson devoted himself to the watchful guidance of the great institution over which he presided with rare zeal and affectionate solicitude for its interests and those of the scholars entrusted to his care, he found time to enrich the classical and educational stores of his country by various works exhibiting alike profound scholar-

department of Christian history and theology. Dr. Donaldson was elected Fellow of the Royal Society of Edinburgh, and received the degree of LL.D. from Aberdeen University ; he has edited at different times various periodical journals, and has contributed several articles to the "Encyclopædia Britannica." In 1881 he was appointed professor of Humanity in the University of Aberdeen.

Among other eminent classical masters in the new High School were John Macmillan, a native of Dumfries-shire, and John Carmichael, a native of Inverness, who was succeeded in 1848 by his nephew, also named John Carmichael, who had won classical distinction both in the Edinburgh Academy and at the University, and who was one of the most brilliant conversationalists and the kindest-hearted of men in Edinburgh.

Among the prizes competed for are the gold medal, value ten guineas, given in 1825 by the Writers to the Signet to the dux of the Senior Humanity Class, and first awarded to Mr. William M. Gunn, classical master of the school in 1843; a gold medal given by Lieut.-Colonel Peter Murray, Adjutant-General in Bengal in 1794, and the name of which was changed to the Macgregor medal in 1831; a gold medal presented by the

medal was first awarded." The appendix to Stevens's history of the famous school contains a most interesting list of 180 boys, medallists or duxes after 1776, with notes, when ascertainable, of their future. His valuable history also contains a catalogue of the persons of eminence and rank educated at this seminary.

Of the distinguished men in every department of life who conned their studies in the class-rooms, even of the new High School, it is impossible to attempt to give a list here; but perhaps no educational

THE HIGH SCHOOL.

city for Greek in the Rector's class; the Ritchie gold medal, presented in 1824, by Mr. William Ritchie, for twenty-three years a master of the school; the Macdonald, a third class medal, given by Colonel John Macdonald, of the regiment of Clan Alpine, son of the celebrated Flora Macdonald, and presented for the first time in 1824.

The College Bailie silver medal for writing, the personal gift of the gentleman holding that office for the year, was first presented in 1814, and for the last time in 1834.

"The head boy or dux of the school, at the yearly examination, till about the close of the eighteenth century," says Dr. Steven, "usually received from the city, as a prize, a copy of the best edition of one of the classics. This was prior to 1794, when a gold

institution in the kingdom has ever sent forth so many pupils who have added fresh laurels to the glory of their country.

In it is still preserved as a relic the carved stone which was over the principal entrance of the first school from 1578 to 1777. It bears within a panel the triple castle of the city, with the initials I. S., and, under the thistle, the date and legend :—

MVSIS : RESPUBLICA
FLORET.   1578.

Above this in a pediment is an imperial crown, with two thistles and the initials I. R. 6.

The High School Club, composed of old scholars, was first instituted in 1849.

At a great entertainment given in the city to Mr. (afterwards Lord) Brougham, on the 25th of April, 1825, presided over by Henry (afterwards Lord)

Cockburn, the former spoke thus affectionately of the High School :—

"In this town it was, as was truly observed by our worthy chairman, that I first imbibed the noble principles of a liberal Scottish education; and it is fit that I should tell you, as many of you may not have heard what I have frequently told to others, in other places, and in other meetings, that I have seen no other plan of education so efficient as that which is established in this city. With great experience and opportunity of observation, I certainly have never yet seen any one system so well adapted for training up good citizens, as well as learned and virtuous men, as the old High School of Edinburgh and the Scottish Universities. Great improvements may, and no doubt will be made, even in these seminaries. But what I have to say of the High School of Edinburgh, and, as the ground of the preference I give it over others, and even over another academy, lately established in this city, on what is said to be a more improved principle—what I say is this: that such a school is altogether invaluable in a free State—in a State having higher objects in view, by the education of its youth, than a mere knowledge of the Latin and Greek languages, and the study of prosody. That in a State like this, higher objects should be kept in view, there can be no doubt; though I confess I have passed much of my time in these studies myself.

"Yet a school like the old High School of Edinburgh is invaluable, and for what is it so? It is because men of the highest and lowest rank of society send their children to be educated together. The oldest friend I have in the world, your worthy vice-president (Lord Douglas Gordon Halyburton of Pitcur, M.P.) and myself were at the High School of Edinburgh together, and in the same class along with others, who still possess our friendship, and some of them in a rank in life still higher than us. One of them was a nobleman who is now in the House of Peers; and some of them were the sons of shopkeepers in the lowest part of the Cowgate—shops of the most inferior description—and one or two of them were the sons of menial servants in the town. *They were sitting side by side*, giving and taking places from each other, without the slightest impression on the part of my noble friends of any superiority on their parts to the other boys, or any ideas of the inferiority on the part of the other boys to them; and this is my reason for preferring the old High School of Edinburgh to other and what may be termed more patrician schools, however well regulated or conducted."

CHAPTER XVI.

THE NEW TOWN.

The Site before the Streets—The Lang Dykes—Wood's Farm—Drumsheugh House—Bearford's Parks—The Houses of Easter and Wester Coates—Gabriel's Road—Craig's Plan of the New Town—John Young builds the First House Therein—Extension of the Town Westward.

LOOKING at the site of the New Town now, it requires an effort to think that there were thatched cottages there once, and farms, where corn was sown and reaped, where pigs grunted in styes or roamed in the yard; where fowls laid eggs and clucked over them, and ducks drove their broods into the North Loch, where the trap caught eels and the otter and water-rat lurked amid the sedges, and where cattle browsed on the upland slopes that were crested by the line of the Lang Dykes; and where the gudeman and his sons left the plough in the furrow, and betook them to steel bonnets and plate sleeves, to jack and Scottish spear, when the bale-fire, flaming out on the Castle towers, announced that "our ancient enemies of England had crossed the Tweed."

Such, little more than one hundred years ago, was the site of "the Modern Athens."

Along the line now occupied by Princes Street lay a straight country road, the Lang Dykes—called the Lang Gait in the "Memorie of the Somervilles," in 1640—the way by which Claverhouse and his troopers rode westward on that eventful day in 1689, and where in 1763, we read in the *Edinburgh Museum* for January of two gentlemen on horseback being stopped by a robber, armed with a pistol, whom they struck down by the butt end of a whip, but failed to secure, "as they heard somebody whistle several times behind the dykes," and were apprehensive that he might have confederates.

The district was intersected by other lonely roads, such as the Kirk Loan, which led north from St. Cuthbert's Church to the wooden, or Stokebridge, and the ford on the Leith at the back of the present Malta Terrace, where it joined Gabriel's Road, a path that came from the east end of the

Lang Dykes; by the old Queensferry Road that descended into the deep hollow, where Bell's Mills lie, and by Broughton Loan at the other end of the northern ridge.

Bearford's Parks on the west, and Wood's Farm on the east, formed the bulk of this portion of the site; St. George's Church is now in the centre of the former, and Wemyss Place of the latter. The hamlet and manor house of Moultray's Hill are now occupied by the Register House; and where the Royal Bank stands was a cottage called "Peace and Plenty," from its signboard near Gabriel's Road, "where ambulative citizens regaled themselves with curds and cream," and Broughton was deemed so far afield that people went there for the summer months under the belief that they were some distance from town, just as people used to go to Powburn and Tipperlinn fifty years later.

Henry Mackenzie, author of "The Man of Feeling," who died in 1831, remembered shooting snipes, hares, and partridges upon Wood's Farm. The latter was a tract of ground extending from Canon Mills on the north, to Bearford's Parks on the south, and was long in possession of Mr. Wood, of Warriston, and in the house thereon, his son, the famous "Lang Sandy Wood," was born in 1725. It stood on the area between where Queen Street and Heriot Row are now, and "many still alive," says Chambers, writing in 1824, "remember of the fields bearing as fair and rich a crop of wheat as they may now be said to bear houses. Game used to be plentiful upon these grounds— in particular partridges and hares . . . . . Wood-cocks and snipe were to be had in all the damp and low-lying situations, such as the Well-house Tower, the Hunter's Bog, and the borders of Canon Mills Loch. Wild ducks were frequently ·shot in the meadows, where in winter they are sometimes yet to be found. Bruntsfield Links, and the ground towards the Braid Hills abounded in hares."

In the list of Fellows of the Royal College of Surgeons, Alexander Wood and his brother Thomas are recorded, under date 1756 and 1775 respectively, as the sons of "Thomas Wood, farmer on the north side of Edinburgh, Stockbridge Road," now called Church Lane.

A tradition exists, that about 1730 the magistrates offered to a residenter in Canon Mills all the ground between Gabriel's Road and the Gallowlee, in perpetual fee, at the annual rent of a crown bowl of punch; but so worthless was the land then, producing only whins and heather, that the offer was rejected. ("Old Houses in Edinburgh.")

The land referred to is now worth more than £15,000 per annum.

Prior to the commencement of the new town, the only other edifices on the site were the Kirk-braehead House, Drumsheugh House, near the old Ferry Road, and the Manor House of Coates.

Drumsheugh House, of which nothing now remains but its ancient rookery in Randolph Crescent, was removed recently. Therein the famous Chevalier Johnstone, Assistant A.D.C. to Prince Charles, was concealed for a time by Lady Jane Douglas, after the battle of Culloden, till he escaped to England, in the disguise of a pedlar.

Alexander Lord Colville of Culross, a distinguished Admiral of the White, resided there subsequently. He served at Carthagena in 1741, at Quebec and Louisbourg in the days of Wolfe, and died at Drumsheugh on the 21st of May, 1770. His widow, Lady Elizabeth Erskine, daughter of Alexander Earl of Kellie, resided there for some years after, together with her brother, the Honourable Andrew Erskine, an officer of the old 71st, disbanded in 1763, an eccentric character, who figures among Kay's Portraits, and who in 1793 was drowned in the Forth, opposite Caroline Park. Lady Colville died at Drumsheugh in the following year, when the house and lands thereof reverted to her brother-in-law, John Lord Colville of Culross. And so lately as 1811 the mansion was occupied by James Erskine, Esq., of Cambus.

Southward of Drumsheugh lay Bearford's Parks, mentioned as "Terras de Barfurd" in an Act in favour of Lord Newbattle in 1587, named from Hepburn of Bearford in Haddingtonshire.

In 1767 the Earl of Morton proposed to have a wooden bridge thrown across the North Loch from these parks to the foot of Warriston's Close, but the magistrates objected, on the plea that the property at the close foot was worth £20,000. The proposed bridge was to be on a line with "the highest level ground of Robertson's and Wood's Farms." In the *Edinburgh Advertiser* for 1783 the magistrates announced that Hallow Fair was to be "held in the Middle Bearford's Park."

Lord Fountainhall, under dates 1693 and 1695, records a dispute between Robert Hepburn of Bearford and the administrators of Heriot's hospital, concerning "the mortified annual rents acclaimed out of his tenement in Edinburgh, called the Black Turnpike," and again in 1710, of an action he raised against the Duchess of Buccleuch, in which Sir Robert Hepburn of Bearford in 1633, is referred to, all probably of the same family.

The lands and houses of Easter and Wester

Coates lay westward of Bearford's Parks and the old Ferry Road. The former edifice, a picturesque old mansion, with turrets, dormer windows, and crowstepped gables, in the Scoto-French style, still remains unchanged among its changed surroundings as when it was built, probably about 1611, by Sir John Byres of Coates, whose town residence was in Byres' Close, in the High Street, and over the door of which he inscribed the usual pious legend, "*Blissit be God in al his giftis*," with the initials of

On the west a dormer gable bears the date 1615, with the initials J. B. and M. B., and a stone built above the western door bears in large letters the word IEHOVA, with the city motto and the date 1614.

According to the inscription on the tomb of " the truly good and excellent citizen John Byres of Coites," in the Greyfriars churchyard, as given by Monteith, it would appear that he was two years city bailie, two years a surburban bailie, six

THE MANSION OF EASTER COATES.

himself and his lady. This lintel was removed by the late Sir Patrick Walker, who had succeeded to the estate, and was rebuilt by him into the present ancient house, which is destined long to survive as the deanery of St. Mary's cathedral. Into the walls of the same house were built some fragments of sculpture from a mansion in the Cowgate, traditionally known as the residence of the French embassy in Mary's time. They are now in the north wing.

On the eastern side of the mansion of Coates are two ancient lintels, one dated 1600, with the initials C. C. I. and K. H. The other bears the same initials with the legend,

I PRAYS YE LORD FOR
ALL HIS BENEFETIS, 1601.

years Dean of Guild, and that he died on the 24th of November, 1629, in his sixtieth year.

Prior to the time of the Byres the property had belonged to the Lindsays, as in the ratification by Parliament to Lord Lindsay, in 1592, are mentioned " the landis of Dene, but the mylnes and mure thereof, and their pertenents lyand within the Sherifdom of Edinburgh, the manes of Drym, the lands of Drymhill, the landis of Coittis and Coitakirs, &c." (Acta Parl., Jacobi VI.)

The mansion of Wester Coates, advertised in the Edinburgh papers of 1783 as " the House of Coates, or White House, belonging to the heirs of the deceased James Finlay of Walliford, and as lately possessed by Lord Covington, situated on the highway leading to Coltbridge," was removed in

1869 to make way for Grosvenor Street, in excavating the foundation of which a number of ancient bronze Caledonian swords were found—the relics of some pre-historic strife. One was specially remarkable for having the hilt and pommel of bronze cast in one piece with the blade—a form very rare, there being only one other Scottish example known —one from Tarves, in Aberdeenshire, and now in the British Museum.

The few houses enumerated alone occupied the lonely site of the New Town when Gabriel's Road,

of the poet Thomson, and who engraved thereon the following appropriate lines from his uncle's poem :—

" August, around, what public works I see !
　　Lo, stately streets ! lo, squares that court the breeze !
　　See long canals and deepened rivers join
　　Each part with each, and with the circling main,
　　The whole entwined isle."

The names given to the streets and squares— the formal array of parallelograms drawn by Craig—were taken from the royal family chiefly,

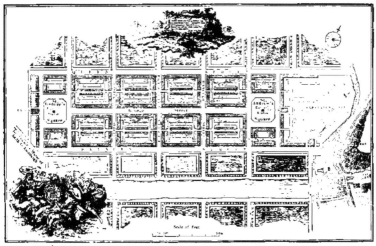

CRAIG'S PLAN OF THE NEW STREETS AND SQUARES INTENDED FOR THE CITY OF EDINBURGH.
(Reduced Facsimile of the Original Engraving.)

latterly a mean, narrow alley, was a delightful country path, " along which," says Wilson, in 1847, " some venerable citizens still remember to have wended their way between green hedges that skirted the pleasant meadows and cornfields of Wood's Farm, and which was in days of yore a favourite trysting place for lovers, where they breathed out their tender tale of passion beneath the fragrant hawthorn."

It ran in an oblique direction through the ancient hamlet of Silvermills, and its course is yet indicated by the irregular slant of the garden walls that separate the little plots behind Duke Street from the East Queen Street Gardens at the lower end.

The plan of the proposed new city was prepared by James Craig, an eminent architect, nephew

and the tutelary saints of the island. The first thoroughfare, now a magnificent terrace, was called St. Giles Street, after the ancient patron of the city ; but on the plan being shown to George III. for his approval, he exclaimed, " Hey, hey !—what, what!—St. Giles Street !—never do, never do !" And so, to escape from a vulgar London association of ideas, it was named Princes Street, after the future George IV. and the Duke of York.

Craig survived to see his plans only partially carried out, as he died in 1795, in his fifty-fifth year. He was the son of Robert Craig, merchant, and grandson of Robert Craig, who in the beginning of that century had been a magistrate of Edinburgh. His mother was Mary, youngest daughter of James Thomson, minister of Ednam, and sister of the author of " The Seasons."

So difficult was it to induce people to build in a spot so sequestered and far apart from the mass of the ancient city, that a premium of £20 was publicly offered by the magistrates to him who should raise the first house; but great delays ensued. The magistrates complimented Mr. James Craig on his plan for the New Town, which was selected from several. He received a gold medal and the freedom of the city in a silver box; and by the end of July, 1767, notice was given that "the plan was to lie open at the Council Chamber for a month from the 3rd of August, for the inspection of such as inclined to become feuars, where also were to be seen the terms on which feus would be granted."

At last a Mr. John Young took courage, and gained the premium by erecting a mansion in Rose Court, George Street—the *first* edifice of New Edinburgh; and the foundation of it was laid by James Craig, the architect, in person, on the 26th of October, 1767. (Chambers's "Traditions," p. 18.)

An exemption from all burghal taxes was also granted to Mr. John Neale, a silk mercer, for an elegant mansion built by him, the first in the line of Princes Street (latterly occupied as the Crown Hotel), and wherein his son-in-law, Archibald Constable, afterwards resided. "These now appear whimsical circumstances," says Robert Chambers: "so it does that a Mr. Shadrach Moyes, on ordering a house to be built for himself in Princes Street, in 1769, held the builder bound to run another farther along, to shield him from the west wind. Other quaint particulars are remembered, as for instance, Mr. Wight, an eminent lawyer, who planted himself in St. Andrew Square, finding that he was in danger of having his view of St. Giles's clock shut up by the advancing line of Princes Street, built the intervening house himself, that he might have it in his power to keep the roof low, for the sake of the view in question; important to him, he said, as enabling him to regulate his movements in the morning, when it was necessary that he should be punctual in his attendance at the Parliament House."

By 1790 the New Town had extended westward to Castle Street, and by 1800 the necessity for a second plan farther to the north was felt, and soon acted upon, and great changes rapidly came over the customs, manners, and habits of the people. With the enlarged mansions of the new city, they were compelled to live more expensively, and more for show. A family that had long moved in genteel or aristocratic society in Blackfriars Wynd, or Lady Stair's Close, maintaining a round of quiet tea-drinkings with their neighbours up the adjoining turnpike stair, and who might converse with lords, ladies, and landed gentry, by merely opening their respective windows, found all this homely kindness changed when they emigrated beyond the North Loch. There heavy dinners took the place of tea-parties, and routs superseded the festive suppers of the closes and wynds, and those who felt themselves great folk when dwelling therein, appeared small enough in George Street or Charlotte Square.

The New Town kept pace with the growing prosperity of Scotland, and the Old, if unchanged in aspect, changed thoroughly as respects the character of its population. Nobles and gentlemen, men of nearly all professions, deserted one by one, and a flood of the lower, the humbler, and the plebeian classes took their places in close and wynd; and many a gentleman in middle life, living then perhaps, in Princes Street, looked back with wonder and amusement to the squalid common stair in which he and his forefathers had been born, and where he had spent the earliest years of his life.

Originally the houses of Craig's new city were all of one plain and intensely monotonous plan and elevation—three storeys in height, with a sunk area in front, enclosed by iron railings, with link extinguishers; and they only differed by the stone being more finely polished, as the streets crept westward. But during a number of years prior to 1840, the dull uniformity of the streets over the western half of the town had disappeared. Most of the edifices, all constructed as elegant and commodious dwelling-houses, are now enlarged, re-built, or turned into large hotels, shops, club-houses, insurance-offices, warehouses, and new banks, and scarcely an original house remains unchanged in Princes Street or George Street.

And this brings us now to the Edinburgh of modern intellect, power, and wealth. "At no period of her history did Edinburgh better deserve her complimentary title of the modern Athens than the last ten years of the eighteenth and the first ten years of the nineteenth century," says an English writer. "She was then, not only nominally, but actually, the capital of Scotland, the city in which was collected all the intellectual life and vigour of the country. London then occupied a position of much less importance in relation to the distant parts of the empire than is now the case. Many causes have contributed to bring about the change, of which the most prominent are the increased facilities for locomotion which have been introduced . . . . . . various causes which contributed to increase the importance of provincial towns were combined in the case of Edinburgh. She was the titular capital of Scotland, and as such, was looked up to with pride and veneration by the nation at large. She was then the residence of many of the old Scottish nobility, and the exclusion of the British from the Continent, during a long, protracted war, made her, either for business, society, or education, the favourite resort of strangers. She was the head-quarters of the legal profession at a time when both the Scottish bench and bar were rendered illustrious by a number of men celebrated for their learning, eloquence, and wit. She was the head-quarters of the Scottish Church, whose pulpits and General Assembly were adorned by divines of great eminence and piety. Lastly, she was the chief seat of scholarship, and the chosen home of literature and science north of the Tweed."

With the Edinburgh of those days and of the present we have now to deal.

CHAPTER XVII.

PRINCES STREET.

A Glance at Society—Change of Manners, &c.—The Irish Giants—Poole's Coffee-house—Shop of Constable & Co.—Weir's Museum, 1794—The Grand Duke Nicholas—North British Insurance Life Association—Old Tax Office and New Club—Craig of Riccarton—"The White Rose of Scotland"—St. John's Chapel—Its Tower and Vaults, &c.—The Scott Monument and its Museum—The Statues of Professor Wilson, Allan Ramsay, Adam Black, Sir James Simpson, and Dr. Livingstone—The General Improvements in Princes Street.

IN 1774 a proposal to erect buildings on the south side of Princes Street—a lamentable error in taste it would have proved—led to an interdict by the Court of Session, which ended in a reference to the House of Lords, on which occasion Lord Mansfield made a long and able speech, and the result was, that the amenity of Princes Street was maintained, and it became in time the magnificent terrace we now find it.

Of the city in 1783 some glimpses are given us in the "Letters of Theophrastus," appended to the second edition of "Arnot." In that year the revenue of the Post Office was only £40,000. There were four coaches to Leith, running every half hour, and there were 1,268 four-wheeled carriages and 338 two-wheeled paying duty. The oyster-cellars had become numerous, and were places of fashionable resort. A maid-servant's wages were about £4 yearly. In 1763 they wore plain cloaks or plaids; but in 1783 "silk, caps, ribbons, ruffles, false hair, and flounced petticoats." In 1783 a number of bathing-machines had been adopted at Leith. People of the middle class and above it dined about four o'clock, after which no business was done, and gentlemen were at no pains to conceal their impatience till the ladies retired. Attendance at church was much neglected, and people did not think it "genteel" to take their domestics with them. "In 1783 the daughters even of tradesmen consume the mornings at the toilet (to which rouge is now an appendage) or in strolling from the perfumer's to the milliner's. They would blush to be seen at market. The cares of the family devolve upon a housekeeper, and Miss employs those heavy hours when she is disengaged from public or private amusements in improving her mind from the precious stores of a circulating library." In that year a regular cock-pit was built for cock-fighting, where all distinctions of rank and character were levelled. The weekly concert of music began at seven o'clock, and mistresses of boarding-schools, &c., would not allow their pupils to go about unattended; whereas, twenty years before "young ladies might have walked the streets in perfect security at all hours." In 1783 six criminals lay under sentence of death in Edinburgh in one week, whereas in 1763 three was an average for the whole kingdom in a year. A great number of the servant-maids still continued "their abhorrence of wearing shoes and stockings in the morning." The Register House was unfinished, "or occupied by pigeons only," and the Records "were kept in a dungeon called the Laigh Parliament House."

The High Street alone was protected by the guard. The New Town to the north, and all the streets and new squares to the south, were totally unwatched; and the soldiers of the guard still preserved "the purity of their native Gaelic, so that few of the citizens understand, or are understood by them;" while the king's birthday and the last night of the year were "devoted to drunkenness, outrage, and riot, instead of loyalty, peace, and harmony," as of old.

One of the earliest improvements in the extended royalty was lighting it with oil lamps; but in the *Advertiser* for 1789 we are told that "while all strangers admire the beauty and regularity of the

New Town, they are surprised at its being so badly lighted and watched at night. The half of the North Bridge next the Old Town is well lighted, while the half next the New remains in total darkness. London and Westminster are lighted all the year through." Among the improvements in the same year, we read of two hackney-coach stands being introduced by the magistrates—one at St. Andrew's Church and another at the Register House ; but sedans were then in constant use, and did not finally disappear till about 1850.

"In Edinburgh there is no trade," wrote a German traveller—said to be M. Voght, of Hamburg, in 1795 ; "but from this circumstance society is a gainer in point both of intelligence and of eloquence. . . . . It is but justice to a place in which I have spent one of the most agreeable winters of my life to declare, that nowhere more completely than there have I found realised my idea of good society, or met with a circle of men better informed, more amicable, greater lovers of truth, or of more unexceptionable integrity. During six months I heard no invectives uttered, no catching at wit practised, no malignant calumnies invented or retailed ; and I seldom left a company without some addition to my knowledge or new incitements to philanthropy. To name and to describe the persons composing this society, and to introduce them to your readers, is a pleasure which I cannot deny myself."

Among those whom he met in the Edinburgh of that day M. Voght mentions Dugald Stewart, "the Bacon of Metaphysics" ; Fraser Tytler, Lord Woodhouselee ; Mackenzie, "The Man of Feeling ;" Drs. Black, Blair, Munro, and Coventry the lecturer on agriculture ; Professor Playfair, Dr. Gregory, and the amiable Sir William Forbes ; Sir John Sinclair of Ulbster, and Colonel Dirom, the historian of Tippoo Sahib, and Sir Alexander Mackenzie ; adding :—"What makes the society in Edinburgh particularly attractive is the crowd of Scotsmen who have been long in the East and West Indies, and have returned thither—old officers who have served in the army and navy, and all of whom in their youth have had the advantage of academical instruction."

Lady Sinclair, he tells us, "is one of the prettiest women in all Scotland," and that Creech, the bookseller, was one of his "most valuable acquaintances." Among others, he enumerates Sir James Hall of Dunglass, Lords Eskgrove, Ancrum, and Fincastle, Professor Rutherford the botanist, Lord Monboddo, and many more, as those making up the circle of a delightful and intellectual society in a city, the population of which, including Leith, was

then only 81,865, of whom 7,206 were in the New Town.

At the close of the century the first academy for classical education was opened there by William Laing, A.M., father of Alexander Gordon Laing, whose name is so mournfully connected with African discovery. In that establishment Mr. Laing laboured for thirty-two years, and was one of the most popular teachers of his day.

In 1811 the population of the city and Leith had increased to 102,987, and exclusive of the latter it was 82,624. By 1881 the estimated population was 290,637.

It was in the year 1805 that the Police Act for the city first came into operation, when John Tait, Esq., was appointed Judge of the Court. Prior to this the guardianship of the city had been entirely in the hands of the old Town Guard, which was then partially reduced, save a few who were retained for limited and special service. The Commissioners of Police first substituted gas for oil lamps ; and in 1823 the papers announce that these officials had "fitted up 341 new gas pillars, chiefly in the New Town ; they are in progress with other forty-two, and have given orders for other 245 gas lights, chiefly in the Old Town. They are to sell the superseded lamp-irons and globes, from which they may realise about £600."

By that time the last traces of ancient manners had nearly departed. "The old claret-drinkers," says a writer in 1824, "are brought to nothing, and some of them are under the sod. The court dresses, in which the nobility and gentry appeared at the balls and first circles in Edinburgh, together with their dress swords or rapiers, are all ' have beens,' for there has been introduced a half-dress —and it is a half-dress : nay, some ladies make theirs less than half ; while the swords of the well-dressed men have been dropped for the fist, and the dashing blades of the present day learn to mill, to fib, and to floor, and to give a facer with their 'mawlies,' and other equally gentleman-like accomplishments." Elsewhere he says :—"To prove the more tenacious adhesion of the Scotch to French manners and old fashions, I can assert that for one cocked hat which appeared in the streets of London within the last forty years, a dozen passed current in Auld Reekie."

The houses first numbered in Princes Street were in the south portion, which caused the legal contention in 1774, and the continuation of which was so fortunately arrested by the Court of Session, and there the numbers run from 1 to 9.

No. 2 was occupied in 1784 by Robertson, "a ladies' hairdresser," where, as per advertisement,

THE OLD TOWN, FROM PRINCES STREET.

(From an Engraving by J. Clark of a Painting by A. Kay, published on August 1, 1814, by D. McIntosh.)

16

two Irish giants—twin brothers—exhibited themselves to visitors at a shilling per head, from four till nine every evening, Sundays excepted. "These wonderful Irish giants are but twenty-three years of age, and measure nearly eight feet high," according to the newspapers. "These extraordinary young men have had the honour to be seen by inches high); and the late Swedish giant will scarce admit of comparison."

Of these Irish giants, whose advent is among the first notabilia of Princes Street, Kay gives us a full-page drawing in his first volume, including, by way of contrast, Lord Monboddo, Bailie Kyd, a wine merchant in the Candlemaker Row, who

ARCHIBALD CONSTABLE. (*After the Portrait by Raeburn.*)

their majesties and the royal family at Windsor, in November, 1783, with great applause, and likewise by gentlemen of the faculty, Royal Society, and other admirers of natural curiosity, who allow them to surpass anything of the kind ever offered (*sic*) to the public. Their address is singularly pleasing; their persons truly shaped and proportioned to their height, and afford an agreeable surprise. They excel the famous Maximilian Miller, born in 1674, shown in London in 1733 (six feet ten died in 1810, Andrew Bell, an engraver (who died in Lauriston Lane in 1809), and others of very small stature.

In 1811 this house and No. 1 were both hotels, the former being named "The Crown," and from them both, the "Royal Eagle" and "Prince Regent" Glasgow stage-coaches started daily at 9 a.m. and 4 p.m. "every lawful day."

Taking the houses of note as they occur *seriatim*, the first on the north side, No. 10—for some time a famous china emporium—has had many and various occupants. In 1783, and before that period, it was Poole's Coffee-house, and till the days of Waterloo was long known as a rendezvous for the many military idlers who were then in Edinburgh—the veterans of Egypt, Walcheren, the Peninsula, and India—and for the officers of the strong garrison maintained there till the general peace. In July, 1783, by an advertisement, "Mathew Poole returns his most grateful acknowledgments to the nobility and gentry for their past favours, and begs leave respectfully to inform them that he has taken the whole of the apartments above his coffee-house, which he has fitted up in the neatest and most genteel manner as a hotel. The airiness of the situation and the convenience of the lodgings, which are perfectly detached from each other, render it very proper for families, and the advantage of the coffee-house and tavern adjoining must make it both convenient and agreeable for single gentlemen."

In the Post Office Directory for 1811, Nos. 3 and 14 appear as the hotels of Walker and Poole; the latter is now, and has been for many years, a portion of the great establishment of Messrs. William Renton and Co.

When, in the summer of 1822, Mr. Archibald Constable, the eminent publisher, returned from London to Edinburgh, he removed his establishment from the Old Town to the more commodious and splendid premises, No. 10, Princes Street, which he had acquired by purchase from the connections of his second marriage, and in that year he was included among the justices of the peace for the city. "Though with a strong dash of the sanguine," says Lockhart—"without which, indeed, there can be no great projector in any walk of life—Archibald Constable was one of the most sagacious persons that ever followed his profession. . . . Indeed, his fair and handsome physiognomy carried a bland astuteness of expression not to be mistaken by any one who could read the plainest of nature's handwriting. He made no pretensions to literature, though he was, in fact, a tolerable judge of it generally, and particularly well skilled in the department of Scotch antiquities. He distrusted himself, however, in such matters, being conscious that his early education had been very imperfect; and, moreover, he wisely considered the business of a critic quite as much out of his proper line as authorship itself. But of that 'proper line,' and his own qualifications for it, his estimation was ample; and as often as I may have smiled at the lofty serenity of his self-complacence, I confess that I now doubt whether he rated himself too

highly as a master in the true science of the bookseller. He was as bold as far-sighted, and his disposition was as liberal as his views were wide."

In January, 1826, the public was astonished by the bankruptcy at No. 10, Princes Street, when Constable's liabilities were understood to exceed £250,000—a failure which led to the insolvency of Ballantyne and Co., and of Sir Walter Scott, who was connected with them both; and when it became known that by bill transactions, &c., the great novelist had rendered himself responsible for debts to the amount of £120,000, of which not above a half were actually incurred by himself. Constable's failure was the result of that of Messrs. Hunt, Robinson, and Co., of London, who had suspended payment of their engagements early in the January of the same fatal year.

At the time of his bankruptcy Constable was meditating a series of publications, which afterwards were issued under the title of "Constable's Miscellany," the precursor of that now almost universal system of cheap publishing which renders the present era one as much of reprint as of original publication; but soon after its commencement he was attacked by a former disease, dropsy, and died on the 21st of July, 1827, in the fifty-third year of his age. His portrait by Raeburn is one of the most successful likenesses of him.

No. 16, farther westward, was, in 1794, occupied as Weir's Museum, deemed in its time a wonderful collection "of quadrupeds, birds, fishes, insects, shells, fossils, minerals, petrifaction, and anatomical preparations . . . . . . One cannot help," says Kincaid, "admiring the birds from Port Jackson, New South Wales, for the extreme beauty of their plumage; their appearance otherwise exhibits them as not deprived of life."

It is of this collection that Lord Gardenstone wrote, in his "Travelling Memoranda":—"I cannot omit to observe that in the whole course of my travels I have nowhere seen the preservation of quadrupeds, birds, fishes, and insects executed with such art and taste as by Mr. Alexander Weir of Edinburgh. He is a most ingenious man, and certainly has not hitherto been so much encouraged by the public as his merit deserves."

No. 27, a corner house, was in 1789 the abode of the Honourable Henry Erskine, who figures prominently in the remarkable collection of Kay; and in the same year No. 47 was occupied by Lady Gordon of Lesmore, in the county of Aberdeen, an old family, created baronets in 1625. It now forms a portion of the great premises of Kennington and Jenner, the latter of whom is brother of Sir William Jenner, Bart., the eminent physician.

Princes Street contains most of the best-stocked, highest-rented, and most handsome business premises and shops in the city. From its magnificent situation it is now, *par excellence*, the street for hotels; and as a proof of the value of property there, two houses, Nos. 49 and 62, were publicly sold on the 12th of February, 1879, for £26,000 and £24,500 respectively.

No. 53 at an early period became the Royal Hotel. In December, 1817, when it was possessed by a Mr. Macculloch, the Grand Duke Nicholas, brother of Alexander I., Emperor of Russia, resided there with a brilliant suite, including Baron Nicolai, Sir William Congreve, Count Kutusoff, and Dr. Crichton—the latter a native of the city, who died so lately as 1856. He was a member of the Imperial Academy of St. Petersburg and that of Natural History at Moscow, K.G.C. of St. Anne and St. Vladimir. He was a grandson of Crichton of Woodhouselee and Newington. A guard of the 92nd Gordon Highlanders was mounted on the hotel, and the Grand Duke having expressed a wish to see the regiment—the costume of which had greatly impressed him—it was paraded before him for that purpose on the 22nd of December, on which occasion he expressed his high admiration of the corps.

No. 64 is now the North British and Mercantile Insurance Company, established in 1809, and incorporated by royal charter, with the Duke of Roxburgh for its present president, and the Dukes of Sutherland and Abercorn, as vice-presidents. A handsome statue of St. Andrew, the patron of Scotland, on his peculiar cross, adorns the front of the building, and is a conspicuous object from the street and opposite gardens.

The Life Association of Scotland, founded in 1839, occupies No. 82. It is a magnificent palatial edifice, erected in 1855-8, after designs by Sir Charles Barry and Mr. David Rhind, and consists of three double storeys in florid Roman style, the first being rusticated Doric, the second Ionic, and the third Corinthian. Over its whole front it exhibits a great profusion of ornament—so great, indeed, as to make its appearance somewhat heavy.

In 1811, and before that period, the Tax Office occupied No. 84. The Comptroller in those days was Henry Mackenzie, author of the "Man of Feeling," who obtained that lucrative appointment from Mr. Pitt, on the recommendation of Lord Melville and Mr. George Rose, in 1804. With No. 85, it now forms the site of the New

Club, a large and elegant edifice, with a handsome Tuscan doorway and projecting windows, erected by an association of Scottish nobles and gentlemen for purposes similar to those of the clubs at the west end of London.

No. 91, which is now occupied as an hotel, was the residence of the aged Robert Craig, Esq., of Riccarton, of whom Kay gives us a portrait, seated at the door thereof, with his long staff and broad-brimmed, low-crowned hat, while his faithful attendant, William Scott, is seen behind, carefully taking "tent" of his old master from the dining-room window. Mr. Craig had been in early life a great pedestrian, but as age came upon him his walks were limited to the mile of Princes Street, and after a time he would but sit at his door and enjoy the summer breeze. He wore a plain coat without any collar, a stock in lieu of a neckcloth, knee-breeches, rough stockings, and enormous brass shoe-buckles. He persisted in wearing a hat with a narrow brim when cocked-hats were the fashion in Edinburgh, until he was so annoyed by boys that he adopted the head-dress in which he is drawn by Kay. He always used a whistle in the ancient manner, and not a bell, to summon his servant. He died on the 13th of March, 1823. Pursuant to a deed of entail, Mr. James Gibson, W.S. (afterwards Sir James Gibson-Craig, Bart., of Riccarton and Ingliston), succeeded to the estate, and assumed the name and arms of Craig; but the house, No. 91, went to Colonel Gibson.

The record of his demise in the papers of the time is not without interest :—" Died at his house in Princes Street (No. 91), on the 13th March, in the 93rd year of his age, Robert Craig, Esq., of Riccarton, the last male heir of Sir Thomas Craig of Riccarton, the great feudal lawyer of Scotland. Mr. Craig was admitted advocate in 1754, and was one of the Commissaries of Edinburgh, the duties of which situation he executed to the entire satisfaction of every one connected with it. He resigned the office many years ago, and has long been the senior member of the Faculty of Advocates. It is a remarkable circumstance that his father's elder brother succeeded to the estate of Riccarton in January, 1681, so that there has been only one descent in the family for 142 years."

No. 100, now occupied as an hotel, was for many years the house of Lady Mary Clerk of Pennicuick, known as "The White Rose of Scotland."

This lady, whose maiden name was Dacre, was the daughter of a gentleman in Cumberland, and came into the world in that memorable year when the Highland army was in possession of Carlisle,

While her mother was still confined to bed a Highland party, under a chieftain of the Macdonald clan, came to her house, but the commander, on learning the circumstances, not only chivalrously restrained his men from levying any contribution, but took from his bonnet his own white rose or cockade, and pinned it on the infant's breast, "that it might protect the household from any trouble by others. This rosette the lady kept to her dying day." In after years she became the wife of Sir James Clerk of Pennicuick, Bart., and who became wife of Hugh, third Viscount Primrose, in whose house in London the loyal Flora Macdonald found a shelter after liberation from the long confinement she underwent for her share in promoting the escape of the prince, who had given it to her as a souvenir at the end of his perilous wanderings.

In the *Edinburgh Observer* of 1822 it is recorded that when George IV. contemplated his visit to Scotland, he expressed a wish to have some relic of the unfortunate prince, on which

PRINCES STREET, LOOKING EAST FROM SCOTT'S MONUMENT.

from time to time, on special occasions, always wore this white rose of the house of Stuart.

Another and more valuable relic of the '45 came into her possession—the pocket-knife, fork, and spoon which Prince Charles used in all his marches and subsequent wanderings. The case is a small one, covered with black shagreen; for portability, the knife, fork, and spoon are made to screw upon handles, so that the three articles form six pieces for close packing. They are all engraved with an ornament of thistle-leaves, and the fork and spoon have the prince's initials, c. s: all have the Dutch plate stamp, showing that they were manufactured in Holland.

It is supposed that this case, with its contents, came to Lady Mary Clerk through Miss Drelincourt, daughter of the Dean of Armagh, in Ireland, who Lady Clerk commissioned Sir Walter Scott to present him with the travelling case, which he accordingly did on the king's arrival in Leith Roads, when he went off to the royal yacht to present him with the silver cross badge, the gift of "the ladies of Scotland."

From the king, the case, with its contents, passed to the Marquis of Conyngham, and from him to his son Albert, first Lord Londesborough, and they are now preserved with great care amidst the valuable collection of ancient plate and *bijouterie* at Grimston Park, Yorkshire. ("Book of Days.")

Sir Walter Scott was a frequent visitor at No. 100, Princes Street, as he was on intimate terms with Lady Clerk, who died several years after the king's visit, having attained a green old age. Till past her eightieth year she retained an

17

THE CASTLE, RAMSAY GARDENS, BANK OF SCOTLAND, AND EARTHEN MOUND, FROM PRINCES STREET.

(From an Engraving by J. Clark of a Painting by A. Kay, published on August 1, 1821, by D. McIntosh.)

erect and alert carriage, together with some old-fashioned peculiarities of costume, which made her one of the most noted street figures of her time.

The editor of "The Book of Days" says that he is enabled to recall a walk he had one day with Sir Walter, ending in Constable's shop, No. 10, Princes Street, "when Lady Clerk was purchasing some books at a side counter. Sir Walter, passing through to the stairs by which Mr. Constable's room was reached, did not recognise her ladyship, who, catching sight of him as he was about to

The University Club, to the westward, was erected in 1866–7, from designs by Peddie and Kinnear, in an ornate Italian style, with Grecian decoration, at the cost of £14,000, and has ample accommodation for 650 members. The new Conservative Club, a minor edifice, stands a little to the east of it.

Nos. 129 and 130 are now extensive shop-premises. In 1811 the former was the residence of Sir Alexander Charles Gibson-Maitland of Clifton Hall, in Lothian, the first baronet of the

PRINCES STREET, LOOKING WEST.   (*From a Photograph by G. W. Wilson and Co.*)

ascend, called out, 'Oh, Sir Walter! are you really going to pass me?' He immediately turned to make his usual cordial greetings, and apologised with demurely waggish reference to her odd dress: 'I'm sure, my lady, by this time I might know your back as well as your face.'"

No. 104 is now connected with the first attempt in arcades in Edinburgh. It forms a six-storey edifice, comprising an hotel, and is an elegant glass-roofed bazaar hall, 105 feet long by 30 feet high. It was completed in 1876. In 1830, No. 105 was the residence of the Honourable Baron Clerk Rattray. It is now a warehouse; and some fifteen years before that, No. 110 was the residence of Drummond of Blair Drummond. It is now Taylor's Repository. Drummond of Gairdrum occupied No. 117.

name, who died in 1820; and in No. 136 dwelt Mr. Henry Siddons of the Theatre Royal.

No. 146 was latterly the Osborne Hotel, which was nearly destroyed by fire in 1879. In the following year it was opened as the Scottish Liberal Club, inaugurated by the Right Hon. W. E. Gladstone, M.P. for Midlothian.

At the extreme west end of the street, and at its junction with the Lothian Road, stands St. John's Episcopal Chapel, erected in 1817, after a design, in the somewhat feeble modern Gothic of that day, by William Burn, though modelled from and partially detailed after St. George's Chapel at Windsor. It is an oblong edifice, consisting of a nave and aisles, 113 feet long by 62 feet wide, and has at its western extremity a square pinnacled tower, 120 feet high. The whole cost, at first, about £18,000.

The tower, as originally designed, terminated in an open lantern, but this fell during a tempest of wind in January, 1818. In a letter to his friend, Willie Laidlaw, Sir Walter Scott refers to the event thus :—" I had more than an anxious thought about you all during the gale of wind. The Gothic pinnacles were blown from the top of Bishop Sandford's Episcopal chapel at the end of Princes Street, and broke through the roof and flooring, doing great damage. This was sticking the horns of the mitre into the belly of the church. The devil never so well deserved the title of Prince of Power of the Air since he has blown down this handsome church, and left the ugly mass of new buildings standing on the North Bridge."

The bishop referred to was the Rev. Daniel Sandford, father of the accomplished Greek scholar, Sir Daniel Keyte Sandford, D.C.L., who was born at Edinburgh in February, 1798, and received all the rudiments of his education under the venerable prelate, who died in 1830.

The interior of St. John's Church is beautiful, and presents an imposing appearance ; it contains a very fine organ, and is adorned with richly-coloured stained-glass windows. The great eastern window, which is thirty feet in height, contains the figures of the twelve apostles, by Eggington of Birmingham, acquired in 1871. There is also a magnificent reredos, designed by Peddie and Kinnear.

In this church ministered for years the late Dean Ramsay, the genial-hearted author of "Reminiscences of Scottish Life and Character." A small cemetery, with two rows of ornamented burial vaults, adjoin the south side of this edifice, the view of which is very striking from the West Churchyard. In these vaults and the little cemetery repose the remains of many persons eminent for rank and talent. Among them are the prince of Scottish portrait painters, Sir Henry Raeburn, the Rev. Archibald Alison, the well-known essayist on "Taste," Dr. Pultney Alison, his eldest son, and brother of the historian, Sir Archibald. The Doctor was professor successively of the theory and practice of physic in the university, author of several works of great authority in medical science, and was one of the most philanthropic men that ever adorned the medical profession, even in Edinburgh, where it has ever been pre-eminently noble in all works of charity ; and he was the able antagonist of Dr. Chalmers in advocating the enforcement of a compulsory assessment for the support of the poor in opposition to the Doctor's voluntary one.

There, too, lie James Donaldson, founder of the magnificent hospital which bears his name ; the Rev. Andrew Thomson, first minister of St. George's Church in Charlotte Square, in his day one of the most popular of the city clergy ; Sir William Hamilton, professor of moral philosophy in the university, and a philosopher of more than European name ; Catherine Sinclair, the novelist ; Macvey Napier, who succeeded Lord Jeffrey as editor of the *Edinburgh Review*, and, together with James Browne, LL.D., conducted the seventh edition of the "Encyclopædia Britannica"; Sir William Arbuthnot, who was Lord Provost in 1823 ; Mrs. Sligo of Inzievar, the sister of Sir James Outram, "the Bayard of India"; and many more of note.

Nearly opposite is a meagre and somewhat obstructive edifice of triangular form, known as the Sinclair Fountain, erected in 1859 at the expense of Miss Catherine Sinclair, the novelist, and daughter of the famous Sir John Sinclair of Ulbster, a lady distinguished for her philanthropy, and is one of the memorials of her benefactions to the city.

Among the many interesting features in Princes Street are its monuments, and taken seriatim, according to their dates, the first—and first also in consequence and magnificence—is that of Sir Walter Scott. This edifice, the design for which, by G. M. Kemp (who lost his life in the canal by drowning ere its completion), was decided by the committee on the 30th of April, 1840, bears a general resemblance to the most splendid examples of monumental crosses, though it far excels all its predecessors in its beauty and vast proportions, being 180 feet in height, and occupying a square area of 55 feet at its base.

The foundation stone was laid in 1840, and in it was deposited a plate, bearing the following inscription by Lord Jeffrey, remarkable for its tenor :—

"This Graven Plate, deposited in the base of a votive building on the fifteenth day of August, in the year of Christ 1840, *and never likely to see the light again till all the surrounding structures have crumbled to dust by the decay of time, or by human or elemental violence,* may then testify to a distant posterity that his countrymen began on that day to raise an effigy and architectural monument, TO THE MEMORY OF SIR WALTER SCOTT, BART., whose admirable writings were then allowed to have given more delight and suggested better feeling to a larger class of readers in every rank of society, than those of any other author, with the exception of Shakespeare alone, and which were therefore thought likely to be remembered long after this act of gratitude on the part of the first generation of his admirers should be forgotten. "HE WAS BORN AT EDINBURGH, 15TH AUGUST, 1771, AND DIED AT ABBOTSFORD, 21ST SEPTEMBER, 1832,"

Engravings have made us familiar with the

features of this beautiful and imposing structure, the design of a self-taught Scottish artisan. The four principal arches supporting the central tower resemble those beneath the rood-tower of a cruciform church, while the lower arches in the diagonal abutments, with their exquisitely-cut details, resemble the narrow north aisle of Melrose.

The groined roof over the statue is of the same design as the roof of the choir of that noble abbey church so much frequented and so enthusiastically admired by Sir Walter. The pillars, canopies of niches, pinnacles, and other details, are chiefly copied from the same ruin, and magnificent views of the city in every direction are to be had from its lofty galleries.

It cost £15,650, and from time to time statuettes of historical and other personages who figure in the pages of Scott have been placed in its numerous niches. Among these are Prince Charles Edward, who directly faces Princes Street, in the Highland dress, with a hand on his sword; the Lady of the Lake; the Last Minstrel and Meg Merrilies—these are respectively on the four centres of the first gallery; Mause Headrigg, Dominie Sampson, Meg Dods, and Dandie Dinmont, are respectively on the south, the west, the north, and the east, of the fourth gallery; King James VI., Magnus Troil, and Halbert Glendinning, occupy the upper tier of the south-west buttress; Minnie Troil, George Heriot, and Bailie Nicol Jarvie, are on the lower tier of it; Amy Robsart, the Earl of Leicester, and Baron Bradwardine, are on the upper tier of the north-west buttress; Hal o' the Wynd, the Glee Maiden, and Ellen of Lorn, are on the lower tier thereof; Edie Ochiltree, King Robert I., and Old Mortality, are on the upper tier of the north-east buttress; Flora MacIvor, Jeanie Deans, and the Laird of Dumbiedykes, are on the lower tier of it; the Sultan Saladin, Friar Tuck, and Richard Cœur de Lion, are on the upper tier of the south-east buttress; and Rebecca the Jewess, Diana Vernon, and Queen Mary, are on its lower tier.

On the capitals and pilasters supporting the roof are some exquisitely cut heads of Scottish poets: those of Robert Burns, Robert Fergusson, James Hogg, and Allan Ramsay, are on the west front; those of George Buchanan, Sir David Lindsay, Robert Tannahill, and Lord Byron, are on the south front; those of Tobias Smollett, James Beattie, James Thomson, and John Home, adorn the west front; those of Queen Mary, King James I., King James V., and Drummond of Hawthornden, are on the north front.

The white marble statue of Scott, from the chisel of Sir John Steel, procured at the cost of £2,000, was inaugurated under the central arches in 1846.

Sir Walter is represented sitting with a Border plaid over his left shoulder, and his favourite highland staghound, Maida, at his right foot.

A staircase in the interior of the south-west cluster of pillars leads to the series of galleries to which visitors are admitted on the modest payment of twopence. It also gives access to the Museum room, which occupies the body of the tower, and therein a number of interesting relics were deposited at its inauguration in April, 1879. These are too numerous to give in detail, but among them may be mentioned a statuette of Sir Walter, by Steel, a bust of George Kemp, the ill-fated architect, with his first pencil sketch of the monument, and a number of models and paintings of historical interest; and on the walls are placed eight alto-relievo portraits in bronze (by J. Hutchison, R.S.A.) of Scottish characters of mark, including James V., James VI., Queen Mary, John Knox, George Buchanan, the Regent Moray, the Marquis of Montrose, and Charles I.

In the collection are some valuable letters in the handwriting of Sir Walter Scott; and the walls are adorned with some of the old flint muskets, swords, and drums of the ancient City Guard.

The statue of Professor John Wilson, "Christopher North," at the western corner of the East Gardens, is the result of a subscription raised shortly after his death in 1854. A committee for the purpose was appointed, consisting of the Lord Justice General (afterwards Lord Colonsay), Lord Neaves, Sir John Watson Gordon, and others, and three years after Sir John Steel executed the statue, which is of bronze, and is a fine representation of one who is fresh in the recollection of thousands of his countrymen. The careless ease of the professor's ordinary dress is adopted; a plaid which he was in the habit of wearing supplies the drapery, and the lion-like head and face, full of mental and muscular power, thrown slightly upward and backward, express genius, while the figure, tall, massive, and athletic, corresponds to the elevated expression of the countenance. At its inauguration the Lord President Inglis said, happily, that there was "in John Wilson every element which gives a man a claim to this personal form of memorial—namely, great genius, distinguished patriotism, and the stature and figure of a demi-god." To his contemporaries this statue vividly recalls Wilson in his every-day aspect, as he was wont to appear in his classroom or on the platform in the fervour of his fiery oratory ; and to succeeding times it will preserve a vivid "representation of one who, apart from all his other claims to such commemoration, was universally recognised as one of the most striking, poetic, and noble-looking men of his time."

About the same period there was inaugurated at the eastern corner of the West Gardens a white marble statue of Allan Ramsay. A memorial of the poet was suggested in the *Scots Magazine* as far back as 1810, and an obelisk to his memory, known as the Ramsay monument, was erected near Pennicuick, nearly a century before that time. The marble statue is from the studio of Sir John Steel, and rather grotesquely represents the poet with the silk nightcap worn by gentlemen of his time as a temporary substitute for the wig, and was

erected by the late Lord Murray, a descendant and representative of Ramsay's. It rises from a pedestal, containing on its principal side a medallion portrait of Lord Murray, and on the reverse side one of General Ramsay (Allan's grandson), on the west one of Mrs. Ramsay, and on the east similar representations of the general's two daughters,

DEAN RAMSAY.   (*From a Photograph by John Moffat.*)

Lady Campbell and Mrs. Malcolm. " Thus we find," says Chambers, " owing to the esteem which genius ever commands, the poet of the *Gentle Shepherd* in the immortality of marble, surrounded by the figures of relatives and descendants who so acknowledged their aristocratic rank to be inferior to his, derived from mind alone."

Next in order was erected, in 1877, the statue to the late Adam Black, the eminent publisher, who represented the city in Parliament, held many

THE SCOTT MONUMENT, PRINCES STREET.

municipal offices, and was twice Lord Provost. It is from the studio of John Hutchison, R.S.A. In the same year there was placed in West Gardens the bronze statue of the great and good physician, Sir James Simpson, Bart. It is from the

PROFESSOR WILSON'S STATUE.

studio of his friend, William Brodie, R.S.A., and is admitted by all to be an excellent likeness, but is unfortunately placed as regards light and shadow.

Another monument erected in these gardens of Princes Street is the bronze statue of Dr. Livingstone, which was inaugurated in August, 1876. It is from the hands of Mrs. D. O. Hill (widow of the well-known artist of that name), sister of Sir Noel Paton. It has the defect of being—though an admirable likeness of the great explorer—far too small for the place it occupies, and is more suitable for the vestibule of a public building.

In the spring of 1877 great improvements were begun in this famous street. These included the widening of the foot pavement along the north side by four feet, the removal of the north line of tramway rails to the south of the previous south line, the consequent inclusion of a belt of gardens about ten feet broad, the shifting of the parapet wall with its iron railing ten feet back, and the erection of an ornamental rail along the whole line

of gardens about two feet from the north edge of the sloping bank, at the estimated cost of about £6,084 from St. Andrew Street to Hanover Street, and £12,160 from thence to Hope Street.

The width of the new carriage-way is sixty-eight feet, as compared with some fifty-seven feet before these improvements commenced, while the breadth of the pavement on the south side has been increased from seven and nine feet, to a uniform breadth of twelve feet, and that on the north to eighteen feet. The contract price of the carriage road was £20,000, a fourth of which was payable by the Tramway Company and the remainder by the Town Council.

Some idea of the extent of this undertaking may be gathered from the fact that about one million of whinstone blocks, nine inches in length, seven in depth, and three thick, have been used in connection with the re-paving of the thoroughfare, which is now the finest in the three kingdoms. On either side of the street square dressed channel stones, from three to four feet in length by one foot

ALLAN RAMSAY'S STATUE.

in breadth, slightly hollowed on the surface, have been laid down, the water in which is carried into the main sewers by surface gratings, placed at suitable intervals along the whole line of this magnificent street.

CHAPTER XVIII.
THE CHURCH OF ST. CUTHBERT.

History and Antiquity—Old Views of it Described—First Protestant Incumbents—The Old Manse—Old Communion Cups—Pillaged by Cromwell—Ruined by the Siege of 1689, and again in 1745—Deaths of Messrs. McVicar and Pitcairn—Early Body-snatchers—Demolition of the Old Church—Erection of the New—Case of Heart-burial—Old Tombs and Vaults—The Nisbets of Dean—The Old Poor House—Kirkbraehead Road—Lothian Road—Dr. Candlish's Church—Military Academy—New Caledonian Railway Station.

IN the hollow or vale at the end of which the North Loch lay there stands one of the most hideous churches in Edinburgh, known as the West Kirk, occupying the exact site of the Culdee Church of St. Cuthbert, the parish of which was the largest in Midlothian, and nearly encircled the whole of the city without the walls. Its age was greater than that of any record in Scotland. It was supposed to have been built in the eighth century, and was dedicated to St. Cuthbert, the Bishop of Durham, who died on the 20th of March, 687.

In Gordon of Rothiemay's bird's-eye view it appears a long, narrow building, with one transept or aisle, on the south, a high square tower of three storeys at the south-west corner, and a belfry. The burying-ground is square, with rows of trees to the westward. On the south of the burying-ground is a long row of two-storeyed houses, with a gate leading to the present road west of the Castle rock, and another on the north, leading to the pathway which yet exists up the slope to Princes Street, from which point it long was known as the Kirk Loan to Stockbridge.

A view taken in 1772 represents it as a curious assortment of four barn-like masses of building, having a square spire of five storeys in height in the centre, and the western end an open ruin—the western kirk—with a bell hung on a wooden frame. Northward lies the bare open expanse, or ridge, whereon the first street of the new town was built.

After the Reformation the first incumbent settled here would seem to have been a pious tailor, named William Harlow, who was born in the city about 1500, but fled to England, where he obtained deacon's orders and became a preacher during the reign of Edward VI. On the death of the latter, and accession of Mary, he was compelled to seek refuge in Scotland, and in 1556 he began "publicly to exhort in Edinburgh," for which he was excommunicated by the Catholic authorities, whose days were numbered now; and four years after, when installed at St. Cuthbert's, Mr. Harlow attended the meeting of the first General Assembly, held in Edinburgh on the 20th of December, 1560. He died in 1578, but four years before that event Mr. Robert Pont, afterwards an eminent judge and miscellaneous writer, was ordained to the ministry of St. Cuthbert's in his thirtieth year, at the time he was, with others, appointed by the Assembly to revise all books that were printed and published. About the same period he drew up the Calendar, and framed the rule to understand it, for Arbuthnot and Bassandyne's famous edition of the Bible. In 1571 he had been a Lord of Session and Provost of the Trinity College.

On Mr. Pont being transferred in 1582, Mr. Nicol Dalgleish came in his place; but the former, being unable to procure a stipend, returned to his old charge, conjointly with his successor. When James VI. insidiously began his attempts to introduce Episcopacy, Mr. Pont, a zealous defender of Presbyterianism, with two other ministers, actually repaired to the Parliament House, with the design of protesting for the rights of the Church in the face of the Estates; but finding the doors shut against them, they repaired to the City Cross, and when the obnoxious "Black Acts" were proclaimed, publicly denounced them, and then fled to England, followed by most of the clergy in Edinburgh.

Meanwhile Nicol Dalgleish, for merely praying for them, was tried for his life, and acquitted, but he was indicted anew for corresponding with the rebels, because he had read a letter which one of the banished ministers had sent to his wife. For this fault sentence of death was passed upon him; but though it was not executed, by a refinement of cruelty the scaffold on which he expected to die was kept standing for several weeks before the windows of his prison.

While Mr. Pont remained a fugitive, William Aird, a stonemason, "an extraordinary witness, stirred up by God," says Calderwood, "and married, learned first of his wife to speak English," was appointed, in the winter of 1584, colleague to Mr. Dalgleish, who, on the return of Mr. Pont in 1585, "was nominated to the principality of Aberdeen."

Pont's next colleague was Mr. Aird. Aware of the ignorance of most of their parishioners concerning the doctrines of the Protestant faith, and that many had no faith whatever, they offered to devote the forenoon of every Thursday to public teaching, and to this end a meeting was held on

the 27th October, 1592, by " the haill elderes, dea-
cones, and honest men of ye parochin . . . .
quha hes agreit, all in ane voice, that in all tymes
coming, thair be ane preaching everie Thursday,
and that it begin at nyne hours in ye morning, and
ye officer of ye kirk to gang with ye bell at aught
hours betwixt the Bow Fut and the Toun-end."
This Thursday sermon was kept up until the middle of the eighteenth century. The " toun-end " is
supposed to mean Fountain Bridge, sometimes of
old called the Causeway-end.

In 1589 the Kirk Session ordained that none in
the parish should have " yair bairnes " baptised,
admitted to marriage, repentance, or alms, but
those who could repeat the Lord's Prayer, the
Belief, and the Commandments, and " gif ane
compt yair of, quhen yai ar examinet, and yis to be
publishit in ye polpete." In the following year a
copy of the Confession of Faith and the National
Covenant was subscribed by the whole parish.

From the proximity of the church to the castle,
in the frequent sieges sustained by the latter, the
former suffered considerably, particularly after the
invention of artillery. At the Reformation it had
a roof of thatch, probably replacing a former one
of stone. The thatch was renewed in 1590, and
new windows and a loft were introduced ; two
parts of the expense were borne by the parish, the
other by Adam, Bishop of Orkney, a taxation
which he vehemently contested. Among other
additions to the church was " a pillar for adulterers,"
built by John Howieson and John Gairns in August,
1591. The thatch was removed and the roof slated.

In 1594 a manse adjoining the church was built
for Mr. Robert Pont, on the site of the present
one, into which is inserted an ancient fragment of
the former, inscribed—

RELIGIONI ET POSTERIS
IN MINISTERIO.
S. R. P. G. A. 1594.

The burying-ground in those days was confined
to the rising slope south-west of the church, and
as " nolt, horse, and scheipe " were in the habit
of grazing there, the wall being in ruins, it was
repaired in 1597. The beadle preceded all funerals with a hand-bell—a practice continued in the
eighteenth century.

In consequence of the advanced age of Messrs.
Pont and Aird, a third minister, Mr. Richard
Dickson, was appointed to the parish in May, 1600,
and in 1606 communion was given on three successive Sundays. On the 8th of May that year the
venerable Mr. Pont passed from the scene of his
labours, and is supposed to have been interred within
the church. To his memory a stone was erected,

which, when the present edifice was built, was removed to the Rev. Mr. Williamson's tomb on the
high ground, in which position it yet remains.
His colleague, Mr. Aird, survived him but a few
months, and their successors, Messrs. Dickson and
Arthur, became embroiled with the Assembly in
1619 for celebrating communion to the people
seated at a table, preventing them from kneeling,
as superstitious and idolatrous. Mr. Dickson was
ordered "to enter his person in ward within the
Castle of Dumbarton," and Mr. Arthur to give
communion to the people on their knees ; but he
and the people declined to " comply with a practice so nearly allied to popery." Mr. Dickson was
expelled in 1620, but Mr. Arthur was permitted to
remain. Among those who were sitters in the
church at this time were William Napier, of the
Wrytes house, and his more illustrious kinsman,
John Napier, of Merchiston, the inventor of logarithms, whose "dasks," or seats, seem to have
been close together.

The old church, like that of Duddingstone, was
furnished with iron jougs, in which it appears that
Margaret Dalgleish was compelled to figure on the
23rd of April, 1612, for her scandalous behaviour;
and in 1622, John Reid, "poltriman," was publicly
rebuked in church for plucking "geiss upon the
Lord his sabbath, in tyme of sermon."

We are told in the " History of the West Church,"
that " in 1622 it was deemed proper to have a bell
hung in the steeple, if the old ruinous fabric which
stood between the old and new kirks might be so
called," for a new church had been added at the
close of the sixteenth century. In 1618 new communion cups of silver were procured. "They were
then of a very peculiar shape, being six inches in
height, gilt, and beautifully chased ; but the cup
itself, which was plated, was only two inches
deep and twenty-four in circumference, not unlike
a small soup-plate affixed to the stalk of a candle-
stick. On the bottom was engraved the following
sentence :—*I wil tak the cvp of salvatiovne and cal
vpone the name of the Lord.* 116 *Pslm.* 1619 ; and
around the rim of the cup these words :—*For the
Vast Kirk ovtwith Edinburghe.*"

The year 1650 saw the church again imperilled
by war. Its records bear, on the 28th July in that
year, that " No sessione was keiped in the monthe
of August, because there lay ane companie at the
church," the seats of which had been destroyed
and the sessioners dispersed, partly by the army
of Cromwell, which lay on the south side of the
parish, and that of the Scots, which lay on the
north ; and on the 13th of that month, after
Cromwell's retreat to Dunbar, the commission of

the General Assembly met in the church, and passed an Act, which, however necessary, perhaps, in those harassing times, concerning "the sine and guilte of the king and his house," caused much suffering to the Covenanters after the Restoration. It was known by the name of the West Kirk Act, and was approved by Parliament the same day.

Subsequently, during his siege of the castle Cromwell made the church a barrack ; hence its roof and windows were destroyed by the guns of the fortress, and soon little was left of it but the bare walls, which were repaired, and opened for service in 1655.

For some years subsequent the sole troubles of the incumbents were breaches of "the Sabbath," such as when William Gillespie, in 1659, was "fund carrying watter, and his wyfe knoking beir," for which they had to make public repentance, or fining people for "taking snuff in tyme of sermon," contrary to the Act of 18th June, 1640 ; till 1665, when the "great mutiny" in the parish occurred, and the minister, William Gordon, for "keeping of festivals," was railed at by the people, who closed the doors against him, for which a man and a woman, according to Wodrow, were scourged through Edinburgh.

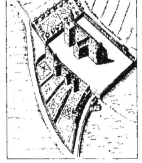

ST. CUTHBERT'S CHURCH.
(From Go don of Rothiemay's Map.)

At the Revolution, those ministers who had been ejected in 1661, and were yet alive, returned to their charges. Among them was Mr. David Williamson, who, in 1689, was settled in St. Cuthbert's manse ; but not quietly, for the castle, defended by the Duke of Gordon, was undergoing its last disastrous siege by the troops of William, and the church suffered so much damage from shot and shell, that for many months after the surrender in June, the people were unable to use it, and the repairs amounted to £1,500. If tradition has not wronged him, Mr. Williamson is the well-known "Dainty Davie" of Scottish song, who had six wives ere the seventh, Jean Straiton, survived him. He died in August, 1706, and was buried in the churchyard, where the vicinity of the grave is alone indicated by the letters D. W. cut on the front of the tomb in which he lies.

The ancient cemetery on the knoll having been found too small for the increasing population and consequent number of interments, in 1701 a piece of ground to the west was added to it (including the garden, with trees, shown in Gordon's Map), from the old boundary to the present west gate at the Lothian Road. About the same time several heritors requested permission to inter their dead in the little or Wester-kirk, which had been a species of ruin since the invasion of Cromwell.

In 1745, after the victory of the Highlanders at Prestonpans, a message was sent to the ministers of the city, in the name of "Charles, Prince Regent," desiring them to preach next day, Sunday, as usual ; but many, alarmed by the defeat of Cope, sought refuge in the country, and no public worship was performed within the city, save by a clergyman named Hog at the Tron.

It was otherwise, however, at St. Cuthbert's, the incumbent of which was then the Rev. Neil McVicar, who preached to a crowded congregation, many of whom were armed Highlanders, before whom he prayed for George II. and also for Charles Edward in a fashion of his own, recorded thus by Ray, in his history of the time, and others :—

"Bless the king ! Thou knowest *what* king I mean. May the crown sit long on his head. As for that young man who has come among us to seek an earthly crown, we beseech Thee to take him to Thyself and give him a crown of glory."

It is said that when the prince heard of McVicar's prayer he laughed heartily, and expressed himself quite satisfied.

Mr. Pitcairn preached in the afternoon to an equally large audience ; and during the brief occupation of the city by the Highlanders no cessation of public worship took place in St. Cuthbert's, though one of the pickets by which they blocked up the castle was posted therein, yet left it always during sermon. It was partially unroofed by cannon-shot, and in this condition was permitted to remain for several years, to the danger and discomfort of the people.

Charles having commenced his march for England on the 31st of October, the parishioners, like those of other sections of the city, took courage, and sought to retrieve their past ill-conduct by noisily preparing to raise forces to defend themselves in case of a second visit from the Highlanders.

When peace came, Messrs. McVicar and Pitcairn, his coadjutor, continued faithfully and successfully to discharge the duties of the ministry.

In 1747 Mr. McVicar, when about to deliver one of the old Thursday sermons, suddenly dropped down dead; and amid a vast concourse of sorrowing parishioners was deposited in his tomb, which has a plain marble monument. A well-painted portrait of him hangs in the vestry of the present church.

His colleague, the Rev. Thomas Pitcairn, followed him on the 13th of June, 1751, and a pyramidal stone, erected to his memory by his youngest daughter, stands in the ancient burying-ground.

So early as 1738 attempts were made to violate graves, for surgical purposes, in the churchyard, which, of course, was then a lonely and sequestered place, and though the boundary walls were raised eight feet high, they failed to be a protection, as watchers who were appointed connived at, rather than prevented, a practice which filled the parishioners with rage and horror.

Hence, notwithstanding all the efforts of the Session to prevent such violation of tombs, several bodies· were abstracted in 1742. George Haldane, one of the beadles, was suspected of assisting in this repulsive practice; and on the 9th of May his house at Maryfield was surrounded by an infuriated mob, and burned to the ground.

The old church, which stood for ages, and had been in succession a Catholic, Presbyterian, Episcopalian, and finally a Presbyterian place of worship again, and which had been gutted and pillaged by Reformers and Cromwellians, and cannon-shotted in civil wars, was found to be dangerous, and condemned to be taken down. Although the edifice was insufficient, and in some parts dangerous, there was no immediate cause for the growing terror that pervaded the congregation, and culminated in a general alarm on Sunday, the 27th September, 1772. Part of a seat in one of the galleries gave way with a crash, on which the entire assembled mass rushed to the doors, and in an instant the church was empty.

A jury of tradesmen met to inspect the church, which they were of opinion should be taken down without delay; but this verdict had hardly been drawn up and read, than a fear seized them that the old church would fall and bury them in its ruins, on which they fled to the adjacent charity workhouse.

The work of demolition was begun forthwith, and when removing this venerable fane, the interior of which now, "formed after no plan, presented a multitude of petty galleries stuck up one above another to the very rafters, like so many pigeons'-nests," a curious example of what is named heart-burial came to light.

The workmen, says the *Scots Magazine* for September, 1773, discovered "a leaden coffin, which contained some bones and a leaden urn. Before opening the urn, a most fragrant smell issued out; on inspecting the cause of it, they found a human heart finely embalmed and in the highest state of preservation. No inscription was upon the coffin by which the date could be traced, but it must have been there for centuries. It is conjectured that the heart belonged to some person who, in the time of the Crusades, had gone to the Holy Land, and been there killed, and the heart, as was customary in those times, embalmed and sent home to be buried with some of the family."

Prior to the erection of the new church, the congregation assembled in a Methodist Chapel in the Low Calton.

In 1775 it was completed in the hideous taste and nameless style peculiar to Scottish ecclesiastical architecture during the times of the first three Georges. It cost £4,231, irrespective of its equally hideous steeple, and is seated for about 3,000 persons, and is now the mother church, associated with ten others, for a parish which includes a great part of the parliamentary burgh of the capital, and has a population of more than 140,000. The church, says a writer, "apart from its supplemental steeple, looks so like a huge stone box, that some wags have described it as resembling a packing-case, out of which the neighbouring beautiful toy-like fabric of St. John's Church has been lifted."

At the base of the spire is a fine piece of monumental sculpture, from the chisel of the late Handyside Ritchie, in memory of Dr. David Dickson, a worthy and zealous pastor, who was minister of the parish for forty years.

Some accounts state that Napier of Merchiston, the inventor of logarithms, was interred in the cemetery; but from an essay on the subject read before the Antiquarian Society by Professor William Wallace in 1832, there is conclusive evidence given, from a work he quoted, "that Napier was buried without the West Port of Edinburgh, in the church of St. Cuthbert," and in a vault, in the month of April, 1617.

The baronial family of Dean had also a vault in the old church, which still remains under the new, entering from the north. Above it is a monumental stone from the old church, to the memory of Henry Nisbet of that ilk, by whom we thus learn the vault was built. The arms of the Dean family are still above this black and gloomy vault; "a memorial alike of the de-molished fane and the extinct race," says Wilson in 1847. "When we last saw it the old oak door was broken in, and the stair that led down to the chamber of the dead was choked up with rank nettles and hemlock—the fittest monument that could be devised for the old barons of Dean, the last of them now gathered to his fathers."

One of the most interesting tombs here is that of Thomas de Quincey, the eccentric "English opium-eater," who was the friend of Professor Wilson, and died at Edinburgh on the 8th of December, 1859. It is reached by taking the first pathway upward to the right at the Lothian Road entrance.

On one of the south walls here, where for more than fifty years it hung unnoticed and forgotten, is a piece of monumental sculpture, by Flaxman, of very rare beauty—a square architectural mural monument, of a mixed Roman and Grecian style, of white and black marble, which was erected to commemorate the death of three infant children.

Two families—the Watsons of Muirhouse, and the Rocheids of Inverleith—retained the right of burial within the new church, under the steeple, which is 170 feet in height. Its bell, which is inscribed "George Watt fecit, St. Ninian's Row, Edin : 1791," was hung in that year.

In the west lobby of the church a handsome tablet bears the following inscription, removed, pro-bably, from the older edifice :—" Here lyes the corpse of the Honble. Sir James Rocheid of Inver-leith, who died the 1st day of May, 1737, in the 71st year of his age."

The last incumbent of the ancient church, Mr. Stewart, having died in April, 1775, was succeeded by the famous Sir Henry Wellwood Moncrieff, D.D., who for more than half a century was one of the greatest ornaments of the Scottish Church.

At St. Cuthbert's he soon became distinguished for his devoted zeal and fidelity in the discharge of his ministerial duties, for the mildness and benevo-lence of his disposition, for his genius, eloquence, and great personal worth. He soon became the leader of the Evangelical section of the church, and in 1785 was unanimously chosen Moderator of the General Assembly. He was appointed collector of the fund for the widows and children of the clergy, and filled that important situation till his death, and received annually the thanks of the Assembly for forty-three years. He was author of several sermons, and the funeral oration he preached on the death of Dr. Andrew Thomson, of St. George's, was long remembered for its power, pathos, and tenderness. He died in 1827 of a lingering illness, in the 78th year of his age and 57th of his ministry.

In its greatest length, *quoad civilia*, in 1835, the parish measured upwards of five miles, and in its greatest breadth three and a half. But in 1834 territories were detached from it and formed into the *quoad sacra* parishes of Buccleuch, St. Bernard's, Newington, and Roxburgh. It was partly land-ward and partly town ; but, as regards population, is chiefly the latter now. The Crown is patron. Each of its two ministers has a manse.

Before quitting the church of St. Cuthbert a reference must be made to its old poor-house, a plain but lofty edifice, with two projecting wings (standing on the south side of what was latterly called Riding School Lane), and now removed.

At an early period a tax of £100 sterling had been laid on the parish to preclude begging, " and maintain those who had been accustomed to live on the charity of others." In 1739, at a meeting of heritors and the Session, the former protested against the levy of this old impost, on the plea " that the poor's funds were sufficient to maintain the poor in the landward part of the parish, with whom only the heritors were concerned ; while the poor living in Pleasance, Potter Row, Bristo, West Port, &c., fell to be maintained by the town in whose suburbs they were."

The assessment was thus abandoned, and an ancient practice was resorted to : the mendicant poor were furnished with metal badges, entitling them to solicit alms within the parish. The number furnished with this unenviable distinction amounted to fifty-eight in 1744, and the number of enrolled poor to 220, for whose support £200 sterling were expended. In 1754 the Kirk Session presented a memorial to the magistrates, craving a moiety of the duty levied on ale for the support of their poor, whereupon a wing was added to the city workhouse for the reception of St. Cuthbert's mendicants.

In June 1759 a subscription was opened for building a workhouse in the West Kirk parish ; the money obtained amounted to £553 sterling for the house, and £196 8s. of annual subscrip-tions for the support of its inmates—a small proof that the incubus or inertia which had so long affected Edinburgh was now passing away ; and the building was commenced on the south side of a tortuous lane, St. Cuthbert's, that then ran be-tween hedgerows from opposite the churchyard gate towards the place named the Grove. It was completed by the year 1761, at a cost of about £1,565 sterling. The expenses of the house were defrayed partly by collections at the church doors and by an assessment on the real property within the parish ; the expense for each inmate in those days was only £4 1s. 6d. On the demolition of the old church, its pulpit, which was of oak, of a very ancient form, and covered with carving, was placed in the hall of the workhouse. The number of the inmates in the first year was eighty-four. The edifice, large and unsightly, was removed, with the Diorama and several other houses, to make space for the Caledonian railway, and the poor of St. Cuthbert's were conveyed to a more airy and commodious mansion, on the site of the old farm-house of Werter.

When the Act of Parliament in 1767 was obtained for extending the royalty of the city of Edinburgh, clauses were inserted in it disjoining a great portion of the ground on which the future new city was to be built, and annexing it to the parish of St. Giles, under the condition that the heritors of the lands should continue liable, as formerly, for tithes, ministers' stipends, and £300 annually of poor's money. Thus the modern parishes of St. Andrew, St. George, St. Mary, and St. Stephen—all formed since that period—have been taken from the great area of the ancient parish of St. Cuthbert.

No very material alteration was made in the burying-ground till April, 1787, when the north side of it, which was bordered by a marsh 2,000 feet in length (to the foot of the mound) by 350 broad—as shown in the maps of that year—was drained and partially filled with earth. Then the walls and gates were repaired. The ground at the east end was raised a few years after, and

enclosed by a wall, on which a line of tombs is now erected.

In the eighteenth century the building of note nearest to the church of St. Cuthbert, on the opposite side of the way, now named Lothian Road, was a tall, narrow, three-storeyed country villa, called, from its situation at the head of the slope, Kirk-braehead House. There the way parted from the straight line of the modern road at the kirk-gate, forming a delta (the upper base of which was the line of Princes Street), in which were several cottages and gardens, long since swept away. A row of cottages lay along the whole line of what is now Queensferry Street, under the name of Kirkbraehead.

OLD WEST KIRK, AND WALLS OF THE LITTLE KIRK, 1772. *(From an Engraving of a Drawing from a Model.)*

The villa referred to was, towards the close of the century, occupied by Lieutenant-General John Lord Elphinstone, who was Lieutenant-Governor of the Castle, with the moderate stipend of £182 10s. yearly, and who died in 1794.

At a subsequent period its occupant was a Mr. John Butler, who figures among "Kay's Portraits," an eccentric character but skilful workman, who was king's carpenter for Scotland; he built Gayfield House and the house of Sir Lawrence Dundas, now the Royal Bank in St. Andrew Square. He was proprietor of several tenements in Carrubber's Close, then one of the most fashionable portions of the old town.

The villa of Kirkbraehead had been built by his father ere the Lothian Road was formed, and concerning the latter, the following account is given by Kay's editor and others.

This road, which leaves the western extremity of Princes Street at a right angle, and runs southward

towards Bruntsfield Links, had long been projected, but owing to the objections raised by the
proprietors of many barns, byres, and sheds which
stood in the way, the plan could not be matured,
till after several years of trouble and speculation;

in length by twenty paces in breadth." This
scheme he concerted with address, and executed
with nautical promptitude. It happened to be the
winter season, when many men were unemployed.
He had no difficulty in collecting several hundreds

ST. CUTHBERT'S CHURCH.

and when at last the proposal was about to be
agreed to by the opposing parties, the broad and
stately road was—to the surprise of the public and
mortification of the opposition—made in one day !
    It so happened that a gentleman, said to be Sir
John Clerk, Bart., of Pennicuik (an officer of the
royal navy, who succeeded his father, Sir George,
in 1784), laid a bet with a friend to the effect
"that he would, between sunrise and sunset,
execute the line of road, extending nearly a mile

of these at the Kirkbraehead upon the appointed
morning before sunrise, when he gave them all a
plentiful breakfast of porter, whisky, and bread and
cheese, after which, just as the sun rose, he ordered
them to set to work; "some to tear down enclosures, others to unroof and demolish cottages,
and a considerable portion to bring earth wherewith to fill up the natural hollow (near the churchyard gate) to the required height. The inhabitants,
dismayed at so vast a force and so summary a

mode of procedure, made no resistance; and so active were the workmen that before sunset the road was sufficiently formed to allow the bettor to drive his carriage triumphantly over it, which he did amidst the acclamations of a great multitude of persons, who flocked from the town to witness the issue of this extraordinary undertaking. Among the instances of temporary distress occasioned to the inhabitants, the most laughable was that of a poor simple woman who had a cottage and small cow-feeding establishment upon the spot. It appears that this good creature had risen early, as usual, milked her cows, smoked her pipe, taken her ordinary matutinal tea, and lastly, recollecting that she had some friends invited to dine with her upon sheep-head and kail about noon, placed the pot upon the fire, in order that it might simmer peaceably till she should return from town, where she had to supply a numerous set of customers with the produce of her dairy. Our readers may judge the consternation of this poor woman when, upon her return from the duties of the morning, she found neither house, nor byre, nor cows, nor fire, nor pipe, nor pot, nor anything that was here upon the spot where she had left them but a few hours before. All had vanished, like the palace of Aladdin, leaving not a wrack behind."

Such was the origin of that broad and handsome street which now leads to where the Castle Barns stood of old.

The Kirkbraehead House was demolished in 1869, when the new Caledonian Railway Station was formed, and with it passed away the southern portion of the handsome modern thoroughfare named Rutland Street, and several other structures in the vicinity of the West Church.

Of these the most important was St. George's Free Church, built in 1845, at the north-east corner of Cuthbert's Lane, the line of which has since been turned into Rutland Street, in obedience to the inexorable requirements of the railway.

During its brief existence this edifice was alone famous for the ministrations of the celebrated Rev. Robert Candlish, D.D., one of the most popular of Scottish preachers, and one of the great leaders of the "Non Intrusion" party during those troubles which eventually led to the separation of the Scottish Church into two distinct sections, and the establishment of that Free Kirk to which we shall have often to refer. He was born about the commencement of the century, in 1807, and highly regarded as a debater. He was author of an "Exposition of the Book of Genesis," works on "The Atonement," "The Resurrection," "Life of

a Risen Saviour," and other important theological books. In 1861 he was Moderator of the Free Church Assembly.

The church near St. Cuthbert's was designed by the late David Cousin in the Norman style of architecture, and the whole edifice, which was highly ornate, after being carefully taken down, was re-constructed in its own mass in Deanhaugh Street, Stockbridge, as a free church for that locality.

While the present Free St. George's in Maitland Street was in course of erection, Dr. Candlish officiated to his congregation in the Music Hall, George Street. He died, deeply regretted by them and by all classes, on the 19th of October, 1873.

The next edifice of any importance demolished at the time was the Riding School, with the old Scottish Naval and Military Academy, so long superintended by an old officer of the Black Watch, and well-known citizen, Captain John Orr, who carried one of the colours of his regiment at Waterloo. It was a plain but rather elegant Grecian edifice, under patronage of the Crown, for training young men chiefly for the service of the royal and East India Company's services, and to all the ordinary branches of education were added fortification, military drawing, gun-drill, and military exercises; but just about the time its site was required by the railway the introduction of a certain amount of competitive examination at military colleges elsewhere rendered the institution unnecessary, though Scotland is certainly worthy of a military school of her own. Prior to its extinction the academy sufficed to send more than a thousand young men as officers into the army, many of whom have risen to distinction in every quarter of the globe.

The new station of the Caledonian Railway, which covered the sites of the buildings mentioned, and with its adjuncts has a frontage to the Lothian Road of 1,100 feet (to where it abuts upon the United Presbyterian Church) by about 800 feet at its greatest breadth, forms a spacious and handsome terminus, erected at the cost of more than £10,000, succeeding the more temporary station at first projected on the west side of the Lothian Road, about half a furlong to the south, and which was cleared and purchased at an enormous cost. It is a most commodious structure, with a main front 103 feet long and 22 feet high, yet designed only for temporary use, and is intended to give place to a permanent edifice of colossal proportions and more than usual magnificence, with a great palatial hotel to adjoin it, according to the custom now so common as regards great railway termini.

CHAPTER XIX.

GEORGE STREET.

Major Andrew Fraser—The Father of Miss Ferrier—Grant of Kilgraston—William Blackwood and his Magazine—The Mother of Sir Walter Scott—Sir John Hay, Banker—Colquhoun of Killermont—Mrs. Murray of Henderland—The Houses of Sir J. W. Gordon, Sir James Hall, and Sir John Sinclair of Ulbster—St. Andrew's Church—Scene of the Disruption—Physicians' Hall—Glance at the History of the College of Physicians—Sold and Removed—The Commercial Bank—Its Constitution—Assembly Rooms—Rules of 1789—Banquet to Black Watch—"The Author of Waverley"—The Music Hall—The New Union Bank—Its Formation, &c.—The Masonic Hall—Watson's Picture of Burns—Statues of George IV., Pitt, and Chalmers.

PREVIOUS to the brilliant streets and squares erected in the northern and western portions of new Edinburgh, George Street was said to have no rival in the world ; and even yet, after having undergone many changes, for combined length, space, uniformity, and magnificence of vista, whether viewed from the east or west, it may well be pronounced unparalleled. Straight as an arrow flies, it is like its sister streets, but is 115 feet broad. Here a great fossil tree was found in 1852.

A portion of the street on the south side, near the west end, long bore the name of the Tontine, and owing to some legal dispute, which left the houses there unfinished, they were occupied as infantry barracks during the war with France.

Nos. 3 and 5 (the latter once the residence of Major Andrew Fraser and of William Creech the eminent bookseller) form the office of the Standard Life Assurance Company, in the tympanum of which, over four fine Corinthian pilasters, is a sculptured group from the chisel of Sir John Steel, representing the parable of the Ten Virgins. In George Street are about thirty different insurance offices, or their branches, all more or less ornate in architecture, and several banks.

In No. 19, on the same side, is the Caledonian, the oldest Scottish insurance company (having been founded in June, 1805). Previously the office had been in Bank Street. A royal charter was granted to the company in May, 1810, and twenty-three years afterwards the business of life assurance was added to that of fire insurance.

No. 25 George Street was the residence (from 1784 till his death, in 1829), of Mr. James Ferrier, Principal Clerk of Session, and father of Miss Susan Ferrier, the authoress of "Marriage," &c. He was a keen whist player, and every night of his life had a rubber, which occasionally included Lady Augusta Clavering, daughter of his friend and client John, fifth Duke of Argyll, and old Dr. Hamilton, usually designated "Cocked Hat" Hamilton, from the fact of his being one of the last in Edinburgh who bore that head-piece. When victorious, he would snap his fingers and caper about the room, to the manifest indignation of Mr. Ferrier, who

would express it to his partner in the words, "Lady Augusta, did you ever see such rediculous leevity in an auld man ?" Robert Burns used also to be a guest at No. 25, and was present on one occasion when some magnificent Gobelins tapestry arrived there for the Duke of Argyll on its way to Inverary Castle. Mrs. Piozzi also, when in Edinburgh, dined there. Next door lived the Misses Edmonstone, of the Duntreath family, and with them pitched battles at whist were of frequent nightly occurrence. These old ladies figure in "Marriage" as Aunts Jacky, Grizzy, and Nicky ; they were grand-nieces of the fourth Duke of Argyll. The eldest Miss Ferrier was one of the Edinburgh beauties in her day ; and Burns once happening to meet her, while turning the corner of George Street, felt suddenly inspired, and wrote the lines to her enclosed in an elegy on the death of Sir D. H. Blair. Miss Ferrier and Miss Penelope Macdonald of Clanronald, were rival belles ; the former married General Graham of Stirling Castle, the latter Lord Belhaven.

In No. 32 dwelt Francis Grant of Kilgraston, father of Sir Francis Grant, President of the Royal Academy, born in 1803 ; and No. 35, now a shop, was the town house of the Blairs of Balthayock, in Perthshire.

No. 45 has long been famous as the establishment of Messrs. Blackwood, the eminent publishers. William Blackwood, the founder of the magazine which stills bears his name, and on the model of which so many high-class periodicals have been started in the sister kingdom, was born at Edinburgh in 1776, and after being apprenticed to the ancient bookselling firm of Bell and Bradfute, and engaging in various connections with other bibliopoles, in 1804 he commenced as a dealer in old books on the South Bridge, in No. 64, but soon after became agent for several London publishing houses. In 1816 he disposed of his vast stock of classical and antiquarian books, 15,000 volumes in number, and removing to No. 17 Princes Street, thenceforward devoted his energies to the business of a general publisher, and No. 17 is to this day a bookseller's shop.

In October, 1817, he brought out the first number of that celebrated magazine which has enrolled among its contributors the names of Wilson, Scott, Henry Mackenzie, J. McCrie, Brewster, De Quincey, Hamilton (the author of "Cyril Thornton"), Aytoun, Alison, Lockhart, Bulwer, Warren, James Hogg. Dr. Moir, and a host of others. This periodical had a predecessor, *The Edinburgh Monthly Magazine*, projected in April, 1817, and edited by Thomas Pringle, a able and interesting papers, contained three calculated to create curiosity, offence, and excitement. The first was a fierce assault on Coleridge's *Biographia Literaria*, which was stigmatised as a "most execrable" performance, and its author "a miserable compound of egotism and malignity." The second was a still more bitter attack on Leigh Hunt, who was denounced as a "profligate creature," one "without reverence for either God or man." The third was the famous

KIRKBRAEHEAD HOUSE. *(After Clerk of Eldin.)*

highly-esteemed poet and miscellaneous writer, the son of a farmer in Teviotdale, and this falling into the hands of new proprietors, became the famous *Blackwood's Magazine*.

This was consequently No. VII. of the series, though the first of *Blackwood.* "In the previous six numbers there had been nothing allowed to creep in that could possibly offend the most zealous partisan of the blue and yellow," says Mrs. Gordon, in her "Life of Professor Wilson." In the first Number the *Edinburgh Review* had been praised for its moderation, ability, and delicate taste. and politics were rather eschewed; but Number seven "spoke a different language, and proclaimed a new and sterner creed," and among

"Chaldee Manuscript," the effect of which upon the then circle of Edinburgh society can hardly be realised now ; but this pungent *jeu d'esprit*, of which it is scarcely necessary to give any account here, is still preserved in Volume IV. of the works of Professor Wilson.

The sensation excited by the new magazine was kept up by all the successive numbers, though for some months no one was attacked ; but the subjects discussed were handled in a masterly manner, and exhibited a variety of talent that could not fail to influence and command the respect of all ; and it has been said that the early defects of the magazine are nowhere better analysed than by the hands of those who did the work—the authors of " Peter's

GEORGE STREET, EDINBURGH.

19

Letters," &c. At what precise period Professor Wilson came into personal communication with old William Blackwood is not quite known, but he had been for some time an anonymous contributor, under the initial N. His last papers, Nos. 9 and 10 of "Dies Boreales," were written, we believe, in the autumn of 1852. William Blackwood himself never wrote more than two or three articles for the earlier numbers, but the whole management and arrangement devolved upon him at No. 17

First there is, as usual, a spacious place set apart for retail business, and a numerous detachment of young clerks and apprentices, to whose management that important department of the concern is entrusted. Then you have an elegant oval saloon, lighted from the roof, where various groups of loungers and literary *dilettanti* are engaged at, or criticising amongst themselves, the publications just arrived by that day's coach from London. In such critical colloquies the voice of the bookseller

THE SALOON IN MESSRS. BLACKWOODS' ESTABLISHMENT.

Princes Street, and he executed the editorial duties with unusual skill, tact, and vigour. He was still there in 1823, when Leigh Hunt threatened legal proceedings against the magazine—"a cockney crow," as Lockhart called it in one of his letters to Wilson; adding, "Who the devil cares for all cockneydom?"

His establishment in 45 George Street is very like what we find it described as having been in "Peter's Letters" (Vol. II.):—"The length of vista presented to one on entering the shop has a very imposing effect, for it is carried back, room after room, through various gradations of light and shadow, till the eye cannot distinctly trace the outline of any object in the farthest distance.

himself may ever and anon be heard mingling the broad and unadulterated notes of its Auld Reekie music; for, unless occupied in the recesses of the premises with some other business, it is here he has his usual station. He is a nimble, active-looking man, of middle age, and moves about from one corner to another with great alacrity, and apparently under the influence of high animal spirits. His complexion is very sanguineous, but nothing can be more intelligent, keen, and sagacious than the expression of the whole physiognomy; above all, the grey eyes and eyebrows, as full of locomotion as those of Catalani. The remarks he makes are, in general, extremely acute—much more so, indeed, than those of any other member of the trade I ever heard speak on such topics. The shrewdness and decision of the man can, however, stand in need of no testimony beyond what his own conduct has afforded—above all, in the establishment of his magazine (the conception of which, I am assured, was entirely his own), and the subsequent energy with which he has supported it through every variety of good and evil fortune."

Like other highly successful periodicals, *Blackwood's Magazine* has paid the penalty of its greatness, for many serial publications have been projected upon its plan and scope, without its inherent originality and vigour.

William Blackwood published the principal works of Wilson, Lockhart, Hogg, Galt, Moir, and other distinguished contributors to the magazine, as well as several productions of Sir Walter Scott. He was twice a magistrate of his native city, and in that capacity took a prominent part in its affairs. He died on the 16th of September, 1834, in his fifty-eighth year.

"Four months of suffering, in part intense," says the *Magazine* for October, 1837, "exhausted by slow degrees all his physical energies, but left his temper calm and unruffled, and his intellect entire and vigorous to the last. He had thus what no good man will consider as a slight privilege : that of contemplating the approach of death with the clearness and full strength of his mind and faculties, and of instructing those around him by the solemn precept and memorable example, by what means humanity alone, conscious of its own frailty, can sustain that prospect with humble serenity."

This is evidently from the pen of John Wilson, in whose relations with the magazine this death made no change.

William Blackwood left a widow, seven sons, and two daughters ; the former carried on—and their grandsons still carry on—the business in the old establishment in George Street, which, since Constable passed away, has been the great literary centre of Edinburgh.

No. 49, the house of Wilkie of Foulden, is now a great music saloon ; and No. 75, now the County Fire and other public offices, has a peculiar interest, as there lived and died the mother of Sir Walter Scott—Anne Rutherford, daughter of Dr. John Rutherford, a woman who, the biographer of her illustrious son tells us, was possessed of superior natural talents, with a good taste for music and poetry and great conversational powers. In her youth she is said to have been acquainted with Allan Ramsay, Beattie, Blacklock, and many other Scottish men of letters in the last century ; and independently of the influence which her own

talents and acquirements may have given her in training the opening mind of the future novelist, it is obvious that he must have been much indebted to her in early life for the select and intellectual literary society of which her near relations were the ornaments—for she was the daughter of a professor and the sister of a professor, both of the University of Edinburgh.

Her demise, on the 24th of December, 1820, is simply recorded thus in the obituary :—" At her house in George Street, Edinburgh, Mrs. Anne Rutherford, widow of the late Walter Scott, Writer to the Signet."

In the same house in George Street is the Scottish Provident Institution, founded by James Cleghorn, a man more fortunate in his financial than his literary undertakings, who, in his day, acquired a certain position as editor of the *Farmer's Magazine*, and who, as he was lame, and went on crutches, like Thomas Pringle (already referred to), was represented in the famous " Chaldee Manuscript " as "skipping on stones." Mr. Cleghorn died in 1838, and a monument has been erected by the institution he founded, over his grave in Warriston cemetery.

No. 78 was, in 1811, the house of Sir John Hay of Smithfield and Hayston, Baronet, banker, who married Mary, daughter of James, sixteenth Lord Forbes. He had succeeded to the title in the preceding year, on the death of his father, Sir James, and is thus referred to in the scarce " Memoirs of a Banking House," by Sir William Forbes of Pitsligo, Bart. :—

" Three years afterwards we made a further change in the administration by the admission of my brother-in-law, Mr. John Hay, as a partner. In the year 1774, at my request, Sir Robert Herries had agreed that he should go to Spain, and serve an apprenticeship in his house at Barcelona, where he continued till spring, 1776, when he returned to London, and was received by Sir Robert into his house in the City—from which, by that time, our separation had taken place—and where, as well as in the banking house in St. James's Street, he acted as a clerk till summer, 1778, when he came to Edinburgh, and entered our country house also, on the footing of a confidential clerk, during three years. Having thus had an ample experience of his abilities and merit as a man of business, on whom we might repose the most implicit confidence, a new contract of co-partnery was formed, to commence from the 1st of January, 1782, in which Mr. Hay was assumed as a partner, and the shares stood as follow : Sir William Forbes, nineteen, Mr. Hunter Blair, nineteen, Mr. Bartlett, six, Mr. Hay, four—in all, forty-eight shares." From that time he grew in wealth and fame with the establishment, which is now merged in the Joint-stock Union Bank of Scotland. Sir John Hay died in 1830, in his seventy-fifth year.

No. 86 was the house of his nephew, Sir William Forbes, Bart., who succeeded to the title on the death of the eminent banker in 1806, and who married the sole daughter and heiress of Sir John Stuart of Fettercairn, whose arms were thus quartered with his own.

In May, 1810, Lord Jeffrey—then at the bar as a practising advocate—took up his dwelling in No. 92, and it was while there resident that, in consequence of some generous and friendly criticism in the *Edinburgh Review*, pleasant relations were established between him and Professor Wilson, which, says the daughter of the latter, "led to a still closer intimacy, and which, though unhappily interrupted by subsequent events, was renewed in after years, when the bitterness of old controversies had yielded to the hallowing influences of time." Lord Jeffrey resided here for seventeen years.

In the second storey of No. 108 Sir Walter Scott dwelt in 1797, when actively engaged in his German translations and forming the Edinburgh Volunteer Light Horse, of which he was in that year, to his great gratification, made quartermaster. Two doors farther on was the house of the Countess of Balcarres, the venerable dowager of Earl Alexander, who died in 1768. She was Anne, daughter of Sir Robert Dalrymple of Castleton.

No. 116, now formed into shops, was long the residence of Archibald Colquhoun of Killermont, Lord Advocate of Scotland in 1807. He was Archibald Campbell of Clathick, but assumed the name of Colquhoun on succeeding to the estate of Killermont. He came to the bar in the same year, 1768, or about the same time as his friends Lord Craig and the Hon. Henry Erskine. He succeeded Lord Frederick Campbell as Lord Clerk Register in 1816. His mind and talents were said to have been of a very superior order; he was a sound lawyer, an eloquent pleader, and his independent fortune and proud reserve induced him to avoid general business, while in his Parliamentary duties as member for Dumbarton he was unremitting and efficient. He died in 1820.

The Edinburgh Association of Science and Arts now occupies the former residence of the Butters of Pitlochry, No. 117. It is an institution formed in 1869, and its title is sufficiently explanatory of its objects.

An interesting lady of the old school abode long in No. 122—Mrs. Murray of Henderland. She was resident there from the early part of the present century. The late Dr. Robert Chambers tells us he was introduced to her by Dr. Chalmers, and found her memories of the past went back to the first years of the reign of George III. Her husband, Alexander Murray, had been, he states, Lord North's Solicitor-General for Scotland. His name appears in 1775 on the list, between those of Henry Dundas and Islay Campbell of Succoth. "I found the venerable lady seated at a window of her drawing-room in George Street, with her daughter, Miss Murray, taking the care of her which her extreme age required, and with some help from this lady we had a conversation of about an hour." She was born before the Porteous Mob, and well remembering the '45, was now close on her hundredth year.

She spoke with affection and reverence of her mother's brother, Lord Chief Justice Mansfield; "and when I adverted," says Chambers, "to the long pamphlet written against him by Athenian Stuart, at the conclusion of the Douglas cause, she said that, to her knowledge, he never read it, such being his practice in respect to all attacks made upon him, lest they should disturb his equanimity in judgment. As the old lady was on intimate terms with Boswell, and had seen Johnson on his visit to Edinburgh—as she was the sister-in-law of Allan Ramsay, the painter, and had lived in the most cultivated society of Scotland all her life—there were ample materials for conversation with her; but her small strength made this shorter and slower than I could have wished. When we came upon the poet Ramsay, she seemed to have caught new vigour from the subject; she spoke with animation of the child-parties she had attended in his house on the Castle Hill during a course of ten years before his death—an event which happened in 1757. He was ' charming,' she said; he entered so heartily into the plays of the children. He, in particular, gained their hearts by making houses for their dolls. How pleasant it was to learn that our great pastoral poet was a man who, in his private capacity, loved to sweeten the daily life of his fellow-creatures, and particularly of the young! At a warning from Miss Murray I had to tear myself away from this delightful and never-to-be-forgotten interview."

From this we may suppose that the worthy publisher never saw the venerable occupant of No. 122 again.

No. 123, on the opposite side, was the residence of the well-known Sir John Watson Gordon, President of the Royal Scottish Academy, who died June 1st, 1863, and to whom reference has already been made in the account of that institution, of which he was the distinguished head. Its site is now occupied by the office of the Scottish-American Company; and the vast Elizabethan edifice near it is the auction rooms of Dowell and Co., built in 1880.

The Mercantile Bank of India, London, and China occupies No. 128, formerly the mansion of Sir James Hall of Dunglass, Bart., a man in his time eminent for his high attainments in geological and chemical science, and author of popular but peculiar works on Gothic architecture. By his wife, Lady Helena Douglas, daughter of Dunbar, Earl of Selkirk, he had three sons and three daughters—his second son being the well-known Captain Basil Hall, R.N. While retaining his house in George Street, Sir James, between 1808 and 1812, represented the Cornish borough of St. Michael's in Parliament. He died at Edinburgh, after a long illness, on the 23rd of June, 1832.

Collaterally with him, another distinguished baronet, Sir John Sinclair of Ulbster, was long the occupant of No. 133, to the print of whom Kay appends the simple title of "The Scottish Patriot," and never was it more appropriately applied. To attempt even an outline of his long, active, and most useful life, would go far beyond our limits; suffice it to say, that his "Code of Agriculture" alone has been translated into nearly every European language. He was born at Thurso in 1754, and so active had been his mind, so vast the number of his scientific pursuits and objects, that by 1797 he began to suffer seriously from the effects of his over-exertions, and being thus led to consider the subject of health generally, he published, in 1803, a quarto pamphlet, entitled "Hints on Longevity" —afterwards, in 1807, extended to four volumes 8vo. In 1810 he was made a Privy Councillor, and in the following year, under the administration of the unfortunate Mr. Perceval, was appointed Cashier of Excise for Scotland. On retiring from Parliament, he was succeeded as member for Caithness by his son. He resided in Edinburgh for the last twenty years of his life, and died at his house in George Street in December, 1835, in his eighty-first year, and was interred in the Chapel Royal at Holyrood.-

Sir John was twice married. By his first wife he had two children; by the second, Diana, daughter of Lord Macdonald, he had thirteen, one of whom, Julia, became Countess of Glasgow. All these attained a stature like his own, so great—being nearly all above six feet—that he was wont playfully to designate the pavement before No. 133 as "The Giants' Causeway."

St. Andrew's church stands 200 feet westward of St. Andrew's Square; it is a plain building of oval form, with a handsome portico, having four great Corinthian pillars, and built, says Kincaid, from a design of Major Fraser, of the Engineers, whose residence was close by it. It was erected in 1785.

It was at first proposed to have a spire of some design, now unknown, between the portico and the body of the church, and for a model of this a young man of the city, named M'Leish, received a premium of sixty guineas from the magistrates, with the freedom of the city; but on consideration, his design "was too great in proportion to the space left for its base." So the present spire, which is 168 feet in height, and for its sky-line is one of the most beautiful in the city, was designed by Major Andrew Fraser, who declined to accept any premium, suggesting that it should be awarded to Mr. Robert Kay, whose designs for a square church on the spot were most meritorious.

The last stone of the spire was placed thereon on the 23rd of November, 1787. A chime of bells was placed in it, 3rd June, 1789, "to be rung in the English manner."

The dimensions of this church, as given by Kincaid, are, within the walls from east to west eighty-seven feet, and from north to south sixty-four feet. "The front, consisting of a staircase and portico, measures forty-one feet, and projects twenty-six feet and a half feet." The entrance is nine feet in height by seven feet in breadth.

This parish was separated from St. Cuthbert's in 1785, and since that date parts of it have been assigned to other parishes of more recent erection as the population increased.

The church cost £7,000, and is seated for about 1,053. The charge is collegiate, and is chiefly remarkable for the General Assembly's meeting in 1843, at which occurred the great Disruption, or exodus of the Free Church—one of the most important events in the modern history of Scotland or of the United Kingdom.

It originated in a zealous movement of the Presbyterian Church, mainly promoted by the great Chalmers, to put an end to the connection between Church and State. In 1834 the Church had passed a law of its own, ordaining that thenceforth no presentee to a parish should be admitted if opposed by the majority of the male communicants—a law which struck at the system of patronage restored after the Union—a system involving important civil rights.

When the Annual Assembly met in St. Andrew's Church, in May, 1843, it was generally understood that a great schism would take place ; but calm onlookers believed that a mere few would relinquish their comfortable stipends, their pleasant manses, and present advantages of position.

Under its moderator, Dr. Welsh, and in presence

protest against further procedure, in consequence of the proceedings affecting the rights of the Church which had been sanctioned by Her Majesty's Government and by the Legislature." After reading a formal protest, signed by 120 ministers and

ST. ANDREW'S CHURCH.

of the Queen's High Commissioner and a brilliant assemblage of spectators, the Assembly met, while a vast multitude thronged the broad area of George Street, breathlessly awaiting the result, and "prepared to see the miserable show of eight or ten men voluntarily sacrificing themselves to what was thought a fantastic principle."

When the time came for making up the roll of members, Dr. Welsh rose, and said that "he must

seventy-two elders, he left his place, followed first by Dr. Chalmers and other prominent men, till the number amounted to *four hundred and seventy*, who poured forth along the streets, where general astonishment, not unmingled with sorrow, admiration, and alarm, prevailed.

When Lord Jeffrey was told of it, an hour after, he exclaimed, "Thank God for Scotland ! there is not another country on earth where such a deed could be done." On leaving the church, the protestors proceeded to Tanfield Hall, Canonmills, where they formed themselves into "The General Assembly of the Free Church of Scotland," and chose Thomas Chalmers, D.D., as their moderator; so "the bush burned, but was not consumed."

It was a remarkable instance of the emphatic assertion of religious principle in an age of material things of which St. Andrew's church was the scene on the 18th of May. It was no sacrifice of blood or life or limb that was exacted, or rendered, as in the days of "a broken covenant;" but it was one well calculated to excite the keenest emotions of the people—for all these clergymen, with their families, cast their bread upon the waters, and those who witnessed the dark procession that descended the long steep street towards Tanfield Hall never forgot it.

Opposite this church there was built the old Physicians' Hall—the successor of the still more ancient one near the Cowgate Port. The members of that college feued from the city a large area, extending between the south side of George Street and Rose Street, on which they erected a very handsome hall, with rooms and offices, from a design by Mr. Craig, the architect of the new city itself.

The foundation stone was laid by Professor Cullen, long a distinguished ornament of the Edinburgh University, on the 27th November, 1775, after a long discussion concerning two other sites offered by the city, one in George Square, the other where now the Scott monument stands. In the stone was placed a parchment containing the names of the then fellows, several coins of 1771, and a large silver medal. There was also another silver medal, with the arms of the city, and an inscription bearing that it had been presented by the city to Mr. Craig, in compliment to his professional talents in 1767, as follows :—

JACOBO CRAIG,
ARCHITECTO,
PROPTER OPTIMUM,
EDINBURGI NOVI
ICHNOGRAPHIUM,
D.D.
SENATUS,
EDINBURGENSIS,
MDCCLXVII.

This building, now numbered among the things that were, had a frontage of eighty-four feet, and had a portico of four very fine Corinthian columns, standing six feet from the wall upon a flight of steps seven feet above the pavement. The sunk floor, which was all vaulted, contained rooms for the librarian and other officials; the entrance floor consisted of four great apartments opening from a noble vestibule, with a centre of thirty-five feet : one was for the ordinary meetings of the college, and another was an ante-chamber; but the principal apartment was the library—a room upwards of fifty feet long by thirty broad, lighted by two rows of windows, five in each row, facing Rose Street, and having a gilded gallery on three sides. On this edifice £4,800 was spent.

In 1781, the library, which had been stored up in the Royal Infirmary, was removed to the hall, when the collection, which now greatly exceeds 6,000 volumes, was still comparatively in its infancy. Dr. Archibald Stevenson was the first librarian, and was appointed in 1683; in 1696 a law was enacted that every entrant should contribute at least one book to the library, which was increased in 1705 "by the purchase of the books of the deceased Laird of Livingstone for about 300 merks Scots;" and the records show how year by year the collection has gone on increasing in extent, and in literary and scientific value.

The two oldest names on the list of Fellows admitted are Peter Kello, date December 11th, 1682, and John Abernethy, whose diploma is dated June 9th, 1683, granted at Orange, and admitted December 4th, 1684, and a wonderful roll follows of names renowned in the annals of medicine. The attempt to incorporate the practitioners of medicine in Scotland, for the purpose of raising alike the standard of their character and acquirements, originated in 1617, when James VI. issued an order in Parliament for the establishment of a College of Physicians in Edinburgh—an order which recites the evils suffered by the community from the intrusion of unqualified practitioners. He further suggested that three members of the proposed college should yearly visit the apothecaries' shops, and destroy all bad or insufficient drugs found therein; but the year 1630 came, and found only a renewal of the proposal for a college, referred to the Privy Council by Charles I. But the civil war followed, and nothing more was done till 1656, when Cromwell issued a patent, still extant, initiating a college of physicians in Scotland, with the powers proposed by James VI.

Years passed on, and by the opposition principally of the College of Surgeons, the universities, the municipality, and even the clergy, the charter of incorporation was not obtained until 1681, when the great seal of Scotland was appended to it on St. Andrew's day. Among other clauses therein was one to enforce penalties on the unqualified who practised medicine; another for the punishment of all licentiates who might violate the laws of the college, which had entire control over the drugs of apothecaries and chemists. It further protected Fellows from sitting on juries.

Under this charter the college continued to discharge its functions for many years, although it eventually abandoned in practice the exclusive rights conferred on it, and ceased to exercise any inspection over the shops of apothecaries as the changes of social position and necessity caused many of the provisions to fall into abeyance. Having become sensible of the advantages that would accrue to it from a new charter, to the end that it might be free from the obligation of admitting to its license all Scottish University graduates without examination, to get rid of the clause prohibiting its connection with a medical school, and further, that it might have the power of expelling unworthy members, a new charter was prepared in 1843, but, after a great many delays and readjustments, was not obtained until the 16th of August, 1861.

The first president of the institution was Dr. Archibald Stevenson, who was elected on the 8th of December, 1681, and held the chair till 1684; his successor was Sir Robert Sibbald (of the house of Balgonie), an eminent physician, naturalist, and antiquary, who graduated in medicine at Leyden in 1661; but from the time of his election there is a hiatus in the records till the 30th of November, 1693, when we again find in the chair Dr. Archibald Stevenson, with the then considerable honour of knighthood.

It was when Sir Thomas Burnet, author of "Thesaurus Medicinæ Practicæ," London, 1673, was president, in 1696-8, that we find it recorded that certain ruinous buildings bordering on the Cowgate were converted by the college "into a pavilion-shaped cold bath, which was open to the inhabitants generally, at a charge for each ablution of twelve shillings Scots, and one penny to the servant; but those who subscribed one guinea annually might resort to it as often as they pleased."

Under the presidency of Dr. John Drummond, in 1722, a new hall was erected in the gardens at Fountain Close; but proving insufficient, the college was compelled to relinquish certain plans for an edifice, offered by Adam the architect, and to find a temporary asylum in the Royal Infirmary. In 1770 the premises at Fountain Close were sold for £800; more money was raised by mortgage and other means, and the hall we have described was erected in George Street, only to be relinquished in time, after about seventy years' occupancy. "The same poverty," says the "Historical Sketch,"

"which had prevented the college from availing itself of the plans of Adam, and which had caused it to desire to part with its new hall in George Street, even before its occupation, still pressed heavily upon it. Having at that time no funded capital, it was entirely dependent on the entrance-fees paid by Fellows, a fluctuating and inadequate source of income. Besides, beautiful as the George Street hall was in its outward proportions, its internal arrangements were not so convenient as might have been desired, and it is therefore not to be wondered at that when the college found their site was coveted by a wealthy banking corporation their poverty and not their will consented; and in 1843 the George Street hall was sold to the Commercial Bank for £20,000—a sum which it was hoped would suffice to build a more comfortable if less imposing, hall, and leave a surplus to secure a certain, though possibly a small, annual income. Although the transaction was obviously an advantageous one for the college, it was not without some difficulty that many of the Fellows made up their minds to part with a building of which they were justly proud."

The beautiful hall was accordingly demolished to the foundation stone, in which were found the silver medals and other relics now in possession of the college, which rented for its use No. 121, George Street till the completion of its new hall, whither we shall shortly follow it.

On its site was built, in 1847, the Commercial Bank, an imposing structure of mingled Greek and Roman character, designed by David Rhind, an architect of high reputation. The magnificent portico is hexastyle. There are ninety-five feet in length of façade, the columns are thirty-five feet in height, with an entablature of nine feet; the pediment is fifteen feet six inches in height, and holds in its tympanum a beautiful group of emblematic sculpture from the chisel of A. Handyside Ritchie, which figures on the notes of the bank. It has a spacious and elegant telling-room, surrounded by tall Corinthian pillars, with a vaulted roof, measuring ninety feet by fifty. The Commercial Bank of Scotland and the National Bank of Scotland have been incorporated by royal charter; but as there is no doubt about their being unlimited, they are considered, with the Scottish joint stock banks, of recent creation.

The deed of partnership of the Commercial Bank is dated 31st October, 1810, but subsequent alterations have taken place, none of which, however, in any way affect the principle named and confirmed in the charter. The capital of the bank was declared at £3,000,000; but only a third of that sum has been called. It is expressly provided by the charter of the bank, granted 5th August, 1831, "that nothing contained in these presents shall be construed as intended to limit the responsibility and liability of the individual partners of the said Corporation for the debts and engagements lawfully contracted by the said Corporation, which responsibility and liability is to remain as valid and effectual as if these presents had not been

most elegant of any in Britain." In addition to the ball-room, "there is to be a tea-room, fifty feet by thirty-six, which will also serve as a ball-room on ordinary occasions; also a grand saloon, thirty-eight feet by forty-four feet, besides other and smaller rooms. The whole expense will be 6,000 guineas, and the building is to be begun immediately. Another Assembly Room, on a smaller scale, is to be built immediately by the

INTERIOR OF ST. ANDREW'S CHURCH, GEORGE STREET.

granted, any law or practice to the contrary notwithstanding."

The branch of the Clydesdale Bank, a little farther westward on the other side, is a handsome building; but the next chief edifice—which, with its arcade of three rustic arches and portico, was long deemed by those obstinately wedded to use and wont both an eyesore and encroachment on the old monotonous amenity of George Street, when first erected—is the Assembly Rooms.

The principal dancing-hall here is ninety-two feet long by forty-two feet wide, and forty feet high, adorned with magnificent crystal lustres. "The New Assembly Rooms, for which the ground is staked out in the new town," says the *Edinburgh Advertiser* for April, 1783, "will be among the

inhabitants on the south side of the town, in George Square." Eventually this room was placed in Buccleuch Place. "Since the peace," continues the paper, "a great deal of ground has been feued for houses in the new town, and the buildings there are going on with astonishing rapidity."

To the assemblies of 1783, the letters of Theophrastus inform us that gentlemen were in the habit of reeling "from the tavern, flustered with wine, to an assembly of as elegant and beautiful women as any in Europe;" also that minuets had gone out of fashion, and country dances were chiefly in vogue, and that in 1787 a master of the ceremonies was appointed. The weekly assemblies here in the Edinburgh season are now among the most brilliant and best conducted in Europe; but the regulations as issued for them a century ago may amuse their frequenters in the present day, and we copy them verbatim.

"NEW ASSEMBLY ROOMS,
GEORGE STREET.

"THE proprietors finding that the mode they proposed for subscribing to the assemblies this winter has not met with general approbation, did, at a general meeting, held 12th January, come to the following resolutions as to the mode of admission in future :—

"Subscription books are open at the house of the Master of the Ceremonies, William Graham, Esq., No. 66, Princes Street, and Mr. William Sanderson, merchant, in the Luckenbooths, to either of whom the nobility and gentry intending to subscribe are requested to send their names and subscription money, when they will receive their tickets. The first assembly (of the season) to be on Thursday, the 29th January, 1789."

Prior to the erection of the adjoining music hall many great banquets and public meetings

OLD PHYSICIANS' HALL, GEORGE STREET, 1829. (*After Shepherd.*)

"I. That the ladies' subscription shall be one guinea.

"II. That subscriptions for gentlemen who are proprietors of the rooms shall be one guinea.

"III. That the subscription for gentlemen who are *not* proprietors of the rooms shall be two guineas.

"IV. That each subscriber shall have twenty-four admission tickets.

"V. Subscribers when absent to have the power of granting two of these tickets for each assembly, either to a lady or gentleman, and no more; when present, only one; and no ticket will procure admittance unless dated and signed by the granter; and the tickets thus granted are not transferable.

"VI. Each non-subscriber to pay 3s. at the door on presenting his ticket.

"VII. Each director is allowed two additional tickets extraordinary for each assembly, which he may transfer, adding the word *Director* to his signature.

"VIII. *No admission without a ticket on any account whatever.*

took place in the great ball-room. One of the most interesting of these was the second ovation bestowed on the famous Black Watch in 1816.

There had been a grand reception of the regiment in 1802, on its return from Egypt, when a new set of colours, decorated with the Sphinx, after a prayer by Principal Baird, were bestowed upon the war-worn Highland battalion on the Castle Hill by General Vyse, amid a vast concourse of enthusiastic spectators; but a still greater ovation and a banquet awaited the regiment on its return to Edinburgh Castle in the year after Waterloo.

It entered the city in two divisions on the 19th and 20th March, 1816. Colonel Dick of Tully-bole, who afterwards fell in India, rode at the head of the first, accompanied by Major-General Hope and that famous old literary officer General Stewart of Garth, who had been wounded under its colours in Egypt; and nothing could surpass the grand, even tearful, enthusiasm with which the veterans had been welcomed "in every town and village through which their route from England lay. Early on the 19th," says the *Scots Magazine*, "vast crowds were collected on the streets, in expectation of their arrival. The road as far as Musselburgh was crowded with people ; and as they approached the city, so much was their progress impeded by the multitude that their march from Piershill to the castle—less than two miles—occupied two hours. House-tops and windows were crowded with spectators, and as they passed along the streets, amid the ringing of bells, waving of flags, and the acclamation of thousands, their red and black plumes, tattered colours—emblems of their well-earned fame in fight—and glittering bayonets, were all that could be seen of these heroes, except by the few who were fortunate in obtaining elevated situations. The scene, viewed from the windows and house-tops, was the most extraordinary ever witnessed in this city. The crowds were wedged together across the whole breadth of the street, and extended in length as far as the eye could reach, and this motley throng appeared to move like a solid body, till the gallant Highlanders were safely lodged in the castle."

To the whole of the non-commissioned officers and privates a grand banquet by public subscription, under the superintendence of Sir Walter Scott, was given in the Assembly Room, and every man was presented with a free ticket to the Theatre Royal. A similar banquet and ovation was bestowed on the 78th or Ross-shire Buffs, who marched in a few days after.

It was in the Assembly Rooms that Sir Walter Scott, on the 23rd February, 1827, at the annual dinner of the Edinburgh Theatrical Fund Association, avowed himself to be "the Great Unknown," acknowledging the authorship of the Waverley Novels—scarcely a secret then, as the recent exposure of Constable's affairs had made the circumstance pretty well known, particularly in literary circles.

In June 1841 a great public banquet was given to Charles Dickens in the Assembly Rooms, at which Professor Wilson presided, and which the novelist subsequently referred to as having been a source of sincere gratification to him.

The rooms underwent considerable improvements in 1871 ; but two shops have always been in the basement storey, and the western of these

is now occupied by the Edinburgh branch of the Imperial Fire and Life Assurance Company.

In immediate connection with the Assembly Rooms is the great music hall, built in 1843, at the cost of more than £10,000. It is a magnificent apartment, with a vast domed and panelled roof, 108 feet long by 91 feet broad, with orchestral accommodation for several hundred performers, and a powerful and splendid organ, by Hill of London.

It is the most celebrated place in the city for public meetings. There, in 1853, was inaugurated by Lord Eglinton and others, the great Scottish Rights Association, the ultimate influence of which procured so many necessary grants of money for Scottish purposes; in 1859 the first Burns Centenary, and in 1871 the first Scott Centenary, were celebrated in this hall. There, too, has the freedom of the city been bestowed upon many great statesmen, soldiers, and others. There has Charles Dickens often read his "Christmas Carols" to delighted thousands ; and there it was that, in 1856, the great novelist and humourist, Thackeray, was publicly hissed down (to the marked discredit of his audience, be it said) in one of his readings, for making disparaging remarks on Mary Queen of Scots.

The new Union Bank of Scotland is on the south side of the street. Commenced in 1874, it was finished in 1878, from designs by David Bryce, R.S.A. It is in the Tuscan style, with a frontage of more than 100 feet, and extends southwards to Rose Street Lane. It exhibits three storeys rising from a sunk basement, with their entrances, each furnished with a portico of Ionic columns. The first floor windows are flanked by pilasters, and furnished with entablatures and pediments; the second floors have architraves, and moulded sills, while the wall-head is terminated by a bold cornice, supporting a balustrade. The telling-room is magnificent—fully eighty feet long by fifty feet broad, and arranged in a manner alike commodious and elegant. In the sunk basement is a library, with due provision of safes for various bank purposes, and thither removed, in 1879, the famous old banking house to which we have more than once had occasion to refer, from its old quarters in the Parliament Square, which were then announced as for sale, with its fireproof interior "of polished stone, with groined arches on the various floors ; its record rooms, book and bullion safes of dressed stone, alike thief and fire proof."

Here we may briefly note that the Union Bank was incorporated in 1862, and its paid-up capital is £1,000,000 ; but this bank is in reality of a much older date, and was originally known as the

Glasgow Union Bank Company, which dates from 1830; in 1843 the name was changed to the Union Bank of Scotland. As was stated by Mr. Gairdner to the Committee of the House of Commons on "Banks of Issue" (1874), several private and public banks were incorporated from time to time in the Union: notably, the Thistle Bank of Glasgow in 1836, the Paisley Union Bank in 1838, the Ayr Bank, the Glasgow Arms and Ship Bank in 1843, Sir William Forbes and J. Hunter and Co. in the same year. The Aberdeen Bank was also absorbed in the Union system in 1849, and the Perth Banking Company in 1857. The special general meeting for "considering whether or not this bank should be registered under the Companies Act, 1862," was called on the 10th December, 1862, but the bank had in fact been so registered on the 3rd November of the same year. At the meeting, Sir John Stuart Forbes, Bart., was in the chair, and it was unanimously agreed "that it is expedient that the bank register itself as an unlimited company under the Companies Act, 1862, and that the meeting do now assent to the bank being so registered, and authorise the directors to take all necessary steps for carrying the motion into effect."

Opposite the Northern Club—a mere plain dwelling-house—is the Masonic Hall and offices of the grand lodge of Scotland, No. 98, George Street. The foundation stone was laid on the 24th of June, 1858, with due masonic honours, by the Grand Master, the Duke of Athole, whose henchman, a bearded Celt of vast proportions, in Drummond tartan, armed with shield and claymore, attracted great attention. The streets were lined by the 17th Lancers and the Staffordshire Militia. The building was finished in the following year,

and, among many objects of great masonic interest, contains the large picture of the "Inauguration of Robert Burns as Poet Laureate of the Grand Lodge of Scotland," by William Stewart Watson, a deceased artist, nephew of George Watson, first president of the Scottish Academy, and cousin of the late Sir John Watson-Gordon. He was an ardent Freemason, and for twenty years was secretary to the Canongate Kilwinning Lodge.

His picture is a very valuable one, as containing excellent portraits of many eminent men who took part in that ceremony. He was the same artist who designed the embellishments of the library at Abbotsford, at the special request of Sir Walter Scott, to whom he was nearly related.

In this office are the rooms and records of the Grand Secretary, and there the whole general business of the entire masonic body in Scotland is transacted.

Three fine bronze pedestrian statues decorate this long and stately street.

The first of these statues, at the intersection of George Street and Hanover Street, to the memory of George IV., is by Chantrey, and was erected in November, 1831. It is twelve feet in height, on a granite pedestal of eighteen feet, executed by Mr. Wallace. The largest of the blocks weighed fifteen tons, and all were placed by means of some of the cranes used in the erection of the National Monument.

The second, at the intersection of Frederick Street, is also by Chantrey, to the memory of William Pitt, and was erected in 1833.

The third, at the intersection of Castle Street, on a red granite pedestal, was erected in 1878 to the memory of Dr. Chalmers, and is by the hand of Sir John Steel.

CHAPTER XX.

QUEEN STREET.

The Philosophical Institution—House of Baron Orde—New Physicians' Hall—Sir James Y. Simpson, M.D.—The House of Professor Wilson—Sir John Leslie—Lord Rockville—Sir James Grant of Grant—The Hopetoun Rooms—Edinburgh Educational Institution for Ladies.

QUEEN STREET was a facsimile of Princes Street, but its grouping and surroundings are altogether different.

Like Princes Street, it is a noble terrace, but not overlooked at a short distance by the magnificent castle and the Dunedin of the Middle Ages. It

looks northward over its whole length on beautiful gardens laid out in shrubs and flowers, beyond which lie fair white terraces and streets that far excel itself—the assembled beauties of another new town spreading away to the wide blue waters of the Firth of Forth. How true are the lines of Scott!—

" Caledonia's queen is changed,
Since on her dusky summit ranged,
Within its steepy limits pent
By bulwark, line, and battlement,
And flanking towers and laky flood,
Guarded and garrisoned, she stood,
Denying entrance or resort,
Save at each tall embattled port ;
Above whose arch suspended hung
Portcullis, spiked with iron prong,
That long is gone ; but not so long,

reading-room in this institution. The library contains above 24,000 volumes of standard works in
every department of literature and science ; and
there is one of reference, kept in a separate department, consisting of a valuable collection of encyclo-
pædias, geographical, biographical, and scientific
dictionaries, atlases, statistical tables, &c., which
are at all times available to the numerous members
on application.

THE MUSIC HALL, GEORGE STREET.

Since early closed, and opening late,
Jealous revolved the studded gate,
Whose task from eve to morning tide
A wicket churlishly supplied.
Stern then and steel-girt was thy brow,
Dun-Edin ! Oh, how altered now !
When safe amid thy mountain court
Thou sitt'st like empress at her sport,
And liberal, unconfined, and free,
Flinging thy white arms to the sea ! "

Near the east end of Queen Street is the Philosophical Institution, the late president of which was
Thomas Carlyle. It was founded in 1848. Here
lectures are delivered on all manner of scientific
and literary subjects. The programme of these
for a session averages about thirty subjects. There
are a library, reading-room, news-room, and ladies'

Classes for Latin, French, German, drawing of
all kinds, mathematics, shorthand, writing, arithmetic, fencing, and gymnastics, are open on
very moderate terms ; and the members of the
Edinburgh Chess Club, who must also be members
of the Philosophical Institution, meet in one of
the apartments, which is open for their use from
11 a.m. to 10 p.m.

Adjoining this edifice are the offices of the
United Presbyterian Church of Scotland.

No. 8 Queen Street was built and occupied by
Chief Baron Orde of the Scottish Exchequer, and
in size considerably exceeds and excels the other
houses in its vicinity. Baron Orde, whose
daughter Elizabeth became the second wife of
Lord Braxfield, died in 1777, and was succeeded in

office by Sir James Montgomery of Stanhope. Early in the next century the house was the residence of Sir William Cunningham, Bart., and in more recent years had as an occupant the gallant Sir Neil Douglas, Commander of the Forces in Scotland and Governor of Edinburgh Castle, who commanded the Cameron Highlanders in the war with France, and was contused by a ball at Quatre Bras. It is now occupied by the Edinburgh Institution for Education, the head of which is Dr. Fergusson, F.R.S.E.

Nos. 9 and 10 were removed in 1844 to make way for the present hall of the Royal College of Physicians, on the demolition of the former one in George Street. The foundation stone was laid on the 8th of August, 1844, by the then president, Dr. Renton, in presence of the Fellows of the college and others. In it were deposited a copy of the first edition of the " Edinburgh Pharmacopœia," containing a list of the Fellows of the college; a work concerning its private affairs, printed several years before; an Edinburgh Almanac for the current year; several British coins, and a silver plate with a suitable Latin inscription.

It was designed by Thomas Hamilton, and is adorned in front with an Attic Corinthian tetrastyle, surmounted by a common Corinthian distyle, and is handsomely adorned by colossal statues of Æsculapius, Hippocrates, and Hygeia; but it was barely completed when, ample though its accommodation appeared to be, the rapid additions to its library and the great increase in the number of Fellows, consequent on a reduction of the money entry, and other changes, seemed to render an extension necessary.

In No. 11 are the offices of the *Edinburgh Gazette*, the representative of the paper started by Captain Donaldson in 1699, and re-issued by the same person in March, 1707.

Sir Henry Wellwood Moncrieff, Bart., D.D., a distinguished divine, who for half a century was one of the brightest ornaments of the Scottish Church, resided in No. 13 during the first years of the present century. He died in August, 1827, and his second son, James, a senator, under the title of Lord Moncrieff, succeeded to the baronetcy, which is one of the oldest in Scotland, having been conferred by Charles I. in 1626.

It was afterwards occupied by the Scottish Heritable Security Company.

The next house westward was the residence, at the same time, of William Honeyman of Graemsay, who was elevated to the bench as Lord Armadale, and created a baronet in 1804. He had been previously Sheriff of the county of Lanarkshire. He mar-

ried a daughter of Lord Braxfield, and died in 1825, leaving behind him a reputation for considerable talent and sound judgment, both as a barrister and judge. He had two sons in the army—Patrick, who served in the old 28th Light Dragoons, and Robert, who died in Jamaica in 1809, Lieutenant-Colonel of the 18th Royal Irish.

His house is now occupied by the site of the Caledonian United Service Club, erected in 1853.

In 1811 No. 27 was the residence of General Graham Stirling, an old and distinguished officer, whose family still occupy it. In the same year Alexander Keith of Ravelston, Hereditary Knight Marshal of Scotland, occupied No. 43. Behind the house line stands St. Luke's Free Church, which has a fictitious street front in the Tudor style, with two richly crocketed finials.

No. 38 was the house of George Paton, Advocate, and afterwards Lord Justice Clerk, whose suicide made much sensation in Edinburgh a few years ago.

In No. 52 lived and died one of the most illustrious citizens of Edinburgh—Professor Sir James Young Simpson, Bart., who came to Edinburgh a poor and nearly friendless student, yet in time attained, as Professor of Midwifery in the University and as the discoverer of extended uses of chloroform, a colossal fame, not only in Europe, but wherever the English language is spoken. He obtained the chair of midwifery in 1840, and seven years after made his great discovery. In 1849 he was elected President of the Edinburgh College of Physicians; in 1852 President of the Medico-Chirurgical Society; and in the following year, under circumstances of the greatest *éclat*, Foreign Associate of the French Academy of Medicine. In 1856 the French Academy of Sciences awarded him the " Monthyon Prize " of 2,000 francs for the benefits he conferred on humanity by the introduction of anæsthesia by chloroform into the practice of surgery and midwifery.

A few weeks earlier, for the same noble cause, he won the royal order of St. Olaf, from Oscar, King of Sweden, and in 1866 was created a baronet of Great Britain. His professional writings are too numerous to be recorded here, suffice it to say that they have been translated into every European language.

No man ever attracted so many visitors to Edinburgh as Sir James Simpson, for many came to see him who were not invalids. His house in Queen Street was the centre of attraction for men of letters and science from all parts of the world—physicians, naturalists, antiquarians, and literati of all kinds were daily to be met at his table. His hospitality was princely, his charity and his philanthropy to the poor were boundless; and amid the crowds of patients and visitors—many of them of the highest rank in Europe—with whom his house overflowed, the grand professor moved with unaffected ease and gaiety, and talking of everything, from some world-wide discovery in the most severe of the severer sciences, to the last new novel. He had a word or a jest for all.

How he carried on his gigantic practice—how he achieved his splendid and apparently unaccountable scientific investigations—how he found time for his antiquarian and literary labours, and yet was able to take a prominent part in every public, and still more in every philanthropic, movement, was ever a mystery to all who knew him.

But during the long and weary watches of the night, beside the ailing or the dying, when watching perilous cases with which he alone could grapple, he sat by the patient's side with book or pen in hand, for not a moment of his priceless time was ever wasted.

"Many of my most brilliant papers," he once said to his students, "were composed at the bedside of my patients." Yet he never neglected them, even the most poor and needy—and they had his preference even to the peers and princes of the land. As a physician he had fewer failures and made fewer mistakes than most men, and he saved the lives of thousands. Simpson was not a specialist—his mind was too broad and great for that; and no one ever excelled him in the ingenuity, simplicity, and originality of his treatment.

When other men shrank from the issues of life and death, he was swift to do, to dare, and to save; and it is a curious fact that on the night Simpson was born in his father's humble abode in the village of Bathgate, the village doctor has marked in his case-book that on that occasion he "arrived too late!"

By the introduction of chloroform into his practice, the labour of 2,000 years of investigation culminated. A new era was inaugurated for woman, though the clergy rose in wrath, and denounced it as an interference with the laws of Providence.

It was on the 28th of November, 1847, that he became satisfied of the safety of using chloroform by experimenting on himself and two other medical men. "Drs. Simpson, Keith, and Duncan," we are told, "sat each with a tumbler in hand, and in the tumbler a napkin. Chloroform was poured upon each napkin, and inhaled. Simpson, after a while, drowsy as he was, was roused by Dr. Duncan snoring, and by Dr. Keith kicking about in a far from graceful way. He saw at once that he must have been sent to sleep by the chloroform. He saw his friends still under its effects. In a word, he saw that the great discovery had been made, and that his long labours had come to a successful end."

Since then how much bodily anguish has vanished under its silent influence! In Britain there are now many manufactories of chloroform; and in Edinburgh alone there is one which makes about three millions of doses yearly—evidence, as Simpson said, of "the great extent to which the practice is now carried of wrapping men, women, and children in a painless sleep during some of the most trying moments and hours of human existence, and especially when our frail brother man is laid upon the operating-table and subjected to the torture of the surgeons' knives and scalpels, his saws and his cauteries."

As to his invention of acupressure in lieu of the ligature, though its adoption has not become general throughout the surgical world, the introduction of this simple method of restraining hæmorrhage would of itself have entitled Simpson to enrol his name among the greatest surgeons of Europe.

The last great movement with which he was connected was hospital reform. He argued that while only one in 180 patients who had even an arm amputated died in the country or in their homes, one in thirty died in hospitals. His idea was that the unit of a hospital was not the ward, but the bed, and the ideal hospital should have every patient absolutely shut off from every other, so that the unhealthy should not pollute or injure the healthy.

As an antiquarian and archæologist he held the highest rank, and for some years was president of the Scottish Society of Antiquaries.

His religious addresses were remarkable for their sweetness, freshness, and fervour; and one which he gave at the last of some special religious services held in the Queen Street Hall during the winter of 1861-2 made a great impression on all who heard him.

He was member of a host of learned societies, the mere enumeration of which would tire the reader. "These were his earthly honours; but their splendour pales when we think that on whatever spot on earth a human being suffers, and is released from anguish by the application of those discoveries his mighty genius has revealed to mankind, his name is remembered with gratitude, and associated with the noblest and greatest of those who, in all ages of the world, have devoted their lives and their genius to enlightening and brightening the lot of humanity."

He died of disease of the heart at 52, Queen Street, on the 6th May, 1870, and never was man more lamented by all ranks and classes of society; and nothing in life so became him, as the calmness and courage with which he left it.

His own great skill had taught him that from the first his recovery was doubtful, and in speaking of a possibly fatal issue, his principal reason for desiring life was that he hoped, if it were God's will, that he might have been spared to do a little more service in the cause of hospital reform; all his plans and prospects were limited by this reference to the Divine will.

"If God takes me to-night," said he to a friend, "I feel that I am resting on Christ with the simple faith of a child." And in this faith he passed away.

His funeral was a great and solemn ovation indeed; and never since Thomas Chalmers was laid in his grave had Edinburgh witnessed such a scene as that exhibited in Queen Street on the 13th May. From the most distant shires, even of the Highlands and the northern counties of England, and from London, people came to pay their last tribute to him whom one of the London dailies emphatically styled "the grand old Scottish doctor."

St. Luke's Free Church, near his house, was made the meeting place of the general public. In front of the funeral car were the Senatus Academicus, headed by the principal, Sir Alexander Grant of Dalvey, and the Royal College of Physicians, all in academic costume; the magistrates, with all their official robes and insignia; all the literary, scientific, legal, and commercial bodies in the city sent their quota of representatives, which, together with the High Constables and students, made altogether 1,700 men in deep mourning.

The day was warm and bright, and vast crowds thronged every street from his house to the grave on the southern slope of Warriston cemetery, and on every side were heard ever and anon the lamentations of the poor, while most of the shops were closed, and the bells of the churches tolled. The spectators were estimated at 100,000, and the most intense decorum prevailed. An idea of the length of the procession may be gathered from the fact that, although it consisted of men marching in sections of fours, it took upwards of thirty-three minutes to pass a certain point.

A grave was offered in Westminster, but declined by his family, who wished to have him buried among themselves. A white marble bust of him by Brodie was, however, placed there in 1879.

No. 53 Queen Street, the house adjoining that of Sir James, was the residence of Mrs. Wilson, mother of Professor John Wilson, widow of a wealthy gauze manufacturer. Her maiden name was Margaret Sym, and her brother Robert figures in the *Noctes Ambrosianæ*, under the cognomen of "Timothy Tickler." "Wilson's Memoirs" contain many of his own letters, dated from there, after 1806 till his removal to Anne Street. There he wrote his "Isle of Palms," prior to his marriage with Miss Jane Penny in May, 1811, and there, with his young wife and her sisters, he was resident with the old lady at the subsequent Christmas. His father left him an unencumbered fortune of £50,000, which had enabled him to cut a good figure at Oxford.

"A little glimpse of the life at 53 Queen Street, and the pleasant footing subsisting between the relatives gathered there, is afforded in a note of young Mrs. Wilson about this time to a sister," says Mrs. Gordon. "She thanks 'Peg' for her note, which, she says, 'was sacred to myself. It is not my custom, you may tell her, to show my letters to John.' She goes on to speak of Edinburgh society, dinners, and evening parties, and whom she most likes. The Rev. Mr. Morehead is 'a great favourite;' Mr. Jeffrey is 'a horrid little man,' but 'held in as high estimation here as the Bible.' Mrs. Wilson senior gives a ball, and 150 people are invited. 'The girls are looking forward to it with great delight. Mrs. Wilson is very nice with them, and lets them ask anybody they like. There is not the least restraint put upon them. John's poems will be sent from here next week. The large size is a guinea, and the small one twelve shillings.'"

Elsewhere we are told that John Wilson's "home was in Edinburgh. His mother received him into her house, where he resided till 1819." She was a lady whose domestic management was the wonder and admiration of all zealous housekeepers. Under one roof, in 53 Queen Street, she contrived to accommodate three distinct families; and there, besides the generosity exercised towards her own, she was hospitable to all, and her charity to the poor was unbounded; and when she died, "it was, as it were, the extinction of a bright particular star, nor can any one who ever saw her altogether forget the effect of her presence. She belonged to that old school of Scottish ladies whose refinement and intellect never interfered with duties the most humble."

In those days in Edinburgh the system of a household neither sought nor suggested a number of servants; thus many domestic duties devolved upon the lady herself: for example, the china —usually a rare set—after breakfast and tea, was always washed and carefully put away by her own delicate hands, and thus breakage was evaded. Marketing was then done in the early morning; and many a time was the stately figure of old Mrs. Wilson, "in her elegantly-fitting black satin dress, seen to pass to and fro from the old market place of Edinburgh, followed by some favourite caddie

peace and harmony reigned supreme, and there are now not a few of her grandchildren who remember this fine old Scottish matron with affection and gratitude.

In 1815 John Wilson had been called to the bar, at the same time with his firm friend Patrick Robertson, Sir William Hamilton, Andrew Rutherford,

SIR JAMES YOUNG SIMPSON.   (From a Photograph by John Moffat.)

(or street porter), bearing the well-chosen meats and vegetables that no skill but her own was permitted to select."

She was a high Tory of the old school; and it is told of her that on hearing it said that her son was contributing to the *Edinburgh Review,* she exclaimed, "John, if you turn Whig this house is no longer big enough for us both!"

In No. 53 she had under her roof for several years two married sons, with their wives, children, and servants, together with her own inmediate household, including two unmarried daughters; yet

Archibald Alison, and others; and in 1819, he, with his wife and children, then five in number, removed from his mother's house in Queen Street to No. 20 Anne Street, Stockbridge. It was in No. 53, however, that the famous "Chaldee Manuscript" was written, amid such shouts of laughter, says Mrs. Gordon, "that the ladies in the room above, sent to inquire in wonder what the gentlemen below were about. I am informed that among those who were met together on that memorable occasion was Sir William Hamilton, who also exercised his wit in writing a verse, and was so amused by his own performance that he tumbled off his chair in a fit of laughter."

No. 62 Queen Street was inhabited by Lord Jeffrey from 1802 till 1810. In the following year it became the residence of Sir John Leslie, K.H., Professor of Mathematics in the University of Edinburgh, who in 1800 invented the differential thermometer, one of the most beautiful and delicate instruments that inductive genius ever contrived as a help to experimental research; and the results of his inquiries concerning the nature and laws of heat, in which he was so much aided by this exquisite instrument, were published in 1804, in his celebrated "Essay on the Nature and Propagation of Heat." Sir John Leslie was one of those many self-made men who are peculiarly the glory of Scotland, for he was the son of a poor joiner in Largo, yet he attained to the highest honours a university can bestow. In 1832, along with Herschel, Brewster, Harris, Nichols, and others, on the recommendation of Lord Brougham, he was created a Knight of the Guelphic Order, but died in the November of that year from an attack of erysipelas.

No. 64 was, and is still, the town residence of the Earls of Wemyss, but has had many other tenants. Among others here resided "Lang Sandy Gordon," as he was named in those days of simple and unassuming familiarity, the son of William, second Earl of Aberdeen, who was admitted an advocate in 1759, and became Stewart-depute of Kirkcudbright in 1764. Twenty years afterwards he was raised to the bench as Lord Rockville, and resided long in the close which bore that name on the Castle Hill, and afterwards in Queen Street. He was remarkable for his manly beauty and handsome figure. He was a member of the Crochallan Club, and a great convivialist. Walking down the High Street one day, when the pavement was unsafe by ice, he fell, and broke his arm. He was conveyed to Provost Elder's shop, opposite the Tron church, where surgical aid was procured and his arm dressed; but, unfortunately, when his friends were conveying him to his new home at No. 64, one of the chairmen fell and overturned the sedan in the street, which unsettled the splinting of his lordship's arm, and ultimately brought on a fever, of which he died on the 13th of March, 1792.

No. 64 was afterwards occupied by Sir James Grant, Bart., of Grant, usually known as "the good Sir James." His town house, with extensive stable-offices, had previously been at the foot of the Canongate, where it was advertised for sale in 1797, as "presently possessed by Professor

Stewart." At a period when the extensive Highland proprietors were driving whole colonies of people from the abodes of their forefathers, and compelling them to seek on distant shores that shelter which was denied them on their own, and "when absenteeism and the vices of courtly intrigue and fashionable dissipation had sapped the morality of too many of our landholders, Sir James Grant escaped the contagion, and during a long life was distinguished for the possession of those virtues which are the surest bulwarks of the peace, happiness, and strength of a country. Possessed of extensive estates, and surrounded by a numerous tenantry, his exertions seemed to be equally devoted to the progressive improvement of the one and the present comfort and enjoyment of the other."

Among his clan he raised two regiments of Highland Fencibles within a few months of each other. One was numbered as the 97th, or Strathspey Regiment, 1,800 strong, and a portion of it joined the 42nd for service in the West Indies. Sir James died at Castle Grant in 1811.

No. 66, now offices, was occupied by Stewart of Castle Stewart; and in No. 68 lived George Joseph Bell, Advocate, Professor of Law, and author of "Principles of the Law of Scotland." No. 71, in 1811, was the residence of Francis, Lord Napier, who served in the American war under General Burgoyne, but left the army in 1789. He took a leading part in many local affairs, was Grand Master Mason of Scotland, Colonel of the Hopetoun Fencibles in 1793, Commissioner to the General Assembly in 1802, and a member of the Board of Trustees for the Encouragement of Scottish Manufactures and Fisheries.

His prominently aquiline face and figure were long remarkable in Edinburgh; though, at a time when gentlemen usually wore gaudy colours—frequently a crimson or purple coat, a green plush vest, black breeches, and white stockings—when not in uniform, he always dressed plainly, and with the nicest attention to propriety. An anecdote of his finical taste is thus given in Lockhart's "Life of Scott":—

"Lord and Lady Napier arrived at Castlemilk (in Lanarkshire), with the intention of staying a week, but next morning it was announced that a circumstance had occurred which rendered it indispensable for them to return without delay to their own seat in Selkirkshire. It was impossible for Lady Stewart to extract any further explanation at the moment, but it afterwards turned out that Lord Napier's valet had committed the grievous mistake of packing up a set of neckcloths which did not correspond *in point of date* with the shirts they accompanied." Lord Napier died in 1823.

His house, together with Nos. 70 and 72 (in the early part of the century the abode of John Mill, Esq., of Noranside), became afterwards one large private hotel, attached to the Hopetoun Rooms. In the former the late Duchess of Kent and others of note frequently put up, and in the latter many important meetings and banquets have been held. Among these notably was the one given to Sir Edward Bulwer Lytton in 1854, on the occasion of his inauguration as President of the Associated Societies of the University. Sir William Stirling of Keir, M.P., occupied the chair, and the croupiers were Sir James Y. Simpson and Professor Blackie. When the army and navy were proposed, Professor Aytoun facetiously responded for the latter as "Admiral of Orkney," being sheriff of those isles, and in reply to an eloquent address of Bulwer's, which he closed by coupling the health of Sir Archibald Alison with the literature of Scotland, the latter replied, and introduced some political and anti-national remarks that caused disapprobation.

The whole street front of the three houses is now occupied by the Edinburgh Educational Institution, or Ladies' College, where above 1,000 pupils (under the care of the Merchant Company) receive a course of study embracing English, French, German, Latin, and all the usual branches of literature, to which are added calisthenics, dancing, needlework, and cookery. The edifice was opened in October, 1876, and has as life governor the Earl of Mar and Kellie.

After the formation of Queen Street, the now beautiful gardens that lie between it and Heriot Row and Abercrombie Place were long a neglected waste. It was not until 1823 that they were enclosed by parapet walls and iron railings, and were laid out in pleasure-walks and shrubberies for the inhabitants of these localities.

CHAPTER XXI.

THE STREETS CROSSING GEORGE STREET, AND THOSE PARALLEL WITH IT.

Rose Street—Miss Burns and Bailie Creech—Sir Egerton Leigh—Robert Pollok—Thistle Street—The Dispensary—Hill Street—Count d'Albany—St. Andrew Street—Hugo Arnot—David, Earl of Buchan—St. David Street—David Hume—Sir Walter Scott and Basil Hall—Hanover Street—Sir J. Graham Dalyell—Offices of Association for the Improvement of the Poor—Frederick Street—Grant of Corrimony—Castle Street—A Dinner with Sir Walter Scott—Skene of Rubislaw—Macvey Napier—Castle Street and Charlotte Street.

In 1784 the magistrates made several deviations from the plan and elevations for building in the New Town; and at that time the names and designs for the two Meuse Lanes, running parallel with George Street, but on the south and north sides thereof, were changed to Rose Street and Thistle Street. These were accordingly built in an inferior style of architecture and of rougher work, for the accommodation of shopkeepers and others, with narrower lanes for stabling purposes behind them.

Rose Street and Thistle Street lie thus on each side of the great central street of the first New Town, at the distance of 200 feet, and are, like it, 2,430 feet long, but only thirty broad.

The first inhabitants were at least people of the respectable class; but one lady who resided in Rose Street in 1789 obtained a grotesque notoriety from the manner in which she became embroiled with the magistrates, and had her named linked with that of Bailie—afterwards Lord Provost—Creech. Miss Burns was a native of Durham, where her father had been a man of wealth, but became unfortunate; thus his family were thrown on the world. His daughter appeared in Edinburgh in 1789, when she had barely completed her twentieth year, and there her youth, her remarkable beauty, and the extreme length to which she carried the then extravagant mode of dress, attracted such notice on the evening promenades that she was brought before the bailies at the instance of some of her neighbours, more particularly Lord Swinton, who died in 1799, and whose back windows faced hers in Rose Street; and she was banished the city, with the threat from Bailie Creech that if she returned she would get six months in the House of Correction, and thereafter be drummed out.

Against this severe decision she appealed to the Court of Session, presenting a Bill of Suspension to the Lord Ordinary (Dreghorn), which was refused; it came before the whole bench eventually, and "the court was pleased to remit to the Lord Ordinary to pass the Bill."

The papers now became filled with squibs at the expense of Bailie Creech, and a London journal announced that Bailie Creech, of literary celebrity, was about to lead Miss Burns of Rose Street " to the hymeneal altar." In his wrath, Creech threatened an action against the editor, whose contradiction made matters worse :—" In a former number we noticed the intended marriage between Bailie Creech of Edinburgh and the beautiful Miss Burns of the same place. We have now the authority of that gentleman to say that the proposed marriage is not to take place, matters having been otherwise arranged, to the mutual satisfaction of both parties and their respective friends." After a few years of unenviable notoriety, says the editor of " Kay," Miss Burns fell into a decline, and died in 1792 at Roslin, where a stone in the churchyard records her name and the date of her demise.

In the same year of this squabble we find a ball advertised in connection with the now unfashionable locality of Rose Street, thus :—" Mr. Sealey (teacher of dancing) begs to acquaint his friends and the public that his ball is fixed for the 20th of March next, and that in order to accommodate his scholars in the New Town, he proposes opening a school in Rose Street, Young's Land, opposite to the Physicians' Hall, the 24th of that month, where he intends to teach on Tuesdays and Fridays from nine in the morning, and the remainder of the week at his school in Foulis's Close, as formerly." In 1796 we find among its residents Sir Samuel Egerton Leigh, Knight, of South Carolina, whose lady " was safely delivered of a son on Wednesday morning (16th March) at her lodgings in Rose Street."

Sir Samuel was the second son of Sir Egerton Leigh, His Majesty's Attorney-General for South Carolina, and he died at Edinburgh in the ensuing January. He had a sister, married to the youngest brother of Sir Thomas Burnet of Leys.

This son, born at Edinburgh in 1796, succeeded in 1818 to the baronetcy, on the death of his uncle, Sir Egerton, who married Theodosia (relict of Captain John Donellan), daughter of Sir Edward, and sister of Sir Theodosius Edward Boughton, for the murder of whom by poison the captain was executed at Warwick in 1781.

It was in Dr. John Brown's Chapel in Rose Street, that Robert Pollok, the well-known author of " The Course of Time," who was a licentiate of the United Secession Church, preached his only sermon, and soon after ordination he was attacked by that pulmonary disease of which he died in 1827.

In 1810 No. 82 was " Mrs. Bruce's fashionable boarding-school," and many persons of the greatest respectability occupied the common stairs, particu-

larly to the westward ; and in Thistle Street were many residents of very good position.

Thus No. 2 was the house, in 1784, of Sir John Gordon, Bart. ; and Sir Alexander Don, Bart., of Newton Don, lived in No. 4, when Lady Don Dowager resided in No. 53, George Street (he had been one of the *détenus* in France who were seized when passing through it during the short peace of 1802), and a Mrs. Colonel Ross occupied No. 17, which is now the New Town dispensary.

Under the name of Hill Street this thoroughfare is continued westward, between Frederick Street and Castle Street, all the houses being " self-contained." The Right Hon. Charles Hope of Granton, Lord Justice Clerk, had his chambers in No. 6 (now writers' offices) in 1808 ; Buchanan of Auchintorlie lived in No. 11, and Clark of Comrie in No. 9, now also legal offices. In one of the houses here resided, and was married in 1822, as mentioned in *Blackwood's Magazine* for that year, Charles Edward Stuart, styled latterly Count d'Albany (whose son, the Carlist colonel, married a daughter of the Earl of Errol), and who, with his brother, John Sobieski Stuart, attracted much attention in the city and Scotland generally, between that period and 1847, and of whom various accounts have been given. They gave themselves out as the grandsons of Charles Edward Stuart, but were said to be the sons of a Captain Thomas Allan, R.N., and grandsons of Admiral John Carter Allan, who died in 1800.

Seven broad and handsome streets, running south and north, intersect the great parallelogram of the New Town. It was at the corner of one of those streets—but which we are not told—that Robert Burns first saw, in 1787, Mrs. Graham, so celebrated for her wonderful beauty, and whose husband commanded in the Castle of Stirling.

From the summit of the ridge, where each of these streets cross George Street, are commanded superb views : on one side the old town, and on the other the northern New Town, and away to the hills of Fife and Kinross.

According to " Peter Williamson's Directory," Hugo Arnot, the historian, had taken up his abode in the Meuse Lane of South St. Andrew Street in 1784. His own name was Pollock, but he changed it to Arnot on succeeding to the estate of Balcormo, in Fifeshire. In his fifteenth year he became afflicted with asthma, and through life was reduced to the attenuation of a skeleton. Admitted an advocate in 1772, he ever took a deep interest in all local matters, and published various essays thereon, and his exertions in promoting the improvements then in progress in Edinburgh were rewarded by the freedom of the city, which was conferred on him by the magistrates.

The house he occupied in St. Andrew's Lane was a small one, and he had an old and very particular lady as a neighbour on the upper floor. She was frequently disturbed by the hasty and impetuous way in which he rang his bell, and often remonstrated with him thereon, but without avail, which led to much ill-feeling between them. At length, on receiving a very imperative and

them by example in buckling on his sword again, as in his youth he had been a lieutenant in the army. In 1787 he retired on account of his health to Dryburgh Abbey, but returning to Edinburgh again, occupied the house 131 George Street, and died in 1829.

In St. Andrew Street lived, and died in 1809, in his sixty-eighth year, Major-General Alexander Mackay, who in 1803 commanded the forces in Scotland, and was thirty years upon the staff there. He was

QUEEN STREET.

petulant message one day, insisting that he should summon his servants in a different manner, great was the old lady's alarm to hear the loud explosion of a heavy pistol in Arnot's house ! But he was simply —as he said—complying with her request by firing instead of ringing for his shaving water.

In 1784 St. Andrew Street was the residence of David, Earl of Buchan, who in 1766 had been Secretary to the British Embassy in Spain, and who formed the Scottish Society of Antiquaries in 1780. Though much engaged in literary and antiquarian pursuits, he was not an indifferent spectator of the stirring events of the time, and when invasion was threatened, he not only used his pen to create union among his countrymen, but essayed to rouse

usually named " Old Buckram," from the stiffness of his gait, for he " walked as if he had swallowed a halbert, and his long queue, powdered hair, and cocked hat, were characteristic of a thoroughbred soldier of the olden time."

Sir James Gibson Craig, W.S., of Riccarton, occupied No. 8 North St. Andrew Street in 1830.

Proceeding westward, at the north-west corner of South St. David Street we find the house of David Hume, whither he came after quitting his old favourite abode in James's Court. The superintendence of the erection of this house, in 1770, was a source of great amusement to the historian and philosopher, and, says Chambers, a story is related in more than one way regarding the manner in which a denomination was conferred upon the street in which his house is situated. "Perhaps, if it be premised that a corresponding street at the other angle of St. Andrew Square is called *St. Andrew Street*—a natural enough circumstance with reference to the square, whose title was determined on the plan—it will appear likely that the choosing of 'St. David Street' for that in which Hume's house stood 'was not originally designed as a jest at his expense, though a second thought and whim of his friends might quickly give it that application."

Burton, in his "Life of Hume," relates that when the house was first inhabited by him, and when the street was as yet without a name—a very dubious story, as every street was named on the original plan—a witty young lady, daughter of Chief Baron Orde, chalked on the wall, ST. DAVID STREET. The allusion was obvious. Hume's servant "lass," judging that it was meant neither in honour nor in reverence, hurried into the house to inform him that he was made game of. "Never mind, lassie," said he; "many a better man has been made a saint before."

Though Hume was a native of Edinburgh, and was born in the Tron parish, the exact spot of his birth is unknown. In six years after it was built, according to Professor Huxley, the house in St. David Street was the centre of the accomplished and refined society which then distinguished Edinburgh. Adam Smith, Blair, and Ferguson, were within easy reach, and what remains of Hume's correspondence with Sir Gilbert Elliot of Minto, Colonel Edmonstone, and Mrs. Cockburn, gives pleasant glimpses of his social surroundings, and enables us to understand his contentment with his absence from the more perturbed, if more brilliant, worlds of Paris and London.

In 1775 his health began to fail, and it was evident that he would not long enjoy his new residence. In the spring of the following year his disorder, which appears to have been a hæmorrhage of the bowels, attained such a height that he knew it must be fatal, so he made his will, and wrote "My Own Life," the conclusion of which is one of the most cheerful and dignified leave-takings of life and all its concerns.

TWO SHADOWS IN CONVERSATION LORD KAMES AND HUGO ARNOT. (*After Kay*)

On Sunday the 25th of August, 1776, Hume died in his new house. On the manner of his death, after the beautiful picture which has been drawn of it by his friend, Adam Smith, we need not enlarge. The coolness of his last moments, unexpected by many, was universally remarked at the time, and is still well known. He was buried in the place selected by himself, in the old burial-ground on the western slope of the Calton Hill. A conflict between vague horror of his imputed opinions and respect for the individual who had passed a life so pure and irreproachable, created a great sensation among the populace of Edinburgh, and a vast concourse attended the body to the grave, which for some time was an object of curiosity to many who were superstitious enough to anticipate for his remains the fate appropriate to those of wizards and necromancers.

"From the summit of this hill," says Huxley, writing of the grave of Hume, "there is a prospect unequalled by any to be seen from the midst of a great city. Westward lies the Forth, and beyond it, dimly blue, the far away Highland hills; eastward rise the bold contours of Arthur's Seat and Salisbury Craigs, along with the grey old town of Edinburgh; while far down below, from a maze of crowded thoroughfares, the hoarse murmur of the toil of a polity of energetic men is borne to the ear. At times a man may be as solitary here as in a veritable wilderness, and may meditate undisturbedly upon the epitome of nature and man—the kingdoms of this world—spread out before him. Surely there is a fitness in the choice of this last resting-place by the philosopher and historian who saw so clearly that these two kingdoms form but one realm, governed by uniform laws, and based alike on impenetrable darkness and eternal silence; and faithful to the last to that profound veracity which was the secret of his philosophic greatness, he ordered that the simple Roman tomb which marks his grave should bear no inscription but, 'DAVID HUME. *Born*, 1711. *Died*, 1776.' Leaving it to posterity to add the rest."

It is a curious fact, sometimes adverted to in Edinburgh, but which cannot be authenticated, according to the *Book of Days*, that in the room in which David Hume died the Bible Society of Edinburgh was many years afterwards constituted, and held its first sitting.

In the early part of the present century, No. 19 was the house of Miss Murray of Kincairnie, in Perthshire, a family now extinct.

In 1826 we find Sir Walter Scott, when ruin had come upon him, located in No. 6, Mrs. Brown's lodgings, in a third-rate house of St. David Street, whither he came after Lady Scott's death at Abbotsford, on the 15th of May in that—to him—most melancholy year of debt and sorrow, and set himself calmly down to the stupendous task of reducing, by his own unaided exertions, the enormous monetary responsibilities he had taken upon himself.

Lockhart tells us that a week before Captain Basil Hall's visit at No. 6, Sir Walter had sufficiently mastered himself to resume his literary tasks, and was working with determined resolution at his "Life of Napoleon," while bestowing an occasional day to the "Chronicles of the Canongate" whenever he got before the press with his historical MS., or felt the want of the only repose he ever cared for—simply a change of labour.

Hanover Street was built about 1786. No. 27, now a shop, was the house of Neilson of Millbank; and in No. 33, now altered and sub-divided, dwelt Lord Meadowbank, prior to 1792, known when at the bar as Allan Maconochie. He left several children, one of whom, Alexander, also won a seat on the bench as Lord Meadowbank, in 1819. No. 39, at the corner of George Street, was the house of Marjoribanks of Marjoribanks and that ilk.

No. 54, now a shop, was the residence of Sir John Graham Dalyell when at the bar, to which he was admitted in 1797. He was the second son of Sir Robert Dalyell, Bart., of Binns, in Linlithgowshire, and in early life distinguished himself by the publication of various works illustrative of the history and poetry of his native country, particularly "Scottish Poems of the Sixteenth Century," "Bannatyne Memorials," "Annals of the Religious Houses in Scotland," &c. He was vice-president of the Antiquarian Society, and though heir-presumptive to the baronetcy in his family, received in 1837 the honour of knighthood, by letters patent under the Great Seal, for his attainments in literature.

A few doors farther down the street is now the humble and unpretentious-looking office of that most useful institution, the Edinburgh Association for Improving the Condition of the Poor, and maintained, like every other charitable institution in the city, by private contributions.

In South Hanover Street, No. 14—of old the City of Glasgow Bank—is now the new hall of the Merchant Company, containing many portraits of old merchant burgesses on its walls, and some views of the city in ancient times which are not without interest. Elsewhere we have given the history of this body, whose new hall was inaugurated on July 9, 1879, and found to be well adapted for the purposes of the company.

The large hall, formerly the bank telling-room, cleared of all the desks and other fixtures, now shows a grand apartment in the style of the Italian Renaissance, lighted by a cupola rising from eight Corinthian pillars, with corresponding pilasters abutting from the wall, which is covered by portraits. The space available here is forty-seven feet by thirty-two, exclusive of a large recess. Other parts of the building afford ample accommodation for carrying on the business of the ancient company and for the several trusts connected therewith. The old manager's room is now used by the board of management, and those on the ground floor have been fitted up for clerks. The premises were procured for £17,000.

All the business of the Merchant Company is now conducted under one roof, instead of being carried on partly in the Old Town and partly in the New, with the safes for the security of papers of the various trusts located, thirdly, in Queen Street.

By the year 1795 a great part of Frederick Street was completed, and Castle Street was beginning to be formed. The first named thoroughfare had many aristocratic residents, particularly widowed ladies—some of them homely yet stately old matrons of the Scottish school, about whom Lord Cockburn, &c., has written so gracefully and so graphically—to wit, Mrs. Hunter of Haigsfield in No. 1, now a steamboat-office; Mrs. Steele of Gadgirth, No. 13; Mrs. Gardner of Mount Charles, No. 20; Mrs. Stewart of Isle, No. 43; Mrs. Bruce of Powfoulis, No. 52; and Lady Campbell of Ardkinglas in No. 58, widow of Sir Alexander, last of the male line of Ardkinglas, who died in 1810, and whose estates went to the next-heir of entail, Colonel James Callender, of the 69th Regiment, who thereupon assumed the name of Campbell, and published two volumes of "Memoirs" in 1832, but which, for cogent reasons, were suppressed by his son-in-law, the late Sir James Graham of Netherby. His wife, Lady Elizabeth Callender, died at Craigforth in 1797.

In Numbers 34 and 42 respectively resided Ronald McDonald of Staffa, and Cunningham of Baberton, and in the common stair, No. 35, there lived for a time James Grant of Corrimony, advocate, who had his town house in Mylne's Court, Lawnmarket, in 1783. This gentleman, the representative of an old Inverness-shire family, was born in 1743, in the house of Corrimony in Urquhart, his mother being Jean Ogilvie, of the family of Findlater. His father, Alexander Grant, was induced by Lord Lovat to join Prince Charles, and taking part in the battle of Culloden, was wounded in the thigh. The cave at Corrimony in which he hid after the battle, is still pointed out to tourists. His son was called to the bar in 1767, and at the time of his death, in 1835, he was the oldest member of the Faculty of Advocates. Being early distinguished for his liberal principles, he numbered among his friends the Hon. Henry Erskine, Sir James Macintosh, Francis Jeffrey, and many others eminent for position or attainments. In 1785 he published his " Essays on the Origin of Society," &c. ; in 1813, " Thoughts on the Origin and Descent of the Gael," &c.: works which, illustrated as they are by researches into ancient Greek, Latin, and Celtic literature, show him to have been a man of erudition, and are valuable contributions to the early history of the Celtic races.

The next thoroughfare is Castle Street, so called from its proximity to the fortress. As the houses spread westward they gradually improved in external finish and internal decoration. By the French Revolutionary war, according to the author of "Old Houses in Edinburgh," writing in 1824, an immense accession of inhabitants of a better class were thrown into the growing city. All the earlier buildings of the new town were rubble-work, and so simple were the ideas of the people at that time, " that main doors (now so important) were not at all thought of, and many of the houses in Princes Street had only common stairs entering from the Mews Lane behind. But within the last twenty years a very different taste has arisen, and the dignity of a front door has become almost indispensable. The later buildings are, with few exceptions, of the finest ashlar-work, erected on a scale of magnificence said to be unequalled ; yet, it cannot be denied that here and there common stairs—a nuisance that seems to cling to the very nature of Edinburgh—have crept in. However, even that objection has in most cases been got over by an ingenious contrivance, which renders them accessible only to the occupants of the various flats," i.e., the crank communicating from each, with the general entrance-door below—a feature altogether peculiar to Edinburgh and puzzling to all strangers.

No. 1 Castle Street, now an hotel, was in 1811

the house of the first Lord Meadowbank, already referred to, who died in 1816. At the same time the adjoining front door was occupied by the Hon. Miss Napier (daughter of Francis, seventh Lord Napier), who died unmarried in 1829. No. 16 was the house of Skene of Rubislaw, the bosom friend of Sir Walter Scott, and the last survivor of the six particular friends to whom he dedicated the respective cantos of " Marmion." He possessed the Bible used by Charles I. on the scaffold, and which is described by Mr. Roach Smith in his " Collectanea Antiqua." Latterly Mr. Skene took up his residence at Oxford. His house is now legal offices.

About 1810 Lady Pringle of Stitchel occupied No. 20, at the corner of Rose Street. She was the daughter of Norman Macleod of Macleod, and widow of Sir James Pringle, Bart., a lieutenant-colonel in the army, who died in 1809. At the opposite corner lived Mrs. Fraser of Strichen; and No. 27, now all sub-divided, was the residence of Robert Reed, architect to the king. No. 37, in 1830, was the house of Sir Duncan Cameron, Bart., of Fassifern, brother of the gallant Colonel Cameron who fell at Quatre Bras, and won a baronetcy for his family. And now we come to the most important house in New Edinburgh, No. 39, on the east side of the northern half of the street, in which Sir Walter Scott resided for twenty-six years prior to 1826, and in which the most brilliant of his works were written and he spent his happiest years, "from the prime of life to its decline." He considered himself, and was considered by those about him, as amassing a large fortune ; the annual profits of his novels alone had not been less than £10,000 for several years. His den, or study, is thus described by Lockhart :—" It had a single Venetian window, opening on a patch of turf not much larger than itself, and the aspect of the place was sombrous. . . . A dozen volumes or so, needful for immediate purposes of reference, were placed close by him on a small movable form. All the rest were in their proper niches, and wherever a volume had been lent its room was occupied by a wooden block of the same size, having a card with the name of the borrower and date of the lending tacked on its front. . . . The only table was a massive piece of furniture which he had constructed on the model of one at Rokeby, with a desk and all its appurtenances on either side, that an amanuensis might work opposite to him when he chose, with small tiers of drawers reaching all round to the floor. The top displayed a goodly array of session papers, and on the desk below were, besides the MS. at which he was working, proof-sheets and so forth, all neatly done up with red tape. . . . His own writing apparatus was a very handsome old box, richly carved, lined with crimson velvet, and containing ink-bottles, taper-stand, &c., in silver. The room had no space for pictures, except one, an original portrait of Claverhouse, which the upper leaves before opening it. I think I have mentioned all the furniture of the room, except a sort of ladder, low, broad, and well carpeted, and strongly guarded with oaken rails, by which he helped himself to books from his higher shelves. On the top step of this convenience, Hinse, a

SIR WALTER SCOTT'S HOUSE, CASTLE STREET.

hung over the chimney-piece, with a Highland target on either side, and broadswords and dirks (each having its own story) disposed star-fashion round them. A few green tin boxes, such as solicitors keep their deeds in, were piled over each other on one side of the window, and on the top of these lay a fox's tail, mounted on an antique silver handle, wherewith, as often as he had occasion to take down a book, he gently brushed the dust off

venerable tom-cat, fat and sleek, and no longer very locomotive, usually lay, watching the proceedings of his master and Maida with an air of dignified equanimity."

Scott's professional practice at the bar was never anything to speak of; but in 1812 his salary and fees as a Principal Clerk of Session were commuted into a fixed salary of £1,600 annually, an income he enjoyed for upwards of twenty-five years. His principal duty as clerk in court was to sit below the bench, watch the progress of the suits, and record the decisions orally pronounced, by reducing them to technical shape.

Prior to living in No. 39 he would appear to have lived for a time in 19 South Castle Street (1798-9), and in the preceding year to have taken his bride to his lodging, 108 George Street.

In 1822 Lord Teignmouth visited Edinburgh, and records in his "Diary" that he dined here with Sir Walter Scott, who on that occasion wore the Highland dress, and was full of the preparations for the forthcoming visit of George IV. To Lord Teignmouth the dinner in all its features was a novelty; and he wrote of it at the time as being the most interesting at which he ever was present, as "it afforded a more complete exhibition of Highland spirit and feelings than a tour of the country might have done."

Four years afterwards saw the melancholy change in Sir Walter's life and affairs, and from his "Diary" we can trace the influence of a darker species of distress than mere loss of wealth could bring to a noble spirit such as his. His darling grandson was sinking apace at Brighton. The misfortunes against which his manhood struggled with stern energy were encountered by his affectionate wife under the disadvantages of enfeebled health; and it would seem but too evident that mental pain and mortification had a great share in hurrying Lady Scott's ailments to a fatal end.

He appears to have been much attached to the house referred to, as the following extract from his "Diary" shows:—"March 15, 1826.—This morning I leave No. 39 Castle Street for the last time! 'The cabin was convenient,' and habit made it agreeable to me. . . . So farewell poor No. 39! What a portion of my life has been spent there! It has sheltered me from the prime of life to its decline, and now I must bid good-bye to it."

On that day the family left Castle Street for Abbotsford, and in Captain Basil Hall's "Diary" he records how he came, by mistake, to 39 Castle Street, and found the door-plate covered with rust, the windows shuttered up, dusty and comfortless, and from the side of one a board projected, with the ominous words "To Sell" thereon. "The stairs were un-

washed," he continues, "and not a footmark told of the ancient hospitality which reigned within. In all nations with which I am acquainted the fashionable world moves westward, in imitation, perhaps, of the civilisation; and, *vice versâ*, those persons who decline in fortune, which is mostly equivalent to declining in fashion, shape their course eastward. Accordingly, by involuntary impulse I turned my head that way, and inquiring at the clubs in Princes Street, learned that he now resided in St. David Street, No. 6."

On the occasion of the Scott Centenary in 1871 the house in Castle Street was decorated, and thrown open to the public by its then tenant for a time. It became the residence of Macvey Napier, editor of the seventh edition of the "Encyclopædia Britannica." He died in 1847, and his "Life and Correspondence" was published in 1879.

Early in the century, No. 49, at the corner of Hill Street, was the residence of Ochterlony of Guynd, in Forfarshire, a family of whom several members have since those days settled in Russia, and a descendant of one, Major-General Ochterlony, fell in the service of the Emperor at Inkerman, after bearing a flag of truce to the British head-quarters.

Charlotte Street and Hope Street lie east and west respectively; but the former is chiefly remarkable for having at its foot on the north-west side a monument, in the shape of a lofty and ornate Eleanor cross, to the memory of Catherine Sinclair, the authoress of "Modern Accomplishments" and many other works. She was born April 17th, 1800, and died August 6th, 1864. Her sister Margaret, one of the best known members of old Edinburgh society, and one of the last survivors of the Abbotsford circle, died on 4th August, 1879, in London, in her eighty-seventh year. She had the curious fortune of being the personal friend of Anne Scott, Sir Walter's daughter, and in her extreme youth of being presented at Court by the beautiful Duchess of Gordon. Miss Margaret Sinclair was intimate with the princesses of the old royal family of "Farmer George," and retained to the last a multitude of recollections of the Scottish world of two generations ago.

CHAPTER XXII.

ST. ANDREW SQUARE.

St. Andrew Square—List of Early Residents—Count Borowlaski—Miss Gordon of Cluny—Scottish Widows' Fund—Dr. A. K. Johnston—
Scottish Provident Institution—House in which Lord Brougham was Born—Scottish Equitable Society—Charteris of Amisfield—Douglas's
Hotel—Sir Philip Ainslie—British Linen Company—National Bank—Royal Bank—The Melville and Hopetoun Monuments—Ambrose's
Tavern.

BEFORE its conversion into a place for public offices, St. Andrew Square was the residence of many families of the first rank and position. It measures 510 feet by 520. Arnot speaks of it as " the finest square we ever saw. Its dimensions, indeed, are small when compared with those in London, but the houses are much of a size. They are of a uniform height, and are all built of free-stone."

The entire square, though most of the original houses still exist, has undergone such changes that, says Chambers, " the time is not far distant when the whole of this district will meet with a fate similar to that which we have to record respecting the Cowgate and Canongate, and when the idea of noblemen inhabiting St. Andrew Square will seem, to modern conceptions, as strange as that of their living in the Mint Close."

The following is a list of the first denizens of the square, between its completion in 1778 and 1784:—

1. Major-General Stewart.
2. The Earl of Aboyne. He died here in his sixty-eighth year, in 1794. He was the eldest son of John, third Earl of Aboyne, by Grace, daughter of Lockhart of Carnwath, afterwards Countess of Murray.
3. Lord Ankerville (David Ross).
5. John, Viscount Arbuthnott, who died 1791.
6. Dr. Colin Drummond.
7. David Hume, afterwards Lord Dreghorn.
8. John Campbell of Errol. (The Earls of Errol have ceased since the middle of the seventeenth century to possess any property in the part from whence they took their ancient title.)
11. Mrs. Campbell of Balmore.
13. Robert Boswell, W.S.
15. Mrs. Cullen of Parkhead.
16. Mrs. Scott of Horslie Hill.
18. Alexander Menzies, Clerk of Session.
19. Lady Betty Cunningham.
20. Mrs. Boswell of Auchinleck (mother of "Corsica Boswell," R. Chambers, 1824).
22. James Farquhar Gordon, Esq.
23. Mrs. Smith of Methven.
24. Sir John Whiteford. (25 in "Williamson's Directory.")
25. William Fergusson of Raith.
26. Gilbert Meason, Esq., and the Rev. Dr. Hunter.
27. Alexander Boswell, Esq.(afterwards Lord Auchinleck), and Eneis Morrison, Esq.
28. Lord Methven.
30. Hon. Mrs. Hope.
32. Patrick, Earl of Dumfries, who died in 1803.

33. Sir John Colquhoun.
34. George, Earl of Dalhousie, Lord High Commissioner, 1777-82.
35. Hon. Mrs. Gordon.
38. Mrs. Campbell of Saddel, Gilbert Kerr of Stodrig, and Sir William Ramsay, Bart., of Banff House, who died in 1807.

By 1784, when Peter Williamson published his tiny " Directory," many changes had taken place among the occupants of the square. The Countess of Errol and Lord Auchinleck were residents, and Thomas, Earl of Selkirk, had a house there before he went to America, to form that settlement in the Gulf of St. Lawrence which involved him in so much trouble, expense, and disappointment. No. 1 was occupied by the Countess of Leven ; the Earl of Northesk, K.C.B., who distinguished himself afterwards as third in command at Trafalgar, occupied No. 2, now an hotel ; and Lord Arbuthnott had been succeeded in the occupancy of No. 5 by Patrick, Lord Elibank, who married the widow of Lord North and Grey.

By 1788 an hotel had been started in the square by a man named Dun. It was there that the celebrated Polish dwarf, Joseph Borowlaski, occasionally exhibited himself. In his memoirs, written by himself, he tells that he was one of a family of five sons and one daughter, "and by one of those freaks of nature which it is impossible to account for, or perhaps to find another instance of in the annals of the human species, three of these children were above the middle stature, whilst the two others, like myself, reached only that of children at the age of four or five years."

Notwithstanding this pigmy stature, the count, by his narrative, would seem to have married, performed many wonderful voyages and travels, and been involved in many romantic adventures. At thirty years of age his stature was three feet three inches. Being recommended by Sir Robert Murray Keith, then British Ambassador at Vienna, to visit the shores of Britain, after being presented, with his family, to royalty in London, he duly came to Edinburgh, where, according to Kay's Editor, " he was taken notice of by several gentlemen, among others by Mr. Fergusson, who generously endeavoured by their attentions to sweeten the bitter cup of life to the unfortunate gentleman."

The count, it would appear, did not exhibit—his "fine feelings" would not have permitted such a thing—he merely *received* in company. He gave a public breakfast, at which the small charge of 3s. 6d. was demanded, and the following is a copy of one of his advertisements :—

"Dun's Hotel, St. Andrew Square. On Saturday next, the 1st August (1788), at twelve o'clock, there will be a public breakfast, for the benefit of Count Borowlaski, in the course of which the count will perform some select pieces on the guitar. Tickets (at 3s. 6d. each) may be had at the hotel or at the count's lodgings, No. 4, St. Andrew Street, where he continues to receive company every day, from ten in the morning till three, and from five till nine. Admittance, one shilling. The count will positively leave this place on Friday."

Count Barrel-of-Whiskey, as he was called in Edinburgh, was still alive in 1838, though close on his hundredth year, and was the occupant of a pretty cottage near the Wear, at Prebend Bridge, in the county of Durham.

Among the earlier residents in the square was Charles Gordon, Esq., of Cluny, in Aberdeenshire, whose daughter Johanna became in 1804 the wife of John, seventh Earl of Stair. His house was No. 4, a large one on the south side, and it was the scene for years of a dark and painful story, still remembered in Edinburgh, and which we will touch with great brevity. The lady was beautiful, brilliant, and witty, but the earl would seem to have tired of her ; and though his marriage was deemed a valid one by the laws of Scotland (as Burke records) and though he was a Scottish peer and she the daughter of a Scottish landholder of ancient descent, he contrived to repudiate the ceremony, and in 1808 contracted another marriage with Louisa, daughter of John Manners, Esq., of Grantham Grange, by Louisa his wife, late Countess of Dysart. In the following year this marriage was dissolved in consequence of the Scottish one with Miss Gordon, and after years of misery and mortification the latter alliance was formally annulled in June, 1820. In this matter a noted gambler who figures in the pages of the "Hermit in Edinburgh" as "Colonel Bobadil," or "Bob Devil," acted an unpleasant part.

The earl died at Paris on the 22nd of March, 1840, when—according to Burke—that line of the Dalrymples became extinct ; and the once beautiful Johanna—the repudiated wife—died seven years afterwards in No. 4, St. Andrew Square, aged, shrivelled, and utterly imbecile. Her tomb may still be seen on the north side of St. Cuthbert's burial-ground, simply inscribed—

JOHANNA, COUNTESS OF STAIR,
WHO DIED 16TH FEB., 1847.

No. 4 was the residence in 1830 of Lieutenant-Colonel John Gordon of Cluny, M.P., but, combined with No. 5, afterwards became the office of the Scottish Widows' Fund, a society instituted in 1815—a period at which there existed scarcely any other life assurance office in Scotland ; but the extraordinary success of the Equitable Society of London, which had then been in existence about half a century, led to the proposal on the part of various individuals to establish an Association in Scotland based upon similar principles. Many difficulties had to be overcome ere the object could be accomplished, and after much consideration, in which some of the most able men in the city lent their assistance and co-operation, the Articles of Constitution were finally adjusted, and the Scottish Widows' Fund Society was founded on the original model of the London Equitable, so far, at least, as regarded the principle of mutual assurance—the policy-holders being members of, and in fact, constituting the Society, each member paying the premium for his assurance into a common fund, the joint property of the whole, and the profits, as from time to time ascertained, being allocated amongst them.

So little, however, was the system of life assurance understood or appreciated during the first years of the Society's existence, that four years after its institution the amount effected by those who had become members, and the accumulated fund and the annual revenue, were comparatively small. Thus at the close of 1818 the total sum of assurances effected had been only £7,900, the realised fund amounted to no more than £3,500, and the annual revenue from premiums to £2,500 ; figures that are in marked contrast with the marvellous business the Society now does.

On the failure of the Western Bank, the handsome and spacious premises in the Florentine style, of that institution in No. 9, on the west side of the square, were taken at a price greatly below the original cost, for the Widows' Fund, where we find it now, and Nos. 4 and 5 became broken up into various chambers and establishments.

No. 4 remained until 1879 the premises of Messrs. W. and A. K. Johnston, the well-known geographical engravers, who have acquired an artistic skill not yet surpassed. A. Keith Johnston, F.R.S., issued his great National Atlas in folio in 1843, which procured his appointment as Geographer to the Queen for Scotland ; but he is best known for having made on a large scale the application of physical science to geography. Founding his researches on the writings of Humboldt and Ritter, and aided by the counsel of the former, he produced "The Physical Atlas of

Natural Phenomena," and many other scientific and geographical works that have won the firm more than European reputation, including the "Royal Atlas of General Geography," dedicated to her Majesty, the only atlas for which a prize medal was awarded at the International Exhibition of London, 1862. Alexander Keith Johnston, LL.D., F.R.S., died on the 9th of July, 1877; but the firm still exists, though removed to more extensive premises elsewhere.

No less than twenty-three Societies and Associations of various kinds have chambers in No. 5, including the Obstetrical, Botanical, Arboricultural, and Geological Societies, together with the Scottish branch of the Army Scripture Readers and Soldiers' Friend Society, the mere description of which would require a volume to themselves.

In the entire square there are above twenty insurance societies or their branches, and several banks, and now it is one of the greatest business centres in the city.

No. 6 was till 1879 the Scottish Provident Institution, established in 1838, and incorporated ten years subsequently. It is a mutual assurance society, in which consequently the whole profits belong to the assured, the policy-holders at the same time, by the terms of the policies and by the deed of constitution, being specially exempt from personal liability.

No. 9 was in 1784 the house of Sir Michael Bruce, Bart., of Stenhouse, in Stirlingshire. He married a daughter of General Sir Andrew Agnew of Lochnaw, heritable sheriff of Galloway, and died in 1795. The whole site is now covered by the Scottish Widows' Fund office.

No 12, once the residence of Campbell of Shawfield, is now the office of the London Accident Company; and No. 14, which no longer exists, was in 1810 the office of the Adjutant-General for Scotland.

In No. 19 (now offices) according to one authority, in No. 21 (now also offices) according to Daniel Wilson, was born on the 19th of September, 1779, Henry, Lord Brougham and Vaux, the future Lord Chancellor of Great Britain, son of Henry Brougham of Scalis Hall, Cumberland, and Brougham Hall, Westmoreland, by Eleanor, daughter of the Rev. James Syme, and maternal niece of Robertson the Scottish historian.

A. and C. Black's "Guide" assigns the third floor of No. 21 as the place where Brougham was born. The birth and existence of this illustrious statesman depended upon a mere chance circumstance, which has in it much that is remarkable. His father was about to be married to a young lady resident near his family seat, to whom he was passionately attached, and every preparation had been made for their nuptials, when the lady died. To beguile his sorrow young Brougham came to Edinburgh, where, when idling on the Castle Hill, he chanced to inquire of a person where he could find a suitable lodging. By this person he was not directed to any fashionable hotel, for at that time scarcely such a thing was known in Edinburgh, but to Mrs. Syme, sister of Principal Robertson, widow of the Rev. Mr. Syme, whilom minister of Alloa, who then kept one of the largest boarding-houses in the city, in the second flat of MacLellan's Land, at the Cowgate Head, the windows of which looked up Candlemaker Row.

There he found quarters, and though it does not appear that he intended to reside permanently in Edinburgh, he soon found occasion to change that resolution by falling in love with Miss Syme, and forgetting his recent sorrow. He married her, and after living for a little space with Mrs. Syme, removed to St. Andrew Square.[*]

The future Lord Brougham received the first seeds of his education at the High School, under Mr. Luke Fraser, and afterwards under Dr. Adam, author of the "Roman Antiquities;" and from there he passed to the University, to become the pupil of Dugald Stewart, Black, Robertson, and other well-known professors, prior to his admission to the Scottish bar in 1800.

No. 22, now the office of the Scottish National Fire and Life Assurance Company, was for years the residence of Dr. James Hamilton, who died in 1835, and whose figure was long remarkable in the streets from his adherence to the three-cornered hat, the collarless coat, ruffles, and knee-breeches, of a past age, with hair queued and powdered; for years too he was in every way one of the ornaments of the metropolis.

His grandfather, the Rev. William Hamilton (a branch of the house of Preston) was Principal of the University in 1730, and his father, Dr. Robert Hamilton, was a distinguished Professor of theology in 1754. At an early age the Doctor was appointed one of the physicians to the infirmary, to Heriot's, the Merchant-maiden and Trades-maiden Hospitals, and he was author of one or two of the most elegant professional works that have been issued by the press. The extreme kindliness of his disposition won him the love of all, particularly of the poor. With the costume he retained much of the gentle courtesy and manly hardihood of the

---

[*] In one of his earlier publications, Robert Chambers states that Brougham was born at No. 8 Cowgate, and that his father afterwards moved to No. 7 George Street.

ST. ANDREW SQUARE.

old Scottish school. His habits were active, and he was fond of all invigorating sports. He was skilled as an archer, golfer, skater, bowler, and curler, and to several kindred associations of those sports he and old Dr. Duncan acted as secretaries for nearly half a century. For years old Eben Wilson, the bell-ringer of the Tron Church, had the reversion of his left-off cocked hats, which he wore, together with enormous shoe-buckles, till his death in 1823. For years he and the Doctor had been the only men who wore the old dress, which the latter retained till he too died, twelve years after.

No. 24 was the house of the famous millionaire, Gilbert Innes of Stowe.

The Scottish Equitable Assurance Society occupies No. 26. It was established in 1831, and was incorporated by royal charter in 1838 and 1846. It is conducted on the principle of mutual assurance, ranks as a first-class office, and has accumulated funds amounting to upwards of £2,250,000, with branch offices in London, Dublin, Glasgow, and elsewhere.

No. 29 was in 1802 the house of Sir Patrick Murray, Bart., of Ochtertyre, Baron of the Exchequer Court, who died in 1837. It is now the offices of the North British Investment Company.

No. 33, now a shop, was in 1784 the house of the Hon. Francis Charteris of Amisfield, afterwards fifth Earl of Wemyss. He was well known during his residence in Edinburgh as the particular patron of "Old Geordie Syme," the famous town-piper of Dalkeith, and a retainer of the house of Buccleuch, whose skill on the pipe caused him to be much noticed by the great folk of his time. Of Geordie, in his long yellow coat lined with red, red plush breeches, white stockings, buckled shoes and blue bonnet, there is an excellent portrait in Kay. The earl died in 1808, and was succeeded by his grandson, who also inherited the earldom of March.

Nos. 34 and 35 were long occupied as Douglas's hotel, one of the most fashionable in the city, and one which has been largely patronised by the royal families of many countries, including the Empress Eugénie when she came to Edinburgh, to avail herself, we believe, of the professional skill of Sir James Simpson. On that occasion Colonel Ewart marched the 78th Regiment or Ross-shire Buffs, recently returned from the wars of India, before the hotel windows, with the band playing *Partant pour la Syrie*, on which the Empress came to the balcony and repeatedly bowed and waved her handkerchief to the Highlanders.

In this hotel Sir Walter Scott resided for a few days after his return from Italy, and just before his death at Abbotsford, in September, 1832.

No. 35 is now the new head office of the Scottish Provident Institution, removed hither from No. 6. It was originally the residence of Mr. Andrew Crosbie, the advocate, a well-known character in his time, who built it. He was the original of Counsellor Pleydell in the novel of "Guy Mannering."

In 1784 Sir Philip Ainslie was the occupant of No. 38. Born in 1728, he was the son of George Ainslie, a Scottish merchant of Bordeaux, who, having made a fortune, returned home in 1727, and purchased the estate of Pilton, near Edinburgh. Sir Philip's youngest daughter, Louisa, became the wife of John Allan of Errol House, who resided in No. 8. Sir Philip's mother was a daughter of William Morton of Gray.

His house is now, with No. 39, a portion of the office of the British Linen Company's Bank, the origin and progress of which we have noticed in our description of the Old Town. It stands immediately south of the recess in front of the Royal Bank, and was mainly built in 1851–2, after designs by David Bryce, R.S.A., at a cost of about £30,000. It has a three-storeyed front, above sixty feet in height, with an entablature set back to the wall, and surmounted above the sixfluted and projecting Corinthian columns by six statues, each eight feet in height, representing Navigation, Commerce, Manufacture, Art, Science, and Agriculture; and it has a splendid cruciform telling-room, seventy-four feet by sixty-nine, lighted by a most ornate cupola of stained glass, thirty feet in diameter and fifty high. With its magnificent columns of Peterhead granite, its busts of celebrated Scotsmen, and its Roman tile pavement, it is all in perfect keeping with the grandeur of the external façade. This bank has about 1,080 partners.

Immediately adjoining, on the south, is the National Bank of Scotland, presenting a flank to West Register Street. It was enlarged backward in 1868, but is a plain almost unsightly building amid its present surroundings. It is a bank of comparatively modern origin, having been established on the 21st March, 1825. In terms of a contract of co-partnership between and among the partners, the capital and stock of the company were fixed at £5,000,000, the paid-up portion of which is £1,000,000. In the royal charter granted to the National Bank on the 5th August, 1831, a specific declaration is made, that "nothing in these presents" shall be construed to limit the responsibility and liability of the individual partners of the bank. The other existing banks have all been constituted by contracts of co-partnery since the year 1825, and, with the exception of the Caledonian Banking Company, are all carrying on business under the Companies Act of 1862. With this office is incorporated No. 41, which, in 1830, was the shop of Messrs. Robert Cadell and Co., the eminent booksellers and publishers.

The Royal Bank of Scotland occupies a prominent position on the west side of the square, in a deep recess between the British Linen Company and the Scottish Provident Institution.

It was originally the town house of Sir Lawrence Dundas, Bart., and was one of the first houses built in the square, on what we believe was intended as the place for St. Andrew's church. The house was designed by Sir William Chambers, on the model of a much-admired villa near Rome, and executed by William Jamieson, mason. Though of an ancient family, Sir Lawrence was the architect of his own fortune, and amassed wealth as a commissary-general with the army in Flanders, 1748 to 1759. He was the second son of Thomas Dundas, a bailie of Edinburgh, whose difficulties brought him to bankruptcy, and for a time Sir Lawrence served behind a counter. He was created a baronet in 1762, with remainder, in default of male issue, to his elder brother, Thomas Dundas, who had succeeded to the estate of Fingask. His son Thomas was raised to the peerage of Great Britain as Baron Dundas of Aske, in Yorkshire, in August, 1794, and became ancestor of the Earls of Zetland.

About 1820 the Royal Bank, which had so long conducted its business in the Old Bank Close in the High Street, removed to the house of Sir Lawrence Dundas.

We have thus shown that St. Andrew Square is now as great a mart for business as it was once a fashionable quarter, and some idea may be had of the magnitude of the interests here at stake when it is stated that the liabilities—that is, the total sums insured—of the six leading insurance houses alone exceed £45,000,000, and that their annual income is upwards of £1,800,000—a revenue greater than that of several States!

Melville's monument, in the centre of the square, was erected in 1821, in memory of Henry Dundas, first Viscount Melville, who was Lord Advocate in 1775, and filled some high official situations in the Government of Britain during the administration of William Pitt. He was raised to the peerage in 1802, and underwent much persecution in 1805 for alleged malversation in his office as treasurer to the navy; but after a trial by his peers was triumphantly judged not guilty.

Designed by William Burn, this monument consists of pedestal, pillar, and statue, rising to the height of 150 feet, modelled after the Trajan column at Rome, but fluted and not ornamented with sculpture; the statue is 14 feet in height. The cost was £8,000, defrayed—as the inverse side of the plate in the foundation stone states —"by the voluntary contributions of the officers, petty-officers, seamen, and marines of these united kingdoms." It was laid by Admirals Sir David Milne and Otway, naval commander-in-chief in Scotland, after prayer by Principal Baird, on the anniversary of Lord Melville's birthday. In the stone was deposited a great plate of pure gold, bearing the inscription. A plate of silver bearing the names of the committee was laid in the stone at the same time.

The Hopetoun monument, within the recess in front of the Royal Bank, is in memory of Sir John Hope, fourth Earl of Hopetoun, G.C.H., Colonel of the 92nd Gordon Highlanders, who died in 1823, a distinguished Peninsular officer, who assumed the command of the army at Corunna, on the fall of his countryman Sir John Moore. It was erected in 1835, and comprises a bronze statue, in Roman costume, leaning on a pawing charger.

West Register Street, which immediately adjoins St. Andrew Square, is a compound of several short thoroughfares, and contains the site of "Ambrose's Tavern," the scene of Professor Wilson's famous "Noctes Ambrosianæ," with a remnant of the once narrow old country pathway known as Gabriel's Road. "Ambrose's Tavern," a tall, three-storeyed edifice, like a country farmhouse, enjoyed much repute independent of the "Noctes," and was removed in 1864. Hogg, the Ettrick Shepherd, who was fond of all athletic sports and manly exercises, was long made to figure conspicuously in these "Noctes" in *Blackwood's Magazine*, which gave his name a celebrity beyond that acquired by his own writings.

At one of the corners of West Register Street is the great palatial paper warehouse of the Messrs. Cowan, one of the most elaborately ornate business establishments in the city, which was erected in 1865, by the Messrs. Beattie, at a cost of about £7,000, and has two ornamental fronts with chaste and elegant details in the florid Italian style.

ST. ANDREW SQUARE.

The Royal Bank of Scotland　　　　　　The British Linen Company's Bank.
The Scottish Provident Institution.　　　　The Scottish Widows' Fund Office.

CHAPTER XXIII.

CHARLOTTE SQUARE.

Charlotte Square—Its Early Occupants—Sir John Sinclair, Bart.—Lamond of that Ilk—Sir William Fettes—Lord Chief Commissioner Adam—Alexander Dirom—St George's Church—The Rev. Andrew Thomson—Prince Consort's Memorial—The Parallelogram of the first New Town.

CHARLOTTE SQUARE, which corresponds with that of St. Andrew, and closes the west end of George Street, as the latter closes the east, measures about 180 yards each way, and was constructed in 1800, after designs by Robert Adam of Maryburgh, the eminent architect; it is edificed in a peculiarly elegant and symmetrical manner, all the façades corresponding with each other. In 1874 it was beautified by ornamental alterations and improvements, and by an enclosure of its garden area, at a cost of about £3,000. Its history is less varied than that of St. Andrew Square.

During the Peninsular war No. 2 was occupied by Colonel Alexander Baillie, and therein was the Scottish Barrack office. One of the earliest occupants of No. 6 was Sir James Sinclair of Ulbster, who, after his marriage with Diana, daughter of Lord Macdonald, continued to reside for a time in the Canongate, after which he removed to Charlotte Square, and finally to that house in George Street in which he died. He was resident in Charlotte Square before 1802, as was also the Earl of Minto. John Lamond of Lamond and that ilk, in Argyleshire, whose son John commanded the second battalion of the Gordon Highlanders from 1809 to 1814, was the first occupant of No. 7, which latterly was the residence of Lord Neaves, who was called

head of Bailie Fyfe's Close ; house 57, Princes Street."

He was for many years a contractor for military stores, and in 1800 was chosen a Director of the British Linen Company, in which he ultimately held stock—the result of his own perseverance and honest industry—to a large amount. He had in the meantime entered the Town Council, in which he filled in 1785 the office of fourth bailie, and in 1799 that of senior bailie. In 1800 he was unani mously elected lord provost of the city, which

CHARLOTTE SQUARE, SHOWING ST. GEORGE'S CHURCH.

to the bar in 1822 and raised to the bench in May, 1854. Mrs. Oliphant of Rossie had No. 10, and No. 13 was at the same time (about 1810) the residence of Sir William Fettes, Bart., of Comely Bank, the founder of the magnificent college which bears his name. He was born at Edinburgh on the 25th of June, 1750, and nine years afterwards attended the High School class taught by Mr. John Gilchrist. At the early age of eighteen he began business as a tea and wine merchant in Smith's Land, High Street, an occupation which he combined for twenty years with that of an underwriter, besides being connected with establishments at Leeds, Durham, and Newcastle. His name appears in Williamson's Directory for 1788-90 as "William Fettes, grocer,

office he held for the then usual period of two years, and for a second time in 1805 and 1806. In 1804, between the two occasions, on the 12th May he was created a baronet. In 1787 he married Maria, daughter of Dr. John Malcolm of Ayr. The only child of this marriage was a son, William, born in 1787. He became a member of the Faculty of Advocates in 1810, and gave early promise of future eminence, but died at Berlin on the 13th of June, 1815.

Retiring from business in 1800, Sir William took up his abode in Charlotte Square, and devoted himself to the management of several estates which he purchased at different times, in various parts of Scotland. The principal of these were Comely

Bank, near Edinburgh; Arnsheen, in Ayrshire; Redcastle, Inverness-shire; Denbrae, Fifeshire; and Gogar Bank in Midlothian. He died on the 27th of May, 1836, Lady Fettes having pre-deceased him on the 7th of the same month.

By his trust disposition and settlement, dated 5th July 1830, and several codicils thereto, the last being dated the 9th of March, 1836, he disponed his whole estates to and in favour of Lady Fettes, his sister Mrs. Bruce, Mr. Corrie, Manager of the British Linen Company, A. Wood, Esq. (afterwards Lord Wood), and A. Rutherford, Esq. (afterwards Lord Rutherford), as trustees; the purposes of the trust, which made ample provision for Lady Fettes in case of her survival, being :—(1) The payment of legacies to various poor relations; (2) Bequests to charitable institutions; and (3) The application of the residue to "form an endowment for the maintenance, education, and outfit of young people whose parents have either died without leaving sufficient funds for that purpose, or who from innocent misfortune during their own lives are unable to give suitable education to their children."

The trust funds, which at the time of the amiable Sir William's death amounted to about £166,000, were accumulated for a number of years, and reached such an amount as enabled the trustees to carry out his benevolent intentions in a becoming manner; and, accordingly, in 1864 contracts were entered into for the erection of the superb college which now very properly bears his name.

Lord Cockburn, that type of the true old Scottish gentleman, "whose dignified yet homely manner and solemn beauty gave his aspect a peculiar grace," and who is so well known for his pleasant and gossiping volume of "Memorials," and for the deep interest he took in all pertaining to Edinburgh, occupied No. 14; and the next house was the residence of Lord Pitmilly. James Wolfe Murray, afterwards Lord Cringletie, held No. 17 in 1811; and the Right Hon. David Boyle, Lord Justice Clerk, and afterwards Lord Justice General, occupied the same house in 1830.

Lieutenant-General Alexander Dirom, of Mount Annan, and formerly of the 44th regiment, when Quartermaster-General in Scotland, rented No. 18 in 1811. He was an officer of great experience, and had seen much service in the old wars of India, and, when major, published an interesting narrative of the campaign against Tippoo Sultan. Latterly his house was occupied by the late James Crawfurd, Lord Ardmillan, who was called to the bar in 1829, and was raised to the bench in January, 1855.

At the same time No. 31 was the abode of the Right Hon. William Adam, Lord Chief Commissioner of the Jury Court, the kinsman of the architect of the Square, and a man of great eminence in his time. He was the son of Adam Blair of Blair Adam, and was born in July, 1751. Educated at Edinburgh, he became a member of the bar, but did not practise then; and in 1774 and 1794 he sat for several places in Parliament. In the latter year he began to devote himself to his profession, and in 1802 was appointed Counsel for the East India Company, and four years afterwards Chancellor for the Duchy of Cornwall. After being M.P. for Kinross, in 1811 he resumed his professional duties, and was deemed so sound a lawyer that he was frequently consulted by the Prince of Wales and the Duke of York.

In the course of a parliamentary dispute with Mr. Fox, about the first American war, they fought a duel, which happily ended without bloodshed, after which the latter remarked jocularly that had his antagonist not loaded his pistols with Government powder he would have been shot. In 1814 he submitted to Government a plan for trying civil causes by jury in Scotland, and in the following year was made a Privy Councillor and Baron of the Scottish Exchequer. In 1816 an Act of Parliament was obtained instituting a separate Jury Court in Scotland, and he was appointed Lord Chief Commissioner, with two of the judges as colleagues, and to this court he applied all his energies, overcoming by his patience, zeal, and urbanity, the many obstacles opposed to the success of such an institution. In 1830, when sufficiently organised, the Jury Court was, by another Act, transferred to the Court of Session, and when taking his seat on the bench of the latter for the first time, complimentary addresses were presented to him from the Faculty of Advocates, the Society of Writers to the Signet, and that of the solicitors before the Supreme Courts, thanking him for the important benefits which the introduction of trial by jury in civil cases had conferred on Scotland. In 1833 he retired from the bench, and died at his house in Charlotte Square, on the 17th February, 1839, in his 87th year.

In 1777 he had married Eleanora, daughter of Charles tenth Lord Elphinstone. She died in 1808, but had a family of several sons—viz., John, long at the head of the Council in India, who died some years before his father; Admiral Sir Charles, M.P., one of the Lords of the Admiralty; William George, an eminent King's Counsel, afterwards Accountant-General in the Court of Chancery; and Lieutenant-General Sir Frederick, who held a command at the battle of Waterloo, and was afterwards successively Lord High Commissioner to the Ionian Isles and Governor of Madras.

His neighbour and brother senator Lord Dundrennan occupied No. 35; and in 1811 William Robertson, Lord Robertson, a senator of 1805, occupied No. 42. He was the eldest son of Dr. Robertson the historian, and in 1779 was chosen Procurator of the Church of Scotland, after a close contest, in which he was opposed by the Hon. Henry Erskine. His personal appearance is described in "Peter's Letters to his Kinsfolk." He retired from the bench in 1826, in consequence of deafness, and died in November, 1835.

On the western side of the Square, and terminating with fine effect the long vista of George Street from the east, is St. George's Church, the foundation of which was laid on the 14th of May, 1811. It was built from a design furnished by Robert Reid, king's architect. The celebrated Adam likewise furnished a plan for this church, which was relinquished in consequence of the expense it would have involved. The whole building, with the exception of the dome, which is a noble one, and seen to advantage from any point, is heavy in appearance, meagre in detail, and hideous in conception, and its ultimate expense greatly exceeded the estimates and the sum for which the more elegant design of Adam could have been carried out. It cost £33,000, is calculated to accommodate only 1,600 persons, and was opened for public worship in 1814. It was intended in its upper part to be a large miniature or reduced copy of St. Paul's in London, and is in a kind of Græco-Italian style, with a lofty but meagre Ionic portico and surmounting an Attic Corinthian colonnade; it rests on a square ground plan measuring 112 feet each way, and culminates in the dome, surmounted by a lantern, cupola, and cross, the last at the height of 160 feet from the ground. The original design included two minarets, which have not as yet been added.

It is chiefly celebrated as the scene of the ministrations of Andrew Thomson, D.D., an eminent divine who was fixed upon as its pastor in 1814. He died suddenly on the 9th of February, 1831, greatly beloved and lamented by the citizens in general and his congregation in particular, and now

he lies in a piece of ground connected with the churchyard of St. Cuthbert.

In Charlotte Place, behind the church, are the atelier of Sir John Steel the eminent sculptor, and a music-room called St. Cecilia's Hall, with an orchestra space for 250 performers and seats for 500 hearers.

In the centre of the Square is the memorial to the Prince Consort, which was inaugurated with much state by the Queen in person, attended by the magistrates and archer guard, &c., in August, 1876. It cost £16,500, and is mainly from the studio of Steel. It is a quasi-pyramidal structure, about thirty-two feet high, with a colossal equestrian statue of the Prince as its central and upper figure; it is erected on an oblong Peterhead granite pedestal, fully seventeen feet high, and exhibiting emblematic bas-reliefs in the panels, with four groups of statues on square blocks, projecting from the corners of the basement; the prince is shown in the uniform of a field marshal. Of all the many statues that have been erected to his memory, this in Charlotte Square is perhaps one of the best and most pleasing.

With this chapter we close the history of what may be regarded as the *first* New Town, which was designed in 1767, laid out, as we have seen, in a parallelogram the sides of which measure 3.900 feet by 1,090.

The year 1755 was the period when Edinburgh seemed really to wake from the sleep and torpor that followed the Union, and a few improvements began in the Old Town. After that period, says Kincaid, writing in 1794, "it is moderate to say that not less than £3,000,000 sterling has been expended in building and public improvements."

"Thirty-five years ago," says the *Edinburgh Advertiser* for 1823, "there were scarcely a dozen shops in the New Town; now, in Princes Street, with the exception of hotels and the Albyn Club Room, they reach to Hanover Street."

In the present day the whole area we have described is mainly occupied by shops, with the exception of Charlotte Square and a small portion of Queen Street.

CHAPTER XXIV.

ELDER STREET—LEITH STREET—BROUGHTON STREET.

Elder Street—Leith Street—The old "Black Bull "- Margaret The Theatre Royal—Its Predecessors on the same Site—The Circus—Corri's Rooms—The Pantheon - Caledonian Theatre Adelphi Theatre—Queen's Theatre and Opera House—Burned and Rebuilt—St. Mary's Chapel—Bishop Cameron.

THE continuation north from East Register Street and St. James's Square, called Elder Street (probably the upper portion of the old Broughton

wine merchant, in premises opposite the Tron church, and died at Forthneth in 1799. He resided long in Princes Street, in the house known as

ADAM'S DESIGN FOR ST. GEORGE'S CHURCH, CHARLOTTE SQUARE.

Loan, which led from the Lang Gate to that village), is named from Thomas Elder of Forneth, who was Lord Provost thrice between 1788 and 1798, at a time when great responsibility attached to his office, when all Lowland Scotland, in which there were only about 2,000 troops, was convulsed by the agitation excited by the "friends of the people." When the memorable British Convention was held on the 5th of December, 1793, Lord Provost Elder suppressed it, and took twelve of the leaders prisoners ; and on the 12th of the same month he crushed another meeting held at the Cockpit in the Grassmarket. For these services to the State, Mr. Elder, in 1795, was appointed Postmaster-General for Scotland. He realised a fortune as a

Fortune's Tontine, and subsequently at No. 85, now a portion of the New Club.

Prior to the erection of the Regent Bridge, and the formation of the roadway eastward therefrom, one line of street, mostly of rough rubble, and nearly all common stairs, extended due south and north from the foot of Shakespeare Square, transversely across Princes Street, to the head of Leith Street, and thence downward at a north-east angle to the corner of St. Ninian's Row, opposite the High and Low Terrace. The latter did not exist in 1787, and the former only partially ; but both follow the curve of the old highway that led from the Lang Gate to Leith Loan or Walk, as it is now called, passing on the left the village of Picardie.

Until recent years the old "Black Bull" was long established here, and an arch on the west side gave access to the stables. In a species of advertisement appended to Kincaid's "View of Edinburgh," in 1794, is the following:—

"English Travellers, on business, are to be found commonly, at Paterson's, Foot of the Pleasance; McFarlane's, Head of the Cowgate; Ramsay's Lodging's, Milne Square; McKay's, Grassmarket; Lee's, Black Bull, Head of Leith

and tried for his life on charges of treason, with Hunter, Muir, and others. He conducted his own case, and the court sentenced him to fourteen years' transportation beyond the seas. "In consequence of the proceedings on the 9th instant," says the *Annual Register* for 1794, "while Mr. Margarot went to the Justiciary Court, every precaution was taken this day by the Lord Provost, magistrates, and sheriff, to prevent any breach of

THE ALBERT MEMORIAL, CHARLOTTE SQUARE.

Walk. N.B.—Strangers can never be at a loss for a guide to any of the above places, as, at the Cross there are always in waiting, running stationers, otherwise *cadies*, that will conduct them to any place wanted, for a small charge."

In style and accommodation the "Black Bull" was one of those old-fashioned inns which were the precursors of the modern hotel, and preserved their style and features unchanged amid the encroachments of private speculation and the rage for public improvement. Now the space on which it stood is covered with shops and dwelling-houses.

In this street lived Margarot, one of the "Friends of the People," who was arrested by Provost Elder,

good order and police. A great crowd assembled at his lodgings in Leith Street about ten o'clock, and he was conducted, with a wreath, or arch, held over him, with inscriptions of *Reason, Liberty,* &c. About the middle of the North Bridge, however, the cavalcade was met by the Lord Provost, sheriff, constable, peace-officers, &c., and immediately dispersed, the arch was demolished, and its supporters taken into custody. A press-gang attended to assist the peace-officers. Mr. Margarot then walked to the court, escorted by the Lord Provost, &c., and no disturbance ensued."

Subsequently we read, that on the 10th of February, Messrs. Margarot, Muir, Skirving, and Palmer—to whose memory the grand obelisk in the Calton burying-ground has been erected—were transmitted from Newgate to a ship bound for Botany Bay.

In those days, and for long after, there was a narrow close or alley named the Salt Backet, which ran between the head of Leith Street and the Low Calton, and by this avenue, in 1806, James Mackoul, *alias* "Captain Moffat," the noted thief, whom we have referred to in the story of Begbie's assassination, effected his escape when pursued for a robbery in the Theatre Royal.

Eastward of the head of Leith Street, and almost in the direct line of the Regent Arch, stood the old Methodist Meeting House.

Facing Leith Walk, at the junction of Little King Street with Broughton Street, is the present Theatre Royal, occupying the site of several places of amusement its predecessors.

About the year 1792 Mr. Stephen Kemble, in the course of his peripatetic life, having failed to obtain the management of the old Theatre Royal at the end of the North Bridge, procured leave to erect a new house, which he called a Circus, in what is described in the titles thereof as a piece of ground bounded by a hedge. Mrs. Esten, an admired actress, the lessee of the Theatre Royal, succeeded in obtaining a decree of the Court of Session against the production of plays at this rival establishment; but it nevertheless was permanently detrimental to the old one, as 'it continued to furnish amusements too closely akin to the theatrical for years; and in the *Scots Magazine* for 1793 we read:—"January 21. The New Theatre of Edinburgh (formerly the Circus) under the management of Mr. Stephen Kemble, was opened with the comedy of the *Rivals*. This theatre is most elegantly and commodiously fitted up, and is considerably larger than the Theatre Royal." By the end of that season, Kemble, however, procured the latter, and retained it till 1800.

A speculative Italian named Signor Corri took up the circus as a place for concerts and other entertainments, while collaterally with him a Signor Pietro Urbani endeavoured to have card and music meetings at the Assembly Rooms. Urbani was an Italian teacher of singing, long settled in Edinburgh, where, towards the close of the eighteenth century, he published "A Selection of Scots Songs, harmonised and improved, with simple and adapted graces," a work extending to six folio volumes. Urbani's selection is remarkable in three respects: the novelty of the number and kind of instruments used in the accompaniments; the filling up of the

pianoforte harmony; and the use, for the first time of introductory and concluding symphonies to the melodies. He died, very poor, in Dublin, in 1816.

Corri's establishment in Broughton Street was eminently unsuccessful, yet he made it a species of theatre. "If it be true," says a writer, "as we are told by an intelligent foreigner in 1800, that very few people in Edinburgh then spent a thousand a year, and that they were considered rather important persons who had three or four hundred; we shall understand how, in these circumstances, neither the theatre, nor Corri's Rooms, nor the Assembly Rooms, could be flourishing concerns."

It is said that Corri deemed himself so unfortunate, that he declared his belief "that if he became a baker the people would give up the use of bread." Ultimately he failed, and was compelled to seek the benefit of the *cessio bonorum*. In a theatrical critique for 1801, which animadverts pretty freely on the public of the city for their indifference to theatrical matters, it is said:—"By a run of the *School for Scandal*, an Italian manager, Corri, was enabled to swim like boys on bladders; but he ultimately sank under the weight of his debts, and was only released by the benignity of the British laws. Neither the universal abilities of Wilkinson, his private worth, nor his full company, could draw the attention of the capital of the North till he was some hundred pounds out of pocket; and though he was at last assisted by the interference of certain public characters, yet, after all, his success did little more than make up his losses in the beginning of the season."

In 1809 Mr. Henry Siddons re-fitted Corri's Rooms as a theatre, at an expense of about £4,000. There performances were continued for two seasons, till circumstances rendered it necessary for Mr. Siddons to occupy the old Theatre Royal.

In 1816 Corri's Rooms, as the edifice was still called, was the scene of a grand *fête* given to the 78th Highlanders, or Ross-shire Buffs, who had just returned from sickly and unhealthy quarters at Nieuport in Flanders. On this occasion, we are told, the rooms were blazing with hundreds of lamps, "shedding their light upon all the beauty and fashion of Edinburgh, enlivened by the uniforms of the officers of the several regiments."

The band of the Black Watch occupied the large orchestra, in front of which was a thistle, with the motto *Prenez garde*. Festoons of the 42nd tartan, and the shields of the Duke of Wellington and the Marquis of Huntly, with cuirasses from the recent field of Waterloo, were among the decorations here. Elsewhere were other trophies, with the mottoes *Egypt* and *Corunna*. At the other end was the band of the 78th, where hung the shields of Picton and Achmuty, and a brilliant star, with the mottoes *Assaye* and *Maida*. " Under this orchestra was a beautiful transparency, representing an old Scotsman with his bonnet, giving a hearty welcome to two soldiers of the 42nd and 78th regiments, while a bonny lassie is peeping out from a cottage door; the background formed a landscape, with Edinburgh Castle in the distance." At eleven o'clock came famous old Neil Gow, with his band of violins, and the ball—which was long remembered in Edinburgh—began.

After some time Corri's Rooms were called the Pantheon, and in December, 1823, the house was again opened under the new appellation of the Caledonian Theatre (which it held for years afterwards), by Mr. Henry Johnstone, an old Edinburgh favourite and luckless native of the city. The papers of the time announce that the dancing and tumbling of the Pantheon "are superseded; and, excepting that melodramas are presented in place of regular tragedies and comedies, the Caledonian Theatre in no respect differs in the nature and style of its entertainments from the regular theatre." One of the first pieces brought out was *The Orphan of Geneva*.

"The house is dingy and even dirty," says the *Weekly Journal* for that year, " and very defectively lighted. This is not at all in harmony with Mr. Johnstone's usual enterprise, and calls for amendment. The name of *Caledonian* is perhaps conceived to be a kind of apology for the clumsy tartan hangings over some of the boxes; but we can by no means comprehend why the house was not re-painted. The visitor cannot fail to be immediately struck with the contrast of its dingy hue, with the freshness and beauty of the Theatre Royal."

Mr. Johnstone's losses compelled him, after a time, to relinquish management. He left Edinburgh, and did not return to it till 1830, when he played four nights at the same theatre, then leased by Mr. Bass. Poor Johnstone, an actor much admired in London, but every way unfortunate, eventually went to America.

The theatre was afterwards called the Adelphi, and was burned in 1853, during the management of Mr. R. H. Wyndham. On its site was rebuilt the Queen's Theatre and Opera House, under the s ime enterprising manager, long one of the greatest theatrical favourites in Edinburgh; but this also was destroyed by fire in 1865, when several lives were lost by the falling of a wall. By a singular fatality it was a third time completely gutted by fire ten years afterwards, but was re-constructed in the latter part of 1875, and reopened in January, 1876, prior to which Mr. and Mrs. Wyndham had taken their farewell of the stage and of Edinburgh.

It is a handsome building, with a portico, and is adorned with medallions of Shakspere, Scott, Molière, and Goethe. Although erected within the walls of the theatre burned on the 6th of February, 1875, it is almost entirely a new building internally, different from all its predecessors, greatly improved, and seated for 2,300 persons. The works have been designed and executed by C. J. Phipps, F.S.A., architect of the Gaiety Theatre, London.

Immediately adjoining this theatre—the gable wall being a mutual one—is St. Mary's Roman Catholic chapel, now the pro-cathedral of the Archbishop of St. Andrews and Edinburgh, whose residence is in the narrow lane to the northward.

It was built in 1813, from designs by James Gillespie Graham, architect, at the expense of £8,000. In the original elevations more ornament was introduced than it was found there were funds to execute, as these were chiefly raised by subscription among the Catholics of Edinburgh, then a small, and still a poor, congregation. The dimensions of this edifice within the walls are 110 feet by 57. The eastern front, in which is the entrance, is ornamented by two central pinnacles 70 feet high, and the adoption of the Gothic style in this small chapel *first* led to the adoption of a similar style in various other religious edifices since erected in the city. It possesses a very good organ, and above the altar is a fine painting of the Saviour dead. It was presented to the church by Miss Chalmers, daughter of Sir G. Chalmers.

Some prelates of the Catholic Church lie buried before the high altar, among them Bishops Alexander Cameron and Andrew Carruthers. The interment of the former excited much interest in Edinburgh in 1828, the funeral obsequies being in a style never seen in Scotland since the Reformation, and also from the general esteem in which the bishop was held by all. He was born in 1747, and went to the Scottish College at Rome in 1760, and bore away all the prizes. Returning to Scotland in 1772, he was Missionary Apostolic in Strathearn till 1780, when he was consecrated at Madeira, and, succeeding Bishop Hay, had resided permanently in Edinburgh since 1806.

REMAINS OF THE VILLAGE OF OLD BROUGHTON, 1852.
(*From a Drawing by George W. Simson.*)

CHAPTER XXV.

THE VILLAGE AND BARONY OF BROUGHTON.

Broughton—The Village and Barony—The Loan—Broughton first mentioned—Feudal Superiors—Witches Burned—Leslie's Head-quarters—Gordon of Ellon's Children Murdered—Taken *Red Hand*—The Tolbooth of the Burgh—The Minute Books—Free Burgesses—Modern Churches erected in the Bounds of the Barony.

ACROSS the once well-tilled slope where now York Place stands, a narrow and secluded way between hedgerows, called the Loan of Broughton, led for ages to the isolated village of that name, of which but a few vestiges still remain.

In a memoir of Robert Wallace, D.D., the eminent author of the "Essay on the Numbers of Mankind," and other works, an original member of the Rankenion Club—a literary society instituted at Edinburgh in 1716—we are told, in the *Scots Magazine* for 1809, that "he died 29th of July, 1771, at his *country* lodgings in Broughton Loan, in his 75th year."

This baronial burgh, or petty town, about a mile distant by the nearest road from the ancient city, stood in hollow ground southward and eastward from the line of London Street, and had its own tolbooth and court-house, with several substantial stone mansions and many thatched cot-

tages, in 1780, and a few of the former are still surviving.

Bruchton, or Broughton, according to Maitland, signified the Castle-town. If this place ever possessed a fortalice or keep, from whence its name seems to be derived, all vestiges of it have disappeared long ago. It is said to have been connected with the Castle of Edinburgh, and that from the lands of Broughton the supplies for the garrison came. But this explanation has been deemed by some fanciful.

The earliest notice of Broughton is in the charter of David I. to Holyrood, *circa* A.D. 1143-7, wherein he grants to the monks, "Hereth, *et Broctunam cum suis rectis divisis*," &c.; thus, with its lands, it belonged to the Church till the Reformation, when it was vested in the State. According to the stent roll of the abbey, the Barony of Broughton was most ample in extent, and, among many other lands, included those of "Lochflatt, Pleasance, St. Leonards, Hillhousefield, Bonnytoun, and Pilrig," &c.

This ancient barony and the surrounding lands comprehended within its jurisdiction were granted by James VI., in 1568, to Adam Bothwell, Bishop of Orkney, in whose time the village tolbooth would seem to have been erected; it remained intact till 1829, and stood at the east of the present Barony Street, a quaint edifice, with crowstepped gables and dormer windows. Over its north door, to which a flight of thirteen steps gave access, was the date 1582. It was flanked on one side by a venerable set of stocks, a symbol of justice rare in Scotland, where the iron *jougs* were always used.

The bishop surrendered these lands to the Crown in 1587, in favour of Sir Lewis Bellenden of Auchnoul, Lord Justice Clerk and Keeper of the Palace of Linlithgow, who obtained a charter uniting them into a free barony and regality. Sir Lewis died in 1591, and was succeeded by his son, who is designated in the public archives as *Jacobo Ballenden de Broughton, filio et heredi apparenti domini Ludovici Ballenden de Auchnoule.*

The Broughton was the scene of some encounters between the Queen's-men and King's-men in the time of the Regent Morton. The latter were in the habit of defying Kirkaldy's garrison in the Castle, by riding about the fields in range of his guns with handkerchiefs tied to the points of their swords. One of these parties, commanded by Henry Stewart, second Lord Methven, in 1571, "being a little too forward, were severely reprimanded for their unreasonable bravery; for, as they stood at a place called Broughton, a cannon bullet knocked his lordship and seven men on the head; he was reputed a good soldier, and had been more lamented had he behaved himself more wisely." (Crawford of Drumsoy.)

Like other barons, the feudal superior of Broughton had powers of "pit and gallows" over his vassals—so-called from the manner in which criminals were executed—hanging the men upon a gibbet, and drowning women in a pit as it was not deemed decent to hang them. Sir Lewis Bellenden

and his successors had the power of appointing bailies and holding courts within the limits of the barony. Sir Lewis, a noted trafficker with wizards, died on the 3rd of November, 1606, and was succeeded by his son Sir William Bellenden, as Baron of Broughton, which in those days was notorious as the haunt of reputed witches and warlocks, who were frequently incarcerated in its old tolbooth. An execution of some of these wretched creatures is thus recorded in the minutes of the Privy Council: "1608, December 1. The Earl of Mar declared to the Council that some women were taken in Broughton as witches, and being put to an assize and convicted, albeit they persevered in their denial to the end, yet they were burned quick (alive) after such a cruel manner that some of them died in despair, renouncing and blaspheming (God); and others, half burned, brak out of the fire, but were cast alive in it again, till they were burned to the death."

In 1623 Sir William borrowed a sum of 3,000 merks Scots from George Heriot, and in security assigned the lands of Dishingflat, Meadowflat, the mills of Canonmills, and other portions of land in the barony of Broughton.

In October, 1627, as the Privy Council was sitting in its chamber at the palace of Holyrood, a strange outrage took place. John Young, a poulterer, attacked Mr. Richard Bannatyne, bailie-depute of Broughton, at the Council-room door, and struck him in the back with his sword, nearly killing him on the spot. In great indignation the Council sent off Young to be tried on the morrow at the tolbooth, with orders: "If he be convict, that his Majesty's justice and his depute cause doom to be pronounced against him, ordaining him to be drawn upon ane cart backward frae the tolbooth to the place of execution at the market cross, and there hangit to the deid and quartered, his head to be set upon the Nether Bow, and his hands to be set upon the Water Yett."

Sir William Bellenden, in 1627, disposed of the whole lands to Robert, Earl of Roxburgh, and by an agreement between him and Charles I. this ancient barony passed by purchase to the Governors of Heriot's Hospital in 1636, to whom the

THE BROUGHTON TOLBOOTH.
(From Wilson's "Memorials of Edinburgh in the Olden Time," published by T. C. Jack, Edinburgh.)

superiority of Broughton was yielded by the Crown, partly in payment of debts due by Charles I. to the hospital. Thenceforward the barony was governed by a bailie, named by the Governors of the Hospital, who possessed to the full the baronial powers of pit and gallows over their tenants therein.

Prior to this, in 1629, Kincaid of Warriston was pursued before the Baron-bailie, but the case was remitted to the Lord Justice General and the Judges, who remitted the affair to the Council.

In 1650, during some portions of the campaign that preceded the battle of Dunbar, General Leslie made Broughton his head-quarters, when he threw up those lines of defence from the base of the Calton Hill to Leith, and so completely baffled Cromwell's advance upon the city.

After the barony came into the possession of Heriot's Hospital, the Common Council of the city, on the 17th of July, 1661, gave a grant to William Johnstone, then Baron-bailie, "of the goods and chattels of women condemned for witchcraft, and which were thereby escheated to the said bailie."

On this remarkable grant, Maitland observes in his History : "Wherefore, it is not to be wondered at that innocent persons should be convicted of a crime they could not be guilty of, when their effects fall to the judge or judges."

In 1715, during the insurrection, a party of Highlanders marching through Broughton were cannonaded from the Castle, and a six-pound shot that went through a barn on this occasion, is preserved in the Antiquarian Museum.

In 1717 Broughton was the scene of the trial and execution in a remarkable case of murder, which made famous the old pathway known as Gabriel's Road. By some strange misconception, in "Peter's Letters to his Kinsfolk," the murderer is called "Gabriel," and in a work called "Celebrated Trials" (in six volumes), he is called the Rev. Thomas Hunter, whereas in reality his name was Robert Irvine. Of this road, to which we have already referred, Chambers gives us the following description :—" Previous to 1767 the eye of a person perched in a favourable situation in the Old Town surveyed the whole ground on which the New Town was built. Immediately beyond the North Loch was a range of grass fields called Bearford's Parks, from the name of the proprietor, Hepburn of Bearford, in East Lothian. Bounding these on the north, in the line of the subsequent Princes Street, was a road enclosed by two dry stone walls, called the Lang Dykes. . . . . The main mass of ground, originally rough with whins and broom, but latterly forming what was called Wood's Farm, was crossed obliquely by a road extending between Silver Mills, a rural hamlet on the mill course of the Leith, and the passage into the Old Town at the bottom of Halkerston's Wynd. There are still some traces of this road. You will see it leave Silver Mills behind West Cumberland Street. Behind Duke Street, on the west side, the boundary wall of the Queen Street garden is oblique, in consequence of its having passed that way. Finally, it terminates in a short oblique passage behind the Register House, wherein stood till lately 'Ambrose's Tavern. This short passage bore the name of Gabriel's Road, and was supposed to do so in connection with a remarkable murder of which it was the scene."

Mr. James Gordon, of Ellon, in Aberdeenshire, a rich merchant of Edinburgh, and once a bailie there, in the early part of the eighteenth century had a villa on the north side of the city, somewhere between this road and the village of Broughton. His family consisted of his wife, two sons, and a daughter, these being all of tender age. He had a tutor for his two boys—John and Alexander—a licentiate of the Church, named Robert Irvine, who was of respectable attainments, but had a somewhat gloomy disposition. Views of predestination, drawn from some work of Flavel's, belonging to the college library, had taken possession of his mind, which had, perhaps, some infirmity ready to be acted upon by external circumstances and dismal impulses.

Having cast eyes of admiration on a pretty servant-maid in Mr. Gordon's house, he was tempted to take some liberties with her, which were observed, and mentioned incidentally by his pupils. For this he was reprimanded by Mr. Gordon, but on apologising, was forgiven. Into Irvine's morbid and sensitive nature the affront, or rebuke, sank deeply, and a thirst for revenge possessed him. For three days he revolved the insane idea of cutting off Mr. Gordon's three children, and on the 28th of April, 1717, he found an opportunity of partially accomplishing his terrible purpose.

It was Sunday, and Mr. and Mrs. Gordon went to spend the afternoon with a friend in the city, taking their little daughter with them. Irvine, left with the two boys, took them out for a walk along the then broomy and grassy slope, where now York Place and St. Andrew Square are situated. While the boys ran about gathering flowers and pursuing butterflies, he sat whetting the knife with which he meant to destroy them!

"Calling the two boys to him, he upbraided them with their informing upon him, and told them that they must suffer for it. They ran off, but he easily overtook and seized them. Then keeping one down upon the grass with his knee, he cut the other's throat, after which he dispatched in like manner the remaining one." *

By a singular chance a gentleman enjoying his evening stroll upon the Castle Hill obtained a perfect view of the whole episode—most probably with a telescope—and immediately gave an alarm. Irvine, who had already attempted, but unsuccessfully, to cut his own throat, now fled from his pursuers towards the Water of Leith, thinking to drown himself, but was taken, brought in a cart to the tolbooth of Broughton, and there chained down to the floor like a wild beast.

In those days there was a summary process in Scotland for murderers, taken as he was—*red hand*. It was only necessary to bring him next day before the judge of the district and have sentence passed upon him. Irvine was tried before the Baron-bailie upon the 30th of April, and received sentence of death.

In his "dying confession," supposed to be unique, it is recorded that "he desired one who was present to take care of his books and conceal his papers, for he said there were many foolish things in them. He imagined that he was to be hung in chains, and showed some concern on that account. He prayed the parents of the murdered children to forgive him, which they, very christianly, consented to. At sight of the bloody clothes in which the children were murdered, and which were brought to him in the prison a little before he went to the place of execution, he was much affected, and broke into groans and tears. When he came to the place of execution the ministers prayed for him, and he also prayed himself, but with a low voice. . . . . Both his hands were struck off by the executioner, and he was afterwards hanged. While he was hanging the wound he gave himself in the throat with the penknife broke out afresh, and the blood gushed out in great abundance."

He was hanged at Greenside, and his hands were stuck upon the gibbet with the knife used in the murders. His body was then flung into a neighbouring quarry-hole.

In February, 1721, John Webster, having committed a murder upon a young woman named Marion Campbell, daughter of Campbell of Kevenknock, near the city wall, but on Heriot's Hospital ground, was taken to Broughton, and condemned to death by the Baron-bailie; and in the same year the treasurer of the hospital complains of the expense incurred in prosecuting offenders in some other cases of murder committed within the barony; but these onerous and costly privileges were eventually abrogated in 1746, by the Act which abolished all hereditable jurisdictions, and a few years afterwards the governors granted the use of the ancient tolbooth to one of their tenants as a storehouse, "reserving to the hospital a room for holding their Baron Courts when they shall think fit." (Steven's "Hist. Heriot's Hospital.")

Though demolished, some fragments of the old edifice still remain in the shape of cellars, in connection with premises occupied as a tavern in Broughton Street.

The minute books of this ancient barony are still preserved, and contain a great number of names of persons of note who were made free burgesses of the burgh, several of these having received that honour in return for good deeds conferred upon it.

During the insurrection of 1715 the inhabitants of the regality obtained leave to form a night-guard for their own protection, but to be under the orders of the captain of the Canongate Guard.

The magistracy of this burgh consisted of a Baron-bailie, a senior and junior bailie, high sheriff, treasurer, clerk, dean of guild, surgeon, bellman, and captain of the tolbooth. The first-named official, "on high occasions, dons a crimson robe and cocked hat, displaying at the same time a grand official chain with medal attached. These, with a bell, ancient musket, sword, and some other articles, compose the moveable property of the corporation."

The lodge of Free Gardeners of the Barony of Broughton was instituted in the year 1845, by a number of citizens of the ward, and as regards the number of its members and finance is said to be one of the most successful of the order in Scotland.

In 21 Broughton Street, there resided about the year 1855 a hard-working and industrious literary man, the late William Anderson, author of "Landscape Lyrics," "The Scottish Biographical Dictionary," "The Scottish Nation," in three large volumes, and other works; but who died old, poor, unpensioned, and neglected.

The village, or little burgh, appears to have been situated principally to the north of where Albany Street stands, comprising within its limits Broughton Place and Street, Barony Street and Albany Street. The houses, with few exceptions, were two-storeyed though small, having outside stairs, thatched roofs, and crow-stepped gables, each having a little garden or kailyard in front. They seem to have

---

* "Domestic Annals," vol. iii.

been placed along both sides of a road that ran east and west; those on the south being more detached, spread away upward nearly to York Place. The western end of the hamlet was demolished when the present Broughton market was constructed. From that portion, which had been a kind of square, a path led through the fields, where now London Street stands, to Canonmills.

One by one the cottages have disappeared, in their rude construction, with forestairs and loop-

building with a graceful spire 180 feet high. It was erected on the site of an ancient quarry, 1859–61, after designs by J. F. Rocheid, at the cost of £13,000, and is in a mixed later English and Tudor style.

Heriot's school, also on the west side of the street, is one of the elementary institutions which the governors of George Heriot's Hospital were empowered by Act of Parliament to erect from their surplus revenues. It is attended by about 3,400 boys and girls, and rises from a spacious and

BROUGHTON BURN, 1850. *From a Drawing by William Channing, in the possession of Dr. J. A. Sidey.*)

hole windows, contrasting strongly with the new and fashionable streets that have replaced them.

In the modern Broughton Street is a plain Ionic edifice, long used as a place of worship by the disciples of Edward Irving, and near it, at the south-east angle of Albany Street, the Independent church was built in 1816, at a cost of £4,000, and improved in 1867 at a cost of more than £200; a plain and unpretending edifice.

The Gaelic church, which adjoins the Independent church, is the old Catholic Apostolic, which was bought in 1875 for about £5,000, improved for about £2,000, and opened in October 1876.

St. Mary's Free church is a beautiful Gothic

airy arcade, under which they can play in wet weather.

At the south-west corner of Broughton Place is St. James's Episcopal chapel, which, in architecture externally, is assimilated with the houses of the street. It was built in 1829, and has attached to it, on the north, a neat school, built in 1869. Fronting Broughton Place, and at the eastern end thereof, stands the United Presbyterian church, built in 1821, at the cost of £7,095. It is a spacious edifice, with a very handsome tetrastyle Doric portico, and underwent repairs in 1853 and 1870, at the united cost of £4,000. It is chiefly remarkable as the scene of the ministrations of the late Dr. John Brown.

The new Catholic and Apostolic church, a conspicuous and spacious edifice, stands north of all those mentioned at the corner of East London Street. It was founded in November, 1873, and opened with much ceremony in April, 1876. It is in a kind of Norman style, after designs by R. Anderson, and measures 200 feet long, is 45 feet in height to the wall-head, and 64 to the apex of the internal roof. It comprises a nave, chancel, and baptistry. The nave measures 100 feet in length, by 45 in breadth; is divided into five bays, marked externally by buttresses, and has at each corner a massive square turret surmounted by a pinnacle rising as high as the ridge of the roof. The chancel measures 61¼ feet, and communicates with the nave.

PICARDY VILLAGE AND GAYFIELD HOUSE. *(After Clerk of Eldin.)*

CHAPTER XXVI.

THE NORTHERN NEW TOWN.

Picardy Place—Lords Eldin and Craig - Sir David Milne—John Abercrombie—Lord Newton—Commissioner Osborne—St. Paul's Church—St. George's Chapel—William Douglas, Artist—Professor Playfair—General Scott of Bellevue—Drummond Place—C. K. Sharpe of Hoddam—Lord Robertson—Abercrombie Place and Heriot Row—Miss Ferrier—House in which H. McKenzie died—Rev. A. Alison—Great King Street—Sir R. Christison—Sir William Hamilton—Sir William Allan—Lord Colonsay, &c.

THE northern New Town, of which we now propose to relate the progress and history, is separated from the southern by the undulating and extensive range of Queen Street Gardens, which occupy a portion of the slope that shelves down towards the valley of the Water of Leith.

It is also in a parallelogram extending, from the quarter we have just been describing, westward to the Queensferry Road, and northward to the line of Fettes Row. It has crescental curves in some of its main lines, with squares, and is constructed in a much grander style of architecture than the original New Town of 1767. Generally, it was begun about 1802, and nearly completed by 1822. In the eastern part of this parallelogram are Picardy Place, York Place, Forth and Albany Streets.

It would appear that so early as 1730 the Governors of Heriot's Hospital, as superiors of the barony of Broughton, had sold five acres of land at the head of Broughton Loan to the city, for the behoof of refugees or their descendants who had come from France, after the revocation of the Edict of Nantes. A colony of these emigrants, principally silk weavers, had been for some time attempting to cultivate mulberry trees on the slope of Moultree's Hill, but without success, owing to the variable nature of the climate.

The position of the houses forming the village of Picardie, as these poor people named it, after their native province, is distinctly shown in the map of 1787, occupying nearly the site of the north side of the present Picardy Place, which after the Scottish Board of Manufacturers acquired the ground, was built in 1809.

More than twenty years before that period the magistrates seem to have contemplated having a square here, as in 1783 they advertised, " to be feued, the several acres, for building, lying on the west side of the new road to Leith, immediately adjoining to Picardy Gardens. The ground is laid out in the form of a square. The situation is remarkably pleasant. . . . According to the plan, the buildings will have plots of background for the purpose of gardens and offices ; and the possessors of these will have the privilege of the area within *the Square*, &c. Further particulars may be had on applying to James Jollie, writer, the proprietor, Royal Bank Close, who will show the plan of the ground." (*Edin. Advert.*, 1783.)

This plan would seem to have been abandoned, and a street, with York Place, in direct communication with Queen Street, substituted.

Among the earliest occupants of a house in Picardy Place was John Clerk, Lord Eldin, who took up his abode in No. 16, when an advocate at the bar. The grandson of Sir John Clerk of Penicuick, and son of John Clerk, author of a celebrated work on naval tactics, Lord Eldin was born in 1757, and in 1785 was called to the bar, and so great were his intellectual qualities—at a time when the Scottish bar was really distinguished for intellect—that, it is said, that at one period he had nearly half of all the court business in his hands ; but his elevation to the bench did not occur until 1823, when he was well advanced in life.

In "Peter's Letters" he is described as the Coryphæus of the bar. " He is the plainest, the shrewdest, and the most sarcastic of men ; his sceptre owes the whole of its power to its weight— nothing to glitter. It is impossible to imagine a physiognomy more expressive of the character of a great lawyer and barrister. The features are in themselves good, at least a painter would call them so, and the upper part of the profile has as fine lines as could be wished. But then, how the habits of the mind have stamped their traces on every part of the face ! What sharpness, razor-like sharpness, has indented itself about the wrinkles of his eyelids; the eyes themselves, so quick, so grey, such bafflers of scrutiny, such exquisite scrutinisers, how they change in expression—it seems almost how they change their colour—shifting from contracted, concentrated blackness, through every shade of brown, blue, green, and hazel, back into their own gleaming grey again. How they glisten into a smile of disdain ! . . . He seems to be affected with the most delightful and balmy feelings, by the contemplation of some soft-headed, prosing driveller, racking his poor brain, or bellowing his lungs out, all about something which he, the smiler, sees so thoroughly, so distinctly."

Lord Eldin, on the bench as when at the bar, pertinaciously adhered to the old Doric Scottish of his boyhood, and in this there was no affectation ; but it was the pure old dialect and idiom of the eighteenth century. He was a man of refined tastes, and a great connoisseur in pictures. He was a capital artist ; and it is said, that had he given himself entirely to art, he would have been one of the greatest masters Scotland has ever produced. He was plain in appearance, and had a halt in his gait. Passing down the High Street one day, he once heard a girl say to her companion, "That is Johnnie Clerk, the lame lawyer." " No, madam," said he ; " I may be a lame man, but not a *lame lawyer.*"

He died a bachelor in his house in Picardy Place, where, old-maid-like, he had contracted such an attachment to cats, that his domestic establishment could almost boast of at least half a dozen of them ; and when consulted by a client he was generally to be found seated in his study with a favourite Tom elevated on his shoulder or purring about his ears.

His death occurred on the 30th May, 1832, after which his extensive collection of paintings, sketches, and rare prints was brought to sale in 16 Picardy Place, where, on the 16th of March, 1833, a very serious accident ensued.

The fame of his collection had attracted a great crowd of men and women of taste and letters, and when the auctioneer was in the act of disposing of a famous Teniers, which had been a special favourite of Lord Eldin, the floor of the drawing-room gave way. " The scene which was produced may be imagined, but can scarcely be described," says the Caledonian Mercury of the 18th March. "From eighty to a hundred persons, ladies as well as gentlemen, were precipitated in one mass into an apartment below, filled with china and articles of vertu. The cries and shrieks, intermingled with exclamations and ejaculations of distress, were heartrending; but what added to the unutterable agony of that awful moment, the density of the cloud of dust, impervious to the rays of light, produced total darkness, diffusing a choking atmosphere, which nearly stifled the terrified multitude, and in this state of suspense they remained several minutes." Among the mass of people who went down with the floor were Lord Moncrieff, Sir James Riddell of Ardnamurchan, and Sir Archibald Campbell of Succoth. Many persons were most severely injured, and Mr. Smith, banker, of Moray Place, on whom the hearth-stone fell, was killed.

York Place, the continuation of this thoroughfare to Queen Street, is nearly all unchanged since it was built, and is broad and stately, with spacious and lofty houses, which were inhabited by Sir Henry Raeburn, Francis Horner, Dr. John Abercrombie, Dr. John Coldstream, Alexander Geddes, A.R.A., and other distinguished men.

No. 10 was the abode of Lord Craig, the successor on the bench of Lord Hailes in 1792, and whose well-known attainments, and especially his connection with the Mirror and Lounger, gave his name an honourable place among local notorieties. He was the cousin-german of the celebrated Mrs. McLehose, the Clarinda of Robert Burns, and to her he bequeathed an annuity, at his death, which occurred in 1813. His house was afterwards occupied by the gallant Admiral Sir David Milne, who, when a lieutenant, took possession of the Pique frigate, after her surrender to the Blanche, in the West Indies; captured La Seine, in 1798, and La Vengeance, of 38 guns, in 1800, and who commanded the Impregnable, in the attack on Algiers, when he was Rear-Admiral, and had 150 of his crew killed and wounded, as Brenton records in his "Naval History." He died a Knight Grand Cross of the Bath, and left a son, Sir Alexander Milne, also K.C.B., and Admiral, more than once commander of fleets, and who first went to sea with his father in the flag-ship Leander, in 1817. Sir David died on board of a Granton steamer, when returning home, in 1845, and was buried at Inveresk.

Doctor John Abercrombie, Physician to Her Majesty, lived in No. 19, and died there in 1844, aged 64. He was a distinguished consulting physician, and moral writer, born at Aberdeen, in 1781; F.R.C.S. in 1823; and was author of "Inquiries concerning the Intellectual Powers," which has gone through many editions, "The Philosophy of the Moral Feelings," &c. His bust is in the museum of the Royal College of Surgeons.

Concerning his death, the following curious story has found its way into print. A Mrs. M., a native of the West Indies, was at Blair Logie at the time of the demise of Dr. Abercrombie, with whom she had been very intimate. He died suddenly, without any previous indisposition, just as he was about to enter his carriage in York Place, at eleven o'clock on a Thursday morning. On the night between Thursday and Friday Mrs. M. dreamt that she saw the whole family of Dr. Abercrombie dressed entirely in white, dancing a solemn funeral dance, upon which she awoke, wondering that she should have dreamt anything so absurd, as it was contrary to their custom to dance on any occasion. Immediately afterwards her maid came to tell her that she had seen Dr. Abercrombie reclining against a wall "with his jaw fallen, and a livid countenance, mournfully shaking his head as he looked at her." She passed the day in great uneasiness, and wrote to inquire for the Doctor, relating what had happened, and expressing her conviction that he was dead, and her letter was seen by several persons in Edinburgh on the day of its arrival.

No. 22 was the house of Lord Newton, known as the wearer of "Covington's gown," in memory of the patriotism and humanity displayed by the latter in defending the Jacobite prisoners on their trial at Carlisle in 1747. His judicial talents and social eccentricities formed the subject of many anecdotes. He participated largely in the bacchanalian propensities so prevalent among the legal men of his time, and was frequently known to put "three lang craigs" (i.e. long-necked bottles of claret) "under his belt" after dinner, and thereafter dictate to his clerk a paper of more than sixty pages. The MS. would then be sent to press, and the proofs be corrected next morning at the bar of the Inner House.

He would often spend the whole night in convivial indulgence at the Crochallan Club, perhaps be driven home to York Place about seven in the morning, sleep for two hours, and be seated on the bench at the usual hour. The French traveller Simond relates his surprise "on stepping one morning into the Parliament House to find in the dignified capacity and exhibiting all the dignified bearing of a judge, the very gentleman with whom he had just spent a night of debauch and parted from only one hour before, when both were excessively intoxicated."

His lordship was so fond of card-playing that he was wont to say, laughingly, "Cards are my profession—the law my amusement." He died at Powrie, in Forfarshire, on the 19th of October, 1811.

In 1795 Sir Henry Raeburn built the large house No. 32, the upper part of which had been lighted from the roof and fitted up as a gallery for exhibiting pictures, while the lower was divided into convenient painting rooms, but his residence was then at Stockbridge.

Mr. Alexander Osborne, a commissioner of the Board of Customs, resided in No. 40 for many years, and died there. He was of great stature, and was the right-hand man of the Grenadiers of the First Regiment of Royal Edinburgh Volunteers, proverbially a battalion of tall men, and his personal appearance was long familiar in the streets of the city. In bulk he was remarkable as well as in stature, his legs in particular being nearly as large in circumference as the body of an ordinary person. The editor of Kay mentions that shortly after the volunteers had been embodied, Lord Melville presented his gigantic countryman to George III., who on witnessing such a herculean specimen of his loyal defenders in Scotland, was somewhat excited and curious. "Are all the Edinburgh volunteers like you?" he asked. Osborne mistaking the jocular construction of the question, and supposing it referred to their status in society, replied, "They are so, please your Majesty." "Astonishing!" exclaimed the King, lifting up his hands in wonder.

In his youth he is said to have had a prodigious appetite, being able to consume *nine pounds* of steak at a meal. His father, who died at Aberdeen, comptroller of the Customs in 1785, is said to have been a man of even more colossal proportions.

Mr. Osborne lived long in Richmond Street prior to removing to York Place, where he died in his 74th year.

During the early years of this century Lady Sinclair of Murkle occupied No. 61, and at the same time No. 47 was the residence of Alexander Nasmyth, landscape painter, father of Peter, who won himself the name of "the English Hobbima," and who, in fact, was the father of the Scottish school of landscape painting. In his youth, the pupil of Allan Ramsay, and afterwards of the best artists in Rome and England, he returned to his native city, Edinburgh, where he had been born in 1758 ; and to his friendship with Burns the world is indebted for the only authentic portrait which exists of our national poet. His compositions were chaste and

elegant, and his industry unceasing ; thus he numbered among his early employers the chief of the Scottish *noblesse*. Most of the living landscape painters of Scotland, and many of the dead ones, have sprung from the school of Nasmyth, who, in his extreme age, became an honorary member of the then new Scottish Academy.

The firmness of his intellect, and the freshness of his fancy continued uninterrupted to the end of his labours ; his last work was the touching little picture called "Going Home;" and he died soon after at Edinburgh in the eighty-third year of his age, in 1840. He married a daughter of Sir James Foulis, Bart., of Colinton and that ilk, by whom he had a large family, all more or less inheriting the genius of their father, particularly his son Peter, who pre-deceased him at London in 1831, aged forty-five years.

On the north side of York Place is St. Paul's Episcopal church, built in that style of Gothic which prevailed in the time of Henry VI. of England, and of which the best specimen may be seen in King's College, Cambridge. The building consists of a nave with four octagon towers at the angles, with north and south aisles. The pulpit is at the east end, and immediately before the communion-table. The organ is at the west end, and above the main entrance, which faces York Lane— a remnant of Broughton Loan. In the north-west angle of the edifice is the vestry. The length of the church is about 123 feet by 73 feet, external measurement. The nave is 109 feet 9 inches in length by 26 feet broad, and 46 feet in height ; and the aisles are 79 feet long by 29 feet in height. The ceiling of the nave is a flat Gothic arch, covered with ornamental tracery, as are also the ceilings of the aisles. The great eastern window is beautifully filled in with stained glass by Egginton of Birmingham. This handsome church—in its time the best example of Gothic erected in Edinburgh since the Reformation—was built from a design by Archibald Elliot, and does considerable credit to the taste and genius of that eminent architect. It was begun in February, 1816, and finished in June, 1818, for the use of the congregation which had previously occupied the great church in the Cowgate, and who contributed £12,000 for its erection. The well-known Archibald Alison, author of "Essays on Taste," and father of the historian of Europe, long officiated here. He was the son of a magistrate of the city of Edinburgh, where he was born in 1757, but graduated at Oxford ; and on the invitation of Sir William Forbes and others, in 1800, became senior incumbent of the Cowgate chapel. After the removal of the congregation to

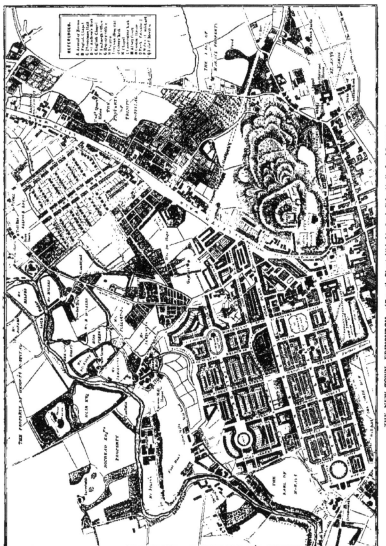

THE NEW TOWN, EDINBURGH. (From the Plan published in 1804 by John Ainslie, Land Surveyor.)

York Place he officiated there, until a severe illness in 1831 compelled him to relinquish all public duties. In "Peter's Letters" we are told that he possessed all the qualifications of a popular orator.

He was elected a Fellow of the Royal Society of Edinburgh in the first year of its formation, and was the intimate friend of many of its most distinguished members, as he was of most of the men of genius and learning of his time in Scotland. His "Essays on Taste" appeared first in 1790, since when it has passed through several editions, and has been translated into French. His theory of taste has met the approval of men of the highest genius in poetry, criticism, and art. He died, universally respected, on the 17th of May, 1839.

St. George's Episcopal chapel, built in 1794, stands on the south side of York Place. It was designed by Robert Adam, and is of no known style of architecture, and is every way hideous in conception and in detail. This dingy edifice cost £3,000.

North of the two streets we have described, and erected coeval with them, are Forth and Albany Streets.

In No. 10 of the former street lived for years, and died on the 27th of August, 1837, in his seventy-first year, George Watson, first president and founder of the Royal Scottish Academy, of whom an account has already been given in connection with that institution, as one of the most eminent artists of his time. In the same house also lived and died his third son, Smellie George Watson, R.S.A., a distinguished portrait painter, named from the family of his mother, who was Rebecca, eldest daughter of William Smellie, the learned and ingenious painter and natural philosopher.

In the little and obscure thoroughfare named Hart Street lived long one who enjoyed considerable reputation in his day, though well-nigh forgotten now: William Douglas, an eminent miniature painter, and the lineal descendant of the ancient line of Glenbervie. "He received a useful education," says his biographer, "and was well acquainted with the dead and living languages. From his infancy he displayed a taste for the fine arts. While yet a mere child he would leave his playfellows to their sports, to watch the effects of light and shade, and, creeping along the furrows of the fields, study the perspective of the ridges. This enabled him to excel as a landscape painter, and gave great beauty to his miniatures."

As a miniature painter he was liberally patronised by the upper ranks in Scotland and England, and his works are to be found in some of the finest collections of both countries. In particular he was employed by the family of Buccleuch, and in 1817 was appointed Miniature Painter for Scotland to the Princess Charlotte, and Prince Leopold afterwards King of the Belgians.

Prior to his removal to Hart Street he lived in No. 17 St. James's Square, a common stair. He possessed genius, fancy, taste, and delicacy, with a true enthusiasm for his art; and his social worth and private virtues were acknowledged by all who had the pleasure of knowing him. He had a vast fund of anecdote, and in his domestic relations was an affectionate husband, good father, and faithful friend. His constant engagements precluded his contributing to the exhibitions in Edinburgh, but his works frequently graced the walls of the Royal Academy at Somerset House. In a note attached to David Malloch's "Immortality of the Soul," he says :—"The author would take this opportunity of stating that if he has been at all successful in depicting any of the bolder features of Nature, this he in a great measure owes to the conversation of his respected friend, William Douglas, Esq., Edinburgh, who was no less a true poet than an eminent artist."

He died at his house in Hart Street on the 20th of January, 1832, leaving a daughter, Miss Ramsay Douglas, also an artist, and the inheritor of his peculiar grace and delicacy of touch.

York Place being called from the king's second son by his English title, Albany Street, by a natural sequence, was named from the title of the second son of the king of Scotland. Albany Row it was called in the feuing advertisements in 1800, and for some twenty years after. In No. 2, which is now broken up and subdivided, lived John Playfair, Professor of Natural Philosophy in the University, a man of whom it has been said that he was cast in nature's happiest mould, acute, clear, comprehensive, and having all the higher qualities of intellect combined and regulated by the most perfect good taste, being not less perfect in his moral than in his intellectual nature. He was a man every way distinguished, respected, and beloved.

When only eighteen years old he became a candidate in 1766 for the chair of mathematics in the Marischal College, Aberdeen, where, after a lengthened and very strict examination, only two out of six rival competitors were judged to have excelled him—these were, Dr. Traill, who was appointed to the chair, and Dr. Hamilton, who subsequently succeeded to it. He was the son of the Rev. James Playfair, minister of Liff and Benvie, and upon the representation of Lord

Gray was ordained his successor to that charge in 1773, but he resigned it ten years afterwards. In 1785 he was appointed joint Professor of Mathematics in the University of Edinburgh with the celebrated Adam Ferguson, LL.D., and discharged the duties of that chair till the death of his friend Professor Robinson, in 1805, when he was appointed his successor. Among his works are " Elements of Geometry " published in 1796; " Illustrations of the Huttonian Theory of the Earth " in 1804; " Outlines of Natural Philosophy;" besides many papers to the scientific department of the *Edinburgh Review* and to various other periodicals.

He died at No. 2, Albany Street, in his seventieth year, on the 20th of July, 1819. An unfinished " Memoir of John Clerk of Eldin," the inventor of naval tactics, left by him in manuscript, was published after his death in the ninth volume of the " Edinburgh Transactions." An interesting account of the character and merits of this illustrious mathematician, from the pen of Lord Jeffrey, was inserted in the " Encyclopædia Britannica " and in the memoir prefixed to his works by his nephew, and a noble monument to his memory is erected on the Calton Hill.

Northwards of the old village of Broughton, in the beginning of the present century, the land was partly covered with trees ; a road led from it to Canonmills by Bellevue to Newhaven, while another road, by the water of Leith, led westward. In the centre of what are now the Drummond Place Gardens stood a country house belonging to the Lord Provost Drummond, and long inhabited by him ; he feued seven acres from the Governors of Heriot's Hospital. The approach to this house was by an avenue, now covered by West London Street, and which entered from the north road to Canonmills.

On the site of that house General Scott of Balcomie subsequently built the large square three-storeyed mansion of Bellevue, afterwards converted into the Excise Office, and removed when the Edinburgh, Perth, and Dundee Railway Company constructed the now disused tunnel from Princes Street to the foot of Scotland Street.

In 1802 the lands of Bellevue were advertised to be sold "by roup within the Justiciary Court Room," for feuing purposes, but years elapsed before anything was done in the way of building. In 1823 the papers announce that "preparations are making for levelling Bellevue Gardens and filling up the sand-pits in that neighbourhood, with a view to finishing Bellevue Crescent, which will connect the New Town with Canonmills on one side, as it is already connected with Stockbridge on the other."

By that year Drummond Place was nearly completed, and the south half of Bellevue Crescent was finished and occupied; St. Mary's parish church was founded and finished in 1824, from designs by Mr. Thomas Brown, at the cost of £13,000 for 1,800 hearers. It has a spire of considerable elegance, 168 feet in height.

General Scott, the proprietor of Bellevue, was one of the most noted gamblers of his time. It is related of him that being one night at Stapleton's, when a messenger brought him tidings that Mrs. Scott had been delivered of a daughter, he turned laughingly to the company, and said, " You see, gentlemen, I must be under the necessity of doubling my stakes, in order to make a fortune for this little girl." He accordingly played rather deeper than usual, in consequence of which, after a few hours' play, he found himself a loser by £8,000. This gave occasion for some of the company to rally him on his " daughter's fortune," but the general had an equanimity of temper that nothing could ruffle, and a judgment in play superior to most gamesters. He replied that he had still a perfect dependence on the luck of the night, and to make his words good he played steadily on, and about seven in the morning, besides clearing his £8,000, he brought home £15,000. His eldest daughter, Henrietta, became Duchess of Portland.

Drummond Place was named after the eminent George Drummond, son of the Laird of Newton, a branch of the Perth family, who was no less than six times Lord Provost of the city, and who died in 1776, in the eightieth year of his age.

The two most remarkable denizens of this quarter were Charles Kirkpatrick Sharpe of Hoddam (previously of 93, Princes Street) and Lord Robertson.

Among the attractions of Edinburgh during the bygone half of the present century, and accessible only to a privileged few, were the residence and society of the former gentleman. Born of an ancient Scottish family, and connected in many ways with the historical associations of his country, by his reputation as a literary man no less than by his high Cavalier and Jacobite tenets, Charles Kirkpatrick Sharpe was long looked up to as one of the chief authorities on all questions connected with Scottish antiquities.

No. 93, Princes Street, the house of Mrs. Sharpe of Hoddam, was the home of her son till the time of her death, and there he was visited by Scott, Thomas Thomson, and those of the next generation, such as David Laing, Robert Chambers, and Cosmo Innes. In his "Diary" Scott writes of him as "a very remarkable man. He has infinite wit and a great turn for antiquarian lore. His drawings are the most fanciful and droll imaginable —a mixture between Hogarth and some of those foreign masters who painted 'Temptations of St. Anthony' and such grotesque subjects. My idea is that Charles Kirkpatrick Sharpe, with his oddities, tastes, satire, and high aristocratic feelings, resembles Horace Walpole."

portraits, some on the walls, but many more on the floor. A small room leading out of this one was the place where Mr. Sharpe gave audiences. Its diminutive space was stuffed full of old curiosities, cases with family bijouterie, &c. One petty object was strongly indicative of character, a calling card of Lady Charlotte Campbell, the once adored beauty, stuck into the frame of a picture. He must have kept it, at that time, about thirty years."

This lady, one of the celebrated Edinburgh beauties, was the second daughter of John, Duke of

THE EXCISE OFFICE, DRUMMOND PLACE. (*From a Drawing by Shepherd, published in 1829.*)

The resemblance in their abodes was more strictly true. The house of Sharpe, No. 28 Drummond Place, was one of the sights of Edinburgh to the select few who found admittance there, with its antique furniture, tapestries, paintings, and carvings —its exquisite enamels, weapons, armour, bronzes, bijouterie, ivories, old china, old books, and cabinets—the mighty collection of a long life, and the sale of which, at his death, occupied six long days at the auction rooms in South Hanover Street.

Robert Chambers describes a visit he paid him in Princes Street. "His servant conducted me to the first floor, and showed me into what is called amongst us the back drawing-room, which I found carpeted with green cloth and full of old family

Argyle, who died in 1806, and the visit referred to took place about 1824.

To Mr. Sharpe Sir Walter owed many of the most graphic incidents which gave such inimitable life to the productions of his pen ; and a writer in the *Gentleman's Magazine* justly remarked that "his collection of antiquities is among the richest which any private gentleman has ever accumulated in the north. In Scottish literature he will be always remembered as the editor of 'Law's Memorials' and of 'Kirkton's History of the Kirk of Scotland.' His taste in music was no less cultivated than peculiar, and the curious variety of singular and obsolete musical instruments which enriched his collection, showed how well the antiquarian taste consorted with the musical skill and critical sagacity of the editor of the ' Minuets and Songs, by Thomas, sixth Earl of Kellie.'"

At his death, in 1851, a desire was felt by many of his friends that his collection of antiquities should, like that of his friend Scott, be preserved as a memorial of him, but from circumstances over which his family had no control this was found to be impossible, so the vast assemblage of rare and curious objects which crowded every room in No. 28 was dispersed. The very catalogue of them, filling upwards of fifty pages, was in some of its features strongly indicative of the character of the man.

Among them we find—" A small box made from a leg of the table at which King James VIII. sat on his first landing here;" "fragment of Queen Mary's bed-curtains;" "hair of that true saint and martyr Charles I., taken from his coffin at Windsor, and given to me by the Hon. Peter Drummond Burrel at Edinburgh, December, 1813;" "piece of the shroud of King Robert the Bruce;" "piece of a plaid worn by Prince Charles in Scotland;" "silk sash worn by the prince;" "pair of gloves belonging to Mary Queen of Scots;" "cap worn by her when escaping from Lochleven;" &c. He had a vast collection of coins, some of which were said to be discovered in consequence of a dream. "The child of a Mr. Christison, in whose house his father was lodging in 1781, dreamt that a treasure was hid in the cellar. Her father had no faith in the dream, but Mr. Sharpe had the place dug up, and a copper pot full of coins was found."

One of the chief features of his drawing-room in Drummond Place was a quaint monstrosity in bronze, now preserved in the British Museum. It was a ewer fashioned in the shape of a tailless lion, surmounted by an indescribable animal, half hound and half fish, found in a vault of his paternal castle of Hoddam, in Dumfries-shire. Charles Kirkpatrick Sharpe was laid amid his forefathers in the family burial-place in Annandale. " May the earth lie light on him," writes one of his friends, " and no plebeian dust invade the last resting-place of a thorough gentleman of the antique type, now wholly gone with other good things of the olden time !"

Patrick Robertson, known as Lord Robertson by his judicial title, was long locally famous as " Peter," one of the most brilliant wits and humorists about Parliament House, and a great friend of " Christopher North." They were called to the bar in the same year, 1815. Robertson was born in 1793. In 1842 he was Dean of Faculty, and

was raised to the bench in the following year. He was famous for his mock heroic speeches on " the general question," and his face, full of grotesque humour, and his rotund figure, of Johnson-like amplitude and cut, were long familiar to all habitués of the law courts. Of his speeches Lockhart gives a description in his account of a Burns dinner in 1818 :—" The last of these presidents (Mr. Patrick Robertson), a young counsellor of very rising reputation and most pleasant manner, made his approach to the chair amid such a thunder of acclamation as seems to issue from the cheeks of the Bacchantes when Silenus gets astride his ass, in the famous picture of Rubens. Once in the chair, there was no fear of his quitting it while any remained to pay homage to his authority. He made speeches, one chief merit of which consisted (unlike epic poems) in their having neither beginning, middle, nor end. He sang songs in which music was not. He proposed toasts in which meaning was not. But over everything that he said there was flung such a radiance of sheer mother wit, that there was no difficulty in seeing that the want of meaning was no involuntary want. By the perpetual dazzle of his wit, by the cordial flow of his good-humour, but, above all, by the cheering influence of his broad, happy face, seen through its halo of purest steam (for even the chair had by this time got enough of the juice of the grape), he contrived to diffuse over us all, for a long time, one genial atmosphere of unmingled mirth."

The wit and humour of Robertson were proverbial, and hundreds of anecdotes used to be current of his peculiar and invincible power of closing all controversy, by the broadest form of *reductio ad absurdum.* At a dinner party a learned and pedantic Oxonian was becoming very tiresome with his Greek erudition, which he insisted on pouring forth on a variety of topics more or less recondite. At length, at a stage of the discussion on some historical point, Lord Robertson turned round, and, fixing his large grey eyes upon the Englishman, said, with a solemn and judicial air, " I rather think, sir, Dionysius of Halicarnassus is against you there." " I beg your pardon," said the other, quickly; "Dionysius did not flourish for ninety years after that period !" " Oh ! " rejoined Robertson, with an expression of face that must be imagined, " I made a mistake—I meant *Thaddeus of Warsaw.*" After that the discussion flowed no longer in the Greek channel.[*]

He was author of a large quarto volume of singu-

* Wilson's " Memoirs," vol ii.

larly weak poems, which were noticed by Lockhart in the *Quarterly Review*, and to the paper he appended in *one* copy, which was sent to the senator, the following distich, by way of epitaph :—

> "Here lies the peerless paper lord, Lord Peter,
> Who broke the laws of God and man and metre."

The joke chiefly lay in Robertson being led to suppose that the lines were in the entire edition, much to his annoyance and indignation ; but Lockhart penned elsewhere the following good wishes concerning him :—

> "Oh! Petrus, Pedro, Peter, which you will,
> Long, long thy radiant destiny fulfil.
> Bright be thy wit, and bright the golden ore
> Paid down in fees for thy deep legal lore ;
> Bright be that claret, brisk be thy champagne,
> Thy whisky-punch, a vast exhaustless main,
> With thee disporting on its joyous shore,
> Of that glad spirit quaffing ever more ;
> Keen be thy stomach, potent thy digestion,
> And long thy lectures on ' the general question ;'
> While young and old swell out the general strain,
> We ne'er shall look upon his like again."

Lockhart wrote many rhyming epitaphs upon him, and is reported to have written, " Peter Robertson is 'a man,' to use his own favourite quotation, 'cast in Nature's amplest mould.' He is admitted to be the greatest corporation lawyer at the Scotch bar, and he is a *vast* poet as well as a *great* lawyer."

Lord Robertson, who lived in No. 32 Drummond Place, died in 1855, in his sixty-second year.

No. 38 was for years the abode of Adam Black, more than once referred to elsewhere as publisher, M.P., and Lord Provost of the city, who died on the 24th January, 1874.

Forming a species of terrace facing the Queen Street Gardens from the north, are Abercrombie Place and Heriot Row—the first named from the hero of the Egyptian campaign, and the latter from the founder of the famous hospital on ground belonging to which it is erected. The western portion of the Row, after it was built, was long disfigured by the obstinacy of Lord Wemyss, who declined to remove a high stone wall which enclosed on the north and east the garden that lay before his house in Queen Street.

Sir John Connel, Advocate and Procurator for the Church, author of a "Treatise on Parochial Law and Tithes," and who figures among Kay's Portraits as one of the "Twelve Advocates," James Pillans, LL.D., Professor of Humanity in the University 1820-63, and Sir James Riddel, Bart., of Ardnamurchan and Sunart, lived respec-

tively in Nos. 16, 22, and 30, Abercrombie Place ; while on the west side of Nelson Street, which opens off it to the north, resided, after 1829, Miss Susan Edmondston Ferrier, authoress of "Marriage," "Inheritance," and "Destiny," one who may with truth be called the *last* of the literary galaxy which adorned Edinburgh when Scott wrote, Jeffrey criticised, and the wit of Wilson flowed into the *Noctes*. She was the friend and confidant of Scott. She survived him more than twenty years, as she died in 1854.

In the house numbered as 6 Heriot Row, Henry Mackenzie, the author of the "Man of Feeling," spent the last years of his long life, surviving all the intimates of his youth, including Robertson, Hume, Fergusson, and Adam Smith ; and there he died on the 14th of January, in the year 1831, after having been confined to his room for a considerable period by the general decay attending old age. He was then in his eighty-sixth year.

No. 44 in the same Row is remarkable as having been for some years the residence of the Rev. Archibald Alison, to whom we have already referred ; in the same house with him lived his sons, Professor Alison, and Archibald the future historian of Europe and first baronet of the name. The latter was born in the year 1792, at the parsonage house of Kenley, in Shropshire. The Rev. Archibald Alison (who was a cadet of the Alisons, of New Hall, in Angus) before becoming incumbent of the Cowgate Chapel, in 1800, had been a prebendary of Sarum, rector of Roddington, and vicar of High Ercal ; and his wife was Dorothea Gregory, grand-daughter of the fourteenth Lord Forbes of that ilk, a lady whose family for two centuries has been eminent in mathematics and the exact sciences.

His sermons were published by Constable in 1817, twenty-seven years subsequent to his work on "Taste," and, according to the *Literary Magazine* for that year and other critical periodicals, since the first publication of Blair's discourses there were no sermons so popular in Scotland as those of Mr. Alison. He enforced virtue and piety upon the sanction of the Gospels, without entering into those peculiar grounds and conditions of salvation which constitute the sectarian theories of religion, regarding his hearers or readers as having already arrived at that state of knowledge and understanding when, "having the principles of the doctrine of Christ, they should go on unto perfection."

Great King Street, a broad and stately thoroughfare that extends from Drummond Place to the

Royal Circus, was built in 1820, and in the following year it was proposed to erect at the west end of it an equestrian statue to the memory of George III., for which subscription lists had been opened, but the project was never carried out.

In Great King Street have resided, respectively in Nos. 3, 16, and 72, three men who are of mark and fame—Sir Robert Christison, Sir William Hamilton, and Sir William Allan.

When the future baronet occupied No. 3, he was Doctor Christison, and Professor of medical jurisprudence. Born in June, 1797, and son of the late Alexander Christison, Professor of Humanity in the University of Edinburgh, he became a student there in 1811, and passed with brilliance through the literary and medical curriculum, and after graduating in 1819, he proceeded to London and Paris, where, under the celebrated M. Orfila, he applied himself to the study of toxicology, the department of medical science in which he became so deservedly famous.

Soon after his return home to Scotland he commenced practice in his native capital, and in 1822 was appointed Professor of Medical Jurisprudence in the University, and was promoted in 1832 to the chair of materia medica. He contributed various articles to medical journals on professional subjects, and wrote several books, among others an exhaustive "Treatise on Poisons," still recognised as a standard work on that subject, and of more than European reputation.

At the famous trial of Palmer, in 1856, Dr. Christison went to London, and gave such valuable evidence that Lord Campbell complimented him on the occasion, and the ability he displayed was universally recognised and applauded. He was twice President of the Royal College of Physicians, Edinburgh—the first time being in 1846—and was appointed Ordinary Physician to the Queen for Scotland. He received the degree of D.C.L. from Oxford in 1866, was created a baronet in 1871, and was made LL.D. of Edinburgh University in 1872. He resigned his chair in 1877, and died in 1882.

In No. 16 lived and died Sir William Hamilton, Bart., of Preston and Fingalton, Professor of Logic and Metaphysics in the University of Edinburgh from 1836 to 1856, and Fellow of the Scottish Society of Antiquaries. He had previously resided in Manor Place. He was called to the Scottish bar in 1815, at the same time with Duncan McNeill, the future Sir Archibald Alison, John Wilson, and others, and in 1816 assumed the baronetcy as twenty-fourth male representative of Sir John Fitz-Gilbert de Hamilton, who was the second son of Sir Gilbert, who came into Scotland in the time of Alexander III., and from whom the whole family of Hamilton are descended. The baronetcy is in remainder to heirs male general, but was not assumed from the death of the second baronet in 1701 till 1806. It was a creation of 1673. With his brother Thomas he became one of the earliest contributors to the columns of *Blackwood's Magazine.*

Besides "Cyril Thornton," one of the best military novels in the language, Thomas Hamilton was author of "Annals of the Peninsular Campaign" and of "Men and Manners in America." In "Peter's Letters" he is described as "a fine-looking young officer, whom the peace has left at liberty to amuse himself in a more pleasant way than he was accustomed to, so long as Lord Wellington kept the field. He has a noble, grand, Spaniard-looking head, and a tall graceful person, which he swings about in a style of knowingness that might pass muster even in the eye of old Potts. The expression of his features is so very sombre that I should never have guessed him to be a playful writer (indeed, how could I have guessed such a person to be a writer at all?). Yet such is the case. Unless I am totally misinformed, he is the author of a thousand beautiful *jeux d'esprit* both in prose and verse, which I shall point out to you more particularly when we meet." He had served in the 29th Regiment of Foot during the long war with France, and died in his fifty-third year, in 1842.

In April, 1820, when the chair of moral philosophy in the University of Edinburgh fell vacant by the death of Dr. Thomas Browne, the successor of Dugald Stewart, Sir William Hamilton became a candidate together with John Wilson. Others were mentioned as possible competitors, among them Sir James MacIntosh and Mr. Malthus, but it soon became apparent that the struggle—one which had few parallels even in the past history of that University—lay between the two first-named. "Sir William was a Whig; Wilson was a Tory of the most unpardonable description," says Mrs. Gordon in her "Memoir," and the Whig side was strenuously supported in the columns of the *Scotsman*—"and privately," she adds, "in every circle where the name of *Blackwood* was a name of abomination and of fear." But eventually, in the year of Dr. Browne's death, Wilson was appointed to the vacant chair, and among the first to come to hear, and applaud to the echo, his earliest lectures, was Sir William Hamilton.

In 1829 the latter married his cousin, Miss Marshall, daughter of Mr. Hubert Marshall, and in July, 1836, was appointed to the chair of logic and metaphysics, in succession to Professor David Ritchie. In the interval between his appointment and the commencement of the college session, in the November of the same year, he was assiduously occupied in preparing to discharge the duties of the chair, which (according to the practice of the University) consist in the delivery of a course of lectures on the subjects assigned to it.

On his appointment at first, Sir William Hamilton would seem to have experienced considerable difficulty in deciding on the character of the course of lectures on Philosophy, which, while doing justice to the subject, would at the same time meet the requirements of his auditors, usually comparatively young students in the second year of their University curriculum. His first course of lectures fell to be written during the currency of the session 1836-7. He was in the habit of delivering three in each week; and each lecture was usually written on the day, or more probably on the evening and night, before its delivery. His "Course of Metaphysics" was the result of this nightly toil.

His lectures on Logic were not composed until the following session, 1837-8. A commonplace book which he left among his papers, exhibits in a very remarkable degree Sir William's power of appreciating and making use of every available hint scattered through the obscurer regions of thought, through which his extensive reading conducted him, says the editor of his collected works, and no part of his writings more completely verifies the remark of his American critic, Mr. Tyler :—"There seems to be not even a random thought of any value which has been dropped along any, even obscure, path of mental activity, in any age or country, that his diligence has not recovered, his sagacity appreciated, and his judgment husbanded in the stores of his knowledge."

The lectures of Sir William Hamilton, apart from their very great intrinsic merit, possess a high academical and historic interest. From 1836 to 1856—twenty consecutive years—his courses of Logic and Metaphysics were the means by which this great, good, and amiable man sought to imbue with his philosophical opinions the young men who assembled in considerable numbers from his native country, from England, and elsewhere ; " and while by these prelections," says his editor in 1870, "the author supplemented, developed, and moulded the National Philosophy—leaving thereon the ineffaceable impress of his genius and learning

—he at the same time and by the same means exercised over the intellects and feelings of his pupils an influence which for depth, intensity, and elevation, was certainly never surpassed by that of any philosophical instructor. Among his pupils are not a few who, having lived for a season under the constraining power of his intellect, and been led to reflect on those great questions regarding the character, origin, and bounds of human knowledge which his teaching stirred and quickened, bear the memory of their beloved and revered instructor inseparably blended with what is highest in their present intellectual life, as well as in their practical aims and aspirations."

At the time of his death, in 1856, he resided, as has been stated, in No. 16 Great King Street, and he was succeeded by his eldest son, William, an officer of the Royal Artillery. Since his death a memoir of him has appeared from the pen of Professor Veitch, of the University of Glasgow.

In No. 72 of the same street lived and died another great Scotsman, Sir William Allan, R.A., whose fame and reputation as an artist extended over many years, and whose works are still his monument. We have already referred to his latter years in our account of the Royal Academy and the *atelier* of his earlier days in the Parliament Close, where, after his wanderings in foreign lands, and in the first years of the century, he was wont to figure " by way of *robe-de-chambre*, in a dark Circassian vest, the breast of which was loaded with innumerable quilted lurking-places, originally, no doubt, intended for weapons of warfare, but now occupied with the harmless shafts of hair pencils, while he held in his hand the smooth cherry-wood stalk of a Turkish tobacco-pipe, apparently converted very happily into a palette guard. A swarthy complexion and profusion of black hair, tufted in a wild but not ungraceful manner, together with a pair of large sparkling eyes looking out from under strong shaggy brows full of vivacious and ardent expressiveness, were scarcely less speaking witnesses of the life of romantic and roaming adventure I was told this fine artist had led." In spite of his bad health, which (to quote "Peter's Letters") "was indeed but too evident, his manners seemed to be full of a light and playful sportiveness, which is by no means common among the people of our nation, and still less among the people of Scotland ; and this again was every now and then exchanged for a depth of enthusiastic earnestness still more evidently derived from a sojourn among men whose blood flows through their veins with a heat and rapidity to which the North is a stranger."

His pictures, the "Sale of Circassian Captives to a Turkish Bashaw," purchased by the Earl of Wemyss and March, and the "Jewish Family in Poland making merry before a Wedding," were among the first of his works that laid the foundation of his future fame. His "Murder of Archbishop Sharp," and other works are too well-known to be referred to here; but the "Battle of Bannockburn," the unfinished work of his old

able lawyer and brilliant pleader. After being junior counsel for the Crown, he was Sheriff of Perth for ten years after 1824, and twice Solicitor-General for Scotland before 1842. From 1842 to 1846 he was Lord Advocate. He was chosen Dean of Faculty in November, 1843, and annually thereafter, till raised to the bench as a Lord of Session and Justiciary in 1851, by the territorial title of Lord Colonsay. In the following

THE RIGHT HON. CHARLES HOPE, COMMANDING THE EDINBURGH VOLUNTEERS. (*After Kay.*)

age, has never been engraved, nor is it likely to be so. Full of years and honour, he died on the 23rd of February, 1850, aged sixty-nine, attended and soothed to the last by the tenderness and affection of an orphan niece.

The house opposite, No. 73, was for some fifty years the residence of Duncan McNeill, advocate, and latterly a peer under the title of Baron Colonsay. The son of John McNeill of Colonsay (one of the Hebrides, at the extremity of Islay), by the eldest daughter of Duncan McNeill of Dunmore, Argyleshire, he was born in the bleak and lonely isle of Colonsay in 1793, and after being educated at the Universities of St. Andrews and Edinburgh, he was called to the Scottish Bar in 1816, and very soon distinguished himself as a sound and

year he was appointed Lord Justice-General and President of the Court, and was created a peer of Britain on retiring in 1867. He was a Deputy-Lieutenant of Edinburgh in 1854, and of Argyle-shire in 1848, and was a member of the Lower House from 1843 to 1851. He died in February, 1874, when the title became extinct.

In the same street, in Nos. 24 and 25 respectively, lived two other legal men of local note: Lord Kinloch, a senator, whose name was William Penny, called to the bar in 1824 and to the bench in 1858 ; and W. B. D. D. Turnbull, advocate, and latterly of Lincoln's Inn, barrister-at-law. He was called to the Bar in 1832, together with Henry Glassford Bell and Thomas Mackenzie, afterwards Solicitor-General.

A noted antiquary, he was *Correspondant du Comité Impérial des Travaux Historiques, et des Sociétés Savants de France, &c.* He was well known in Edinburgh for his somewhat coarse wit, and as a collector of rare books, whose library in Great King Street was reported to be the most valuable private one in the city, where he was called—but more especially among legal men—"Alphabet Turnbull," from the number of his initials. He removed to London about 1853, and became seriously embroiled with the authorities concerning certain historical documents in the State Paper Office, when he had his chambers in 3 Stone Buildings, Lincoln's Inn Fields.

He died at London on the 22nd of April, 1863, in his fifty-second year; and a story went abroad that a box of MS. papers was mysteriously buried with him.

CHAPTER XXVII.

NORTHERN NEW TOWN (*concluded*).

Admiral Fairfax—Bishop Terrot—Brigadier Hope—Sir T. M. Brisbane—Lord Meadowbank—Ewbank the R.S.A.—Death of Professor Wilson—Moray Place and its District—Lord President Hope—The Last Abode of Jeffrey—Baron Hume and Lord Moncrieff—Forres Street—Thomas Chalmers, D.D.—St. Colme Street—Captain Basil Hall—Ainslie Place—Dugald Stewart—Dean Ramsay—Great Stuart Street—Professor Aytoun—Miss Graham of Duntroon—Lord Jerviswoode.

IN the narrow and somewhat sombre thoroughfare named Northumberland Street have dwelt some people who were of note in their time.

In 1810 Lady Emily Dundas, and Admiral Sir William George Fairfax, resided in Nos. 46 and 53 respectively. The admiral had distinguished himself at the battle of Camperdown as flag-captain of the *Venerable*, under Admiral Duncan; and in consideration of his acknowledged bravery and merit on that occasion—being sent home with the admiral's despatches—he was made knight-banneret, with an augmentation to his coat-of-arms in chief, a representation of H.M.S. *Venerable* engaging the Dutch admiral's ship *Vryheid*; and to do justice to the memory of "departed worth," at his death his son was made a baronet of Great Britain in 1836. He had a daughter named Mary, who became the wife of Samuel Greig, captain and commissioner in the imperial Russian navy.

No. 19 in the same street was for some years the residence of the Right Rev. Charles Hughes Terrot, D.D., elected in 1857 *Primus* of the Scottish Episcopal Church, and whose quaint little figure, with shovel-hat and knee-breeches, was long familiar in the streets of Edinburgh. He was born at Cuddalore in the East Indies in 1790. For some reasons, though he had not distinguished himself in the Cambridge Tripos list of University honours, his own College (Trinity College) paid him the highest compliment in their power, by electing him a Fellow on the first occasion after he had taken his degree of B.A. in mathematical honours, and subsequently proceeded to M.A. and D.D. He did not remain long at college, as he soon married and went to Scotland, where he continued all his life attached to the Scottish Episcopal Church, as successively incumbent of Haddington, of St. Peter's, and finally St. Paul's, York Place, Edinburgh. In 1841 he was made bishop of Edinburgh, on the death of Bishop Walker. He was author of several works on theology. During the latter years of his life, from extreme age and infirmity, he had been entirely laid aside from his pastoral and episcopal labours; but during the period of his health and vigour few men were more esteemed in his pastoral relations as their minister, or by his brethren of the Episcopal Church for his acuteness and clever judgment in their discussions in church affairs.

The leading features of Dr. Terrot's intellectual character were accuracy and precision rather than very extensive learning or great research. It was very striking sometimes after a subject had been discussed in a desultory and commonplace manner, to hear him coming down upon the question with a clear and cutting remark which put the whole matter in a new and distinct point of view.

He was long a Fellow and Vice-President of the Royal Society of Edinburgh, to which he communicated some very able and acute papers, especially on logical and mathematical subjects. So also in his moral and social relations, he was remarkable for his manly, fair, and honourable bearing. He had what might essentially be called a pure and honest mind. He was devotedly attached to his own Church, and few knew better how to argue in favour of its polity and forms of service, never varying much in externals; but few men were more ready to concede to others the liberality of judgment which he claimed for himself. Hence it was that few men were more esteemed and respected by others than Dr. Terrot of the Episcopal Church. He died at 9 Carlton Street, Stockbridge, in April, 1872, in his eighty-second year.

No. 57 Northumberland Street was the residence of the gallant Sir John Hope (afterwards Lord Niddry and Earl of Hopetoun), while serving as Brigadier-General, after Corunna, on the staff in Scotland, from 1810 till he rejoined the Peninsular army and took command of the left wing at the battle of Nivelles.

The northern New Town is intersected by four steep thoroughfares that run north and south, being continuations of the corresponding streets south of Queen Street, and all, save in one instance, affording far-stretching views of the villas, woods, and fields that lie between them and the shore of the Forth, with the undulations of the Fifeshire hills beyond.

· Dundas and Pitt Streets form the most stately of these thoroughfares. From them the view southwards is bounded by the distant spire of the Assembly Hall, and the double towers of the Free Church College, which present a singularly noble and striking aspect when beheld from the foot of the long descent of upwards of 1,300 yards.

In Dundas Street, in 1811, there were resident in Nos. 9, 26, and 31, respectively, Miss Macfarlane of that ilk, Munro of Culrain, and Thomas Brisbane of Brisbane and that ilk, the father of the eminent Lieut.-General Sir Thomas Macdougall Brisbane, Bart., latterly colonel of the 34th Regiment, and who distinguished himself greatly with the Duke of York's army in Holland, in the West Indies under Abercrombie, and in several general actions in the Peninsula, and who died after being G.C.B., G.C.H., LL.D., and President of the Royal Society of Edinburgh.

North-westward of this, built on each side of the way which curved down towards Stockbridge, and where of old stood a farm with its steading, is the broad, spacious, and stately Royal Circus, with its gardens, the houses of which were finished and inhabited about the end of 1823. The late Lord Meadowbank, son of Allan Maconochie (also Lord Meadowbank), and the successor on the bench of Lord Reston in 1819, had his residence here in No. 13. As Lord Advocate in prior years his duties were of a most harassing and arduous description. In 1817, during what was named "the Radical era," when the greatest political excitement, amounting in some instances to open insurrection, prevailed throughout the country, he had to defend himself in the House of Commons against a charge preferred by Lord Archibald Hamilton, and Henry (afterwards Lord) Brougham, of "oppression in the exercise of his duties," an accusation made in the course of a warm discussion on the further suspension of the "Habeas Corpus Act," and having reference to the case of a prisoner named Mackinlay, who, it was alleged, had been thrice put upon his defence.

No. 11 Howe Street, or a part thereof, was for some years the abode of an unfortunate English genius, John Ewbank, R.S.A., who was famous in his time as a marine and landscape painter. He was the son of Michael Ewbank of Gateshead, innkeeper, and was born at Darlington on the 4th May, 1799, and he removed to Gateshead in the year 1804. After being bound apprentice to Mr. Thomas Coulson, of Newcastle, he became a journeyman house-painter. He was the fellow-apprentice of Thomas Fenwick, the landscape painter. He accompanied his master to Edinburgh in 1816, and was encouraged by him to take lessons of Mr. Alexander Nasmyth, who resided in 47, York Place, after which he devoted his time to the higher department of painting. He lived long in No. 5 Comely Bank, where many of his finest pictures were painted; and it is in his declension that we find him at 11 Howe Street, in the years 1830 and 1831. He might have attained fame, and acquired opulence, as he painted well and quickly pictures that sold rapidly, but he fell into irregular habits, and sank into utter obscurity, and a somewhat untimely grave. Several of the views in this work have been engraved from drawings by John Ewbank.

In Gloucester Place, which adjoins the Circus on the west, we come upon the house No. 6, where genial Professor Wilson lived from 1826 till his death. In a letter written in the preceding year to Mr. Finlay of Easter Hill, one of his friends, he says :—

"I am building a house in Gloucester Place, a small street leading from the circus into Lord Moray's grounds. This I am doing because I am poor, and money yielding no interest. If Jane (Mrs. Wilson) is better next winter I intend to carry my plan into effect of taking into my house two or three young gentlemen. Mention this in any quarter. Remember me kindly to your excellent wife."

Thither he removed with his family from 29 Anne Street, but the project of having boarders was never put in execution, and the house became the centre of that cluster of home-bred authors whom he drew around him, and chiefly as contributors to *Blackwood*—"The Ettrick Shepherd,"

Galt, and "Delta," with the brilliant but short-lived nautical novelist, Michael Scott, who penned "Tom Cringle's Log," and the "Cruise of the Midge," and other writers of greater note—Lockhart, Samuel Warren, De Quincey, Mrs. Hemans, Caroline Bowles, Jerrold, Dr. Maguire, and others, even while the "Waverley" radiance blazed elsewhere.

In the prime of his life, at the age of thirty-four, he had obtained the important chair of Moral Philosophy, in the greatest university of his native country, and that post is associated with his best fame. In Gloucester Place his career was a pleasant and prosperous one, marked chiefly by the rich articles which flowed from his pen monthly (though there he lost his amiable wife, a loss which he felt keenly, and which cast a gloom over all his actions at the time), the college lectures, and the award at each session end, to his rival essayists, the retreat in summer to sylvan Elleray and its circle of poets, or a visit to the Burns festival in Ayrshire.

The death of Mrs. Wilson affected him deeply, nigh to depriving him of reason, and when he resumed his duties next session it was with a solemn and crushed spirit; but when he saw the sympathy of his students, who worshipped him, he fairly broke down, and leaning his lion-like head upon his desk, exclaimed in a low voice, never forgotten by those who heard it, "Oh, gentlemen, forgive me! But since we last met I have been in the valley of the shadow of death!"

He was elected first President of the Edinburgh Philosophical Institution at its formation, and in 1852 he resigned the college chair, after an honorary pension from Government had been conferred upon him by Lord John Russell.

Many are the personal anecdotes still remembered of the Professor in his Edinburgh circle, or elsewhere, from jocose colloquy with Lord Robertson, to the incident of the unfortunate printer, who lost some editorial "copy" in his hat on the way to Blackwood's, and returning to Gloucester Place to narrate the mishap, was so crushed by Wilson's silent look as to take forthwith to his bed, so that his terrified wife, able to draw no explanation from him, went to the printing-office to ask what had been done to her husband. "I'll shake my tawny mane at you," was another expression which he often used; and, indeed, his magnificent head of hair looked like enough a lion's.

After a long and severe illness John Wilson died at No. 6 Gloucester Place, on the 3rd of April, 1854, exactly as St. Stephen's clock struck midnight. Failure of memory had been one of the precursors of his dissolution, which was more im-

mediately preceded by a stroke of paralysis. He had barely gained the allotted term of threescore and ten. He was buried in the beautiful Dean Cemetery, on the 7th of April, and seldom has such a procession passed in the bright sunshine of a spring afternoon as that which went up Doune Terrace, by Moray Place and Randolph Crescent, to that sequestered spot, where lie a goodly company of Scottish men whose names will never die. On this day old students were there, who had come from distant places to pay their last tribute "to the old Professor." The coffin was borne shoulder high, and followed by the Scottish Academy, the directors of the Philosophical Institution, the high constables, magistrates, members of the College of Justice, and all the officials of the University.

In his love of dumb animals his house at Gloucester Place was a rendezvous for dogs of all kinds. Of his own pets, "their name was legion," says his daughter. "I remember Bronte, Rover, Fury, Paris, Charlie, Fido, Tip, and Grog." Some of them and a hecatomb of others, besides gallant game-cocks, lie in the green behind No. 6, Gloucester Place, at the present hour.

But a few doors distant from the house of the Professor was the last Edinburgh abode, after he had risen to wealth and fame, and prior to his retirement to St. Andrews, of Robert Chambers—1, Doune Terrace—the distinguished and well-known historical writer, and junior partner in the great publishing firm of W. and R. Chambers.

The local papers for October, 1823, announce that "the plan of the elegant octagon in Lord Moray's ground is beginning to develop itself, and at the west end of Queen Street, on the north side, several noble houses (Albyn Place), are newly finished as to masonry." The ground to the westward from the end of the Queen's Street Gardens to the old Queensferry Road, and the crest of the high rocks that overhang the deep ravine, where Leith runs brawling towards the sea, a great tabular tract, now occupied by Moray Place, Great Stuart Street, Ainslie Place, and Randolph Crescent, was all, until 1823, open country, or verdant and beautifully wooded park, in the centre of which stood the Earl of Moray's seat of Drumsheugh. The scenery there was charming then; in 1783 it was the abode of Francis, Earl of Moray, who died in 1810 in his house of Drumsheugh. Here also died in 1791, Lord Doune, eldest son of the Earl of Moray, and M.P. for Bedwin, Wilts.

The edificed places now upon it were erected in 1822-3 and following years, according to plans and designs by Gillespie Graham; and though stately, have been—perhaps justly—regarded by some

1, HERIOT ROW; 2, ROYAL CIRCUS; 3, INDIA PLACE; 4, AINSLIE PLACE; 5, MORAY PLACE.

critic ias, "beautifully monotonous, and magnificently dull;" and by others as the beau-ideal of a fashionable west-end quarter; but whatever may be their intrinsic elegance, they have the serious and incurable fault of turning their frontages inwards, and shutting out completely, save from their irregular rows of back windows, the magnificent prospect over the valley of the Water of Leith and away to the Forth.

Moray Place, which reaches to within seventy yards of the north-west quarter of Queen Street, is a pentagon on a diameter of 325 yards, with an ornate and central enclosed pleasure ground. It displays a series of symmetrical, confronting façades, adorned at regular intervals with massive, quarter-sunk Doric columns, crowned by a bold entablature.

No 28, on the west side, divided afterwards, was reserved as the residence of Francis tenth Earl of Moray, who married Lucy, second daughter of General John Scott, of Balcomie and Bellevue.

For years the Right Hon. Charles Hope, of Granton, Lord President of the Court of Session, and his son, John Hope, Solicitor-General for Scotland in 1822, and afterwards Lord Justice Clerk in 1841, lived in Moray Place, No. 12.

The former, long a distinguished senator and citizen, was born in 1763. His father, an eminent London merchant, and cadet of the house of Hopetoun, had been M.P. for West Lothian. Charles Hope was educated at the High School, where he attained distinction as dux of the highest class, and from the University he passed to the bar in 1784, and two years afterwards was Judge-Advocate of Scotland. In 1791 he was Steward of the Orkney and Shetland Isles, and in the first year of the century was Lord Advocate, and as such drew out and aided the magistrates in obtaining a Poor's Bill for the city, on which occasion he was presented with a piece of plate valued at a hundred guineas.

When the warlike spirit of the country became roused at that time by the menacing aspect of France, none was more active among the volunteer force than Charles Hope. He enrolled as a private in the First Edinburgh Regiment, and was eventually appointed Lieut.-Colonel, and from 1801, with the exception of one year when the the corps was disbanded at the Peace of Amiens, he continued to command till its final dissolution in 1814. Kay gives us an equestrian portrait of him in 1812, clad in the now-apparently grotesque uniform of the corps, a swallow-tailed red coat, faced with blue and turned up with white; brass wings, and a beaver-covered helmet-hat with a side hackle, jack boots, and white breeches, with a leopard-skin saddle-cloth and crooked sabre. The corps presented him with a superb sword in 1807. He personally set an example of unwearied exertion; his speeches on several occasions, and his correspondence with the commander-in-chief, breathed a Scottish patriotism not less pure than hearty in the common cause. "We did not take up arms to please any Minister or set of Ministers," he declared on one occasion, "but to defend our native land from foreign and domestic enemies."

After being M.P. for Dumfries, on the elevation of Mr. Dundas to the peerage in 1802, he was unanimously chosen a member for the city of Edinburgh, and during the few years he continued in Parliament, acted as few Lords Advocate have ever done, and notwithstanding the pressure of imperial matters and the threatening aspect of the times, brought forward several measures of importance to Scotland; but his parliamentary career was rendered somewhat memorable by an accusation of abuse of power as Lord Advocate, brought against him by Mr. Whitbread, resulting in a vast amount of correspondence and debating in 1803. The circumstances are curious, as stated by the latter :—

"Mr. Morrison, a farmer in Banffshire, had a servant of the name of Garrow, who entered a volunteer corps, and attended drills contrary to his master's pleasure; and on the 13th of October last, upon the occasion of an inspection of the company by the Marquis of Huntly, he absented himself entirely from his master's work, in consequence of which he discharged him. The servant transmitted a memorial to the Lord Advocate, stating his case, and begging to know what compensation he could by law claim from his late master for the injury he had suffered. His lordship gave it as his opinion that the memorialist had no claim for wages after the time he was dismissed, thereby acknowledging that he had done nothing contrary to law; but he had not given a bare legal opinion, he had prefaced it by representing Mr. Morrison's act as unprincipled and oppressive, and that without proof or inquiry. Not satisfied with this, he next day addressed a letter to the Sheriff-substitute of Banffshire, attributing Mr. Morrison's conduct to *disaffection and disloyalty*."

The letter referred to described Morrison's conduct as "atrocious," and such as could only have arisen from a spirit of treason, adding, "it is my order to you as Sheriff-substitute of the county, that on the first Frenchman landing in Scotland, you do immediately apprehend and secure

Morrison as a suspected person, and you will not liberate him without a communication with me; and you may inform him of these, my orders. And further, I shall do all I can to prevent him from receiving any compensation from any part of his property which may either be destroyed by the enemy or the King's troops to prevent it falling into their hands."

In the debate that ensued, Fox and Pitt took animated parts, and Charles Hope ably defended himself, saying that had Mr. Whitbread made such an accusation against him in Edinburgh, "there would be 100,000 tongues ready to repel the charge, and probably several arms raised against him who made it." He described the defence-less state of the country, and the anomalous duties thrown upon the Lord Advocate since the Union, after which the Privy Council, Lord Chancellor, and Secretary of State, were illegally abolished, adding that Morrison was influenced by the Chairman of the "Society of Friends of Uni-versal Liberty," in Portsoy, one of whose favourite measures was to obstruct and discourage the for-mation of volunteer corps to repel the expected invasion.

Pitt spoke eloquently in his defence, contend-ing that "great allowances were to be made for an active and ardent mind placed in the situation of Advocate-General." He voted for the order of the day, and against the original motion. When the House divided, 82 were for the latter, and 159 against it; majority, 77.

On the death of Sir David Rae of Eskgrove, in 1804, he was appointed Lord Justice Clerk, and on taking his seat addressed the Bench in a concise and eloquent speech, which was long one of the traditions of the Court. During seven years that he administered justice in the Criminal Court, his office was conducted with ability, dignity, and solemnity.

On the death of the Lord President Blair, in 1811, Charles Hope was promoted in his place, and when taking his seat, made a warm and pa-thetic panegyric on his gifted predecessor, and the ability with which he filled his station for a period of thirty years is still remembered in the Col-lege of Justice. He presided, in 1820, at the special commission for the trial of the high treason cases in Glasgow and the West; and sixteen years after-wards, on the death of James Duke of Montrose, K.G., by virtue of an act of parliament, he was ap-pointed Lord Justice-General of Scotland, and as such, having to preside in the Justiciary Court, he went back there after an absence of twenty-five years. At the proclamation of Queen Victoria he wore the robes of Lord Justice-General. He died and was succeeded in office, in 1841, by the Right Hon. David Boyle of Shewalton; and his son John, who in that year had been appointed Lord Justice Clerk, after being Dean of Faculty, also died at Edinburgh in 1858.

No. 24 Moray Place was the last and long the town residence of Lord Jeffrey, to whom we have had often to refer in his early life elsewhere. Here it was, that those evening reunions (Tuesdays and Fridays) which brightened the evening of his life, took place. "Nothing whatever now exists in Edinburgh that can convey to a younger generation any impression of the charms of that circle. If there happened to be any stranger in Edinburgh worth seeing you were sure to meet him there."

The personal appearance of the first recognised editor of the *Edinburgh Review* was not remarkable. His complexion was very swarthy; his features were good and intellectual in cast and expression; his forehead high and lips firmly set. He was very diminutive in stature—a circumstance that called forth innumerable jokes from his friend Sydney Smith, who once said, "Look at my little friend Jeffrey; he hasn't body enough to cover his mind decently with; his intellect is indecently exposed." On another occasion, Jeffrey having arrived unex-pectly at Foston when Smith was from home, amused himself by joining the children, who were riding a donkey. After a time, greatly to the de-light of the youngsters, he mounted the animal, and Smith returning at the time, sang the following impromptu:—

> "Witty as Horatius Flaccus,
> Great a Jacobin as Gracchus,
> Short, but not as fat as Bacchus,
> Riding on a little Jackass!"

His fondness for children was remarkable. He was never so happy as when in their society, and was a most devoted husband and father.

He was Dean of Faculty, and prior to his eleva-tion to the Bench, when he came to 24 Moray Place, had some time previously resided in 92 George Street. Deemed generally only as a crusty and uncompromising critic, he possessed great good-ness of heart and domestic amiability. In his latter years, when past the psalmist-appointed term of life, he grew more than ever tender-hearted and amiable, praised nursery songs, patronised medio-crities, and wrote letters that were childish in their gentleness of expression. "It seemed to be the natural strain of his character let loose from some stern responsibility, which made him sharp and critical through all his former life."

In their day his critical writings had a brilliant

reputation, but he was too much a votary of the regular old rhetorical style of poetry to be capable of appreciating the Lake school, or any others among his own contemporaries; and thus he was apt to make mistakes, draw wrong deductions as to a writer's future, and indulge in free-and-easy condemnation.

He was passionately attached to his native city, Edinburgh, and was always miserable when away from it. It was all the same through life — he never could reconcile himself to new places, new people, or strange habits; and thus it was that his letters, in age, from Oxford, from London, and America, teem with complaints, and longing for home. His industry was indefatigable, and his general information of the widest range, perfectly accurate, and always at command. He died in 1850, in his seventy-seventh year, and was borne from Moray Place to his last home in the cemetery at the Dean.

In No. 34 lived the Hon. Baron David Hume, of the Scottish Exchequer in 1779 and 1780, nephew of the historian, and an eminent writer on the criminal jurisprudence of the country, one of the correspondents of the Mirror Club, and who for many years sat with Sir Walter Scott, at the Clerks' table in the first Division of the Court of Session. No. 47 was long the abode of Sir James Wellwood Moncreiff, Bart., of Tullibole in Kinross-shire, who was called to the Scottish bar in 1799, and was raised to the bench in 1829, under the title of Lord Moncreiff, and died in 1851.

His contemporary Baron Hume, filled various important situations with great ability, having been

FRANCIS, LORD JEFFREY.   (*After the Portrait by Colvin Smith, R.S.A.*)

successively Sheriff of Berwickshire and of West Lothian, Professor of Scots Law in the University of Edinburgh, and Baron of Exchequer till the abolition of the Court in 1830. His great work on the Criminal Law of Scotland has been deemed the text-book of that department of jurisprudence, and is constantly referred to as an authority, by bench and bar. It was published in 2 vols. quarto in 1799. He died at Edinburgh on the 30th August, 1838, and left in the hands of the secretary of the Royal Society of Edinburgh a valuable collection of MSS. and letters belonging to, or relating to his celebrated uncle, the historian of England.

In Forres Street —a short and steep one opening south from Moray Place—No. 3 was the residence of the great Thomas Chalmers, D.D., the leader of the Free Church movement, a large-hearted, patriotic, and devout man, and of whom it has been said, that he was pre-eminently in the unity of an un-divided life, at once a man of God, a man of science, and a man of the world. He was born on the 17th of March, 1780. As a preacher, it is asserted, that there were few whose eloquence was capable of producing an effect so strong and irresistible as his, without his ever having recourse to any of the arts of common pulpit enthusiasm.

His language was bold and magnificent; his imagination fertile and distinct, gave richness to his style, while his arguments were supplied with a vast and rapid diversity of illustration, and all who ever heard him, still recall Thomas Chalmers with serious and deep-felt veneration.

He is thus described in his earlier years, and

long before he took the great part he did in the storm of the Disruption :—

"At first sight his face is a coarse one—but a mysterious kind of meaning breathes from every part of it, that such as have eyes cannot be long without discovering. It is very pale, and the large half-closed eyelids have a certain drooping melancholy about them, which interested me very much, I understood not why. The lips, too, are singularly pensive in their mode of falling down at the sides, although there is no want of richness and vigour in their central fulness of curve. The upper lip from the nose downwards, is separated by a very deep line, which gives a sort of leonine firmness of expression to all the lower part of the face. The cheeks are square and strong, in texture like pieces of marble, with the cheek bones very broad and prominent. The eyes themselves are light in colour, and have a strange, dreamy heaviness, that conveys any idea than that of dulness, but which contrasts in a wonderful manner with the dazzling watery glare they exhibit when expanded in their sockets and illuminated into all their flame and fervour in some moment

DR. CHALMERS IN 1821. (*From the Portrait by Andrew Geddes.*)

of high entranced enthusiasm. But the shape of the forehead is perhaps the most singular part of the whole visage ; and indeed it presents a mixture so very singular, that I should have required some little time to comprehend the meaning of it. . . . In the forehead of Dr. Chalmers there is an arch of imagination, carrying out the summit boldly and roundly, in a style to which the heads of very few poets present anything comparable—while over this again there is a grand apex of veneration and love, such as might have graced the bust of Plato himself, and such as in living men I had never beheld equalled in any but the majestic head of Canova. The whole is edged with a few crisp locks, which stand boldly forth and afford a fine relief to the death-like paleness of those massive temples."

He died on the 31st May, 1847, since when his Memoirs have been given to the world by Dr. William Hanna, with his life and labours in Glasgow, his residence in St. Andrews, and his final removal to Edinburgh, his visits to England, and the lively journal he kept of what he saw and did while in that country.

St. Colme Street, the adjacent continuation of Albyn Place, is so named from one of the titles of the Moray family, a member of which was commendator of Inchcolm in the middle of the 16th century.

Here No. 8 was the residence of Captain Basil Hall, R.N., the popular writer on several subjects. He was the second son of Sir James Hall of Dunglass, Bart., and Lady Helena Douglas, daughter of Dunbar, third Earl of Selkirk.

He was made captain in 1817, but in the preceding year, when in command of the *Lyra*, he visited the islands on the coast of Corea, which in honour of his father, his friend Captain (afterwards Sir Murray) Maxwell, named Sir James Hall's Group ; and in 1818 he published his voyage to Corea and the Great Loochoo Island in the Sea of Japan. In 1824 he published at Edinburgh his experience on the coasts of Chili, Peru, and Mexico, during the three preceding years. His travels in North America followed ; but the work by which he is best known—his pleasant " Fragments of Voyages and Travels, including Anecdotes of Naval Life," in three volumes, he published at Edinburgh in 1831, during his residence in St. Colme Street where some of his children were born. " Patchwork," a work in three volumes, he published in England in 1841. He married Margaret, daughter of Sir John Hunter, Consul-general in Spain, and died at Portsmouth in 1844, leaving behind him the reputation of having been a brave and intelligent officer, a good and benevolent man, and a faithful friend.

Ainslie Place is an expansion of Great Stuart Street, midway between Moray Place and Randolph Crescent. It forms an elegant, spacious, and symmetrical double crescent, with an ornamental garden in the centre, and is notable for containing the houses in which Dugald Stewart and Dean Ramsay lived and died, namely, Nos. 5 and 23.

To the philosopher we have already referred in our account of Lothian Hut, in the Horse Wynd. In 1792 he published the first volume of the "Philosophy of the Human Mind," and in the following year he read before the Royal Society of Edinburgh his account of the life and writings of Adam Smith; and his other works are too well-known to need enumeration here. On the death of his wife, in 1787, he married Helen D'Arcy Cranstoun, daughter of the Hon. George Cranstoun, who, it is said, was his equal in intellect, if superior in blood. She was the sister of the Countess Purgstall (the subject of Basil Hall's "Schloss Hainfeldt") and of Lord Corehouse, the friend of Sir Walter Scott.

Though the least beautiful of a family in which beauty is hereditary, she had (according to the *Quarterly Review*, No. 133) the best essence of beauty, expression, a bright eye beaming with intelligence, a manner the most distinguished, yet soft, feminine, and singularly winning. On her ill-favoured Professor she doted with a love-match devotion; to his studies and night lucubrations she sacrificed her health and rest; she was his amanuensis and corrector at a time when he was singularly fortunate in his pupils, who never forgot the charm of her presence, the instruction they won, and the society they enjoyed, in the house of Dugald Stewart. Among these were the Lords Dudley, Lansdowne, Palmerston, Kinnaird, and Ashburton. In all his after-life he maintained a good fellowship with them, and, in 1806, obtained the sinecure office of *Gazette* writer for Scotland, with £600 per annum.

Her talent, wit, and beauty made the wife of the Professor one of the most attractive women in the city. "No wonder, therefore," says the *Quarterly*, "that her saloons were the resort of all that was the best of Edinburgh, the house to which strangers most eagerly sought introduction. In her Lord Dudley found indeed a friend, she was to him in the place of a mother. His respect for her was unbounded, and continued to the close; often have we seen him, when she was stricken in years, seated near her for whole evenings, clasping her hand in both of his. Into her faithful ear he poured his hopes and his fears, and unbosomed his inner soul; and with her he maintained a constant correspondence to the last."

Her marriage with the Professor came about in a singular manner. When Miss Cranstoun, she had written a poem, which was accidentally shown by her cousin, the Earl of Lothian, to Dugald Stewart, then his private tutor, and unknown to fame; and he was so enraptured with it, and so warm in his commendations, that the authoress and her critic fell in love by a species of second-sight, before their first interview, and in due time were made one.

Dugald Stewart died at his house in Ainslie Place, on Wednesday, the 11th June, 1828, after a short but painful illness, when in the seventy-fifth year of his age, having been born in the old College of Edinburgh in 1753, when his father was professor of mathematics. His long life had been devoted to literature and science. He had acquired a vast amount of information, profound as it was exact, and possessed the faculty of memory in a singular degree. As a public teacher he was fluent, animated, and impressive, with great dignity and grace in his manner.

He was buried in the Canongate churchyard. The funeral procession proceeded as a private one from Ainslie Place at three in the afternoon; but on reaching the head of the North Bridge it was joined by the Senatus Academicus in their gowns (preceded by the mace bearer) two and two, the junior members in front, the Rev. Principal Baird in the rear, together with the Lord Provost, magistrates and council, with their officers and regalia.

He left a widow and two children, a son and daughter, the former of whom, Lieutenant-Colonel Matthew Stewart, published an able pamphlet on Indian affairs. His widow, who holds a high place among writers of Scottish song, survived him ten years, dying in July, 1838.

The Very Rev. Edward Bannerman Ramsay, LL.D. and F.R.S.E., a genial writer on several subjects, but chiefly known for his "Reminiscences of Scottish Life and Character," was long the occupant of No. 23. He was the fourth son of Sir Alexander Ramsay, Bart., of Balmaine, in Kincardineshire, and was a graduate of St. John's College, Cambridge. His degree of LL.D. was given him by the University of Edinburgh, on the installation of Mr. Gladstone as Lord Rector in 1859. He held English orders, and for seven years had been a curate in Somersetshire. His last and most successful contribution to literature was derived from his long knowledge of Scottish character. He was for many years Dean of the Episcopal Church in Scotland, and as a Churchman he always advocated moderate opinions, both in ritual and doctrine. He died on the 27th December, 1872, in the seventy-ninth year of his age.

In the summer of 1879 a memorial to his memory was erected at the west end of Princes Street, eastward of St. John's Church, wherein he so long officiated. It is a cross of Shap granite, twenty-six feet in height, having a width of eight feet six inches from end to end of the arms. At the height of sixteen feet there spring curves which bend round into the arms, while between those arms and the upright shaft are carried four arcs, having a diameter of six feet.

On each of its main faces the cross is divided into panels, in which are inserted bronze bas-reliefs, worked out, like the whole design, from drawings by R. Anderson, A.R.S.A. Those occupying the head and arms of the cross represent the various stages of our Lord's Passion, the Resurrection and the Ascension; in another series of six, placed thus on either side of the shaft, are set forth the acts of charity, while the large panels in the base are filled in with sculptured ornament of the fine twelfth-century type, taken from Jedburgh abbey.

Three senators of the College of Justice have had their abodes in Ainslie Place—Lord Barcaple, raised to the bench in 1862, Lord Cowan, a judge of 1851, and George Cranstoun, Lord Corehouse, the brother of Mrs. Dugald Stewart, who resided in No. 12. This admirable judge was the son of the Hon. George Cranstoun of Longwarton, and Miss Brisbane of that ilk. He was originally intended for the army, but passed as advocate in 1793, and was Dean of Faculty in 1823, and succeeded to the bench on the death of Lord Hermand, three years after. He was the author of the famous Court of Session *jeu d'esprit*, known as "The Diamond Beetle Case," an amusing and not overdrawn caricature of the judicial style, manners, and language, of the judges of a bygone time.

He took his judicial title from the old ruined castle of Corehouse, near the Clyde, where he had built a mansion in the English style. He was an excellent Greek scholar, and as such was a great favourite with old Lord Monboddo, who used to declare that "Cranstoun was the only scholar in all Scotland," the scholars in his opinion being all on the south side of the Tweed.

He was long famed for being the beau-ideal of a judge; placid and calm, he listened to even the longest debates with patience, and was an able lawyer, especially in feudal questions, and his opinions were always received with the most profound respect.

Great Stuart Street leads from Ainslie Place into Randolph Crescent, which faces the Queensferry Road, and has in its gardens some of the fine old trees which in former times adorned the Earl of Moray's park.

In No. 16 of the former street lived and died, after his removal from No. 1, Inverleith Terrace, the genial and patriotic author of the "Lays of the Scottish Cavaliers," a Scottish humourist of a very high class. William Edmondstoune Aytoun, Professor of Rhetoric in the University of Edinburgh, was born in 1813, of a fine old Fifeshire family, and in the course of his education at one of the seminaries of his native capital, he became distinguished among his contemporaries for his powers for a poem on "Judith." In his eighteenth year he published a volume entitled "Poland and other Poems," which attracted little attention; but after he was called to the bar, in 1840, he became one of the standing wits of the Law Courts, yet, save as a counsel in criminal cases, he did not acquire forensic celebrity as an advocate.

Five years afterwards he was presented to the chair of Rhetoric and Belles Lettres in the University, and became a leading contributor to *Blackwood's Magazine*, in which his famous "Lays," that have run through so many editions, first appeared. Besides these, he was the author of many brilliant pieces in the "Book of Ballads," by Bon Gaultier, a name under which he and Sir Theodore Martin, then a solicitor in Edinburgh, contributed to various periodicals.

In April, 1849, he married Jane Emily Wilson, the youngest daughter of "Christopher North," in whose class he had been as a student in his early years, a delicate and pretty little woman, who predeceased him. In the summer of 1853 he delivered a series of lectures on "Poetry and Dramatic Literature," in Willis's Rooms, to such large and fashionable audiences as London alone can produce; and to his pen is ascribed the mock-heroic tragedy of "Firmilian," designed to ridicule, as it did, the rising poets of "The Spasmodic School." With all his brilliance as a humourist, Aytoun was unsuccessful as a novelist, and his epic poem "Bothwell," written in 16 Great Stuart Street, did not bring him any accession of fame.

In his latter years, few writers on the Conservative side rendered more effective service to their party than Professor Aytoun, whom, in 1852, Lord Derby rewarded with the offices of Sheriff and Vice-Admiral of Orkney.

Among the many interesting people who frequented the house of the author of "The Lays" few were more striking than an old lady of strong Jacobite sentiments, even in this prosaic age, Miss Clementina Stirling Graham, of Duntrune, well worthy of notice here, remarkable for her historical connections as for her great age, as she died in her ninety-fifth year, at Duntrune, in 1877. Born in the Seagate of Dundee, in 1782, she was the daughter of Stirling of Pittendreich, Forfarshire, and of Amelia, daughter of Alexander Graham, of Duntrune, who died in 1804, and was thus the *last* lineal representative of Claverhouse.

In addition to her accomplishments, she possessed wit and invention in a high degree, and was always lively, kind, and hospitable. She had a keen perception of the humorous, and was well known in Edinburgh society in the palmy days of Jeffrey. Gifted with great powers of mimicry, her personifications at private parties were so unique, that even those who knew her best were deceived. One of the most amusing of these took place in 1821, at the house of Jeffrey.

He asked her to give a personation of an old lady, to which she consented, but, in order to have a little amusement at *his* expense, she called upon him in the character of a "Lady Pitlyal," to ask his professional opinion upon an imaginary law plea, which she alleged her agent was misconducting.

On this occasion she drove up to his house in the carriage of Lord Gillies, accompanied by a young lady as her daughter, and so complete was the personification, that the acute Jeffrey did not discover till next day that he had been duped! This episode created so much amusement in Edinburgh that it found its way into the pages of *Blackwood*. Sir Walter Scott, who was a spectator of Miss Graham's power of personation, wrote thus regarding it :—

"March 7. Went to my Lord Gillies to dinner, and witnessed a singular exhibition of personification. Miss Stirling Graham, a lady of the family from which Claverhouse was descended, looks like thirty years old, and has a face of the Scottish cast, with good expression, in point of good sense and

WILLIAM EDMONSTOUNE AYTOUN.
(From a Photograph by Messrs. Ross and Thomson.)

good humour. Her conversation, so far as I have had the advantage of hearing it, is shrewd and sensible, but noways brilliant. She dined with us, went off as to the play, and returned in the character of an old Scottish lady. Her dress and behaviour were admirable, and her conversation unique. I was in the secret of course, and did my best to keep up the ball, but she cut me out of all feather. The prosing account she gave of her son, the antiquary, who found an old ring in a slate quarry, was extremely ludicrous, and she puzzled the professor of agriculture with a merciless account of the succession of crops in the parks around her old mansion house. No person to whom the secret was not entrusted had the least guess of an impostor, except the shrewd young lady present, who observed the hand narrowly, and saw that it was plumper than the age of the lady seemed to warrant. This lady and Miss Bell, of Coldstream, have this gift of personation to a much greater degree than any person I ever saw." Miss Graham published in 1829 the "Bee Preserver," translated from the work of M. de Gelieu, for which she received the medal of the Highland Society. She possessed a large circle of friends, and never had an enemy.

Her friend William Edmondstoune Aytoun died on the 4th August, 1865, sincerely regretted by all who knew him, and now lies under a white marble monument in the beautiful cemetery at the Dean.

Charles Baillie, Lord Jerviswoode, who may well be deemed by association one of the *last* of the historical Lords of Session, for years was the occupant of No. 14, Randolph Crescent, and his name is one which awakens many sad and gentle memories. He was the second son of George Baillie of Jerviswoode, and a descendant of that memorable Baillie of Jerviswoode, who, according to Hume, was a man of merit and learning, a cadet of the Lamington family, and called "The Scottish Sidney," but was executed as a traitor on the scaffold at Edinburgh, in 1683, having identified himself with the interests of Monmouth and Argyle.

Lord Jerviswoode was possessed of more than average intellectual gifts, and still more with charms of person and manners that were not confined to the female side of his house. One sister, the Marchioness of Breadalbane, and another, Lady Polwarth, were both celebrated for their beauty, wit, and accomplishments. On the death of their cousin, in the year 1859, his eldest brother became tenth Earl of Haddington, and then Charles, by royal warrant, was raised to the rank of an earl's brother.

Prior to this he had a long and brilliant course in law, and in spotless honour is said to have been "second to none." He was called to the Bar in 1830, and after being Advocate Depute, Sheriff of Stirling, and Solicitor-General, was Lord Advocate in 1858, and M.P. for West Lothian in the following year, and a Lord of Session. In 1862 he became a Lord of Justiciary. He took a great interest in the fine arts, and was a trustee of the Scottish Board of Manufactures; but finding his health failing, he quitted the bench in July, 1874.

He died in his seventy-fifth year, on the 23rd of July, 1879, at his residence, Dryburgh House, in Roxburghshire, near the ruins of the beautiful abbey in which Scott and his race lie interred. For the last five years of his life little had been heard of him in the busy world, while his delicate health and shy nature denied him the power of taking part in public matters.

CHAPTER XXVIII.

THE WESTERN NEW TOWN—HAYMARKET—DALRY—FOUNTAINBRIDGE.

Maitland Street and Shandwick Place—The Albert Institute—Last Residence of Sir Walter Scott in Edinburgh—Lieutenant-General Dundas —Melville Street—Patrick F. Tytler—Manor Place—St. Mary's Cathedral—The Foundation Laid—Its Size and Aspect—Opened for Service—The Copestone and Cross placed on the Spire—Haymarket Station—Winter Garden—Donaldson's Hospital—Castle Terrace - Its Churches—Castle Barns--The U. P. Theological Hall—Union Canal—First Boat Launched—Dalry—The Chieslies—The Caledonian Distillery—Fountainbridge—Earl Grey Street—Professor G. J. Bell—The Slaughter-houses—Bain Whyt of Bainfield—North British India Rubber Works—Scottish Vulcanite Company—Their Manufactures, &c.—Adam Ritchie.

THE Western New Town comprises a grand series of crescents, streets, and squares, extending from the line of East and West Maitland Streets and Athole Crescent northward to the New Queensferry Road, displaying in its extent and architecture, while including the singularly picturesque ravine of the Water of Leith, a brilliance and beauty well entitling it to be deemed, par excellence, "The West End," and was built respectively about 1822, 1850, and 1866.

Lynedoch Place, so named from the hero of Barossa, opposite Randolph Crescent, was erected in 1823, but prior to that a continuation of the line of Princes Street had been made westward towards the lands of Coates. This was finally effected by the erection of East and West Maitland Streets, Shandwick Place, and Coates and Athole Crescents. In the latter are some rows of stately old trees, which only vigorous and prolonged remonstrance prevented from being wantonly cut down, in accordance with the bad taste which at one time prevailed in Edinburgh, where a species of war was waged against all growing timber.

The Episcopal chapel of St. Thomas is now compacted with the remaining houses at the east end of Rutland Street, but presents an ornamental front in the Norman style immediately east of Maitland Street, and shows there a richly-carved porch, with some minutely beautiful arcade work.

Maitland Street and Shandwick Place, once a double line of front-door houses for people of good style, are almost entirely lines of shops or other new buildings. In the first years of the present century, Lockhart of Castlehill, Hepburn of Clerkington, Napier of Dunmore, Tait of Glencross, and Scott of Cauldhouse, had their residences in the former; and No. 23, now a shop, was the abode, about the year 1818, of J. Gibson Lockhart, the son-in-law and biographer of Sir Walter Scott. He died at Abbotsford in 1854.

In Shandwick Place is now the Albert Institute of the Fine Arts, erected in 1876, when property to the value of £25,000 was acquired for the purpose. The objects of this institute are the advancement of the cause of art generally, but more especially contemporary Scottish art; to

75

promote the pleasant intercourse of those who practise art either professionally or privately; to increase facilities for the study and observation of art, and to obtain more general attention to its claims.

The association is composed of artists, professional and amateur, and has exhibitions of paintings, sculpture, and water-colour drawings, at intervals during the year, without being antagonistic in any way to the Royal Scottish Academy. Lectures are here delivered on art, and the entire institute is managed by a chairman and executive council.

In No. 6 Shandwick Place Sir Walter Scott resided from 1828 to 1830, when he relinquished his office as clerk of session in the July of the latter year. This was his *last* permanent residence in Edinburgh, where on two future occasions, however, he resided temporarily. On the 31st of January, 1831, he came to town from Abbotsford for the purpose of executing his last will, and on that occasion he took up his abode at the house of his bookseller, in Athole Crescent, where he resided for nine days. At that time No. 6 was the residence of Mr. Jobson.

No. 11, now a hotel, was for about twenty years the residence of Lieutenant-General Francis Dundas, son of the second President Dundas, and brother of the Lord Chief Baron Dundas. He was long a colonel in the old Scots Brigade of immortal memory, in the Dutch service, and which afterwards came into the British in 1795, when his regiment was numbered as the 94th of the line. In 1802-3 he was Governor of the Cape of Good Hope. During the brief peace of Amiens, in accordance with his instructions to evacuate the colony, he embarked his troops on board the British squadron, but on the same evening, having fortunately received counter orders, he re-landed the troops and re-captured the colony, which has ever since belonged to Britain.

In 1809 he was colonel of the 71st Highlanders, and ten years after was Governor of Dumbarton Castle. He died at Shandwick Place on the 4th of January, 1824, after a long and painful illness, "which he supported with the patience of a Christian and the fortitude of a soldier."

At the east end of Shandwick Place is St. George's Free Church, a handsome and massive Palladian edifice, built for the congregation of the celebrated Dr. Candlish, after a design by David Bryce, R.S.A., seated for about 1,250 persons, and erected at a cost, including £13,600 for the site, of £31,000.

In No. 3 Walker Street, the short thoroughfare between Coates Crescent and Melville Street, Sir Walter Scott resided with his daughter during the winter of 1826-7, prior to his removal to Shandwick Place.

Melville Street, which runs parallel with the latter on the north, at about two hundred yards distance, is a spacious thoroughfare symmetrically and beautifully edificed; and is adorned in its centre, at a rectangular expansion, with a pedestrian bronze statute of the second Viscount Melville, ably executed by Steel, on a stone pedestal; it was erected in 1857.

This street contains houses which were occupied by two eminent divines, the Rev. David Welsh and the Rev. Andrew Thomson, already referred to in the account of St. George's parish church. In No. 36, Patrick Fraser Tytler, F.R.S.E., the eminent Scottish historian, resided for many years, and penned several of his works. He was the youngest son of Alexander Fraser Tytler, Lord Woodhouselee, and thus came of a race distinguished in Scottish literature. Patrick was called to the bar in 1813, and six years after published, at Edinburgh, a "Life of the Admirable Crichton," and in 1826, a "Life of Wicliff." His able and laborious "History of Scotland" first appeared in 1828, and at once won him fame, for its accuracy, brilliance, and purity of style; but his writings did not render him independent, as he died, when advanced in life, in receipt of an honorary pension from the Civil List.

In Manor Place, at the west end of Melville Street, lived Mrs. Grant of Laggan, the well-known authoress of "Letters from the Mountains," and whose house was, in her time, the resort of select literary parties; of whom Professor Wilson was always one. She had for some time previous resided in the Old Kirk Brae House. In 1825 an application was made on her behalf to George IV. for a pension, which was signed by Scott, Jeffrey, Mackenzie—"The Man of Feeling"—and other influential persons in Edinburgh, and in consequence she received an annual pension of £100 from the Civil Establishment of Scotland.

This, with the emoluments of her literary works, and liberal bequests by deceased friends, made easy and independent her latter days, and she died in Manor Place, on the 7th of November, 1838, aged 84.

It was not until 1868 that this street was edificed on its west side partially. Westward and northward of it a splendid new extension of the city spreads, erected subsequently to that year, comprising property now worth nearly £1,000,000.

This street is named from the adjacent mansion house of the Walkers of Coates, and is on the property of the latter name. Lying immediately westward of Princes Street, this estate includes the sites of Coates Crescent, Melville, Walker, Stafford Streets, and other thoroughfares, yielding a rental of about £20,000 yearly, and representing a capital of £400,000, the whole of which, in 1870, was bequeathed by the late Misses Walker of Coates and Drumsheugh, for the erection of a cathedral for the Scottish Episcopal Church, dedicated to St. Mary, facing the west end of Melville Street.

Miss Mary Walker—the last of an old Episcopalian family—died in 1871, her sister Barbara having pre-deceased her. The foundation-stone was laid with impressive ceremony, by the Duke of Buccleuch, assisted by some 200 clergy and laymen of the Episcopal communion on the 21st of May, 1874; and when fully completed it will be the largest and most beautiful church that has been erected in Scotland, or perhaps in Great Britain since the Reformation. The total cost, when finished, will be about £132,567.

The architect, Sir Gilbert Scott, founded his design on the early Pointed style of architecture.

The axis of this cathedral coincides with the centre of Melville Street, its site being immediately to the south of Coates House, the sole example of an old Scottish mansion surviving in the New Town. The form adopted is that of a cruciform church, the general effect being enhanced by the introduction to the central tower of two minor, though still lofty, towers at the western end. The plan embraces a choir with north and south aisles; at the intersection of the transepts rises the central or rood tower, 275 feet in height; the total length of the edifice externally is 278 feet 2 inches, and the breath 98 feet 6 inches. The choir is 60 feet 9 inches long and 29 broad, with aisles 16 feet wide, divided into two great and four minor bays by beautifully clustered columns. From the floor to the key-stones of the vaulting, which is all of stone, the height is 58 feet. The transepts, which project by one bay beyond the nave and choir, are 35 feet 4 inches long, by 30 feet 9 inches broad, with aisles above 13 feet wide. This unusual proportion of breadth was given to the transepts to provide ample accommodation for congregational purposes. To the north of the north chancel aisle is the library, an apartment measuring 30 feet by 19 feet. The main entrance of the church is from Palmerston Place, opposite what are grotesquely named Grosvenor Gardens. This elevation is the most imposing modern Gothic façade in Scotland, severe in its purity, and rich in elaboration. The most important features here are the portal and great west window. The shafts and flanking arches of the former are of red granite, from Shap in Westmoreland, harmonising well with the fine Dunmore

and Polmaise freestone of which the edifice is built. In the vesica of the centre pediment is a seated figure of the Saviour, supporting with the left hand a lamb, and with the outstretched right holding a key. Around is the legend :—

"EGO SUM OSTIUM ; PER ME SI QUIS INTROIERIT SALVABITUR."

In the spandrils are figures of St. Peter and John the Baptist. Below this grouping are ranged along the door lintel angels bearing a scroll inscribed—

"TU ES CHRISTUS FILIUS DEI."

The side elevations of the nave present the usual features of the early Pointed style, the walls of the aisle being substantially buttressed, dividing the length into five bays, in each of which is a double window. Above the clerestory runs a bold cornice, and from the wall head there springs a high pitched roof. In the gable of the south transept is another portal, the mouldings of which are exquisitely carved. The window consists of three lancets separated by massively clustered buttress shafts. Above it is a rose window 24 feet in diameter, filled in with geometrical tracery. Above it are five pointed niches, containing statues of St. Paul and St. Luke, Titus, Silas, and Timotheus.

Though treated in a somewhat similar manner, the gable of the north transept has some features peculiarly its own. The wheel window, 24 feet in diameter, is of a later period than that in the south gable. Over it is a statue of David. As usual in cathedrals, the choir has been treated with greater elaboration of design and detail than the nave, especially in the triforium and clerestory. The gable fronting Melville Street is nearly occupied by a triple lancet window, the apex of the arches being 54 feet from the ground. Above is an arcade, the arches of which are filled by statues of the mother of our Lord and the four Evangelists. In the vesica is a figure of the Saviour surrounded by angels in the act of adoration. The four shafted and clustered pillars of the rood-tower, though framed to support a superincumbent mass of no less than 6,000 tons, are finely proportioned and even light in appearance. The tower rises square from the roof in beautiful proportions, the transition to the octagonal form taking place at the height of 120 feet from the foundation.

Viewed from any point, the nave, with its long-drawn aisles and interlacing arches, has a peculiarly grand and impressive effect. Designed in the style of the twelfth century, the font stands in the baptistery under the south-west tower. It is massive, of yellowish alabaster streaked with red veins, and is placed on a pedestal of three steps; the basin, which is supported by four red marble columns, shows in carved panels round its sides the ark, dove, fishes, and a floriated cross.

The cathedral, before its completion, was opened for service on the 25th of January, 1879, by the streets. In attendance upon the bishop were the Lord Provost, Lord Teignmouth, and others.

The senior and junior chaplains of the cathedral, together with the clerk of works, ascended the spire to place the stone and cross in position with certain religious rites—from its vast height a some-

ST. MARY'S CATHEDRAL, EXTERIOR VIEW.

Right Rev. Henry Cotterill, Episcopal bishop of Edinburgh, in presence of a great congregation assembled in the nave, and consecrated 30th October, 1879.

On the 9th of June, 1879, the copestone and finial cross of the great central spire were placed in position with befitting ceremony, in presence of a vast assemblage of ladies and gentlemen in the cathedral grounds, and even in the adjacent what perilous and difficult task for these gentlemen to undertake. They spread the mortar, and the copestone and cross, which were fifteen feet in height and about a ton in weight, were lowered into position by tackle; the Rev. Mr. Meredith tapped them with a mallet and declared them to have been duly laid " in the name of the Blessed Trinity." The company aloft then joined in the doxology.

A shot fired from the belfry apprised the multitude far down below of the close of the ceremony, and immediately the choir, along with other officials of the church in surplices stationed in the garden, sung the hymn "Praise ye the Lord, ye Heavens in the nave and clerestory bear the arms of many ancient Scottish families.

Away to the westward of the quarter we have described, at the delta of the old Glasgow and Dalry roads, where for several generations stood

ST. MARY'S CATHEDRAL, INTERIOR VIEW.   (*From a Photograph by G. W. Wilson and Co., Aberdeen.*)

adore Him," after which the people were addressed by the Lord Provost.

Sir Gilbert Scott did not live to see the completion of this cathedral, which is one of the many lasting monuments of his skill as an architect. Among the gifts to the cathedral are a peal of ten bells presented by Dean Montgomery; the great west window by Mrs. Gordon of Cluny, as a memorial of her deceased husband; the windows a solitary roadside inn—where regiments coming from Glasgow by wings upon the two roads, formed a junction and halted, while the officers had breakfast or dinner before pushing on to the Castle by the Lang Dykes and latterly by Princes Street and the Earthern Mound—is the Haymarket Railway Station, the first or original terminus of the Edinburgh and Glasgow Railway, a neat two-storeyed Italian edifice facing transversely the line of Athole

Place, and now chiefly used as a coal depôt. Some of the merchants having coal offices here are among the oldest and most extensive firms in the city, one having been established so far back as 1784, and having now business ramifications so ample as to require a complete system of private telegraphs for the transmission of orders between their various offices and coal stores throughout Edinburgh and the suburbs.

This station is reached from the East Princes Street Gardens by a tunnel 3,000 feet in length, passing under the West Church burial ground and the foundations of several streets, and serves as a port for the North British system at the West End.

In its vicinity, on the north side of the way, is a large Winter Garden at the corner between the Glasgow Road and Coates Gardens. It was formed in 1871, and has a southern front 130 feet in length, with a main entrance 50 feet wide, 30 feet long, and surmounted by a dome 65 feet in height.

A little westward of it is West Coates Established Church, built in the later Pointed style, in 1869, with a tower and spire 130 feet in height. It cost £7,500, and is seated for 900 persons.

The United Presbyterian Churches in Palmerston Place (the old line of Bell's Mills Loan) and Dalry Road were opened in 1875, and cost respectively £13,000 and £5,000. The former is an imposing edifice in the classic Italian style, with a hexastyle portico, carrying semicircular headed arches and flanked by towers 100 feet in height.

On the gentle swell of the ground, about 600 yards westward of the Haymarket, amid a brilliant urban landscape, stands Donaldson's Hospital, in magnitude and design one of the grandest edifices of Edinburgh, and visible from a thousand points all round the environs to the westward, north, and south. It sprang from a bequest of about £210,000 originally by James Donaldson of Broughton Hall, a printer, at one time at the foot of the ancient West Bow, who died in the year 1830.

It was erected between the years 1842 and 1851, after designs by W. H. Playfair, at a cost of about £100,000, and forms a hollow quadrangle of 258 feet by 207 exteriorly, and 176 by 164 interiorly. It is a modified variety of a somewhat ornate Tudor style, and built of beautiful freestone. It has four octagonal five-storeyed towers, each 120 feet in height, in the centre of the main front, and four square towers of four storeys each at the corners; and most profuse, graceful, and varied ornamentations on all the four façades, and much in the interior.

It was specially visited and much admired by Queen Victoria in 1850, before it was quite completed, and now maintains and educates poor boys and girls. The building can accommodate 150 children of each sex, of whom a considerable per centage are both deaf and dumb. According to the rules of this excellent institution, those eligible for admission are declared to be—"1. Poor children of the name of Donaldson or Marshall, if appearing to the governors to be deserving. 2. Such poor children as shall appear to be in the most destitute circumstances and the most deserving of admission." None are received whose parents are able to support them. The children are clothed and maintained in the hospital, and are taught such useful branches of a plain education as will fit the boys for trades and the girls for domestic service. The age of admission is from seven to nine, and that of leaving the hospital fourteen years. The Governors are the Lord Justice-General, the Lord Clerk Register, the Lord Advocate, the Lord Provost, the Principal of the University, the senior minister of the Established Church, the ministers of St. Cuthbert's and others ex-officio.

The Castle Terrace, of recent erection, occupies the summit of a steep green bank westward of the fortress and overhanging a portion of the old way from the West Port to St. Cuthbert's. A tenement at its extreme north-western corner is entirely occupied by the Staff in Scotland. Here are the offices of the Auxiliary Artillery, Adjutant-General, Royal Engineers, the medical staff, and the district Commissariat.

Southward of this stands St. Mark's Chapel, erected in 1835, the only Unitarian place of worship in Edinburgh. It cost only £2,000, and is seated for 700. It has an elegant interior, and possesses a fine organ. Previous to 1835 its congregation met in a chapel in Young Street.

Near it, in Cambridge Street, stands the new Gaelic Free Church, a somewhat village-like erection, overshadowed by the great mass of the United Presbyterian Theological Hall. The latter was built in 1875 for the new Edinburgh or West End Theatre, from designs by Mr. Pilkington, an English architect, who certainly succeeded in supplying an edifice alike elegant and comfortable. In its first condition the auditorium measured 70 feet square within the walls, and the accommodation was as follows—pit and stalls, 1,000; dress circle and private boxes, 400; second circle, 600; gallery, 1,000; total, 3,000. The stage was expansive, and provided with all the

DONALDSON'S HOSPITAL.

newest mechanical appliances, including hydraulic machinery for shifting the larger scenes. The proscenium was 32 feet wide by 32 feet in height, with an available width behind of 74 feet, expanding backwards to 114 feet.

The lighting was achieved by a central sunlight and lamps hung on the partition walls. The ventilation was admirable, and the temperature was regulated by steam-pipes throughout the house.

But the career of this fine edifice as a theatre was very brief, and proved how inadequate Edinburgh is, from the peculiar tastes and wishes of its people, to supply audiences for more than two or three such places of entertainment. It speedily proved a failure, and being in the market was purchased by the members of the United Presbyterian Church, who converted it into a theological hall, suited for an audience of 2,000 in all.

The total cost of the building to the denomination, including the purchase of the theatre, amounted to £47,000. Two flats under the street floor are fitted up as fireproof stores, which will cover in all an area of 3,500 square yards.

In connection with this defunct theatre it was proposed to have a winter garden and aquarium. Near it the eye is arrested by a vast pile of new buildings, fantastic and unique in design and detail, the architect of which has certainly been fortunate, at least, in striking out something original, if almost indescribable, in domestic architecture.

Free St. Cuthbert's Church is in Spittal Street, which is named from Provost Sir James Spittal, and is terminated by the King's Bridge at the base of the Castle Rock.

All this area of ground and that lying a little to the westward have the general name of the Castle Barns, a designation still preserved in a little street near Port Hopetoun. A map of the suburbs, in 1798, shows Castle Barns to be an isolated hamlet or double row of houses on the Falkirk Road, distant about 250 yards from the little pavilion-roofed villa still standing at the Main Point. Maitland alleges that somewhere thereabout an edifice was erected for the accommodation of the royal retinue when the king resided in the Castle; and perhaps such may have been the case, but the name implies its having been the grange or farm attached to the fortress, and this idea is confirmed by early maps, when a considerable portion of the ground now lying on both sides of the Lothian Road is included under the general term.

On the plateau at the head of the latter, bordered on the south-east by the ancient way to Fountain-bridge, stands one of the most hideous features of Edinburgh—the Canal Basin, with its surrounding stores and offices.

In 1817 an Act of Parliament was procured, giving power to a joint stock company to cut a canal from Edinburgh to the Forth and Clyde Canal at a point about four miles before the communication of the latter with the Forth. The canal was begun in the following year and completed in 1822. The chief objects of it were the transmission of heavy goods and the conveyance of passengers between the capital and Glasgow—a system long since abandoned; the importation to the former of large coal supplies from places to the westward, and the exportation of manure from the city into agricultural districts. The eastern termination, called Port Hopetoun, occasioned the rapid erection of a somewhat important suburb, where before there stood only a few scattered houses surrounded by fields and groves of pretty trees; but the canal, though a considerable benefit to the city in pre-railway times, has drained a great deal of money from its shareholders.

Though opened in 1822 the canal was considerably advanced in the year preceding. In the *Weekly Journal* for November 7, 1821, we read that "from the present state of the works, the shortening of the days, and the probability of being retarded by the weather, it seems scarcely possible that the trade of this navigation can be opened up sooner than the second month of spring, which will be exactly four years from its commencement. Much has been done within the last few months on the west end of the line, while at the east end the forming of the basin, which is now ready to receive the water, together with the numerous bridges necessary in the first quarter of a mile, have required great attention. Of the passage boats building at the west end of Lochrin distillery, two of which we mentioned some time ago as being in a forward state, one is now completed; she is in every respect an elegant and comfortable vessel, and is called the *Flora Mac Ivor*; the second is considerably advanced, and a third boat after the same model as the others is commenced building."

In the same (now defunct) periodical, for 1st January, 1822, we learn that the *Flora*, "the first of the Union Canal Company's passage boats, was yesterday launched from the company's building yard, at the back of Gilmore Place."

One of the best features of street architecture that sprung up in this quarter after the formation of the canal was Gardiner's Crescent, with its chapel, which was purchased from the United Secession Congregation by the Kirk Session of St.

Cuthbert's, in 1831, for £2,500, and seated for 1,300.

The church was built in 1827, and is now named St. David's, the parish being *quoad sacra*, and disjoined from St. Cuthbert's.

The United Secession Congregation, which formerly sat here, have now their place of worship, seated for 1,284, on the west side of the Lothian Road. In architecture, externally, it is assimilated with the street.

charters granted by the Scottish kings between 1309 and 1413 the lands of Dalry, near Edinburgh, are mentioned in several instances. Under Robert I. "the lands of Merchinstoun and Dalry" were granted to William Bisset. Under David II., Roger Hog, burgess of Edinburgh, had "one annual forth of Dalry;" and there was a charter given by William More, of Abercorn, to William Touris and Helenor Bruce, Countess of Carrick, of the lands of Dalry, in the county of Edinburgh.

EDINBURGH CASTLE FROM PORT HOPETOUN, 1825. (*After Ewbank.*)

Westward of this quarter lies the old historic suburban district named Dalry. The quaint old manor house of that name, which stood so long embosomed among its ancient copsewood, on the east side of the Dalry Road, with its projecting towers crowned by ogee roofs, is now incorporated with one of the somewhat humble class of streets, which hereabout have covered the whole estate, even to Wester Dalry, near the cemetery of that name.

Of Celtic origin, it takes its name from Dal, a vale, and righ, "a king," like a place of the same name in Cunningham, near which there is also a spot named, like that at Holyrood, Croft an Righ, "the croft of the king." In the roll of missing

This Helenor was the only daughter of Alexander, fifth Earl of Carrick (who fell at the battle of Halidon Hill, in 1333), and was the wife of Sir William Cunningham, of Kilmaurs.

In the sixteenth century this fertile and valuable barony became the property of the Chieslies, wealthy burgesses of Edinburgh.

In 1672 there was a "ratification" by Parliament in favour of the notorious John Chieslie (son of Walter Chieslie of Dalry) of the lands of Gorgie; and the inscription on the tomb of his mother in the Greyfriars is thus given in Monteith's "Theatre of Mortality," 1704—

Memoriæ charissimæ suæ conjugis, Catharinæ Tod, quæ decessit 27th January, 1679 Monumen-

tum hoc extrui curavit marius superstes Walterus Chieslie de Dalry, mercator et civis Edinburgensis.

Burnet describes his father as "a noted fanatic at the time of the civil war." In 1675-9 there was a manufactory of paper at his mills of Dalry, on the Water of Leith.

In April, 1682, John Chieslie complained to the Privy Council that Davis, Clark, and some other gentlemen of the Royal Life Guards (the regiment of Claverhouse) had committed "hame-sucken,"

they were certainly guilty of, is death," says Fountainhall (Vol. I.).

We have related in its place how this man, the father of the famous Rachel Chieslie, Lady Grange, assassinated the Lord President, Sir George Lockhart of Carnwath, in 1689, for which his right hand was struck off, after he had been put to the torture and before his execution, and also how his body was carried away and secretly buried.

About 1704 his heir, Major Chieslie, sold the

DALRY MANOR HOUSE.

by invading him in his own house at Dalry, where they beat and wounded him and his servants, and took possession of his stables, out of which they turned his horses. "They had also," records Fountainhall, "a recrimination against him, viz., that they being come to fetch his proportion of straw for their horses, conform to the late Acts of Parliament and Council, he with sundry of his servants and tenants fell on them with (pitch) forks, grapes, &c., and had broken their swords and wounded some of them."

The dispute was referred to the Criminal Court, by sentence of which Davis was banished Scotland, never to return, and Clark was expelled from the Guards. "The punishment of hame-sucken, which

lands of Dalry to Sir Alexander Brand, whose memory yet lingers in the names of Brandfield Street and Place on the property. Afterwards the estate belonged to the Kirkpatricks of Allisland, and latterly to the Walkers, one of whom, James, was a Principal Clerk of Session, whose son Francis, on his marriage with the heiress of Hawthornden, assumed the name of Drummond.

This once secluded property is now nearly all covered with populous streets. One portion of it, at the south end of the Dalry Road, is now a public cemetery, belonging to the Edinburgh Cemetery Company, and contains several handsome monuments.

The same company have established an additional cemetery, a little to the south, beyond Ardmillan Terrace, near the new Magdalene Asylum, a lofty, spacious, and imposing edifice, recently erected in lieu of the old one, established in 1797. Adjoining it is the Girls' House of Refuge, or Western Reformatory, another noble and humane institution, the directors of which are the Lord Provost and magistrates of the city.

These edifices stand near the ancient toll of Tynecastle, and may be considered the termination of the city as yet, in this direction.

On removing an old cottage close by this toll, in April, 1843, the remains of a human skeleton were found buried close to the wall. The skull had been perforated by a bullet, and in the plastered wall of the edifice a bullet was found flattened against the stone.

On the western side of the Dalry Road, about 500 yards from the ancient mansion house, is the Caledonian Distillery, one of the most extensive in Scotland, and one of those which produce " grain whisky," as some make malt whisky only. It was built in 1855, covers five acres of ground, and occupies a situation most convenient for carrying on a great trade. In every part it has been constructed with all the most recent improvements by its proprietors, the Messrs. Menzies, Bernard, and Co. All the principal buildings are five storeys in height, and so designed that the labour of carrying the materials through the various stages of manufacture is reduced to the smallest amount, while branch lines from the Caledonian and North British Railways converge in the centre of the works, thus affording the ready means of bringing in raw material and sending out products.

The extent of the traffic here may be judged from the facts that 2,000 quarters of grain and 200 tons of coal are used every week, while the quantity of spirits sent out in the same time is 40,000 gallons, the duty on which is £20,000, or at the rate of £1,040,000 a year. The machinery is propelled by five steam-engines, varying from 5 to 150 horse-power, for the service of which, and supplying the steam used in distillation, there are nine large steam boilers.

The Caledonian distillery contains the greatest still in Scotland. In order to meet a growing demand for the variety of whisky known as "Irish," the proprietors of the Caledonian distillery, about 1867 fitted up two large stills of an old pattern, with which they manufacture whisky precisely similar to that which is made in Dublin. In connection with this branch of their business, stores capable of containing as many as 5,000 puncheons were added to their works at Dalry, and in

these various kinds of whisky have been permitted to lie for some time before being sent out.

Fountainbridge, a long and straggling suburb, once among fields and gardens, at the close of the last century and the beginning of the present contained several old-fashioned villas with pleasure-grounds, and was bordered on its northern side by a wooded residence, the Grove, which still gives a name to the streets in the locality.

Some of the houses at its southern end, near the present Brandfield Place, were old as the time of William III. In the garden of one of them an antique iron helmet, now in the Antiquarian Museum, was dug up in 1781. In one of them lived and died, in 1767, Lady Margaret Leslie, third daughter of John Earl of Rothes, Lord High Admiral of Scotland on the accession of George I. in 1714.

A narrow alley near its northern end still bears the name of the Thorneybank, i.e., a ridge covered with thorns, long unploughed and untouched. In its vicinity is Earl Grey Street, a name substituted for its old one of Wellington after the passing of the great Reform Bill, by order of the Town Council.

This quarter abuts on Lochrin, " the place where the water from the meadows (i.e. the burgh loch) discharges itself," says Kincaid, but "rhinn" means a flat place in Celtic in some instances; and near it is another place with the Celtic name of Drumdryan.

George Joseph Bell, Professor of Scottish Law in the University of Edinburgh, was born in Fountainbridge on the 26th March, 1770. A distinguished legal writer, he was author of " Commentaries on the Law of Scotland," " Principles of the Law," for the use of his students, and other works, and held the chair of law from 1822 to 1843, when he was succeeded by Mr. John Shankmore.

Among the leading features in this locality are the extensive city slaughter-houses, which extend from the street eastward to Lochrin, having a plain yet handsome and massive entrance, in the Egyptian style, adorned with great bulls' heads carved in freestone in the coving of the entablature. These were designed by Mr. David Cousin, who brought to bear upon them the result of his observations made in the most famous abattoirs of Paris, such as du Roule, de Montmartre, and de Popincourt.

In 1791 there died in Edinburgh John Strachan, a flesh-caddie, in his 105th year. " He recollected," says the Scots Magazine, " the time when no flesher would venture to kill any beast till all the different parts were bespoke, butcher meat being then a very unsaleable article."

At the southern extremity of Fountainbridge stood, till within the last few years, an antique villa, a little way back from the road, named Bainfield, for years the residence of an old and well-known citizen, Bain Whyt, a W.S. of 1789, who was senior lieutenant and afterwards adjutant of the First Edinburgh Volunteers formed in 1794, and who is still remembered in Edinburgh as the founder of the Wagering Club in 1775. Yearly, on the night of the 30th January, the members of this club meet and solemnly drink to the memory of "Old Bain Whyt," in whose honour songs are occasionally sung, the character of which may be gathered from the following two verses of one sung at the ninetieth anniversary :—

" Come all ye jolly wagerers, and listen unto me,
  And I will sing a little song, composed in memorie
  Of the fine old Scottish gentleman, who in 1775,
  Did plant the tree that still we see, right hearty and
  alive.
  Chorus—Right hearty and alive,
      In this its ninetieth year !
      Then drink to-night, to old Bain Whyt,
      With mirth and hearty cheer !
" When haughty Gaul did fiercely crow and threaten sword
  in hand,
  Bain Whyt among the foremost rose to guard our native
  land ;
  A soldier good, full armed he stood, for home and
  country dear,
  The pattern of a loyal man, a British volunteer !
  Chorus—A British volunteer,
      And an adjutant was he !
      Then fill the cup, and quaff it up,
      To him with three times three !"

The wagers, for small sums, a bottle of wine, a dinner, perhaps, are made on the probable course of current public events. They are then noted and sealed up, to be opened and read from the chair that night twelvemonth—the club holding no meetings in the interim ; and the actual results are often so far wide of all human speculation as to excite both amusement and interest.

North of Bainfield, in what is still called Gilmore Park, are two of the largest and finest manufactories of India-rubber in the world, and the operations conducted therein illustrate most ably the nature and capabilities of caoutchouc. They stand near each other on the western bank of the Union Canal, and belong respectively to the North British Rubber Company, and the Scottish Vulcanite Company.

In 1855 an enterprising American brought to Edinburgh the necessary capital and machinery for an India-rubber manufactory, and acquired possession of a great quadrangular block of fine buildings, known as the Castle Silk Mills, which had long been vacant, the projectors having failed in their expectations. This edifice consists of two large blocks of five floors each, with a number of adjacent buildings.

Here the India-rubber arrives in different forms, according to the fashion of the countries that produce it, some shaped like quaint bottles, and some in balls, of five inches diameter, and it is carefully examined with a view to the detection of foreign substances before it is subjected to the processes of manufacture. After being softened in hot water, the balls are crushed into thin pieces between cylinders, the rubber being sent through and through again and again, until it is thoroughly crushed and assumes the form of a web. If further reduction is necessary, it is sent through a third set of rollers, and to rid it completely of foreign matter, leaves or bark, &c., washing and cleansing machines are employed. So adhesive is its nature, that cleansing would prove abortive in a dry state, and consequently jets of water flow constantly on the rubber and cylinders when the machines referred to are in operation. After being thus cleansed, the webs are hung in the warm atmosphere of the drying-room for several weeks.

From thence they are taken to " the mill," which occupies two entire floors of the main building. The grinding machines, to the operation of which the rubber is subjected, consist of two cylinders, one of which is moderately heated by steam, and the webs formed by the washing-machines are kept revolving round and round the cylinders, until the material becomes quite plastic. At this stage, sulphur, or other chemical substances, are incorporated with it, to determinate its ultimate character, and it is then made up into seven or eight pound rolls, while all further treatment depends upon the purpose to which it is to be applied.

Great is the variety of goods produced here. One of the upper floors is occupied by shoemakers alone. There are boots and shoes of all sizes are made, but more especially the goloshes for wearing over them; another floor is occupied by the makers of coats, leggings, cushions, bags, and so forth. The light-coloured coats for India are the finest articles made here.

The North British Rubber Company have paid much attention to that department which includes the manufacture of tubes, springs, washers, driving-belts, tires for wheels, &c. They made the latter for the wheels of the road steamer invented by Mr. R. W. Thomson, of Edinburgh—huge rings of vulcanised rubber—the largest pieces of the material ever manufactured, as each tire weighed 750 lbs.

The company employ at an average 600 work-people in their establishment ; but in the preparation of the cloth, thread, &c., used in the manufacture, as many more are employed in an indirect way. The health and comfort of all are carefully provided for ; and in no department can it be said that the labour is heavy, while that assigned to the women is peculiarly well suited to them.

washing, kneading, and cleansing the rubber is precisely similar to that used by the North British Company. There are other departments which produce respectively combs, jewellery, and miscellaneous articles. In the comb department the steam cutters are so expert—rising and falling with rapidity, and fed by skilled workmen—that each produces some hundred dozens of combs per day. Besides dressing and fine combs, a variety of others are made, and much taste and ingenuity are ex-

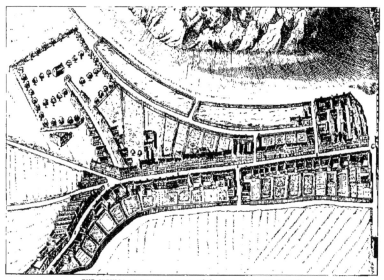

THE SUBURBS OF THE WEST PORT, 1646. (*After Gordon of Rothiemay.*)
c, The West Port ; *i*, The Suburbs.

The adjacent Scottish Vulcanite Company was formed in 1861 by several shareholders of the preceding establishment ; but the two are every way distinct. At the commencement many difficulties had to be overcome. The chief of these was the training of the people to a work so novel, and the waste thereby of material ; but now the original factory has had a fourfold increase, and employs about 500 souls.

The factory consists of a large central block, 230 feet long, and seven detached buildings. The former is four storeys in height. A remarkably beautiful engine, of 120 horse-power, erected in one of the most elegant of engine-rooms, supplies the motive power. The machinery used in breaking,

pended on ladies' back combs, which are often mounted with metal, glass, porcelain, or carving in vulcanite. The company was created chiefly for the manufacture of combs.

In Kay's work we have an interesting and quaint portrait of an aged denizen of Fountainbridge in the Scottish Lowland costume of his day, " Adam Ritchie, born 1683 ; died 1789 ; drawn from the life." This old man, who died at the age of 106 years and two months, had followed the humble occupation of a cow-feeder ; but his life was not an uneventful one ; he had been under arms in 1715, " on the side of the House of Hanover, not from choice (as he said) but necessity, he having been forced into the ranks to supply the place of his master's son." This centenarian died with " all his teeth fresh and complete, and made it his boast that he could crack a nut with the youngest and stoutest person in the parish."

The *Edinburgh Magazine* for 1792 records the death of his brother William, in his 106th year, adding, that " he was twice married and had twenty-two children, alternately sons and daughters."

PORTSBURGH COURT HOUSE.

CHAPTER XXIX.

WEST PORT.

The West Port—Its Boundaries—Malefactors' Heads—The City Gates—Royal Entrances—Mary of Guise—Anne of Denmark—Charles I. -
General Assembly Expelled—A Witch—Jesuit Church—The Lawsons of the Highriggs—Lady Lawson's Wynd—The Tilting Ground—
King's Stables—The Vennel—Tanner's Close—Burke and Hare—Their Native Country—Their " Den," Log's Lodgings—Their Murders
—The Mode of them - Trial and Sentence—Execution and Dismemberment.

The ancient Burgh of Barony, called Portsburgh, comprehended two districts, the Easter and Wester, which are discontiguous ; but it is of the latter, or West Port, we mean to treat just now. This district lies wholly to the westward of Wharton Lane and the ancient Vennel, and may be described as comprehending the main street of the West Port (the link between Fountainbridge and the Grassmarket), the whole of Lauriston from the Corn-market and foot of the Vennel to the Main Point, including Portland Place on the west, and to Bruntsfield Links on the east, including Home and Leven Streets.

In 1160 John Abbot of Kelso granted to Lawrence, the son of Edmund of Edinburgh, a toft situated between the West Port and the Castle, on the left of the entrance into the city. In this little burgh there were of old eight incorporated trades, deriving their rights from John Touris of Inverleith.

Many of the houses here were roofed with thatch in the sixteenth century, and the barrier-gate by which the whole of the district was cut off from the city was built in 1513, as a port in the Flodden wall.

Some gate may, however, have existed previously, as Balfour in his "Annales," tells that the head of Robert Graham, one of the assassins of James I., in 1437, "was sett ouer the West Port of Edinburgh;" and in 1515 the head of Peter Moffat, "ane greit swerer and thief," was spiked in the same place, after the reins of government were assumed by John Duke of Albany. ("Diurnal of Occurrents.")

In the same year it was ordained by the magistrates and council that only three of the city gates were to be open daily, viz., "the West Port, Nether Bow, and the Kirk-of-Field—and na ma. And ilk port to haif twa porteris daylie quhill my Lord Governoure's hame coming. [Albany was then on the Borders, putting down Lord Home's rebellion.] And thir porteris suffer na maner of person on hors nor fute, to enter within this toune without the President or one of the bailies knaw of their cuming and gif thame licence. And the said personis to be convayit to thair lugings be one of the said porteris, swa that gif ony inconvenient happenis, that thair hoste mycht answer for thame as efferis." (Burgh Records.) It was also ordained that a fourth part of the citizens should form a watch every night till the return of Albany, and

HIGHRIGGS HOUSE, 1854. (*After a Drawing by the Author.*)

that every man in the city "be reddy boddin for weir," in his best armour at "the jow of the common bell" for its defence if necessary. Nearly similar orders were issued concerning the gates in 1547, and the warders were to be well armed with jack, steel helmet, and halberd or Jedwood axe, finding surety to be never absent from their posts. (*Ibid.*)

In 1538 Mary of Guise made her first entry by the West Port on St. Margaret's day, "with greit trivmphe," attended by all the nobility (Diurnal of Occ.). There James VI. was received by "King Solomon" on his first state entry in 1579; and by it Anne of Denmark entered in 1590, when she was received by a long Latin oration, while the garrison in the Castle "gave her thence a great volley of shot, with their banners and ancient displays upon the walls" ("Marriage of James VI.," Bann. Club). Here also in 1633, Charles I. at his grand entrance was received by the nymph Edina, and again at the Overbow by the Lady Caledonia, both of whom welcomed him in copious verse from the pen, it is said, of the loyal cavalier and poet, Drummond of Hawthornden.

Fifteen years before this period the Common Council had purchased the elevated ridge of ground lying south of the West Port and Grassmarket, denominated the Highriggs, on a part of which Heriot's Hospital was afterwards built, and the most recent extension of the city wall then took place for the purpose of enclosing it. A portion of this wall still forms the boundary of the hospital grounds, terminating at the head of the Vennel, in the only tower of the ancient fortifications now remaining.

In 1648 the superiority of the Portsburgh was bought by the city from Sir Adam Hepburn for the sum of 27,500 merks Scots; and in 1661 the king's stables were likewise purchased for £1,000 Scots, and the admission of James Baisland to the freedom of Edinburgh.

In 1653 the West Port witnessed a curious scene, when Lieutenant-Colonel Cotterel, by order of Cromwell, expelled the General Assembly from Edinburgh, literally *drumming* the members out at that gate, under a guard of soldiers, after a severe reprimand, and ordering that never more than three of them should meet together.

Marion Purdy, a miserable old creature, "once a milkwife and now a beggar," in the West Port, was apprehended in 1684 on a charge of witchcraft, for "laying frenzies and diseases on her neighbours," says Fountainhall; but the King's Advocate failed to bring her to the stake, and she was permitted to perish of cold and starvation in prison about the Christmas of the same year.

Five years subsequently saw the right hand of Chieslie, the assassin of Lockhart, placed above the gate, probably on a spike; and in the street close by, on the 5th September, 1695, Patrick Falconar, a soldier of Lord Lindsay's regiment, was murdered by George Cumming, a writer in Edinburgh, who deliberately ran him through the body with his sword, for which he was sentenced to be hanged and have his estates forfeited. From the trial, it appears that Cumming was much to blame, and had previously provoked the unoffending soldier by abusive language. (Crim. Trials.)

The tolls collected at the West Port barrier in 1690 amounted to £105 11s. 1½d. sterling. (Council Register.)

In the year of the Union the Quakers would seem to have had a meeting-house somewhere in the West Port, as would appear from a dispute recorded by Fountainhall—"Poor Barbara Hodge" against Bartholomew Gibson, the king's farrier, and William Millar, the hereditary gardener of Holyrood.

On the south side of this ancient burgh, in an opening of somewhat recent formation, leading to Lauriston, the Jesuits have now a very large church, dedicated to "The Sacred Heart," and capable of holding more than 1,000 hearers. It is in the form of a great lecture hall rather than a church, and was erected in 1860, by permission of the Catholic Bishop Gillis, in such a form, that if ever the order was suppressed in Scotland the edifice might be used for educational purposes. Herein is preserved a famous image that once belonged to Holyrood, but was lately discovered by E. Waterton, F.S.A., in a shop at Peterborough.

Almost opposite to it, and at the northern corner of the street, stood for ages the then mansion house of the Lawsons of the Highriggs, which was demolished in 1877, and was undoubtedly one of the oldest, if not the very oldest, houses in the city. When built in the fifteenth century it must have

been quite isolated. It had crowstepped gables, dormers on the roofs, and remarkably small windows.

It was the residence of an old baronial family, long and intimately connected with the city. "Mr. Richard Lawson," says Scott of Scotstarvet, "Justice Clerk, conquest a good estate about Edinburgh, near the Burrow Loch, and the barony of Boighall, which his grandson, Sir William Lawson of Boighall, dilapidated, and went to Holland to the wars." He was Justice Clerk in the time of James IV., from 1491 to 1505.

In 1482 his name first appears in the burgh records as common clerk or recorder, when Sir John Murray of Tulchad was Provost, a post which the former obtained on the 2nd May, 1492. He was a bailie of the city in the year 1501, and Provost again in 1504. Whether he was *the* Richard Lawson who, according to Pitscottie, heard the infernal summons of Pluto at the Market Cross before the army marched to Flodden we know not, but among those who perished on that fatal field with King James was Richard Lawson of the Highriggs; and it was his daughter whose beauty led to the rivalry and fierce combat in Leith Loan between Squire Meldrum of the Binns and Sir Lewis Stirling, in 1516.

In 1555 we find John Lawson of the Highriggs complaining to the magistrates that the water of the burgh loch had overflowed and "drownit ane greit pairt of his land," and that he could get no remedy therefor.

Lady Lawson's Wynd, now almost entirely demolished, takes its name from this family. The City Improvement Trustees determined to form it into a wide thoroughfare, running into Spittal Street. In one of the last remaining houses there died, in his 95th year, in June, 1879, a naval veteran named M'Hardy, supposed to be the last survivor of the actual crew of the *Victory* at Trafalgar. He was on the main-deck when Nelson received his fatal wound.

One of the oldest houses here was the abode of John Lowrie, a substantial citizen, above whose door was the legend—SOLI DEO. H.G. 1565, and a shield charged with a pot of lilies, the emblems of the Virgin Mary. "John Lowrie's initials," says Wilson, "are repeated in ornamental characters on the eastern crowstep, separated by what appears to be designed for a baker's peel, and probably indicating that its owner belonged to the ancient fraternity of Baxters."

The West Port has long been degraded by the character of its inhabitants, usually Irish of the lowest class, and by the association of its name with the dreadful Irish murders in 1828 ; but its repute was very different in the last century. Thus we find in the Edinburgh papers for 1764, advertised as to let there, " the new-built house, beautifully situated on the high ground south of the Portsburgh, commanding an extensive prospect every way, with genteel furniture, perfectly clean, presently possessed by John Macdonald, Esq., of Lairgie," with chaise-house and stabling.

remained intact up till so recently as 1881, while around the large cupola and above the chief seat were panels of coats of arms of the various city crafts, and that also of the Portsburgh—all done in oil, and in perfect condition. This court-room was situated in the West Port. In its last days it was rented from the city chamberlain by the deacons' court of Dr. Chalmers' Territorial Church. Mission meetings and Sunday-schools were held in it, but

OLD HOUSES IN THE WEST PORT, NEAR THE HAUNTS OF BURKE AND HARE, 1869.
(From a Drawing by Mrs. J. Stewart Smith.)

Near the Territorial Church is a door above which are the arms of the Cordiners of the Portsburgh—a cordiner's cutting-knife crowned, within a circle, with the heads of two winged cherubim, and the words of Psalm 133, versified :—

> " Behold how good a thing it is,
> And how becoming well,
> Together such as brethren are,
> In unity to dwell.
> 1696."

One of the most complete of the few rare relics of the City's old municipal institutions was the court-room where the bailies of the ancient Portsburgh discharged their official duties. The bailies' bench, seats, and other court-room fittings

the site upon which it was built was sold by roup for city improvements.

In the middle of the West Port, immediately opposite the Chalmers Territorial Free Church and Schools, and running due north, is a narrow alley, called the Chapel Wynd. Here, at the foot thereof, stood in ancient times a chapel dedicated to the Virgin Mary, some remains of which were visible in the time of Maitland about 1750. Near it is another alley—probably an access to it—named the Lady Wynd. Between this chapel and the Castle Rock there exists, in name chiefly, an ancient appendage of the royal palace in the fortress—the king's stables, "although no hoof of the royal stud has been there for well-nigh three centuries," and the access thereto from the Castle must have been both inconvenient and circuitous.

It has been supposed that the earliest buildings on this site had been erected in the reign of James IV., when the low ground to the westward was the scene of those magnificent tournaments, which drew to that princely monarch's court the most brilliant chivalry in Europe, and where those combats ensued of which the king was seldom an idle spectator.

This tilting ground remained open and unen-

appointed for triell of suche matters." Latterly the place bore the name of Livingstone's Yards.

We have mentioned the acquisition by the city of the king's stables at the Restoration. Lord Fountainhall records, under date 11th March, 1685, a reduction pursued by the Duke of Queensberry, as Governor of the Castle, against Thomas Boreland and other possessors of these stables, as part of the Castle precincts and property. Boreland and others asserted that they held their property in

THE GRASSMARKET, FROM THE WEST PORT, 1825. (*After Ewbank.*)

closed when Maitland wrote, and is described by him as a pleasant green space, 150 yards long, by 50 broad, adjoining the Chapel of Our Lady ; but this "pleasant green" is now intersected by the hideous Kingsbridge ; one portion is occupied by the Royal Horse Bazaar and St. Cuthbert's Free Church, while the rest is made odious by tan-pits, slaughter-houses, and other dwellings of various descriptions.

Calderwood records that in the challenge to mortal combat, in 1571, between Sir William Kirkaldy of Grange, and Alexander Stewart younger of Garlies, they were to fight "upon the ground, the Baresse, be-west the West Port of Edinburgh, the place accustomed and of old

virtue of a feu granted in the reign of James V., but the judges decided that unless the defenders could prove a legal dissolution of the royal possession, they must be held as the king's stables, and be accordingly annexed to the crown of Scotland.

Thomas Boreland's house, one which long figured in every view of the Castle from the foot of Vennel (see Vol. I., p. 80), has recently been pulled down. It was a handsome and substantial edifice of three storeys in height, including the dormer windows, crow-stepped, and having three most picturesque gables in front, with a finely moulded door, on the lintel of which were inscribed a date and legend :—

FEAR . GOD.　　HONOR . THE . KING.
T. B. V. B.　1675.

"From the date 1675, over the main doorway, we may presume," says Wilson, "that this substantial mansion had its full influence in directing the attention of the Duke of Queensberry to this pendicle of the royal patrimony." The initials are supposed to be those of the proprietor, and probably of his brother or wife. The houses that adjoined it were of much greater antiquity. Their last reflection of royal prerogative was that of affording sanctuary for a brief period to debtors, a right of protection pertaining to the precincts of royal residences now entirely fallen into desuetude, though (according to Chambers's "Traditions") they are affirmed to have proved available for this purpose within the memory of some aged persons. Gordon's map shows a dense mass of houses in the quarter where Boreland's mansion was afterwards built, all lying westward of the Lady Wynd.

Human heads would seem to have been deemed an essential decoration for the West Port. Fountainhall, after noting the execution of three Covenanters in 1681, says, that in about eight days two of their heads were stolen from the West Port. "The criminal lords, *to supply that want*, ordained two of their criminals' heads to be struck off, and to be affixed in their place."

Overshadowed in part by the city wall, the steep, narrow, and ancient Vennel terminates the Portsburgh on the south-east.

In Tanner's Close, a narrow and filthy alley on the north side of the West Port, and in its most unsavoury quarter, was the abode, or den, of those terrible Irish Thugs, William Burke and William Hare, whose murders—roughly stated to average between sixteen and thirty, for the number was never precisely known—in 1827, startled all Europe—crimes on which a vivid light was first thrown by the powerful articles in the *Caledonian Mercury* for that year, from the pen of James Browne, LL.D.

Burke was born in the parish of Orrery, in the county of Cork, in 1792; his countryman, William Hare, was a native of Londonderry; both were vagabonds from their birth, and both came to Scotland as labourers; and the former, abandoning his wife and family in Ireland, associated himself with an infamous woman, named McDougal, with whom he became acquainted when working on the Union Canal at Mediston. Hare was also a labourer on the same canal, and used to work at the loading and unloading of boats at Port Hopetoun. Here he become acquainted with a man named Log, whose widow he afterwards married, or with whom he lived, at all events.

After the canal work was ended he became a travelling huckster, with an old horse and cart, selling fish or crockery, or bartering them for old clothes, old iron, &c. He quarrelled with Log, who expelled him from the low Irish lodging-house he occupied in Tanner's Close; but when Log was dead and buried, he returned to the close, where he assumed all the rights of a landlord over the seven bed-rooms of the so-called lodging-house, as well as the privileges of a husband, though Mrs. Log was never called by his name.

Always addicted to intoxication, the miserable drawings of twopence or threepence nightly from the wretched and obscure Irish tramps who sought quarters at Log's lodgings made him more drunken and dissolute than ever. Though no pugilist, he was always ready to fight, and Mrs. Log, also a drunkard, was ready to encounter him at any time; thus rows, quarrels, oaths, and noise of all kinds, perpetually prevailed in Tanner's Close; and such was the life led by this congenial couple when Burke and McDougal, two congenial spirits, came to live with them, the former calling himself a shoemaker.

The place which went by the name of Log's lodging-house was situated near the foot of Tanner's Close. The entry from the West Port Street to the alley begins with a descent of a few steps, and is dark from the superincumbent mass of building. On proceeding downwards you came—for the house, as an accursed place, has been rased to the ground—to a small self-contained dwelling of one flat, containing three apartments, and ticketed, "Beds to Let," an invitation to the passing vagrants, so many of whom were destined never to leave those fatal beds alive. "The outer apartment was large, occupied all round by those structures called beds, composed of knocked-up fir stumps and covered with a few grey sheets and brown blankets, among which the squalid wanderer sought rest, and the profligate snored out his debauch under the weight of nightmare."

There was a small closet, the window of which overlooked a dead wall and pig-stye, into which were introduced all those who were doomed to death. The character of the house, the incessant rows and "shindies," real or pretended, always proceeding there, caused no surprise or alarm when actual cries of murder and suffering rang out upon the night, while the extraordinary mode in which the assassins extinguished life enabled them to pursue their terrible traffic for the dissecting-rooms without exciting suspicion.

Neither Burke nor Hare was a resurrectionist, but their cupidity was first excited, and their diabolical trade suggested, by the sum paid to them by a distinguished anatomist for the body of a poor old pensioner, named Donald, who died in their hands, a short time before his pension became due. Hare, who expected to be reimbursed for £4 owing to him by Donald, was exasperated by the loss, and filling the coffin with bark from the adjacent tannery, it was buried, while the corpse in a sack was carried alternately by Burke and Hare, through College Street, to Surgeon Square, and sold for seven pounds ten shillings, to Dr. Knox and his assistants.

The money so easily won seemed to exert a magnetic influence over the terrible quaternion in Tanner's Close. The women foresaw that other lodgers *might* die, and hoped to flaunt in finery before the poor denizens of the Portsburgh; and the steady and studied career of assassination began, and was continued, by Burke's own confession, from Christmas, 1827, to the end of October, 1828. —(*Weekly Journal*, Jan. 6th, 1829.)

The *modus operandi* was very simple: the unknown and obscure wayfarer was lured into the "lodging-house," weary and hungry, perhaps, then generally well dosed with coarse raw whisky, preparatory to strangulation, glass after glass being readily and cordially filled in contemplation of the value of the future corpse, as in the case of one unfortunate creature named Mary Haldane. Then, "all is ready—the drooping head—the closing eye—the languid helpless body. The women get the hint. They knew the unseemliness of being spectators—nay, they were delicate! A repetition of a former scene, only with even less resistance. Hare holds again the lips, and Burke presses his twelve stone weight on the chest. Scarcely a sigh; but on a trial if dead a long gurgling indraught. More is not required—and all is still in that dark room, with the window looking out on the dead wall." By twelve the same night the body of Mary Haldane was in the hands of "the skilled anatomist," who made no inquiries; and as the supply from Log's lodgings increased, the value for each subject seemed to increase also, as the partners began to get from £12 to £14 for each—nearly double what they had received for the body of the poor Highland pensioner.

The attempt to rehearse in detail all the crimes of which these people were guilty, would only weary and revolt the reader. Suffice it to say, that the discovery of the dead body of a woman, quite nude, and with her face covered with blood, among some straw in an occupied house of Burke and another Irishman named Broggan, caused the arrest of the four suspects. Hare turned King's evidence, and

on the 24th December, 1828, amid such excitement as Edinburgh had not witnessed for ages, William Burke and Helen McDougal were arraigned at the bar of the Justiciary Court, charged with a succession of murders! Among these were the murder of a very handsome girl named Mary Paterson in the house of Burke's brother, Constantine Burke, a scavenger residing in Gibb's Close, Canongate; that of a well-known idiot, named James Wilson ("Daft Jamie"), at the house in Tanner's Close; of Mary McGonegal, or Docherty, at the same place. These were selected for proof as sufficient in the indictment; but the real list was never known or exhausted. Among the cases was supposed to be that of a little Italian boy named Ludovico, who went about the city with white mice. Two little white mice were seen for long after haunting the dark recesses of Tanner's Close, and in Hare's house a cage with the mice's turning-wheel was actually found. Of this murder Burke was supposed to be guiltless, and that it had been a piece of private business done by Hare on his own account. The libel contained a list of a great number of articles of dress, &c., worn or used by the various victims, and among other things were Daft Jamie's brass snuff-box and spoon, objects which excited much interest, as Jamie was a favourite with the citizens, and his body must have been recognised by Dr. Knox the instant he saw it on the dissecting table. The presiding judge of the court was the Lord Justice-Clerk Boyle; the others were the Lords Pitmilly, Meadowbank, and M'Kenzie; the prosecutor was Sir William Rae, Lord Advocate. The counsel for Burke was the Dean of Faculty; that for M'Dougal the celebrated Henry Cockburn. The witnesses were fifty-five in number—the two principal being Hare and the woman Log, received as evidence in the characters of *socii criminis*.

When all had been examined, and the cases were brought fatally home to Burke, while his paramour escaped with a verdict of "not proven," a loud whisper ran through the court of "Where are the doctors?" as it was known the names of Knox and others were placed on the back of the indictment as witnesses; yet they could scarcely have appeared but at the risk of their lives, so high was the tide of popular indignation against them.

Burke was sentenced to death in the usual form, the Lord Justice-Clerk expressing regret that his body could not be gibbeted in chains, but was to be publicly dissected, adding, "and I trust that if it is ever customary to preserve skeletons yours will be preserved, in order that posterity may keep in remembrance your atrocious crimes." So the body of Burke was sent appropriately where he had sent so many others; and his skeleton now hangs in the Museum of the University. The Parliament Square rang with reiterated cheers as if the city held jubilee, when sentence was pronounced; but the people were greatly dissatisfied with the verdict of "not proven" in the case of M'Dougal; and had Hare not effected his escape secretly by the mail home to Ireland, the people would infallibly have torn him limb from limb. In prison, and with death before him, Burke's thoughts were ever recurring to earth. Once he was observed (says Alexander Leighton) to be silent and medi-

viously he had been unaccustomed to. The fact is," continues the editor of the *Weekly Journal,* "that the wretch, when awake, by means of ardent spirits steeped his senses in forgetfulness. . . . At night he had short fits of sleep, during which he raved, but his expressions were inarticulate, and he ground his teeth in the most fearful manner."

In the morning he was removed to the Calton gaol, and secured by a chain to the massive iron gaud. On the 27th January he was unchained and conveyed to the lock-up in Liberton's Wynd, at the heap of which the gallows was erected. He was

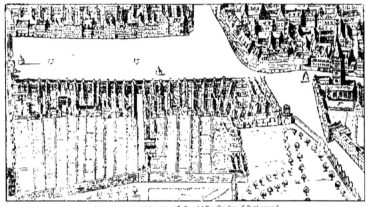

THE GRASSMARKET IN 1646. *(After Gordon of Rothiemay.)*
15, The Horse Market Street, *r*, St. Mary Magdalen's Chapel.

tative, and a pious attendant took it as a sign of contrition; but Burke said suddenly—"I think I am entitled to and ought to get that five pounds from Dr. Knox, which is still unpaid, on the body of the woman Docherty."

"Why," replied the astonished pietist, "Dr. Knox lost by the transaction, as the body was taken from him."

"That was not my business," said Burke; "I delivered the subject, and he ought to have kept it."

He confessed in the lock-up house that he "had participated in many more murders than those he had been indicted for; and said that after his mind was composed he would make disclosures, which would implicate several others, besides Hare and his wife, in the same crimes for which he was doomed to die. He was asked how did he feel when pursuing his horrible avocation? He replied, that in his waking moments he had no feeling, but that when he slept he had frightful dreams, which pre-

attended by two Catholic priests and two Presbyterian ministers, for his ideas of religion were somewhat vague and cloudy. When his heavy fetters were removed and they fell with a clank on the floor, "So may all earthly chains fall from me!" he exclaimed, but went to die evidently with the hopeless secret feeling "that he was too deeply sunk in crime even to think of the infinite mercy of Heaven." Yet was he eager to be dead, and ascended the scaffold with his eyes half closed, as if anxious to be beyond the roar of the vast assemblage that thronged the great thoroughfare far as the eye could reach, and filled every window, roof, and foot of vantage ground. The deep hoarse roar of voices rose into a terrible and prolonged yell, on which he threw around him a fierce glance of desperate defiance and hatred; and again rose the prolonged yell of disgust and half-glutted vengeance when, after hanging the usual time, the body was conveyed to the College.

The sight of the execution instead of allaying the passions of the justly-excited people, inflamed them with a desire to drag his body out and tear it to pieces; but a grand public exhibition was arranged for the morrow, and the white, naked corpse, so loathed, was laid on the black narrow escape from an infuriated mob, according to the *Weekly Journal.* "In the den of murder occupied by Burke," continues the paper, "several objects strengthen the general persuasion that many other wretches had fallen a sacrifice under the same roof. The bloody straw in the corner, a

BALLANTYNE'S CLOSE, GRASSMARKET, 1850. (*From a Drawing by W. Channing.*)

marble table of the theatre, and displayed to thousands who streamed through the entire day.

Burke was cut up and put in strong pickle and in small barrels for the dissecting-table, and part of his skin was tanned.

The woman M'Dougal after the execution had the daring effrontery to present herself in Tanner's Close again; but the people of the Portsburgh rose, and she only found in the watch-house a heap of bloody clothes on the floor, and a pile of old boots and shoes, chiefly those of females, amounting to several dozens, for which the pretended trade of a shoemaker never can account, furnish ample food for suspicion! The idea suggests itself that the clothes and shoes belonged to the unfortunate girls whom this monster decoyed to his house, intoxicated, and murdered, as he did the poor old wanderer. . . . The two houses which were inhabited by this gang were well chosen for the purpose to which they were put. Burke's dwelling, in which he has only resided since June last, is at the end of a long passage, and separated from every other house except one. After going through the close from the street there is a descent by a stair to the passage, at the end of which is to be found this habitation of wickedness. It consists of one apartment, an oblong square, at the end of which is a miserable bed, under which may still be seen some straw in which his murdered victims were con-

cealed. The house of Hare is in a more retired situation. The passage to it is by a dark and dirty close, in which there are no inhabitants, except in the flat above. Both houses are on the ground floor."

Tanner's Close still exists, but the abodes of those two wretches—the most cold-blooded criminals in history—are now numbered, as we have stated, among the things that were.

At the head of Liberton's Wynd three reversed stones indicate where, on this and on other occasions, the last sentence of the law was carried out.

CHAPTER XXX.

THE GRASSMARKET.

The Grassmarket—The Mait of 1477—Margaret Tudor—Noted Executions—"Half Hangit Maggie Dickson"—Italian Mountebanks—Grey Friary Founded by James I.—Henry VI. of England a Fugitive—The Grey Friars Port—New Corn Exchange—The White Horse Inn—Carriers—The Castle Wynd—First Gaelic Chapel there—Currie's Close—The Cockpit—Story of Watt and Downie, "The Friends of the People "—Their Trial and Sentence—Execution of Watt.

THE Grassmarket occupies that part of the southern valley which lies between the eastern portion of the Highriggs and the ridge of the Castle Hill and Street. It is a spacious and stately rectangle, 230 yards in length, communicating at its south-east corner with the ancient Candlemaker Row and southern portion of the old town, and at its north-east angle with the acclivitous, winding, narrow, and more ancient alley, the West Bow, or that fragment of it which now runs into Victoria Street, and the steps near the (now demolished) Land of Weir the wizard.

The Grassmarket is darkly overhung on the north by the precipitous side of the Castle Esplanade, the new west approach, and the towering masses of Johnstone Terrace and the General Assembly Hall, but on the south is the gentler slope, crowned by the turrets of Heriot's Hospital and the heavy mass of the Greyfriars churches.

The western end of this rectangle was long closed up and encroached upon by the Corn Market, an unsightly arcaded edifice, 80 feet long by 45 broad, with a central belfry and clock, now swept away, and its eastern end, where the old Corn Market is shown in Edgar's map, is deeply associated with much that is sad, terrible, and deplorable in Scottish history, as the scene of the fervid testimony and dying supplications of many a martyr to "the broken covenant," in defence of that Church, every stone of which may be said to have been cemented by the blood of the people.

Now the Grassmarket is the chief rendezvous of carriers and farmers, and persons of various classes connected with the county horse and cattle markets, and presents a remarkably airy, busy, and imposing appearance, with its infinite variety of architecture, crow-stepped gables, great chimneys, turnpike stairs, old signboards, and projections of many kinds.

The assignment of this locality as the site of a weekly market dates from the year 1477, when King James III. by his charter for the holding of markets, ordained that wood and timber be sold "fra Dalrimpill yarde to the Grey Friars and westerwart; alswa all old graith and geir to be vsit and sold in the Friday market before the Greyfriars lyke as is usit in uthir cuntries."

In 1503, on the marriage of Margaret of England to James IV., the royal party were met at the western entrance to the city by the whole of the Greyfriars—whose monastery was on the south side of the Grassmarket—bearing in procession their most valued relics, which were presented to the royal pair to kiss; and thereafter they were stayed at an embattled barrier, erected for the occasion, at the windows of which appeared angels singing songs of welcome to the English bride, while one presented her with the keys of Edinburgh.

In 1543 we first hear of this part of the city having been causewayed, or paved, when the Provost and Bailies employed Moreis Crawfurd to mend "the calsay," at 26s. 8d. per rood from the Upper Bow to the West Port.

In 1560 the magistrates removed the Corn

Market, from the corner of Marlin's Wynd (where Blair Street is now) to the east end of the Grassmarket, where it continued to be held until within the last few years.

It was not until about a century later that this great market place began to acquire an interest of a gloomy and peculiar character, as the scene of the public execution of many victims of religious intolerance, who died heroically here, and as the spot where many criminals met their doom.

Prior to the adoption of this place for public executions, the Castle Hill and Market Cross had been the spots chosen; and a sword, as in France and elsewhere on the Continent, was used, before the introduction of the Maiden, for beheading. Thus we find that in 1564, the magistrates, because the old beheading sword had become worn out, received from William Macartnay "his tua-handit sword, to be usit for ane heiding sword," and gave him the sum of five pounds therefor.

Among some of the most noted executions in the Grassmarket were those of the fanatic Mitchel in 1676, for attempting to shoot Archbishop Sharp in 1668; of Sergeant John Nisbett, of Hardhill, in 1685, who had received seventeen wounds at the battle of Pentland, and fought at Drumclog, according to the Wodrow Biographies; of Isabel Alison and Marion Harvey—the latter only twenty years of age—two young women, for merely having heard Donald Cargill preach. The human shambles in this place of wailing witnessed executions of this kind almost daily till the 17th of February, 1688, when James Renwick, the celebrated field preacher, and the last martyr of the Covenant, was found guilty, on his own confession, of disowning an uncovenanted king, and executed in the twenty-sixth year of his age. Most of the hundred and odd pious persons who suffered for the same cause in Edinburgh breathed their last prayers on this spot. Hence arose the Duke of Rothes' remark, when a covenanting prisoner proved obdurate, "Then let him glorify God in the Grassmarket"—the death of that class of victims always being accompanied by much psalm-singing on the scaffold. In the time of Charles II., Alexander Cockburn, the city hangman, having murdered a King's Bluegown, died here the death he had so often meted out to others.

In 1724 the same place was the scene of the partial execution of a woman, long remembered in Edinburgh, as "Half-hangit Maggie Dickson." She was a native of Inveresk, and was tried under the Act of 1690 for concealment of pregnancy, in the case of a dead child; and the defence that she was a married woman, though living apart from her husband, who was working in the keels at New-

castle, proved of no avail, and a broadside of the day details her execution with horrible minuteness: how the hangman did his usual office of dragging down her legs, and how the body, after hanging the allotted time, was put into a coffin, the *cooms* of which were nailed firmly to the gibbet-foot.

After a scuffle with some surgeon-apprentices who wished to possess themselves of the body, her friends conveyed it away by the Society Port, but the jolting of the cart in which the coffin lay had stirred vitality and set the blood in motion. Thus she was found to be alive when passing Peffermiln, and was completely restored at Musselburgh, where flocks of people came daily to see her. She had several children after this event, and lived long as the keeper of an ale-house and as a crier of salt in the streets of Edinburgh. ("Dom. Ann." III., Stat. Acct., Vol. XVI).

In the account of the Porteous Mob (Vol I., pp. 128–131), we have referred to the executions of Wilson and of Porteous, in 1736, in this place—the street "crowded with rioters, crimson with torchlight, spectators filling every window of the tall houses—the Castle standing high above the tumult amidst the blue midnight and the stars." It continued to be the scene of such events till 1784; and in a central situation at the east end of the market there remained until 1823 a massive block of sandstone, having in its centre a quadrangular hole, which served as the socket of the gallows-tree; but instead of the stone there is now only a St. Andrew's Cross in the causeway to indicate the exact spot.

The last person who suffered in the Grassmarket was James Andrews, hanged there on the 4th of February, 1784, for a robbery committed in Hope Park; and the first person executed at the west end of the old city gaol, was Alexander Stewart, a youth of only fifteen, who had committed many depredations, and at last had been convicted of breaking into the house of Captain Hugh Dalrymple, of Fordell in the Potterrow, and Neidpath Castle, the seat of the Duke of Queensberry, from which he carried off many articles of value. It was expressly mentioned by the judge in his sentence, that he was to be hanged in the Grassmarket, "or any other place the magistrates might appoint," thus indicating that a change was in contemplation; and accordingly, the west end of the old Tolbooth was fitted up for his execution, which took place on the 20th of April, 1785.

In 1733 the Grassmarket was the scene of some remarkable feats, performed by a couple of Italian mountebanks, a father and his son. A rope being fixed between the half-moon battery of the Castle, and a place on the south side of the market, 200 feet below, the father slid down it in half a minute. The son performed the same feat, blowing a trumpet all the way, to the astonishment of a vast crowd of spectators.

Three days afterwards there was a repetition of the performance, "at the desire of several people of quality," when after sliding down, the father made his way up to the battery again, firing a pistol,

striking." These houses were not so old, however, as the order of the Templars, but having been built upon their land, and being also the heritage of the Hospitallers, and forming, as such, a portion of the barony of Drem, had affixed to them the iron cross in remembrance of certain legal titles and privileges which are to this day productive of solid benefits.

With the Temple Close, which was entered by a

THE TEMPLE LANDS, GRASSMARKET.   (*From a Drawing by George W. Simson.*)

beating a drum, and proclaiming that while up there he could defy the whole Court of Session.

The whole of the south side of the Grassmarket had been pulled down and re-built at intervals before 1879.

Among the oldest edifices that once stood here were unquestionably the Temple tenements and the Greyfriars Monastery. In describing the execution of Porteous, which took place in front of the former, Scott says :—" The uncommon height and antique appearance of these houses, some of which were formerly the property of the Knights Templar and the Knights of St. John, and still exhibit on their fronts and gables the iron cross of their orders, gave additional effect to a scene in itself so

narrow arch beneath them, they have been entirely swept away since 1870.

Immediately to the westward of them was one of the most modern houses in this quarter, through which entered Hunter's Close, above the arch of which was inscribed ANNO DOM. MDCLXXI., and it was from the dyer's pole in front of this tenement that Porteous was hanged in 1736. "The long range of buildings that extend beyond this," says Wilson, writing in 1847, "presents as singular and varied a group of antique tenements as either artist or antiquary could desire. Finials of curious and grotesque shapes surmount the crowstepped gables, and every variety of form and elevation diversifies the skyline of their roofs and chimneys, while behind the noble pile of Heriot's Hospital towers above them, as a counterpart to the old Castle that rises majestically over the north side of the same area. Many antique features are discernible here. Several of the older houses are built with bartizaned roofs and ornamental copings, designed to afford their inmates an uninterrupted view of the magnificent pageants that were wont of old to defile through the wide area below, or of the gloomy tragedies that were so frequently enacted here between the Restoration and the Revolution."

Towards the south-east end of the market place stood the ancient monastery of Grey Friars, opposite where the Bow Foot Well, erected in 1681, now stands. James I., a monarch, who by many salutary laws and the encouragement of learning, endeavoured to civilise the country, long barbarised by wars with England, established this monastery. In obedience to a requisition made by him to the Vicar-General of the Order at Cologne, a body of Franciscans came hither under Cornelius of Zurich, a scholar of great reputation. The house prepared for their reception proved so magnificent for the times, says Arnot, that in the spirit of humility and self-denial they declined to live in it, and could only be prevailed upon to do so at the earnest request of the Archbishop of St. Andrews; consequently a considerable time must have elapsed ere they were finally established in the Grassmarket. There they taught divinity and philosophy till the Reformation, when their spacious and beautiful gardens, that extended up the slope towards the town wall, were bestowed on the citizens as a cemetery by Queen Mary.

That the monastery was a sumptuous edifice according to the times, is proved by its being assigned for the temporary abode of the Princess Mary of Gueldres, who after her arrival at Leith in June, 1449, rode thither on a pillion behind the Count de Vere, and was visited by her future husband, James II., on the following day.

In 1461, after the battle of Towton, its roof afforded shelter to the luckless Henry VI. of England when he fled to Scotland, together with his heroic Queen Margaret and their son Prince Edward. The fugitives were so hospitably entertained by the court and citizens, that in requital

thereof, Henry granted to them a charter empowering the latter to trade to any part of England, subject to no other duties than those payable by the most highly favoured natives of that country, in acknowledgment, as he states, of the humane and honourable treatment he met with from the

EAST END OF THE GRASSMARKET, SHOWING THE WEST BOW, THE GALLOWS, AND OLD CORN MARKET.
(Fac-simile of an Etching by Jame Skene of Rubislaw.)

Provost and burgesses of Edinburgh. As the house of Lancaster never regained the English throne, the charter survives only as an acknowledgment of Henry's gratitude. How long the latter resided in the Grassmarket does not precisely appear. Balfour states that in 1465, Henry VI., "having lurked long under the Scotts King's wing as a privat man, resolves in a disgyssed habit to enter England." His future fate belongs to English history, but his flight from Scotland evidently was the result of a treaty of truce, in Feb., 1464.

Some English writers have denied that Henry was ever in Edinburgh at any time; and that the Queen alone came, while he remained at Kirkcudbright. But Sir Walter Scott, in a note to "Marmion," records, that he had seen in possession of Lord Napier, "a grant by Henry of forty merks to his lordship's ancestor, John Napier (of Merchiston), subscribed by the King himself *at Edinburgh*, the 28th August, in the thirty-ninth year of his reign, which exactly corresponds with the year of God, 1461."

Abercrombie, in his "Martial Achievements," after detailing some negociations between the Scottish ministry of James III. (then a minor) and Henry VI., says, that after they were complete, "the indefatigable Queen of England left the King, her husband, at his lodgings in the Greyfriars of Edinburgh, where his own inclinations to devotion and solitude made him choose to reside, and went with her son into France, not doubting but that by the mediation of the King of Sicily, her father, she should be able to purchase both men and money in that kingdom."

That a church would naturally form a most necessary appendage to such a foundation as this monastery can scarcely be doubted, and Wilson says that he is inclined to infer the existence of one, and of a churchyard, long before Queen Mary's grant of the gardens to the city, and of this three proofs can be given at least.

A portion of the treaty of peace between James III. and Edward IV. included a proposal of the latter that his youngest daughter, the Princess Cecilia, then in her fourth year, should be betrothed to the Crown Prince of Scotland, then an infant of two years old, and that her dowry of 20,000 merks should be paid by annual instalments commencing from the date of the contract. On this basis a peace was concluded, the ceremony of its ratification being performed, along with the betrothal, "in the church of the Grey Friars, at Edinburgh, where the Earl of Lindsay and Lord Scrope appeared as the representatives of their respective sovereigns."

The "Diurnal of Occurrents" records that on the 7th July, 1571, the armed craftsmen made their musters "in the Gray Friere Kirk Yaird," and, though the date of the modern church, to which we shall refer, is 1613, Birrel, in his diary, under date 26th April, 1598, refers to works in progress by "the Societie at the Gray Friar Kirke."

In 1559, when the storm of the Reformation broke forth, the Earl of Argyle entered Edinburgh with his followers, and "the work of purification" began with a vengeance. The Trinity College Church, St. Giles's, St. Mary-in-the-Field, the monasteries of the Black and Grey Friars, were pillaged of everything they contained. Of the two latter establishments the bare walls alone were left standing. In 1560 the stones of these two edifices were ordered to be used "for the bigging of dykes;" and other works connected with the Good Town; and in 1562 we are told that a good crop of corn was sown in the Grey Friars' Yard by "Rowye Gairdner, fleschour," so that it could not have been a place for interment at that time.

The Greyfriars' Port was a gate which led to an unenclosed common, skirting the north side of the Burgh Muir, and which was only included in the precincts of the city by the last extension of the walls in 1618, when the land, ten acres in extent, was purchased by the city from Towers of Inverleith.

In 1530 a woman named Katharine Heriot, accused of theft and bringing contagious sickness from Leith into the city, was ordered to be drowned in the Quarry Holes at the Greyfriars' Port. In the same year, "Janet Gowane, accused of haiffand the pestilens apone hir," was branded on both cheeks at the same place, and expelled the city.

This gate was afterwards called the Society and also the Bristo Port.

Among the edifices removed in the Grassmarket was a very quaint one, immediately westward of Heriot's Bridge, which exhibited a very perfect specimen of a remarkably antique style of window, with folding shutters and transom of oak entire below, and glass in the upper part set in ornamental patterns of lead.

Near this is the New Corn Exchange, designed by David Cousin, and erected in 1849 at the cost of £20,000, measuring 160 feet long by 120 broad; it is in the Italian style, with a handsome front of three storeys, and a campanile or belfry at the north end. It is fitted up with desks and stalls for the purpose of mercantile transactions, and has been, from its great size and space internally, the scene of many public festivals, the chief of which were perhaps the great Crimean banquet, given there on the 31st of October, 1856, to the soldiers of the 34th Foot, 5th Dragoon Guards, and Royal Artillery; and that other given after the close of the Indian Mutiny to the soldiers of the Ross-shire Buffs, which elicited a very striking display of high national enthusiasm.

On the north side of the Market Place there yet stands the old White Hart Inn, an edifice of considerable antiquity. It was a place of entertainment as far back perhaps as the days when the Highland drovers came to market armed with sword and target, and no gentleman took the road without pistols in his holsters, and was the chief place for carriers putting up in the days when all the country traffic was conducted by their carts or waggons. In 1788 forty-six carriers arrived weekly in the Grassmarket, and this number increased to ninety-six in 1810. In those days the Lanark coach started from George Cuddie's stables there, every Friday and Tuesday at 7 a.m.; the Linlithgow and Falkirk flies at 4 every afternoon, "Sundays excepted;" and the Peebles coach from "Francis M'Kay's, vintner, White Hart Inn," thrice weekly, at 9 in the morning.

Some bloodshed occurred in the Castle Wynd in 1577. When Morton's administration became so odious as Regent that it was resolved to deprive him of his power, his natural son, George Douglas of Parkhead, held the Castle of which he was governor, and the magistrates resolved to cut off all supplies from him. At 5 o'clock on the 17th March their guards discovered two carriages of provisions for the Castle, which were seized at the foot of the Wynd. This being seen by Parkhead's garrison, a sally was made, and a combat ensued, in which three citizens were killed and six wounded, but only one soldier was slain, while sixteen others pushed the carriages up the steep slope. "The townsmen, greatly incensed by the injury," says Moyse, "that same night cast trenches beside Peter Edgar's house for enclosing of the Castle."

Latterly the closes on the north side of the Market terminated on the rough uncultured slope of the Castle Hill; but in the time of Gordon of Rothiemay a belt of pretty gardens had been there from the west flank of the city wall to the Castle Wynd, where a massive fragment of the wall of 1450 remained till the formation of Johnstone Terrace. On the west side of the Castle Wynd is an old house, having a door only three feet three inches wide, inscribed:

BLESSIT . BE . GOD . FOR . AL . HIS . GIFTIS.
16.   1637.   10.

The double date probably indicated a renewal of the edifice.

The first Gaelic chapel in Edinburgh stood in the steep sloping alley named the Castle Wynd. Such an edifice had long been required in the Edinburgh of those days, when such a vast number of Highlanders resorted thither as chairmen, porters, water-carriers, city guardsmen, soldiers of the Castle Company, servants and day-labourers, and when Irish immigration was completely unknown. These people in their ignorance of Lowland Scottish were long deprived of the benefit of religious instruction, which was a source of regret to themselves and of evil to society.

Hence proposals were made by Mr. William Dickson, a dyer of the city, for building a chapel wherein the poor Highlanders might receive religious instruction in their own language; the contributions of the benevolent flowed rapidly in; the edifice was begun in 1767 and opened in 1769, upon a piece of ground bought by the philanthropic William Dickson, who disposed of it to the Society for the Propagation of Christian Knowledge. The church cost £700, of which £100 was given by the Writers to the Signet.

It was soon after enlarged to hold about 1,100 hearers. The minister was elected by the subscribers. His salary was then only £100 per annum, and he was, of course, in communion with the Church of Scotland, when such things as the repentance stool and public censure did not become things of the past until 1780. "Since the chapel was erected," says Kincaid, "the Highlanders have been punctual in their attendance on divine worship, and have discovered the greatest sincerity in their devotions. Chiefly owing to the bad crops for some years past in the Highlands, the last peace, and the great improvements carrying on in this city, the number of Highlanders has of late increased so much that the chapel in its present situation cannot contain them. Last Martinmas above 300 applied for seats who could not be accommodated, and who cannot be edified in the English language."

The first pastor here was the Rev. Joseph Robertson MacGregor, a native of Perthshire, who was a licentiate of the Church of England before he joined that of Scotland. "The last levies of the Highland regiments," says Kincaid, "were much indebted to this house, for about a third of its number have, this last and preceding wars, risqued (sic) their lives for their king and country; and no other church in Britain, without the aid or countenance of Government, contains so many disbanded soldiers."

Mr. MacGregor was known by his mother's name of Robertson, assumed in consequence of the proscription of his clan and name; but, on the repeal of the infamous statute against it, in 1787, on the day it expired he attired himself in a full suit of the MacGregor tartan, and walked conspicuously about the city.

The Celtic congregation continued to meet in the Castle Wynd till 1815, when its number had so much increased that a new church was built for them in another quarter of the city.

The Plainstanes Close, with Jamieson's, Beattie's,

Currie's, and Dewar's Closes on the north side of the market, were all doomed to destruction by the late City Improvement Act.

In the vicinity of the first-named alley, whose distinctive title implied its former respectability as a paved close, was a tenement, dated 1634, with a fine antique window of oak and ornamental leaden tracery, and an adjacent turnpike stair has the same date, with the common legend, "Blissit . be .

of December, 1793, so many members of the memorable British Convention were seized and made prisoners, with several English delegates, when holding a political meeting for revolutionary purposes and correspondence with the French Republic.

In these transactions and meetings, Robert Watt, a wine merchant, and David Downie, became so deeply involved that they were condemned to

THE CORN EXCHANGE, GRASSMARKET.

God . for . all . his . Giftis," and the initials, "L. B. G. K."

In Currie's Close was an ancient door, only two feet nine inches broad, with the half-defaced legend :

GOD . GIVES THE . . . . RES . . . .

and the initials, "G. B." and "B. F." and a shield charged with a chevron and something like a boar's head in base.

In 1763 such a diversion as cockfighting was utterly unknown in Edinburgh, but in twenty years after, regular matches or *mains*, as they were technically termed, were held, and a regular cockpit for this school of gambling and cruelty was built in the Grassmarket, and there it was that, on the 12th

death for high treason. After the dispersion of the British Convention in the Grassmarket, they became active members of a "Committee of Union," to collect the sense of the nation, and of another body styled "the Committee of Ways and Means," of which Downie, who was a goldsmith in the Parliament Close, and an office-bearer of his corporation, was appointed treasurer. In unison with the London Convention, the "Friends of the People" in Edinburgh had lost all hope of redress for their alleged political wrongs by constitutional means, and designs of a dangerous nature were considered—wild schemes, of which Watt was the active promoter.

Their first attempt was to suborn the Hopetoun Fencibles, then at Dalkeith, and under orders for

THE GRASSMARKET.

1. Head of Cowgate, from Grassmarket, 1825 (*after Ewbank*) ; 2. Grassmarket, from Cowgate ; 3. The Vennel ; 4. South Side of Grassmarket, 1820 (*after Storer*) ; 5. Grassmarket, looking west (*after Storer and Shepherd*).

England, but they failed to excite mutiny; yet a plan was formed by which it was expected that the Castle and city would both fall into the hands of the Friends of the People, who were secretly arming. The design was this :—

"A fire was to be raised near the excise office, which would require the attendance of the soldiers, who were to be met on their way by a body of the Friends of the People, another party of whom were

committee of "Sense and Money" was formed to procure them. Two smiths, named Robert Orrock and William Brown, who had enrolled, received orders to make 4,000 pikes, some of which were actually completed, delivered to Watt, and paid for by Downie in his capacity as treasurer.

Meanwhile the trials of Skirving, Margarot, and Gerald, had taken place, for complicity to a certain extent in the same movements; but it was not

THE WHITE HART INN, GRASSMARKET.

to issue from the West Bow, confine the soldiers between two forces, and cut off all retreat. The Castle was next to be attempted, the judges and magistrates were to be seized, and all the public banks to be secured. A proclamation was then to be issued, ordering all farmers to bring in their grain to the market as usual, and enjoining all country gentlemen unfriendly to the cause to keep within their houses, or three miles of them, under penalty of death. Then an address was to be sent to his Majesty, commanding him to put an end to the war, to change his ministers, or take the consequences!" Similar events were to take place in Dublin and London on the same night.

Before this startling scheme could be effected, arms of all descriptions were necessary, and a third

until about the 15th of May, 1794, that Watt and Downie were apprehended. On that day it chanced that two sheriff officers when searching the house of the former for the secreted goods of a bankrupt, found some pikes, which they conveyed to the sheriff's chambers. A warrant was issued to search the whole premises, and in the cellars a form of types from which the address to the troops had been printed, and a great quantity of pikes, were discovered, while in the house, thirty-three in various stages of completion were found. Hence, early on the morning of June 2nd, Watt, Downie, and Orrock, were conveyed from the old Tolbooth to the Castle, as State prisoners, and lodged in the strong apartment above the portcullis.

True bills of indictment being found against

Watt and Downie, they were brought to trial respectively in August and September, and the facts were fully proved against them. A letter from Downie, treasurer of the Committee of Ways and Means, to Walter Millar, Perth, acknowledging the receipt of £15, on which he gave a coloured account of the recent riots in the theatre on the performance of "Charles I." was produced and identified; and Robert Orrock stated that Downie accompanied Watt to his place at the Water of Leith, where the order was given for the pikes.

William Brown said that he had made fifteen of these weapons, by order of Watt, to whom he delivered them, receiving 22s. 6d. for the fifteen. Other evidence at great length was led, a verdict of guilty was returned, and sentence of death was passed upon the prisoners—to have their bowels torn out, and to be hanged, drawn, and quartered. The punishment of Downie was commuted to transportation; and on the royal clemency being announced to him he burst into tears, and kneeling on the floor of the vault above the portcullis he exclaimed, in ecstasy, "Oh, glory be to God, and thanks to the king! Thanks to him for his goodness! I will pray for him as long as I live!" He had a wife and children, and for years had enjoyed the reputation of being a sober and respectable mechanic.

Previous to his execution Watt made a full confession of the aims and objects contemplated by the committees and their ramifications throughout Britain. He was in his thirty-sixth year, and was the natural son of a gentleman of fortune in Angus. He was executed on the 15th October, 1794. The magistrates, Principal Baird, the city guard, and town officers, with their halberds, conducted him from the Castle to the place of death at the end of the Tolbooth about two o'clock. The sheriff and his substitute were there, in black, with white gloves and rods. The hurdle was painted black, but drawn by a snow-white horse. It was surrounded by constables and 200 of the Argyle Fencible Highlanders, stepping to the "Dead March."

Watt was a picture of the most abject dejection. He was wrapped up in an old great-coat, and wore a red night-cap, which, on the platform, he exchanged for a white one and a round hat; but his whole appearance was wretched and pitiful in the extreme, and all unlike that of a man. willing to die for conscience, or for country's sake. After his body had hung for thirty minutes, it was cut down lifeless and placed on a table; the executioner then came forward with a large axe, and with two strokes severed from the body the head, which fell into a basket, and was then held up by the hair, in the ancient form, by the executioner, who exclaimed, "This is the head of a traitor!"

The crowd on this occasion was slow in collecting, but became numerous at last, and showed little agitation when the drop fell; "but the appearance of the axe," says the *Annual Register*, "a sight for which they were totally unprepared, produced a shock instantaneous as electricity; and when it was uplifted such a general shriek or shout of horror burst forth as made the executioner delay his blow, while numbers rushed off in all directions to avoid the sight." The remains were next put into a coffin and conveyed away. The handcuffs used to secure Watt while a prisoner in the Castle were, in 1841, presented by Miss Walker of Drumsheugh to the Antiquarian Museum, where they are still preserved.

CHAPTER XXXI.

THE COWGATE.

The Cowgate—Origin and General History of the Thoroughfare—First Houses built there—The Vernour s Tenement—Alexander Alesse—Division of the City in 1512—"Dichting the Calsay" in 1518—The Cowgate Port—Beggars in 1616—Gilbert Blakhal—Names of the most Ancient Closes—The North Side of the Street—MacLellan's Land—Mrs. Syme—John Nimmo—Dr. Graham—The House of Sir Thomas Hope and Lady Mar—The Old Back Stairs--Tragic Story of Captain Cayley—Old Meal Market—Riots in 1763—The Episcopal Chapel, now St. Patrick's Roman Catholic Church—Trial of the Rev. Mr Fitzsimmons.

THE Cowgate is, and has always been, one of the most remarkable streets in the ancient city. A continuation of the south back of the Canongate it runs along the deepest part of a very deep gorge, into which Blair, Niddry, and St. Mary's Streets, with many other alleys, descend rapidly from the north and others from the south, and though high in its lines of antique houses, it passes underneath the over-spanning central arch of the South Bridge and the more spacious one of George IV. Bridge, and, though very narrow, is not quite straight.

For generations it has been the most densely peopled and poorest district in the metropolis, the most picturesque and squalid, and, when viewed from the two bridges named, it seems to cower in its gorge, a narrow and dusky river of quaint and black architecture, yet teeming with life, bustle, and animation. Its length from where the Cowgate Port stood to the foot of the Candlemaker Row is about 800 yards.

It is difficult to imagine the time when it was probably a narrow country way, bordered by hedgerows, skirting the base of the slope whereon lay the churchyard of St. Giles's, ere houses began to appear upon its line, and it acquired its name, which is now proved to have been originally the Sou'gate, or South Street.

One of the earliest buildings immediately adjacent to the Cowgate must have been the ancient chapel of the Holyrood, which stood in the nether kirkyard of St. Giles's till the Reformation, when the materials of it were used in the construction of the New Tolbooth. Building here must have begun early in the 15th century.

In 1428 John Vernour gave a land (i.e., a tenement) near the town of Edinburgh, on the south side thereof, in the street called Cowgate, to Richard Lundy, a monk of Melrose, for twenty shillings yearly. He or his heirs were to have the refusal of it if it were sold. ("Monastic Ann.," Teviotdale.)

In 1440 William Vernour, according to the same authority, granted this tenement to Richard Lundy, then Abbot of Melrose, without reserve, for thirteen shillings and fourpence yearly; and in 1493, Patrick, Abbot of Holyrood, confirmed the monks of Melrose in possession of their land called the Holy Rood Acre between the common Vennel, and another acre which they had beside the highway near the Canongate, for six shillings and eightpence yearly.

On the 31st May, 1498, James IV. granted to Sir John Ramsay of Balmain (previously Lord Bothwell under James III.) a tenement and orchard in the Cowgate. This property is referred to in a charter under the Great Seal, dated 19th October, 1488, to Robert Colville, director of chancery, of lands in the Cowgate of Edinburgh, once the property of Sir James Liddell, knight, "*et postea Johannis Ramsay, olim nuncupati Domini Boithvele*," now in the king's hands by the forfeiture first of Sir James Liddell, and of tenements of John Ramsay.

Many quaint timber-fronted houses existed in the Cowgate, as elsewhere in the city. Such mansions were in favour throughout Europe generally in the 15th century, and Edinburgh was only influenced by the then prevailing taste of which so many fine examples still remain in Nuremberg

and Chester; and in Edinburgh open piazzas and galleries projecting from the actual ashlar or original front of the house were long the fashion—the former for the display of goods for sale, and the latter for lounging or promenading in; and here and there are still lingering in the Cowgate mansions, past which James III. and IV. may have ridden, and whose occupants buckled on their mail to fight on Flodden Hill and in Pinkey Cleugh.

Men of a rank superior to any of which modern Edinburgh can boast had their dwellings in the Cowgate, which rapidly became a fashionable and aristocratic quarter, being deemed open and airy. An old author who wrote in 1530, Alexander Alesse, and who was born in the city in 1500, tells us that "the nobility and chief senators of the city dwell in the Cowgate—*via vaccarum in quâ habitant patricii et senatores urbis*," and that "the palaces of the chief men of the nation are also there; that none of the houses are mean or vulgar, but, on the contrary, all are magnificent—*ubi nihil humile aut rusticum, sed omnia magnifica!*"

Much of the street must have sprung into existence before the wall of James II. was demolished, in which the High Street alone stood; and it was chiefly for the protection of this highly-esteemed suburb that the greater wall was erected after the battle of Flodden.

A notarial instrument in 1509 concerning a tenement belonging to Christina Lamb on the south side near the Vennel (or wynd) from the Kirk of Field, describes it as partly enclosed with pales of wood fixed in the earth and having waste land adjoining it.

In the division of the city into three quarters in 1512, the first from the east side of Forester's Wynd, on both sides of the High Street, and under the wall to the Castle Hill, was to be held by Thomas Wardlaw. The second quarter, from the Tolbooth Stair, "quhair Walter Young dwellis in the north part of the gaitt to the Lopley Stane," to be under the said Walter; and the third quarter from the latter stone to Forester's Wynd "in the sowth pairt of the gaitt, with part of the Cowgate, to be under George Dickson."

In 1518, concerning the "Dichting of the Calsay," it was ordained by the magistrates, that all the inhabitants should clean the portion thereof before their own houses and booths "als weill in the Kowgaitt venellis as on the Hie Gaitt," and that all tar barrels and wooden pipes be removed from the streets under pain of escheat. In 1547 and 1548 strict orders were issued with reference to the guards at the city gates, and no man who was skilled in any kind of gunnery was to quit the town on any pretext, under pain of forfeiture of all he possessed and final banishment—measures rendered necessary by the recent defeat at Pinkey.

In 1555 the magistrates assigned the care of the Cowgate Port—the gate which closed the street on a line with the Pleasance—to Luke Moresoun for

In 1558 the causeway of the Cowgate was ordered to be raised and re-laid level at the expense of the heritors, from the (Black) Friars Wynd to Marlin's Wynd.

The gorge through which the Cowgate runs must once have been much deeper than it is now become,

OLD HOUSES IN THE COWGATE, NEAR THE SOUTH BRIDGE, 1850. (*From a Drawing by William Channing.*)

thirty shillings yearly, with orders "to steik and oppin the samyn," from Michaelmas to Candlemas between 6 a.m. and 5 p.m., and from Candlemas to Michaelmas between 6 a.m. and 8 p.m. ; and in the same year they paid fourteen shillings to Mungo Hunter, smith, for a new great hanging lock and key for the gate, because "the auld loke was first brokin and mendit that it could nocht be eftir mendit."

by the accumulation of soil and successive causeways. As a proof of this, in 1836 the blade of a large knife or dagger was found eleven feet below the present surface, while a drain was being dug ; and in the October of the same year an ancient iron hammer was found six feet below the surface, lying close to a thick stone wall, which had once crossed the Cowgate diagonally towards the west side of the Candlemaker Row.

Both these relics are now preserved in the Museum of Antiquities.

An act of the Privy Council in 1616 describes Edinburgh as infested by strong and idle vagabonds, having their resorts "in some parts of the Cowgate, Canongate, Potterrow, West Port, &c., where they ordinarily convene every night, and pass their time in all kind of riot and filthy lechery, to the offence and displeasure of God," lying all day on

Close in 1514; Todrig's Wynd is mentioned in 1456, when Patrick Donald granted two merks yearly from his tenement therein for repairing the altar of St. Hubert, and in 1500 a bailie named Todrig, was assaulted with drawn swords in his own house by two men, who were taken to the Tron, and had their hands stricken through.

Carrubber's Close was probably named from "William of Caribris," one of the three bailies in

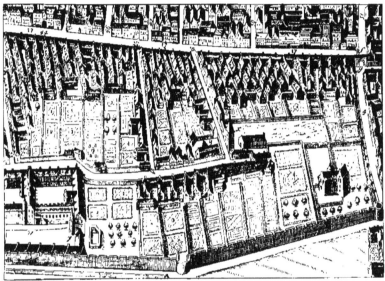

THE COWGATE, FROM THE PORT TO COLLEGE WYND, 1646. (*After Gordon of Rothiemay.*)

17, The Cowgate ; 44, Peebles Wynd ; 45, Merlin's Wynd ; 46, Niddry's Wynd ; 47, Dickson's Close ; 50, Gray's Wynd ; 51, St. Mary's Wynd ; 4, St. Mary's Wynd Suburbs ; *f*, Cowgate Port ; *g*, St. Mary's Wynd Port ; 53, The College Wynd ; 54, Robertson's Wynd ; 55, High School Wynd ; *q*, Lady Yester's Kirk ; *x*, The High School ; *w*, The College ; *y*, St. Mary of the Fields, or the Kirk of Fields ; 25, The Town Wall.

the causeway, extorting alms with "shameful exclamations," to such an extent that passengers could neither walk nor confer in the streets without being impeded and pestered by them ; hence the magistrates gave orders to expel them wholesale from the city and keep it clear of them.

The Burgh Records throw some light on the names of certain of the oldest closes—those running between the central street and the Cowgate, as being the residences or erections of old and influential citizens. Thus Niddry's Wynd is doubtless connected with Robert Niddry, a magistrate in 1437 ; Cant's Close with Adam Cant, who was Dean of Guild in 1450, though it is called Alexander Cant's

1454, as doubtless Con's Close was from John Con, a wealthy flesher of 1508. William Foular's Close is mentioned in 1521, when Bessie Symourtoun is ordered to be burned there on the cheeks and banished for passing gear infected with the pest ; and Mauchan's Close was no doubt connected with the name of John Mauchane, one of the bailies in 1523 ; Lord Borthwick's Close is frequently mentioned before 1530, and Francis Bell's Close occurs in the City Treasurer's Accounts, under date 1554. Liberton's Wynd is mentioned in a charter by James III. in 1474, and the old protocol books of the city refer to it frequently in the twelve years preceding Flodden ; William Liberton's heirs are mentioned as residents in it in 1501. He was Provost in 1425, and was succeeded in 1434 by Sir Henry Preston of Craigmillar.

Other alleys are mentioned as having existed in the sixteenth century : Swift's Wynd, Aikman's Close, and "the Eirle of Irgyllis Close," in the Dean of Guild's Accounts in 1554, and Blacklock's Close, where the unfortunate Earl of Northumberland was lodged in the house of Alexander Clarke, when he was betrayed into the hands of the Regent Moray in December, 1569. In a list of citizens, adherents of Queen Mary, in 1571, are two *glassier-wrights*, one of them named Steven Loch, probably the person commemorated in Stevenlaw's Close, in the High Street.

From Palfrey's bustling inn, at the Cowgate-head, the Dunse fly was wont to take its departure twice weekly at 8 a.m. in the beginning of the century ; and in 1780 some thirty carriers' wains arrived there and departed weekly. Wilson says that " Palfrey's, or the King's Head Inn, is a fine antique stone land of the time of Charles I. An inner court is enclosed by the buildings behind, and it long remained one of the best frequented inns in old Edinburgh, being situated at the junction of two of the principal approaches to the town from the south and west."

In this quarter MacLellan's Land, No. 8, a lofty tenement which forms the last in the range of houses on the north side of the street, has peculiar interest from its several associations. Towards the middle of the last century this edifice—the windows of which look straight up the Candlemaker-row—had as the occupant of its third floor Mrs. Syme, a clergyman's widow, with whom the father of Lord Brougham came to lodge, and whose daughter became his wife and the lady of Brougham Hall. He died in 1810, and is buried in Restalrig churchyard. Mrs. Brougham's maiden aunt continued to reside in this house at the Cowgate-head till a period subsequent to 1794.

In his father's house, one of the flats in MacLellan's Land, Henry Mackenzie, "the Man of Feeling," resided at one time with his wife and family.

In the flat immediately below Mrs. Syme dwelt Bailie John Kyd, a wealthy wine merchant, who made no small noise in the city, and who figures among Kay's etchings. He was a Bailie of 1769, and Dean of Guild in 1774.

So lately as 1824 the principal apartments in No. 8 were occupied by an aged journeyman printer, the father of John Nimmo, who became conspicuous as the nominal editor of the *Beacon,* as his name appeared to many of the obnoxious articles therein. This paper soon made itself notorious by its unscrupulous and scurrilous nature,. and its attacks on the private character of the leading Whig nobles and gentlemen in Scotland, which ended in Stuart of Dunearn horsewhipping Mr. Stevenson in the Parliament Square. The paper was eventually suppressed, and John Nimmo, hearing of the issue of a Speaker's warrant against him, after appearing openly at the printing office near the old back stairs to the Parliament House,. fled the same day from Leith in a smack, and did not revisit Edinburgh for thirty-one years. He worked long as a journeyman printer in the service of the great Parisian house of M. Didot, and for forty years he formed one of the staff of *Galignani's Messenger,* from which he retired with a pension to Asnières, where he died in his eighty-sixth year in February, 1879.

In this quarter of the Cowgate was born, in 1745,. Dr. James Graham (the son of a saddler), who was a man of some note in his time as a lecturer and writer on medical subjects, and whose brother William married Catharine Macaulay, authoress of a "History of England" and other works forgotten now. In London Dr. Graham started an extraordinary establishment, known as the Temple of Health, in Pall Mall, where he delivered what were termed Hymeneal Lectures, which in 1783 he redelivered in St. Andrew's Chapel, in Carrubber's Close. In his latter years he became seized with a species of religious frenzy, and died suddenly in his house, opposite the Archer's Hall, in 1794.

In Bailie's Court, in this quarter, lived Robert Bruce, Lord Kennet, 4th July, 1764, successor on the bench to Lord Prestongrange, and who died in 1786. This court—latterly a broker's yard for burning bones—and Allison's Close, which adjoins it—a damp and inconveniently filthy place, though but a few years ago one of the most picturesque alleys in the Cowgate—are decorated at their entrances with passages from the Psalms, a custom that superseded the Latin and older legends towards the end of the seventeenth century.

In Allison's Close a door-head bears, but sorely defaced, in Roman letters, the lines from the 120th Psalm :—"In my distress I cried unto the Lord, and he heard me. Deliver my soul, O Lord, from lying lips and from a deceitful tongue."

In Fisher's Close, which led directly up to the Lawnmarket, there is a well of considerable antiquity, more than seventy feet deep, in which a man was nearly drowned in 1823 by the flagstone that covered it suddenly giving way.

The fragment of a house, abutting close to the northern pier of the centre arch of George IV.

Bridge, with a boldly moulded doorway, inscribed,

TECUM HABITA, 1616,

(*i.e.*, "keep at home" or "mind your own affairs ") indicates the once extensive tenement occupied by the celebrated Sir Thomas Hope, King's Advocate of Charles I. in 1626, and one of the foremost men in Scotland, and who organised that resolute opposition to the king's unwise interference with the Scottish Church, which ultimately led to the great civil war, the ruin of Charles and his English councillors.

This mansion was one of the finest and most spacious of its day, and possessed a grand oak staircase. "AT HOSPES HUMO" was carved upon one of the lintels, an anagram on the name of the sturdy old Scottish statesman. In the Coltness Collections, published by the Maitland Club, is the following remark :—" If the house near Cowgeat-head, north syde that street, was built by Sir Thomas Hope, the inscription on one of the lintall-stones supports this etymologie—(viz., that the Hopes derive their name from Houblon, the Hop-plant, and not from *Esperance*, the virtue of the mind), for the anagram is *At hospes humo*, and has all the letters of Thomas Houpe." But Hope is a common name, and the termination of many localities in Scotland.

In the tapestried chambers of this old Cowgate mansion were held many of the Councils that led to the formation of the noble army of the Covenant, the camp of Dunselaw, and the total rout of the English troops at Newburnford. Hope was held by the Cavaliers in special abhorrence. "Had the d——d old rogue survived the Restoration he would certainly have been hanged," wrote C. Kirkpatrick Sharpe. "My grandfather's grandfather, Sir Charles Erskine of Alva, disgraced himself by marrying his daughter, an ugly slut."

Honours accorded to him by Charles failed to detach him from the national cause ; in 1638 he was one of the framers of the Covenant, and in 1645 was a Commissioner of Exchequer. Two of his sons being raised to the bench while he was yet Lord Advocate, he was allowed to wear his hat when pleading before them, a privilege which the King's Advocate has ever since enjoyed.

He died in 1646, but must have quitted his Cowgate mansion some time before that, as it became the residence of Mary, Countess of John, seventh Earl of Mar, guardian of Henry Duke of Rothesay (afterwards Prince of Wales). She was the daughter of Esme Stuart, Lord D'Aubigne and Duke of Lennox, and she died in Hope's house on the 11th May, 1644.

These and the adjacent tenements, removed to make way for the new bridge, were all of varied character and of high antiquity, displaying in some instances timber fronts and shot windows.

A little farther eastward were the old Back Stairs, great flights of stone steps that led through what was once the Kirkheugh, to the Parliament Close. Here resided the young English officer, Captain Cayley, whose death at the hands of the beautiful Mrs. Macfarlane, on the 2nd October, 1716, made much noise in its time, and was referred to by Pope in one of his letters to Lady Mary Wortley Montagu.

Captain John Cayley, Commissioner of Customs, was a conspicuous member of a little knot of unwelcome and obnoxious English officials, whom new arrangements subsequent to the Union had brought into Edinburgh. He seems to have been a vain and handsome fellow, whose irregular passions left him little prudence or discretion. Among his new acquaintances in the Scottish capital was a young married woman of uncommon beauty, the daughter of Colonel Charles Straiton—a well-known adherent of James VIII.—and wife of John Macfarlane, Writer to the Signet, at one time agent to Simon Lord Lovat. By her mother's side she was the grand-daughter of Sir Andrew Forester.

One Saturday forenoon Mrs. Macfarlane, then only in her twentieth year, and some months *enceinte*, was exposed by the treachery of Captain Cayley's landlady to an insult of the most atrocious kind on his part, in his house adjacent to the Back Stairs—one account says opposite to them. On the Tuesday following he visited Mrs. Macfarlane at her own house, and was shown into the drawing-room, anxious—his friends alleged—to apologise for his recent rudeness. Other accounts say that he had meanly and revengefully circulated reports derogatory to her honour, and that she was resolved to punish him. Entering the room with a brace of pistols in her hand, she ordered him to leave the house instantly.

"What, madam," said he, "d'ye design to act a comedy?" "If you do not retire instantly you will find it a tragedy!" she replied, sternly.

As he declined to obey her command, she fired one of the pistols—Cayley's own pair, borrowed but a few days before by her husband—and wounded his left wrist. With what object—unless self-preservation—it is impossible to say, Cayley drew his sword, and the moment he did so, she shot him through the heart. So close were they together that Cayley's shirt was burned at the left sleeve by one pistol, and at the breast by the other.

In wild terror Mrs. Macfarlane now rushed from the room, locked the door, and sending for her husband showed him the body, and told him all that had transpired. "Oh, woman!" he exclaimed, in misery, "what have you done?" His friends whom he consulted advised her instant flight, and at six o'clock that evening she walked down the High Street, followed by her husband at a little distance, and disappeared.

By ten that night—deeming her safe—Mr. Mac-farlane sent for the magistrates, who secured the house and servants. A contemporary says :— "I saw his (Cayley's) corpse after he was unclothed, and saw his blood where he lay on the floor for 24 hours after he died just as he fell, so it was difficult to straighten him." ("Dom. Ann.," Vol. III.)

Criminal letters were raised against Mrs. Macfar-lane by the Lord Advocate, Sir David Dalrymple, and the father and brother of the deceased, who was a native of York. Not appearing for trial she was declared an outlaw, while her husband was absolved from all blame.

Mrs. Murray, Cayley's landlady, who kept a grocery shop in the Cowgate, vindicated herself in a pamphlet from imputations which Mrs. Mac-

farlane's accusations had thrown upon her character, and denying that the lady had been in the house on the Saturday before the murder; "but evidence was given that she was seen issuing from the close in which Mrs. Murray resided, and after ascending the Back Stairs was observed passing through the Parliament Square towards her own house."

Of this Scottish Lucretia the future is unknown, and the only trace seems something of the marvellous. Margaret Swinton, a grand-aunt of Sir Walter Scott, related to him more than once, that when she, a little girl, was once left alone in Swinton House, Berwickshire, she wandered into the dining-room, and there saw an unknown lady, "beautiful as an enchanted queen, pouring out tea at a table. The lady seemed equally surprised as herself, but addressed the little intruder kindly, in particular desiring her to speak first to her mother *by herself* of what she had seen." Margaret for a moment looked out of the window, and when she turned the beautiful lady had vanished! On the return of the family from church, she told her mother of what she had seen, was praised for her discretion, and pledged to secresy in what seemed to be a dream. Sub-

OLD HOUSES IN THE COWGATE.

sequently she was informed that the lady was Captain Cayley's slayer, who had found a temporary shelter in the house of the Swintons as a kinswoman, and had a hiding-place concealed by a sliding panel. Sir Walter Scott, who introduced the incident into "Peveril of the Peak," states in a

was laid bare, proving it to have been a solid and magnificent piece of masonry, when compared with the hasty erection of 1513. On the slope nearer the Cowgate, at fourteen feet below the present surface, there was found a range of strong oak coffins, lying close together, and full of human

EAST END OF THE COWGATE, LOOKING TOWARDS THE SOUTH BACK OF CANONGATE.
(*After a Painting in Sepia by George Manson in possession of Dr. J. A. Sidey*).

note to that work, that she afterwards returned to Edinburgh, where she lived and died.

When excavations were made for the erection of the new Courts of Law in 1844, and the site of the old Back Stairs was cleared, some curious discoveries were made, illustrative of the changes that had taken place in the Cowgate during the preceding 400 years.

A considerable fragment of the wall of James II.

remains. In form these coffins were remarkable, being quite straight at the sides, with lids ridged in the centre. The same operatioins brought to light, beyond the first city wall, and at the depth of eighteen feet below the present level of the Cowgate, a common shaped barrel, six feet high, standing upright, embedded eighteen inches deep in a stratum of blue clay, and with a massive stone beside it. The appearance of the whole showed that the barrel had been placed so as to collect the rain water from the eaves of a long defunct house, with a stepping-stone to enable any one to reach its contents.

The old Meal Market was the next locality of importance on this side. In 1477 James III. ordained this market to be held " fra the Tolbooth up to Liberton's Wynd, alsua fra thence upward to the treviss ; " but the meal market of 1647, as shown in Gordon's map, directly south of the Parliament House, seems to have been a long, unshapely edifice, with two high arched gates. In 1690 the meal market paid to the city, £77 15s. 6d. sterling. As we have related elsewhere, all this quarter was destroyed by the " Great Fire " of 1700, which " broke out in the lodging immediately under Lord Crossrig's lodging in the meal market," and from which he and his family had to seek flight in their night-dress. One of his daughters, Jean Home, died at Edinburgh in Feb. 1769.

Edgar's map shows the new meal market, a huge quadrangular mass, with 150 feet front by 100 in depth, immediately eastward of the Back Stairs. This place was the scene of a serious riot in 1763. In November there had been a great scarcity of meal, by which multitudes of the poor were reduced to great suffering; hence, on the evening of the 21st, a great mob proceeded to the girnels in the meal market, carried off all that was there, rifled the house of the keeper, and smashed all the furniture that was not carried off. At midnight the mob dispersed on the arrival of some companies of infantry from the Castle, to renew their riotous proceedings, however, on the following day, when they could only be suppressed "by the presence of the Provost (George Drummond), bailies, trainband, constables, party of the military, and the city guard." Many of the unfortunate rioters were captured at the point of the bayonet, and lodged in the Castle, and the whole of the Scots Greys were quartered in the Canongate and Leith to enforce order. "The magistrates of Edinburgh, and Justices of Peace for the County of Midlothian," says the *North British Magazine* for 1763, "have since used every means to have this market supplied effectually with meal ; but from whatever cause it may proceed, certain it is that the scarcity of oatmeal is still severely felt by every family who have occasion to make use of that commodity."

The archiepiscopal palace and the mint, which were near each other, on this side of the street, have already been described (Vol. I., pp. 262—4 ; 267—270) ; but one of the old features of the locality still remaining unchanged is the large old gateway, recessed back, which gave access to the extensive pleasure-grounds attached to the residence of the Marquises of Tweeddale, and which seem to have measured 300 feet in length by 250 in breadth, and been overlooked in the north-west angle by the beautiful old mansion of the Earls of Selkirk, the basement of which was a series of elliptical arcades. These pleasure grounds ascended from the street to the windows of Tweeddale House, by a succession of terraces, and were thickly planted on the east and west with belts of trees. In Gordon's map for 1647, the whole of this open area had been—what it is now becoming again—covered by masses of building, the greatest portion of it being occupied by a huge church, that has had, at various times, no less than three different congregations, an Episcopal, Presbyterian, and, finally, a Catholic one.

For a few years before 1688 Episcopacy was the form of Church government in Scotland— illegally thrust upon the people ; but the self-constituted Convention, which transferred the crown to William and Mary, re-established the Presbyterian Church, abolishing the former, which consisted of fourteen bishops, two archbishops, and 900 clergymen. An Act of the Legislature ordered these to conform to the new order of things, or abandon their livings; but though expelled from these, they continued to officiate privately to those who were disposed to attend to their ministrations, notwithstanding the penal laws enacted against them—laws which William, who detested Presbyterianism, and was "an uncovenanted King," intended to repeal if he had lived. The title of archbishop was dropped by the scattered few, though a bishop was elected with the title *Primus*, to regulate the religious affairs of the community. There existed another body attached to the same mode of worship, composed of those who favoured the principles which occasioned the Revolution in Scotland, and, adopting the ritual of the Church of England, were supplied with clergy ordained by bishops of that country. Two distinct bodies thus existed— designated by the name of Non-jurants, as declining the oaths to the new Government. The first of these bodies — unacknowledged as a legal association, whose pastors were appointed by bishops, who acknowledged only the authority of their exiled king, who refused to take the oaths prescribed by law, and omitted all mention of the House of Hanover in their prayers—were made the subject of several penal statutes by that House.

An Episcopal chapel, whose minister was qualified

to preach openly, by taking the oaths to Government, had been founded in Edinburgh by Baron Smith, and two smaller ones were founded about 1746, in Skinner's and Carrubber's Closes; but as these places were only mean and inconvenient apartments, a plan was formed for the erection of a large and handsome church. The Episcopalians of the city chose a committee of twelve gentlemen to see the scheme executed. They purchased from the Royal College of Physicians the area of what had formerly been the Tweeddale gardens, and opened a subscription, which was the only resource they had for completing the building, the trifling funds belonging to the former obscure chapels bearing no proportion to the cost of so expensive a work. But this impediment was removed by the gentlemen of the committee, who generously gave their personal credit to a considerable amount.

The foundation stone was laid on the 3rd of April, 1771, by the Grand Master Mason, Lieutenant-General Sir Adolphus Oughton, K.B., Colonel of the 31st Foot, and Commander of the Forces in Scotland. The usual coins were deposited in the stone, under a plate, inscribed thus:—

EDIFICII SAC. ECCLESIÆ EPISC. ANGLIÆ,
PRIMUM POSUIT LAPIDEM,
I. ADOLPHUS OUGHTON,
IN ARCHITECTONICA SCOTIÆ REPUB.
CURIO MAXIMUS,
MILITUM PRÆFECTUS,
REGNANTE GEORGIO III.
TERTIO APR. DIE,
A.D. MDCCLXXI.

Towards this church the Writers to the Signet subscribed 200 guineas, and the Incorporation of Surgeons gave 40 guineas, and on Sunday, the 9th of October, 1774, divine service was performed in it for the first time. "This is a plain, handsome building," says Arnot, "neatly fitted up in the inside somewhat in the form of the church of St. Martin's-in-the-Fields, London. It is 90 feet long by 75 broad over the walls, and is ornamented with a neat spire of a tolerable height. In the spire hangs an excellent bell, formerly belonging to the Chapel Royal at Holyrood, which is permitted to be rung for assembling the congregation, an indulgence that is not allowed to the Presbyterians in England. This displays a commendable liberality of sentiment in the magistrates of Edinburgh; but breathes no jealousy for the dignity of their national Church. In the chapel there is a fine organ, made by Snetzler of London. In the east side is a niche of 30 feet, with a Venetian window, where stands the altar, which is adorned with paintings by Runciman, a native of

Edinburgh. In the volta is the Ascension; over the small window on the right is Christ talking with the Samaritan woman; on the left the Prodigal returned. In these two the figures are half-length. On one side of the table is the figure of Moses; on the other that of Elias."

At the time Arnot wrote £6,800 had been spent on the building, which was then incomplete. "The ground," he adds, "is low; the chapel is concealed by adjacent buildings; the access for carriages inconvenient, and there is this singularity attending it, that it is the only Christian church standing north and south we ever saw or heard of. . . . . There are about 1,000 persons in this congregation. Divine service is celebrated before them according to all the rites of the Church of England. This deserves to be considered as a mark of increasing moderation and liberality among the generality of the people. Not many years ago that form of worship in all its ceremonies would not have been tolerated. The organ and paintings would have been downright idolatry, and the chapel would have fallen a sacrifice to the fury of the mob."

Upon the death of Mr. Carr, the first senior clergyman of this chapel, he was interred under its portico, and the funeral service was sung, the voices of the congregation being accompanied by the organ. In Arnot's time the senior clergyman was Dr. Myles Cooper, Principal of New York College, an exile from America in consequence of the revolt of the colonies.

In the middle of February, 1788, accounts reached Scotland of the death and funeral of Prince Charles Edward, the eldest grandson of James VII., at Rome, and created a profound sensation among people of all creeds, and the papers teemed with descriptions of the burial service at Frascati; how his brother, the Cardinal, wept, and his voice broke when singing the office for the dead prince, on whose coffin lay the diamond George and collar of the Garter, now in Edinburgh Castle, while the militia of Frascati stood around as a guard, with the Master of Nairn, in whose arms the prince expired.

In the subsequent April the Episcopal College met at Aberdeen, and unanimously resolved that they should submit " to the present Government of this kingdom as invested in his present Majesty George III.," death having broken the tie which bound them to the House of Stuart. Thenceforward the royal family was prayed for in all their churches, and the penal statutes, after various modifications, were repealed in 1792. Eight years afterwards the Rev. Archibald Alison (father of

the historian) became senior minister of the Cowgate chapel.

One of his immediate predecessors, the Rev.
Mr. Fitzsimmons, an Englishman, became seriously
embroiled with the authorities, and was arraigned

Two of these four, Vanvelde and Jaffie, had
escaped from the Castle by sawing through their
window bars with a sword-blade furnished to them
by John Armour, a clerk in the city. The other
two were on parole. The Hon. Henry Erskine

THE MEAL MARKET, COWGATE.

before the High Court of Justiciary in July, 1799,
on the charge of aiding the escape of Jean Bap-
tiste Vanvelde, Jean Jacques Jaffie, Réné Griffon,
and Hypolite Depondt, French prisoners, from the
Castle of Edinburgh, by concealing them in his
house, and taking them in the Newhaven fishing
boat of Neil Drysdale to the Isle of Inchkeith,
where they remained hidden till taken to a cartel
ship, commanded by Captain Robertson, in Leith
Roads.

defended Mr. Fitzsimmons, who was sentenced to
three months' imprisonment in the Tolbooth. In
the following September 600 French prisoners (including the crew of the *Victorieux*) were marched
from the Castle, under a guard of the North York
Militia, to Leith, where they embarked for England in care of 150 bayonets of the 71st Highlanders.

After the erection of St. Paul's Church, in York
Place, the Cowgate Chapel was purchased by the

United Secession congregation. It was then seated for 1,792, with a stipend of £210 and £12 allowance for sacramental purposes. And in 1856, it became, by purchase, the property of the Roman Catholic body, with whom it still remains. It was Wynd, or street, has been pulled down; also, the east side of the High School Wynd, with all its picturesque and overhanging timber fronts and dovecot gables.

In 1784 Mr. John Francis Erskine, of the at-

THE EPISCOPAL CHAPEL, COWGATE. (*After an Engraving in the "Scots' Magazine," 1774.*)

dedicated to St. Patrick, and the then adjacent mansion of the Earls of Selkirk was repaired and restored with admirable taste by the late Rev. Dr. Marshal, as a chapel-house; but it has since been uselessly and recklessly removed by the Improvement Trust, and a hideous edifice substituted in its place.

Since then, with the exception of the Tweeddale archway, the whole north side of the street from the Blackfriars' Wynd to the foot of St. Mary's tainted house of Mar, who died in 1825, resided in the Cowgate, but in what part we have no means of ascertaining.

That the ancient name of this street was the Southgate is proved by the title-page of a work presented to the Advocate's Library in 1788—

"𝔥eir endis the maying and disport of 𝔠haucer. 𝔦mprentit in the 𝔰outhgaitt of 𝔈dinburgh be 𝔚alter 𝔠hepman and 𝔞ndrew 𝔪ollar the fourth day of 𝔞prile the ȝheir of 𝔊od 𝔐.𝔠𝔠𝔠𝔠𝔠 and viii ȝheirs.

CHAPTER XXXII.

C O W G A T E (conclud.d).

The South Side of the Street—The High School Wynd—"Claudero"—Robertson's Close—House of the Bishops of Dunkeld—Tomb of Gavin Douglas—Kirk-of-Field and College Wynd—House of the Earls of Queensberry—Robert Monteith—Oliver Goldsmith—Dr. Joseph Black—House in which Sir Walter Scott was born—St. Peter's Pend—House of Andro Symson, the Printer, 1697—The Horse Wynd—Galloway House—Guthrie Street—Tailors' Hall—French Ambassador's Chapel and John Dickison's House—Tam o' the Cowgate and James VI.—The Hammermen's Land and Hall—Magdalene Chapel—John Craig—A Glance at the Ancient Corporations—The Hammermen—Their Charter—Seal and Progress—The Cordiners—First Strike in the Trade—Skinners and Furriers—Websters—Hat and Bonnet-makers—Fleshers—Coopers—Tailors—Candle-makers—Baxters—Barbers—Chirurgeons.

PROCEEDING westward from the point we have left, the mutilated range of buildings on the south side, between George Heriot's School (the site of the old Cowgate Port) and the foot of what was the High School Wynd, show fragments of what were, in their day, exceedingly picturesque old timber-fronted tenements, of a very early date, but which were far inferior in magnificence to the Mint which stood opposite to them. This Wynd was originally a narrow and rather lonely road or path, that led towards the Dominican monastery, and westward to the house of the Kirk-of-Field. A finely-carved lintel, which surmounted the doorway of an antique range of tenements, is described by Wilson, as having been replaced over the entrance of a modern building erected on the same site in 1801. The inscription, he shows, cut in very unusual character, having in the centre a shield charged with a barrel, the device of its more recent occupant, a brewer, substituted for the armorial bearings of his predecessors :—

AL . MY . TRIST . I — S . IN . YE . LORD.

"We have found," he adds, "on examining ancient charters and title-deeds referring to property in the Cowgate, much greater difficulty in assigning the exact tenements referred to, from the absence of such marked and easily recognisable features as serve for a guide in the High Street and Canongate. All such evidence, however, tends to prove that the chief occupants of this ancient thoroughfare were eminent for rank and station, and their dwellings appear to have been chiefly in the front street, showing that, with patrician exclusiveness, traders were forbid to open their booths within its dignified precincts."

Latterly the High School Wynd was chiefly remarkable for the residence, in an old tenement at its foot, of an obscure local poet, whose real name was James Wilson, but whose nom de plume was "Claudero," and who by his poetic effusions upon local subjects continued to eke out a precarious subsistence, frequently by furnishing sharp lampoons on his less gifted fellow-citizens. He latterly added to his income by keeping a little school, and by performing "half-merk marriages, an occupation which, no doubt, afforded him additional satisfaction, as he was thereby taking their legitimate duties out of the hands of his old enemies the clergy," for Claudero, who was a cripple, is said to have been rendered so, in youth, by a merciless beating he received from "the pastoral staff" of the minister of his native parish, Cumbernauld, in Dumbartonshire. A satirist by profession, Claudero made himself a source of terror by his pungent wit, for in the Edinburgh of the eighteenth century there lived a number of wealthy old men who had realised large fortunes in questionable manners abroad, and whose characters, as they laboured under strange suspicions of the slave trade—even buccaneering perhaps—" were wonderfully susceptible of Claudero's satire ; and these, the wag," we are told, "used to bleed profusely and frequently, by working upon their fears of public notice."

In 1766 appeared his "Miscellanies in Prose and Verse, by Claudero, son of Nimrod the mighty Hunter," dedicated to the renowned Peter Williamson, "from the other world." In this volume are "The Echo of the Royal Porch of Holyrood," demolished in 1753 ; "The last Speech and Dying Words of the Cross," executed, &c., "for the horrid crime of being an encumbrance to the street ;" "Scotland's Tears over the Horrid Treatment of her Kings' Sepulchres ;" "A Sermon on the Condemnation of the Netherbow ;" and other kindred subjects. With all his eccentricity, Claudero seems to have felt genuine disgust at the wanton destruction of many beautiful and historical edifices and monuments in Edinburgh, under the reckless fiat of a magistracy of the most tasteless age in British history—the epoch of George III. In the year 1755 he was wandering about London, but returned to Edinburgh, where he lived for thirty years consecutively, and died in 1789.

The wynd led straight up the slope to the old High School, which with its tower and spire stood on the east side of it. Robertson's Close adjoined it on the west—in 1647, a long and straight street, with lofty houses on both sides, and spacious gardens lying westward, behind the line of the Cowgate, close up to the College Wynd. Latterly it was occupied on one side by Dick's extensive brewery, and it leads to the modern Infirmary Street.

The house of the Bishops of Dunkeld stood a little westward of this, on the south side of the Cowgate, near the bottom of where South Niddry Street ascends the slope. So early as 1449, Thomas Lauder, Canon of Aberdeen, granted an endowment of forty shillings annually, to a chaplain in St. Giles's Church, "out of his own house lying in the Cowgate, betwixt the land of the Abbot of Melrose on the east, and of George Cochrane on the west."

This divine was the same Thomas Lauder who was preceptor to James II., and was Bishop of Dunkeld between 1452 and 1476; and it is recorded (in Mylne's lives of the bishops of that see) that besides many other acts of munificence, he purchased a house in Edinburgh for himself and his successors in the diocese—evidently the mansion in question. "That its situation is the same as that above described," says Chambers, "appears from a charter of Thomas Cameron, in 1498, referring to a house on the south side of the Cowgate ' betwixt the Bishop of Dunkeld's land on the east, the common street on the north, and the gait that leads to the Kirk-of-Field on the south.'" Cameron bequeathed the tenement referred to to the chaplain of St. Catharine's altar in St. Giles's, and Robertson's Close now marks the boundary of the bishop's garden, which must have extended up the slope—the line of the present Infirmary Street.

Here then was the abode of Gavin Douglas, Bishop of Dunkeld, in 1515, one of the most distinguished Scottish poets, the third son of Archibald fifth Earl of the warlike and glorious house of Angus. Of the part he bore in the memorable skirmish known as "Cleanse the Causeway" we have recorded in our account of the archiepiscopal palace, which stood (nearly opposite his own) till 1878.

Before 1501 he had completed a translation of Ovid, and at the request of Henry first Lord Sinclair, he rendered the Æneid into the Scots vernacular. He wrote his "Palace of Honor" in the days of his exile—an apologue in which, under the similitude of a vision, he depicts the vanity and inconstancy of all worldly glory.

The Regent Albany, in 1515, prevented him from taking possession of his see, and made him a prisoner in the Castle of Edinburgh, under a charge of procuring bulls from Rome, thereby contravening the laws of the realm. In 1521 he was compelled, by the disputes between the Earls of Arran and Angus, to seek shelter in England, where he formed the acquaintance of Polydor Virgil, and received a pension from Henry VIII. He died of the plague in London, in 1522, in his forty-eighth year, and was buried in the old Savoy chapel, near the Strand, where in October, 1878, a long missing brass was found by the chaplain, the Rev. Henry White, with the following inscription:—"*Hic jacet Gavan Dolkglas, natione Scotus, Dunkellensis Præsul patriâ suâ exul. Anno Christi,* 1522."

His lodging in the Cowgate has long since disappeared, and its once pleasant garden is now covered by humble plebeian edifices. By the City Improvement Trust of 1866 nearly the whole tenements and closes on the south side of the street, between the South Bridge and Minto House, were doomed to be swept away, with a very few and nameless exceptions.

We now come to the birthplace of Sir Walter Scott, in the alley named of old, in hundreds of charters and records, " The Wynd of the Blessed Virgin Mary in the Field "—the College Wynd in later times. Here, until several years after the Improvement Act, remained unchanged, or nearly so, the straight and steep alley which ascended to the southern side of the town, the avenue to the church of St. Mary—an avenue full of wonderful associations since the days when Dominicans and Grey Friars, with the prebends and choristers of St. Mary, clomb the ascent together, and since the great, the grave, and the learned professors went by the same path to the ancient and to the new colleges.

Some of the buildings here were of great antiquity; and among the charters of property acquired by the city for the establishment of the college is one connected with " Shaws tenement in the Wynd of the Blessed Mary-in-the-Field, now the College Wynd. Item, an instrument of sasine, dated 30th June, 1525, of a land built and waste, lying in the Wynd of the Blessed Virgin Mary-in-the-Field, on the west side thereof, &c., in favour of Alex. Schaw, son of Wm. Schaw, of Polkemet."

Wilson gives us the best description of some of the features of this old street of so many memories as it existed shortly before its destruction, and where every feature was as Scott had seen it in infancy, boyhood, and old age. "About the middle of the wynd, on the east side, a curious and antique edifice retained many of its original features, notwithstanding its transmutation from a *Collegium Sacerdotum,* or prebendal building of the neighbouring collegiate church, to a brewer's granary and spirit vault! The ground floor had been entirely re-paved with hewn stone; but over a large window on the first floor there was a sculptured lintel, which is mentioned by Arnot as having

interesting remains, so characteristic of the obsolete faith and habits of a former age, afforded undoubted evidence of the importance of this building in early times, when it formed a part of the extensive collegiate establishment of St. Mary-in-the-Fields

TAILORS' HALL, COWGATE.

surmounted the gateway into the inner court. It bore the following inscription, cut in beautiful and very early characters :—

    " Abe Maria, gratia plena, Dominus tecum."

A most beautiful Gothic niche was in the front of this building. " It is said to have stood originally over the main gateway," he continues, " above the carved lintel we have described, and without a doubt it contained a statue of the Virgin, to whom the wayfarer's supplications were invited. These

founded and endowed apparently by the piety of the wealthy citizens of the capital. To complete the ecclesiastical feature of this ancient edifice, a boldly-cut shield on the lower crowstep bore the usual monogram of our Saviour, I.H.S., and the window presented the common feature of broken mullions and transoms with which they had been originally divided."

Internally it would seem that this edifice presented features of a more recent date, indicating that its occupants were worthy neighbours of the aristocratic tenants of the Cowgate. The stucco ornaments were all of the era of Charles I., and most prominent among them was the crowned heart of the house of Douglas.

From this it has been supposed to have been the one of the doors of the stair possessed the old-fashioned appendage of a tirling-pin. Many of the buildings which remained till the total demolition of the wynd bore the initials of their builders on an ornamental shield, sculptured on the lowest crowstep, with the date—1736."

HIGH SCHOOL WYND.   (*After Ewbank.*)

town residence of one of the first Earls of Queens-berry—probably William, whose title was created by Charles I. on his visit to Scotland in 1633. " The projecting staircase of the adjoining tene-ment to the south had a curious ogee-arched win-dow, evidently of early character, and fitted with the antique oaken transom and folding shutters below. A defaced inscription and date were deci-pherable over the lintel of the outer doorway, and

When Scott was a little boy some of the houses opposite his father's windows would be barely forty years old.

It is not improbable that the land or tenement referred to so elaborately by Wilson was connected in some way with that referred to in the Burgh Records, under date August 30th, 1549, when the Town Council consented to the feuing of a land (in the wynd) pertaining to the chaplaincy of the high altar in the Kirk-of-Field, of which they were patrons, and concerning which Master Archibald Barrie, the chaplain thereof, "declairit thair wes ane land called Cliddisdail andis lyand in the Kirk-of-Field Wynd, on the *eist* side of the trans thereof, quhilk gaif yeirlie to him the sowm of ten merks of meal allanarlie," &c., but which was then ruinous and about to fall; so the site was given in feu to Marion Craig, widow of "vmquhille Jhon Foularton."

In 1712, when Mr. Robert Monteith, M.A., was preparing the second edition of his curious "Theater of Mortality" (the first appeared in 1704)—a grim collection of Scottish sepulchral inscriptions which had already cost him "eight years sore travel and at vast charges and expenses"—he was resident in the College Wynd, whither he, by advertisement in the *Courant*, requested the copies to be sent to him, in the hope that "all generous persons will cheerfully submit his proposals in a matter so pious, *pleasant*, profitable, and national." ("Dom. Ann.," III.)

SIR WALTER SCOTT.
(After the Drawing by G. S. Newton, R.A., in the Illustrated Edition of "Waverley," by permission of Messrs. A. & C. Black).

The middle of the same century saw a more eminent *littérateur* resident in the College Wynd, when Oliver Goldsmith, an unknown and unheeded young Irish student, took up his abode in some airy tenement thereof in 1752, while attending the medical classes prior to the completion of his education at Leyden, whither he went in 1754. The Duke of

SIR WALTER SCOTT'S ARMS.
(From the Illustrated Edition of "Waverley," by permission of Messrs. A. & C. Black.)

Hamilton—Duke James, who married the beautiful Miss Gunning—had engaged the services of the young Irishman apparently as a tutor, and with an eye, it is supposed, to his reputed scholarship as an alumnus of Trinity College, Dublin; and it has been supposed that a curious tailor's bill which came recently to light in Edinburgh, had some reference to his expected visits to the Duke's apartments in Holyrood, of which the Hamilton family are hereditary keepers.

An old ledger was being torn up for waste paper (says Wilson in his "Reminiscences"), when happily one of its leaves attracted the quick eye of the late David Laing, and there he found preserved an account, for the year 1753, between "Mr. Oliver Goldsmith" and Mr. Filby, a tailor of Edinburgh; it indicates the passion which poor Oliver had for fine clothes, and which—according to Dr. Strain —caused him to miss ordination by appearing before the Bishop of Elphin (in Roscommon) in scarlet breeches. "The fragment of the Edinburgh tailor's ledger thus snatched from oblivion illustrates the marvellous change since that olden time, when a medical student's wardrobe shone resplendent in 'sky-blue satin, rich black Genoa velvet fine sky-blue shalloon, and the best superfine high claret-coloured cloth,' to which has to be added 'a superfine small hatt,' laced with '8s. worth of silver hatt-lace,' duly charged by its weight of the precious metal in ounces and drachms. The first bill was paid 'by cash in full,' before the end of the year; the second is carried over 'to folio 424,' which, unfortunately, has vanished with the superfine high claret-coloured suit, which stands charged against Oliver for £3 6s. 6d., like later unsettled accounts of the poet's wardrobe."

And doubtless many a time and oft must young Oliver have made his way, attired in Mr. Filby's finery, with a small sword by his side, down the College Wynd to the Old Assembly Close, and to those assemblies over which the Hon. Miss Nicky Murray presided as Lady Directress.

In a house close to the old College gate, on the east side of the wynd, lived for years the illustrious Joseph Black, M.D., the founder of pneumatic chemistry, who was completing his medical studies in the Edinburgh University in 1751, collaterally with Goldsmith; and Forster tells us in his life of the latter, that "he was fond of chemistry, and was remembered favourably by the celebrated Black." The doctor graduated here as M.D. in 1754, his inaugural thesis containing an outline of his cele-brated discovery of fixed air, or carbonic gas, which with his discovery of latent heat laid the foundation of modern pneumatic chemistry, and has opened to the investigation of the philosopher a fourth kingdom of nature, viz., the gaseous kingdom. Other brilliant achievements in science followed fast before and after Dr. Black's appointment to a chair in Glasgow in 1756. Ten years after he became Professor of Chemistry in Edinburgh, and was so for twenty-nine years. He died in 1799, while sitting at table, with his usual fare, a few prunes, some bread, and a little milk diluted with water. Having the cup in his hand, and feeling the approach of death, he set it carefully down on his knees, which were joined together, and kept it steadily in his hand, in the manner of a person perfectly at ease, and in this attitude, without spilling a drop, and without a writhe on his coun-tenance, Joseph Black, styled by Lavoisier "the illustrious Nestor of the chemical revolution," ex-pired placidly, as if an experiment had been wanted to show his friends the ease with which he could die.

In another house at the wynd head, but exactly opposite, Sir Walter Scott was born on the 15th of August, 1771. It belonged to his father Walter Scott, W.S., and was pulled down to make room for the northern front of the New College. According to the simple fashion of the Scottish gentry of that day, on another floor of the same building—the first flat—dwelt Mr. Keith, W.S., father of the late Sir Alexander Keith, of Ravelston, Bart. ; and there, too, did the late Lord Keith reside in his student days.

Scott's father, deeming his house in the College Wynd unfavourable to the health of his family—for therein died several brothers and sisters of Sir Walter, born before him—removed to an airier mansion, No. 25, George Square ; but the old wynd he never forgot. "In the course of a walk through this part of the town in 1825," says genial Robert Chambers, "Sir Walter did me the honour to point out the site of the house in which he had been born. On his mentioning that his father had got a good price for his share of it, I took the liberty of jocularly expressing my belief that more money might have been made of it, and the public certainly much more gratified, if it had remained to be shown as the birthplace of the man who had written so many popular books. 'Ay, ay,' said Sir Walter, 'that is very well ; but I am afraid I should have required to be dead first, and that would not have been so comfortable, you know.'"

The house of Mr. Scott, W.S., on the flat of the old tenement, was approached by a turnpike stair, within a little court off the wynd head ; in another corner of it resided Mr. Alexander Murray, the future solicitor-general, who afterwards sat on the Bench as Lord Henderland, and died in 1795.

It was up this narrow way, on Sunday the 15th of August, 1773—when Scott was exactly a baby of two years old—that Boswell and Principal Robertson conducted Dr. Johnson to show him the College.

Within the narrow compass of this ancient wynd —so memorable as the birthplace of Scott—were representatives of nearly every order of Scottish society, sufficient for a whole series of his Waverley novels. No wonder is it then, beyond the expe-rience of "Auld Reekie," that we should find one of Kay's quaintest characters, "Daft Bailie Duff," a widow's idiot boy, long regarded as the in-dispensable appendage of an Edinburgh funeral, dwelling in a little den at the foot of the alley, where he died in 1788.

Most picturesque were the venerable edifices that stood between the foot of the College and the Horse Wynds, though between them lay St. Peter's Close, which, in its latter days, led only to a byre, and a low, dark, filthy, and horrible place, "full of holes and water."

On the east side of St. Peter's Pend was a very ancient house, the abode of noble proprietors in early times, but which had been remodelled and enlarged in the days of James VI. Three large and beautiful dormer windows rose above its roof, the centre one surmounted by an escallop shell, while a smaller tier of windows peeped out above them from the "sclaited roof," and the lintel of its projecting turnpike stair, bore all that remained of its proprietors, these initials, V. P. and A. V.

On the other side of the Pend, and immediately abutting on the Horse Wynd, was that singularly picturesque timber-fronted stone tenement, of which drawings and a description are given in the "Edin-burgh Papers," on the ancient architecture of the city published in 1859, and referred to as "another of the pristine mansions of the Cowgate—the houses where William Dunbar and Gavin Douglas may have paid visits, and probably sent forth mailed warriors to Flodden. . . . . Here, besides the ground accommodation and gallery floor, with an outside stair, there is a contracted second floor, having also a gallery in front with a range of small windows. On the gallery floor at the head of the outside stair, is a finely-moulded door, at the base of an inner winding or turnpike stair leading up to the second floor. Such is the style or door to be seen in all these early wooden houses—a style which must unhesitatingly be pronounced to be superior in elegance to almost any other doors given to modern houses either in Edinburgh or in London. On a frieze between the mouldings is a legend in a style of lettering and orthography which speaks of the close of the fifteenth century:—

GIF . YE . DEID . AS . YE . SOULD . YE
MYCHT . HAIF . AS . YE . VULD.

In modern English, 'If we died as we should, we the sacred story, and digested into English verse.'. Before, this, however, he had acted as amanuensis to the famous Lord Advocate, Sir George Mackenzie of Rosehaugh, and of "bluidie memorie;" and in 1699 he edited and published a new folio edition of Sir George's work on "The Laws and Customs of Scotland," which bears on its title-page that it is "Printed by the heirs and successors of Mr. Andrew Anderson, printer to the King's most Excellent Majesty, for Mr. Andrew Symson, and

COLLEGE WYND. (From a Drawing by William Channing.)

might have as we would.' There is unfortunately no trace of the man who built the house and put upon it this characteristic apophthegm; but it is known that the upper floors were occupied about (before?) 1700 by the worthy Andro Symson, who having been ousted from his charge as an episcopal minister at the Revolution, continued to make a living here by writing and printing books."

Symson had been curate of Kirkinner, in Galloway, a presentation to him by the earl of that title, and was the author of an elaborate work, and mysterious poem of great length, issued from his printing-house at the foot of the Horse Wynd, entitled, "Tripatriarchicor; or the lives of the three patriarchs, Abraham, Isaac, and Jacob, extracted forth of are to be sold by him in the Cowgate, near the foot of the Hose Wynd, Anno Dom. 1699."

The Horse Wynd which once connected the Cowgate with the open fields on the south of the city, and was broad enough for carriages in days before such vehicles were known, is supposed to have derived its name from an inn which occupied the exact site of the Gaelic church which was erected there in 1815, after the building in the Castle Wynd was abandoned, and which ranked as a *quoad sacra* parish church after 1834, though it was not annexed to any separate territory. It was seated for 1,166, and cost £3,000, but was swept away as being in the line of the present Chambers Street.

Although the name of this wynd is as old as the middle of the seventeeth century, none of the buildings in it latterly were older than the middle of the eighteenth. They had all been removed by those who were anxious for the benefit of such fine air as its surroundings afforded, for in the map of 1647 the *Vicus Equorum* is shown as having to the westward gardens in plenitude, divided by four long hedgerows, and closed on the south by the

became remarkable for piety, mingled with great stateliness and pride ; and she is thus referred to in the Ridotto of Holyrood, partly written by her sister-in-law, Lady Bruce of Kinloss :--

"And there was Bob Murray, though married, alas !
 Yet still rivalling Johnstone in beauty and grace.
 And there was *my lady*, well known by her airs,
 Who ne'er goes to revel but after her prayers."

The Bob herein referred to was Sir Robert

SYMSON THE PRINTER'S HOUSE, 1873. (*After a Photograph by Alexander A. Inglis.*)

crenelated wall of the city, and it terminated by a bend eastward at the Potterrow Port.

Respectable members of the bar were always glad to have a flat in some of the tall edifices on the east side of the wynd. About the middle of it, on the west side, was a distinct mansion called Galloway House, having a large pediment, and ornamented on the top by stone vases. This residence was built by Alexander, sixth Earl of Galloway, one of the Lords of Police, who died in 1773. His countess Catharine, daughter of John Earl of Dundonald, colonel of the Scottish Horse Guards, was mother of Captain George Stewart, who fell at Ticonderoga. She had been a beauty in her youth, and formed the subject of one of Hamilton of Bangour's poetical tributes, and in her old age

Murray of Clermont. Among all the precise grand-dames of her time in Edinburgh, Lady Galloway was noted for her pre-eminent pomp and formality, and would order out her coach with six horses, if but to pay a visit to a friend at the corner of the wynd, or to Lord Minto, whose house was a few yards westward of it. "It was alleged that when the countess made calls, the leaders were sometimes at the door she was going to when she was stepping into the carriage at her own door. This may be called a *tour de force* illustration of the nearness of friends to each other in Old Edinburgh."

New College Wynd, which strikes from the eastern part of Chambers Street, runs first 110 feet northward, then 180 feet westward, and then northward again in the line of the lower part of the

Horse Wynd, and, in honour of the Rev. Dr. Guthrie, is named Guthrie Street.

"Nearly opposite the site of the Old Parliament Stairs," says Wilson, 1847, "a uniform and lofty range of handsome tenements forms the front of an enclosed quadrangle, which includes within its precincts the Tailors' Hall, by far the most stately of all the corporation halls, if we except St. Magdalene's Chapel, and one interestingly associated with important national and civic events. A handsome broad archway considerably ornamented forms the entrance through the front tenement to the inner quadrangle. The gateway is surmounted by an ornamental tablet, decorated with a huge pair of shears, the insignia of the craft, and bearing the date 1644, with the following elegant distich :—

"ALMIGHTIE GOD WHO FOUND-
ED BVILT AND CROVND
THIS WORK WITH BLESSINGS
MAK IT TO ABOVND."

The corporation, however, had a hall on the same site at an earlier period. An assembly of about three hundred clergymen, together with the Earls of Rothes, Lindsay, and Loudon, met in it on the 27th of February, 1638, to consider the terms of the National Covenant, which was to be presented to the public next day in the Greyfriars' churchyard. The Earl of Rothes records that some there were who objected to certain points in the document, but they were taken aside into the garden attached to the hall, and there addressed specially on the necessity of mutual concession for the general good of the national cause, and they soon gave their entire consent. Until a recent period, comparatively, the garden in which these dissentients met retained its early character, but now it is merely a yard for brewers' barrels.

The Tailors' Hall occupies the south and east sides of the court, off the deep browed arch from the Cowgate, and ere it received an additional storey to adapt it for its modern use as a brewer's granary, it exhibited an ornamental pediment, with the shears of the corporation, and the date 1621, with the inscription — *God . give . the . blising . to . the . Tailzer . craft . in . the . Good . Tovn . of . Edinburgh ;* and, little foreseeing that in the eighteenth century this hall would be devoted to the profane use of a theatre, the pious tailors placed over the main entrance the following lines :—

TO THE GLORE OF GOD AND VIRTEWIS RENOWNE,
AND THE CWMPANIE OF TAILZEOVRS WITHIN THIS GOOD
TOVNE,
FOR MEITING OF THAIR CRAFT THIS HAL HAS BEEN ERECTED
WITH TRUST IN ALL GOD'S GOODNES TO BE BLIST AND
PROTECTED.

This hall was used in 1656 as the court-house of the Scottish Commissioners appointed by Cromwell for the administration of the forfeited estates of the Royalists, and from a period subsequent to 1727, till after the year 1753, it was used as a theatre by itinerating companies, who met with some success, notwithstanding the bitter and incessant denunciations of the clergy. It was a house which, in a theatrical sense, held from £40 to £45, and it was a split in the company here which led to the erection of the rival theatre in 1746-7 in the Canongate.

It is supposed that the last regular representation which took place in the Tailors' Hall is one referred to in "Minor Antiquities," as advertised for the 20th March, 1747.

To the westward of it is a house of the time of Charles I., with a moulded doorway, bearing this inscription in Roman letters :—

R . H . O . MAGNIFIE . THE . LORD . WITH . ME . J . H .
AND . LET . US . EXALT . HIS . NAME . TOGETHER.
ANNO DOMINI. 1643.

But no record of the building remains save the piety that inspired the legend for the exclusion of evil and sorcery. This door is only 3 feet 3 inches wide.

Above this very narrow door there is sculptured the device of two men bearing a barrel between them, slung from a pole resting on their shoulders.

On the same side of the street, where now George IV. Bridge passes, there was a house possessing strange features, and a traditionary history. Over the ground floor was one of good elevation, having several elegant windows, including two square and heavily moulded, which were said to have lighted the private chapel of the French ambassador during the reign of Mary. On the uppermost floor, above these, was a large double dormer window, the sill of which was on a line with the eaves, on the acute angles of which were the heads of the Twelve Apostles, and on its apex a set of limbs said to represent those of our Saviour, set astride the summit. A square projecting tower with three square windows, containing a common stair, was entered by a handsomely-moulded door, surmounted by a shield, the chief figure in which was that creature of mediæval superstition a *wehr-wolf*—a wolf with a man's face, from a once prevalent belief that men, under a peculiar affection, were transformed into wolves, by animosity, known as lycanthropy, in which character they howled, and devoured their fellow creatures. There were also three stars in chief, and beneath the motto— "*Speravi et Inveni.*"

This was the house of Dickison, of Winkston, in Peebles-shire, whose armorial bearings then were derived from Dickson by the stars, according to Nisbet in his "Heraldry." A John Dickison of Winkston, who was provost of Peebles, was assassinated in the High Street of that town, on the 1st of July, 1572, and James Tweedie, burgess of Peebles, and four other persons, were tried for the crime and acquitted. This is supposed to be the John Dickison who built the house, and had placed upon it these remarkable devices as a bold proof of his adherence to the ancient faith. "The hand- some antique form of this house, the strange armorial device of the original proprietor, the tradi- tion of the Catholic chapel, the singular figures over the double dormer window, and Dickison's own tragic fate, in the midst of a frightful civil war, when neither party gave quarter to the other, all combine to throw a wild and extraordinary interest over it, and make us greatly regret its removal." ("Ancient Arch. of Edin.")

The peculiar pediment, as well as the sculptured lintel of the front door, were removed to Coates' House, and are now built into different parts of the northern wing of that quaint and venerable château in the New Town.

In the middle of the last century, and prior to 1829, a court of old buildings existed in the Cow- gate, on the ground now occupied by the southern piers of George IV. Bridge, which were used as the Excise Office, but, even in this form, were somewhat degraded from their original character, for there resided Thomas Hamilton of Priestfield, Earl of Melrose in 1619, and first Earl of Hadding- ton in 1627, Secretary of State in 1612, King's Advocate, and Lord President of the Court of Session in 1592.

He rented the house in question from Macgill of Rankeillor, and from the popularity of his cha- racter and the circumstance of his residence, he was endowed by his royal master, King James, whose chief favourite he was, with the sobriquet of *Tam o' the Cowgate*, under which title he is better remembered than by his talents as a statesman or his Earldom of Haddington.

He was famous for his penetration as a judge, his industry as a collector of decisions—drawing up a set of these from 1592 to 1624—and his talent for creating a vast fortune. It is related of him, in one of many anecdotes concerning him, communicated by Sir Walter Scott to the indus- trious author of the "Traditions of Edinburgh," that, after a long day's hard labour in the public service, he was one evening seated with a friend over a bottle of wine near a window of his house in the Cowgate, for his ease attired in a *robe de chambre* and slippers, when a sudden disturbance

was heard in the street. This turned out to be a *bicker*, one of those street disturbances peculiar to the boys of Edinburgh, till the formation of the present police, and referred to in the Burgh Re- cords so far back as 1529, anent "gret bikkyrringis betwix bairns;" and again in 1535, when they were to be repressed, under pain of scourging and banishment.

On this occasion the strife with sticks and stones was between the youths of the High School and those of the College, who, notwithstanding a bitter resistance, were driving their antagonists before them.

The old Earl, who in his youth had been a High School boy, and from his after education in Paris, had no sympathy for the young collegians, rushed into the street, rallied the fugitives, and took such an active share in the combat that, finally, the High School boys—gaining fresh courage upon discover- ing that their leader was Tam o' the Cowgate, the great judge and statesman—turned the scale of victory upon the enemy, despite superior age and strength. The Earl, still clad in his robe and slippers, assumed the command, exciting the lads to the charge by word and action. Nor did the hubbub cease till the students, unable by a flank movement to escape up the Candlemaker Row, were driven headlong through the Grassmarket, and out at the West Port, the gate of which he locked, compelling the vanquished to spend the night in the fields beyond the walls. He then returned to finish his flask of wine. And a rare jest the whole episode must have been for King James, when he heard of it at St. James's or Windsor.

When, in 1617, the latter revisited Scotland, he found his old friend very rich, and was informed that it was a current belief that he had discovered the Philosopher's Stone. James was amused with the idea of so valuable a talisman having fallen into the hands of a Judge of the Court of Session, and was not long in letting the latter know of the story. The Earl immediately invited the king, and all who were present, to dine with him, adding that he would reveal to them the mystery of the Philosopher's Stone.

The next day saw his mansion in the Cowgate thronged by the king and his Scottish and English courtiers. After dinner, James reminded him of the Philosopher's Stone, and then the wily Earl addressed all present in a short speech, concluding with the information that his whole secret of suc- cess and wealth, lay in two simple and familiar maxims :—"Never put off till to-morrow what can be done to-day ; nor ever trust to the hand of another that which your own can execute."

Full of years and honours, Tam o' the Cowgate died in 1637. At Tynninghame, his family seat, there are two portraits of him preserved, and also his state dress, in the crimson velvet breeches of which there are no less than nine pockets. Among many of his papers, which remain at Tynninghame House, one contains a memorandum which throws a curious light upon the way in which political matters were then managed in Scotland. This paper details the heads of a petition in his own

each way, and had a border of trees upon its east and south sides. Latterly it bore the name of Thomson's Green, from the person to whom it was leased by the Commissioners of Excise.

The Hammerman's Close, Land, and Hall, adjoined the site of this edifice on the westward.

The Land was in 1711 the abode of a man named Anthony Parsons, among the last of those who followed the ancient practice of vending quack medicines on a public stage in the streets. In the

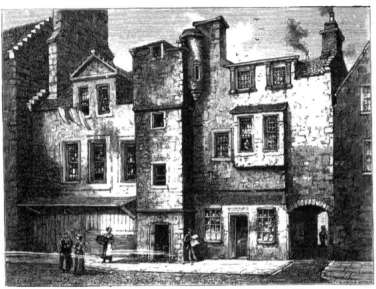

THE FRENCH AMBASSADOR'S CHAPEL. (*From a Drawing by W. Geikie.*)

hand-writing to the Privy Council with a prayer to "gar the Chancellor" do something else in his behalf

The Excise Office was removed about 1730 from the Parliament Square to the house so long occupied by the Earl of Haddington, which afforded excellent accommodation for so important a public institution. The principal room on the second floor, the windows of which opened to the Cowgate, was one of great magnificence, having a stucco ceiling divided into square compartments, each of which contained an elegant device, and there was also much fine paneling. At the back of the house, extending to where the back of Brown Square was built, and entered by a gate from the Candlemaker Row, it measured nearly 200 feet

October of that year he advertised in the *Scots Postman*—"It being reported that Anthony Parsons is gone from Edinburgh to mount public stages in the country, this is to give notice that he hath left off keeping stages, and still lives in the Hammerman's Land, near the head of the Cowgate, where may be had the *Orviet n*, a famous antidote against infectious distempers, and helps barrenness," &c. Four years subsequently Parsons—an Englishman, of course—announced his design of bidding adieu to Edinburgh, and in that prospect offered his quack medicines at reduced rates, and likewise, by auction, "a fine cabinet organ."

The last of these English quacks was Dr. Green, gauger, of Doncaster, who made his appearance in

1725, accompanied by a servant, "or tumbler," who robbed him, and against whom he warned the people of certain country towns in the *Courant* of December, 1725.

Arnot records that in early times there existed in the Cowgate an ancient *Mais·n Dieu* which had fallen into decay; but it was re-founded in the reign

the latter was used as a hall for their meetings. The foundation was augmented in 1541 by two donations from Hugh Lord Somerville, who was taken prisoner by the English in the following year, and had to ransom himself for 1,0co merks.

If the edifice suffered in the general sack of the city during the invasion of 1544 it must have been

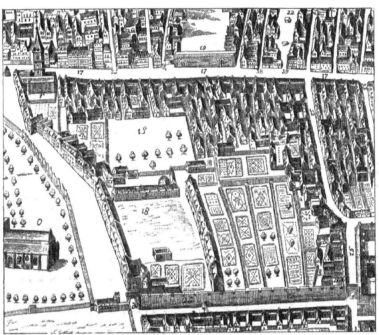

THE COWGATE, FROM THE COLLEGE WYND TO THE GRASSMARKET.   (*After Gordon of Rothiemay's Plan.*)

d, The Society Port; *e*, The Potterrow Port; *o*, The West Kirk, or Greyfriars Kirk, with the burial-place; *r*, Magdalene Chapel; 3, Potterrow Suburbs; 17, Cowgate; 18, The Society, with the Gardens; 19, Meal Market; 25. City Wall; 35, Liberton's Wynd; 36, Foster's Wynd; 38, St. Monan's Wynd; 39, Fishmarket Wynd; 52, Horse Wynd; 56, Beth's Wynd.

of James IV., chiefly by the pious contributions of Michael Macqueen (or Macquhen), a wealthy citizen, and afterwards by his widow, Janet Rhynd.

The hospital—designed to accommodate a chaplain and seven poor men—and the chapel, the little square spire of which (with its gargoyles formed like cannon, each with a ball stuck in its mouth) is nearly lost amid the towering modern edifices which surround it—were dedicated to St. Mary Magdalene, and by the will of the founders were left in trust to the Corporation of Hammermen, by whom

quickly repaired, as the windows are still adorned with ancient painted glass—the only fragments in all Scotland which have survived the Reformation, and contain the royal arms of Scotland, encircled by a wreath of thistles, and those of the Queen Regent Mary of Guise, within a wreath of laurel, with the shields of the founder and foundress within ornamental borders. These probably date from 1556, in which year we find that "The baillies and counsale ordainis the thesaurer to mak ane powpet to Maister Alexander Sym to reid in the Magdalene

Chapel, and quhat expensis he makis thaeron sal be allowit to him in his accomptis."

In one window, a Saint Bartholomew has strangely escaped the destructive mobs of 1559 and 1688; but its tints are far inferior to the deep crimson and gold of the royal arms. It is remarkable that one other feature has also escaped destruction, the tomb of Janet Rhynd, with the following inscription in ancient Gothic characters :—

Heir lyis ane honorabil woman, Janet Rynd, ye Spous of umquhil Micel Makquhen, burgess of Ed. founder of yis place, and deceasit ye iiii day of Decemr., Ao dno Mc.v.bli.

Impaled in one shield, the arms of the husband and wife are in the centre of the sculptured stone, which is now level with a platform at the east end of the chapel for the accommodation of the officials of the Corporation.

The hospital was founded in 1504—nine years before Flodden ; but the charter by which its permanent establishment is secured by Janet Rhynd, who gave personally £2,000 Scots, is supposed to have been dated about 1545 in the reign of Mary, and as one of the last deeds executed for a pious purpose, is now remarkable in its tenor.

The chapel is decorated at its east end with the royal arms, those of the city, and of the twenty-two corporations forming the ancient and honourable Incorporation of Hammermen, " the guardians of the sacred banner, the Blue Blanket, on the unfurling of which every liege burgher of the kingdom is bound to answer the summons."

On the walls are numerous tablets recording the names and gifts of benefactors. The oldest of these is supposed to be a daughter of the founders, " Isabel Macquhane, spouse to Gilbert Lauder, merchant burgess of Edinburgh, who bigged ye cross-house, and mortified £50 out of the Caussland, anno 1555." " John Spens, burgess of Edinburgh," tells another tablet, " bestowed 100 lods of Wesland lime for building the stipel of this chapell, anno 1621."

Eleven years after the quaint steeple was built a bell was hung in it, which bears round it, in large Roman characters,—

SOLI DEO GLORIA MICHAEL BURGERHUYS ME FECIT. ANNO 1632.

And underneath, in letters about half the size, is the legend,

God blis the Hammermen of Magdalen Chapel.

The bell is still rung, though not for the objects detailed in the will of Janet Rhynd, and in 1641 it was used to summon the congregation of the Greyfriars, who paid for its use £40 Scots yearly.

When the distinguished Reformer John Craig returned to Scotland at the Reformation—escaping from Rome on the very day before he was to perish in a great *auto-da-fe*—after an absence of twenty-four years, he preached for some time in this chapel in the Latin language, to a select congregation of the learned, being unable from long disuse to hold forth in the Scottish tongue. He was subsequently appointed colleague to John Knox, and is distinguished in history for having defied even Bothwell, by refusing to publish the banns of his marriage with Mary, and also for having written the National Covenant of 1589.

The General Assembly of 1578 met in the Magdalene Chapel, and on the 30th of June, 1685, the headless body of the Earl of Argyle—whose skull was placed on the north gable of the Tolbooth —was deposited here, prior to its conveyance to Kilmun—the tomb of the Campbells—in Argyleshire.

Among the sculpture above the door of the chapel there remains an excellent figure of an Edinburgh hammerman of 1555 in the costume of the period, in doublet and trunk-breeches, with peaked beard and moustache, with a hammer in his right hand. The arms of the corporation are *azure*, a hammer proper, ensigned with the imperial crown.

St. Eligius, Bishop and Confessor, was the patron of the Edinburgh hammermen ; but, as the Scots always followed the French mode and terms, he has always been known as St. Eloi, whose altar in St. Giles's Church was the property of the corporation. It was the most eastern of the chapels in that ancient fane. The keystone of this chapel alone is preserved. It is a richly-sculptured boss formed of four dragons with distended wings, each different in design. The centre is formed by a large flower, in which is inserted the iron hook, whereat hung the votive lamp over the altar of St. Eloi, who is referred to in all the historical documents of the corporation.[*] According to the Bollandists, he had been a goldsmith early in life, and became master of the Mint to Clotaire II., on some of whose gold coins his name appears. He died Bishop of Noyon about 659, and Kincaid in his history (1794) says that in the Hammermen's Hall a relic of him is shown, " called St. Eloi's gown." This was probably some garment which had clothed a statue.

The chapel proper has latterly become the property of the Protestant Institute of Scotland, whose chambers are close by at 17, George IV. Bridge.

It is impossible to quit this locality without some

* An engraving of this keystone will be found on p. 147, Vol. I.

reference to those trades which form the United Incorporation of Hammermen, and to the old city companies and trades in general.

"The Hammerer's Seill of Cause," was issued on the 2nd May, 1483, by Sir Patrick Baron of Spittalfield, Knight, Provost of the City, Patrick Balbirnie of that ilk, David Crawford of St. Giles's Grange, and Archibald Todrig, being bailies ; and under the general name are included at that time, blacksmiths, goldsmiths, lorimers, saddlers, cutlers, buckler-makers, armourers, "and all others within the said burgh of Edinburgh." Pewterers were afterwards included, and a heckle-maker so lately as 1609. By the rule of the corporation it was statute and ordained, that "na hammerman, maister, feitman, servand, nor utheris, tak vpon hand fra this tyme furth, to exercise or use ony mair craftis but alanerly ane, and to live thairupon, sua that his brether craftismen be not hurt throu his large exercitation and exceeding of boundis," &c. And all the privileges of the hammermen were ratified by Act of Parliament so recently as September, 1681, when shearsmiths appear as members of the corporation. In those days all the operations of industry were treated as secrets. Each trade was a *craft*, and those who followed it were called craftsmen ; and skilled artisans were "cunning men." (Smiles.)

The Hammermen's seal bears the effigy of St. Eloi, in apostolical vestments, in a church porch surmounted by five pinnacles, holding in one hand a hammer, and in the other a key, with the legend, "*Sigillum commune artis tudiatorum.*"

By the end of the 16th century the manufacture of offensive weapons predominated over all other trades in the city. The *essay-piece* of a cutler, prior to his admission to the corporation, was a well-finished "quhinzier," or sword ; and there were gaird-makers, whose business consisted in fashioning the hilts ; dalmascars, who gilded weapons and armour. In 1582 sword blades were damascened at Edinburgh ; but "Hew Vans, dalmascar, was ordained not to buy blades to sell again," his business being confined to gilding steel. There were also the belt-makers, who wrought military girdles ; dag-makers, who made hackbutts (short guns), and dags, or pistols ; but all these various trades became associated in the general one of armourers or gunsmiths, as the wearing of weapons began to fall into desuetude, and other arts connected with civilisation and luxury began to take their places.

In 1586 a locksmith is first found in Edinburgh, where he was the only one, and could only make a "kist-lock." Tirling-pins, wooden latches, and transom bars, were the appurtenances of doors before his time generally. But by 1609, "as the security of property increased," says Chambers, "the essay was a kist-lock and a hing and bois lock with ane double plate lock ;" and, in 1644, "a key and sprent band were added to the essay." In 1682 "a cruik and cruik band" were further added ; and in 1728, for the safety of the lieges, the locksmiths' essay was appointed to be "a cruik and cruik-band, a pass-lock with a round filled bridge, not cut or broke in the backside, with nobs and jamb bound." The trade of a shearsmith appears first in 1595 in Edinburgh, and in 1613 Thomas Duncan, the first tinkler in the city was admitted a hammerman. The trade of a pewterer is found as far back as 1588 ; the first knock-maker (or clockmaker) appears in 1647, but his business was so limited that he added thereto the making of locks. ("Traditions of Edin.") In 1664 the first white iron smith was admitted a hammerman, and the first harness-maker, though lorimers—manufacturers of the iron-work used in saddlery—were members since 1483. The first maker of surgical instruments in Edinburgh was Paul Martin, a French Protestant refugee, in 1691. In 1720 the first pin-maker appears ; and in 1764 the first edge-tool maker, and the first manufacturer of fish-hooks.

By the first charter of the hammermen all applicants for admission were examined by the deacons and masters of their respective arts, as to their qualifications ; and any member found guilty of a breach of any one of the articles contained in their charter, was fined eight shillings Scots towards the support of the corporation's altar of St. Eloi in St. Giles's Church and the chaplain thereof. The goldsmiths were separated from the hammermen in 1581 ; but since then many other crafts have joined them, including gunsmiths, watchmakers, founders, braziers, and coppersmiths.

The cordiners, or shoemakers, were first created into a society by the magistrates on the 28th of July, 1449 (according to Maitland), in terms of which each master of the trade who kept a booth within the town, paid one penny Scots, and their servants one halfpenny, towards the support of their altar of St. Crispin, in St. Giles's Church. A new seal of cause was granted to them in 1509, and another in 1586, which enacted that their shops were not to be open on Sundays after 9 A.M., and that no work was to be done on that day under pain of twenty shillings fine. It also regulated the days of the week on which leather boots and shoes could be sold by strangers in booths. This charter was confirmed on 6th March, 1598, by James VI., in consideration of "the goodwill and thankful service done to us by our servitor, Alexander Crawford, present deacon of the said cordiners and his brethren." We first hear of a kind of "strike," in the trade in 1768, when the cordiners entered into a combination not to work without an increase of wages, and reduction of hours. The masters prosecuted their men, many of whom were fined and imprisoned, for "entering into an unlawful combination," as the sheriff termed their trade union.

under the paine of confiscation of the same for His Majesty's use." Edinburgh has always been the chief seat of the leather trade in Scotland, and the troops raised after the American War were entirely supplied with shoes from there.

In 1475 the wrights and masons were granted the aisle and chapel of St. John in the same church, when their seal of cause was issued. Their charter was confirmed in 1517 by the Archbishop of St. Andrews, in 1527 by James V., and in 1635 by

THE CHAPEL AND HOSPITAL OF ST. MARY MAGDALENE. (*After an Etching published in 1816.*)

The skinners would seem to have been created into a corporation in 1474, but references to the trade occur in the Burgh Records at an earlier date. Thus, in 1450, there is recorded an obligation by the skinners, undertaken by William Skynner, in the name of the whole, to support the altar of St. Crispin in St. Giles's Church, "in the fourth year of the pontificate of Nicholas the Fifth;" and a seal of cause was issued to the skinners and furriers conjointly in 1533, wherein they were bound to uphold the shrine of St. Christopher in St. Giles's, and several Acts of Parliament were passed for their protection. One, in 1592, prohibits "all transporting and carrying forth the realm, of calves-skinnes, huddrones, and kidskins, packing and peilling thereof, in time coming,

Charles I. In 1703, by decree of the Court of Session, the bow-makers, plumbers, and glaziers, were added to the masons; and to the wrights were added the painters, slaters, sieve-wrights, and coopers. These incorporated trades held their meetings in St. Mary's Chapel, Niddry's Wynd, and were known as "The United Incorporation of St. Mary's Chapel."

In 1476 the websters were incorporated, and bound to uphold the altar of St. Simon in St. Giles's, and it was specially stipulated that "the priest shall get his meat." Cloth was made in those days by the weavers much in the same fashion that is followed in the remote Highland districts, where the wool is carded and spun by the females of the household; but Edinburgh was one of the first places where woollen goods were made, and had, at one time, the most important wool market in Britain.

The hatmakers were formed into a corporation in 1473, when ten masters of the craft presented a petition to that effect; but the bonnet-makers did not receive their seal of cause till 1530, prior to which they had been united with the walkers and shearers, with whom they were bound to uphold the altar of St. Mark in St. Giles's Church. In

the articles and conditions it contained; but it is said that a seal was issued. In 1508, Thomas Greg, "Kirk-master of the flescheour craft," on behalf of the same, brought before the Council a complaint, that certain persons, not freemen of the craft or the burgh, interfered with their privileges, and had them forbidden to sell meat, except on Sunday and Monday, the free market days, "quhill thai obtene thair fredome."

The coopers were incorporated in 1489, binding

INTERIOR OF THE CHAPEL OF ST. MARY MAGDALENE.

1685 an Act of Parliament confirmed all their privileges, together with those of the litsters, or dyers. About the middle of the seventeenth century, owing to the spread of the use of hats, instead of the national bonnet, among the upper classes, this society was reduced to so low a condition that its members could neither support their families or the expense of a society.

The fleshers were a very old corporation, but the precise date of their charter is not very clear. In 1483 regulations concerning the fleshers dealing in fish in Lent, &c., were issued by the magistrates, whom they petitioned in 1488 for a seal of cause, which petition was taken into consideration by the Council, who ratified and confirmed the whole of

themselves to uphold the altar of St. John in St. Giles's Church.

The walkers obtained their seal of cause in August, 1500. They had an altar in the same church dedicated to SS. Mark, Philip, and Jacob, to which the following among other fees were paid :—

Each master, on taking an apprentice paid ten shillings Scots; and on any master taking into his service, either the apprentice or journeyman of any other master, he paid twenty shillings Scots; if any craftsman was found working with cards in the country, he was to forfeit the sum of fifteen shillings Scots, to be equally divided between the work of St. Giles's, their altar, and the informer. It is also provided by the said charter, that each person commencing business for himself shall be worth three pairs of shears, and of ability to pay for one stock of white cloth, whereby he may be in a condition to make good any damages to those who employ him.

In the same year (1500) the tailors were incorporated on the 26th August, prior to which, as a society, they possessed the altar of St. Anne in St. Giles's, and they only had their old rules and regulations embodied in their charter from the Council. Another seal of cause was issued to them thirty years afterwards, in the reign of James V.

The Corporation of Candlemakers first appears in 1517. They had no altar of their own in St. Giles's, but certain fines provided by their charter were to be paid towards the sustenance of any "misterfull alter within the College Kirk of Sanct Geils." The craftsmen were forbidden to send boys or servants to sell candles in the streets, under pain of forfeit, and paying "ane pund of walx to Our Lady altar, after the first fault;" two pounds of wax for the second, and such punishment as the magistrates may award for the third. No member was to take an apprentice for less than four years, and all women were to be "expellit the said craft, bot freemennis wyffes of the craft allanerlie."

The above charter was confirmed by James VI. in 1597, though the corporation lost the privilege in 1582 of sending a member to the Common Council, by failing to produce their charter, and signing the reference made in that year to the arbiters appointed by James, at the time the late constitution of the burgh was established, and remained unchanged till the passing of the Reform Bill in 1832.

We may here mention that a manufactory for soap is first mentioned, 23rd November, 1554, when the magistrates granted a "license to Johnne Gaittis, Inglisman, to brew saip within the fredome of this burgh for the space of ane yeir nixt heirafter;" and to sell the same in lasts, half-lasts, barrels, half-barrels, and firkins. But after this, till about 1621, it was chiefly imported from Flanders.

The Baxters (or bakers) obtained their charter on the 20th of March, 1522, but the trade must have possessed one before, as it sets forth that in times of trouble the original document had been lost. By this seal of cause it appears that they had in St. Giles's an altar dedicated to "Sanct Cubart." But the chaplain thereof, instead of being supported by fines, as the priests of the other corporations were, obtained his food by going from house to house among the members of the guild in rotation.

The sole privilege of baking bread within the city was vested in its members, but bread baked without the walls might be sold, the corporation having, however, control over it, or the power of examining the weight and quality of "the flour baiks and fadges that cumes fra landwart into this toune to sell."

The city records contain many references to the Baxters before the date above given. Thus in 1443, the time when they might bake and sell "mayne breid," was only at "Whitsunday, St. Giles's Mass, Yule and Pasche." In 1482, in buying flour from beyond the sea they were to pay multure, as if from the common mills. In 1503 Baxters convicted of baking cakes that were under weight were threatened with penalties. In 1510 there was an agreement between the farmers of the city mills and the Baxters as to grinding at the mills, with reference to the quantities to be ground when water was scarce. In 1523 the Baxters were ordained to "baik thair breid sufficientlie and weill dryit;" the twopenny loaf to weigh ten ounces from thenceforward, "under pain of tynsale of their fredome," and escheat of the bread, which is to be marked with their irons as heretofore. In April, 1548, the city Baxters were ordered to furnish bread for the army in the field at a given rate, and the corporation promised to do so, in the presence of the Lords Dunkeld, Rothes, Galloway, Dunfermline, and Seaton; but in July the troops would seem to have declined to receive the bread which the trade had on hand; thus "outland Baxters were charged not to bring any bread to market for three days."

We have elsewhere (Vol. I., 382-3) had occasion to refer to the Corporation of Barber-surgeons, whose charter, dated 1st July, 1505, binds them to "uphold ane altar in the College Kirk of Sanct Geill, in honour of God and Sanct Mongow." They were bound to know something of anatomy, the "nature and complexioun of every member of humanis (sic) body," and all the veins of the same, and "in quhilk member the *signe has domination for the time*," &c.

In 1542 we read of four surgeons sent from the city to the borders, for the care of those wounded by the English. ("Pitcairn's Trials," I.) And in 1558 the corporation sent twenty-five of their number, including apprentices, to join the force raised for the defence of Edinburgh against "our auld inemyes of Ingland." ("List of Fellows, R.C.S. Edin.") By Queen Mary they were exempted from serving on assizes.

The arms of this corporation were azure, on a fesse argent, a naked man fesse-ways, between a dexter hand palmed, and in its palm an eye. In the dexter canton, a saltire argent, under the imperial crown, surmounted by a thistle ; and in base a castle argent, masoned sable, within a border, charged with instruments used by the society. To the surgeons were added the apothecaries.

James IV., one of the greatest patrons of art and science in his time, dabbled a little in surgery and chemistry, and had an assistant, John the Leeche, whom he brought from the Continent. Pitscottie tells us that James was "ane singular guid chirurgione," and in his daily expense book, singular entries occur in 1491, of payments made to people to let him bleed them and pull their teeth :—

"Item, to ane fallow, because the King pullit furtht his twtht, xviii shillings.

"Item, to Kynnard, ye barbour, for tua teith drawin furtht of his hed be the King, xviii sh."

The barbers were frequently refractory, and brought the surgeons into the Court of Session to adjust rights, real or imagined. But after the union of the latter with the apothecaries, they gave up the barber craft, and were formed into one corporation by an Act of Council, on the 25th February, 1657, as already mentioned in the account of the old Royal College of Surgeons.

The first admitted after the change, was Christopher Irving, recorded as "ane free chirurgone," without the usual words "and barber," after his name. He was physician to James VII., and from him the Irvings of Castle Irving, in Ireland, are descended.

CHAPTER XXXIII.
THE SOCIETY.

The Candlemaker Row—The "Cunzie Nook"—Time of Charles I.—The Candlemakers' Hall—The Affair of Dr. Symons—The Society, 1598—Brown Square—Proposed Statue to George III., 1764—Distinguished Inhabitants—Sir Islay Campbell—Lord Glenlee—Haig of Beimerside—Sir John Leslie—Miss Jeannie Elliot—Argyle Square—Origin of it—Dr. Hugh Blair—The Sutties of that Ilk—Trades Maiden Hospital—Minto-House and the Elliots—New Medical School—Baptist Church—Chambers Street—Industrial Museum of Science and Art—Its Great Hall and adjoining Halls—Aim of the Architect—Contents and Models briefly glanced at—New Watt Institution and School of Arts—Phrenological Museum—New Free Tron Church—New Training College of the Church of Scotland—The Dental Hospital—The Theatre of Varieties.

THE Candlemaker Row is simply the first portion of the old way that led from the Grassmarket and Cowgate-head, where Sir John Inglis resided in 1784, to the lands of Bristo, and thence on to Powburn ; and it was down this way that a portion of the routed Flemings, with Guy of Namur at their head, fled towards the Castle rock, after their defeat on the Burghmuir in 1335.

In Charles I.'s time a close line of street with a great open space behind occupied the whole of the east side, from the Greyfriars Port to the Cowgate-head. The west side was the boundary wall of the churchyard, save at the foot, where two or three houses appear in 1647, one of which, as the Cunzie Nook, is no doubt that referred to by Wilson as "a curious little timber-fronted tenement, surmounted with antique crow-steps ; an open gallery projects in front, and rude little shot-windows admit the light to the decayed and gloomy chambers therein." This, we presume, to be the Cunzie Nook, a place where the Mint had no doubt been established at some early period, possibly during some of the strange proceedings in the Regency of Mary of Guise, when the Lords of the Congregation "past to Holyroodhous, and tuik and intromettit with the ernis of the Cunzehous."

On the west side, near the present entrance to the churchyard of the Greyfriars, stands the hall of the ancient Corporation of the Candlemakers, which gave its name to the Row, with the arms of the craft boldly cut over the doorway, on a large oblong panel, and, beneath, their appropriate motto,

Omnia manifesta luce.

Internally, the hall is subdivided into m residences, smaller accommodation sufficing for the fraternity in this age of gas, so that it exists little more than in name. In 1847 the number of its members amounted to only *three*, who met periodically for various purposes, connected with the corporation and its funds.

Edgar's plan shows, in the eighteenth century, the close row of houses that existed along the whole of the west side, from the Bristo Port to the foot, and nearly till Forrest Road was opened up in a line with the central Meadow Walk.

Humble though this locality may seem now, Sir James Dunbar, Bart., of Durn, rented No. 21 in 1810, latterly a carting office. In those days the street was a place of considerable bustle ; the Hawick dilligence started twice weekly from Paterson's Inn, a well-known hostel in its time, and weekly thirty-two carriers put up in the same quarter.

In that year the Candlemaker's Row was the scene of a tragedy that excited great attention at the time—the slaughter of a noted ruffian named John Boyd, an inhabitant of the street, by Dr. Symons of the 51st or Edinburgh Regiment of Militia, on the night of the 2nd August, for which, after being out on bail under £500, he was brought before the High Court of Justiciary on a charge of murder.

It would appear that about midnight Dr. Symons, after being at a dinner-party in Buccleuch Place, was on his way through the Row to the Castle, accompanied by Lieutenant Ronaldson of the same regiment, when opposite Paterson's Inn they were attacked by two men, one of whom, a notorious disturber of the peace, struck the doctor a blow behind the neck, and subsequently attempted to wrest his sword away, knocking him down and kicking him at the same time.

Staggering to his feet, and burning with rage, the doctor drew his sword and pursued his assailant down the Row to Merchant Street, when a fresh struggle ensued, and Boyd was run through the body and left bleeding in the gutter, where he was found dead, while the doctor was totally ignorant that he had injured him so severely. The generally infamous character of the deceased being proved, the Lord Justice Clerk, Charles Hope, summed up to the effect, " that the charge of murder was by no means brought home to the prisoner ; that what he had done was altogether in self-defence, and the natural impulse of the moment, from being attacked, beaten, knocked down, and grievously insulted." The jury returned a verdict of "Not Guilty," and the doctor was dismissed from the bar, and lived long years after as a practitioner in the country.

TABLET ON THE CHAPEL OF ST. MARY MAGDALENE.
(From a Photograph by Alexander A. Inglis.)

In the open space referred to, eastward of Candlemaker Row, Gordon of Rothiemay shows us (see p. 261) the ancient buildings known as the Society, forming an oblong quadrangle, lying east and west, with open ground to the north and south, the former sloping down to the Cowgate, and planted with trees. These buildings, the last of which —a curiously picturesque group, long forming the south-east quarter of what was latterly Brown Square — were only removed when Chambers Street was made in 1871, and were built by a society of brewers established in 1598.

It was built upon a piece of ground that belonged of old to the convent of Sienna (at the Sciennes), and was a corporation for the brewing of ale and beer, commodities which have ever been foremost among the staple productions of Edinburgh, and the name of "Society" accorded to that quarter, remained as a tradition of the ancient company long after it had passed away. An Englishman who visited Edinburgh in 1598, wrote :—" The Scots drink pure wines, not with sugar as the English ; yet at feasts they put comfits in the wine, after the French manner, but they had not our vintners' fraud to mix their wines. I did never see nor hear that they have any public inns ; but the better sort of citizens brew ale, their usual drink, which will distemper a stranger's body."

The usual allowance of ale at table then, was a chopin, equal to about an imperial pint, to each person. Though Edinburgh ale is still famous, private brewing is no longer practised.

A curious fragment of the old town wall was built into the southern edifices of the Society, and portions of them may remain, where an old established inn once stood, long known as the *Hole in the Wall.*

In this quarter a fashionable boarding-school for young ladies was established in the middle of the last century by Mrs. Janet Murray, widow of Archibald Campbell, collector of the customs at Prestonpans. She died in the Society in 1770, and the establishment was then conducted by her friends under the name of " Mrs. Murray's Boarding School."

To those who remember it in its latter days the locality seems a strange one for a young ladies'

Dykes. This might have been prevented had the magistrates contrived to acquire a piece of ground south of the Old Town, which was offered to them for only £1,200, but which was purchased by a builder and architect named George Brown, a brother of Brown of Lindsaylands and Elliston. He was the projector and builder of George Square, and also built the large house of Bellevue (for General Scott of Balcomie), which stood so long in Drummond Place.

THE CUNZIE HOUSE, CANDLEMAKER ROW, 1850.   (*From a Drawing by William Channing.*)

school; but Lord Hailes, after removing from Todrig's Wynd, occupied a house in "The Society," before locating himself in New Street.

Brown Square, now nearly swept away, was a small oblong place, about 200 feet east and west, by 150 north and south. During the long delay which took place between the first project of having a New Town, and building a bridge that was to lead to it, a rival town began to spring up in another quarter, which required neither a bridge nor an Act of Parliament, nor even the unanimity of several interested proprietors to mature it, and it soon became important enough to counteract for some years the extension by the ridge of the Lang

On the ground acquired so cheaply he proceeded at once to erect, in 1763-4, houses that were deemed fine mansions, and found favour with the upper classes, before a stone of the New Town was laid. Repenting of their mistake, the magistrates offered Mr. Brown £2,000 for the ground; but he, perceiving the success of his scheme, demanded £20,000, so the city relinquished the idea. The square was quickly finished on nearly three sides, including the Society, and one old mansion having an octagon turnpike stair, dated 1718, at the north-east corner next Crombie's Close, and became filled with inhabitants of a good class while George Square rose collaterally with it.

Till about 1780 the inhabitants of these districts formed a distinct class of themselves, and had their own places of amusement, independent of all the rest of the city. Nor was it until the New Town was rather far advanced that the *south side* lost its attractions; and we are told that, singular as it may appear, there was one instance, if not more, of a gentleman living and dying in this southern district without having once visited, or even seen, the New Town, although at the time of his death it had extended westward to Castle Street. (Scott's " Provincial Antiquities.")

In the notes to " Redgauntlet," the same author tells us, that in its time Brown Square was hailed "as an extremely elegant improvement " on Edinburgh residences, even with its meagre plot of grass and shabby iron railings. It is here he places the house of Saunders Fairford, where Alan is described as first beholding the mysterious *Lady Greenmantle*, and as being so bewildered with her appearance, that he stood as if he had been senseless. " The door was opened, out she went, walked along the pavement, turned down the close (at the north-east end of the square leading into the Cowgate), and put the sun, I believe, into her pocket when she disappeared, so suddenly did dulness and darkness sink down on the square when she was no longer visible."

To show how much this new locality was thought of, we will here quote a letter in the *Edinburgh Advertiser* of 6th March, 1764 (Vol. I.) :—

" Sir,—With pleasure I have observed of late the improvements we are making in this metropolis, and there is nothing which pleases me more than the taste for elegant buildings, than which nothing can be a greater ornament to a city, or give a stranger a greater impression of the improvement of the inhabitants in polite and liberal arts.

" That very elegant square, called Brown Square, which, in my opinion, is a very great beauty to the town, is now almost finished, and last day the green pasture was railed in. Now, I think, to complete the whole, an elegant statue in the middle would be well worth the expense; and I dare say the gentlemen who possess houses there would not grudge a small sum to have that part adorned with an equestrian statue of his present Majesty George the Third, and which I should think, would be contributed to by public subscriptions, set a-foot for that purpose. While we are thus making such improvements, I am surprised nobody has ever mentioned an improvement on our College [the old one was then extant] which, as it now is, gives strangers but an unfavourable idea of our University, which, however, is at present so

flourishing. . . . . To have a handsome building for that purpose is surely the desire of every good citizen. This could be easily accomplished by various means. Suppose a lottery should be proposed, every student I dare say would take a ticket, and I would venture to ensure the success of it."

But George III. was fated not to have a statue either in Brown Square or Great King Street, according to a suggestion some sixty years afterwards ; yet as a proof that the square was deemed alike fashionable and elegant, we may enumerate some of those who resided there. Among them were the Dowager Lady Elphinstone (daughter of John sixth Earl of Wigton) who had a house here in 1784 ; Henry Dundas (afterwards Viscount Melville), when a member of the Faculty of Advocates ; Sir Islay Campbell, Bart., of Succoth, in the days when it was the custom of the senators to walk to court in the morning, with nicely powdered wigs, and a small cocked hat in the hand—a practice retained nearly to the last by Lord Glenlee : he was afterwards Lord President. He bought Lord Melville's house in Brown Square, and after a time removed to York Place.

His successor in the same residence, No. 15, was John Anstruther of that ilk, Advocate, with whom resided the family of Charles Earl of Traquair, whose mother was a daughter of Sir Philip Anstruther of Anstrutherfield. Other residents were Lord Henderland and the future Lord President Blair of Avontoun, both when at the bar, and William Craig, afterwards a Lord of Justiciary in 1792 ; Sir John Forbes-Drummond, when a captain of the Royal Navy, and before he became Baronet of Hawthornden ; Henry Mackenzie, the ubiquitous " Man of Feeling ; " Lord Woodhouselee, and the Lord President Miller, whose residence was the large house (No. 17) with the painted front, on the north side, the interior of which, with its frescoes and panelings, is now one of the finest specimens remaining of a fashionable Edinburgh mansion of the eighteenth century ; and therein lived and died his son Lord Glenlee, who (*ultimus Scotorum !*) resisted the attraction of three successive New Towns, to which all his brethren had long before fled.

He retained, until within a few years of his death, the practice referred to, of walking daily to Court, hat in hand, with a powdered wig, through Brown Square, down Crombie's Close, across the Cowgate, and up the Back Stairs to the Parliament House, attended by his valet, and always scrupulously dressed in black. In 1838, when nearly eighty years of age, this grand lord of the old school, was compelled to have recourse to a sedan chair by which he was wont to be carried to Court by George IV. Bridge. He died in No. 17, in 1846, surviving for thirty-one years the death of his favourite and lamented son, Colonel William Miller of the 1st Foot Guards, who fell mortally wounded at Quatre Bras.

No. 3 was the residence, in 1811, of James Haig, of Beimerside and that ilk, who is mentioned in the "Minstrelsy of the Scottish Border," with reference to the old prophecy said to have been made by Thomas the Rhymer, that,

"Tide tide, whatever betide,
There 'll aye be a Haig in Beimerside."

The family have possessed the estate for many centuries. "The grandfather of the present proprietor of Beimerside," wrote Scott in 1802, "had twelve daughters before his lady brought him a male heir. The common people trembled for their favourite soothsayer. The late Mr. Haig was at length born, and their belief in the prophecy confirmed beyond the shadow of a doubt."

No. 14 was the residence of stout and portly Sir John Leslie, Bart., K.H., Professor of Natural History in the University, the celebrated mathematician, the successor of Playfair, who died in 1832; and though mentioned last, not least, this now nearly defunct square held the residence of Miss Jeannie Elliot, authoress, about the middle of the last century, of the song "The Flowers of the Forest," who is said to have composed it in consequence of a wager with her brother that she could not write a ballad on the subject of Flodden as they were driving homeward one evening in the carriage. "Yielding," says the biographer of the "Songstresses of Scotland," "to the influence of the moment, Jean accepted the challenge. Leaning back in her corner with all the most mournful stories of the country-side for her inspiration, and two lines of an old ballad which had often rung in her ears and trembled on her lips for a foundation, she planned and constructed the rude framework of her 'Flowers of the Forest,' in imitation of the older song to the same air."

Miss Elliot of Minto dwelt on the first floor of a house beside the archway or pend which gave access to Brown Square from the Candlemaker Row, in the south-west corner, opposite the Greyfriars' Gate. She spent the latter part of her life chiefly in Edinburgh, where she mingled a good deal in the better sort of society. "I have been told," says Chambers in his "Scottish Songs," "by one who was admitted in youth to the privileges of her conversation, that she was a remarkably

agreeable old lady, with a prodigious fund of Scottish anecdote, but did not appear to have been handsome." Miss Tytler describes her, when advanced in years, to have been a little delicate old woman, in a close cap, ruffle, and ample snow-white neckerchief; her eyebrows well arched, but having a nose and mouth that belonged to an expressive, rather than a handsome face. She generally went abroad in a sedan.

Eastward of this quarter lay Argyle Square (now swept away to make room for Chambers Street), an open area of 150 feet long, by the same in breadth, including the front gardens of the houses on the north side. The houses were all massive, convenient, and not inelegant, and in some instances, three storeys in height. The exact date of its being built seems doubtful, tradition takes it back nearly to 1730, and it is said to have been named from the following circumstances :—A tailor named Campbell having got into the graces of his chief, the great John Duke of Argyle and Greenwich, was promised the first favour that peer's acquaintance or interest might throw in his way. Accordingly, on the death of George I., the Duke having early intelligence of the event, let his clansman, the tailor, instantly know it, and the latter, before his brethren in the trade were aware, bought up all the black cloth in the city, and forthwith drove such a trade in supplying the zealous Whigs with mourning suits at his own prices, that he shortly realised a little fortune, wherewith he laid the foundation of a greater.

He began to build the first houses of this square, and named it Argyle in honour of his patron, and much of it appears to have been finished when Edgar drew his first plan of the city in 1742. In the plan of 1765 the whole of the south side was still called Campbell's New Buildings. But prior to any edifice being erected here, a retired bookseller of the Parliament Close, who had once been Lord Provost, built himself a mansion in what he deemed a very rustic and suburban quarter, at the head of Scott's Close, latterly used as a ministers' hall. Prior to that, and after the Provost's death, it had been the family mansion of Sir Andrew Agnew of Lochnaw.

Lord Cullen dwelt here in a flat above what was in 1824 a grocery store; and in the central house, on the north side, lived Dr. Hugh Blair, the eminent divine and sermon writer, one of the greatest ornaments of the Scottish Church and of his native capital; and in that house (when he was Professor of Rhetoric) died his wife, on the 9th February, 1795; she was his cousin Catharine, daughter of the Rev. James Bannatyne, a city minister.

Many professors succeeded Blair as tenants of the same house; among them, Alexander Christison, Professor of Humanity, between 1806 and 1820, father of the great chemist, Professor Sir Robert Christison, Bart.

In the north-western extremity of the square was the mansion of Sir George Suttie, Bart. of that ilk, and Balgone in Haddingtonshire, who married Janet, daughter of William Grant, Lord

the two squares which was described as prevailing in their amusements—tea-drinking and little fêtes at a time when manners in Edinburgh were starched, stately, and old-fashioned, as the customs and ideas that were retained, when dying out elsewhere.

On the east side of this square was the old Trades Maiden Hospital, a plain substantial edifice, consisting of a central block, having a great arched door, to which a flight of steps ascended,

OLD HOUSES, SOCIETY, 1852. (*From a Drawing by George W. Simson.*)

Prestongrange; and here also resided his son, Sir James, who, in 1818, succeeded his aunt, Janet Grant, Countess of Hyndford, as heir of the line of Prestongrange, and assumed thereby in consequence the additional name and arms of Grant. Their neighbour was Lady Mary Cochrane, daughter of Thomas sixth Earl of Dundonald, who died unmarried at an old age.

In 1795 among the residents in Argyle Square were Sir John Dalrymple, the Ladies Rae, Sutton (dowager), and Reay, Elizabeth Fairlie (dowager of George Lord Reay, who died in 1768). Isolated from the rising New Town on the north by the great mass of the ancient city, and viewing it with a species of antagonism and rivalry, we may well imagine the exclusiveness of the little coteries in

and wings, with a frontage of about 150 feet. It was intended for the daughters of decayed tradesmen, and was a noble institution, founded in 1704 by the charitable Mrs. Mary Erskine, the liberal contributor to the Merchant Maiden Hospital, and who was indeed the joint foundress of both.

In 1794 fifty girls were maintained in the hospital, paying £1 13s. 4d. on entrance, and receiving when they left it a bounty of £5 16s. 6½d., for then its revenue amounted to only £600 per annum. In the process of making Chambers Street this edifice was demolished, and the institution removed to Rillbank near the Meadows.

It stood immediately opposite Minto House, a handsome and spacious edifice on the north side of the square, forty-five feet square, on the slope down towards the Cowgate, surrounded by trees, and recessed back, within, latterly, a pillared carriage entrance, ninety feet from the line of the street.

This was the first town lodging of the family of Lord Minto, whose race were wont of old to take their share in the rough moss-trooping work of the Borders, but changed with the new world of things. Sir Gilbert Elliot, when constituted a senator in

"And had it no been for *me*, Willie," retorted Lord Minto, "the pyets wad hae pyked your pow on the Netherbow Port."

He was succeeded by his son Sir Gilbert, who was also bred to the bar, and on being appointed Lord Justice Clerk, assumed the title of Minto, and died in 1766. His son, the third baronet, was a man of considerable political and literary abilities, and filled several high official situations.

THE FIRST TRADES MAIDEN HOSPITAL. (*After Storer and Shepherd.*)

1705, assumed the title of Lord Minto. He had made his hit at the bar in rescuing William Veitch, a Covenanting minister, from the Scottish Government, in the last days of the persecution, and is said to have had a hand in the escape of the Earl of Argyle from his captivity in Edinburgh; however, he was compelled to take refuge in Holland; but with the Revolution came the days of change, and seventeen years subsequent thereto he found himself on the bench. On the Dumfries circuit he met his old client Veitch, then a parish minister, and they playfully reverted to the terrible times of the past.

"Had it no been for me, my lord," said Veitch, "ye 'd been writing papers yet, at a plack a page."

83

He was author of the well-known pastoral beginning, in the affected style peculiar to his day—

"My sheep I neglected, I left my sheep-hook,
  And all the gay haunts of my youth I forsook;
  No more for Amynta fresh garlands I wove,
  For ambition, I said, would soon cure me of love;
  Oh! what had my youth with ambition to do,
  Why left I Amynta? why broke I my vow?"

He also wrote a monody on the death of Colonel Gardiner at Prestonpans, which is only singular for being almost the only song of the period not on the Jacobite side. His philosophical correspondence with David Hume is quoted with commendation by Dugald Stewart in "Philosophy of the Human Mind," and in his "Dissertation prefixed to the seventh edition of the Encyclopædia

Britannica." In 1763 he was Treasurer of the Navy, and died at Marseilles in 1777.

For some years after that period Minto House was the residence of Sir William Nairne of Dunsinnan, a Judge of the Court of Session, who removed there from one he had long occupied, before his promotion to the bench, at the head of the Back Stairs, and in which he had lived as Mr. Nairne, at that terrible period of his family history, when his niece, the beautiful Mrs. Ogilvie, was tried and convicted for murder in 1766.

He was the last of his line; and when he died, in 1811, at an advanced age, his baronetcy became extinct, and a nephew, his sister's son, assumed the name and arms of Nairne of Dunsinnan.

The principal entrance to Minto House in those days was from the Horse Wynd, when it was noted chiefly as a remnant of the dull and antiquated grandeur of a former age. It was next divided into a series of small apartments, and let to people in the humblest rank of life. But it was not fated to be devoted long to such uses, for the famous surgeon, Mr. (afterwards Professor) Syme, had it fitted up in 1829 as a surgical hospital for street accidents and other cases. Mr. Syme retained the old name of Minto House, and the surgery and practice acquired a world-wide celebrity. Long the scene of demonstrations and prelections of eminent extra-mural lecturers, it was swept away in the city improvements, and its successor is now included in Chambers Street, and has become the "New Medical School of Minto House," so that the later traditions of the site will be perpetuated.

Among other edifices demolished in Argyle Square, together with the Gaelic Church, was the Meeting House of the Scottish Baptists, seated for 240—one of two sections of that congregation established in 1766.

Proceeding westward, from the broad site of what was once Adam Square, and the other two squares of which we have just given the history, Chambers Street opens before us, a thousand feet in length, with an average of seventy in breadth, extending from the South Bridge to that of George IV.

It was begun in 1871 under the City Improvement Act, and was worthily named in honour of the Lord Provost Chambers, the chief promoter of the new city improvement scheme. With the then old squares it includes the sites of North College Street, and parts of sites of the Horse and College Wynds, and is edificed into four large blocks, three or four storeys high, in ornate examples of the Italian style, with some specimens of the French.

Chambers Street was paved with wooden blocks in 1876, at a cost of nearly £6,000, and on that occasion 322,000 blocks were used.

On the south side three hundred and sixty feet of Chambers Street are occupied by the north front of the University. Over West College Street—of old, the link between the Horse Wynd and Potterrow—is thrown a glass-covered bridge, connecting the University with the Museum of Science and Art, which, when completed, will occupy the remaining 400 feet of the north side to where "The Society"—besides one of Heriot's schools—exists now in name.

This great and noble museum is in the Venetian Renaissance style, from a design by Captain Fowkes of the Royal Engineers. The laying of the foundation-stone of this structure, on the 23rd of October, 1861, was the last public act of His Royal Highness the Prince Consort. It is founded on plans similar to those of the International Exhibition buildings in London, and, by the year 1870, contained—a great hall, 105 feet long, seventy wide, and seventy-seven in height; a hall of natural history, 130 feet long, fifty-seven feet wide, and seventy-seven in height; a south hall, seventy feet long, fifty feet wide, and seventy-seven in height; and two other great apartments. When completed it will be one of the noblest buildings in Scotland.

In 1871-4 the edifice underwent extension, the great hall being increased to the length of 270 feet, and other apartments being added, which, when finished, will have a measurement of 400 feet in length, 200 feet in width, with an average of ninety in height. Already it contains vast collections in natural history, in industrial art, in manufacture, and in matters connected with physical science.

The great aim of the architect has been to have every part well-lighted, and for this purpose a glass roof with open timberwork has been adopted, and the details of the whole structure made as light as possible. Externally the front is constructed of red and white sandstone, and internally a more elaborate kind of decoration has been carried out. Altogether the effect of the building is light, rich, and elegant. In the evenings, when open, it is lighted up by means of horizontal iron rods in the roof studded with gas burners, the number of jets exceeding 5,000.

The great hall or saloon is a singularly noble apartment, with two galleries. The collection of industrial art here comprises illustrations of nearly all the chief manufactures of the British Isles and foreign countries, and the largest collection in the world of the raw products of commerce. It possesses sections for mining and quarrying, for

THE INDUSTRIAL MUSEUM.

1, EXTERIOR; 2, THE GREAT HALL; 3, THE NATURAL HISTORY ROOM.

metallurgy and constructive materials, for ceramic and vitreous manufactures, the decorative arts, textile manufactures, food, education, chemistry, materia medica, photography, &c.

The whole floor is covered with articles illustrative of the arts of construction, such as products of the clay-fields, fire and brick clays, and terra-cottas. Cements and artificial stones stand next in order, followed by illustrations of the mode of quarrying real stone; adjoining these are stones dressed for building purposes, and others carved for ornamental uses.

Oriental stone carving is illustrated by a set of magnificent plaster casts from one of the most famous gates of Delhi, made by order of the Indian Government. The sanitary appliances used in building are likewise exhibited here; also slate and its uses, with materials for surface decorations, and woods for house timber and furniture.

Among the more prominent objects are large models of Scottish lighthouses, presented by the Commissioners of Northern Lights, of St. Peter's at Rome, St. Paul's at London, and the Bourse in Berlin, together with a singularly elegant carton-pierre ceiling ornament, and finely designed mantel-piece, that were originally prepared for Montagu House.

In the centre of the hall are some beautiful specimens of large guns and breechloading field-pieces, with balls and shells, and a fine model of the bridge over the Beulah in Westmoreland.

A hall devoted to the exhibition of flint and clay products, and illustrations of glass and pottery, is in the angle behind the great and east saloons. The art potteries of Lambeth are here represented by beautiful vases and plaques, made by the same articles in the style of old Flemish stoneware. There are also fine examples of the French *faïence*, by Deck of Paris, including a splendid dish painted by Anker, and very interesting samples of Persian pottery as old as the fourteenth century.

There is a magnificent collection of Venetian glass, comprising nearly 400 pieces, made by the Abbot Zanetti of Murano, in Lombardy; while modern mosaic work is exemplified by a beautiful reredos by Salviati, representing the Last Supper. The beauty of ancient tile work is here exhibited in some exquisite fragments from Constantinople. These formed, originally, part of the several decorations of the mosque of Broussa, in Anatolia, which was destroyed by an earthquake. In rich blue on a white ground they display a variety of curious conceptions, one of which represents the human soul shooting aloft as a tall cypress tree, while good and evil spirits, under the

guise of various animals, seek to aid or hinder its ascent.

Near these are placed, first, illustrations of colliery work, then of metallurgical operations, and lastly, the manufacture of metals. The first, or lower gallery of this hall, contains specimens of the arts in connection with clothing, and the textile fabrics generally and their processes; wood, silk, cotton, hemp, linen, jute, felt, silk, and straw-hat making, leather, fur, and also manufactures from bone, ivory, horn, tortoise-shell, feathers, hair-gut, gutta-percha, india-rubber, &c.; and the upper gallery contains the collection illustrative of chemistry, the chemical arts, materia medica, and philosophical instruments.

The department of machinery contains a specimen, presented by the inventor, of Lister's wool-combing machine, which, by providing the means of combing long wools mechanically, effected an enormous change in the worsted trade of Yorkshire. *

In the front of the east wing is the lecture room, having accommodation for 800 sitters. Above it is a large apartment, seventy feet in length by fifty broad, containing a fine display of minerals and fossils. One of the most interesting features in this department is the large and valuable collection of fossils which belonged to Hugh Miller.

The ethnological specimens are ranged in hand-some cases around the walls. The natural history hall contains on its ground floor a general collection of mammalia, including a complete grouping of British animals. The first gallery contains an ample collection of birds and shells, &c.; the upper gallery, reptiles and fishes. In the hall is suspended the skeleton of a whale seventy-nine feet in length.

On the north side of Chambers Street is the new Watt Institution and School of Arts, erected in lieu of that of which we have already given a history in Adam Square. (Vol. I., pp. 379, 380.) It was erected in 1872-3 from designs by David Rhind, and is two storeys in height, with a pavilion at its west end, and above its entrance porch the handsome statue of James Watt which stood in the demolished square.

Beside this institution stands the Phrenological Museum, on the north side, forming a conjoint building with it, and containing a carefully assorted collection of human skulls some of them being of great antiquity. It was formerly in Surgeon Square, High School Yard.

The new Free Tron Church stands here, nearly

---

* See "Great Industries of Great Britain," Vol. I., pp. 107-8; II., 8-9.

opposite the east wing of the Museum of Science and Art. It was erected in 1876-7, and presents a central block with two side pavilions; and has also a deeply recessed principal entrance, with four massive columns on each side, and a bold surmounting pediment, projected on massive corbels or trusses.

Here, too, stands the new Training College of the

The architecture, by Mr. David Rhind, of this new College, which is opposite the Industrial Museum, is simple in character, the more conspicuous features of the elevations being large bay windows and effective Mansard pavilion roofs.

On the second floor is the lecture hall, which measures forty-eight feet by forty, and has a ceiling which, so far as decorative art is concerned, may

OLD MINTO HOUSE, 1873. (*From a Drawing in the possession of Dr. Robert Paterson.*)

Church of Scotland, destined to supplement, and eventually to supersede, the edifice in Johnstone Terrace, the arrangements and accommodation of which have proved somewhat defective.

The principal object aimed at in the new premises is to provide a separate college entirely devoted to the training of male students, while the present school will thus be enlarged, and the seventh and eighth standards instituted in addition to those recognised in the Code, enabling the committee to form an upper elementary, or lower secondary school, for the instruction of advanced English, elementary Latin, French, and Mathematics.

be considered one of the chief features in the building. A noteworthy circumstance in connection with the site of this new Training College is that the staircase is said to stand exactly over the spot where stood the room in which Sir Walter Scott was born. But this seems doubtful.

In this street is the new Dental Hospital and School, inaugurated in October, 1879, and which bids fair to become the headquarters of dentistry in Scotland.

At the east end of Chambers Street is the Theatre of Varieties, seated for 1,200 persons, and opened in 1875.

CHAMBERS STREET.

CHAPTER XXXIV.

THE LORD PROVOSTS OF EDINBURGH.

The First Magistrate of Edinburgh—Some noted Provosts—William de Dederyk, Alderman—John Wigmer and the Ransom of David II.—John of Quhitness, First Provost—William Bertraham—The Golden Charter—City Pipers—Archibald Bell-the-cat—Lord Home—Arran and Kilspindie—Lord Maxwell—"Greysteel s" Penance—James VI. and the Council—Lord Fyvie—Provost Tod and Gordon's Map—The First Lord Provost—George Drummond—Freedom of the City given to Benjamin Franklin—Sir Lawrence Dundas and the Parliamentary Contest—Sir James Hunter Blair——Riots of 1792—Provost Coulter's Funeral—Lord Lynedoch—Recent Provosts—The First Englishman who was Lord Provost of Edinburgh.

THE titles by which the chief magistrate is known are "The Right Honourable the Lord Provost of the City of Edinburgh, Her Majesty's Lieutenant and High Sheriff within the same and Liberties thereof, Justice of the Peace for the County of Midlothian, and Admiral of the Firth of Forth," &c. A sword and mace are always borne before him.

It has been suggested that at some early period the chief magistrate had an official residence, and Lawson, in his Gazetteer, gives us a tradition that it was in the well-known alley from the High Street to the Public Markets, "now called the Fleshmarket Close, but formerly the *Provost's Close.*"

Few Highland names appear among those of the chief magistrates before the fifteenth century, while in the earlier ages many Norman and Saxon are to be found, as these elements existed largely in the Lowlands. We have the son of Malcolm III. addressing his subjects thus:—"*Eadgarus Rex Scotorum, omnibus per regnum suum Scotis et Anglis, salutem,*" with reference no doubt to the English Border counties, then a portion of the realm.

Although seven aldermen and three provosts appear among the first men in authority over Edinburgh, it is probable that the office of bailie, bailiff, or rent-gatherer, is more ancient than either, as such an officer was originally appointed by the king to collect revenues and administer justice within the burghs.

In 1296 the first magistrate, whose name can be traced to Edinburgh, was William de Dederyk, *alderman ;* he appears as such in "Prynne's Records of the Tower, and the Ragman Rolls." In the preceding year John Baliol held a Parliament at Edinburgh, and a convention of the burgesses of the city, Berwick, Roxburgh, and Stirling, met in Holyrood Abbey.

After a gap of forty-eight years we find John Wigmer *alderman* in 1344. Thirteen years subsequently certain burgesses of Edinburgh and other burghs are found negotiating for the ransom of King David II., taken in battle by the English.

In 1362 William Guppeld was alderman, 9th April, and till 1369, in which year a council sat at Edinburgh, when the king granted a charter to the abbey of Melrose.

In 1373 the *alderman* was Sir Adam Forrester, said to be of Whitburn and Corstorphine, a man possessed of immense estates, for which he obtained no less than six charters under the great seal of Robert II., and was several times employed in treaties and negotiations with the English, between 1394 and 1404.

In 1377 John of Quhitness first appears as *Provost*, or *Prepositus*, on the 18th of May, and in the following year Adam Forrester was again in office. In 1381 John de Camera was provost, and in 1387 Andrew Yutson (or Yichtson), between whom, with "Adam Forster, Lord of Nether Libberton," the Burgh of Edinburgh, and John of Stone, and John Skayer, masons, an indenture was made, 29th November, for the erection of five new chapels in St. Giles's, with pillars and vaulted roofs, covered with stone, and lighted with windows. These additions were made subsequent to the burning of the city by the invaders under Richard of England two years before.

In 1392 John of Dalrymple was provost, and the names of several bailies alone appear in the Burgh Records (Appendix) till the time of Provost Alexander Napier, 3rd October, 1403, whom Douglas calls first Laird of Merchiston. Under him Symon de Schele was Dean of Guild and Keeper of the Kirk Work, when the first head guild was held after the feast of St. Michael in the Tolbooth.

Alan of Fairnielee was provost 1410-1, and again in 1419, though George of Lauder was provost in 1413.

So lately as 1423 John of Levyntoun was styled alderman, with Richard Lamb and Robert of Bonkyl bailies, when the lease of the Canonmills was granted by Dean John of Leith, sometime Abbot of Holyrood, to "the aldermen, baylyes, and dene of the gild," 12th September, 1423. His successor was Thomas of Cranstoun, *Prepositus*, when the city granted an obligation to Henry VI. of England, for 50,000 merks English money, on account of the expenses of James I., while detained in England by the treasonable intrigues of his uncle. William of Liberton, George of Lauder,

and John of Levyntoun, appear as provosts successively in 1425, 1427, and 1428.

In 1434 Sir Henry Preston of Craigmillar was appointed provost; but no such name occurs in the Douglas peerage under that date. After John of Levyntoun, Sir Alexander Napier appears as provost after 1437, and the names of Adam Cant and Robert Niddry are among those of the magistrates and council. Then Thomas of Cranstoun was provost from 1438 till 1445, when Stephen Hunter succeeded him.

With the interval of one year, during which Thomas Oliphant was provost, the office was held from 1454 to 1462 by Sir Alexander Napier of Merchiston, a man of considerable learning, whom James II. made Comptroller of Scotland. In 1451 he had a safe-conduct from the King of England to visit Canterbury as a pilgrim, and by James III. he was constituted Vice-Admiral. He was also ambassador to England in 1461 and 1462.

In succession to Robert Mure of Polkellie, he was provost again in 1470, and until the election of James Creichton of Rothven, or Rowen, in 1477, when the important edict of James III. concerning the market-places and the time of holding markets was issued.

In 1481 the provost was William Bertraham, who, in the following year, with "the whole fellowship of merchants, burgesses, and community" of Edinburgh, bound themselves to repay to the King of England the dowry of his daughter, the Lady Cecil, in acknowledgment for which loyalty and generosity, James III. granted the city its Golden Charter, with the banner of the Holy Ghost, locally known still as the Blue Blanket. In 1481 the provost was for the first time allowed an annual fee of £20 out of the common purse; but some such fee would seem to have been intended three years before.

His successor was Sir John Murray of Touchadam, in 1482; and in the same year we find Patrick Baron of Spittlefield, under whose *régime* the Hammermen were incorporated, and in 1484 John Napier of Merchiston, eldest son of Provost Alexander Napier. He was John Napier of Rusky, and third of Merchiston, whom James III., in a letter dated 1474, designates as *cur louite familiar sqwiar*, and he was one of the lords auditors in the Parliament of 1483. Two of his lineal heirs fell successively in battle at Flodden and Pinkie.

The fourth provost in succession after him was Patrick Hepburn, Lord Hailes, 8th August. He was the first designated "My *Lord* Provost," probably because he was a peer of the realm. He had

"James of Creichtoun of Felde," as a deputy provost under him; and the first entry in the Records under that date is a statute that "the commoun pyperis of the towne" shall be properly feed, for the honour thereof, and that they get their food, day about, from all honest persons of substance, under a penalty of 9d. per day, "that is to ilk pyper iijd at least."

The fifth provost after this was Sir Thomas Tod, 22nd August, 1491, and again in 1498, with Richard Lawson of the Highriggs, and Sir John Murray in the interval during 1492.

From this date to 1513, with a little interval, Richard Lawson was again provost; the office was held by Sir Alexander Lauder of Blythe, who in the last named year was also Justice Depute.

He fell in the battle on the fatal 9th of September, 1513, and the affairs of the city, amid the consternation and grief that ensued, were managed by George of Tours, who with Robert Bruce, William Lockhart, William Adamson, and William Clerk, all bailies, had been, on the 19th of August, chosen by the provost and community to rule the city after his departure with the army for England.

The aged Archibald Douglas, Earl of Angus (better known as Archibald Bell-the-cat)—whose two sons, George Master of Angus, and Sir William Douglas of Glenbervie, with more then 200 knights and gentlemen of his surname, found their tomb on Flodden Hill—was elected provost on the 30th of September, twenty-one days after the battle; and at the same time his son, Gawain the Poet, provost of St. Giles's, was "made burgess, gratis, for the common benefit of the town." It was he of whom Scott makes the grim old Earl say, with reference to the English knight's act of forgery,

> "Thanks to St. Bothan, son of mine,
> Save Gawain, ne'er could pen a line."

He was succeeded on the 24th July, 1514, by Alexander Lord Home, Great Chamberlain of Scotland in 1507, and baron of Dunglas and Greenlaw, under whom preparations for the defence of the city, in expectation of a counter-invasion, went on. An Act was passed for the furnishing "of artailyerie for the resisting of our auld innemies of Ingland;" a tax was laid upon all—even the widows of the fallen, so far as their substance permitted them to pay—and all persons having heidyaird dykes, "were to build them up within fifteen days, under pain of six pounds to the Kirk-werk." In August of the same year David Melville was provost, and the pestilence caused the division of the city into four quarters, each under a bailie and quarter-master to attend to the health of the people.

Except the interval, during which Sir Patrick Hamilton of Kincavil and Archibald Douglas were Provosts, Melville was in office till 1517, when James Earl of Arran, Regent of Scotland, took it upon him, and was designated *Lord Provost*. In consequence of the influence it conferred, the office was at this time an object of ambition among the nobility. His enemies, the Douglases, taking advantage of his temporary absence from the city, procured the election of Archibald Douglas of Kilspindie, the uncle of the Earl of Angus, in his place; and when Arran returned from the castle of Dalkeith, where the court was then held, he found the gates of Edinburgh shut against him. His followers attempted to force an entrance sword in hand, but were repulsed, and a number were killed and wounded on both sides. Similar scenes of violence and bloodshed were of almost daily occurrence, and between the rival factions of Hamilton and Douglas the Lowlands were in a complete state of demoralisation; and on the 21st of February, 1519, in consequence of the bitter feud and bloody broils between the houses of Douglas and Hamilton, he was ordered by the Regent, then absent, to vacate his office, as it was ordained that no person of either of those names was eligible as provost, till the "Lord Governor's home coming, and for a year."

Thus, in 1520, Robert Logan of Coitfield was provost, and in October he was granted by the Council 100 merks of the common good, beside his ordinary fee, for the sustentation of four armed men, to carry halberds before him, "because the warld is brukle and troublous."

The fourth provost after this was Robert Lord Maxwell, 18th August, 1524, who was made so by the Queen-mother, when she "tuik the haill government of the realm and ruele of the king (James V.) upoun her." This was evidently an invasion of the rights of the citizens; yet on the same day the Lord Justice Clerk appeared before the Council, and declared "that it was the mind and will" of the king, then in his minority, that Mr. Francis Bothwell, provost, "cedit and left his office of provostier in the town's hand," and the said provost protested that the leaving of his office thus should not be derogatory to the city, nor injurious to its privileges. Lord Maxwell was afterwards Governor of Lochmaben, Captain of the Royal Guard, Warden of the West Marches, and Ambassador to France to negotiate the king's marriage with Mary of Lorraine; but long ere all that he had been succeeded as provost by Allan Stuart.

In 1526 Archibald Douglas of Kilspindie, Lord High Treasurer, was provost again. In this year it was ordained that through the resort to Edinburgh of great numbers of His Majesty's subjects and strangers, there should be three weekly market days for the sale of bread, when it should be lawful for dealers, both buyers and landward, to dispose of bread for ready money; three market days for the sale of meat under the same circumstances, were also established—Sunday, Monday, and Thursday.

In 1528 the Lord Maxwell became again provost of Edinburgh, and when, some years after, his exiled predecessor, Douglas of Kilspindie, became weary of wandering in a foreign land he sought in vain the clemency of James V., who, in memory of all he had undergone at the hands of the Douglases, had registered a vow never to forgive them. The aged warrior—who had at one time won the affection of the king, who, in admiration of his stature, strength, and renown in arms, had named him " Greysteel," after a champion in the romance of " Sir Edgar and Sir Guion "—threw himself in James's way near the gates of Stirling Castle, to seek pardon, and ran afoot by the side of his horse, encumbered as he was by heavy armour, worn under his clothes for fear of assassination. But James rode in, and the old knight, sinking by the gate in exhaustion, begged a cup of water. Even this was refused by the attendants, whom the king rebuked for their discourtesy; but old Kilspindie turned sadly away, and died in France of a broken heart.

In the year 1532 the provost and Council furnished James V. with a guard of 300 men, armed on all "pointts for wayr," to serve against his " enimies of Ingland," in all time coming.

In 1565, when Mary was in the midst of her most bitter troubles, Sir Simon Preston of Craigmillar and that ilk was provost, and it was in his house, the Black Turnpike, she was placed a prisoner, after the violated treaty of Carberry Hill; and four years after he was succeeded in office by the celebrated Sir William Kirkaldy of Grange.

In 1573 Lord Lindsay was provost, the same terrible and relentless noble who plotted against Rizzio, led the confederate lords, conducted Mary to Lochleven, who crushed her tender arm with his steel glove, and compelled her under terror of death to sign her abdication, and who lived to share in the first Gowrie conspiracy.

In 1578 the provost was George Douglas of Parkhead. who was also Governor of the Castle ; a riot having taken place in the latter, and a number of citizens being slain by the soldiers, the Lords of the Secret Council desired the magistrates to remove him from office and select another. They craved delay, on which the Council deposed Douglas, and sent a precept commanding the city to

choose a new provost within three hours, under pain of treason. In obedience to this threat Archibald Stewart was made interim provost till the usual time of election, Michaelmas ; previous to which, the young king, James VI., wrote to the magistrates desiring them to make choice of certain persons whom he named to hold their offices for the ensuing year. On receiving this peremptory command the Council called a public meeting of the citizens, at which it was resolved to allow no interference with their civic privileges. A deputation consisting of a bailie, the treasurer, a councillor, and two deacons, waited on His Majesty at Stirling and laid the resolutions before him, but received no answer. Upon the day of election another letter was read from James, commanding the Council to elect as magistrates the persons therein named for the ensuing year ; but notwithstanding this arbitrary command, the Council, to their honour, boldly upheld their privileges, and made their own choice of magistrates.

Alexander Home, of North Berwick, was provost from 1593 to 1596. He was a younger son of Patrick Home of Polwarth, and his younger sister was prioress of the famous convent at North Berwick, where strange to say she retained her station and the conventual lands till the day of her death.

In 1598 a Lord President of the College of Justice was provost, Alexander Lord Fyvie, afterwards Lord Chancellor, and Earl of Dunfermline in 1606. Though the time was drawing near for a connection with England, a contemporary writer in 1598 tells us that "in general, the Scots would not be attired after the English fashion *in any sort ;* but the men, especially at court, followed the French fashion."

Sir William Nisbet, of Dean, was provost twice in 1616 and 1622, the head of a proud old race, whose baronial dwelling was long a feature on the wooded ridge above Deanhaugh. His coat of arms, beautifully carved, was above one of the doors of the latter, his helmet surmounted by the crest of the city, and encircled by the motto,

" HIC MIHI PARTIVS HONOS."

It was in the dark and troublesome time of 1646-7, when Sir Archibald Tod was provost, that James Gordon, the minister of Rothiemay, made his celebrated bird's-eye view of Edinburgh—to which reference has been made so frequently in these pages, and of which we have engraved the greater part.

James Gordon, one of the eleven sons of the Laird of Straloch, was born in 1615. He was M.A. of Aberdeen, and in April, 1647, he submitted his view of the city—a work wonderful for its minuteness and fidelity—to provost Tod and the Council, who made him a free burgess, and paid him £333 6s. 8d. Scots, or £27 16s. 8d. sterling for the drawing, which was engraved in Holland by De Witt, and dedicated to the provost and magistrates, who appear by the city accounts to have had a collation on the occasion.

The provost who was present at and presided over the barbarous execution of Montrose, in 1650, was Sir James Stewart of Coltness, who suffered therefor a long imprisonment after the Restoration, and was only rescued from something worse by the intercession of a Cavalier gentleman, whose son's life he had saved by his humane intercession some years before.

Sir Andrew Ramsay, of Abbots Hall, was then provost, and it was during his second term of office in 1667, that Charles II. wrote him a letter stating that the chief magistrate of Edinburgh should have the same freedom in Scotland as the mayor of London had in England, and should have the permanent title of "Lord Provost." In 1672, when last in office, a salary was settled upon him of £200 sterling annually—the first that seems ever to have been regularly paid to a magistrate of the city. He had been ten years altogether provost, his re-elections having been secured by the influence of the Duke of Lauderdale, in return for his having obtained for his Grace £6,000 as the price of the citadel of Leith. Sir Andrew while in the civic chair conducted himself so tyrannically, by applying the common good of the city for the use of himself and his friends, and by inventing new employments and concessory offices within it, to provide for his dependents, that the citizens, weary of his yoke, resolved to turn him out at the next election; but he having had a majority the burgesses were forced to "intent a reduction of the election."

This case being submitted to the Chancellor and President, they ordered an Act to be passed in the Common Council of the city, declaring that none should hereafter continue in office as provost for more than two years. But this regulation has not been strictly observed, and the Lord Provosts of the city are now elected for three years.

In 1683 Sir George Drummond was Lord Provost; but in August, 1685, he became a bankrupt, and took refuge in the Sanctuary at Holyrood, the first, says Fountainhall, "that during his office has broke in Edinburgh." A week or two afterwards, a riot having taken place at the Town Guard-house, the Lord Chancellor, the Earl of Perth, who was bound to do what he could to protect the provost,

got a protection to enable him to appear in this matter. "Thus he was brought to the street again."

His predecessor in 1676 was a Sir William Binny, who, in 1686 had a curious case before the Court of Session, against Hope of Carse, on the testament of Colonel Gordon, who with Leslie and Walter Butler of the Irish Musketeers, slew the great Wallenstein, Duke of Friedland.

Sir Hugh Cunningham was provost when Anne was proclaimed by the heralds at the Cross, on the 8th of March, 1702, Queen of Scotland; and she in her first letter to Parliament pressed them to consider the advantages which might accrue to both countries by a union; and Sir Samuel MacLellan was provost in the year of stormy dissension in which it was ultimately achieved.

We have elsewhere (Vol. I, p. 318) referred to the unfortunate Archibald Stewart, who was Lord Provost in the next memorable epoch of Scottish history, the insurrection of 1745.

William Alexander was Lord Provost when the first great breach was made in the ancient city, and the first appearance of some vitality began to brighten in 1753, when the New Exchange was founded on the north side of the Luckenbooths; but one of the most distinguished chief magistrates of the seventeenth century was George Drummond, who was elected no less than six times Lord Provost of the city. A cadet of the noble house of Perth, he was born in 1687, and when only eighteen years of age was employed by the Committee of the Scottish Parliament to give his assistance in the arrangement of the national accounts prior to the Union; and in 1707, on the establishment of the Excise, he was rewarded with the office of Accountant-General, and in 1717 he was a Commissioner of the Board of Customs. In 1725 he was elected Lord Provost for the first time, and two years after was named one of the commissioners and trustees for improving the fisheries and manufactures of Scotland. He was the principal agent in the erection of the Royal Infirmary; and in 1745 he served as a volunteer with Cope's army at the Battle of Prestonpans. As grand-master of the freemasons he laid the foundation-stone of the Royal Exchange, and in 1755 was appointed to that lucrative—if dubious —office, a trustee on the forfeited estates of the Jacobite lords and landholders. We have related (in its place) how he laid the foundation-stone of the North Bridge. He died in 1766 in the eightieth year of his age, and was honoured, deservedly, with a public funeral in the Canongate. To Provost Drummond Dr. Robertson the historian owed his appointment as Principal of the University, which was also indebted to him for the institution of five new professorships. A few years after his death a bust of him by Nollekens was erected in their public hall by the managers of the Royal Infirmary.

In 1754 the Lord Provost, dean of guild, bailies, and city treasurer, appeared in November, for the first 'time, with gold chains and medals, in lieu of the black velvet coats, which were laid aside by all save the provost, and which had been first ordered to be worn by an Act of the Council in 1718.

In 1753, on the 17th February, died Patrick Lindsay, Esq., late Lord Provost of Edinburgh, and Governor of the Isle of Man.

In 1768 the Lord Provost was James Stuart. In the following year, during spring, the great Benjamin Franklin and his son spent six weeks in Scotland, and the University of St. Andrews conferred upon him the honorary title of Doctor, by which he has since been generally known. On his coming to Edinburgh, Provost Stuart and the Corporation bestowed upon him the freedom of the city, when every house was thrown open to him, and the most distinguished men of letters crowded round him. Hume, Robertson, and Lord Kames, became his intimate friends; but Franklin was not unduly elated. "On the whole," he wrote, "I must say the time I spent there (in Scotland) was six weeks of the *dearest* happiness I have met with in any part of my life."

Stuart's successor in office was John Dalrymple, whose eldest son succeeded to the baronetcy of Hailes (which is now extinct) on the death of Lord Hailes, the distinguished judge and writer.

In the year 1774 there was considerable political strife in the city, originating in the general parliamentary election, when exertions were made to wrest the representation from Sir Lawrence Dundas, who unexpectedly found as opponents Loch of Carnbie, and Captain James Francis Erskine of Forrest. A charge of bribery being preferred against Sir Lawrence, some delay occurred in the election, and the then Lord Provost Stoddart came forward as a candidate. The votes of the Council were—for Sir Lawrence, twenty-three; for Provost Stoddart, six; and for Captain Erskine, three. One of the Council, Gilbert Laurie (who had been provost in 1766) was absent. Messrs. Stoddart and Loch protested that the election had been brought about by undue influence.

The opposition to Sir Lawrence became still greater, and a keen trial of strength took place when the election of deacons and councillors came in 1776, and many bitter letters appeared in the public prints; but the friends of the Dundas family proved again triumphant, and united in the choice of Alexander Kincaid, as Lord Provost, His Majesty's Printer for Scotland. He died in office in 1777, in a house situated in the Cowgate, in a small court westward of the Horse Wynd, and known as Kincaid's Land, and was succeeded by Provost Dalrymple.

Two years afterwards the city was assessed in the sum of £1,500 to repay damage done by a mob to the Roman Catholic place of worship, for the destruction of furniture, ornaments, books, and altar vessels. In this year, 1779, there were 188 hackney sedan chairs in the city, but very few hackney coaches; and the umbrella first appeared in the streets. By 1783 there were 1,268 four-wheeled carriages entered to pay duty, and 338 two-wheeled.

At Michaelmas, 1784, Sir James Hunter Blair, Bart., was elected Lord Provost, in succession to David Stuart, who resided in Queen Street, and who was a younger son of Stuart of Dalguise. The second son of Mr. John Hunter of Ayr, Sir James, commenced life as an apprentice with Coutts and Co., the Edinburgh bankers, in 1756, when Sir William Forbes was then a clerk, and both became ultimately the principal partners. He married the eldest daughter of Blair of Dunskey, who left no less than six sons at the time of this event, all of whom died, and on her succession to the estates. Sir James assumed the name and arms of Blair. As Lord Provost he was indefatigable in the activity of his public spirit, and set afoot the great operations for the improvement of Edinburgh, and one object he had specially in view when founding the South Bridge was the rebuilding of the University.

Sir James lived only to see the commencement of the great works he had projected in Edinburgh, as he died of fever at Harrogate in July, 1787, and was honoured with a public funeral in the Greyfriars' churchyard. In private life he was affable and cheerful, attached to his friends and anxious for their success. In business and in his public exertions he was upright, liberal, and, as a Scotsman, patriotic; he possessed in no small degree those talents which are requisite for rendering benevolence effectual, uniting great knowledge of the world with sagacity and sound understanding.

Sir James Stirling, Bart., elected Lord Provost, after Elder of Forneth, had a stormy time when in office. He was the son of a fishmonger at the head of Marlin's Wynd, where his sign was a wooden *Black Bull*, now in the Antiquarian Museum. Stirling, after being secretary to Sir Charles Dalling, Governor of Jamaica, became a partner in the bank of Mansfield, Ramsay, and Co. in Cantore's Close, Luckenbooths, and married the daughter of the head of the firm. When he took office politics ran high. The much-needed reform of the royal burghs had been keenly agitated for some time previous, and a motion on the subject, negatived in the House of Commons by a majority of 26, incensed the Scottish public to a great degree, while Lord Melville, Secretary of State, by his opposition to the question, rendered himself so obnoxious, that in many parts of Scotland he was burned in effigy. In this state of excitement Provost Stirling and others in authority at Edinburgh looked forward to the King's birthday—the 4th of June, 1792—with considerable uneasiness, and provoked mischief by inaugurating the festival by sending strong patrols of cavalry through the streets at a quick pace with swords drawn. Instead of having the desired effect, the people became furious at this display, and hissed and hooted the cavalry with mocking cries of "Johnnie Cope." In the afternoon, when the provost and magistrates were assembled in the Parliament House to drink the usual loyal toasts, a mob mustered in the square, and amused themselves after a custom long peculiar to Edinburgh on this day, of throwing dead cats at each other, and at the City Guard who were under arms to fire volleys after every toast.

Some cavalry officers incautiously appeared at this time, and, on being insulted, brought up their men to clear the streets, and, after considerable stone-throwing, the mob dispersed. Next evening it re-assembled before the house of Mr. Dundas in George Square, with a figure of straw hung from a pole. When about to burn the effigy they were attacked by some of Mr. Dundas's friends—among others, it is said, by his neighbours, the naval hero of Camperdown, and Sir Patrick Murray of Ochtertyre. These gentlemen retired to Dundas's house, the windows of which were smashed by the mob, which next attacked the residence of the Lord Advocate, Dundas of Arniston. On this it became necessary to bring down the 53rd Regiment from the Castle; the Riot Act was read, the people were fired on, and many fell wounded, some mortally, who were found dead next day in the Meadows and elsewhere. This put an end to the disturbances for that night; but on Wednesday evening the mob assembled in the New Town with the intention of destroying the house of Provost Stirling at the south-east corner of St. Andrew Square, where they broke the City Guards' sentry boxes to pieces. But, as an appointed signal, the ancient beacon-fire, was set aflame in the Castle, the *Hind* frigate sent ashore her marines at Leith, and the cavalry came galloping in from the eastward, on which the mob separated finally.

By this time Provost Stirling had sought shelter in the Castle from the mob, who were on the point of throwing Dr. Alexander Wood (known as Lang Sandy) over the North Bridge in mistake for him. For his zeal, however, he was made a baronet of Great Britain. The year 1795 was one of great distress in the city; Lord Cockburn tells us that 16,000 persons (about an eighth of the population) were fed by charity, and the exact quantity of food each family should consume was specified by public proclamation. In 1793 a penny post was established in Edinburgh, extending to Leith, Musselburgh, Dalkeith, and Prestonpans. Sir James Stirling latterly resided at the west end of Queen Street, and died in February, 1805.

Sir William Fettes, Lord Provost in 1800 and 1804, we have elsewhere referred to; but William Coulter, a wealthy hosier in the High Street, who succeeded to the civic chair in 1808, was chiefly remarkable for dying in office, like Alexander Kincaid thirty years before, and for the magnificence with which his funeral obsequies were celebrated. He died at Morningside Lodge, and the cortège was preceded by the First R. E. Volunteers, and the officers of the three Regiments of Edinburgh local militia, and the body was in a canopied hearse, drawn by six horses, each led by a groom in deep mourning. On it lay the chain of office, and his sword and sash as colonel of the volunteers. A man of great stature, in a peculiar costume, bore the banner of the City. When the body was lowered into the grave, the senior herald broke and threw therein the rod of office, while the volunteers, drawn up in a line near the Greyfriars' Church, fired three funeral volleys.

Sir John Marjoribanks, Bart., Lord Provost in 1813, was the son of Marjoribanks of Lees, an eminent wine merchant in Bordeaux, and his mother was the daughter of Archibald Stewart, Lord Provost of the city in the memorable '45. Sir John was a partner in the banking-house of Mansfield, Ramsay, and Co., and while in the civic chair was the chief promoter of the Regent Bridge and Calton Gaol, though the former had been projected by Sir James Hunter Blair in 1784. When the freedom of the city was given to Lord Lynedoch, "the gallant Graham," Sir John gave him a magnificent dinner, on the 12th of August, 1815—two months after Waterloo. There were present the Earl of Morton, Lord Audley, Sir David Dundas, the Lord Chief Baron, the Lord Chief Commissioner, Sir James Douglas, Sir Howard Elphinstone, and about a hundred of the most notable men in Edinburgh, the freedom of which was presented to Lord Lynedoch in a box of gold; and at the conclusion of the banquet he gave as a toast, "May the Ministry not lose by their pens what the army has won by their swords!"

Sir John was succeeded as Lord Provost by William Arbuthnot, who twice held the chair in 1815, and again in 1821. He was created a baronet by the King in person on the 24th of August, 1822, at the banquet given to his Majesty by the City in the Parliament House; but the patent bore date, 3rd April, 1823. He was a son of Arbuthnot of Haddo, who, like himself, had been an official in the Trustees office. In the interim Kincaid Mackenzie and John Manderston had been Lords Provost—the former in 1817. He was a wine merchant in the Lawnmarket, and while in office had the honour of entertaining at his house in Gayfield Square, first, the Russian Grand Duke Michael, and subsequently Prince Leopold, the future King of the Belgians.

Among the most eminent Lords Provost of later years we may refer to Sir James Forrest, Bart., of Comiston, who received his title on the occasion of the first visit of Queen Victoria to her Scottish metropolis in 1838, and who was worthily succeeded in 1843 by the late Adam Black, M.P., the distinguished publisher.

In 1848 the Lord Provost was the eminent engraver William Johnstone, who was knighted in 1851, when he was succeeded by Duncan M'Laren, a wealthy draper in the High Street, afterwards M.P. for the city, and well known as a steady upholder of Scottish interests in the House.

On the 7th August, 1860, during the provostry of Francis Brown Douglas, Advocate, there took place the great review before the Queen and Royal Family in Holyrood Park of 22,000 Scottish Volunteers,

one of the grandest and most successful public spectacles ever witnessed by Old or New Edinburgh.

In 1862 the Lord Provost was Charles Lawson of Borthwick Hall, one of the most extensive seed merchants perhaps in Scotland, and who had the honour to entertain at his house, 35, George Square, the Prince and Princess of Wales. It was during Mr. Lawson's reign that, on the 10th of March, 1863, the Prince's marriage took place, an occasion that gave rise to the great and magnificent illumination of the city—a spectacle the like of which has never been seen, before or since, in this country. His successor, in 1865, was William Chambers, LL.D., the well-known Scottish writer, and member of the eminent publishing firm of W. and R. Chambers, High Street, during whose double tenure of office the work of demolition in connection with the city improvements commenced in the block of buildings between St. Mary's Wynd and Gullan's Close, Cannongate, on the 15th June, 1868. A grand review and sham-fight of volunteers and regulars, to the number of 10,000 men, took place in the royal park on the 4th July; and subsequently the freedom of the City was bestowed upon Lord Napier of Magdala, and upon that far-famed orator, John Bright, M.P. In 1874 James Falshaw was elected to the chair, the *first* Englishman who ever held such an office in Edinburgh. He was created a baronet of the United Kingdom in 1876 on the occasion of the unveiling by the Queen of the Scottish National Memorial of the late Prince Consort in Charlotte Square. He was preceded in the chair by William Law, and succeeded in 1877 by Sir Thomas Jamieson Boyd, the well-known publisher, who was knighted in 1881 on the occasion of the Volunteer Review.

CHAPTER XXXV.

INFIRMARY STREET AND THE OLD HIGH SCHOOL.

Blackfriars Monastery—Its Foundation—Destroyed by Fire—John Black the Dominican—The Friary Gardens—Lady Yester: her Church and Tomb—The Burying Ground—The Old High School—The Ancient Grammar School—David Vocat—School Founded—Hercules Rollock—Early Classes—The House Destroyed by the English—The Bleis-Silver—David Malloch—The Old High School—Thomas Ruddiman, Rector—Barclay's Class—Henry Mackenzie's Reminiscences—Dr. Adam, Rector: his Grammar—New Edifice Proposed and Erected—The School-boy Days of Sir Walter Scott—Allan Masterton—The School in 1803—Death of Rector Adam—James Pillans, M.A.,' and A. R. Carson, Rectors—The New School Projected—The Old one Abandoned.

INFIRMARY STREET is now a continuation of Chambers Street to the eastward, and is a thoroughfare of great antiquity, as it led from the north side of the Kirk-of-field, past the Dominican Monastery and into the Old High School Wynd. In 1647 it was a double street with one long continuous line of houses, occupying the whole front-

age of the future infirmary, and having six long abutments (or short closes) running south towards the south-eastern flank of the City wall.

On the exact site of the Old Surgical Hospital there stood for nearly four hundred years a great edifice of which now not a trace remains, the Dominican or Blackfriars' Monastery, founded in

1230 by King Alexander II., and in its earliest charters named *Mansio Regis*, as he had bestowed upon
the monks a royal residence as their abode.

The church built by Alexander was a large cruciform edifice with a central rood-tower and lofty
spire. It was renowned for being the scene of the
great meeting of all the bishops, abbots, and priors

bishop of Glasgow and Lord High Chancellor,
fled from the Douglases during the terrible street
conflict or tulzie in 1519, and, as Pitscottie records,
was dragged " out behind the altar, and his rockit
riven aff him, and had been slaine," had not Gavin
Douglas, Bishop of Dunkeld, interceded for him,
" saying, it was shame to put hand on an conse-

SIR JAMES FALSHAW, BART., AND H.M. LIEUTENANT OF EDINBURGH.
(From a Photograph by John Moffat.)

in the realm, summoned in 1512 by the Papal
Legate, Cardinal Bagimont, who presided. In
this synod, says Balfour, all ecclesiastical benefices
exceeding forty pounds per annum were taxed in
the payment of ten pounds to the Pope by way of
pension, and to the King of Scotland such a tax as
he felt disposed to levy. This valuation, which
is still known by the name of Bagimont's Roll,
was made thereafter the standard for taxing the
Scottish ecclesiastics at the Vatican.

It was to this church that James Beaton, Arch-

crate bishop." And here we may remark that the
Scottish word *tulzie*, used by us so often, is derived
from the French *touill-er*, to confuse, or to mix.

The monastery was destroyed by an accidental
fire in 1528, but the church would seem to have
been uninjured by the view of it in 1544, though
no doubt it would suffer, like all the others in the
city, at the hands of the English in that year.

In 1552 the Provost and Council ordered Alex.
Park, city treasurer, to deliver to " the Dene of
Gild x li., that he may thairwith pay the Blak

Freirs xx li. owing to them, at this last Fasterns evin, for thair bell, conform to the act maid thairupon" (Burgh Records).

In 1553 another Act ordains "John Smyson" to pay them the sum "of xx li. compleit payment of thair silver bell;" and in 1554-5 in the Burgh Accounts is the item—"To the Blackfriars and Greyfriars, for their preaching yeirlie, ilk ane of thame self ane last of sownds beir; price of ilk boll xxviij s. summa, xvj li. xvj s."

When John Knox, after his return to Scotland, began preaching against the Mass as an idolatrous worship, he was summoned before an ecclesiastical judicatory held in the Blackfriars' church on the 15th May, 1556. The case was not proceeded with at the time, as a tumult was feared; but the summons so greatly increased the power and popularity of Knox, that on that very 15th of May he preached to a greater multitude than he had ever done before. In 1558 the populace attacked the monastery and church, and destroyed everything they contained, leaving the walls an open ruin.

In 1560 John Black, a Dominican friar, acted as the permanent confessor of Mary of Guise, during her last fatal illness in the Castle of Edinburgh, and Knox in his history indulges in coarse innuendoes concerning both. His name is still preserved in the following doggerel verse :—

" There was a certain Black friar, always called Black,
  And this was no nickname, for *black* was his work ;
  Of all the Black friars he was the blackest clerk,
  Born in the Black Friars to be a black mark."

This Dominican, however, was a learned and subtle doctor, a man of deep theological research, who in 1561 maintained against John Willox the Reformer, and ex-Franciscan, a defence of the Roman Catholic faith for two successive days, and gave him more than ordinary trouble to meet his arguments. He was afterwards stoned in the streets " by the rabble," on the 15th December, or, as others say, the 7th of January.

By 1560 the stones of the Black Friary were used "for the bigging of dykes," and other works connected with the city. The cemetery was latterly the old High School Yard, and therein a battery of cannon was erected in 1571 to batter a house in which the Parliament of the king's men held a meeting, situated somewhere on the south side of the Canongate.

The Dominican gardens, in which the dead body of Darnley was found lying under a tree, and their orchard, lay to the southward, and in 1513 were intersected, or bounded by the new city wall, in which there remained—till July, 1854, when some six hundred yards of it were demolished, and a

parapet and iron railing substituted—an elliptically arched doorway, half buried in the pavement, three feet three inches wide, and protected by a round gun-port, splayed out four feet four inches wide. Through this door the unscathed body of Darnley must have been borne by his murderers, ere they blew up the house of the Kirk-of-field. It was an interesting relic, and its removal was utterly wanton.

The next old ecclesiastical edifice on the other side of the street was Lady Yester's church, which in Gordon's map is shown as an oblong barn-like edifice surrounded by a boundary wall, with a large window in its western gable.

Lady Yester, a pious and noble dame, whose name was long associated with ecclesiastical charities in Edinburgh, was the third daughter of Mark Kerr, Commendator of Newbattle Abbey, a Lord of Session, and founder of the house of Lothian. Early in life she was married to James Lord Hay of Yester, and had two sons, John Lord Yester, afterwards Earl of Tweeddale, and Sir William, for whom she purchased the barony of Linplum. After being a widow some years she married Sir Andrew Kerr younger of Fernyhurst.

In 1644 she built the church at the south-east corner of the High School Wynd, at the expense of £1,000 of the then money, with 5,000 merks for the salary of the minister. It was seated for 817 persons, and in August, 1655, the Town Council appointed a district of the city a parish for it. Shortly before her death, Lady Yester "caused joyne thereto an little isle for the use of the minister, yr she lies interred." This aisle is shown by Gordon to have been on the north side of the church, and Monteith (1704) describes the following doggerel inscription on her "tomb on the north side of the vestiary" :—

" It 's needless to erect a marble tomb :
   The daily bread that for the hungry womb,
   And bread of life thy bounty hath provided
   For hungry souls, all times to be divided ;
   World-lasting monuments shall reare,
   That shall endure, till Christ himself appear.
   Pood was thy life, prepared thy happy end ;
   Nothing in either was without commend.
   Let it be the care of all who live hereafter,
   To live and die, like Margaret Lady Yester."
   Who dyed 15th March, 1647. Her age 75.

" Blessed are the dead, which die in the Lord ; they rest from their labours, and their works do follow them."—Rev. xiv. 13.

After Cromwell's troops rendered themselves houseless in 1650 by burning Holyrood, quarters were assigned them in the city churches, including Lady Yester's; and in all of these, and part of the college, the pulpits, desks, lofts, and seats, were, says Nicol, "dung down by these English sodgeris, and burnt to asses."

When the congregation of the abbey church were compelled by James VII. to leave it in 1687, they had to seek accommodation in Lady Yester's till another place of worship could be provided for them. A small cemetery adjoined the church; it is now covered with buildings, but was still in use about the close of the last and beginning of the present century, and many seamen of the Russian fleet, which lay for a time at Leith, and who died in the infirmary, were buried there.

In 1803 the old church was taken down, and a new one erected for 1,212 sitters, considerably to the westward of it, was opened in the following year. Though tasteless and nondescript in style, it was considered an ornament to that part of the city.

The tomb of the foundress, and the tablet recording her good works, are both re-built into this new fane; but it seems doubtful whether her body was removed at the same time. The parish is wholly a town one, and situated within the city; it contains 64,472 square yards.

With diffidence, yet with ardour and interest, we now approach the subject of the old High School of Edinburgh—the famous and time-honoured *Schola Regia Edinensis*—so prominently patronised by James VI., and the great national importance of which was recognised even by George IV., who gave it a handsome donation.

Scott, and thousands of others, whose deeds and names in every walk of life and in every part of the globe have added to the glory of their country, have conned their tasks in the halls of this venerable institution. "In the roll of its scholars," says Dr. Steven, "are the names of some of the most distinguished men of all professions, and who have filled important situations in all parts of the world, and it is a fact worth recording that it includes the names of three Chancellors of England, all *natives* of Edinburgh—Wedderburn, Erskine, and Brougham."

Learning, with all the arts and infant science too, found active and munificent patrons in the monarchs of the Stuart line; thus, so early as the sixth Parliament of James IV., it was ordained that all barons and freeholders of substance were to put their eldest sons to school after the age of six or nine years, there to remain till they were perfect in Latin, "swa that they have knowledge and understanding of the lawes, throw the quhilks justice may remaine universally throw all the realme." Those who failed to conform to this

Act were to pay a fine of twenty pounds. But Scotland possessed schools so early as the twelfth century in all her principal towns, though prior to that period scholastic knowledge could only be received within the walls of the monasteries. The Grammar School of Edinburgh was originally attached to the abbey of Holyrood, and as the demand for education increased, those friars whose presence could be most easily dispensed with at the abbey, were permitted by the abbot and chapter to become public teachers within the city.

The earliest mention of a regular Grammar School in Edinburgh being under the control of the magistrates is on the 10th January, 1519, "the quhilk day, the provost, baillies, and counsall statutis and ordains, for resonable caussis moving thame, that na maner of nychtbour nor indweller within this burgh, put thair bairins till ony particular scule within this toun, *bot to the principal Grammer Scule* of the samyn," to be taught in any science, under a fine of ten shillings to the master of the said principal school.

David Vocat, clerk of the abbey, was then at the head of the seminary, enjoying this strange monopoly; and on the 4th September, 1524, George, Bishop of Dunkeld, as abbot of Holyrood, with consent of his chapter, appointed Henry Henryson as assistant and successor to Vocat, whose pupil he had been, at the Grammar School of the Canongate.

By a charter of James V., granted under the great seal of Scotland, dated 1529, Henryson had the sole privilege of instructing the youth of Edinburgh; but he was also to attend at the abbey in his surplice on all high and solemn festivals, there to sing at mass and evensong, and make himself otherwise useful in the chapel.

According to Spottiswood's Church History, Henryson publicly abjured Romanism so early as 1534, and thus he must have left the High School before that year, as Adam Melville had become head-master thereof in 1531. The magistrates of the city had as yet no voice in the nomination of masters, though the whole *onus* of the establishment rested on them as representing the citizens; and in 1554, as we have elsewhere (Vol. I. p. 263) stated, they hired that venerable edifice, then at the foot of Blackfriars Wynd—once the residence of Archbishop Beaton and of his nephew the cardinal—as a school; but in the following year they were removed to another house, near the head of what is named the High School Wynd, which had been built by the town for their better accommodation.

The magistrates having obtained from Queen

Mary in March, 1566, a gift of all the patronages and endowments in the city, which had belonged to the Franciscan and Dominican priories, including the ancient school, which, till then, had been vested in the abbey of the Holy Cross, in January, 1567, they resolved to erect a suitable schoolhouse on the land of the Blackfriars monastery; and this edifice, which was built for £250 Scots (about £40 sterling) was ready for occupation in the following year.

ascertained, and they were obliged to teach *grat.;* the sons of all freemen of the burgh.

For the ultimate completion of its buildings, which included a tall square tower with a conical spire, the school was indebted to James Lawson, who succeeded John Knox as one of the city clergy; but it did not become what it was originally intended to be—an elementary seminary for logic and philosophy as well as classics; but it led to the foundation of the University in its vicinity, and

LADY YESTER'S CHURCH, 1820. (*After Storer.*)

This edifice, which was three-storeyed with crowstepped gables, stood east and west, having on its front, which faced the Canongate, two circular towers, with conical roofs, and between them a square projection surmounted by a gable and thistle. The main entrance was on the east side of this, and had over it the handsome stone panel, which is still preserved in the last new school, and which bears the city arms, the royal cypher, and the motto.

MVSIS . RES PUBLICA . FLORET . 1578.

At that time, says Arnot, there appears to have been only two teachers belonging to this school, with a small salary, the extent of which cannot be

hence, says Dr. Steven, "they may be viewed as portions of one great institution."

The encouragement received by the masters was so small that they threatened to leave the school if it were not bettered, on which they were ordered to receive a quarterly fee from the sons of the freemen; the masters of three, and the usher of two shillings Scots (nearly 6s. and nearly 4s. sterling) from each; and soon after four teachers were appointed with fixed salaries and fees, which were augmented from time to time as the value of money changed, and the cost of living increased (Arnot).

In 1584, a man of superior attainments and considerable genius, named Hercules Rollock, a native of Dundee, after undergoing a full course of study at St. Andrews, became head-master, and among his pupils the name of one alone has come down to us, William Drummond of Hawthornden, the historian of the Jameses, the poet and Cavalier. "In those days," says Steven, "frequent tumults took place, which seldom or never characterise modern times. The rude behaviour of the boys towards their teachers, particularly manifested in what has been termed a *barring-out*, was frequently practised both in England and in Scotland in the sixteenth and seventeenth centuries."

In 1580 the scholars were so turbulent that nine of them were put in the common prison; and during Rollock's term of office the boys rose in absolute rebellion, and arming themselves with those deadly weapons which then abounded in every Scottish household, they threatened the lives of their teachers. "Rollock being determined not to suffer his authority to be trampled upon with impunity, dispatched a messenger to the Council Chamber for aid. The provost, with other functionaries, repaired to the spot. It was soon discovered that the malcontents would not be so easily subdued, and that they were as much disposed to resist the civic authorities as they had already disdainfully rejected the advice and commands of their excellent preceptor."

By order of the provost, William Little, the principal door was battered to pieces, the school entered, and the scholars were overawed, though fire-arms of every description, with swords and halberds, were found in their possession; but in such lawless proceedings the boys only imitated the conduct of their seniors, who were daily engaged in raids, brawls, and street tulzies.

As a teacher Rollock was well supported by his countrymen; and in 1591, by the patronage of Queen Anne, some Danes were entrusted as pupils to his care. Save Greek and Latin, nothing had been taught as yet at the High School, but in 1593 a teacher of penmanship, named William Murdoch, was appointed; yet no salary was allowed, though the master was authorised to charge ten shillings

CARVED STONE WHICH WAS OVER THE MAIN ENTRANCE TO THE HIGH SCHOOL FROM 1578 TO 1777.

Scots quarterly for each pupil "writter." In 1595 the school was the scene of that famous *barring-out* and tragic tumult in which Bailie MacMorran was shot, and of which a full relation is given in the account of his residence.

This fatal event greatly affected the sensitive mind of Rollock, while the expulsion of some scholars, and the withdrawal of others by their parents, thinned his classes, and at the same time he lost the favour of the Town Council, and became involved in a litigation, which made such inroads on his slender funds, that at his death in 1599 he left his family in such poverty that the Council in 1600 made a small grant to his widow.

His successor was Alexander Hume, B.A. of St. Andrews in 1574, and for some years a tutor at Oxford; but the precise mode that was daily followed in the High School during the sixteenth century is now quite unknown.

In 1597-8 the studies of the school underwent a thorough revision, and the leading members of the legal and clerical professions willingly aided the somewhat unlettered Town Council, and recommended that in all time coming there should be four regents or masters, "learned and godly men."

The fourth regent was Principal, and his duties were distinctly defined in a document drawn up in October, 1598.

The quarterly examinations, at which were present the magistrates, ministers, and members of the Bar, took place at Candlemas, Beltane, Lammas, and Martinmas. By all these officials and the masters "nothing was left undone to impress on the minds of the young the abhorrence of the tenets of the Roman Catholics," says Dr. Steven; "but publicly to caricature the ecclesiastics of another communion was surely unworthy of Protestant magistrates and teachers. In the summer of 1598 the city treasurer was directed to purchase grey cloth sufficient for five dresses resembling those worn by friars, and likewise coarse red cloth to represent (in burlesque) the official costume of his Holiness and the college of cardinals. The Corporation agreed to this outlay on the distinct understanding that at the close of this theatrical display the dresses so used should be given to the poor."

For many years the history of the school is little more than a biographical list of the various masters and teachers. A fifth class was established in 1614 for the rudiments of Greek during the rectorship of John Ray (the friend of Zachary Boyd), who after being Professor of Humanity in the university for eight years, regarded it promotion to leave it to take full charge of the High School; and when he died, in February, 1630, his office was again conferred upon a Professor of Humanity, Thomas Crawford, who figured prominently amid the pageants with which Charles I. was welcomed to the city in 1633, and with Hawthornden and others composed and delivered some of the bombastic speeches on that occasion.

In his time the number of pupils fluctuated greatly; he complained to the Council that though they had led him to expect "400 bairns at the least," he had only 180 when he began office. But there is no authentic record of attendance at that early period; and it is curious that the abstract of the annual enrolment of scholars goes no farther back than the Session of 1738-9, while a general matriculation register was not commenced till 1827.

In December, 1640, Crawford returned to the university, and was succeeded by William Spence, schoolmaster of Prestonpans; but to give all the successive masters of the institution would far exceed our space. The masters and scholars had very indifferent accommodation during the invasion of Cromwell after Dunbar. His troops made a barrack of the school-house, and while there broke and burned all the woodwork, leaving it in such a state of ruin that the pupils had to meet in Lady Yester's Church till it was repaired by funds drawn from the masters of the Trinity Hospital at the foot of Leith Wynd.

A library for the benefit of the institution was added to it in 1658, and it now consists of many thousand volumes. Among the first donors of books were John Muir the rector, all the masters, Patrick Scott of Thirlstane, and John Lord Swinton of that ilk. At present it is supported by the appropriation of one half of the matriculation fund to its use, and every way it is a valuable classical, historical, geographical, and antiquarian collection. The rector and masters, with the assistance of the janitor, discharge in rotation the duties of librarian.

An old periodical source of income deserves to be noticed. In 1660, on the 20th January, the Town Council ordered "the casualty called the *bleis-silver*" to be withheld until the 1st of March.

This was a gratuity presented to the masters by their pupils at Candlemas, and he who gave the most was named the King. "Bleis" being the Scottish word for *blaze*, the origin of the gratuity must have been a Candlemas offering for the lights and candles anciently in use; moreover, the day was a holiday, when the boys appeared in their best apparel accompanied by their parents.

The roll was then called over, and each boy presented his offering. When the latter was less than the quarterly fee no notice was taken of it, but if it amounted to that sum the rector exclaimed with a loud voice, *Vivat;* to twice the ordinary fee, *Floreat bis;* for a higher sum, *Floreat ter;* for a guinea and upwards, *Gloriat!* The highest donor was named the *Victor*, or King.

The Council repeatedly issued injunctions against the levy of any "*Bleis-sylver*, or *Bent-sylver*," but apparently in vain. The latter referred to the money for collecting *bent*, or rushes, to lay down on the clay floor to keep the feet warm and dry; and so lately as the commencement of the seventeenth century, during the summer season, the pupils had leave to go forth with hooks to cut bent by the margins of Duddingston and the Burgh lochs, or elsewhere. "Happily," says Steven, of a later date, "all exactions are now unknown; and at four regular periods in the course of each session, the teachers receive from their pupils a fixed fee, which is regarded as a fair remuneration for their professional labour."

In those days the pupils attended divine service, accompanied by their masters, and were frequently catechised before the congregation. A part of Lady Yester's Church, was set apart for their use, and afterwards the eastern gallery of the Trinity College church.

In 1680, the Privy Council issued a proclamation prohibiting all private Latin schools to be opened within the city or suburbs, and thus the High School enjoyed an almost undisturbed monopoly; and sixteen years after, in the proceedings of the Town Council, we find the following enactment:—

"*Edinburgh, Sept.* 11, 1696.—The Council considering that the High School of this city being situate in a corner at some distance, many of the inhabitants, whose children are tender, being unwilling to expose them to the cold winter mornings, and send them to the said school before the hour of seven, as use is; therefore, the Council ordain the masters of the said school in all time coming, to meet and convene at nine of the clock in the morning during the winter season, viz., from the 1st of November to the 1st March yearly, and to teach the scholars till twelve, that which they were in use to teach in those mornings and forenoons. And considering that the ordinary Latin rudiments in use to be taught children at their beginning to the Latin tongue is difficult and hard for beginners, and that Wedderburn's Rudiments are more plain and easy, the Council ordain the said masters in time coming, to teach and begin their scholars with Wedderburn's Rudiments in place of the Latin Rudiments in use as taught formerly. Ro. CHIESLIE, *Provost.*"

David Wedderburn, whose work is thus referred to, was born about 1570, and was the accomplished author of many learned works, and died, it is supposed, about 1644, soon after the publication of his "Centuria Tertia."

In 1699 £40 Scots was voted by the magistrates to procure books as a reward for the best scholars, and when the century closed the institution was in a most creditable condition, and they—as patrons —declared that "not a few persons that are now eminent for piety and learning, both in Church and State, had been educated there."

In the year 1716 there was an outbreak among the scholars for some reason now unknown; but they seem to have conducted themselves in an outrageous manner, demolishing every pane of glass in the school, and also of Lady Yester's church, levelling to the earth even the solid stone wall which enclosed the school-yard. About this time the janitor of the institution was David Malloch, a man distinguished in after life as author of the beautiful ballad of "William and Margaret," a poet and miscellaneous writer, and under-secretary to the Prince of Wales in 1733; to please the English ear, he changed his name to Mallet, and became an avowed infidel, and a venal author of the worst description. Dr. Steven refers to his receipt as being extant, dated 2nd February, 1718, "for sixteen shillings and eight pence sterling, being his full salary for the preceding half-year. That was the exact period he held the office."

In 1736 we again hear of the *Bleis-silver,* "a profitable relic of popery, which it seemed difficult to relinquish." Heartburnings had arisen because it had become doubtful in what way the Candlemas offerings should be apportioned between the rector and masters; thus, on the 28th January in that year, the Council resolved "that the rector himself, and no other, shall collect, not only his own quarterly fees, but also the fee of one shilling from each scholar in the other classes. The Council also transferred the right from the master of the third, to the master of the first elementary class, to demand a shilling quarterly from each pupil in the rector's class; and declared that the rector

and four masters should favourably receive from the scholars themselves whatever benevolence or Candlemas offerings might be presented."

Thomas Ruddiman, the eminent grammarian and scholar, who was born at Boyndie in 1674, and who in 1724 began to vary his great literary undertakings by printing the ancient *Caledonian Mercury,* about 1737 established—together with the rector, the masters, and thirty-one other persons—a species of provident association for their own benefit and that of their widows and children, and adopting as the title of the society, "The Company of the Professors and Teachers of liberal arts and sciences, or any branch or part thereof, in the City of Edinburgh and dependencies thereof."

The co-partners were all taxed equally; but owing to inequalities in the yearly contributions, a dissolution nearly took place after an existence of fifty years; but the association rallied, and still exists in a flourishing condition.

One of the most popular masters in the early part of the eighteenth century was Mr. James Barclay, who was appointed in June, 1742, and whose experience as a teacher, attainments, and character, caused him to be remembered by his scholars long after his removal to Dalkeith, where he died in 1765.

When Henry Mackenzie, author of the "Man of Feeling," was verging on his eightieth year, he contributed to Dr. Steven's "History," his reminiscences of the school in his own early years, between 1752 and 1757, which we are tempted to quote at length:—

"Rector Lees, a very respectable, grave, and gentlemanlike man, father or uncle, I am not sure which, of Lees, the Secretary for Ireland. He maintained great dignity, treating the other masters somewhat *de haut en bas*; severe, and rather too intolerant of dulness, but kind to more promising talents. It will not be thought vanity, I trust—for I speak with the sincerity and correctness of a third person—when I say that I was rather a favourite with him, and used for several years after he resigned his office to drink tea with him at his house in a large land or building at the country end of the suburb called Pleasance, built by one Hunter, a tailor, whence it got the name of 'Hunter's Folly,' or 'the Castle o' Clouts.'

"MASTERS continued.—*First,* or youngest class, when I was put to school, Farquhar, a native of Banffshire, cousin-german of Farquhar, author of admired—and indeed they may be called admirable—sermons, and of Mr. Farquhar, the Vicar of Hayes, a sort of 'Parson Adams,' a favourite of the great William Pitt, afterwards Lord Chatham. My master was a great favourite of his pupils, about sixty in number.

" *Second.*—Gilchrist, a good-humoured man, with a great deal of comedy about him ; also liked by the class, in number somewhat exceeding Farquhar's.

" *Third.*—Rae, a severe, harsh-tempered man, but an excellent scholar, a rigid disciplinarian, and very frequent flogger of the school, consequently very unpopular with the boys, though from the reputation

were then removed to the Rector's class, where they read portions of Livy, along with the other classics above mentioned.   The hours of attendance were from seven to nine a.m., and after an interval of an hour for breakfast, from ten to twelve ; then after an interval of two hours (latterly, I think, in my time, three) for dinner, returned for two hours in the afternoon. The scholars wrote versions, translations from Latin into English ; and at the annual examination in August recited speeches, as

THE HIGH SCHOOL ERECTED IN 1578. *(After the Engraving in Dr. Steven's History of the School.)*

of his superior learning, he had more scholars than either of the above masters.

" *Fourth.*—Gib, an old man, short and squabby, with a flaxen three-tailed wig, verging towards dotage, though said to be in his younger days a very superior scholar, and particularly conversant in Hebrew. He had then only twenty-five or thirty pupils, who liked him from the indulgence which his good-natured weakness and laxity of discipline produced.

" The scholars went through the four classes taught by the under-masters, reading the usual elementary Latin books—for at that time no Greek was taught in the High School—and so up to Virgil, Horace, Sallust, and parts of Cicero. They

they were called, being extracts of remarkable passages from some of the Roman poets.

" Of eminent men educated at the High School were most of the leading lawyers of Scotland. In modern times were President Hope, Mr. Brougham, Mr. Francis Horner, Mr. Wilde, the great favourite of Mr. Burke, Mr. Reddie, town clerk of Glasgow, who, during the short time he was at the Edinburgh bar had a high reputation for his ability and knowledge of law. Lord Woodhouselee was at the school with me, in the class below mine ; so was Lord Meadowbank, who had for his tutor Mr. Adam, afterwards rector. The Chief Commissioner Adam was of the same standing and class."

In 1765 began the connection of the eminent

Alexander Adam, LL.D., with this seminary, when he was appointed joint-rector with Alexander Matheson, who died in Merchant's Court in 1799; and of the many distinguished men who have presided over it, few have left a higher reputation for learning behind them.

Born at the Coates of Burghie in Elgin, in 1741, he was the son of humble parents, whose poverty was such, that during the winter mornings, in boyhood, he conned his little Elzevir edition of Livy and other tasks by the light of bog-splinters found in the adjacent morass, having to devote to manual labour the brighter hours of day. In 1757 he obtained a bursary at Aberdeen, and after attending a free course of lectures at the Edinburgh University, he was employed at the sum of one guinea per quarter, in the family of Alan Maconochie, afterwards Lord Meadowbank. "At this time," says Anderson in his biography of Adam, "he lodged in a small room at Restalrig, for which he paid fourpence per week. His breakfast consisted of oatmeal porridge with small beer ; his dinner often of a penny loaf and a drink of water." Yet, at the age of nineteen, so high were his attainments, he obtained—after a competitive examination—the head-mastership of Watson's Hospital; and in 1765, by the influence of the future Lord Provost Kincaid, he became joint-rector of the High School with Mr. Matheson, whose increasing infirmities compelled him to retire on a small annuity ; and thus, on the 8th of June, 1768, Adam succeeded him as sole rector, and most assiduously did he devote himself to his office.

To him the school owes much of its high reputation, and is entirely indebted for the introduction of Greek, which he achieved in 1772, in spite of the powerful opposition of the Senatus Academicus. Into his class he introduced a new Latin grammar of his own composition, as a substitute for Ruddiman's, causing thereby a dispute between himself and the masters, and also the Town Council, in defiance of whose edict on the subject in 1786 he continued to use his own rules till they ceased to interfere with him. In 1780 the degree of LL.D. was conferred upon him by the College of Edinburgh, chiefly at the suggestion of Principal Robertson ; and before his death he had the satisfaction of seeing his own grammar finally adopted in the seminary to which he had devoted himself.

By 1774 it was found that the ancient school house, built in 1578, was incapable of accommodating the increased number of pupils ; its unsuitable state had frequently been brought before the magistrates ; but lack of revenue prevented them from applying the proper remedy of the growing evil.

At last several of the leading citizens, including among others, Sir William Forbes, Bart., of Pitsligo, Professor John Hope, William Dalrymple, and Alexander Wood, surgeon, set afoot a subscription list to build a new school, and on March 8, 1775, the Council contributed thereto 300 guineas. The Duke of Buccleuch gave 500, Lord Chancellor Wedderburn, 100, and eventually the sum of £2,000 was raised —but the building cost double that sum ere it was finished—and plans were prepared by Alexander Laing, architect. The managers of the Royal Infirmary presented the projectors with a piece of ground from their garden to enlarge the existing area, and the Corporation of Surgeons also granted a piece from the garden before their hall.

On the 24th June, 1777, the foundation-stone of the second High School was laid by Sir William Forbes, as Grand Master Mason of Scotland. The procession, which was formed in the Parliament Square, and which included all the learned bodies in the city, moved off in the following order :— The magistrates in their robes of office ; the Principal of the University (Robertson, the historian) and the professors in their academic gowns ; the Rector Adams in his gown at the head of his class, the scholars marching by threes—the smallest boys in front ; the four masters, each with his class in the same order ; sixteen masonic lodges, and all the noblesse of the city. There was no South Bridge then ; so down the High Street and Blackfriars Wynd, and from the Cowgate upward, the procession wound to the High School yard.

The total length of the building erected on this occasion—but now turned to other uses—was a hundred and twenty feet long, by thirty-eight. The great hall, which was meant for prayers, measured sixty-eight feet by thirty, and at each end was a library of thirty-two feet by twenty. The second floor was divided into five apartments or class-rooms, with a ceiling of seventeen feet. It was all built of smoothly-dressed ashlar, and had a Doric portico of four columns, with a pediment.

This, then, was the edifice most intimately associated with the labours of the learned Rector Adams, and one of the chief events in the history of which was the enrolment of Sir Walter Scott as a scholar there when the building was barely two years old.

"In 1779," says Sir Walter in his Autobiography, "I was sent to the second class of the grammar school, or High School, then taught by Mr. Luke Fraser, a good Latin scholar and a very worthy man. Though I had received with my brothers, in private, lessons of Latin from Mr. James French, now a minister of the Kirk of Scotland, I was nevertheless behind the class in which I was placed both in years and progress. This was a real disadvantage, and one to which a boy of lively temper ought to be as little exposed as one who might be less expected to make up his leeway, as it is called. The situation has the unfortunate effect of reconciling a boy of the former character (which in a posthumous work I may claim for my own) to holding a subordinate station among his class-fellows, to which he would otherwise affix disgrace. There is also, from the constitution of the High School, a certain danger not sufficiently attended to. The boys take precedence in their *places*, as they are called, according to their merit, and it requires a long while, in general, before even a clever boy (if he falls behind the class, or is put into one for which he is not quite ready) can force his way to the situation which his abilities really entitle him to hold. . . . . It was probably owing to this circumstance that, although at a more advanced period of life I have enjoyed considerable facility in acquiring languages, I did not make any great figure at the High School, or, at least, any exertions which I made were desultory, and little to be depended upon."

In the class with Scott, at this time, were several clever boys among whom he affectionately enumerates, the first *dux*, who retained that place without a day's interval during "all the while we were at the High School"— James Buchan, afterwards head of the medical staff in Egypt, where amid the wards of the plague-hospitals, " he displayed the same well-regulated and gentle, yet determined perseverance, which placed him most worthily at the head of his class-fellows ;" his personal friends were David Douglas, and John Hope, W.S., who died in 1842.

"As for myself," he continues, " I glanced like a meteor from one end of the class to the other, and commonly disgusted my master as much by negligence and frivolity, as I occasionally pleased him by flashes of intellect and talent. Among my companions my good nature and a flow of ready imagination rendered me very popular. Boys are uncommonly just in their feelings, and at least equally generous. I was also, though often negligent of my own task, always ready to assist my friends, and hence I had a little party of staunch partisans and adherents, stout of heart and hand, though somewhat dull of head—the very tools for raising a hero to eminence. So, on the whole, I made a brighter figure in the *Yards* than in the *Class*."

After being three years in Luke Fraser's class, Scott, with other boys of it, was turned over to that of the Rector Adam's, under whose tuition he benefited greatly in the usual classic course ; and in the years to come he never forgot how his heart swelled with pride when the learned Rector announced that though many boys "understood the Latin better, *Gualterus Scott* was behind few in following and enjoying the author's meaning. Thus encouraged, I distinguished myself by some attempts at poetical versions from Horace and Virgil. Dr. Adam used to invite his scholars to write such essays, but never made them tasks. I gained some distinction on these occasions, and the Rector in future took much notice of me, and his judicious mixture of censure and praise went far to counterbalance my habits of indolence and inattention. I saw that I was expected to do well, and I was piqued in honour to vindicate my master's favourable opinion. . . . . . Dr. Adam, to whom I owe so much, never failed to remind me of my obligations when I had made some figure in the literary world."

In 1783 Scott quitted the High School, intent —young though he was—on entering the army ; but this his lameness prevented. His eldest son, Lieut.-Col. Sir Walter Scott, who died in 1847, on board the *Wellesley*, near the Cape of Good Hope, was also a High School pupil, under Irwin and Pillans, between 1809 and 1814.

In the spring of 1782, David, Earl of Buchan, the active founder of the Scottish Society of Antiquarians, paid a formal visit to the school, and harangued the teachers and assembled scholars, after which Dr. Adam made an extempore reply in elegant Latin ; and nine years subsequently the latter gave to the world one of his most important works, " The Roman Antiquities," which has been translated into many languages, and is now used as a class book in many English schools, yet for which he only received the sum of £600.

In 1795 we find among the joint writing-masters at the High School the name of Allan Masterton, who was on such terms of intimacy with Robert Burns, and composed the music for his famous bacchanalian song,

" Oh, *Willie* brewed a peck o' maut,
    And *Rab* and *Allan* cam' to prie ;
    Three blyther lads that lee lang nicht,
    Ye wadna find in Christendie !"

"Willie" was William Nicol, M.A., another schoolmaster and musical amateur, afterwards a private teacher in Jackson's Land, on the north side of the High Street, in 1795. "The air is Masterton's," says Burns ; "the song is mine. . . . . We had such a joyous meeting that Mr. Masterton and I agreed, each in our own way, to celebrate the business."

Of the Rector and other teachers we have the following description by Mr. B. Mackay, M.A., in Steven's work :—" I first saw the High School in 1803. I was then a youth of sixteen, and had come from Caithness, my native county, with a view to prosecute the study of medicine . . . . . The first master to whom I was introduced was the celebrated Dr. Adam. He was sitting at his study table with ten or twelve large old volumes spread out before him. He received us with great kindness, invited me to visit his class, and obligingly offered to solve any difficulties that might present themselves in the course of my classical reading, but held out no prospect of private teaching. His appearance was that of a fresh, strong, healthy old man, with an exceedingly benevolent countenance. Raeburn's portrait of him, hung up in the school, is an admirable likeness, as well as the print engraved from it. He wore a short threadbare spencer, or jacket, which gave him rather a droll appearance, and, as I then thought, indicated economical habits. I was successively introduced to all the other masters, and visited their classes. The first day I entered Dr. Adam's class he came forward to meet me, and said, ' Come away, sir ! You will see more done here in an hour than in any other school in Europe.' I sat down on one of the cross benches. The Doctor was calling up pupils from all parts of it ; taking sometimes the head, sometimes the foot of the forms ; sometimes he examined the class downwards from head to foot, and sometimes from foot to head. . . . . The next class I visited was that of Mr. Alexander Christison, afterwards Professor of Humanity. He was seated quite erect in his desk, his chin resting on his thumb, and his fore-finger turned up towards his temple, and occasionally pressed against his nose. When we entered he took no notice of us. He was giving short sentences in English, and requiring the boys to turn them *extempore* into Latin, and vary them through all the moods and tenses, which they did with great readiness and precision. His class was numerous, but presented the stillness of death. You might have heard a pin drop. . . . . . The next master to whom I was introduced was Mr. Luke Fraser, whom we found standing on the floor examining his class. He was, I think, the strongest built man I ever beheld. He was then old, and wore a scratch wig. The class, like the rest, was numerous and in fine order. In changing books, however, the boys made a little noise, which he checked by a tremendous stamp on the floor that made both them and me quake, and enveloped his own legs in a cloud of dust."

During all the years of his rectorship Adam was contributing from time to time to the classical literature of the country. The least popular of his many works is the " Classical Biography," published in 1800 ; and the last and most laborious of his useful compilations was his abridged " *Lexicon Lingua Latina Compendiarium*," 8vo, published in 1805. Through life he had been a hard student and an early riser. On leaving his class at three p.m., his general walk was round by the then tree-shaded Grange Loan ; but in earlier years his favourite ramble was up the green slopes of Arthur's Seat. Having been seized in school with an apoplectic attack, he languished for five days, and as death was approaching, fancying himself during the wanderings of his mind, as the light faded from his eyes, still among his pupils, he said, "*But it grows dark*—boys, you may go !" and instantly expired, in the 68th year of his age, on the 18th December, 1809.

His remains were laid in the gloomy little ground attached to St. Cuthbert's chapel of ease, where a monument was erected to his memory with a Latin inscription thereon, written by Dr. James Gregory of the Edinburgh University. He was among the last who adhered to the old-fashioned dress, breeches and silk stockings, with knee and shoe-buckles and the queue, though he had relinquished the use of hair-powder.

A successor was found to him in the person of Mr. James Pillans, M.A. (the "paltry Pillans" of Byron's "English Bards and Scotch Reviewers "), who was elected rector on the 24th of January, 1810. As one of the Doctor's early pupils, and ranking next to Francis Horner, who had borne off the highest honours, he entered upon his duties with enthusiasm, and the ardour with which he was received in the hall of the High School on his appearance there, augured well for the future. In 1812 he published a selection from the school exercises of his best pupils, a volume, which, excepting imperfections, was most honourable to the boyish authors, the oldest of whom had not reached his fifteenth year. A favourable critique of this unique work—which was in Latin metre—appeared in the *Quarterly Review* from the pen of the then poet laureate, Southey. ·

To the cultivation of Greek literature great attention was now paid, and the appearance made by the pupils at their periodical examinations was so brilliant, that on the motion of Sir John Marjoribanks, Bart., the Lord Provost, the Town Council unanimously resolved on the 27th July, 1814, "that there be annually presented by the City of Edinburgh to the boy at the head of the Greek class, taught by the Rector of the High

School, a gold medal of the same value (five guineas) as that annually presented to the Latin class."

"Several circumstances, to which I shall briefly advert," wrote an old pupil to Dr. Steven, "seemed, in my time, to distinguish the High School, and could not fail to give a peculiar character to many of its scholars in after life. For instance, the variety of ranks : for I used to sit between a youth of a ducal family and the son of a poor cobbler.

Humanity in the University, which he filled long and with the highest honour.

He was succeeded as Rector by Aglionby-Ross Carson, M.A., LL.D , a native of Dumfries-shire, who in 1806 had obtained a mastership in the school, and laboured in it assiduously and successfully. Three months before his appointment as Rector he had declined the Greek chair in the University of St Andrews, to which, though not a candidate, he had been elected. It was while he

THE SECOND HIGH SCHOOL, 1820. (*After Storer.*)

Again, the variety of nations : for in our class under Mr. Pillans there were boys from Russia, Germany, Switzerland, the United States, Barbadoes, St. Vincent's, Demarara, the East Indies, England, and Ireland. But what I conceive was the chief characteristic of our school, as compared at least with the great English schools, was its semi-domestic, semi-public constitution, and especially our constant intercourse at home with our sisters and other folk of the other sex, these, too, being educated in Edinburgh ; and the latitude we had for making excursions in the neighbourhood."

In June, 1820, the connection ceased between the school and Mr. Pillans, who, on the death of Professor Christison, was awarded the Chair of

was in office that the third and last High School— that magnificent building which has been described in our account of the Calton Hill—was erected ; and the closing examination in the old school-house at the foot of Infirmary Street took place in the autumn of 1828, and that interesting locality, where the successive youth of Edinburgh for more than two hundred and seventy years had flocked for the acquisition of classical learning—a school-boy scene enshrined in the memories of many generations of men, was abandoned for ever.

In 1828 the disused school-house was sold to the managers of the Royal Infirmary for £7,500, and was adapted to form part of the Surgical Hospital, externally, however, remaining unchanged.

DR. ADAM. (*After the Portrait by Raeburn.*)

CHAPTER XXXVI.

THE OLD ROYAL INFIRMARY—SURGEON SQUARE.

The Old Royal Infirmary—Projected in time of George I.—The First Hospital Opened—The Royal Charter—Second Hospital Built—
Opened 1741—Size and Constitution—Benefactors' Patients—Struck by Lightning—Chaplain's Duties—Cases in the Present Day—The
Keith Fund—Notabilities of Surgeon Square—The House of Curriehill—The Hall of the Royal and Medical Society—Its Foundation—
Bell's Surgical Theatre.

THOUGH the ancient Scottish Church had been during long ages distinguished for its tenderness and charity towards the diseased poor, a dreary interval of nearly two centuries, says Chambers, intervened between the extinction of its lazar-houses and leper-houses, and the time when a merely civilised humanity suggested the establishment of a regulated means for succouring the sickness-stricken of the poor and homeless classes.

A pamphlet was issued in Edinburgh in 1721 suggesting the creation of such an institution, and there seems reason to suppose that the requirements of her rising medical schools demanded it; but the settled gloom of the "dark age" subsequent to the Union, usually stifled everything, and the matter went to sleep till 1725, when it was revived by a proposal to raise £2,000 sterling to carry it out.

In that year a fishing company was dissolved, and the partners were prevailed upon to assign part of their stock to promote this benevolent institution, which the state of the poor in Edinburgh rendered so necessary, as hitherto the members of the Royal College of Physicians had given both medicines and advice to them gratis.

A subscription for the purpose was at the same time urged, and application made to the General Assembly to recommend a subscription in all the parishes under its jurisdiction; but Arnot records, to the disgrace of the clergy of that day, that "ten out of eleven utterly disregarded it."

Aid came in from lay purses, and at the second meeting of contributors, the managers were elected, the rules of procedure adjusted, and in 1729, on the 6th of August, the Royal Infirmary—one of the grandest and noblest institutions in the British Isles, was opened, but in a very humble fashion—in a small house hired for the sick poor, near the old University—a fact duly recorded in the *Monthly Chronicle* of that year, on the 18th of the month. This edifice had been formerly used by Dr. Black, Professor of Chemistry, as the place for delivering his lectures, says Kincaid, but this must have been before his succession to the chair. It was pulled down when the South Bridge was built. Six physicians and surgeons undertook to give, as before, medicines and attendance gratis; and the total number of patients received in the first year amounted to only thirty-five, of whom nineteen were dismissed as cured. The six physicians, whose names deserve to be recorded with honour, were John M'Gill, Francis Congalton, George Cunninghame, Robert Hope, Alexander Munro, and John Douglas. " Such was the origin of the Edinburgh Infirmary, which, small as it was at first, was designed from its very origin as a benefit to the whole kingdom, no one then dreaming that a time would come when every considerable county town would have a similar hospital."

In the year 1736, by a royal charter granted by George II., at Kensington palace, on the 25th of August, the contributors were incorporated, and they proposed to rear a building calculated to accommodate 1,700 patients per annum, allowing six weeks' residence for each at an average; and after a careful consideration of plans a commencement was made with the east wing of the present edifice, the foundation-stone of which was laid on the 2nd of August, 1738, by George Mackenzie, the gallant Earl of Cromarty, who was then Grand Master Mason of Scotland, and was afterwards attainted for leading 400 of his clan at the battle of Falkirk. The Royal College of Physicians attended as a body on this occasion, and voted thirty guineas towards the new Infirmary.

This portion of the building was, till lately, called the Medical House. Supplies of money were promptly rendered. The General Assembly—with a little better success—again ordered collections to be made, and the Established clergy were now probably spurred on by the zeal of the Episcopalians, who contributed to the best of their means; so did various other public bodies and associations. Noblemen and gentlemen of the highest position, merchants, artisans, farmers, carters—all subscribed substantially. Even the most humble in the ranks of the industrious, who could not otherwise aid the noble undertaking, gave their personal services at the building for several days gratuitously.

Many joiners gave sashes to the windows. A Newcastle glass-making company glazed the whole house gratis; and by personal correspondence money was obtained, not only from England and Ireland, but from other parts of Europe, and even from America, as Maitland records; but this would be, of course, from Scottish colonists or exiles.

So the work of progression went steadily on, until the present great quadrangular edifice on the south side of Infirmary Street was complete. It consists of a body and two projecting wings, all four storeys in height. The body is 210 feet long, and in its central part is thirty-six feet wide; in the end portions, twenty-four. Each wing is seventy feet long, and twenty-four wide. The central portion of the edifice is ornate in its architecture, having a range of Ionic columns surmounted by a Palladian cornice, bearing aloft a coved roof and cupola. Between the columns are two tablets having the inscriptions, "I was naked and ye clothed me;" "I was sick and ye visited me;" and between these, in a recess, is, curiously enough, a statue of George II. in a Roman costume, carved in London.

The access to the different floors is by a large staircase in the centre of the building, so spacious as to admit the transit of sedan chairs, and by two smaller staircases at each end. The floors are portioned out into wards fitted up with beds for the patients, and there are smaller rooms for nurses and medical attendants, with others for the manager, for consultations, and students waiting.

Two of the wards devoted to patients whose cases are deemed either remarkable or instructive, are set apart for clinical lectures attended by students of medicine, and delivered by the professors of clinical surgery in the adjacent University. Within the attic in the centre of the building is a spacious theatre, capable of holding above 200 students to witness surgical operations. The Infirmary has separate wards for male and female patients, and a ward which is used as a Lock hospital; but even in ordinary periods the building had become utterly incompetent for the service of Edinburgh, and during the prevalence of an epidemic afforded but a mere fraction of the required accommodation, and hence the erection of its magnificent successor, to which we shall refer elsewhere.

The Earl of Hopetoun, in 1742, and for the last twenty-five years of his life, generously contributed £400 per annum to the institution when it was young and struggling. In 1750 Dr. Archibald Kerr of Jamaica bequeathed to it an estate worth £218 11s. 5d. yearly; and five years afterwards the Treasury made it a gift of £8,000; yet it has never met with the support from Government that it ought to have done, and which similar institutions in London receive.

But the institution owed most of its brilliant success to Lord Provost Drummond. Among his associates in this good work he had the honoured members of the Colleges of Physicians and Surgeons in Edinburgh, ever first in all works of goodness and charity; and the first Dr. Munro, Professor of Anatomy, was singularly sanguine of the complete success of the undertaking.

That portion of the house which was founded by the Earl of Cromarty was opened for the reception of patients in December, 1741. The theatre described was made to serve the purposes also of a chapel, and twelve cells on the ground floor, for cases of *delirium tremens*, being found unnecessary, were converted into kitchens and larders, &c. The grounds around the house, consisting of two acres, and long bounded on the south by the city wall, were laid out into grass walks for the convalescents, and ultimately the house was amply supplied with water from the city reservoir.

In the years 1743-4 the sick soldiers of the regiments quartered in the Castle were accommodated in the Infirmary; and in the stormy period of the '45 it was of necessity converted into a great military hospital for the sick and wounded troops of both armies engaged at Prestonpans and elsewhere; and in 1748 the surgeon-apothecaries, who since 1729 had given all manner of medical aid gratis, were feed for the first time. Wounded from our armies in Flanders have been sent there for treatment.

In 1748, after paying for the site, building, furniture, &c., the stock of the institution amounted to £5,000; and sick patients not wishing to be resident were invited to apply for advice on Mondays and Fridays, and were in cases of necessity admitted as supernumeraries at the rate of 6d. per day. About this time there was handed over an Invalid Grant made by Government to the city, on consideration of sixty beds being retained for the use of all soldiers who paid 4d. per diem for accommodation. This sum, £8,270, was fully made over to the managers, who, for some time after, found themselves called upon to entertain so many military patients, that a guard had to be mounted on the house to enforce order; and liberty was obtained to deposit all dead patients in Lady Yester's churchyard, on the opposite side of the street.

Hitherto the physicians had, with exemplary fidelity, attended the patients in rotation; but in January, 1751, the managers on being empowered by the general court of contributors, selected Dr. David Clerk and Dr. Colin Drummond, physicians in ordinary, paying them the small honorarium of £30 annually.

The University made offer to continue its services, together with those of the ordinary physicians, which offer was gladly accepted; and though the practice fell into disuse, they were long continued in monthly rotation. To the option of the two ordinary physicians was left the visiting of the patients conjointly, or by each taking his own department. "It was their duty to sign the tickets of admission and dismission. In case of any unforeseen occurrences or dangerous distemper, the matron or clerks were permitted to use this authority; the physicians on their arrival, however, were expected to append their signatures to the tickets. The good and economy of the house from the first, induced the managers to appoint two of their number to visit the institution once every month, who were enjoined to inquire how far the patients were contented with their treatment, and to note what they found inconsistent with the ordinary regulations: their remarks to be entered in a book of reports, to come under review at the first meeting of managers." ("Journal of Antiq.," Vol. II.)

In 1754 some abuses prevailed in the mode of dispensing medicines to the out-door patients, detrimental to the finances; an order was given for a more judicious and sparing distribution. In the following year application was made to the Town Council, as well as to the Presbytery of the Church, to raise money at their several churches to provide a ward for sick servants—which had been found one of the most useful in the house. From its first institution the ministers of the city had, in monthly rotation, conducted the religious services; but in the middle of 1756 the managers appointed a regular chaplain, whose duty it was to preach every Monday in the theatre for surgical operations.

He had, moreover, to say prayers twice weekly, and be ever ready to attend the dying when summoned by them.

In 1763 a number of Scottish soldiers disbanded on the great reduction of the army in that year, sick, lame, and destitute, applied for admission to the hospital. On this, an extraordinary meeting of the managers was summoned, and their application was granted, though the former did not consider themselves bound in any way to do so ; and in that year,

Three were struck down ; two recovered, but one became delirious. (*Scot. Mag.* Vol. XXX.)

The Colleges of Physicians and Surgeons had been in the habit of giving medical attendance in monthly rotation ; but the managers, finding this to prove inconvenient, selected two regular physicians and four expert surgeons, to whom various departments were committed. The four latter were named substitutes, and divided the year equally, so that each had his own quarter.

THE OLD ROYAL INFIRMARY. (*After the Drawing by Paul Sandby, in Maitland's "History of Edinburgh."*)

in pursuance of an order he received from the Commander-in-chief, Dr. Adam Austin commenced a regular visitation of the military wards, on the state of which he was bound to report to the Adjutant-General in Scotland. The Doctor was a Fellow of the Royal College of Surgeons. He married Anne, daughter of Hugh Lord Semple, and left a daughter who died so lately as March, 1864, aged 100 years and more. (*Scotsman*, 7th March, 1864.)

In 1768 the whole edifice narrowly escaped destruction, apparently not being provided with a lightning conductor. On the 30th of July the south wing was struck furiously by lightning ; many of the windows were destroyed and the building much damaged ; several of the patients felt the shock.

The other surgeons, or ordinaries of the Incorporation, attended by monthly rotation. The four substitutes, besides their quarterly attendance, had their monthly tour of duty with the rest ; "and when the month of any of the four fell in with his quarter, then, either the next substitute in order was to become his assistant, or he was to apply for the assistance of another for that month, that the attendance of two might at no time be wanting in the Infirmary."

Such was the organised system of attendance ; besides all this, the managers enjoined these substitutes to be present at all consultations, to take charge of all dresses and dressings, of the record of surgical cases kept by the surgeons' clerks, and of the instruments for the use of the wards; and to each of these four surgeons, after 1766, was assigned a salary in proportion to what the funds of the institution admitted.

Distinct as these regulations were, they did not work well, and a committee was appointed to confer with the managers in 1769 to adjust certain matters that were in dispute, and new arrangements were made. Under these " one of the substitutes was to be changed annually, and his place supplied by a brother duly elected by the Incorporation of Surgeons according to seniority—at least in the order in which they could find any disposed to accept of the trust: all this was to be done under the authority of the managers, and to continue in force until they saw cause to alter it."

About 1769 the ordinary patients, exclusive of soldiers and servants, averaged about sixty; but the funds having grown apace, eighty were accommodated. "If the physicians, on a due consideration of certain cases thought otherwise, no more were to be admitted, and those taken in, so long as they remained supernumeraries, were expected to pay sixpence per day."

Dr. John Stedman, on the 2nd of August, 1773, was elected in place of Dr. Drummond, who had emigrated to Bristol; but his health was so infirm, that in 1775 Dr. Black was chosen in his place, and afterwards Dr. James Hamilton senior, one of the ornaments of the city; and after obtaining also the office of physician to George Heriot's, the Trades Maiden, and Merchant Maiden Hospitals, he superintended these benevolent institutions for upwards of fifty years.

As an estimate of the good accomplished it may

THE OLD ROYAL INFIRMARY, 1820. (*After Storer.*)

be mentioned that between 1770 and 1775 the numbers admitted yearly at an average amounted to 1,567⅙, and the number of deaths 63⅙, and, omitting fractional parts, the deaths were to the numbers admitted as 1 to 25.

In 1778 the total number of patients with their attendants made up a family of 230, but so rapid has been the increase of the population, that between October 1846 and October 1847 no fewer than 7,576 patients sought refuge within its walls. Of these 1,059 died—"a large number no doubt," says a report, "still, but for such a house of refuge, how many more would have breathed out their last amidst the noxious abodes of our city, spreading wider and wider the pestilential calamity which has swept away its thousands of victims in all parts of the country."

In the year 1848 the chaplain was required by new regulations to read a portion of the Scriptures, and engage in devotional exercises in every ward in the house—a duty which generally occupied about five hours; he had to meet the convalescent patients in chapel for religious duty every evening; to be ready to attend the dying, and he had to preach twice on Sunday to the nurses, servants, and all patients who could attend.

In the old house over 5,000 patients were admitted annually, of whom about 2,300 were surgical cases. The average number of out-door patients yearly was about 12,000, obtaining the benefit of the highest professional skill of the medical and surgical officers, and receiving all the necessary dressings, appliances, and comforts at the expense of the house, which has an admirable staff of nurses under a lady-superintendent.

We may close our notice of the Old Royal Infirmary by a reference to the Keith Fund, established by the late Mrs. Janet Murray Keith and her sister Ann for the relief of incurable patients who have been in the house. These generous ladies by trust-deed left a sum of money, the interest of which was to be applied for the behoof of all who were discharged therefrom as incurable by the loss of their limbs, or so forth. The fund, which consists of Bank of Scotland stock, is held for this purpose by trustees, who are annually appointed by the managers of the Royal Infirmary, the annual dividend to which amounts to £250. In 1877 there were on the list of recipients 101 patients receiving allowances varying from £1 to £4; and in their deed of settlement the donors express a hope that the small beginning thus made for the relief of such sufferers, if well managed, may encourage richer persons to follow their example. Although this trust is appointed to be kept separate for ever from the affairs of the Royal Infirmary, the trustees are directed to publish annually, with the report of the managers, an abstract of the fund, with such other information as they may deem desirable.

In the account of the west side of the Pleasance we have briefly adverted to the ancient hall of the Royal College of Surgeons,* which, bounded by the eastern flank of the city wall, was built by that body when they abandoned their previous place of meeting, which they rented in Dickson's Close for £40 yearly, and acquired Curriehill House and grounds, the spot within the angle of the wall referred to. This had anciently belonged to the Black Friars, but was secularised, and passed successively into the hands of Sir John and Sir James Skene, judges of the Court of Session, both under the title of Lord Curriehill. Sir James Skene "succeeded Thomas, Earl of Melrose, as President on the 14th Feb., 1626, in which office he continued till his death, which took place on the 15th October, 1633, in his own lodging beside the Grammar School of Edinburgh."

After them it became the property of Samuel Johnstoun of the Sciennes; and after him of the patrons of the university, who made it the house of their professor of divinity, and he sold it to the surgeons for 3,000 merks Scots in 1656.

This house, which should have been described in its place, is shown by Rothiemay's plan (see p. 241) in 1647 to have been a large half-quadrangular four-storeyed house, with dormer windows, a circular turnpike stair with a conical roof on its north front,

and surrounded by a spacious garden, enclosed on the south and east by the battlemented wall of the city, and having a doorway in the boundary wall of the High School yard on the north. On the site of this edifice there was raised the future Royal College of Surgeons, giving still its name to the adjacent Square.

On the west side of that square stood the hall of the Royal Medical Society, which, Arnot says, was coeval with the institution of a regular school of medicine in the University "by the establishment of professors in the different branches of that science. Dr. Cullen, Dr. Fothergill, and others of the most eminent physicians in Britain, were among the first of its members. None of its records, however, of an earlier date than A.D. 1737, have been preserved."

Since that year the greater number of the students of medicine at the University, who have been distinguished in after years by their eminence, diligence, and skill, have been members of this Society, to which none are admitted until they have made some progress in the study of physic.

In May, 1775, the foundation stone of their new hall in Surgeon Square was laid by Dr. Cullen in the presence of the other medical professors, the presidents of the learned societies, and a large audience.

This Society was erected into a body corporate by a royal charter granted on the 14th of December, 1778, and "is intended," says Arnot, writing of it in his own time, "as a branch of medical education, and a source of further discoveries and improvements in that science, and those branches of philosophy intimately connected with it. The members at their weekly meetings read in rotation discourses on medical subjects, which, at least six months previous to their delivery, had been assigned to them by the Society, either at their own request or by lot. And before any discourse be publicly read it is communicated in writing to every member, three of whom are particularly appointed to impugn, if necessary, its doctrines. From these circumstances the author of every discourse is induced to bestow the utmost pains in rendering it as complete as possible; and the other members have an opportunity of coming prepared to point out every other view in which the subject can be rendered. Thus, emulation and industry are excited, genius is called forth, and the judgment exercised and improved. By these means much information is obtained respecting facts and doctrines already published; new opinions are often suggested, and further inquiries pointed out. And it is acknowledged by all who are acquainted with the Univer-

---

* Vol. I., pp. 382-3.

sity of Edinburgh that the Medical Society has contributed much to the prosperity and reputation of this school of physic."

Such are still the objects of the Royal Medical Society, which has now, however, quitted its old hall and chambers for newer premises in 7 Melbourne Place. Its staff consists of four presidents, two honorary secretaries, curators of the library and museum, with a treasurer and sub-librarian.

Many old citizens of good position had residences in and near the High School yards and Surgeon Square. Among these was Mr. George Sinclair of Ulbster, who married Janet daughter of Lord Strathmore, and who had a house of seven rooms in the yard, which was advertised in the *Courant* of 1761. His son was the eminent agriculturist, and first baronet of the family.

In 1790 a theatre for dissections and an anatomical museum were erected in Surgeon Square by Dr. John Bell, the eminent anatomist, who was born in the city on the 12th May, 1763, and who most successfully applied the science of anatomy to practical surgery—a profession to which, curiously enough, he had from his birth been devoted by his father. The latter, about a month before the child's birth, had—when in his 59th year—undergone with success a painful surgical operation, and his gratitude led him to vow he would rear his son John to the cause of medicine for the relief of mankind; and after leaving the High School the boy was duly apprenticed to Mr. Alexander Wood, surgeon, and soon distinguished himself in chemistry, midwifery, and surgery, and then anatomy, which had been somewhat overlooked by Munro.

In the third year after his anatomical theatre had been opened in the now obscure little square, he published his " Anatomy of the Human Body," consisting of a description of the action and play of the bones, muscles, and joints. In 1797 appeared the second volume, treating of the heart and arteries. During a brilliant career, he devoted himself with zeal to his profession, till in 1816 he was thrown from his horse, receiving a shock from which his constitution never recovered.

CHAPTER XXXVII.

ARTHUR'S SEAT AND ITS VICINITY.

The Sanctuary—Geology of the Hill—Origin of its Name, and that of the Craigs—The Park Walls, 1554—A Banquet *al fresco*—The Pestilence —A Duel—"The Guttit Haddie"—Mutiny of the Old 78th Regiment—Proposed House on the Summit—Muschat and his Cairn— Radical Road Formed—May Day—Skeletons found at the Wells o' Wearie—Park Improvements—The Hunter's Bog—Legend of the Hangman's Craig—Duddingston—The Church—Rev. J. Thomson—Robert Monteith—The Loch—Its Swans—Skaters—The Duddingston Thorn—The Argyle and Abercorn Families—The Earl of Moira—Lady Flora Hastings—Cauvin's Hospital—Parson's Green—St. Anthony's Chapel and Well—The Volunteer Review before the Queen.

TAKING up the history of the districts of the city in groups as we have done, we now come to Arthur's Seat, which is already well-nigh surrounded, especially on the west and north, by streets and mansions.

Towering to the height of 822 feet above the Forth, this hill, with the Craigs of Salisbury, occupies the greater portion of the ancient Sanctuary of Holyrood, which included the royal park (first enclosed and improved from a condition of natural forest by James V. and Queen Mary), St. Anne's Yard and the Duke's Walk (both now obliterated), the Hermitage of St. Anthony, the Hunter's Bog, and the southern parks as far as Duddingston, a tract of five miles in circumference, in which persons were safe from their creditors for twenty-four hours, after which they must take out a *Protection*, as it was called, issued by the bailie of the abbey; the debtors were then at liberty to go where they pleased on Sundays, without molestation; but later legal alterations have rendered retirement to the Sanctuary to a certain extent unnecessary.

The recent formation of the Queen's Drive round the hill, and the introduction of the rifle ranges in the valley to the north of it, have destroyed the wonderful solitude which for ages reigned there, even in the vicinity of a busy and stormy capital. Prior to these changes, and in some parts even yet, the district bore the character which Arnot gave it when he wrote :—" Seldom are human beings to be met in this lonely vale, or any creature to be seen, but the sheep feeding on the mountains, or the hawks and ravens winging their flight among the rocks." The aspect of the lion-shaped mountain and the outline of the craigs are known to every one. There is something certainly grand and awful in the front of mighty slope and broken rock and precipice, which the latter present to the city. Greenstone, which has been upheaved through strata surfaced with sandstone and clay, forms the body of this mighty mass; and in places where the sandstone has been quarried (as the craigs were for years to pave the streets of London), beautiful specimens have been obtained of radiated hæmatites, intermixed with steatites, green fibrous iron ore, and calcareous spar, a most uncommon mixture.

In many parts of the craigs have been found

them tearing the rock away in masses. Marks of the glacier are to be found all over these craigs and Arthur's Seat, and on various parts are found rounded boulders, some of which have been worked backwards and forwards till left at last, stranded by the farewell ebb of an ancient sea.

The rocky cone of Arthur's Seat is strongly magnetic. Mr. William Galbraith first called the atten-

PLAN OF ARTHUR'S SEAT (THE SANCTUARY OF HOLYROOD).

veins of calcareous spar, talc, zoolite, and amethystine quartzose crystals; and strange to say several large blocks of the same greenstone of which they are composed are to be found on Arthur's Seat, at elevations of from eighty to 200 feet above the craigs.

In ascending the steep path which leads from Holyrood to the top of the latter, we pass over layers of sandstone which show ripple marks—the work of the ice—of unknown ages, grinding and depositing pebbles, coarse sand, and sedimentary rock. The bluffs above the path must have had many a hard struggle, when glaciers crashed against

tion of men of science to this circumstance in 1831, when he stated that at some points he found the needle completely reversed. (*Edin. Phil. Journal*, No. XXII.)

Concerning the origin of the name of this remarkable mountain, and that of the adjacent craigs, there have been many theories. Arthur is a name of frequent occurrence in Scottish, as well as Welsh and English topography, and is generally traced by tradition to the famous Arthur of romance, and who figures so much in half-fabulous history. From this prince, who is said to have reigned over Strathclyde from 508 to 542, when he was slain at the battle of Camelon, unsupported tradition has always alleged that Arthur's Seat obtained its name ; while with equal veracity the craigs are said to have been so entitled · from the Earl of Salisbury, who accompanied Edward III. in one of his invasions of Scotland, an idle story told by Arnot, and often repeated since.

Maitland, a much more acute writer, says, "that the idea of the mountain being named from Arthur, a British or Cimrian king, I cannot give into," and

"Do thou not thus, brigane, thou sall be brynt,
　With pik, tar, fire, gunpoldre, and lynt
　On Arthuris-Sete, or on a hyar hyll."

And this is seventy-seven years before the publication of Camden's "Britannia," in which it is so named. But this is not the only Arthur's Seat in Scotland, as there is one near the top of Loch Long, and a third near Dunnichen in Forfarshire.

Concerning the adjacent craigs, Lord Hailes in a note to the first volume of his Annals, says of "the

THE HOLYROOD DAIRY.* (*From a Calotype by Dr. Thomas Keith.*)
[The circular structure in the background to the right was a temporary Government store.]

adds that he considers "the appellation of Arthur's Seat to be a corruption of the Gaelic *Ard-na-Said*, which implies the 'Height of Arrows ;' than which nothing can be more probable ; for no spot of ground is fitter for the exercise of archery, either at butts or rovers, than this ; wherefore *Ard-na-Said*, by an easy transition, might well be changed to Arthur's Seat."

Many have asserted the latter to be a name of yesterday, but it certainly bore it at the date of Walter Kennedy's poem, his "flyting," with Dunbar, which was published in 1508 :—

precipice now called Salisbury Craigs ; some of my readers may wish to be informed of the origin of a word so familiar to them. In the Anglo-Saxon language, *saer*, *sere*, means dry, withered, waste. The Anglo-Saxon termination of *Burgh*, *Burh*, *Barrow*, *Bury*, *Biry*, implies a castle, town, or habitation ; but in a secondary sense only, for it is admitted that the common original is *Beorg* a *rock*. . . . . Hence we may conclude, *Saerisbury*, *Serisbury*, *Salisbury*, is the *waste or dry habitation*. An apt description, when it is remembered that the hills which now pass under the general but corrupted

* Dr. J. A. Sidey writes : "The Holyrood Dairy, which stood at the entrance to St. Anne's Yard, had no reference to the Palace (from which it was 150 feet distant) except in regard to name. It was taken down about 1858, and was kept by Robert McBean, whose son was afterwards one of the 'Keepers' of the Palace(as Mr. Andrew Kerr tells me) and had the old sign in his possession. Mr. Kerr says the dairy belonged to the Corporation of Perth, and was held for charitable purposes, and sold for the sum of money that would yield the same amount as the rental of the dairy."

name of Arthur's Seat were anciently covered with wood. The other eminences in the neighbourhood of Edinburgh had similar appellations. Calton, or *Caldoun*, is admitted to be the hill covered with 'trees." But there is another hill named thus—. *Choilledun*, near the Loch of Monteith.

The rough wild path round the base of the Salisbury Craigs, long before the present road was formed, was much frequented for purpose of reverie by David Hume and Sir Walter Scott. Thither Scott represents Reuben Butler as resorting on the morning after the Porteous mob :—"If I were to choose a spot from which the rising or setting sun could be seen to the greatest possible advantage, it would be that wild path winding round the foot of the high belt of semicircular rocks, called Salisbury Craigs, and marking the verge of the steep descent which slopes down into the glen on the southeastern side of the city of Edinburgh. The prospect in its general outline commands a close-built high-piled city, stretching itself out beneath in a form, which to a romantic imagination may be supposed to represent that of a dragon ; now a noble arm of the sea, with its rocks, isles, distant shores, and boundary of mountains ; and now a fine and fertile champaign country varied with hill and dale. . . . . This path used to be my favourite evening and morning resort, when engaged with a favourite author or a new subject of study."

The highest portion of these rocks near the Catnick, is 500 feet above the level of the Forth ; and here is found a vein of rock different in texture from the rest. "This vein," says a writer, "has been found to pierce the sandstone below the footpath, and no doubt fills the vent of an outflow of volcanic matter from beneath. A vein of the same nature has probably fed the stream of lava, which forced its way between the strata of sandstone, and formed the Craigs."

A picturesque incident, which associates the unfortunate Mary with her turbulent subjects, occurred at the foot of Arthur's Seat, in 1564. In the romantic valley between it and Salisbury Craigs there is still traceable a dam, by which the natural drainage had been confined to form an artificial lake ; at the end of which, in that year, ere her wedded sorrows began, the beautiful young queen, in the sweet season, when the soft breeze came laden with the perfume of the golden whin flowers from the adjacent Whinny Hill, had an open-air banquet set forth in honour of the nuptials of John, fifth Lord Fleming, Lord High Chamberlain, and Elizabeth the only daughter and heiress of Robert Master of Ross.

In 1645, when the dreaded pestilence reached

Edinburgh, we find that in the month of April the Town Council agreed with Dr. Joannes Paulitius that for a salary of £80 Scots per month he should visit the infected, a vast number of whom had been borne forth from the city and hutted in the King's Park, at the foot of Arthur's Seat ; and on the 27th of June the Kirk Session of Holyrood ordered, that to avoid further infection, all who died in the Park should be buried there, and not within any churchyard, " except they mortified (being able to do so) somewhat, *ad pios usus*, for the relief of other poor, being in extreme indigence." (" Dom. Ann.," Vol. II.)

In November, 1667, we find Robert Whitehead, laird of Park, pursuing at law John Straiton, tacksman of the Royal Park, for the value of a horse, which had been placed there to graze at 4d. per night, but which had disappeared—no uncommon event in those days ; but it was urged by Straiton that he had a placard on the gate intimating that he would not be answerable either for horses that were stolen, or that might break their necks by falling over the rocks. Four years afterwards we read of a curious duel taking place in the Park, when the Duke's Walk, so called from its being the favourite promenade of James Duke of Albany, was the common scene of combats with sword and pistol in those days, and for long after. In the case referred to the duellists were men in humble life.

On the 17th June, 1670, William Mackay, a tailor, being in the Castle of Edinburgh, had a quarrel with a soldier with whom he was drinking, and blows were exchanged. Mackay told the soldier that he dared not use him so if they were without the gates of the fortress, on which they deliberately passed out together, procured a couple of sharp swords in the city, and proceeded to a part of the King's Park, when after a fair combat, the soldier was run through the body, and slain. Mackay was brought to trial ; he denied having given the challenge, and accused the soldier of being the aggressor ; but the public prosecutor proved the reverse, so the luckless tailor—not being a gentleman—was convicted, and condemned to die.

A beacon would seem to have been erected on the cone of Arthur's Seat in 1688 to communicate with Fifeshire and the north (in succession from Garleton Hill, North Berwick, and St. Abb's Head) on the expected landing of the Prince of Orange. On one occasion the appearance of a large fleet of Dutch fishing vessels off the mouth of the Firth excited the greatest alarm, being taken for a hostile armament.

The *Edinburgh Evening Courant* of the 29th of October, 1728, contains the following reference to the Craigs, or the chasm, there named the Catnick:—"A person who frequents the (King's) Park, having noticed a man come from a cleft towards the north-west of Salisbury Rocks, had the curiosity to climb the precipice, if possibly he might discover something that could invite him there. He found a shallow pit, which delivered him into a little snug room or vault hung with dressed leather, lighted from the roof, the window covered with a bladder. It is thought to have been the cave of a hermit of ancient times, though now the hiding-place of a gang of thieves."

The long, deep, and tremendous rift in the western slope of Arthur's Seat (locally known as the *Guttit Haddie*) was caused by a mighty waterspout, on the 13th of September, 1744. "Dividing its force"—says the "Old Statistical Account"—"it discharged one part upon the western side, and tore up a channel or chasm, which still remains a monument of its violence; the other division took its direction towards the village of Duddingston, carried away the gable of the most westerly cottage, and flooded the loch over the adjacent meadows."

On the steep sloping shoulder of Arthur's Seat, south-westward, under the Rock of Dunsappie, the Highland army encamped in September before the battle of Prestonpans, and from thence it was —after the Prince had held a council of his chiefs and nobles—the march began at daybreak on the morning of the 20th through the old hedgerows and woods of Duddingston, with pipes playing and colours flying, after Charles, in front of the line, had significantly drawn his claymore and flung away the scabbard.

From a letter which appears in the *Advertiser* for the 15th of January, 1765, the entrance to the Park from St. Anne's Yard to the Duke's Walk having become impassable, was privately repaired at the expense of a couple of classical wits, whose names were unknown, but who placed upon the entrance the following inscription :—

Ite nunc faciles per gaudia vestra,
QUIRITES
B Cque secun sua reficiendum cur.
Cal. Jan. MD.C.CLXV.
Dii faciant ut hæc sæpius fiant.

Mungo Campbell (formerly officer of Excise at Saltcoats), who shot Archibald, tenth Earl of Eglinton, committed suicide in the Tolbooth in 1770, on the day after he had been sentenced to death, when the judge also directed that his body should be given to the professor of anatomy. His counsel having interposed on the plea that dis-section was not a legal penalty for self-murder, it was privately interred at the foot of Salisbury Craigs. But the Edinburgh mob, who were exasperated by the manner in which he had shot the earl in a poaching affray, took the body out of the grave, tossed it about till they were tired, and eventually flung it over the cliffs. After this, to prevent further indecency and outrage, Campbell's friends caused the body to be conveyed in a boat from Leith and sank it in the Firth of Forth. (Caldwell Papers ; *Scots Mag.*, Vol. XXXII.)

Southward of the cone of Arthur's Seat are the Raven's Craig and the Nether Hill, or Lion's Haunch ; between the latter and the cone can still be traced the trench and breastwork formed by the Seaforth Highlanders when they revolted in 1778— an event which created a profound sensation in Scotland.

In the July of that year they had marched into the Castle, replacing the Royal Edinburgh Volunteers, or 80th Regiment of the Line, a corps which was raised by General Sir William Erskine in 1777, and was disbanded in 1783-5.

Kenneth Mackenzie, Earl of Seaforth, had recently raised his noble regiment, which was then numbered as the 78th (but is now known as the Duke of Albany's Own Highlanders), among his clansmen in the district of Kintail and Applecross, Kilcoy, and Redcastle ; of these 500 were from his own estate ; the rest were all from the others named, and the corps mustered 1,130 bayonets at its first parade in Elgin in the May of 1778 ; but from a great number of another sept who were in its ranks, the subsequent mutiny was known at first as *the affair of the Wild Macraas.*

The latter was an ancient but subordinate tribe of the west, who had followed the "Caber Feigh," or banner of Seaforth, since the days when Black Murdoch of Kintail carried it in the wars of Robert I., and now many of its best men were enrolled in Earl Kenneth's new Fencible regiment, perfect subordination in the ranks of which was maintained in the Castle until the 5th of August, when an order was issued for marching at an hour's notice. A landing of a French force being expected near Greenock, 200 of them, with seven 9-pounders, marched there with the greatest enthusiasm to meet the foe, who never appeared ; but by the time these two companies returned, transports to convey the whole for foreign service had come to anchor in Leith Roads.

Where the scene of that service lay the men knew not. It was kept a mystery from them and their officers. The former would not believe a rumour spread that it was to be the Isle of Guernsey, and a deep excitement prevailed, when it was whispered—none knew how—that they were under secret orders for the distant East Indies—in other words, that they had been *sold* to the East India Company by the Government, and that, worse than the authorities basely having an idea that the poor clansmen of Kintail "were ignorant, unable to comprehend the nature of their stipulations, and incapable of demanding redress for any breach of trust." But the Seaforth men were neither so ignorant

CLOCKMILL HOUSE, 1780.*
(From a Print by Robert and Andrew Riddell, in possession of Dr. J. A. Sidey.)

all, they had been sold by their officers and by the chief, whom they had looked upon as a father and leader.

All their native jealousy and distrust of the Saxon was now kindled and strengthened by their love of home. General David Stewart, in his "Sketches of the Highlanders," boldly asserts that the regiment was secretly under orders for India, nor so confiding as the Government supposed, and they were determined at all hazards not to submit to the least infraction of the terms on which they were enlisted as Fencible Infantry—limited service and within the British Isles ; and when the day for embarkation came, the 22nd September, their long-smothered wrath could no longer be hidden.

"The regiment paraded on the Castle hill, and

---

* This eighteenth-century building (which was in the shape of the letter L, with the door in the corner), has already been alluded to, see *ante*, p. 41.

all remained quiet until the order was given to march, when, to the astonishment of the Earl and his officers the greatest confusion ensued. A shout burst from the ranks; several hundred men loaded their muskets with ball; the whole fixed their bayonets; a scuffle ensued; some of the officers were wounded, and one was repeatedly fired on. The latter displayed the colours with their Gaelic mottoes, and by their efforts so far soothed the less refractory, that five hundred of them under Lord

Ere Lord Seaforth's portion had passed the Tron Church, it was assailed by the Macraas, who, with bayonet and claymore, wounded several officers and men; after which they made a rapid circuit through the Abbey Hill, down the Easter Road, and then advancing in line westward across Leith Links sought again to oppose his march to the harbour. Several shots were fired, and two hun' dred more joined the Macraas, who, with this accession of force, now marched direct to the

DUDDINGSTON VILLAGE, FROM THE QUEEN'S DRIVE. (*Partly after a Photograph by A. A. Inglis.*)

Seaforth marched for Leith; while four hundred (chiefly Macraas), deaf alike to threats and remonstrances, displayed two tartan plaids on pikes for standards, and with the pipers playing before them, marched down the Canongate, where they assailed the guard-house, and liberated some of their comrades who were confined there. ("Memorials of Edin. Castle.")

Kay relates the latter episode differently, stating that a party came from Arthur's Seat to demand their release, when Captain Mackenzie of Redcastle, commanding the Tolbooth guard there, on finding his life threatened, bared his breast, and told the mutineers to strike if they dared, but he would not release a man—on which the men recovered arms, and retired to the encampment.

summit of Arthur's Seat, accompanied by a vast concourse of sympathisers, from whom they received every encouragement, much applause, and what proved of more value—fuel, provisions, and ammunition.

They selected a strong position at the point mentioned, threw up a redoubt, and judiciously set watchers at all the approaches for the autumn night, amid a mountain solitude then as wild and silent as their native homes in Kintail. That night a sentinel fell over the Craigs, and was killed.

The revolt caused the greatest excitement in the city, where all were favourable to the Highlanders, many regiments of whom had been previously deluded by the Government. Sir Adolphus Oughton, Commander-in-chief in Scotland, and Major-

General Robert Skene, the Adjutant-General there, summoned all the troops they could collect to attack "the wild Macraas," and next day the 11th Dragoons, under Colonel Ralph Dundas, 200 of the Fencible Regiment of Henry Duke of Buccleuch, and 400 of the Royal Glasgow Regiment of Volunteers, or old 83rd Foot, commanded by Colonel Alexander Fotheringham Ogilvie, all marched into Edinburgh, and were deemed sufficient to storm Arthur's Seat.

On that day the Earl of Dunmore, Duncan Lord Macdonald and General Oughton, visited the revolters, who received them with military honours, while they ceased not to inveigh against their officers, whom they accused of peculation, and of having basely sold them to the India Company.

In their ranks at this time there was an unfortunate fellow named Charles Salmon, who had been born in Edinburgh about 1745, and had filled a subordinate position in the Canongate theatre, after being in the service of Ruddiman the printer. He was a companion of the poet Fergusson, and became a local poet of some note himself. He was laureate of the Jacobite Club, and author of many Jacobite songs; but his irregular habits led to his enlistment in the Seaforth Highland Regiment.

His superior education and address now pointed him out as a fit person to manage for his comrades the negotiations which ultimately led to a peaceful sequel to the dispute; but after the corps went to India poor *Stewart* Salmon, as he called himself, was heard of no more. On the 29th of September this revolt, which promised to have so tragic an end, was satisfactorily adjusted by the temperate prudence of the Duke of Buccleuch and others.

The Earl of Dunmore again visited the revolters, presented them with a bond containing a pardon, and promise of all arrears of pay. They then formed in column by sections of threes, and with the Earl and the pipers at their head, they descended by the Hunter's Bog to the Palace Yard, where they gave Sir Adolphus Oughton three cheers, and threw all their bonnets in the air. He then formed them in hollow square, and addressed them briefly, but earnestly exhorting them to behave well and obediently. On that night they all sailed from Leith to Guernsey, from whence they were soon after despatched to India—a fatal voyage to the poor 78th, for Lord Seaforth died ere St. Helena was in sight; then a great grief, with the *mal du pays*, fell upon his clansmen, and of 1,100 who sailed from Portsmouth, 230 perished at sea, and only 390 were able to carry arms, when, in April 1782, they began the march for Chingleput.

In 1783 an eccentric named Dr. James Graham, then lecturing in Edinburgh, in Carrubber's Close chiefly, the projector of a Temple of Health, and a man who made some noise in his time as a species of talented quack, who asserted that our diseases were chiefly caused by too much heat, and who wore no woollen clothes, and slept on a bare mattress with all his windows open, was actually in terms with the tacksman of the King's Park for liberty to build a huge house on the summit of Arthur's Seat, in order to try how far the utmost degree of cold in the locality of Edinburgh could be borne; but, fortunately, he was not permitted to test his cool regimen to such an extent.

Two localities near Arthur's Seat, invariably pointed out to tourists, are Muschat's Cairn, and the supposed site of Davie Deans' cottage, where an old one answering the description of Scott still overlooks the deep grassy and long sequestered dell, where gallants of past times were wont to discuss points of honour with the sword, and where Butler, on his way to visit Jeanie, encounters Effie's lover, and receives the message to convey to the former to meet him at Muschat's Cairn "when the moon rises."

Muschat's Cairn, a pile of stones adjacent to the Duke's Walk, long marked the spot where Nicol Muschat of Boghall, a surgeon, and profligate wretch, murdered his wife in 1720. On arraignment he pled guilty, and his declaration is one of the most horrible tissues of crime imaginable. He married his wife, whose name was Hall, after an acquaintance of three weeks, and, soon tiring of her, he with three other miscreants, his aiders and abettors in schemes which we cannot record, resolved to get rid of her. At one time it was proposed to murder the hapless young woman as she was going down Dickson's Close, for which the perpetrators were to have twenty guineas.

Through Campbell of Burnbank, then storekeeper in Edinburgh Castle, one of his profligate friends, Muschat hoped to free himself of his wife by a divorce, and an obligation was passed between them in November, 1719, whereby a claim of Burnbank, for an old debt of 900 merks, was to be paid by Muschat, as soon as the former should be able to furnish evidence to criminate the wife. This scheme failing, Burnbank then suggested poison, which James Muschat and his wife, a couple in poor circumstances undertook to administer, and several doses were given, but in vain. The project for criminating the victim was revived again, but also without effect.

Then it was that James undertook to kill her in Dickson's Close, but this plan too failed. These terrible schemes occupied Nichol Muschat, his brother, and his sister-in-law, together with Burnbank, "in the Christian city of Edinburgh, during a course of many months, without any one, to appearance, ever feeling the slightest compunction towards the poor woman, though it is admitted she loved her husband, and no real fault on her side has ever been insinuated."

At length it would seem that Nicol, infatuated and lured by evil fate, at the suggestion of "the devil, that cunning adversary"—as his confession has it—borrowed a knife, scarcely knowing for what purpose, and, inviting his unsuspecting wife to walk with him as far as Duddingston one night, cut her throat near the line of trees that marked the Duke's Walk. He then rushed in a demented state to tell his brother what he had done, and thereafter sank into a mood of mind that made all seem blank to him. Next morning the unfortunate victim was found "with her throat cut to the bone," and many other wounds received in her dying struggle.

In the favourite old Edinburgh religious tract, which narrates the murderous story, in telling where he went before doing the deed, he says that he passed "through the Tirlies," at the end of a lane which was near the Meadows. The entrance to the Park, near the Gibbet Fall, was long known as "the Tirlies," implying a sort of stile.

Nicol Muschat was tried, and confessed all. He was hanged, on the 6th of the ensuing January in the Grassmarket, while his associate Burnbank was declared infamous, and banished ; and the people, to mark their horror of the event, in the old Scottish fashion raised a cairn on the spot where the murder was perpetrated, and it has ever since been a well-remembered locality.

The first cairn was removed during the formation of a new footpath through the park, suggested by Lord Adam Gordon, who was resident at Holyrood House in 1789, when Commander of the Forces in Scotland ; but from a passage in the *Weekly Journal* we find that it was restored in 1823

ST MARGARET'S WELL.

by a cairn near the east gate and close to the north wall. "The original cairn is said to have been several paces farther west than the present one, the stones of which were taken out of the old wall when it was pulled down to give place to the new gate that was constructed previous to the late royal visit"—that of George IV.

In 1820 the pathway round Salisbury Craigs was formed, and named the "Radical Road" from the circumstance of the destitute and discontented west-country weavers being employed on its construction under a committee of gentlemen. At that time it was proposed to "sow the rocks with wall-flowers and other odoriferous and flowering plants." It was also suggested "to plant the cliffs above the walk with the rarest heaths from the Cape of Good Hope and other foreign parts." (*Weekly Journal*, XXIV.)

The papers of this time teem with bitter complaints against the Earl of Haddington, who, as a keeper of the Royal Park, by an abuse of his prerogative, was quarrying away the craigs, and selling the stone to pave the streets of London ; and the immense gaps in their south-western face still remain as proofs of his selfish and unpatriotic rapacity.

As a last remnant of the worship of Baal, or Fire, we may mention the yearly custom that still exists of a May-day observance, in the young of the female sex particularly, ascending Arthur's Seat on Beltane morning at sunrise. "On a fine May morning," says the "Book of Days," "the appearance of so many gay groups perambulating the hill sides and the intermediate valleys, searching for dew, and rousing the echoes with their harmless mirth, has an indescribably cheerful effect." Many old citizens adhered to this custom with wonderful tenacity, and among the last octogenarians who did so we may mention Dr. Andrew Duncan of Adam Square, the founder of the Morningside Asylum, who paid his last annual visit to the hill top on May-day, 1826, in his eighty-second year, two years before his death ; and James Burnet, the last captain of the old Town Guard, a man who weighed *nineteen* stone, ascended to the cone from the base by the way of St. Anthony's Well, for a wager, in fifteen minutes, on a hot summer's day—a feat in which he was timed by the eminent naturalist William Smellie.

In 1828 the operations connected with the railway tunnel, under the brow of the columnar mass of basalt known as Samson's Ribs, commenced, and near to the springs so well known in tradition as the Wells of Wearie. Close by these wells, and near a field named Murder Acre, in May the work-

In 1843 the sum of £40,000 was paid to Thomas Earl of Haddington, for the surrender of his office of Hereditary Keeper of the Royal Park, and thereafter extensive improvements were carried out under the supervision of the Commissioners for Woods and Forests. Among these not the least was the Queen's Drive, which winds round the park, passes over a great diversity of ground from high to low, slope to precipice, terrace to plateau, and commands a panorama second to none in

DUDDINGSTON CHURCH (EXTERIOR).

men came upon three human skeletons, only three and a half feet below the surface of the smooth green turf. As a very large dirk was found near one of them, they were conjectured to be the remains of some of Prince Charles's soldiers, who had died in the camp on the hill. The "Wells," are the theme of more than one Scottish song, and a very sweet one runs thus :—

"And ye maun gang wi' me, my winsom Mary Grieve ;
    There is nought in the world to fear ye ;
For I have asked your minnie, and she has gi'en ye leave,
    To gang to the Wells o' Wearie.

"Oh, the sun winna blink in your bonnie blue een,
    Nor tinge your white brow, my dearie ;
For I will shade a bower wi' rashes lang and green,
    By the lanesome Wells o' Wearie."

Europe. All the old walls which had intersected the park in various places, in lots as the Hamilton family had rented it off for their own behoof, were swept away at this time, together with the old powder magazine in the Hause, a curious little edifice having a square tower like a village church ; and during these operations there was found at the base of the craigs one of the most gigantic boulders ever seen in Scotland. It was blown up by gunpowder, and, by geologists, was alleged to have been torn out of the Corstorphine range during the glacial period.

Among the improvements at this time may be included the removal, in 1862, and re-erection (in the northern slope of the craigs) of St. Margaret's

Well from Restalrig, where it had been all but buried under the workshops of the North British Railway; but now a limpid perennial rill from the Craigs flows into its ancient basin, the Gothic archway to which is closed by an open iron gate.

The old solitude and amenity of the Hunter's Bog, after 1858, were destroyed by the necessary erection of four rifle ranges, two of 300 yards, and two of 600 yards, for the use of the garrison and family that had long possessed an estate near Melrose. His earlier years had been passed in profligacy; his patrimony was gone, and at length, for the sake of food, he was compelled to accept this degrading office, "which, in those days," says Chambers, "must have been unusually obnoxious to popular odium, on account of the frequent executions of innocent and religious men. Notwithstanding his extreme degradation, this unhappy

DUDDINGSTON CHURCH (INTERIOR).

volunteers, and the construction of two unornamental powder magazines. The danger signal is always hoisted in the gorge known as the Hause; the rocky ridge named the Dasses overlooks these ranges on the east.

Leaving the Echoing Rock, an isolated eminence, and following the old road round the hill, under Samson's Ribs, a superb range of pentagonal greenstone columns sixty feet long by five in diameter, the Fox's Holes, and the rugged stony slope named the Sclyvers, we come to a lofty knoll named the Girnel Craig, and another named the Hangman's Craig or Knowe, from the following circumstance. About the reign of Charles II., the office of public executioner was taken by a reduced gentleman, the last member of an old reprobate could not altogether forget his former tastes and habits. He would occasionally resume the garb of a gentleman, and mingle in the parties of citizens who played at golf in the evenings on Bruntsfield Links. Being at length recognised, he was chased from the ground with shouts of execration and loathing, which affected him so much that he retired to the solitude of the King's Park, and was next day found dead at the bottom of a precipice, over which he is supposed to have thrown himself in despair. The rock was afterwards called the *Hangman's Craig.*"

The deep gorge between it and the Sclyvers is named the Windy Goule, and through it winds the ancient path that leads direct to the hamlet of Duddingston, which, with the loch of that name, lies directly at the south-eastern base of Arthur's Seat, and has long been one of the daily postal districts of the city.

Overhung by the green slopes and grey rocks of Arthur's Seat, and shut out by its mountainous mass from every view of the crowded city at its further base in Duddingston, says a statist, writing in 1851, a spectator feels himself sequestered from the busy scenes which he knows to be in his immediate vicinity, as he hears their distant hum upon the passing breezes by the Willow Brae on the east, or the gorge of the Windy Goule on the south; and he looks southward and west over a glorious panorama of beautiful villas, towering castles, rich coppice, hill and valley, magnificent in semi-tint, in light and shadow, till the Pentlands, or the lonely Lammermuir ranges, close the distance.

The name of this hamlet and parish has been a vexed subject amongst antiquaries, but as a surname it is not unknown in Scotland: thus, among the missing charters of Robert Bruce, there is one to John Dudingstoun of the lands of Pitcorthie, in Fife; and among the gentlemen slain at Flodden in 1513 there was Stephen Duddingston of Kildinington, also in Fife. Besides, there is another place of the same name in Linlithgowshire, the patrimony of the Dundases.

GATEWAY OF DUDDINGSTON CHURCH, SHOWING THE JOUGS AND LOUPING-ON-STONE.

The ancient church, with a square tower at its western end, occupies a green and rocky peninsula that juts into the clear and calm blue loch. It is an edifice of great antiquity, and belonged of old to the Tyronensian Monks of Kelso, who possessed it, together with the lands of Eastern and Western Duddingston; the chartulary of that abbey does not say from whom they acquired these possessions, but most probably it was from David I.

Herbert, first abbot of Kelso, a man of great learning and talent, chamberlain of the kingdom under Alexander I. and David I., in 1128, granted the lands of Eastern and Western Duddingston to Reginald de Bosco for an annual rent of ten marks, to be paid by him and his heirs for ever.

From the style of the church and the structure of its arches, it is supposed to date from the epoch of the introduction of Saxon architecture. A semi-circular arch of great beauty divides the choir from the chancel, and a Saxon doorway, with fantastic heads and zig-zag mouldings, still remains in the southern face of the tower. The entrance-gate to its deep, grassy, and sequestered little burying-ground, is still furnished with the antique chain and collar of durance, the terror of evil-doers, named the jougs, and a time-worn *louping-on-stone*, for the use of old or obese horsemen.

Some interesting tombs are to be found in the burying-ground; among these are the marble obelisk erected to the memory of Patrick Haldane of Gleneagles by his unfortunate grandson, whose fate is also recorded thereon; and that of James Browne, LL.D., Advocate, the historian of the Highlands and Highland clans, in the tower of the church.

In the register of assignations for the minister's stipends in the year 1574, presented in MS. by Bishop Keith to the Advocates' Library, Duddingston is said to have been a joint dependence with the Castle of Edinburgh upon the Abbey of Holyrood. The old records of the Kirk Session are only of the year 1631, and in the preceding year the lands of Prestonfield were disjoined from the kirk and parish of St. Cuthbert, and annexed to those of Duddingston.

On the 18th of May, 1631, an aisle was added to the church for the use of the Laird of Prestonfield, his tenants and servants.

David Malcolme, minister here before 1741, was an eminent linguist in his time, whose writings were commended by Pinkerton, and quoted with respect by Gebelin in his *Monde Primitif*, and Bullet in his *Mémoires Celtiques*; but the church is chiefly famous for the incumbency of the Rev. John Thomson, a highly distinguished landscape painter, who from his early boyhood exhibited a strong predilection for art, and after being a pupil of Alexander Nasmyth, became an honorary member of the Royal Scottish Academy. He became incumbent of Duddingston in 1805. His favourite subjects were to be found in the grand and sublime of Nature, and his style is marked chiefly by vigour, power, and breadth of effect—strong light and deep shadow. As a man and a Christian minister, his life was simple, pure, and irreproachable, his disposition kind, affable, and benevolent. He died of apoplexy in 1840, in his sixty-second year.

The city must have had some interest in the loch, as in the Burgh accounts for 1554 we read :—
" Item : twa masons twa weeks to big the Park Dyke at the loch side of Duddingston, and foreanent it again on Priestfield syde, ilk man in the week xv'. summa iij".

" Item : for ane lang tree to put in the wall that lyes far in the loch for outganging of *wyld beistis* vj'." (" Burgh Records.")

The town or lands of Duddingston are included in an act of ratification to James, Lord Lindsay of the Byers, in 1592.

In the Acts of Sederunt for February, 1650, we find Alexander Craig, in-dweller in the hamlet, pilloried at the Tron of Edinburgh, and placarded as being a " lying witness " in an action-at-law concerning the pedigree of John Rob in Duddingston ; but among the few reminiscences of this place may be mentioned the curious hoax which the episcopal incumbent thereof at the Restoration played upon Cardinal de Retz.

This gentleman, whose name was Robert Monteith, had unfortunately become involved in an amour with a lady in the vicinity, the wife of Sir James Hamilton of Prestonfield, and was compelled to fly from the scene of his disgrace. He was the son of a humble man employed in the salmon-fishing above Alloa ; but on repairing to Paris, and after attaching himself to M. de la Porte, Grand Prior of France, and soliciting employment from Cardinal de Retz, he stated he was "one of the Monteith family in Scotland." The cardinal replied that he knew the family well, but asked to which branch he belonged. " To the Monteiths of Salmon-net," replied the unabashed adventurer.

The cardinal replied that this was a branch he had never heard of, but added that he believed it was, no doubt, a very ancient and illustrious family. Monteith was patronised by the cardinal, who bestowed on him a canonry in Notre Dame, and made him his secretary, in which capacity he distinguished himself by his elegance and purity, in the French language. This strange man is author of a well-known work, published in folio, entitled, " *Histoire des Troubles de Grand Bretagne,*

depuis l'an 1633 *jusqu'à l'an* 1649, *par Robert Mentet de Salmonet. Paris,* 1661."

It was dedicated to the Coadjutor Archbishop of Paris, with a portrait of the author ; and a translation of it, by Captain James Ogilvie, was published in 1735 by G. Strachan, at the "Golden Ball," in Cornhill.

In the year of the Revolution we find the beautiful loch of Duddingston, as an adjunct to the Royal Park, mentioned in a case before the Privy Council on the 6th March.

The late Duke of Lauderdale having placed some swans thereon, his clever duchess, who was carrying on a legal contest with his heirs, deemed herself entitled to take away some of those birds when she chose ; but Sir James Dick, now proprietor of the loch, broke a lock-fast place in which she had put them, and set them once more upon the water. The irate dowager raised an action against him, which was decided in her favour, but in defiance of this, the baronet turned all the swans off the loch ; on which the Duke of Hamilton, as Heritable Keeper of the palace, came to the rescue, as Fountainhall records, alleging that the loch bounded the King's Park, and that all the wild animals belonged to him ; they were, therefore, restored to their former haunts.

Of the loch and the lands of Priestfield (or Prestonfield), Cockburn says, in his "Memorials" :—"I know the place thoroughly. The reeds were then regularly cut over by means of short scythes with very long handles, close to the ground, and this (system) made Duddingston nearly twice its present size." Otters are found in its waters, and a solitary badger has at times provoked a stubborn chase. The loch is in summer covered by flocks of dusky coots, where they remain till the closing of the ice excludes them from the water, when they emigrate to the coast, and return with the first thaw. Wild duck, teal, and water-hens, also frequent it, and swans breed there prolifically, and form one of its most picturesque ornaments. The pike, the perch, and a profusion of eels, which are killed by the barbed sexdent, also abound there.

In winter here it is that skating is practised as an art by the Edinburgh Club. "The writer recalls with pleasure," says the author of the "Book of Days," "skating exhibitions which he saw there early in the present century, when Henry Cockburn, and the philanthropist James Simpson, were conspicuous amongst the most accomplished of the club for their handsome figures and great skill in the art. The scene of that loch 'in full bearing' on a clear winter day, with its busy and stirring multitude of sliders, skaters, and curlers, the snowy hills around glistening in the sun, the ring of the ice, the shouts of the careering youth, the rattle of the curling-stones, and the shouts of the players, once heard and seen, would never be forgotten."

It was to Duddingston, in 1736, that the fugitive, "Geordie Robertson," the stabler at Bristo Port, after effecting that escape from St. Giles's Church by the generous courage of Wilson, which led to the catastrophe of the Porteous mob, and after passing through the East Cross Causeway,

Not far from it, and nearly opposite the gate of the Manor House, stood for ages a memorable thorn, known as Queen Mary's Tree. It was one of the oldest in Scotland, and of great proportions, being over nine feet in circumference. It formerly stood within the park, but on widening the carriage-way, it remained outside, and many fissures being found in its root, they were filled up with lime and stone by order of the road trustees ; but too late : a storm in 1840 tore it up by the roots. A

DUDDINGSTON LOCH.

took his breathless flight. When reaching the village, he fainted from exhaustion, but after receiving some refreshment—the first he had obtained for three days—he procured a horse, rode away, and was never heard of again.

Western Duddingston, at the north end of the loch, was once a populous village, wherein some forty looms were at work in the Loan, making a coarse linen stuff, then known as Duddingston hardings. It is surrounded by gardens and plantations, and in it is still shown the house in which Prince Charles slept, with his staff, on the night before he marched to Prestonpans. It was then thatched, but has now a tiled roof, and consists of two storeys.

well-known and justly-reputed statist, who resided in the neighbourhood, ascertained that the Duddingston Thorn existed so far back as the reign of Alexander I. (1107), when it was one of the landmarks of the property on which it grew. It is mentioned in the title-deeds of the Abercorn estate, and hence the desire of the family to preserve a precise knowledge of the spot where it stood.

The barony of Duddingston, which comprehends the greatest part of the whole parish, was long in possession of a family named Thomson, created baronets of Nova Scotia, 1636, in the person of Sir Thomas Thomson of Duddingston, by Charles I. Sir William Thomson—his son, probably—was a

Commissioner for the Plantation of Kirks and Valuation of Benefices in 1672; but the title is now extinct, and in 1674 the barony had become the property of the atrocious Duke of Lauderdale, from whom it passed with a daughter of his first duchess, as pin money, to her husband, Archibald, tenth earl, and first Duke of Argyle.

This lady was Elizabeth, daughter of Sir Lionel Talmash of Helingham, and her mother was the daughter and heiress of William Murray, Earl of

mansion house upon it. It was completed in 1768, from designs furnished by the architect of Somerset House, in the Strand, Sir William Chambers, the son of Scottish parents, but born in Stockholm in 1726. It cost £30,000, and is an elegant edifice of a somewhat Grecian style, surrounded by plantations, canals, and gardens, but in a situation too low for any extensive view.

Duddingston House was for years the favourite residence of Francis, Earl of Moira, a veteran of

PRINCE CHARLIE'S HOUSE, DUDDINGSTON.
(From the Engraving in the Roxburgh Edition of "Waverley," published by Messrs. A. & C. Black.)

Dysart. The celebrated John and Archibald, successively Dukes of Argyle, passed much of their time here, and it is said received most of their education from their mother, who resided constantly in this, then, secluded village prior to 1734.

In 1745 Duddingston was sold by Archibald, Duke of Argyle, to James, Earl of Abercorn, whose ducal descendants still hold it; but it was not until 1751 that this beautiful and valuable estate was sub-divided, enclosed, and improved by James, the eighth earl, who built commodious farm-houses, planted hedgerows and coppice in places where the land, prior to 1746, rented at only ten shillings per acre !

In 1763, after the estate had been thoroughly enclosed, the earl began to build the present

the American War, who, in 1803, was appointed Commander-in-chief in Scotland, where he was long deservedly popular with the people, and where he married, in 1804, Flora Mina Campbell (in her own right), Countess of Loudon, who was the first, north of the Tweed, to introduce those laconic invitation cards now so common, and the concise style of which—"The Countess of Loudon and Moira at Home"—so puzzled the Edinburgh folk to whom they were issued.

On the 14th of June, 1805, one of these "At Homes" is thus noticed in a print of the day :—

"On Friday evening the Countess of Loudon and Moira gave a grand fête at Duddingston House, to receive three hundred of the nobility and gentry in and about the city—among whom were the Duke of Buccleuch, the Earl of Errol, the Earl of Dalhousie, the Earl of Roden, Lord Elcho, Count Piper, Sir John Stuart, Sir William Forbes, Admiral Purves, Sir James Hall, the Countesses of Errol and Dalhousie, Lady Charlotte Campbell (the famous beauty), Lady Elizabeth Rawdon, Lady Helen Hall, Lady Stuart, Lady Fettes, Admiral Vashon (who conquered the Jygate pirates), and a great number of naval and military gentlemen, most of the judges, &c. The saloon was brilliantly fitted up with festoons of flowers, and embellished with a naval pillar, on which were the names of *Howe, Duncan, St. Vincent,* and *Nelson.* The dancing commenced at ten o'clock, and was continued till two in the morning."

In this year the earl also had a residence in Queen Street (where Lady Charlotte Campbell also resided in Argyle House), but whether it was there or at Duddingston that his daughter, the celebrated Lady Flora Hastings, was born, there are now no means of ascertaining, as no other record of her birth seems to remain but its simple announcement in the *Scots Magazine:* "At Edinburgh, 11th March, 1806, the Countess of Loudon and Moira of a daughter." The story of this amiable and unfortunate lady, her poetical talent, and the inhumanity with which she was treated at Court, are too well known to need more than mention here. On his appointment as Governor-General of India, in 1813, the earl, to the regret of all Scotland, bade farewell to it, and, as the song has it, to "Loudon's bonnie woods and braes," whither he did not return till the summer of 1823; he was then seventy-one years of age, but still erect and soldierly in form. "The marchioness is forty-six," says the editor of the *Free Press* on this occasion, "and seems to have suffered little from the scorching climate. She has all the lady in her appearance—modest, dignified, kind, and affectionate. Lady Flora is a young lady of most amiable disposition, mild and attractive manners." The earl died and was buried at Malta; but Lady Flora lies beside her mother in the family vault at Loudon, where she was laid in 1839, in her thirty-third year. An edition of her poems, seventy in number, many of them full of touching pathos and sweetness, was published in 1842 by her sister, who says in her preface that the profits of the volume would be dedicated "to the service of God in the parish where her mother's family have so long resided . . . . to aid in the erection of a school in the parish of Loudon, as an evidence of her gratitude to Almighty God and her good will to her fellow creatures."

Prior to the purchase of Sandringham, the estate of Duddingston, it is said, would have been purchased by H.R.H. the Prince of Wales, but for some legal difficulties that were in the way.

At the south-east end of Duddingston Loan, where the road turns off towards the Willow Brae and Parson's Green, stands, at the point of the eastern slope of Arthur's Seat, Cauvin's Hospital, the founder of which, Louis Cauvin (Chauvin or Calvin), was a teacher of French in Edinburgh, whose parents were Louis Cauvin and Margaret Edgar. "It is not correctly ascertained," says Kay's editor, "on what account the father was induced to leave his native country and settle in the metropolis of Scotland. According to some accounts, he was forced to expatriate himself, in consequence of the fatal issue of a duel in which he had been implicated. According to others, he was brought over to Edinburgh as a witness in the 'Douglas Cause,' having served in the capacity of a footman in the family of Lady Jane Douglas for a considerable time during her residence in Paris. A portrait of him in his youth, in military garb, is still preserved."

After teaching for a time, he became tenant of a small farm near the hamlet of Jock's Lodge, where he died in 1778, and was buried in Restalrig.

His son Louis, after being educated at the High School and the Universities of Edinburgh and of Paris, became a teacher of French in the former city, where he retired from work in 1818 with a handsome fortune, realised by his own exertions. Imitating his father, for twenty years before relinquishing his scholastic labours he rented a large farm in Duddingston, now named the Woodlands, and during his occupation of it he built, on the opposite side of the Loan, then, as now, wooded and bordered by hedges, the house of Louisfield, which forms the central portion of his hospital. He died in 1824, and was laid beside his father in Restalrig.

By a codicil to his will, dated Duddingston Farm, 28th April, 1823, he thus arranges for his sepulture:—"My corpse is to be deposited in Restalrig churchyard, and watched for a proper time. The door of the tomb must be taken off, and the space built up strongly with ashlar stones. The tomb must be shut for ever, and never to be opened. There is a piece of marble on the tomb door, which I put up in memory of my father; all I wish is that there may be put below it an inscription mentioning the time of my death. I beg and expect that my trustees will order all that is written above to be put in execution."

The hospital he founded resembles a large and elegant villa, and was opened in 1833, for the maintenance of twenty boys, sons of teachers and farmers, who are maintained in it for six years; "whom failing, the sons of respectable master printers or booksellers, and the sons of respectable servants in the agricultural line," and who, when admitted, must be of the age of six, and not more than eight, years. They are taught the ordinary branches of education, and Latin, Greek, French, German, and mathematics.

The management of this institution is in the survivor of certain individuals nominated by the founder, and in certain *ex-officio* trustees, viz., the Lord Provost, the Principal of the University, the Rector of the High School, the Ministers of Duddingston, Liberton, Newton, the Laird of Niddrie, and the factor of the Duke of Abercorn.

On the north-east side of Arthur's Seat, overlooked by those portions of it known as the Whinny Hill and Sampson's Grave, is the Mansion House of Parson's Green, which was terribly shaken by three distinct shocks of an earthquake on the 30th September, 1789, that caused a dinner party there to fly from the table, while the servants also fled frm the kitchen.

Here the hand of change has been at work, and though the mansion house and much of its surrounding timber have been retained, streets have been run along the slope and close to Piershill Tollbar, and westward of these was the great dairy, long known as the Cow palace, and the temporary railway station for the use of the royal family.

Above the curious little knoll, named the Fairies' or Haggis Knowe, on a plateau of rock overlooking St. Margaret's artificial loch, on the northern slope of Arthur's Seat, we find the ruined chapel and hermitage of St. Anthony—a familiar feature in the landscape.

The former, which terminated in a square tower, with two gables at its summit—as shown in the view of the city in 1544—is 36 feet long by 12 inside the walls, and was roofed by three sets of groined arches that sprang from corbels. It had two entrance doors, one on the south and one on the north, where the hole yet remains for the bar that secured it. Near it was the elegantly-sculptured font. A press, grooved for shelves, yet remains in the north-east corner; and a stair ascended to the tower, which rose on groins about forty feet high.

Nine yards south-east is the ruin of the hermitage, partly formed of the rock, irregular in shape, but about 17 feet by 12 in measurement. The hermit who abode here must, in the days when it was built, have led a lonely life indeed, though beneath him lay a wealthy abbey and a royal palace, from whence a busy city, girt by embattled walls, covered all the slope to the castled rock. More distant, he could see on one side the cheerful fields and woods that spread away towards the Firth of Forth, but elsewhere only the black basaltic rocks; and, as a writer has excellently expressed it, he had but to step a few paces from the brow of the rock on which his cell and chapel stood to immure himself in such a grim mountain solitude as Salvator Rosa might have thought an appropriate scene for the temptations of that saint of the desert to whom the chapel was dedicated. Kincaid says that a handsome stone seat projected from the outside of the wall at the east end, and the whole appeared to have been enclosed by a stone wall.

So simple is the architecture of the edifice that it is difficult to assign any precise date for it. There remains not a single vestige of record to say when, or by whom, it was erected or endowed, though it stands in the centre of a tract that for ages has been a royal park. No reference to it occurs in the muniments of the Abbey of Holyrood, nor is there any evidence—though it has often been asserted—that it was a chaplaincy or pendicle of the Knights Hospitallers of St. Anthony in Leith. Yet it is extremely probable that it was in some way connected with them.

Tradition says it was merely founded for the guardianship of the holy well in its vicinity, and that it was a spot for watching vessels, the impost on which formed part of the revenues of the adjacent abbey, and also that a light was hung in the tower to guide mariners in the Firth at night, that, as Grose says in his "Antiquities," they might be induced to make vows to its titular saint.

At the foot of the rock there still bubbles up the little spring named St. Anthony's Well, which flows pleasantly down through the rich grass of the valley. Originally the spring flowed from under the little stone arch, but about the year 1674 it dried up, and after a time broke out lower down, where we now find it. The well is referred to in the old song which begins "O waly, waly!" the Scottish exclamation for "Alas!" In Robert Chambers's "Scottish Songs" there is a note upon it, from which we may give the following passage :—

"This beautiful old song has hitherto been supposed to refer to some circumstance in the life of Queen Mary, or at least to some unfortunate love affair which happened at her Court. It is now discovered, from a copy which has been found as forming part of a ballad in the Pepysian Library at Cambridge (published in Motherwell's 'Minstrelsy,' 1827, under the title of 'Lord Jamie Douglas '), to have been occasioned by the affecting tale of Lady Barbara Erskine, daughter of John (sixteenth Lord Erskine), ninth Earl of Mar, and wife of James II.,

Marquis of Douglas. This lady, who was married in 1670, was divorced, or at least expelled from the society of her husband, in consequence of some malignant scandals which a former and disappointed lover, Lowrie of Blackwood, was so base as to insinuate into the ear of the marquis."

Her father took her home, and she never again saw her husband, who married Mary, daughter of the Marquis of Lothian, and died in 1700. Lady Barbara's only son, James, Earl of Angus, fell

Martinmas wind, when wilt thou blaw,
   An' shake the green leaves aft the tree ?
O gentle death, when wilt thou come ?
   For o' my life I am wearie."

A public event of great importance in this locality was the Royal Scottish Volunteer Review before the Queen on the 7th of August, 1860, when Edinburgh, usually so empty and dull in the dog days, presented a strange and wonderful scene. For a few days before this event regiments from all

RUINS OF ST. ANTHONY'S CHAPEL, LOOKING TOWARDS LEITH. (*From a Photograph by Alex. A. Inglis.*)

bravely at Steinkirk, in his twenty-first year, at the head of the 26th, or Cameronian Regiment. Two verses of the song run thus :—

> " Oh, waly ! waly ! gin love be bonnie
>   A litttle time while it is new ;
> But when it 's auld it waxeth cauld,
>   And fades away like morning dew.
> Oh, wherefore should I busk my heid?
>   Or wherefore should I kame my hair ?
> For my true love has me forsook,
>   And says he 'll never love me mair.
>
> " Now Arthur's Seat shall be my bed,
>   The sheets shall ne'er be pressed by me ;
> St. Anton's Well shall be my drink,
>   Since my true love 's forsaken me !

parts of Scotland came pouring into the city, and were cantoned in school-houses, hospitals, granaries, and wherever accommodation could be procured for them. The Breadalbane Highlanders, led by the white-bearded old marquis, attracted especial attention, and, on the whole, the populace seemed most in favour of kilted corps, all such being greeted with especial approbation.

Along the north wall of the park there was erected a grand stand capable of containing 3,000 persons. The royal standard of Scotland—a splendid banner, twenty-five yards square—floated from the summit of Arthur's Seat, while a multitude of other standards and snow-white bell-tents covered all the inner slopes of the Craigs. By

THE VOLUNTEER REVIEW IN THE QUEEN'S PARK, 1860.
(From the Print published by Messrs. McFarlane & Erskine, Edinburgh.)

23

one o'clock all the regiments were in Edinburgh, and defiled into the park by four separate entrances at once, and were massed in contiguous close columns, formed into divisions and brigades of artillery, engineers, and infantry, the whole under the command of Lieutenant-General Sir G. A. Wetherall, K.C.B.

The scene which burst upon the view of these volunteers as they entered the park, and the vast

was magnificent, when more than two-and-twenty thousand rifles and many hundred sword-blades flashed out the royal salute, and then the arms were shouldered as she drove slowly along the line of massed columns. The ground was kept by the 13th Hussars, the 29th Regiment, 78th Highlanders (the recent heroes of Lucknow), and the West York Rifle Militia. The Queen seemed in the highest spirits, wore a tartan dress, and bowed and smiled as

ST. ANTHONY'S CHAPEL IN 1544 AND 1854.

(From a Drawing by the Author; the Chapel as in 1544 being restored from a View in a Print of the Period as shown in top left-hand corner.)

slopes of Arthur's Seat came in sight, will never be forgotten by those who were there, and made many a strong man's heart beat high and his eyes glisten. The vast hilly amphitheatre was crowded by more than 100,000 spectators, who made the welkin ring with their reiterated cheers, as the deep and solid columns, with all their arms glittering in the sun, were steadily forming on the grassy plain below. Every foot of ground upon the northern slopes not too steep for standing on was occupied, even to the summit, where the mighty yellow standard with the red lion floated out over all.

When the Queen, accompanied by the Prince Consort, the aged Duchess of Kent, and the royal children, came in front of the grand stand, the sight

the Volunteers passed the saluting point in quick time, to the number of 250 regiments, the Highland corps being played past by the pipers of the Ross-shire Buffs.

"So admirable was the arrangement," wrote one at the time, "by which the respective corps were brought back to their original ground, that not ten minutes had elapsed after the marching-past of the last company before all was ready for the advance in line, the officers having taken post in review order, and the men standing with shouldered arms. On the signal being given, the whole line (of columns) advanced, the review bands playing. The effect of this was, in one word, indescribable, and when the whole was simultaneously halted, and the royal salute given, the silent grandeur of the scene, broken only by the National Anthem, sent a thrill of heart-stirring awe through the assembled multitude. But on a sudden the death-like silence is broken, and the pent-up enthusiasm of the Volunteers breaks forth like the bursting of some vast reservoir. A cheer, such as only Britons have in them to give, goes forth with the full power of 22,000 loyal throats— a cheer such as old Holyrood never heard before, caught up by the crowds on the hill, and rolled back to the plain, again and again to burst forth with redoubled energy, until it merges into one prolonged, heart-stirring, joyous roar — shakoes, caps, and busbies, being held high on swords, rifles, and carbines ; and then it was that the Queen spoke long to Sir George Wetherall, expressing her delight."

By six p.m. all was over, and by the four exits the whole 22,000 men had left the park in about half an hour, and the columns moved like long glittering snakes through the streets of the city, on their journey home by road or rail ; and so admirable were the municipal arrangements, that not the slightest accident occurred, and

ST. ANTHONY'S WELL.
(From a Photograph by Alex. A. Inglis.)

the slopes of the great hills were bared of their multitudes as if by magic. The great review was over, and in due time came the following order from the Adjutant-General Sir J. Yorke Scarlett :—

"Horse Guards, August 10th, 1860.

"The Adjutant-General has received the Queen's commands to convey her thanks to the several corps of Artillery and Rifle Volunteers assembled at Edinburgh on the 7th instant, and to assure them of the satisfaction and gratification with which Her Majesty beheld the magnificent spectacle presented to her.

"Her Majesty could not see without admiration the soldier-like bearing of the different corps as they passed before her ; and she finds in the high state of efficiency to which they have attained in an incredibly short space of time another proof that she may at all times surely rely on the loyalty and patriotism of her people for the defence, in

the hour of need, of the freedom and integrity of the empire."

On the same ground, in August 1881, and before a vast multitude, Her Majesty reviewed a force of 40,000 Scottish Volunteers. So many men under arms had not been massed together in Scotland since James IV. marched to Flodden. "Although unhappily marred by continuous rain," says the Duke of Cambridge's order, dated Edinburgh Castle, August 26th, "the spectacle yesterday presented to her Majesty was an admirable sequel to the great review held recently at Windsor, and the Queen has observed with much gratification, the same soldierlike bearing, progress in discipline, and uniform good conduct, which distinguished the Volunteers there assembled, were conspicuous in a like degree on the present occasion. . . . . The Field Marshal Commanding in Chief has been commanded by the Queen to express to the Volunteers of all ranks her entire satisfaction with the appearance of the troops assembled."

The whole force was commanded by Major General Alastair Macdonald ; and perhaps none were more applauded in the march past than the London Scottish, led by Lord Elcho. The bands of the Black Watch and 5th Fusileers were placed beside the saluting post, whereon was hoisted the royal standard, as borne in Scotland, the lion rampant being first and fourth in the quarterings.

Undeterred by the incessant deluge of rain, the Queen remained till the last, and so did the rest of the royal party ; but even ere the second division had defiled before her the vast slopes of Arthur's Seat had been greatly denuded of spectators, "and the great mass of umbrellas slipped down and gathered about the Holyrood gates, egress through which was still denied," owing to certain instructions adapted evidently to a fair-weather gathering.

It was greatly to the credit of these Scottish troops, and a proof of their excellent discipline, that to the very close of that trying and harassing day, their behaviour was quiet, orderly, and admirable to the last, and not a single accident occurred.

CHAPTER XXXVIII.

BRISTO AND THE POTTERROW.

Bristo Street—The Darien House—The Earl of Rosebery—Old Charity Workhouse—A Strike in 1764—Old George Inn—U. P. Church—Dr. Peddie –Sir Walter Scott's First School—The General's Entry and the Dalrymples of Stair—Burns and Clarinda—Crichton Street—Alison Rutherford of Farnielee—The Eastern Portsburgh—The Duke of Lennox Men—The Plague—The Covenanters' Gun Foundry—A Witch—A Contumacious Barber—Tailors' Hall—Story of Jean Brown—Duke of Douglas's House—Thomas Campbell the Poet—Earl of Murray's House—Charles Street and Field.

THOSE who see Forrest Road now—a broad and handsome thoroughfare—can form no conception of the features of its locality for more than a hundred years before 1850.

A great archway, in a modern addition to the city wall, led from the Bristo Port by a winding pathway, a hundred yards long, and bordered by trees to a wicket, or klinket-gate, in the city wall, opposite the centre walk of the meadows. On its west side rose the enormous mass of the old Charity Workhouse, with a strong box at its gate, inscribed, " He that giveth unto the poor lendeth unto the Lord," and having an orifice, wherein the charitable passer might drop a coin. On its east side were the ancient offices of the Darien Company, the Correction House, and Bedlam, to which another pathway diverged south-eastward from before the Workhouse gate. On the east and south rose the mass of the embattled city wall, black with smoke and years, and tufted with grass.

A group of mansions of vast antiquity, their dark chimneys studded by glistening oyster-shells, were on the west side of the Bristo Port, the name of which is still retained by two or three houses of modern construction.

In 1647 the whole of the area referred to here was an open grass park of oblong form, about 250 paces long by 200 broad, according to Gordon's map.

Till lately the west side of Bristo Street, from the Port to Teviot Row, was entirely composed of the dead angle of the city wall. Immediately within this, facing the south, stood the office of the Darien Company, a two-storeyed and substantial edifice, built of polished freestone, with the high-pitched roof that came into fashion with William of Orange ; but till the last " it was a melancholy and desolate memorial of that unfortunate enterprise." A row of eight arched niches were along its upper storey, but never held busts in them, though intended for such.

This edifice was built in 1698, as an ornamental tablet above the main entrance bore, together with a sun-dial, and within, a broad flight of handsome stairs, guarded by balustrades, led to the first floor. Here, then, was transacted the business of that

grand national project, the Darien Expedition, formed for establishing a settlement on the isthmus of that name, and fitting out ships to trade with Africa and the Indies. By this the highest anticipations were raised ; the then large sum of £400,000 was subscribed, and an armed expedition sailed from Scotland for the new settlement.

Apart from people of all ranks who were subscribers to this scheme, we may mention that the Faculty of Advocates, the Merchant Company of Edinburgh, with Sir Robert Christie the Provost, the Cities of Edinburgh and Perth, joined it as communities ; but " meanwhile, the furious denunciations of the English Parliament proved a thorough discouragement to the project in London, and nearly the whole of the stockholders there silently withdrew from it. Under the same influence the merchants of Hamburg were induced to withdraw their support and co-operation, leaving Scotland to work out her own plans by herself. She proceeded to do so with a courage to be admired." (" Dom. Ann.," Vol. III.) The house described was built, and schemes for trade with Greenland, Archangel, and the Gold Coast, were considered, and, under the glow of a new and great national object, all the old feuds and antipathies of Covenanter and Cavalier were forgotten, till pressure from without crushed the whole enterprise.

When intelligence reached Edinburgh that the company had planted the Scottish flag on Darien, formed Fort St. Andrew, and successfully repulsed the Spaniards, who were urged to the attack by William of Orange, thanksgivings were offered up in St. Giles's and all the other churches ; the city was illuminated ; but the mob further testified their joy by seizing all the ports, setting fire to the Tolbooth door, and liberating all the prisoners incarcerated there for issuing seditious prints against the king and the English Court.

No less vehement was the fury of the populace on the destruction of this national enterprise, than their joy at its first brief success. The Tolbooth was again forced, the windows of all adherents of King William were broken, and such rage was exhibited, that his commissioner and the officers of State had to fly the city to escape from the exasperated people.

In the days of its declension, the Darien House was abandoned to the uses of a lunatic asylum for the paupers of the adjoining workhouse. South of it stood a square edifice, which was latterly used for the same purpose. In the early part of the eighteenth century this was the mansion house of a wealthy quaker, named Buntin (or Bontein), whose daughter was locally known as "the beautiful

Darien House, in 1871, and the site of both is now occupied by several blocks of new buildings, in making the excavations for which the labourers found that nearly the whole area had been an ancient and forgotten cemetery, the bones and coffins in which lay at an average depth of six feet below the surface.

The first Merchant Maiden Hospital was built in 1707, on the east side of Bristo Street; and in 1739 we find James, second Earl of Rosebery,

THE CHARITY WORKHOUSE, 1820. (*After Storer.*)

Mally." To see her leave the meeting-house in the Pleasance, all the bucks and gay fellows of the city were wont to crowd; but from her father's house, at Bristo (in its last years a dispensary), she eloped with Mr. Craig, the minister of Currie, in the churchyard of which her tombstone still remains.

To this latter house, as a Bedlam, a peculiarly melancholy interest attached, as it was there that Robert Fergusson, the ill-fated poet, died a raving lunatic in his twenty-fourth year, in 1774, after a contusion received by a fall down-stairs; and when his last hours came, his piteous shrieks for his "mother" often rang out upon the night. This house was removed about the same time as the

living in Denham's Land, in the same thorough-fare. This peer was one who carried the follies and fantastic vices of the age to such an extravagant length as led people to doubt his sanity. During the lifetime of his father, Earl Archibald, he had been frequently a debtor in the Tolbooth, and on the 28th January, 1726, was incarcerated there for "deforcement, riot, and spulzie."

In 1739 there occurs in the public journals a singular advertisement, issued by this ornament to the Scottish peerage, relative to the elopement of one Polly Rich, who had been engaged by him for a year. She is described as being about eighteen five feet six inches high, "fine-shap'd, blue-ey'd, with black hair or nut-brown; all her linnen or cambrick", bears the earl's coronet above his initial R. Three guineas' reward was offered for any one who would return Polly "to her owner," either at John's Coffee House, "or the Earl of Roseberrie at Denham's Land, Bristow, and no questions will be asked. She is a London girl, and what they call a *Cockney*." There are in the advertisement a great many arguments and inducements used by the earl to induce the fair

was a park called Forglens Park, upon part of which the New Bridge is built," says a writer in 1775, "and the rest feued out by the magistrates to different persons, upon which there are now many good houses erected. This park used to pay £10 yearly."

At midsummer, in 1743, this house was opened for the reception of the poor, who were employed according to their ability, and allowed twopence

DARIEN HOUSE, 1750.

one to return, and the whole are wound up by the following elegant couplet :—

" My Lord desires Polly Rich,
To mind on Lord Roseberrie's dear little Fish."
(*Scottish Journal*, Vol. I.)

Westward of Bristo Street, in the large open field described, there was erected in 1743 the Workhouse. It was four storeys in height, very spacious, but plain, massive, and dingy, with a pedimented or gabled centre, whereat hung a huge bell, and in which there were three tall arched windows of the chapel or hall. It stood 200 feet south-west of the Bristo Port, on a part of the ground then denominated the High Riggs, and the expense of the edifice was defrayed by the voluntary contributions of the inhabitants ; and for its use, " among other subjects,

out of every shilling they earned. The annual expense of maintaining each person in those days amounted to £4 10s., and was defrayed by a tax of two per cent. on the valued rents of the city, the dues of the dead, or the passing bell, burial warrants, green turfs, half the profits of the Ladies' Assembly Room, the collections at the church doors, and other voluntary contributions. It was early proposed to establish a permanent poor rate, but this was opposed by the members of the College of Justice, on the plea that they were not liable to local burdens.

The number maintained in this now defunct edifice from the 1st of January, 1777, to the 1st of January, 1778, was only 484 adults, of both sexes, of whom 52 died ; 180 children, of whom

9 died; but Scotland was not then, nor for long after, subjected to the incessant immigration of the Irish poor. The government of this house was vested in ninety-six persons, who met quarterly, and fifteen managers, who met weekly. There were also a treasurer, chaplain, surgeon, and other officials.

This unsightly edifice survived the Darien House for some years, but was eventually removed to make way for the handsome street in a line with George IV. Bridge, containing the Edinburgh Rifle Volunteer Hall, and the hall of the Odd Fellows.

At the acute angle between Forrest Road and Bristo Street is the New North Free Church, erected in 1846. It presents Gothic fronts to both thoroughfares, and has a massive projecting front basement, adorned with a small Gothic arcade.

In 1764 we first hear of something like a trade strike, when a great number of journeyman masons met in July in Bristo Park (on the open side of the street, near Lord Ross's house), where they formed a combination "not to work in the ensuing week unless their wages were augmented. This, it seems, they communicated to their masters on Saturday night, but had no satisfactory answer. Yesterday morning they came to work, but finding no hopes of an augmentation, they all, with one consent, went off. The same evening the master-masons of the city, Canongate, Leith, and suburbs, met in order to concert what measures may be proper to be taken in this affair." (*Edin. Advert.*, Vol. II.)

They resolved not to increase the wages of the men, and to take legal advice "to prevent undue combinations, which are attended with many bad effects." The sequel we have no means of knowing. The same print quoted records a strike among the sweeps, or tronmen, in the same park, and elsewhere adds that "an old soldier has lately come to town who sweeps chimneys after the English manner, which has so disgusted the society of chimney-sweepers that they refuse to sweep any unless this man is obliged to leave the town, upon which a number of them have been put in prison to-day. They need not be afraid of this old soldier taking the bread from them, as few chimneys in this place will admit of a man going through them." (*Edin. Advert.*, Vol. III.)

In the Bristo Port, or that portion of the street so called, stood long the Old George Inn, from whence the coaches, about 1788, were wont to set forth for Carlisle and London, three weekly—fare to the former, £1 10s., to the latter, £3 10s. 6d—and from whence, till nearly the railway era, the waggons were despatched every lawful day to

London and all parts of England; "also every day to Greenock, Glasgow, and the west of Scotland."

Southward of where this inn stood is now St. Mary's Roman Catholic school, formerly a church, built in 1839. It is a pinnacled Gothic edifice, and was originally dedicated to St. Patrick, but was superseded in 1856, when the great church in the Cowgate was secured by the Bishop of Edinburgh.

Lothian Street opens eastward from this point. In a gloomy *cul-de-sac* on its northern side is a circular edifice, named Brighton Chapel, built in 1835, and seated for 1,257 persons. Originally, it was occupied by a relief congregation. The continuation of the thoroughfare eastward leads to College Street, in which we find a large United Presbyterian church.

In a court off the east side of Bristo Street, a few yards south from the east end of Teviot Row, is another church belonging to the same community, which superseded the oldest dissenting Presbyterian church in Edinburgh. In a recently-published history of this edifice, we are told that early in the century, "when the old church was pulled down, within the heavy canopy of the pulpit" (the sounding-board) "were found three or four skeletons of horses' heads, and underneath the pulpit platform about twenty more. It was conjectured that they had been placed there from some notion that the acoustics of the place would be improved."

The church was built in 1802, at a cost of £4,084, and was enlarged afterwards, at a further cost of £1,515, and interiorly renovated in 1872 for £1,300. It is a neat and very spacious edifice, and was long famous for the ministry of the Rev. Dr. James Peddie, who was ordained as a pastor of that congregation on the 3rd April, 1783. On his election, a large body of the sitters withdrew, and formed themselves into the Associate Congregation of Rose Street, of which the Rev. Dr. Hall subsequently became minister; but the Bristo Street congregation rapidly recruited its numbers under the pastoral labours of Dr. Peddie, and from that time has been in a most flourishing condition.

In 1778, when six years of age, Sir Walter Scott attended the school of Mr. John Luckmore, in Hamilton's Entry, off Bristo Street, a worthy preceptor, who was much esteemed by his father, the old Writer to the Signet, with whom he was for many years a weekly guest. The school-house, though considerably dilapidated, still exists, and is occupied as a blacksmith's shop. It is a small cottage-like building with a red-tiled roof, situated on the right-hand side of the court called Hamilton's Entry, No. 36, Bristo Street. As to the identity of the edifice there can be no doubt, as it was pointed out by Sir Walter himself to the late Dr. Robert Chambers. In 1792 Mr. Luckmore was appointed one of the four English masters of the High School on the city's establishment, and continued to hold that office till his death, in 1811. Sir Walter Scott, on leaving his school in Hamilton's Entry, was placed under the domestic tutelage of Mr. James French, who prepared him to join Mr. Luke Fraser's second class at the High School, in October, 1779.

Another interesting locality in Bristo Street, at its junction with the Potterrow, was long known as the General's Entry, No. 58, though now it exists but in name. This was a desolate-looking court of ancient buildings. The south and east sides of the quadrangle were formed by somewhat ornate edifices. The crowstepped gable at the south-east angle bore an antique sun-dial, with the quaint legend—

"WE SHALL DIE ALL ;"

and beyond this was a row of circular-headed dormer windows, in the richly decorated style of James VI. One of these bore a shield, charged with a monkey and three mullets-in-chief, surrounded by elaborate scroll-work of the same reign and bearing the initials J.D.

Unvarying tradition has assigned this mansion to General Monk as a residence while commanding in Scotland, but there is not much probability to support it. The house was furnished with numerous out-shots and projections, dark, broad, and bulky stacks of chimneys, reared in unusual places, all blackened by age and encrusted with the smoke of centuries. It is said to have been built by Sir James Dalrymple, afterwards first Viscount Stair, one of the Breda Commissioners, and who continued his practice at the bar with great reputation after the battles of Dunbar and Worcester.

That he was a particular favourite with General Monk, and even with Cromwell, to whom the former recommended him as the fittest person for the bench in 1657, is well known ; and under such circumstances, it may be supposed that Monk would be his frequent visitor when he came from his quarters at Dalkeith to the capital. Tradition has assigned the house as the permanent residence in those days of the Commander of the Forces in Scotland. But there is sufficient proof that it was the town abode of the Stair family, till, like the rest of the Scottish nobility, they abandoned Edinburgh, after the Treaty of Union. "It is not unlikely," says Wilson, "that the present name of the old court is derived from the more recent residence there of John, second Earl of Stair, who served during the protracted campaigns of the

Duke of Marlborough, and was promoted to the rank of lieutenant-general after the bloody victory of Malplaquet. He shared in the fall of the great duke, and retired from Court until the accession of George I., during which interval it is probable that the family mansion in the Potterrow formed the frequent abode of the disgraced favourite."

But General's Entry is perhaps now most intimately associated with one of Burns's heroines, Mrs. McLehose, the romantic Clarinda of the notorious correspondence, in which the poet figured as Sylvander. He was introduced to her in the house of a Miss Nimmo, on the first floor of an old tenement on the north side of Alison Square.

A little parlour, a bed-room, and kitchen, according to Chambers, constituted the accommodation of Mrs. Agnes McLehose, "now the residence of two, if not three, families in the extreme of humble life."

In December, 1787, Burns met at a tea-party this lady, then a married woman of great beauty, about his own age, and who, with her two children, had been deserted by a worthless husband. She had wit, could use her pen, had read "Werther" and his sorrows, was sociable and flirty, and possessed a voluptuous loveliness, if we may judge by the silhouette of her in Scott Douglas's edition of the poet's works. She and Burns took a fancy to each other on the instant. She invited him to tea, but he offered a visit instead. An accident confined him for about a month to his room, and this led to the famous Clarinda and Sylvander correspondence. At about the fifth or sixth exchange of their letters she wrote : "It is really curious, so much *fun* passing between two persons who saw each other only *once*."

During the few months of his fascination for this fair one in General's Entry, Burns showed more of his real self, perhaps, than can be traced in other parts of his published correspondence. In his first letter to her after his marriage, he says, in reply to her sentimental reproaches, "When you call over the scenes that have passed between us, you will survey the conduct of an honest man struggling successfully with temptations the most powerful that ever beset humanity, and preserving untainted honour in situations where the severest virtue would have forgiven a fall." But had Clarinda been less accessible, she might have discovered eventually that much of the poet's warmth was fanciful and melodramatic. From their correspondence it would appear that she was in expectation of Burns visiting her again in Alison Square in 1788.

She was the cousin-german of Lord Craig, who,

at his death in York Place, in 1813, left her an annuity, and thirty years after still found her living in Edinburgh.

"She is now nearly eighty years of age, but enjoys excellent health," says Kay's editor in February,

(Lord Craig), about whom you have been inquiring. He was the best friend I ever had.' After a little conversation about his lordship, she directed our attention to a picture of Burns by Horsburgh, after Taylor. 'You will know who

THE MERCHANT MAIDEN'S HOSPITAL, BRISTO, 1820. (*After Storer.*)

1837. "We found her sitting in the parlour, with some papers on the table. Her appearance at first betrayed a little of that languor and apathy which attend age and solitude ; but the moment she comprehended the object of our visit, her countenance—which even *yet* retains the lineaments of what Clarinda may be supposed to have been— became animated and intelligent. 'That,' said she, rising up, and pointing to an engraving over the mantelpiece, 'is a likeness of my relative

that is ; it was presented to me by Constable and Co., for having simply declared what I know to be true—that the likeness was good.' We spoke of the correspondence between the poet and Clarinda, at which she smiled, and pleasantly remarked on the great change which the lapse of so many years had produced in her personal appearance. Indeed, any observation respecting Burns seemed to afford her pleasure. Having prolonged our intrusion to the limits of courtesy, and conversed on various topics, we took leave of the venerable lady, highly gratified by the interview. To see and talk with one whose name is so indissolubly associated with the fame of Burns, and whose talents and virtues were so much fare, where, in the days of her widowhood, as Mrs. Cockburn of Ormiston, resided Alison Rutherford of Fairnielee, Roxburghshire, authoress of the modern version of the "Flowers of the Forest" and other Scottish songs—in her youth a "forest flower

BRISTO PORT, 1820.　(*After Storer.*)

esteemed by the bard—who has now (in 1837) been sleeping the sleep of death for upwards of forty years—may well give rise to feelings of no ordinary description. In youth Clarinda must have been about the middle size. Burns, she said, if living, would have been about her own age, probably a few months older."

Off Bristo Street there branches westward Crichton Street, so named from an architect of the time, a gloomy, black, and old-fashioned thorough-

of rare beauty." She removed hither from Blair's Close in the Castle-hill, and her house was the scene of many happy and brilliant reunions. Even in age her brown hair never grew grey, and she wore it combed over a toupee, with a lace band tied under her chin, and her sleeves puffed out in the fashion of Mary's time. "She maintained," says Scott, "that rank in the society of Edinburgh which French women of talent usually do in that of Paris; and in her little parlour used to assemble a very distinguished and accomplished circle, among whom David Hume, John Home, Lord Monboddo, and many other men of name, were frequently to be found."

Now she lies not far from Crichton Street, in the north-east corner of the old burying-ground of the Chapel of Ease; her tombstone is near the graves of the poet Blacklock and old Rector Adam of the High School.

"Except a mean street called Potterrow, and a very short one called Bristo, there were, till within these twelve years, hardly any buildings on the south side of the town," says Arnot in 1779; and with these lines he briefly dismisses the entire history of one of the oldest thoroughfares in Edinburgh—the Eastern Portsburgh, which lies wholly to the eastward of Bristo Street, and may be described as comprehending the east side of that street from the Bristo Port southward, the Potterrow, Lothian and South College Streets, Drummond Street to opposite Adam Street, and Nicolson Street to nearly the entry to the York Hotel on the west, and to the Surgeons' Hall on the east. But jurisdictions had long ceased to be exercised in either of the Portsburghs by the baron or resident bailies; yet there are eight incorporated trades therein, who derive their rights from John Touris of Inverleith.

In Edgar's map the main street of the Potterrow is represented as running, as it still does, straight south from the Potterrow Port in the city wall, adjacent to the buildings of the old college, its houses on the east overlooking the wide space of Lady Nicolson's Park, between which and the west side of the Pleasance lay only a riding-school and some six or seven houses, surrounded by gardens and hedgerows.

It has always been a quaint and narrow street, and the memorabilia thereof are full of interest. A great doorway on its western side, only recently removed, in 1870, measured six feet six inches wide, and was designed in heavy Italian rustic-work, with the date 1668, and must have given access to an edifice of considerable importance.

In 1582 the Potterrow, together with the West Port, Restalrig, and other suburbs, was occupied by the armed companies of the Duke of Lennox, who, while feigning to have gone abroad, had a treasonable intention of seizing alike the palace of Holyrood and the city of Edinburgh; but "straitt watche," says Calderwood, "was keeped both in the toun and the abbey."

In November, 1584, it was enacted by the Council that none of the inhabitants of the city, the Potterrow, West Port, Canongate, or Leith,

harbour, stable, or lodge strangers, for dread of the plague, without reporting the same within an hour to the commissary within whose quarter or jurisdiction they dwell. ("Privy Council Register.")

In the year 1639 a gun foundry was established in the Potterrow to cast cannon for the first Covenanting war, by order of General Leslie. These guns were not exclusively metal. The greater part of the composition was leather, and they were fabricated under the eye of his old Swedish comrade, Sir Alexander Hamilton of the Red House, a younger son of the famous "Tam o' the Cowgate," and did considerable execution when the English army was defeated at Newburnford, above Newcastle, on the 28th August, 1640.

These cannon, which were familiarly known among the Scottish soldiers as "Dear Sandie's stoups," were carried slung between two horses.

About the same time, or soon after this period, witches and warlocks began to terrify the locality, and in 1643 a witch was discovered in the Potterrow—Agnes Fynnie, a small dealer in groceries, who was tried and condemned to be "worried at the stake," and then burned to ashes—a poor wretch, who seems to have had no other gifts from Satan than a fierce temper and a bitter tongue. Among the charges against her, the fifth was, while "scolding with Bettie Currie about the changing of a sixpence, which she alleged to be ill (bad), ye in great rage threatened that ye would make the devil take a bite of her."

The ninth is that, "ye ending a compt with Isabel Atchesone, and because ye could not get all your unreasonable demands, ye bade the devil ride about the town with her and hers; whereupon *the next day* she broke her leg by a fall from a horse, and ye came and saw her and said, 'See that ye say not I have bewitched ye, as the other neighbours say.'" The eighteenth clause in her *dittay* is, "that ye, having fallen into a controversie with Margaret Williamson, ye most outrageously wished the devil to blaw her blind; after which, she, by your sorcerie, took a grievous sickness, whereof she went blind." The nineteenth is, "for laying a madness on Andrew Wilson conform to your threating, *wishing the devil to rive the soul out* of him." (Law's "Memorialls," 1638-84.)

At the utmost, this unfortunate creature had only been guilty of bad wishes towards certain neighbours, and if such had any sequel, it must have been through superstitious apprehensions. It is fairly presumable, says a writer, that while the community was so ignorant as to believe that malediction would have actively evil results, it would occasionally have these effects by its influence on *imagination*, and thus become a positive evil. Her indictment consisted of twenty articles, all similar to those given, and "she confest before the Kirk Session that for twenty-eight years past she has been defamed for a witch."

There was a learned argument upon the relevancy of her indictment, but it was, as may be supposed, unsuccessful. The jury, says Pitmedden, was composed "of cordiners, tailyeors, and other inhabitants of the Potterrow," where she lived, and who must have known her well. Rosehaugh notices this case, and concurs in thinking her sentence to the stake a hard one.

In 1650, when an English invasion was expected, many houses in Potterrow, as well as the West Port, were demolished by order of the magistrates, that the guns of the castle, and those on the city wall might have free action to play upon the enemy; and we are told that "the four prickes bigged on the Neddir Bow, quhilk was ane verry great ornament," were demolished, and cannon put in their places. ("Nicolls' Diary.")

In July, 1671, William Wood, a barber in the Portsburgh, was found to have transgressed his act of admission by working as a barber within Heriot's Hospital, which was without the bounds of the Portsburgh, and having been disobedient to the Deacon, he was incarcerated in the Tolbooth of Edinburgh, so sharp was the practice of those days; and afterwards he persisted "malitiouslie in his disobedience without making application unto the calling; therefore the saidis deacon, masters, and brethren suspends the said William Wood from the exercise of his calling, and ordains his signe to be taken down during the callings' pleasure." ("Hist. R. Coll. Surgeons.")

Two years after this, the Hall of the Incorporation of Tailors in the Eastern Portsburgh was built, on the east side of the street. Above the entrance-door of the turnpike stair are the shears of the craft within a wreath, and a large open volume, well carved in stone, bearing the following inscription on its leaves :—

Behold	How good
a thing	it is,
and how be-	coming weel
Together	such as
Brit	hern ar
In Unitie	to Dwel.

1673.

In the revenue of the city for 1690, the tolls collected at the Society and Potterrow Ports amounted to £66 13s. 4d. sterling; but the tolls taken at the West Port nearly doubled that sum.

That the Potterrow was not, at one time, deemed

an unaristocratic quarter may be inferred from the fact that, so lately as 1716, Robert, seventh Earl of Morton, a man who, Douglas says, "was well versed in the knowledge of the antiquities of our country," had his residence there; and later still, in 1760, Archibald, Duke of Douglas, had a stately mansion, surrounded by extensive grounds, immediately on the west side of the Potterrow, near the north end of which was his carriage entrance, a gate within a recess, overlooked by the city wall. Lady Houston lived in the Potterrow in 1784.

In the *Diary* of Lord Grange, we are told of Jean Brown, a woman in humble life, residing in the Potterrow in 1717, who had some curious experiences, which, while reminding us of those of St. Teresa, the Castilian, the foundress of the Barefooted Carmelites, were not, singular to say, inconsistent with orthodox Presbyterianism.

Being taken, together with Mr. Logan, the incumbent of Culross, to see this pious woman, at Lady Aytoun's lodging behind the College, he found her to be between thirty and forty years of age; when, having Communion administered to her at Leith, in the October of that year, she had striven to dwell deeply on the thought of Christ and all His sufferings. Then she had a vision of Him extended on the cross and in His rocky sepulchre, "as plainly as if she had been actually present when these things happened, though there was not any visible representation thereof made to her bodily eyes. She also got liberty to speak to Him, and asked several questions at Him, to which she got answers, as if one had spoken to her audibly, though there was no audible voice."

Lord Grange admits that all this was somewhat like delusion or enthusiasm, but deemed it far from him to say it was either. Being once at Communion in Kirkcaldy, a voice called to her, "Arise and eat; for thou hast a journey to make—a Jordan to pass through."

The latter proved to be the Firth of Forth, where she was upset in the water, but floated till rescued by a boat. Lord Grange called frequently to see her at her little shop in the Potterrow, but usually found it so crowded with children buying her wares that his wishes were frustrated. "Afterwards," he states, "I employed her husband (a shoemaker) to make some little things for me, mostly to give them business, and that I might thereby get opportunity now and then to talk with such as, I hope, are acquainted with the ways of God."

Middleton's Entry, which opened westward off the Potterrow, was associated with another of Burns's heroines, Miss Jean Lorimer, the flaxen-haired

Chloris of some of his finest lyrics, the daughter of a prosperous farmer at a place called Kemmis Hall, on the banks of the Nith, and who, after undergoing many vicissitudes, and having for a time "had her portion with weeds and outworn faces," was seized with consumption, and retired to an obscure abode in that narrow and gloomy lane.

" If Fortune smile, be not puffed up,
　And if it frown, be not dismayed ;
　For Providence governeth all,
　Although the world 's turned upside down."

It was in Alison Square that Thomas Campbell, the poet, resided when writing the " Pleasures of Hope." He occupied the second floor of a stair

CLARINDA'S HOUSE, GENERAL'S ENTRY.

There she lingered long in loneliness and suffering, supported by the charity of strangers, till she found a final home in Newington burying-ground.

Alison Square, which lay farther south, and through which a street has now been run, was built in the middle of the eighteenth century, upon a venture, by Colin Alison, a joiner, who in after life was much reduced in circumstances by the speculation. In his latter days he erected two boards on different sides of his buildings, whereon he had painted a globe in the act of falling, with this inscription :—

on the north side of the central archway, with windows looking partly into the Potterrow, and partly into Nicolson Street. The poem is said to have been written here in the night, his master's temper being so irritable that it was then only he could find peace for his task.

Alison Square was completely transformed in 1876, when Marshall Street was constructed through it. A Baptist church, in a most severe Lombardic style, stands on the north side of this new street. It was built in 1876-7, at the cost of £4,000.

Between 1773 and 1783, Francis, eighth Earl of

Moray, who died in 1810, lived in the Potterrow, in a large mansion, which was entered through a garden "at the east end of the row, and another by Chapel Street." An advertisement, offering it for sale in 1783, says the earl had occupied it "for these ten years past;" that it consists of fifteen apartments, with servants' hall, vaulted cellar, and ample stabling. This was, in all probability, the house formerly occupied by the Duke of Douglas.

The Original Seceder Congregation, afterwards located in Richmond Street, was established in the Potterrow about 1794, and removed to the former quarter in 1813.

We get an idea of the class of humble Edinburgh merchant, as the phrase was understood in Scotland. On Sundays, too, Mrs. Flockhart's little visage might have been seen in a front gallery seat in Mr. Pattieson's chapel in the Potterrow. Her abode, situated opposite to Chalmers' Entry, in that suburban thoroughfare, was a square, about fifteen feet each way."

A mere screen divided her dwelling-house from her tavern, and before it, every morning, the bottles containing whisky, rum, and brandy, were placed on the bunker-seat of a window, with glasses and a salver of gingerbread biscuits. Anon an elderly gentleman would drop in, saluting her with " Hoo d'ye do, mem ?" and then proceed to

ROOM IN CLARINDA'S HOUSE, GENERAL'S ENTRY.

taverns of the old school from the description that Chambers gives us of a famous one, Mrs. Flockhart's—otherwise " Lucky Fykie's "—in the Potterrow, at the close of the last century.

It was a small as well as obscure edifice, externally having the appearance of a huckster's shop. Lucky Fykie was a neat little elderly woman, usually clad in an apron and gown of the same blue-striped stuff, with a black silk ribbon round her mutch, the lappets of which were tied under her chin. "Her husband, the umquhile John Flucker, or Flockhart, had left her some ready money, together with his whole stock-in-trade, consisting of a multifarious variety of articles— ropes, tea, sugar, whipshafts, porter, ale, beer, yellow-sand, camstane, herrings, nails, cotton-wicks, thread, needles, tapes, potatoes, lollipops, onions, and matches, &c., constituting her a respectable

help himself from one of the bottles ; another and another would drop in, till the tiny tavern was full, and, strange to say, all of them were men of importance in society, many of them denizens of George Square — eminent barristers or wealthy bankers—so simple were the habits of the olden time.

In No. 7, Charles Street, which runs into Crichton Street, near the Potterrow, Lord Jeffrey, the eminent critic, was born in 1773, in the house of his father, a Depute-Clerk of Session, though some accounts have assigned his birthplace to Windmill Street. Lady Duffus was resident in Charles Street in 1784. Where this street is now, there was an old locality known as Charles's Field, which on Restoration Day, 1712, was the scene of an ingenious piece of marked Jacobitism, in honour of the exiled Stuarts.

There was then in Edinburgn a merchant, named Charles Jackson, to whom Charles II. had acted as godfather in the Kirk of Keith, and Jackson was a name assumed by Charles after his escape in the *Royal Oak*. In consideration of all this, by an advertisement in the *Courant*, Mr. Jackson, as being lineally descended from a stock of royalists. "invited all such to solemnise that memorable day (29th May) at an enclosure called Charles's Field, lying a mile south from this city (where he hath erected a very useful bleaching-field), and there entertained them with a diversity of liquors, fine music, &c."

He had a huge bonfire lighted, and a tall pole erected, with a large banner displayed therefrom, and the royal oak painted on it, together with the bark in which his sacred majesty made his escape, and the colonel who accompanied him. "The company around the bonfire drank Her Majesty Queen Anne's health, and the memory ot the happy Restoration, with great mirth and demonstrations of loyalty. The night concluded with mirth, and the standard being brought back to Mr. Jackson's lodgings, was carried by *loyal* gentlemen bareheaded, and followed by several others with trumpets, hautboys, and bagpipes playing before them, where they were kindly entertained." (*Reliquiæ Scoticæ.*)

CHAPTER XXXIX.

NICOLSON STREET AND SQUARE.

Lady Nicolson—Her Pillar—Royal Riding School—M. Angelo—New Surgeons' Hall—The Earl of Leven—Dr. Borthwick Gilchrist—The Blind Asylum—John Maclaren—Sir David Wilkie—Roxburgh Parish—Lady Glenorchy's Chapel.

NICOLSON STREET, which runs southward to the Cross Causeway, on a line with the South Bridge, was formed about the middle of the eighteenth century, on the grounds of Lady Nicolson, whose mansion stood on an area now covered by the eastern end of North College Street ; and a writer in a public print recently stated that the house numbered as 82 in Nicolson Street, presently occupied as a hotel, was erected for and occupied by her after the street was formed.

In Shaw's "Register of Entails" under date of Tailzie, 7th October, 1763, and of Registration, 4th December, 1764, is the name of Lady Nicolson (Elizabeth Carnegie), relict of Mr. James Nicolson, with note of the lands and heritable subjects in the shire of Edinburgh that should belong to her at her death.

In Edgar's plan for 1765, her park, lying eastward of the Potterrow, is intersected by the "New Road," evidently the line of the present street, and at its northern end is her mansion, some seventy feet distant from the city wall, with a carriage gate and lodge, the only other building near it being the Royal Riding School, with its stables, on the site of the present Surgeons' Hall.

On the completion of Nicolson Street, Lady Nicolson erected at its northern end a monument to her husband. It was, states Arnot, a fluted Corinthian column, twenty-five feet two inches in height, with a capital and base, and fourteen inches diameter. Another account says it was from thirty to forty feet in height, and had on its pedestal an inscription in Latin and English, stating that Lady Nicolson having been left the adjacent piece of ground by her husband, had, out of regard for his memory, made it to be planned into "a street, to be named from him, Nicolson Street."

On the extension of the thoroughfare and ultimate completion of the South Bridge, from which it was for some years a conspicuous object, it was removed, and the affectionate memorial, instead of being placed in the little square, with that barbarous want of sentiment that has characterised many improvements in Edinburgh and elsewhere in Scotland in more important matters, was thrown aside into the yard of the adjacent Riding School, and was, no doubt, soon after broken up for rubble.

One of the first edifices in the newly-formed thoroughfare was the old Riding School, a block of buildings and stables, measuring about one hundred and fifty feet each way.

The first "master of the Royal Riding Menage" was Angelo Tremamondo, a native of Italy, as his name imports, though it has been supposed that it was merely a mountebank assumption, as it means the tremor of the world, a universal earthquake ; but be that as it may, his Christian name in Edinburgh speedily dwindled down to *Ainslie.* He was in the pay of the Government, was among the earliest residents in Nicolson Square, and had a salary of £200 per annum.

In the account given of the formation of the school in the *Scots Magazine* for December, 1763, he is called M. Angelo; and it was agreed at a meeting of the subscribers that the institution should be opened in the subsequent January. "Each scholar pays four guineas the first month, and two every other month; sixteen teaching days in the month. Gentlemen whose business will not allow them to attend regularly, get sixteen tickets for a month, and pay three guineas for the first, and £2 16s. for every other month." The sum raised to build this edifice was only £2,733 15s., and in 1776 it received a royal charter. The actual school was 124 feet long by 42 broad.

The *Weekly Magazine* for 1776 describes "a carousal" held at the Royal Riding School, at which the gentlemen performed their various equestrian exercises with great dexterity, and at which "a gold medal, with a suitable device and motto, given by M. Angelo," was presented by the Countess of Selkirk, as the prize of successful merit, to Robert Cay, Esq., of Northumberland.

Kay gives us an equestrian portrait of Angelo, in a Kevenhuller hat and long riding-boots. He died at Edinburgh in April, 1805, in his eighty-fourth year.

The edifice in which he so long officiated was pulled down to make way for the new Surgeons' Hall, and the scene of equestrian exercise was removed to the now defunct school at the back of the Royal Scottish Naval and Military Academy, so long superintended by the veteran Captain John Orr, in St. Cuthbert's Lane.

Its successor, the new Surgeons' Hall, on the east side of Nicolson Street, and a little south of Drummond Street, is a remarkably chaste and beautiful building, in the Grecian style, with a noble portico and pediment, supported by six great fluted Ionic columns, after a design by W. H. Playfair, at a cost of £20,000.

It was opened in 1832, during the presidency of John Gairdner, M.D., whose portrait, painted by order of the College, is in the hall, the committee rooms of which are adorned by many of the old oak panels of 1697, from the former hall in Surgeon Square; and some of the sculptured stones and armorial bearings which belonged to that edifice are now to be seen in the front of the Medical Lecture Rooms, behind the hall in Nicolson Street. ("Hist. Sketch R. C. S.")

The extensive museum here contains a valuable collection of anatomical and surgical preparations, and may be seen almost daily free.

Nearly opposite, on the west side, is Nicolson Square, containing a house occupied by Lady Sinclair of Stevenson in 1784, and another at its north-west corner, long occupied by David, Earl of Leven and Melville, who in 1782 became Commissioner to the General Assembly, an office which he held with honour till his eightieth year, in 1801. He married in 1747 Wilhelmina, the *nineteenth* child of William Nisbet of Dirleton, and after years of conjugal affection and happiness, he celebrated the fiftieth anniversary of his marriage with her at Melville House in 1797, and there she died in the following year. He died at 2, St. Andrew Square, in 1802. In the Directory for 1784, Sir John Dalrymple, Baron of Exchequer, appears among the residents in Nicolson Street, the Countess of Aberdeen in No. 25, and Robert, Lord Colville, and Lady Nisbet of Dean, in No. 26.

Sir Charles Preston, Bart., of Valleyfield, one of the Commissioners of Customs for Scotland, died at his house in Nicolson Square, 23rd March, 1800; and in No. 3 of the same square there lived long the celebrated Orientalist, John Borthwick Gilchrist, LL.D., a native of the city, born in 1759, and who, from Heriot's Hospital, passed into the service of the East India Company, when he devoted himself with ardour and industry to the acquirement of all Oriental languages, for which purpose he travelled in Indian garb wherever he deemed them to be spoken with the greatest purity.

From his pen issued many most valuable works on these languages; and after resigning his chair as Professor of Hindostanee and Persian in the new College of Fort William, he returned to take up his residence in Edinburgh in 1804, and among other schemes, instituted a bank in 7, Hunter Square, under the name of "Inglis, Borthwick Gilchrist, and Co.;" but as other banks refused the notes, the establishment was relinquished.

He quitted his house in Nicolson Square in 1815, and after engaging in many literary publications, all of an Oriental nature, he spent the latter years of his life in retirement and died at Paris, in his eighty-first year, in 1841.

At the south-west corner of the square is a Wesleyan Methodist church, with a handsome Roman front. It was built in 1814, measures 80 feet by 60, with a minister's house and schools attached. It was regularly attended by the President of the United States, General U. S. Grant, during his sojourn in Edinburgh.

The most interesting building in the street is undoubtedly the Royal Blind Asylum and School, instituted in 1793; nor is this lessened by the recollection that it long formed the residence of the celebrated chemist, Dr. Joseph Black, who, as we have elsewhere stated, was found dead in his chair in November, 1799, and whose high reputation contributed so largely in his time to the growing fame of our University.

The institution was first suggested by the celebrated Dr. Thomas Blacklock, who lost his sight before he was six months old, and by Mr. David Miller, also a sufferer from blindness; but it was chiefly through the exertions of Dr. David John-

sales of the above kinds of work have in some years amounted to £10,000, and in 1880 to £18,724 8s., notwithstanding the general depression of trade; but this was owing to the Government contract for brushes. Hence the directors have been enabled to make extensive alterations and improvements to a large amount.

The asylum has received a new and elegant façade, surmounted by stone-faced dormer windows, a handsome cornice, and balustrade, with a large

THE MAHOGANY LAND, POTTERROW, 1821. (*After a Painting by W. McEwan, in the possession of Dr. J.A. Sidey.*)

stone, the philanthropic minister of North Leith, aided by a subscription of £20 from the great Wilberforce, that the asylum was founded in 1793, in one of the dingy old houses of Shakespeare Square, into which nine blind persons were received; but the public patronage having greatly increased, in 1806 the present building, No. 58, was purchased, and in 1822 another house, No. 38, was bought for the use of the female blind.

The latter are employed in sewing the covers for mattresses and feather beds, knitting stockings, &c. The males are employed in making mattresses, mats, brushes, baskets of every kind, in weaving sacking, matting, and "rag-carpets." No less than eighteen looms are employed in this work. The

central doorway, in a niche above which is a bust of Dr. David Johnstone, the founder, from the studio of the late Handyside Ritchie.

The inmates seem to spend a very merry life, for though the use of their eyes has been denied them, they have no restriction placed upon their tongues; thus, whenever two or three of them are together, they are constantly talking, or singing their national songs.

A chapel is attached to the works, and therein, besides regular morning worship, the blind hold large meetings in connection with the various benefit societies they have established among themselves. The younger lads who come from the Blind School at Craigmillar, and are employed here, spend a portion of each day in education, often passing an hour or more daily in learning to read by means of raised letters, under the direction of the chaplain.

One of the most remarkable inmates here was John Maclaren, who deserves to be recorded for his wonderful memory. He was a native of Edinburgh, and lost his sight by small-pox in infancy. He was admitted into the first asylum in Shakespeare Square in 1793, and was the last survivor

In West Richmond Street, which opens off the east side of Nicolson Street, is the McCrie Free Church, so named from being long the scene of the labours of Dr. Thomas McCrie, the zealous biographer of Knox and Melville. Near it, a large archway leads into a small and dingy-looking court, named Simon Square, crowded by a humble, but dense population ; yet it has associations intimately connected with literature and the fine arts, for there a poor young student from Annandale, named

SURGEONS' HALL.

of the original members. With little exception, he had committed the whole of the Scriptures to memory, and was most earnest in his pious efforts to instruct the blind boys of the institution in portions of the sacred volume. He could repeat an entire passage of the Bible, naming chapter and verse, wherever it might be opened for him. As age came upon him the later events of his life eluded his memory, while all that it had secured of the earlier remained distinct to the last. Throughout his long career he was distinguished by his zeal in promoting the spiritual welfare and temporal comfort of the little community of which he was a member, and also for a life of increasing industry, which closed on the 14th of November, 1840.

Thomas Carlyle, lodged when he first came to Edinburgh, and in a narrow alley called Paul Street David Wilkie took up his abode on his arrival in Edinburgh in 1799.

He was then in his fourteenth year ; and so little was thought of his turn for art, that it required all the powerful influence of the kind old Earl of Leven to obtain him admission as a student at the Academy of the Board of Trustees. The room he occupied in Paul Street was a little back one, about ten feet square, at the top of a common stair on the south side of the alley, and near the Pleasance.

From this he removed to a better lodging in East Richmond Street, and from thence to an attic in Palmer's Lane, West Nicolson Street, where he occupied the same apartment as that in which resided, till the year before his death, in 1785, Alexander Runciman, one of the most eminent Scottish artists of his day, and where, no doubt, he must have entertained the poet Robert Fergusson, " while with ominous fitness he sat as his model for the Prodigal Son."

Nicolson Street church, erected in 1819-20, at a cost of £6,000, has a handsome Gothic front, with two turreted pinnacles ninety feet in height. It is built upon the site of the old Antiburgher Meeting-house, and is notable for the ministry of Dr. John Jamieson, author of several theological works, and of the well-known " Etymological Dictionary of the Scottish Language." It was among the first efforts at an improved style of church architecture in Edinburgh, where, as elsewhere in Scotland after the Reformation, the accommodation of the different congregations in the homeliest manner was all that was deemed necessary.

The *quoad sacra* parish called Lady Glenorchy's lies eastward of Nicolson Street, and therein quite a cluster of little churches has been erected. The parish church was built as a relief chapel in 1809, by the Rev. Mr. Johnstone, and altered in 1814, when it was seated for 900 persons. The Independent congregation in Richmond Court was established in 1833 ; but their place of worship till 1840 was built about 1795 by the Baptists. The Hebrew congregation was established in 1817, but has never exceeded 100 souls. The Episcopal congregation of St. Peter's, Roxburgh Place, was established in 1791, and its place of worship consisted of the first and second flats of a five-storeyed tenement, and was originally built, at the sole expense of the clergyman, for about 420 persons.

To Roxburgh Place came, in 1859, the congregation of Lady Glenorchy's church, which had been demolished by the operations of the North British Railway. The Court of Session having found that

this body must be kept in full communion with the Established Church, authorised the purchase of Roxburgh Place chapel in lieu of the old place of worship, and trustees were appointed to conduct their affairs.

The chapel handed over to them was that of the Relief Communion just mentioned. Externally it has no architectural pretensions ; but many may remember it as the meeting-place of the " Convocation " which preceded the ever-memorable secession in 1843, after which it remained closed and uncared for till it came into the hands of the Glenorchy trustees in 1859, in so dilapidated a condition that their first duty was to repair it before the congregation could use it.

The remains of the pious Lady Glenorchy, which had been removed from the old church near the North Bridge, were placed, in 1844, in the vaults of St. John's church ; but the trustees, wishing to comply as far as was in their power with the wishes of the foundress, that her remains should rest in her own church, had a suitable vault built in that at Roxburgh Place. It was paved and covered with stone, set in Roman cement, and formed on the right side of the pulpit.

Therein her body was laid on the evening of Saturday, 31st December, 1859. The marble tablet, which was carefully removed from the old church, was placed over her grave, with an additional inscription explaining the circumstance which occasioned her new place of interment.

The portion of St. Cuthbert's parish which was disjoined and attached to Lady Glenorchy's is bounded by Nicolson Street and the Pleasance on the west and east, by Drummond Street on the north, and Richmond Street on the south, with an average population of about 7,000 souls.

Roxburgh Terrace is built on what was anciently called Thomson's Park ; and the place itself was named the Back Row in the city plan of 1787.

CHAPTER XL.

GEORGE SQUARE AND THE VICINITY

Ross House—The last Lord Ross—Earlier Residents in the Square—House of Walter Scott, W.S.—Sir Walter's Boyhood—Bickers—Green Breeks—The Edinburgh Light Horse—The Scots Brigade—Admiral Duncan—Lord Advocate Dundas—The Grants of Kilgraston—Baron Dundas—Sedan Chairs—Campbells of Succoth—Music Class Room—The Eight Southern Districts—Chapel of Ease—Windmill Street—Buccleuch Place—Jeffrey's First House there—The Burgh Loch—Society of Improvers—The Meadows.

Ross Park and House, a massive suburban mansion, belonging to the Lords Ross and to the age of stately ceremony and stately manners, occupied till the middle of the eighteenth century the site

of this square, which is one of the largest in the city. In those days the mansion, which was a square block with wings, was approached by an avenue through a plantation upwards of sixty yards long, from where the north-east end of Teviot Row was latterly. There were the stable offices; in front of the house was a tree of great size, while its spacious garden was bordered by Bristo Street.

When offered for sale, in March, 1761, it was described in a newspaper of the period as "Ross House, with the fields and gardens lying around it, consisting of about twenty-four acres, divided as follows : About an acre and a half in a field and court about the house ; seventeen acres in one field lying to the south-west, between it and Hope Park ; the rest into kitchen-gardens, running along Bristo Street and the back of the wall. The house consists of dining, drawing, and dressing rooms, six bed-chambers, several closets and garrets; in the ground storey, kitchen, larder, pantry, milk-house, laundry, cellars, and accommodation for servants, &c."

This house, which was latterly used as a lying-in hospital, was occupied for some time prior to 1753 by George Lockhart of Carnwath, during whose time it was the scene of many a gay rout, ball, and ridotto ; but it was, when the family were in Edinburgh, the permanent residence of the Lords Ross of Halkhead, a family of great antiquity, dating back to the days of King William the Lion, 1165.

In this house died, in June, 1754, in the seventy-third year of his age, George, twelfth Lord Ross, Commissioner of the Customs, whose body was taken for interment to Renfrew, the burial-place of the family. His chief seats were Halkhead and Melville Castle. He was succeeded by his son, the Master of Ross, who was the last lord of that ilk, and who died in his thirty-fourth year, unmarried, at Mount Teviot, the seat of his uncle, the Marquis of Lothian, in the following August, and was also taken to Renfrew for purposes of interment. His sister Elizabeth became Countess of Glasgow, and eventually his heiress, and through her the Earls of Glasgow are also Lords Ross of Halkhead, by creation in 1815.

Another sister was one of the last persons in Scotland supposed to be possessed of an evil spirit—Mary, who died unmarried. A correspondent of Robert Chambers states as follows:— "A person alive in 1824 told me that, when a child, he saw her clamber up to the top of an old-fashioned four-post bed. In her fits it was impossible to hold her."

At the time Ross House was offered for sale the city was almost entirely confined within the Flodden Wall, the suburbs being of small extent— Nicolson Street and Square, Chapel Street, the southern portion of Bristo Street, Crichton Street, Buccleuch Street, and St. Patrick Square; though some were projected, the sites were nearly all fields and orchards. The old Statistical Account says that Ross Park was purchased for £1,200, and that the ground-rents of the square yield now (i.e., in 1793) above £1,000 sterling per annum to the proprietor.

James Brown, architect, who built Brown Square, having feued from the city of Edinburgh the lands of Ross Park, built thereon most of the houses of the New Square, which measures 220 yards by 150, and is said to have named it, not for the king, but Brown's elder brother George, who was the Laird of Lindsaylands and Elliestown. It speedily became a more popular place of residence than Brown Square, being farther from town, and possessing houses that were greatly superior in style and accommodation.

Among the early residents in the square in 1784, and prior to that year, were the Countesses of Glasgow and Sutherland, the Ladies Rae and Philiphaugh, Anthony, Earl of Kintore, eighth Lord Falconer of Halkertoun, Sir John Ross Lockhart, and the Lords Braxfield, Stonefield, and Kennet ; and in 1788, Major-General Sir Ralph Abercrombie, who died of his wounds in Egypt.

It has been recorded as an instance of Lord Braxfield's great nerve that during the great political trials in 1793-4, when men's blood was almost at fever heat, after each day's proceedings closed, usually about midnight, he always walked home, alone and unprotected, through the dark or ill-lighted streets, to his house in George Square, though he constantly commented openly upon the conduct of the Radicals, and more than once announced in public that "They wad a' be muckle the better o' bein' hung !"

Here, too, resided in 1784 the Hon. Henry Erskine (brother of the Earl of Buchan), the witty advocate, who, after being presented to Dr. Johnson by Mr. Boswell, and having made his bow in the Parliament House, slipped a shilling into Boswell's hand, whispering that it was for the sight of his English bear.

To those named, Lord Cockburn, in his "Memorials," adds the Duchess of Gordon, Robert Dundas of Arniston, Lord Chief Baron of Exchequer, the hero of Camperdown, Lord President Blair, Dr. John Jamieson, the Scottish lexicographer, and says, "a host of other distinguished people all resided here. The old square, with its pleasant trim-kept gardens, has still an air of antiquated grandeur about it, and retains not a few traces of its former dignity and seclusion."

Among the documents exhibited at the Scott

Centenary celebration in 1872 was a "Contract between James Brown, architect in Edinburgh, and Walter Scott, W.S., to feu and build a dwelling-house, with cellars, coach-house, &c., on the west side of the great square, called George Square (No. 25), at the annual feu of £5 14s., the first payment to commence on Whit Sunday, 1773. Six pages, each signed *Walter Scott*."

In this house, then, with its back windows overlooking the Meadow Walk, beneath its happy

my infirmity (his lameness) as she lifted me coarsely and carelessly over the flinty steps which my brother traversed with a shout and bound. I remember the suppressed bitterness of the moment, and, conscious of my own infirmity, the envy with which I regarded the elastic steps of my more happily-formed brethren."

In No. 25 Scott received, from private tutors, the first rudiments of education; and he mentions that "our next neighbour, Lady Cumming, sent

THE BLIND ASYLUM (FORMERLY THE HOUSE OF DR. JOSEPH BLACK), NICOLSON STREET, 1820.   (*After Storer.*)

parental roof, were spent the bright young years of Scott, who there grew up to manhood under the eye of his good mother. Among his papers, after death, there was found a piece of verse, penned in a boyish hand, endorsed in that of his mother, "*My Walter's first lines.*"

"My father's house in George Square," says Scott, "continued to be my most established place of residence (after my return from Prestonpans in 1776) till my marriage in 1797."

Writing of an incident of his childhood, he says:—
"Every step of the way (the Meadow Walk, behind George Square) has for me something of an early remembrance. There is the stile at which I recollect a cross child's maid upbraiding me with

to beg that the boys might not be all flogged at the same hour, as though she had no doubt the punishment was deserved, yet the noise was dreadful!"

There, too, he had that long illness which confined him to bed, and during which the boy, though full of worldly common sense, was able to indulge in romantic and poetical longings after a mediæval age of his own creation, and stored his mind with those treasures of poesy and romance which he afterwards turned to such wondrous account.

During the weary weeks of that long illness he was often enabled to see the vista of the Meadow Walk by a combination of mirrors so arranged that while lying in bed he could witness the troops marching out to exercise in the Links, or any other incident which occurred in that then fashionable promenade.

It was in this square, and in the adjoining suburbs of Bristo Street, the Potterrow, and Cross Causeway, that those " bickers " of stones, or street fights between boys of different ranks and localities—New Town and Old Town boys, Herioters and Watsoners—took place—juvenile exploits, to which he refers in his general preface to the "Waverley Novels." These dangerous rows were bickers which took place between the aristocratic youths of George Square and the plebeian fry of its vicinity, and it runs thus :—" It followed, from our frequent opposition to each other, that, though not well acquainted with their appearance, and had nicknames for the most remarkable of them. One very active and spirited boy might be considered leader in the cohort of the suburbs. He was, I suppose, thirteen or fourteen years old, finely made,

GEORGE SQUARE, SHOWING HOUSE (SECOND ON THE LEFT) OF SIR WALTER SCOTT'S FAtHER.

difficult of suppression, as the parties always kept pretty far apart, and the fight was often a running one, till the Town Guard came on the ground, and then all parties joined against that force as a common foe, and clouds of stones were hurled at them. These bickers, as an Edinburgh feature, were of great antiquity, and we have already cited an act of the Town Council published *anent* them in 1529; and Calderwood tells us that "upon the Lord's Day, the 20th (January, 1582-3), the Lord Heries departed this life suddonlie, in time of the afternoone's preaching, going to an upper chamber in William Fowllar's lodging *to see the boyes bicker*."

Scott has told us an anecdote of his share in the tall, blue-eyed, with long fair hair, the very picture of a Goth. This lad was always the first in the charge and last in retreat—the Achilles and Ajax of the Cross Causeway." From an old pair of green livery breeches which he wore, he was named Green Breeks. " It fell once upon a time," he added, "when the combat was at the thickest, this plebeian champion headed a sudden charge, so rapid and furious that all fled before him. He was several paces before his comrades, and had actually laid his hands on the patrician standard, when one of our party, whom some misjudging friend had entrusted with a *couteau de chasse*, inspired with a zeal for the honour of the corps worthy of Major Sturgeon himself, struck poor Green Breeks over the head with sufficient strength to cut him down. When this was seen, the casualty was so far beyond what had ever taken place before that both parties fled different ways, leaving poor Green Breeks, with his bright hair plentifully dabbled in blood, to the care of the watchman, who (honest man) took care *not* to know who had done the mischief. The bloody hanger was flung into one of the meadow ditches, and solemn secrecy sworn on all hands; but the remorse and terror of the actor were beyond all bounds, and his apprehensions of the most dreadful character. The wounded hero was for a few days in the infirmary, the case being only a trifling one; but though inquiry was strongly pressed on him, no argument could make him indicate the person from whom he had received the wound, though he must have been perfectly well known to him. When he recovered, the author and his brother opened a communication with him, through the medium of a popular gingerbread baker, with whom both parties were customers, in order to tender a subsidy in the name of smart-money. The sum would excite ridicule were I to name it; but I am sure that the pockets of the noted Green Breeks never held so much money of his own. He declined the remittance, saying he would not sell his blood; but at the same time repudiated the idea of being an informer, which he said was *clam*—that is, base or mean. With much urgency he accepted a pound of snuff for the use of some old woman—aunt, grandmother, or the like—with whom he lived. We did not become friends, for the bickers were more agreeable to both parties than any other pacific amusement; but we conducted them ever after under mutual assurances of the highest consideration for each other."

Lockhart tells us that it was in No. 25 that, at a later period, an acquaintance took place which by degrees ripened into friendship with Francis Jeffrey, born, as we have said, at No. 7, Charles Street, about 150 yards distant from Scott's house. Here one evening Jeffrey found him in a small den on the sunk floor, surrounded by dingy books, and from thence they adjourned to a tavern and supped together. In that "den" he was collecting "the germ of the magnificent library and museum of Abbotsford." "Since those days," says Lockhart, "the habits of life in Edinburgh have undergone many changes; and 'the convenient parlour' in which Scott first showed Jeffrey his collection of minstrelsy is now, in all probability, thought hardly good enough for a menial's sleeping-room."

There it was, however, that his first assay-piece as a poet—his bold rendering of Burger's weird *Lenore*—was produced; and there it was, too, that by his energy his corps of Volunteer Horse was developed. The *Edinburgh Herald and Chronicle* for 20th February, 1797, announced the formation of the corps thus:—

"An offer of service, subscribed by sixty gentlemen and upwards of this city and neighbourhood, engaging to serve as a Corps of Volunteer Light Dragoons during the present war, has been presented to His Grace the Duke of Buccleuch, Lord Lieutenant of the county, who has expressed his high approbation of the plan. Regular drills have in consequence been established.

"Such gentlemen as wish to become members of this corps will make their application through *Mr. Walter Scott, Advocate, George Square,* secretary to the committee of management.

"The service is limited to Midlothian, unless in case of actual invasion or the imminent hazard, when it extends to all Scotland. No member of the corps can be required to join unless during his residence within the county."

Of this corps Scott was the quartermaster.

In one of his notes to "Wilson's Memorials," the cynical C. K. Sharpe says:—" My grand-aunt, Mrs. Campbell of Monzie, had the house in George Square that now belongs to Mr. Borthwick (of Crookston). I remember seeing from the window Walter limping home in a cavalry uniform, the most grotesque spectacle that can be conceived. Nobody then cared much about his two German ballads. This was long before I personally knew him."

In 1797 Scott ceased to reside in No. 25 on his marriage, and carried his bride to a lodging on the second floor of No. 108, George Street; however, the last roof he was under in his "own romantic town" was that of the Douglas Hotel, St. Andrew Square, where, on his return from Italy, on the 9th of July, 1832, he was brought from Newhaven in a state of unconsciousness, and after remaining there two nights, was taken home to Abbotsford to die. His signature, in a boyish hand, written with a diamond, still remains on a pane in one of the windows in 25, George Square, or did so till a recent date.

On the 19th of June, 1795, Lord Adam Gordon, Commander of the Forces in Scotland, had the honour of presenting, in George Square, a new set of British colours to the ancient Scots Brigade of immortal memory, which, after being two hundred years in the Dutch service, had—save some fifty who declined to leave Holland—joined the British army as the 94th Regiment, on the 9th October in the preceding year, under Francis Dundas.

Lord Adam, who was then a very old man, having entered the 18th Royal Irish in 1746, said, with some emotion:—" General Dundas and officers of the Scots Brigade, I have the honour to present these colours to you, and I am very happy in having this opportunity of expressing my wishes that the brigade may continue by good conduct to merit the approbation of our gracious sovereign, and to maintain that high reputation which all Europe knows that ancient and respectable corps has most deservedly enjoyed."

His address was received with great applause, and many of the veterans who had served since their boyhood in Holland were visibly affected.

We have already referred to the tragic results of the Dundas riots in this square during 1792, when the mob broke the windows of the Lord Advocate's house, and those of Lady Arniston and Admiral Duncan, who, with a Colonel Dundas, came forth and assailed the rabble with their sticks, but were pelted with stones, and compelled to fly for shelter.

The admiral's house was No. 5, on the north side of the square, and it was there his family resided while he hoisted his flag on board his ship the *Venerable*, and blockaded the Texel, till the mutiny at the Nore and elsewhere compelled him to bear up for the Yarmouth Roads; and in the October of that year (1797) he won the great battle of Camperdown, and with it a British peerage. The great ensign and sword of the Dutch admiral he brought home with him, and instead of presenting them to Government, retained them in his own house in George Square; and there, if we remember rightly, they were shown by him to Sir James Hall of Dunglass, and his son, the future Captain Basil Hall, then an aspirant for the navy, to whom the admiral said, with honest pride, as he led him into the room where the Dutch ensign hung—

"Come, my lad, and I'll show you something worth looking at."

The great admiral died at Kelso in 1804, but for many years after that period Lady Duncan resided in No. 5.

It was while the Lord Advocate Dundas was resident in the square that, at the trial of Muir and the other "political martyrs," he spoke of the leaders of the United Irishmen as "wretches who had fled from punishment." On this, Dr. Drennan, as president, and Archibald Hamilton Rowan of Killileagh, demanded, in 1793, a recantation of this and other injurious epithets. No reply was accorded, and as Mr. Rowan threatened a hostile visit to Edinburgh, measures for his apprehension were taken by the Procurator Fiscal.

Accompanied by the Hon. Simon Butler, Mr. Rowan arrived at Dumbreck's Hotel, St. Andrew Square, when the former, as second, lost no time in visiting the Lord Advocate in George Square, where he was politely received by his lordship, who said that, "although not bound to give any explanation of what he might consider proper to state in his official capacity, yet he would answer Mr. Rowan's note without delay." But Mr. Butler had barely returned to Mr. Rowan when they were both arrested on a sheriff's warrant, but were liberated on Colonel Norman Macleod, M.P., becoming surety for them, and they left Edinburgh, after being entertained at a public dinner by a select number of the Friends of the People in Hunter's Tavern, Royal Exchange.

In No. 30 dwelt Lord Balgray for about thirty years, during the whole time he was on the bench, one of the last specimens of the old race of Scottish judges ; and there he died in 1837.

In No. 32 lived for many years Francis Grant of Kilgraston, whose fourth son, also Francis, became President of the Royal Academy, and was knighted for great skill as an artist, and whose fifth son, General Sir James Hope Grant, G.C.B., served with such distinction under Lord Saltoun in China, and subsequently in India, where he led the 9th Lancers at Sobraon, and who further fought with such distinction in the Punjaub war, and throughout the subsequent mutiny, under Lord Clyde, and whose grave in the adjacent Grange Cemetery is now so near the scenes of his boyhood.

In No. 36 lived Admiral Maitland of Dundrennan, and in No. 53 Lady Don, who is said to have been the last to use a private sedan chair.

No. 57 was the residence of the Lord Chief Baron Dundas, and therein, on the 29th of May, 1811, died, very unexpectedly, his uncle, the celebrated Lord Melville, who had come to Edinburgh to attend the funeral of his old friend the Lord President Blair, who had died a few days before, and was at that time lying dead in No. 56, the house adjoining that in which Melville expired.

No. 58 was the house of Dr. Charles Stuart of Dunearn in the first years of the present century. His father, James Stuart of Dunearn, was a great-grandson of the Earl of Moray, and was Lord Provost of the city in 1764 and 1768. The doctor's eldest son, James Stuart of Dunearn, W.S., a well-known citizen of Edinburgh, died in 1849.

The private sedan, so long a common feature in the areas or lobbies of George Square, is no longer to be seen there now. In the Edinburgh of the eighteenth century there were far more sedans than coaches in use. The sedan was better suited for the narrow wynds and narrower closes of the city, and better fitted, under all the circumstances, for transporting a finely-dressed lady in a powdered toupee. The public sedans were, for the most part, in the hands of Highlanders, who generally wore short tartan coats, and whose strange jargon and fiery irritability of temper, amid the confusion of a dissolving assembly or a dismissed theatre, were deemed highly amusing. Now there is no such thing as a private sedan in Edinburgh any more than in London, and the use of public ones has entirely ceased.

North of George Square, No. 1, Park Place (now removed to make way for the new university Medical Schools), was the town house of the Campbells of Succoth. Sir Islay, the first baronet, was Lord

distance from the east end of Teviot Row, the class-room of the chair of music. This handsome hall, though inadequate to the purposes for which it is required, is in the Italian style, and is the finest of the university class-rooms. It was erected by order of the Court of Session, in 1861, from funds which were bequeathed for the purpose by General John Reid, the composer of the spirited march, "The Garb of Old Gaul," to words written by General Sir Harry Erksine, and it has a museum containing an almost unique collection of instruments, both acoustic and musical, together with various other objects of interest. There is also a library of musical compositions

PARK PLACE, SHOWING CAMPBELL OF SUCCOTH'S HOUSE.

President of the Court of Session, under the title of Lord Succoth, and was descended from the house of Argyle, and his mother was the only daughter and heiress of John Wallace of Elderslie. He was one of the counsel for the defence in the great Douglas cause, and brought to Edinburgh the first tidings of Lord Douglas's victory in the House of Lords. A baronetcy was conferred upon the Lord President when he retired from office in 1808, and he died in 1823, after being long resident on his estate of Garscube, whither his son, Sir Archibald—who in 1809 became a senator under the title of Lord Succoth—also retired in 1824; and his great house in Park Place was latterly occupied as the Edinburgh Ladies' Institution for Education, and near it was the new Jewish Synagogue.

In Park Place (where Dr. Tait, the present Archbishop of Canterbury, was born) stands, about ninety yards west of Charles Street and the same

and treatises, which is one of the most complete at present existing.

Perhaps the special feature is the magnificent organ by Messrs. Hill and Son, which in some points is unsurpassed. It contains four manuals and sixty-six stops, of which latter eleven belong to the "pedal organ." In this department of the instrument are two specimens, both in wood and in metal, of the rare register of "32 feet." These pedal stops, and several on the manuals, of the most exquisite softness and delicacy, are the great points of this renowned instrument, which has been completed by the present occupant of the chair of music, Professor Sir Herbert Oakeley, who, during the university term, gives fortnightly open "recitals," which are much prized by students and citizens. During late years the interior of the hall has been much improved. Under ten panels the name and date of the ten greatest composers have been inscribed. Figures of two of these—Mozart and Beethoven—have been already painted by a Munich artist, and it is understood to be Sir Herbert's hope that the remaining eight will be added.

Towards the middle of the eighteenth century an

II. The streets of Bristo and Potterrow, from their two ports to where they join (near the General's Entry), and the cross streets between them, to be the district of Bristo and Potterrow.

III. George Square, with Charles and Crichton Streets (exclusive of the corner house of the latter),

THE ORGAN IN THE MUSIC-CLASS ROOM. *(From a Photograph by John Moffat.)*

attempt was made to have the royalty extended over all the southern suburbs of Edinburgh; but, as that was strenuously opposed, they were afterwards, by an Act of George III. in 1771, divided into eight districts in the following manner :—

I. The road leading from Bristo Street westward by Teviot Row and Lauriston, "to the Twopenny Custom" (in Old Toll Cross), to be called the district of Lauriston.

with other thoroughfares leading into it, to be George Square district.

IV. Nicolson Park, including the cross-ways intersecting it, from the Chapel Street to the Pleasance, and the street along the back of the City Wall from Potterrow to Pleasance, to be Nicolson Park district.

V. The Cross Causeway, from the south end of the Potterrow to the east end of the said causeway, and from thence along the Gibbet Street northward, to where it is divided from the burgh of the Canongate, to be the Cross Causeway district. By a subsequent Act of George III. there was added to it all the tract on the north-east of the road leading from the Wright's-houses to the Grange Toll-bar, and from thence along the Mayfield Loan to the old Dalkeith Road, and from thence in a straight line eastward to the March Dyke of the King's Park nearest to the said loan; and the whole ground west of the dyke to where it joins the Canongate—all to be called the Causeway-side district.

VI. From the east end of the Cross Causeway southward to the Gibbet Toll, including the Gibbet Loan, to be called Gibbet Street district.

VII. From the chapel of ease south to the Grange Toll, including the Sciennes, to be the Causeway-side district.

VIII. From the south end of the property of the late Joseph Gavin on the west, and that of John Straiton in Portsburgh on the east of the road leading from the Twopenny Custom southward to the Wright's-house Toll, to be the Toll Cross district.

The chapel of ease in Chapel Street, originally a hideous and unpretending structure, was first projected in January, 1754, when the increasing population of the West Kirk parish induced the Session to propose a chapel somewhere on the south side of it. The elders and deacons were furnished with subscription lists, and these, by March, 1755, showed contributions to the amount of £460; and in expectation of further sums, "a piece of ground at the Wind Mill, or west end of the Cross Causeway, was immediately feued," and estimates, the lowest of which was about £700, were procured for the erection of a chapel to hold 1,200 persons. By January, 1756, it was opened for divine service, and a bell which had been used in the West Church was placed in its steeple in 1763; it weighs nineteen stone, cost £366 Scots, and bears the founder's name, with the words, "*For the Wast Kirk*, 1700."

In 1866 this edifice was restored and embellished by a new front at the cost of more than £2,000, and has in it a beautiful memorial window, erected by the Marquis of Bute to the memory of his ancestress, Flora Macleod of Raasay, who lies interred in the small and sombre cemetery attached to the building. There, too, lie the remains of Dr. Thomas Blacklock "the Blind Poet," Dr. Adam of the High School, Mrs. Cockburn the poetess, and others.

Buccleuch Free Church is situated at the junction of the Cross Causeway and Chapel Street. It was built in 1850, and has a fine octagonal spire, erected about five years after, from a design by Hay of Liverpool.

Lady Dalrymple occupied one of the houses in Chapel Street in 1784; Sir William Maxwell, Bart., of Springkell, who died in 1804, occupied another; and in the same year Lady Agnew of Lochnaw was resident in the now obscure St. Patrick Street, close by.

In this quarter there is an archway at the top of what is now called Gray's Court, together with an entrance opposite the chapel of ease. These were the avenues to what was called the Southern Market, formed about 1820 for the sale of butcher-meat, poultry, fish, and vegetables; but as shops sprang into existence in the neighbourhood, it came to an end in a few years.

The Wind Mill—a most unusual kind of mill in Scotland—from which the little street in this quarter takes its name, was formed to raise the water from the Burgh Loch to supply the Brewers of the Society, a company established under James VI. in 1598; and near it lay a pool or pond, named the Goose Dub, referred to by Scott in the "Fortunes of Nigel." From this mill the water was conveyed in leaden pipes, on the west side of Bristo Street as far as where Teviot Row is now, and from thence in a line to the Society, where there was a reservoir that supplied some parts of the Cowgate. In 1786, when foundations were dug for the houses from Teviot Row to Charles Street, portions of this pipe were found. It was four-and-a-half inches in diameter and two-eighths of an inch thick. The Goose Dub was drained about 1715, and converted into gardens.

In the year 1698 Lord Fountainhall reports a case between the city and Alexander Biggar, brewer, heritor of "the houses called Gairnshall, beyond the Wind Mill, and built in that myre commonly called the Goose-dub," who wished to be freed from the duties of watching and warding, declaring his immunity from "all burghal prestations," in virtue of his feu-charter from John Gairns, who took the land from the city in 1681, "bearing a *reddendo* of ten merks of feu-duty *pro omni alio onere*, which must free him from watching, warding, outreiking militia, or train bands, &c." The Lords found that he was not liable to the former duties, but as regarded the militia, "ordained the parties to be further heard."

In February, 1708, he reports another case connected with this locality, in which Richard Howison, minister at Musselburgh, "having bought some acres near the Wind-milne of Edinburgh," took the rights thereof to himself and his wife in liferent, and to his children in fee, and a dispute in law occurred about the division of the property.

Buccleuch Place, branching westward off the old Carlisle Road, as it was named, was formed between 1766 and 1780, as part of a new and aristocratic quarter, and in rivalry to the New Town. Among the first residents there was Elizabeth Fairlie, dowager of George, fifth Lord Reay, who died in 1768. She died in Buccleuch Place on the 10th November, 1800.

The street is of uniform architecture, 270 yards long, but has a chilling and forsaken aspect. The large and isolated tenement facing the south-east entrance to George Square was built, and used for many years as Assembly Rooms for the aristocratic denizens of this quarter. "In these beautiful rooms," says Lord Cockburn, "were to be seen the last remains of the stately ball-room discipline of the preceding age." Now they are occupied as dwelling-houses.

Jeffrey, on marrying a second cousin of his own in 1801, began housekeeping in the third flat of a common stair here, No. 18, at a time when, as he wrote to his brother, his profession had never brought in a hundred a year; and there he and his wife were living in 1802, when in March, Brougham and Sydney Smith met at his house, and it was proposed to start the *Edinburgh Review*; and these, the first three, were joined in meeting with Murray, Horner, Brown, Lord Webb Seymour, and John and Thomas Thomson, and negotiations were opened with Manners and Millar, the publishers in the Parliament Close; and—as is well known—Jeffrey was for many years the editor of, as well as chief contributor to, that celebrated periodical.

Where the Meadows now lie there lay for ages a loch coeval with that at Duddingstone, some three-quarters of a mile long from Lochrin, and where the old house of Drumdryan stands on the west, to the road that led to the convent of Sienna on the east, and about a quarter of a mile in breadth [*] —a sheet of water wherein, in remote times, the Caledonian bull, the stag, and the elk that roamed in the great oak forest of Drumsheugh, were wont to quench their thirst, and where, amid the deposit of marl at its bottom, their bones have been found from time to time during trenching and draining operations. The skull and horns of one

gigantic stag (*Cervus elephas*), that must have found a grave amidst its waters, were dug up below the root of an ancient tree in one of the Meadow Parks in 1781, and are now in the Antiquarian Museum.

In 1537 the land lying on its south bank was feued by the sisters of the Cistercian convent, and in July, 1552, the provost, bailies, and council, ordered that no person should "wesch ony claithis at the Burrow Loch in tyme cummyng, and dischargis the burnmen to tak ony burn at ony wells in the burgh under sic pains as the jugis ples imput to them." ("Burgh Records.")

On the 25th of May, 1554, the magistrates and council ordained that the Burgh Loch should be inclosed, "biggit up" in such a manner as would prevent its overflow (Ibid). In April, 1556, they again ordained the city treasurer to build up the western end of it, "and hold the watter thairof," though in the preceding January they had ordered its water "to be lattin forth, and the dyke thairof stoppit, so that it may ryn quhair it ran before" (into Dalry Burn, doubtless), "quhill the first of Pasche nixt to cum," when they should consider whether the water, which seemed to occasion some trouble to the bailies, "be lattin furth or holden in as it is now."

In 1690 the rental of the loch and its "broad meadows" is given at £66 13s. 4d. sterling, in *common good* of the city. Early in the seventeenth century an attempt was boldly made to drain this loch, and so far did the attempt succeed that in 1658 the place, with its adjacent marshes, was let to John Straiton, on a lease of nineteen years, for the annual rent of £1,000 Scots, and from him it for a time received the name of Straiton's Loch, by which it was known in 1722, when it was let for £800 Scots to Mr. Thomas Hope of Rankeillor, on a fifty-seven years' lease.

Hope was president of "The Honourable Society of Improvers in the Knowledge of Agriculture in Scotland," who met once a fortnight in a house near what is now called Hope Park, where they received and answered queries from country people on farming subjects. Mr. Hope had travelled in Holland, France, and England, where he picked up the best hints on agriculture, and was indefatigable in his efforts to get them adopted in Scotland.

In consideration of the moderate rent, he bound himself to drain the loch entirely, and to make a walk round it, to be enclosed with a hedge, a row of lime-trees, and a narrow canal, nine feet broad, on each side of it; and in this order the meadows remained unchanged till about 1840, always a

---

[*] Dr. J. A. Sidey kindly supplies a description of the original of the engraving on p. 349, taken from the Merchant Company's Catalogue. "View of George Watson's hospital and grounds from the south, with the castle and a portion of the town of Edinburgh in the distance. One of the two fine frescoes which originally adorned the walls of the Governor's Board Room in said hospital. . . The painter is believed to have been Alexander Runciman, the celebrated Scottish artist. He died on the 21st October, 1785. His younger brother John died in 1768, aged 24."

damp and melancholy place, even in summer, though much frequented as a public walk.

The western end obtains still the name of Hope Park, and a more modern street close by bears the name of his Fifeshire estate—Rankeillor—now passed to another family.

Among these Improvers were the Earls of Stair, Islay, and Hopetoun, the Lords Cathcart and Drummore, with Dalrymple of Cousland and Cockburn of Ormiston. Lord Stair was the first to raise turnips

end of the central walk, and a little, but once famous, cottage and stable, where asses' milk was sold, long disfigured the upper walk at Teviot Row.

A few old-fashioned villas were on the south side of the Meadows; in one of these, in 1784, dwelt Archibald Cockburn, High Judge Admiral of Scotland. No. 6 Meadow Place was long the residence of David Irving, LL.D., author of "The Lives of the Scottish Poets" and other works, librarian to the Faculty of Advocates; and in Warrender

THE MEADOWS, ABOUT 1810. (*From a Painting in the possession of Dr. J. A. Sidey.*)

in the open fields, and so laid the foundation of the most important branch of the store-husbandry of modern times.

The Meadows were long a fashionable promenade. "There has never in my life," says Lord Cockburn, "been any single place in or near Edinburgh which has so distinctly been the resort at once of our philosophy and our fashion. Under these poor trees walked, and talked, and meditated, all our literary and scientific, and many of our legal, worthies of the last and beginning of the present century."

They still form the shooting ground of the Royal Company of Archers. A species of ornamental arbour, called "The Cage," stood long at the south

Lodge, Meadow Place, lived and died James Ballantine, the genial author of "The Gaberlunzie's Wallet" and other works of local notoriety, but more especially a volume of one hundred songs, with music, many of which are deservedly popular. Celebrated in his own profession as a glass-stainer, he was employed by the Royal Commissioners on the Fine Arts, to execute the stained glass windows for the House of Lords at Westminster.

Now the once sequestered Meadows, save on the southern quarter, which is open to Bruntsfield Links, are well-nigh completely encircled by new lines of streets and terraces, and are further intersected by the fine modern drive named from Sir John Melville, who was Lord Provost in 1854-9.

THE BURGH LOCH.   (*After a Photograph of the Original, by permission of the Merchant Company of Edinburgh.*)

CHAPTER XLI.

HOPE PARK END.

"The Douglas Cause," or Story of Lady Jane Douglas-Stewart—Hugh Lord Semple—"The Chevalier"—The Archers' Hall—Royal Company of Archers formed—Their Jacobitism—Their Colours—Early Parades—Constitution and Admission—Their Hall built—Messrs. Nelsons' Establishment—Thomas Nelson.

HOPE PARK END is the name of a somewhat humble cluster of unpretending houses which sprang up at the east end of the Meadows ; but the actual villa latterly called Hope Park was built on the south bank of the former loch, "immediately eastward of the Meadow Cage," as it is described in the prints of 1822. In character Hope Park End has been improved by the erection of Hope Park Crescent and Terrace, with the U. P. church in their vicinity ; but when its only adjuncts were the Burgh Loch Brewery, the dingy edifices known as Gifford Park, and an old house of the sixteenth century, pulled down by the Messrs. Nelson, it was a somewhat sombre locality. Another old house near the Archers' Hall showed on the lintel of its round turnpike stair the date 1704, and the initials A. B. —J. L. ; but in which old mansion in this quarter the celebrated and unfortunate Lady Jane Douglas-Stewart resided we have no means of ascertaining, or whether before or after she occupied a garret in the East Cross Causeway, and only know from her letters that she lived here during a portion of the time (1753) when her long vexed case was disputed in Scotland and in England.

Having referred to this case so often, it is necessary, even for Edinburgh readers, to say something of what it was—one in which the famous toady Boswell, though little inclined to exaggeration, is reported by Sir Walter Scott to have been so ardent a partisan that he headed a mob which smashed the windows of the adverse judges of the Court of Session, when, "For Douglas or Hamilton ? " was the question men asked each other in the streets, at night, and swords instantly drawn if opinions were hostile ; for " the Douglas cause," as Scott says, "shook the security of birthright in Scotland, and was a cause which, had it happened before the Union, when there was no appeal to a

British House of Lords, would have left the fortress of honours and of property in ruins." The decision of the Court of Session in 1767 led to serious disturbances and much acrimony; thus the reversal of it, two years subsequently, was received in Scotland with the greatest demonstrations of joy.

Archibald, third marquis, and first Duke of Douglas, created so in 1703, was the representative of that long and illustrious line of warriors whose race and family history are second to none in Europe.

His father, the second marquis, had been twice married—first to a daughter of the Earl of Mar, by whom he had the gallant Earl of Angus, who fell at Steinkirk in 1692; and secondly, to Lady Mary Kerr, of the house of Lothian, by whom he had Archibald, afterwards Duke of Douglas, his successor, and Lady Jean, or Jane, celebrated, like most of the women of her family, for her remarkable beauty, but still more so for her singularly evil fate.

In the first flush of her womanhood she was betrothed to Francis, Earl of Dalkeith, who succeeded his grandmother in the ducal title of Buccleuch; but the marriage was broken off, and he chose another bride, also a Jane Douglas, cf the house of Queensberry, and for many years after this, the heroine of our story persistently refused all offers that were made for her hand.

At length, in the eventful year 1746, when residing at Drumsheugh, when she was in her forty-eighth year, she was secretly married to Colonel John Stewart, brother of Sir George Stewart, Bart., of Grantully, but a somewhat penniless man. Thus the sole income of the newly-wedded pair consisted of only £300 per annum, given rather grudgingly by the Duke of Douglas to his sister, with whom he was on very indifferent terms.

For economy the couple repaired to France for three years, and on returning, brought with them two boys, of whom they alleged Lady Jane had been delivered in Paris. Six months before their return their marriage was only made known, on which the duke, already referred to in our account of the Potterrow, though childless, at once withdrew the usual allowance, and thus plunged them in the direst distress; and to add thereto, Colonel Stewart's creditors cast him into prison, while his sons were declared spurious.

With womanly heroism Lady Jane bore up against her troubles, and addressed the following letter to Mr. Pelham, the Secretary of State:—"Sir,—If I meant to importune you, I should ill deserve the generous compassion which I was informed, some months ago, you expressed on being acquainted with my distress. I take this as the least troublesome way of thanking you, and desiring you to lay my application before the king in such a light as your own humanity will suggest. I cannot tell my story without seeming to complain of one of whom I *never will complain.* I am persuaded my brother wishes me well, but from a mistaken resentment, upon a creditor of mine demanding from him a trifling sum, he has stopped the annuity which he has always paid me—my father having left me, his only younger child, in a manner unprovided for. Till the Duke of Douglas is set right—which I am confident he will be—*I am destitute.* Presumptive heiress to a great estate and family, with two children, I want bread. Your own nobleness of mind will make you feel how much it costs me to beg, though from the king. My birth and the attachment of my family, I flatter myself, His Majesty is not unacquainted with. Should he think me an object of his royal bounty, my heart won't suffer any bounds to my gratitude; and, give me leave to say, my spirit won't suffer me to be burdensome to His Majesty longer than my cruel necessity compels me. I little thought of ever being reduced to petition in this way; your goodness will therefore excuse me if I have mistaken the manner or said anything improper. Though personally unknown to you, I rely on your intercession. The consciousness of your own mind in having done so good and charitable a deed will be a better return than the thanks of JANE DOUGLAS-STEWART."

A pension of £300 per annum was the result of this application; but, probably from the accumulation of past debts, the couple were still in trouble. The colonel remained in prison, and Lady Jane had to part with her jewels, and even her clothes, to supply him with food, lest he might starve in the King's Bench. Meanwhile she resided in a humble lodging at Chelsea, and the letters which passed between the pair, many of which were touching in their tenor, and which were afterwards laid before the Court of Session, proved that their two children were never absent from their thoughts, and were the objects of the warmest affection.

Accompanied by them, Lady Jane came to Edinburgh, and in the winter of 1752 took up her residence at Hope Park, in the vicinity of her brother's house. She sought a reconciliation, but the duke sternly refused to grant her even an interview. In a letter dated from there 8th December, 1752, to the minister of Douglas, she complains of the conduct of the Duke of Hamilton in her affairs, and of some mischief which the Marquis of Lothian had done to her cause at Douglas Castle, and adds in a postscript:—

"My dear little ones, Archy and Sholto, are, I bless God, in very good health. I beg your prayers for them and me, which I set a high value on. Mrs. Hewitt (her faithful attendant) sends you her best compliments and good wishes. My address is at Hope Park, near Edinburgh, to the care of Mr. Walter Colville, at his house at the foot of Niddry's Wynd."

She returned to London in the summer of 1753, leaving the children in the care of their faithful nurse ; but, notwithstanding all the care of the latter, Sholto Thomas Stewart, the younger of the twins, who had always been feeble and sickly, died at Hope Park, "near the Meadow." This child was said to be the image of his mother. She hurried to Edinburgh, worn out by hardship, fatigue, starvation, and, as Dr. Pringle of the Guards alleged, dying of a broken heart. She expired on the 22nd of November, 1753.

Four hours before her death she desired Archibald, the future Lord Douglas, to be brought before her, and laying her hands on the weeping boy's head, she said—

"God bless you, my child ! God make you a good and honest man, for riches I despise." Then, as the old Douglas spirit glowed within her, she added: "Take a sword in your hand, and you may one day be as great a hero as some of your ancestors."

Archibald, though barbarously expelled from the carriages at his mother's funeral, found friends, who educated and supported him as befitted his rank ; and his father having succeeded to the baronetcy and estates of Grantully, though he married a daughter of Lord Elibank, executed a bond of provision in his favour for upwards of £2,500, and therein acknowledged him as his son by Lady Jane Douglas. Still the duke, more rancorous than ever, repudiated him as his nephew, and in the hope of having heirs of his own body, in 1758 he married Miss Douglas of Mains, who, to his increased indignation, became so warm an adherent of the alleged foundling, that His Grace separated from her for a considerable time.

In 1761 a fatal illness fell upon the duke, and as death came nigh, he repented of all his conduct to his dead sister, and as reparation he executed a deed of entail of his entire estates in favour of the heirs of his father, James, Marquis of Douglas, with remainder to Lord Douglas Hamilton, brother of the Duke of Hamilton, "and supplemented it by another deed, which set forth that, as in the event of his death without heirs of his body, Archibald Douglas, alias Stewart, a minor, and son of the deceased Lady Jane Douglas, his sister, would

succeed him, he appointed the Duchess of Douglas, the Duke of Queensberry, and certain others whom he named, the lad's tutors and guardians."

Thus the penniless waif of Hope Park End became the heir of a peerage and a long rent-roll ; but the house of Hamilton repudiated his claims, while his guardians resolved to enforce them. It was suggested by the former that the whole story of the birth of twins was a fabrication, and all Paris was ransacked in support of this allegation, and that the two children had been stolen from their French parents. The *Edinburgh Advertiser* for June, 1764, records the death of Sir John Stewart of Grantully, at Murthly. Prior to this, he affirmed on oath before competent witnesses, "as one slipping into eternity, that the defendant (Archibald Stewart) and his deceased twin-brother were both born of the body of Lady Jane Douglas, his lawful spouse, in the year 1748." In 1767 the case came before the whole fifteen judges ; seven voted for the claimant, and seven against him. The Lord President, who had no vote save in such a dilemma, voted for the Hamilton or illegitimacy side, and thus deprived Archibald Douglas-Stewart of fortune and rank ; but this decision was reversed in 1769 by the House of Lords, and the son of Lady Jane succeeded to the princely estate of his uncle, the Duke of Douglas, whose name he assumed, and was created a peer of the United Kingdom as Baron Douglas of Douglas Castle, in Lanarkshire, in 1790. He died in 1827.

Another waif of the nobility was resident at Hope Park End in the early years of this century —at least, before 1811. This was Hugh, thirteenth Lord Semple, who had lost his estates and come signally down in the world in many ways. He was born in 1758, and succeeded his father in 1782. He was a lieutenant of the Scots Guards in 1778, and a captain in 1781, and was said to have been obliged to leave the regiment through having incurred the displeasure of George III. by his political opinions. He died in very indifferent circumstances in 1830, in his seventy-second year.

In "The Hermit in Edinburgh," 1824, a writer, who sketched with fidelity the real characters of his own time, tells us of a recluse, or mysterious old gentleman, who dwelt at Hope Park End, and was known as "the Chevalier." He was pensive and sweet in manner, and wore a garb of other years, with a foreign military order; his locks were white, but his face was Scottish ; he had the bearing of a soldier, and, like the Baron of Bradwardine, used French phrases. He had lost nearly his all in the French Funds at the Revolution in 1789.

His lodgings consisted of one room in a flat ;

"a broadsword, a real Andrea Ferrara blade, hung by his bed-side, and over the clock (a very old French one), on the chimney-piece, were attached a broken pipe and withered rose." The pipe was the gift of a comrade, and a secret story attached to the withered rose ; but, the writer adds, "when he handed me his snuff-box, the *miniature* on the lid told everything—a blue bonnet, a white rose in it, the graceful flowing tartan, and the *star* upon the breast." He was the son of a Jacobite exile, whom

having perished by fire about the beginning of the eighteenth century, little is known of its constitution prior to the time of Queen Anne. A society for the encouragement of archery was first formed in the reign of Charles II., by order of the Secret Council, in 1676, though with what military utility at that time is not very apparent; its seal bore Cupid and Mars, with the motto, IN PEACE AND WARR. They were ordered to "be modelled and drawn up in a formal company, with drums and

THE ARCHERS' HALL.

none knew ; but when he died, he had nothing to bequeath to his friend but his foreign cross, the snuff-box, the claymore, and the pipe, and his story, whatever it was, died with him.

The Archers' Hall, in this district, is famous as being the head-quarters of the Royal Company of Archers, or King's Body Guard for Scotland.

This remarkable corps, which takes precedence of all royal guards and troops of the line, is composed entirely of nobles and gentlemen of good position, under a captain-general, who is always a peer of the highest rank, with four lieutenants-general, four majors-general, four ensigns-general, sixteen brigadiers, an adjutant, and surgeon.

The ancient records · of the Royal Company

colours, whereof the officers are to be chosen by the said Counsill, and which company, so formed, shall meet on the Links of Leith," or elsewhere ; each archer, "with sufficient shuting graith, carrying the Company's seal and arms in their hatts or bonnets as their proper cognisance."

The Marquis of Athole, with the Earl of Kinghorn and Lord Elphinstone, commanded, and the Scottish Treasury gave a prize worth £20 sterling to be shot for. This corps, sometimes called the King's Company of Archers, frequently met during the reigns of Charles II. and James VII., but little can be traced of it after the Revolution.

Upon the accession of Queen Anne and the death of the Marquis of Athole, they elected as a captain-general the famous Sir George Mackenzie, then Lord Tarbat, and Secretary of State, and afterwards Earl of Cromartie. Having judiciously chosen a leader of powerful influence and approved fidelity, they obtained from Queen Anne, on the 6th March, 1704, a charter under the Great Seal of Scotland, erecting them into a royal company, receiving and ratifying in their behalf the old laws and acts in favour of archery; giving them power to enrol members, to select a council, and choose

for the Jacobites to omit utilising it for eventual military purposes, and thus when, in 1714, the critical state of the country and the hopes and fears of opposite factions were roused by the approaching death of Queen Anne and the distracted state of her ministry, an unusual amount of vigour inspired the Royal Company of Archers. Their laws were extended on vellum, adorned with festoons of ribbon, and subscribed by all the members; and they did not hesitate to engross in their minute

ARCHERS' HALL: THE DINING HALL.

their own leaders; "as also of convening in military fashion, by way of weapon-shaw, under the guidance of their own officers . . . . and of going forth as often as to it shall seem proper, at least once in each year, about Midsummer, to shoot arrows with a bow at a butt." ("Laws, &c., of the Royal Company of Archers "—J. B. Paul's Hist., &c.). The magistrates of Edinburgh soon after gave them a silver arrow, to be shot for yearly.

These new rights and privileges they were appointed to possess after the mode of a feudal tenure, and to hold them in free gift of her Majesty and her successors, paying therefor an annual acknowledgment of a pair of barbed arrows.

Such an organisation as this proved too tempting

book, in terms not to be misunderstood, that on his birthday they drank to the health of the exiled James VIII.

They still carry a pair of colours. The first bears on one side Mars and Cupid within a wreath of thistles, with the motto mentioned; on the other is a yew-tree, supported by two archers, with the motto, *Dat gloria vires.* The second colour has on one side the royal standard, or lion rampant, with a crowned thistle and the national motto, *Nemo me impune lacessit.* On the other side is St. Andrew on his cross, with a crown over all, and the then very significant motto, *Dulce pro patria periculum.*

On the 14th of June the Earl of Cromartie, then

upwards of eighty years of age, as captain-general, and the Earl of Wemyss as lieutenant-general, marched at the head of the Royal Archers, with colours flying, from the Parliament Square to Holyrood, and thence to Leith, where they shot for the Edinburgh Arrow, and returned with similar parade, receiving from all guards and troops the honours that are paid to the regular army ; but in the following year (1715), the Earl of Cromartie being dead, they were led by the Earl of Wemyss to a similar parade.

On the 16th of June a letter addressed to Wodrow says :—" Upon Monday last the Royal Company of Archers, consisting of about 200, all clad in the old Scottish garb, made their parade through this town and in Leith ; they *all* consist of Jacobites, except five or six. At night they came to the playhouse, and betwixt the acts they desired Sir Thomas Dalzell (who is mad) to order the musicians to play that air called ' Let the King enjoy his own again.' After it was over, the whole house clapp'd 3 times lowd, but a few hissed."

These facts serve to show that what was called the Royal Company of Archers all through the reigns of Anne and George I. was really a sodality, composed exclusively of the Jacobite aristocracy— in short, a marked muster for the House of Stuart. Their leaders were, and have been always, nobles of the highest rank ; they had " their adjutant and other officers, their colours, music, and uniforms, and pretty effective military organisation and appearance." (" Dom. Ann.")

Their dress was tartan, trimmed with green silk fringe ; their bonnets were trimmed with green and white ribbons, with St. Andrew's cross in front ; their horns and swords were decorated with green and white ribbons, and the dresses of the officers were laid over with rich silver lace. We are told that " the cavalier spirit of Allan Ramsay glowed at seeing these elegant specimens of the *Aristoi* of Scotland engaged at butts and rovers, and poured itself forth in verses to their praise."

After the futile insurrection of 1715, the Archers made no parade for nine years ; but on James, Duke of Hamilton, K.T., being chosen captain-general, they marched to Musselburgh in 1724, and afterwards occasionally till the 10th July, 1732, when they had a special parade, in which the Jacobite element greatly predominated. A guard of honour brought the colours from the Duke of Hamilton's apartments at Holyrood, when the march to the Links began under his Grace as captain-general, preceded by Lord Bruce " on horseback, with fine Turkish furniture, as major-general, in absence of the Earl of Crawford."

" The Lord Provost and magistrates saw the procession from a window, and were saluted by the several officers, as did General Wade from a balcony in the Earl of Murray's lodgings in the Canongate. The Governor of Damascus came likewise to see the ceremony. Betwixt one and two the company arrived in the Links, whence, after shooting for the arrow (which was won by Balfour of Foret), they marched into Leith in the same order, and after dinner returned to the city, and saw acted the tragedy called *Macbeath*." (*Caledonian Mercury*, 1732.)

Including the sovereign's prize, there are seventeen shot for annually by the archers. Among these are the City of Edinburgh silver arrow, given in 1709, and the Musselburgh silver arrow, which appears to have been shot for so far back as 1603. As in the instance of many of the other prizes, the victor retains it only for a year, and returns it with a medal appended, and engraved with a motto, device, or name. The affairs of the Guard are managed by a preses, six councillors, a secretary, and treasurer. The rules say " That all persons possessed of Scottish domicile or of landed estate in Scotland, or younger sons, though not domiciled in Scotland, of a Scottish landed proprietor qualified to act as a commissioner of supply, are eligible for admission to the royal company."

After the battle of Culloden and the decay of Jacobitism, the vigour of the Archer Guard declined, till some new life was infused into its ranks by William St. Clair of Roslin, and then it was that the present Archers' Hall, near Hope Park End, was built. There an acre of ground was feued from the city, at a feu of £12 yearly, with double that sum every twenty-fifth year, and the foundation stone was laid by Mr. St. Clair on August the 15th, 1776.

The dining-hall measures 40 feet by 24, and is 18 feet in height. There are two other rooms about 18 feet square, with other apartments, kitchen, &c. The last most important appearances of the Royal Archers have been on the occasion of George IV.'s visit in 1822—when they wore the old tartan costume, which was afterwards replaced by tunics of Lincoln green,—on the visit of Queen Victoria, and the first great volunteer review in the Royal Park.

An old gable-ended house, the windows of which looked westward along the vista of the Meadows, and their predecessor, the Burgh Loch, was traditionally said to have been inhabited by George Heriot, but was removed in 1843, when the Messrs. Nelson built there an establishment, which, for printing, publishing, and bookbinding together, was the most extensive in Scotland. His initials,

G. H., cut in wood, remained in several parts of the house. The Rev. Dr. Steven, governor of the hospital, presented a coloured drawing of the house to the Messrs. Nelson, as "the country residence of the founder of the hospital." It perished in the fire of 1878, but another is preserved.

The house was also, about 1800, the abode of an aged lady, well known to those of Jacobite proclivities in Edinburgh, Mrs. Hannah Robertson, an alleged grand-daughter of Charles II., and whose sister was ancestress of the Mercers of Gorthy. She died in 1808.

The well-known firm of the Messrs. Nelson and Sons was originally established by the late Mr. Thomas Nelson, whose first business premises were in a small corner shop at the head of the West Bow, only lately removed, where he published cheap editions of the "Scots Worthies," Baxter's "Saints' Rest," and similar works; but it was not until his sons entered the business that the work of the firm was placed upon a wider basis.

Mr. Nelson was born at a village called Throsk, near Stirling, in 1780. When twenty years of age he went to London, and after experiencing his own share of difficulties, familiar to young men in pushing their way in the world, he at last entered the service of a publishing house in Paternoster Row. This determined the course of his career. One of his early associates in London was the late Mr. Kelly, publisher, afterwards raised to the Lord Mayor's chair. Mr. Nelson had begun by this time to show that love for the standard works of the old theological school which characterised him in after life. He remained for some years in London, and then came to Edinburgh, where he soon signalized himself as a publisher.

Cheap issues are a common feature of the publishing trade of the country now, but it was otherwise in the beginning of the century, and he was among the first to introduce the new order of things by the publication of works like those of

Paley, Leighton, Romaine, Newton, and many others.

For several years in the latter part of his life he was more or less of an invalid. He died, at the age of eighty, on the 23rd of March, 1861. He lies buried in Edinburgh in the Grange cemetery, next to the grave of Hugh Miller.

The Messrs. Nelsons' range of offices at Hope Park were on a scale surpassing any similar place of business in Edinburgh, as it consisted of three conjoined blocks of neat and plain design, forming as many sides of a square. In the main building were three floors, and machinery was used wherever it was available, and by means of that and an admirably organised system of the division of labour, the amount of literary work turned out was enormous. The process of stereotyping, which was invented by Mr. William Ged, a goldsmith in Edinburgh, and has been brought to the highest perfection in the place of its birth, was here greatly in practice. By 1870 the Messrs. Nelson employed fully 600 workpeople, the half of whom were young women, and on their own premises they manufactured all the inks used in printing, and the varnishes for bookbinding.

The whole of their extensive premises were destroyed by a calamitous fire, after which the Messrs. Nelson erected new offices and workshops upon several acres of land, known as Parkside, with a fine frontage to the old Dalkeith Road, south of "The Castle of Clouts," and near what was called of old the Gibbet Toll.

Erected by the Messrs. Nelson in 1881, two handsome pillars, surmounted respectively by the Unicorn and Lion, now ornament the entrance to the Melville Drive at the east end of the Meadows. These pillars stand near the site of their former premises, and were erected as a gift to the city, in commemoration of the kindness and sympathy shown to them by the magistrates at the time of the great fire.

CHAPTER XLII.

LAURISTON.

The New University Buildings—The Estimates and Accommodation—George Watson's Hospital—Founded—Opened and Sold—The New Royal Infirmary—Its Capabilities for Accommodation—Simpson Memorial Hospital—Sick Children's Hospital—Merchant Maiden Hospital—Watson's Schools—Lauriston United Presbyterian Church—St. Catharine's Convent.

IN the district of Lauriston we find quite a cluster of charitable institutions; but before treating of the more ancient one—Heriot's Hospital—we shall describe those edifices which lie between the street and the northern walk of the Meadows.

In the city map of 1787, after Watson's Hospital,

the most prominent edifice to the westward, and nearly opposite the head of Lady Lawson's Wynd and the present cattle market, is Lauriston House, a large mansion, with a lodge and circular carriage approach. Here, at Lauriston, in 1763, died Sir

erect thereon in immediate vicinity of the new infirmary, a vast edifice, with complete class-rooms, theatres, and museums, with all the latest scientific improvements, for the medical faculty of the metropolitan university; to re-organise the existing

THOMAS NELSON.   *(From a Sketch in possession of the Family.)*

John Rutherford, baronet of that ilk, and the whole space between that house and Leven Lodge was covered by open fields and gardens, till after the beginning of the present century.

Owing to the increasing necessity for the further accommodation at the old college, the Edinburgh University Buildings scheme was developed to purchase the sites of Park Place and Teviot Row, at the cost of about £33,000, and to

class-rooms of the latter, and to improve them in direct adaptation to the wants of the several professors of arts, law, and theology; to provide increased and more convenient accommodation for the University Library; and to erect a University Hall for the conferring of degrees, the holding of examinations, and for all public academical ceremonials.

Trustees for this purpose were appointed, among

THE EDINBURGH UNIVERSITY MEDICAL SCHOOLS, LAURISTON.

whom were the Duke of Buccleuch, the Earl of Stair, and Sir William Stirling-Maxwell, of Pollock and Keir, with an acting committee, at the head of whom were the Lord Provost, the Principal, Sir Alexander Grant, Bart., and Professor Sir Robert Christison, Bart., D.C.L.

The project was started in 1874, and commenced fairly in 1878. The architect was Mr. R. Rowand Anderson, and the cost of the whole, when finished, was estimated at about £250,000.

The first portion erected was the southern block, comprising the departments of anatomy, surgery, practice of physic, physiology, pathology, midwifery, and a portion of the chemistry. The frontage to the Meadow Walk presents a bold and semicircular bay, occupied by the pathology and midwifery department. An agreeable variety, but general harmony of style, characterises the buildings as a whole, and this arose from the architect adhering strictly to sound principle, in studying first his interior accommodation, and then allowing it to express itself in the external elevations.

The square block at the southern end of the Meadow Walk, near the entrance to George Square, is chiefly for the department of physiology; whilst the south front is to a large extent occupied by anatomy.

The hall for the study of practical anatomy is lighted by windows in the roof and an inner court facing to the north, a southern light being deemed unnecessary or undesirable. The blank wall thus left on the south forms an effective foil to the pillared windows of the physiology class-room, at one end, and to some suitable openings, similarly treated, which serve to light hat and coat rooms, &c., at the other.

In the eastern frontage to Park Place, where the departments of anatomy, physic, and surgery, are placed, a prominent feature in the design is produced by the exigencies of internal accommodation. As it was deemed unnecessary in the central part of the edifice to carry the ground-floor so far forward as the one immediately above, the projecting portion of the latter is supported by massive stone trusses, or brackets, which produce a series of deep shadows with a bold and picturesque effect. The inner court is separated from the chief quadrangle of the building by a noble hall upwards of 100 feet long, for the accommodation of the University anatomical museum. It has two tiers of galleries, and is approached by a handsome vestibule with roof groined in stone, and supported by pillars of red sandstone. The quadrangle is closed in to the west, north, and east,

by extensive ranges of apartments for the accommodation of chemistry, materia medica, and medical jurisprudence. The north front faces Teviot Row, and in it is the chief entrance to the quadrangle by a massive gateway, which forms one of the leading architectural features of the design. When the building devoted to educational purposes shall have been completed, there will only remain to be built the great college hall and campanile, which are to complete the east face of the design. Including the grant of £80,000 obtained from Government, the whole amount at the disposal of the building committee is about £180,000.

For the erection of the hall and tower a further sum of about £50,000 or £60,000 is supposed to be necessary.

The new Royal Infirmary, on the western side of the Meadow Walk, occupies the grounds of George Watson's Hospital, and is engrafted on that edifice. The latter was built in what was then a spacious field, lying southward of the city wall. The founder, who was born in 1650, the year of Cromwell's invasion, was descended from a family which for some generations had been merchants in Edinburgh; but, by the death of his father, John Watson, and the second marriage of his mother, George and his brother were left to the care of destiny. A paternal aunt, Elizabeth Watson, or Davidson, however, provided for their maintenance and education; but George being her favourite, she bound him as an apprentice to a merchant in the city, and after visiting Holland to improve his knowledge of business, she gave him a small sum wherewith to start on his own account. He returned to Scotland, in the year 1676, when he entered the service of Sir James Dick, knight, and merchant of Edinburgh, as his clerk or book-keeper, who some time after allowed him to transact, in a mercantile way, certain affairs in the course of exchange between Edinburgh and London on his own behalf. In 1695 he became accountant to the Bank of Scotland, and died in April, 1723, and by his will bequeathed £12,000 to endow a hospital for the maintenance and instruction of the male children and grandchildren of decayed merchants in Edinburgh; and by the statutes of trustees, a preference was given to the sons and grandsons of members of the Edinburgh Merchant Company. The money left by the prudent management of the governors was improved to about £20,000 sterling before they began the erection of the hospital in 1738, in a field of seven acres belonging to Heriot's Trust.

George Watson, in gratitude for the benefits conferred upon him in his friendless boyhood by his aunt Elizabeth, ordered that on application for taking children into his hospital, those of the name of Davidson should have a preference, as well as those of Watson. In June, 1741, twelve boys were admitted into it; in three years the number amounted to thirty; and in 1779 that number was doubled.

Watson's Merchant Academy, as it was named in 1870, underwent a great change in that year. The governors of the four hospitals connected with the Merchant Company, taking advantage of the Endowed Institutions (Scotland) Act, applied for and obtained provisional orders empowering them to convert the foundation into day-schools, and it was opened as one. The edifice was sold to the Corporation of the Royal Infirmary, and the building formerly occupied as the Merchant Maiden Hospital was acquired for, and is now being used as, George Watson's College School for boys.

The building was long conspicuous from several points by its small spire, surmounted by a ship, the emblem of commerce. Here, then, we now find the new Royal Infirmary, one of the most extensive edifices in the city, which was formally opened on Wednesday, the 29th of October, 1879, the foundation stone having been laid in October, 1870, by H.R.H. the Prince of Wales.

The situation of the infirmary is alike excellent and desirable, from its vicinity to the open pasture of the Meadows and Links, the free breezes from the hills, and to the new seat of university medical teaching. The additions and improvements at the old Royal Infirmary, and the conversion of the old High School into a Surgical Hospital, were still found unfitted for the increasing wants of the Corporation as the city grew in extent and population, as the demands of medical science increased, and the conditions of hospital management became more amplified and exacting; and the necessity for some reform in the old edifice in Infirmary Street led to the proposal of the managers for rebuilding the entire Medical House. When those contributors met to whom this bold scheme was submitted, complaints were urged as to the wants of the Surgical Hospital, and it was also referred to the committee appointed to consider the whole question.

The subscription list eventually showed a total of £75,000, and a proposed extension of the old buildings, by the removal of certain houses at the South Bridge, was abandoned, when a new impetus was given to the movement by the late Professor James Syme, who had won a high reputation as a lecturer and anatomist.

His strictures on the state of the Surgical Hospital led to a discussion on the wiser policy of rebuilding the whole infirmary, coupled with a proposal, which was first suggested in the columns of the *Scotsman*, that a site should be found for it, not near the South Bridge, but in the open neighbourhood of the Meadows. The Governors of Watson's Hospital, acting as we have stated, readily parted with the property there, and plans for the building were prepared by the late David Bryce, R.S.A., and to his nephew and partner, Mr. John Bryce, was entrusted the superintendence of their completion.

In carrying out his plans Mr. Bryce was guided by the results of medical experience on what is known now as the cottage or pavilion system, by which a certain amount of isolation is procured, and air is freely circulated among the various blocks or portions of the whole edifice. "When it is mentioned that of an area of eleven and a half acres— the original purchase of Watson's ground having been supplemented by the acquisition of Wharton Place—only three and a half are actually occupied with stone and lime, and that well distributed in long narrow ranges over the general surface, it will be understood that this important advantage has been fully turned to account. While the primary purpose of the institution has been steadily kept in view, due regard has been had to its future usefulness as a means of medical and surgical education."

Most picturesque is this now grand and striking edifice from every point of view, by the great number and wonderful repetition of its circular towers, modelled after those of the Palaces of Falkland and Holyrood, while the style of the whole is the old Scottish baronial of the days of James V., the most characteristic details and features of which are completely reproduced in the main frontage, which faces the north, or street of Lauriston.

The façade here presents a central elevation 100 feet in length, three storeys in height, with a sunk basement. A prominent feature here is a tower, buttressed at its angles, and corbelled from the general line of the block, having its base opened by the main entrance, with a window on either side to light the hall.

The tower rises clear of the wall-head in a square form, with round corbelled Scottish turrets at the corners, one of them containing a stair, and over all there is an octagonal slated spire, terminating in a vane, at the height of 134 feet from the ground. On the east and west rise stacks of ornamental chimneys. The elevations on each side of this tower are uniform, with turrets at each corner, and three rows of windows, the upper gableted above the line of the eaving-slates.

From each side of this central mass there are three floors of corridors, affording access to the wards of the Surgical Hospital, and to the front view appear as so many ranges of triple-windows surmounted by a balustrade of stone. Each of these passages is twelve feet wide, and run from end to end of the buildings ; and there branch out towards Lauriston four blocks of wards, 128 feet long by 33 wide. Each comes to within some 35 feet of the

It consists of four pavilions lying east and west, parallel to each other, at distances of about 100 feet apart, with their eight towers facing the Meadows, repeating the architectural features of the Lauriston front at their northern ends, all connected by a corridor, the flat roof of which becomes available as an open gallery.

Each of all these separate blocks or pavilions, besides their attics and basements, have three floors,

GEORGE WATSON'S HOSPITAL.
(Reduced Facsimile of R. Scott's Engraving of the Drawing by Andrew Scott Mason, aged 13, published in 1819.)

pavement, presenting a front of eight Holyrood towers, with four crowstepped gables between. The masonry is hammer-dressed stone and dressed ashlar.

On the south side of the main corridors are two blocks that project to the south, and between them are two class-rooms, also entering from these corridors, with a theatre for operations in rear of the central block, while immediately to the south of all this are the old buildings of Watson's Hospital, re-modelled for administrative purposes.

The Surgical Hospital forms a pile of building with a frontage of 480 feet, combining a picturesque group of round towers, and corbelled tourelles, over all of which rises the lofty spire.

The Medical Hospital occupies that portion of the ground nearest to the northern walk of the Meadows, and most simple are its arrangements.

each of which constitutes a ward, or separate and independent hospital, capable, if necessary, of complete isolation. The floors are connected by a spacious staircase, and each opens out from the wide corridor, at right angles to its upper end ; and two hydraulic hoists run from the basement to the top of the block—one for sending up meals from the general kitchen, and the other large enough to hold a bed for the conveyance, up or down, of a helpless patient. There are also shoots for soiled linen and sweepings and ashes. In short, everything is considered, and no comfort seems to have been forgotten, even to a complete set of fire-extinguishing apparatus.

For the nurse in charge of each department there are comfortable apartments, one of which, by a glazed opening, commands a view of the ward.

BIRD'S-EYE VIEW OF THE NEW ROYAL INFIRMARY, FROM THE NORTH-EAST, 1878.

As a precaution against the germs of disease, the walls are cemented and faced with parian, while the floors are of well-varnished Baltic pine. Galton grates are extensively used, with a view of obtaining the fullest benefit of all the fires.

A well-lighted class-room enters from the south side of a ground-floor corridor, where 300 students may have the advantage of clinical demonstrations; while a similar room, with accommodation for 200, holds a corresponding situation on the female side. A short passage from the entrance hall leads southward to the great operating theatre, which is capable of holding about 500 students, and has retiring rooms in it, one specially for the administration of chloroform. A wing of Watson's Hospital has been allocated as the nurses' kitchen and dining-hall, the housekeeper's rooms, and those of the lady superintendent and her assistant. In the west wing are the dining-room, library, and private apartments of the resident medical staff.

In the north-west corner of the grounds, and apart from the general edifice, is a group of buildings, with a frontage to Lauriston of 150 feet, which though detailed in a less florid style, yet harmonise with the general design. This is the department for Pathology, the principal feature of which is an ample-sized theatre for lectures, seated for 220 students, and having microscopic and chemistry rooms, &c., attached. Near it is the mortuary, the walls of which are lined with white glazed bricks. It is in direct communication with the Surgical and Medical Hospitals, from both of which the bodies of the dead can be conveyed thereto, unseen by the other patients, through an underground passage.

To the washing-house, in another building, the soiled linen is conveyed through a tunnel, and subjected to a washer worked by steam, a mechanical wringer, and a drying chamber of hot air. Beside it is the boiler-house, for working the heating apparatus generally and the hydraulic machinery of the hoists, which latter is effected by a steam-engine of 32 horse-power.

A residence for the superintendent, commodious, and harmonising with the general buildings, has been erected near the Meadow Walk, in rear of the Surgical Hospital.

In regard to its capabilities for accommodation, we may state that of the eighteen wards in the surgical departments there are fifteen which will accommodate sixteen patients, including private beds. In the medical house are twelve wards, each capable of receiving twenty-three patients. Including the ophthalmic, accident, and D. T. wards, together with the reserved beds, there is a total of 600, or

140 over the daily average of patients treated in the last year of the old infirmary. The amount of space provided for each patient varies from 2,350 feet to 2,380, as compared to the 1,800 cubic feet allowed in St. Thomas's Hospital, London, and 1,226 cubic feet in Fort Warren, Massachusetts. (*Scotsman*, 1879, &c.)

The Infirmary was inspected by the Queen on the occasion of her visit to Edinburgh in connection with the Volunteer Review of 1881.

The Edinburgh Royal Maternity and Simpson Memorial Hospital—so called as a tribute to the noble name and memory of the late Sir James Y. Simpson—was erected in 1878, for the accommodation of this most important charity, at the corner of Lauriston Place and Lauriston Park.

Meadow-side House, the hospital specially devoted to sick children, is in Lauriston Lane, and in the most sunny portion of the grounds. It is a humane and useful charity; its directors chiefly consist of medical men, a matron, and a committee of ladies, with a complete medical staff of resident, ordinary, and consulting physicians.

Immediately adjoined to where this edifice stands, there was erected in 1816 the Merchant Maiden's Hospital, the successor of that establishment which was endowed by Mrs. Mary Erskine, incorporated by Act of Parliament in 1702, and which we have described in a preceding chapter, as being in the vicinity of Argyle Square. That old building had long been found inadequate to its objects, and its vicinity having become crowded with houses, the governors, zealous for the comfort of the young ladies under their care, purchased three acres to the west of Lauriston Lane, which is a southern continuation of the ancient Vennel in a spot, which we are told, in 1816, "united all the advantages of retirement and pure air, without an inconvenient distance from town." (*Scots Mag.*, 1816).

Erected from designs by Mr. Burn, this edifice is still a very elegant one, 180 feet long by 60 deep, with a bow of 36 feet radius in its north front. Its style is purely Grecian. The central portico of four fine Ionic columns faces the West Meadow, and is detailed from a small temple on the Ilyssus, near Athens. The windows on the lower storey are double arched, and the superstructure has an aspect of strength and solidity. The foundation-stone was laid on the 2nd of August, 1816, in presence of the governors and the preses, William Ramsay, a well known banker, and the total expense was about £9,000.

On the principal floor, as it was then laid out, was an elegant chapel and governors' room, 30 feet in diameter and 22 feet high; one school-room, 52 feet long by 26 wide; and two others of 42 feet by 24; with, on the upper floors, the nursery, bed-rooms, music, store and governesses' rooms. The building was opened in 1819, and two years after contained 80 girls, its annual revenue being then about £3,000 sterling.

In 1871 another hospital for the girls was erected elsewhere, and the edifice described was appropriated for the use of George Watson's College Schools, with an entrance from Archibald Place. The design of these schools is to provide boys with a liberal education, qualifying them for commercial or professional life, and for the universities. Their course of study includes the classics, English, French, and German, and all the other usual branches of a most liberal education, together with chemistry, drill, gymnastics, and fencing. The number of foundationers has been reduced to 60, at least one fourth of whom are elected by competitive examination from boys attending this and the other schools of the Merchant Company, and boys attending these schools have the following benefits, viz. 1: A presentation to one of the foundations of this, or Stewart's Hospital, tenable for six years; 2. A bursary, on leaving the schools of £25 yearly for four years.

The foundationers are boarded in a house belonging to the governors, with the exception of those who are boarded with families in the city. When admitted, they must be of the age of nine, and not above fourteen years. On leaving each is allowed £7 for clothes; he may receive for five years £10 annually; and on attaining the age of twenty-five a further sum of £50, to enable him to commence business in Edinburgh.

The Chalmers Hospital, at the south side of the west end of Lauriston Place, is a large edifice, in a plain Italian style, and treats annually about 180 in-door, and over 2,500 out door patients. It was erected in 1861. George Chalmers, a plumber in Edinburgh, who died on the 10th of March, 1836, bequeathed the greater part of his fortune, estimated at £30,000, for the erection and the endowment of this "Hospital for the Sick and Hurt."

The management of the charity is in the hands of the Dean and Faculty of Advocates, who, after allowing the fund to accumulate for some years, in conformity to the will of the founder, erected the building, which was fully opened for patients in 1864; and adjoining it is the new thoroughfare called Chalmers Street.

The Lauriston Place United Presbyterian church, a large and handsome Gothic structure at the corner of Portland Place, was built in 1859; and near it, in Lauriston Gardens, is the Catholic convent of St. Catharine of Sienna—the same saint to whom the old convent at the Sciennes was devoted—built in 1859, by the widow of Colonel Hutchison. It is in the regular collegiate style, and the body of the foundress is interred in the grounds attached to it, where stands an ancient thorn-tree coeval with the original convent.

CHAPTER XLIII.

GEORGE HERIOT'S HOSPITAL AND THE GREYFRIARS CHURCH.

Notice of George Heriot—Dies Childless—His Will—The Hospital founded—Its Progress—The Master Masons—Opened—Number of Scholars —Dr. Balcanquall—Alterations—The Edifice—The Architecture of it—Heriot's Day and Infant Schools in the City—Lunardi's Balloon Ascent—Royal Edinburgh Volunteers—The Heriot Brewery—Old Greyfriars Church—The Covenant—The Cromwellians—The Covenanting Prisoners—The Martyrs' Tomb—New Greyfriars—Dr. Wallace—Dr. Robertson—Dr. Erskine—Old Tombs in the Church—Grant by Queen Mary—Morton Interred—State of the Ground in 1779—The Graves of Buchanan and others—Bones from St. Giles's Church.

AMONG the many noble charitable institutions of which Edinburgh may justly feel proud one of the most conspicuous is Heriot's Hospital, on the north side of Lauriston—an institution which, in object and munificence, is not unlike the famous Christ's Hospital in the English metropolis.

Of the early history of George Heriot, who, as a jeweller and goldsmith was the favourite and humble friend of James VI. and who was immortalised in one way by Scott in the "Fortunes of Nigel," but scanty records remain.

He is said to have been a branch of the Heriots of Trabroun, in East Lothian, and was born at Edinburgh in June, 1563, during the reign of Mary, and in due time he was brought up to the profession of a goldsmith by his father, one of the craft, and a man of some consideration in the city, for which he sat as Commissioner more than once in Parliament. A jeweller named George Heriot, who was frequently employed by James V., as the Treasury accounts show, was most likely the elder Heriot, to whose business he added that of a banker. On the 28th of May, 1588, he was admitted a member of the corporation of Goldsmiths.

The first material notice of George Heriot is connected with his marriage, when his father furnished him with the means of starting in business, by "ye setting up of ane buith to him." In all he received from his father, and the relations of his wife—Christian, daughter of Simon Marjoribanks, burgess of Edinburgh—a sum of about £214 11s. 8d. sterling, and the *buith* we have noticed already

thing for her to pledge the most precious of her jewels with Heriot, and James was often at his wits' end to redeem the impledged articles, to enable the queen to appear in public.

On the 4th of April, 1601, Heriot was appointed jeweller to the king, and it has been computed, says Dr. Steven, that during the ten years which immediately *preceded* the accession of James to the Crown of Great Britain, Heriot's bills for Queen Anne's jewels alone did not amount to less than

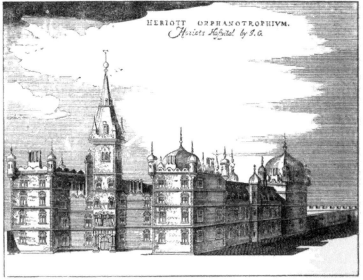

HERIOTT ORPHANOTROPHIVM.

Heriots Hospital by J. G.

REDUCED FACSIMILE OF A VIEW OF HERIOT'S HOSPITAL BY GORDON OF ROTHIEMAY.

as being in the vicinity of St. Giles's church. There he acquired an extensive connection as a goldsmith and money-lender, and soon recommended himself to the notice of his sovereign, by whom he was constituted, as Birrel records, on the 17th of July, goldsmith to his consort the gay Queen Anne, which "was intimat at the crosse, be opin proclamatione and sound of trumpet ; and ane Clic, the Frenchman, dischargit, quha was the Queen's Goldsmythe befor."

Anne was extravagant, fond of jewellery and splendour, thus never had tradesman a better customer. She loved ornaments for the decoration of her own person, and as presents to others, and when desirous of procuring money, it was no uncommon

£50,000 sterling—an enormous sum for those days.

Imitating the extravagance of the Court, the nobles vied with each other in their adornment with precious jewels, many of which found their way back again to " Jingling Geordie ;" and Anne's want of discretion and foresight is shown in one of her letters found by Dr. Steven, when she lacked money, on the occasion of having to pay a hurried visit to her son the Duke of Rothesay and Crown Prince of Scotland, at Stirling :—

"GEORDG HERIOTT, I ernestlie dissyr youe present to send me twa hundrethe pundis vithe all expidition becaus I man hest me away presentlie."   "ANNA R."

When James became king of England, Heriot

followed him to London, and transferred his double
business from his *krame* by St. Giles's, to somewhere
in Cornhill, opposite the Exchange, where his business became so great that on one occasion, by
royal proclamation, all the mayors of England, and

in the flower of her days, leaving Heriot once more
a childless widower. He felt her death keenly,
and a scrap of paper has been preserved, on which
he traced, two months after, the brief, but significant sentence, never meant for the public—"*She*

GEORGE HERIOT. *(From the Portrait by Scougal.)*

justices of the peace, were required to assist him in
procuring workmen at the current rate of wages.
Here, amid his prosperity, his wife died, without
children.

Five years afterwards he married Alison, one of
the nineteen children of James Primrose, who for
forty years was clerk to the Privy Council, and
ancestor of the Earls of Rosebery; but Alison,
who brought him a dowry of £333, died soon after

*cannot be too mutch lamented, who culd not be too
mutch loved.*" Her death occurred on the 16th
April, 1612.

He now devoted himself entirely to the prosecution of his greatly extended business, and in de-
vising plans for the investment of his property at his
decease; and having no relations for whom he felt
any regard, save two natural daughters, and friends
to whom he left legacies, his mind became filled

with the idea of founding an institution in his native city, somewhat like Christ's Hospital, and in the arrangements for this he was assisted by his cousin Adam Lautie, a notary in Edinburgh. Having thus set his house in order, he died peacefully in London on the 12th of February, 1624, a year before his royal master James VI., and was buried at St. Martins in-the-Fields.

The whole of his large property, the legacies excepted, was by him bequeathed to the civic authorities and clergy of Edinburgh, for the erection and maintenance of a hospital "for the education, nursing, and upbringing of youth, being puir orphans and fatherless children of decayet burgesses and freemen of the said burgh, destitute, and left without means."

Of what wealth Heriot died possessed is uncertain, says Arnot; but probably it was not under £50,000. The town council and clergy employed Sir John Hay of Barns, afterwards Lord Clerk Register, to settle accounts with Heriot's English debtors. Among these we find the famous Robin Carr, Earl of Somerset, the dispute being about a jewelled sword, valued at between £400 and £500 by the Earl, but at £890 by the executors.

Heriot had furnished jewels to Charles I. when the latter went to Spain in 1623, and when he ascended the throne, his debt for these, due to Heriot, was paid to the trustees in part of the purchase-money of the Barony of Broughton, the crown lands in the vicinity of the city.

The account settled between Sir John Hay and the Governors of the Hospital, 12th of May, 1647, and afterwards approved by a decree of the Court of Session, after deducting legacies, bad debts, and compositions for debts resting by the Crown, amounted to £23,625 10s. 3½d. sterling (Arnot), and on the 1st July, 1628, the governors began to rear the magnificent hospital on the then open ridge of the High Riggs; but the progress of the work was interrupted by the troubles of subsequent years.

Who designed Heriot's Hospital has been more than once a vexed question, and though the edifice is of a date so recent, this is one of the many architectural mysteries of Europe. Among other fallacies, a popular one is that the architect was Inigo Jones, but for this assertion there is not the faintest shadow of proof, as his name does not appear in any single document or record connected with Heriot's Hospital, though the names of several "Master Masons," are commemorated in connection with the progress of the work, and the house contains a portrait of William Aytoun, master mason, engraved in Constable's memoir of Heriot, published in 1822,

a cadet of the house of Inchdairnie in Fifeshire.

When the edifice was first founded the master of works was William Wallace, who had under him an overseer or foreman named Andrew Donaldson, who, says Billings, seems to have been in reality the master mason, while William Wallace was the architect.

On his death the Governors recorded their high sense of "his extraordinay panes and grait cair he had in that wark baith by his advyce, and in the building of the same." The contract made in the year 1632, with William Aytoun, his successor, has been preserved; and it appears to be just the sort of agreement that would be made with an architect in the present day, whose duty it was to follow up, wholly or in part, the plans of his predecessor. Thus, Aytoun became bound "to devyse, plott, and sett down what he sall think meittest for the decorment of the said wark and pattern thereof alreddie begun, when any defect is found; and to make with his awin handis the haill mowlds, alsweil of tymber, as of stane, belanging generally to the said wark, and generally the said William Aytoun binds and obliges him to do all and quhatsumevir umquhile William Wallace, last Maister Maissone at the said wark, aither did or intended to be done at the same."

The arrangements for the erection of the building were originally conducted by a Dr. Balcanquall, a native of the city, one of the executors under Heriot's last will, and who drew up the statutes. He had been a chaplain to James VI., and Master of the Savoy in the Strand. The edifice progressed till 1639, when there was a stoppage from want of funds; the tenants of the lands in which the property of the institution was vested being unable to pay their rents amid the tumult of the civil war. In the records, however, of the payments made about this period, we find the following extraordinary items:—

31st *March.*—To ye 6 wemen yt drew ye cairt　　xxviijs.
　For 6 shakellis to ye wemeinis hands,
　　wit ye chainyeis to zame　　　　　　vii lib. ijs.
　Mair for 14 lokis for yair waists
　　ond yair handis　　　　　　　　iiij lib. iiijs.
　For ane qwhip for ye gentlwemen
　　in ye cairt　　　　　　　　　　　xijs.

What species of "gentlwemen" they were who were thus shackled, chained, whipped, and harnessed to a cart, it is difficult to conceive.

In 1642 the work was recommenced in March, and there is an instruction that the two front towers be plat-formed, "with ane bartisane about ilk ane of them." And in July, 1649, "George

Wauchop Thesauer," is ordained "to take down the stonewark of the south-west tower, and to make (it) the same as the north-west and north-east towers ar, and this to be done with all diligence."

In Rothiemay's view of the Hospital, published in 1647, he shows it enclosed by the crenelated ramparts of the city from the present tower in the Vennel, and including the other three on the west and south.

A high wall, with a handsome gateway, bounds it above the Grassmarket, and on the west a long wall separates it from the Greyfriars churchyard, and the entire side of the present Forrest Road. Gordon's view is still more remarkable for showing a lofty spire above the doorway, and the two southern towers surmounted by cupolas, which they certainly had till about 1692.

A somewhat similar view (which has been reproduced here,* on p. 368) will be found in Slezer's "Theatrum Scotiæ," under the title of Boghengieght. How this name (which is the name of one of the Duke of Gordon's seats) came to be applied by the engraver to Heriot's Hospital is not known.

The hospital was filled with the wounded of the English army, brought thither from the battle-field of Dunbar by Cromwell. And it was used for sick and wounded soldiers by General Monk, till about 1658, when the governors prevailed upon him to remove them, accommodation being provided for them elsewhere.

During this period the governors granted an annual pension of £55 to a near relation of Heriot, but not until they had received two urgent notes from Cromwell. This pension was afterwards resigned. Many improvements and additions were made, and the total expenses amounted then to upwards of £30,000, when in 1659 it was opened for the reception of boys on the 11th April, when 30 were admitted. In August they numbered forty. In 1660 the number was 52; in 1693 it was 130; and in 1793 140.

Fifteen years before the opening of the hospital, the life of Dr. Walter Balcanquall, the trustee whom Maitland curiously calls its architect, had come to a grievous end. The son of the Rev. Walter Balcanquall, a minister of Edinburgh for forty-three years, he had graduated at Oxford as Bachelor of Divinity, and was admitted a Fellow on the 8th September, 1611; in 1618 he represented—while royal chaplain—the Scottish Church at the Synod of Dort, and his letters concerning that convocation, addressed to Sir Dudley Carleton,

are preserved in Hale's "Golden Remains." It was after he had been successively Dean of Rochester and of Durham that he was one of Heriot's three trustees. In 1638 he accompanied the Marquis of Hamilton, Royal Commissioner, as chaplain; and some doubts of his dealings on this and subsequent occasions rendered him obnoxious to the Presbyterians of Scotland and the Puritans of England; and in July, 1641, he and five others having been denounced as incendiaries by the Scottish Parliament, after being persecuted, pillaged, and sequestrated by the Puritans, he shared the falling fortunes of Charles I. He was thrown into Chirk Castle, Denbighshire, where he died on Christmas Day, 1645, just after the battle of Naseby, and a splendid monument to his memory was subsequently erected in the parish church of Chirk, by Sir Thomas Myddleton.

In the hospital records for 1675 is the following, under date May 3rd:—"There is a necessity that the steeple of the hospital be finished, and a top put thereon. Ro. Miln, Master Mason, to think on a drawing thereof against the next council meeting." But nothing appears to have been done by the king's master mason, for on the 10th July, Deacon Sandilands was ordered to put a roof and top on the said steeple in accordance with a design furnished by Sir William Bruce, the architect of Holyrood Palace.

In 1680, about the time that the obnoxious test was made the subject of so much mockery, Fountainhall mentions that " the children of Heriot's Hospitall, finding that the dog which keiped the yards of that hospitall had a public charge and office, ordained him to take the test, and offered him the paper; but he, loving a bone rather than it, absolutely refused it. Then they rubbed it over with butter (which they called an Explication of the Test in imitation of Argile), and he licked off the butter and did spit out the paper, for which they held a jurie on him, and in derision of the sentence against Argile, they found the dog guilty of treason, and actually hanged him."

In 1692 the Council Records refer to the abolition of the cupolas, the appearance of which in old views of the hospital have caused some discussion among antiquaries.

"The council having visited the fabric of the hospital, and found that the south-east quarter thereof is not yet finished and completed, and that the south-west quarter is finished and completed by a pavilion turret of lead, and that the north-east and north-west corners of the said fabric are covered with a pavilion roof of lead; therefore, and for making the whole fabric of the said

---

* The Editor is indebted to Mr. D. F. Lowe, M.A., House-Governor of Heriot's Hospital, for assistance very kindly rendered in the matter of illustrations.

REDUCED FACSIMILE OF AN OLD ENGRAVING OF HERIOT'S HOSPITAL. (After 1700.)

HERIOT'S HOSPITAL FROM THE SOUTH-WEST.

94

hospital regular and uniform, and for the more easy finishing and completing thereof, they give warrant and order, to the present treasurer, to finish and complete the south-west quarter of the said hospital with a platform roof, in the same way and manner nished by Inigo Jones; and yet, as a whole, the building is remarkable for its bold beauty and symmetry.

The windows are two hundred in number, and richly ornamented with curious devices; and not-

THE CHAPEL, HERIOT'S HOSPITAL. *(From an Engraving published in 1817.)*

as the north-east and north-west quarters thereof are covered; and with all conveniency to take down the pavilion turret in the north-west quarter, and to rebuild and cover the same with a platform roof, regularly with the other three quarters of the fabric."

Prolix as this quotation may be, it seems, with the other references to Wallace, Aytoun, Donaldson, and Brown, as master masons and architects, that any uniform design could never have been fur-

withstanding that there are so many, no two are to be found precisely similar.

The hospital is quadrangular, and measures externally 162 feet each way, and 94 each way in the court, which is paved; it has on the north and east sides a piazza six feet and a half broad. Over the gateway, which is on the north side, facing the Grassmarket, is a tower projecting from the main line, surmounted by a small dome and lantern, provided with a clock. The corners of the four blocks at each angle of the quadrangle are furnished with corbelled turrets, having cupola roofs and vanes. Each of these is four storeys in height; the other parts are three.

On the south, opposite the entrance, and facing Lauriston, is the chapel, 61 feet by 22, neatly fitted up, and occasioning a projection, surmounted by a small spire, which balances the tower on the north. For a long period it remained in a comparatively unfinished state, when it was fitted up in what Dr. Steven calls a "flimsy species of Italian architecture," excepting the pulpit and end galleries, which were a kind of Early English, but meagre in their details. But forty years ago or so, Mr. Gillespie Graham, the architect, suggested that the chapel should be entirely renovated in a style worthy of the building, and he offered to prepare the designs gratuitously. This generous offer was accepted, and it was fitted up in its present elegant style. It has a handsome pulpit, a richly adorned ceiling, and many beautiful carvings of oak.

In an architectural point of view this famous hospital is full of contradictions, but when viewed from distant points, its turrets, chimneys, and pinnacles stand up against the sky in luxuriant confusion, yet with singular symmetry, though no two portions are quite alike. A professional writer says, "we know of no other instance in the works of a man of acknowledged talent, where the operation of changing styles is so evident. In the chapel windows, though the outlines are fine Gothic, the mouldings are Roman. In the entrance archways, although the principal members are Roman, the pinnacles, trusses, and minute sculptures partake of the Gothic."

This building has another marked peculiarity, in the segment of an octagonal tower in front—that of the chapel—lighted through its whole extremity by a succession of Gothic windows divided by mullions alone, which produce a singularly rich and pleasing effect.

The hospital is surrounded by a stately and magnificent balustraded terrace, from which noble flights of at least twelve steps descend to the ground.

In the wall over the gateway is a statue of George Heriot, the founder, in the costume of the time of James VI. This, the boys on "Heriot's Day," the first Monday of June, decorate with flowers, in honour of their benefactor, of whom several relics are preserved in the hospital, particularly his bellows and cup. There is also a portrait of him, said to be only the copy of an original. It represents him in the prime of life, with a calm, thoughtful, and penetrating countenance, and about the mouth an expression of latent humour.

Heriot's foundation has continued to flourish and enjoy a well-deserved fame. "With an annual revenue," says a writer in 1845, "of nearly £15,000, it affords maintenance, clothing, and education for, also pecuniary presents to, one hundred and eighty boys, such being all that the house large as it is, is able conveniently to accommodate. Instead of increasing the establishment in correspondence with the extent of the funds, it was suggested a few years ago, by Mr. Duncan MacLaren, one of the governors, to devote an annual overplus of about £3,000 to the erection and maintenance of free schools throughout the city, for the education of poor children, those of poor burgesses being preferred, and this judicious proposal being forthwith adopted and sanctioned by an Act of Parliament (6 and 7 William IV.), there have since been erected, and are now (1845) in operation, five juvenile and two infant schools, giving an elementary education to 2,131 children." This number has greatly increased since then.

The management of the hospital is vested in the Lord Provost, Bailies, and Council of the city, and the clergy of the Established Church, making in all fifty-four governors, with a House Governor, Treasurer, Clerk, Superintendent of Property, Physician, Surgeon, Apothecary, Dentist, Accountant, a matron, and a staff of masters.

In 1880 the revenue of the hospital amounted to £24,000. In it are maintained 180 boys, of whom 60 are non-resident. The age of admission is between 7 and 10 years, though in exceptional cases, non-residents may be taken at 12. All leave at 14, unless they pass as "hopeful scholars." They are taught English, French, Latin, Greek, and all the usual branches of a liberal education, with music and drawing.

Those who manifest a desire to pursue the learned professions are sent to the adjacent University, with an allowance for four sessions of £30 per annum; and apprentices may also receive bursary allowances to forward them in their trades; while ten out-door bursaries, of £20 each yearly, are likewise bestowed on deserving students at college.

On leaving the hospital the "poore fatherless boyes, freemen's sonnes," as Heriot calls them in his will, are provided with clothes and suitable books; and such of them as become apprentices for five years or upwards, receive £50 divided into equal annual payments during their term of service, besides a gratuity of £5 at its end. Those who are apprenticed for a shorter term than five years receive a correspondingly less allowance.

One master is resident, as is the house governor, but all the rest are non-resident.

By the Act of Parliament referred to, the governors were empowered to erect from this surplus revenue their elementary schools within the city, for educating, free of all expense: 1st, the children of all burgesses and freemen in poor circumstances; 2nd, the children of burgesses and freemen who were unable to provide for their support; 3rd, the children of poor citizens of Edinburgh, resident within its boundaries. They were also empowered by the same Act, "to allow to any boys, in the course of their education at such schools, being sons of burgesses and freemen, uniform fixed sum of money, in lieu and place of maintenance, and such uniform fixed sum for fee as apprentices after their education at the said schools is completed, as shall be determined."

There are now sixteen of these free Heriot schools, in different quarters of Edinburgh, all more or less elegant and ornate in the details of their architecture copied from the parent hospital. These schools are attended by upwards of 4,400 boys and girls.

There are also nine schools in various parts of the city, open for free instruction in reading, writing, arithmetic, grammar, French, German, and drawing, attended by about 1,400 young men and women.

There are five infant schools maintained from the surplus funds of the same noble and generous institution. "On the report of the Bursary Committee being given in," at the meeting of governors in November 1879, "Bailie Tawse stated that they had at present eighteen of their young men at college. For the month ending 20th October last, there were 4,907 pupils on the roll in George Heriot's schools, and 1,075 in connection with the Hospital evening classes."

In the old volunteering times, about the last years of the eighteenth century and the first years of the present, the green before the hospital was the favourite place for the musters, parades, and other displays of the civic forces. Here their colours were presented, from here they were trooped home to the Colonel's house, when Edinburgh possessed, per cent. of the population, a much greater number of enrolled volunteers than she has now.

But other exhibitions took place in Heriot's Bowling Green, such as when the famous aëronaut, Vincent Lunardi, made his ascent therefrom, on the 5th of October, 1785. On that occasion, we are told, above 80,000 spectators assembled, and all business in the city was suspended for the greatest portion of the day. At noon a flag was hoisted on the castle, and a cannon, brought from

Leith Fort, was discharged in Heriot's Green, to announce that the process of filling the balloon had begun, and by half-past two it was fully inflated.

Lunardi—attired, strange to say, in a scarlet uniform faced with blue, sword, epaulettes, powdered wig, and three-cocked hat—entered the cage, with a Union Jack in his hand, and amid a roar of acclamation from the startled people, who were but little used to strange sights in that dull time, he ascended at ten minutes to three P.M.

He passed over the lofty ridge of the old town, at a vast height, waving his flag as the balloon soared skyward. It took a north-easterly direction near Inch Keith, and came down almost into the Forth; but as he threw out the ballast, it rose higher than ever. The wind bore him over North Berwick, and from there to Leven and Largo, after which a SSW. breeze brought him to where he descended, a mile east from Ceres in Fifeshire. Where the balloon was at its greatest altitude —three miles—the barometer stood at eighteen inches five tenths, yet Lunardi experienced no difficulty in respiration. He passed through several clouds of snow, which hid from him alike the sea and land.

Some reapers in a field near Ceres, when they heard the sound of Lunardi's trumpet, and saw his balloon, the nature of which was utterly beyond their comprehension, were filled with dreadful alarm, believing that the end of all things was at hand; and the Rev. Mr. Arnot, the minister of Ceres, who had been previously aware of Lunardi's ascent, required some persuasion to convince them that what they beheld was not supernatural.

A number of gentlemen who collected at Ceres, set the church bell ringing, and conveyed the bold aëronaut with all honour to the manse, where a crowd awaited him. His next ascent was from Kelso.

On the 26th of September, 1794, there mustered on Heriot's Green, to receive their colours, the Royal Regiment of Edinburgh Volunteers, under Lieutenant-Colonel Elder (the old provost) and Colonel William Maxwell, afterwards a general. The corps consisted of eight companies with thirty-two officers, fifteen of whom had belonged to the regular army; but all ranks were clothed alike, the sergeants being indicated by their pikes and the officers by their swords. The corps numbered about 785, all told.

Their uniform was a blue coat, lapelled with black velvet, cut away from below the breast, with broad heavy square skirts, a row of buttons round the cuff, gold epaulettes for all ranks, white cassimere vest and breeches, with white cotton stockings, a round hat, with a cockade and black feather on the left side, buttons having on them the arms of the city and inscribed, *Edinburgh Volunteers (Scots Mag.*, 1794, &c.), their oval belt plates also bearing the city arms. Two of the companies were grenadiers, and all men of unusual stature. They wore bearskin caps, with the grenade thereon, and on their skirts.

The belts, black at first, were afterwards painted white; but, as the paint scaled off, plain buff was

A second regiment of Edinburgh volunteers was formed in the same manner in 1797, when a landing of the French was expected in Ireland, and the first battalion volunteered to garrison the Castle, to permit the withdrawal of the regular troops. This offer was renewed in 1801, when the Lieutenant-Colonel, the Right Hon. Charles Hope, afterwards Lord President, wrote thus to General Vyse, commanding the forces :—

HERIOT'S HOSPITAL: THE COUNCIL ROOM.

substituted, and the first showy uniform underwent changes.

The colours presented to them were very handsome; the King's bore a crown and the letters G.R. ; the regimental bore the arms of Edinburgh. The magistrates, the senators, Academicians and the whole Town Council, were on the ground in their robes of office. From the green the battalion marched by the bridges to Princes Street, where the colours were presented to them by Mrs. Elder, after which they went to the house of the Lord Provost, Sir James Stirling, Bart., in Queen's Street.

The latter, in virtue of his office, was honorary colonel of the regiment; but all the other commissions were conferred by the king, on the recommendation of the volunteers themselves.

"In the event of an enemy appearing on our coast, we trust that you will be able to provide for the temporary safety of Edinburgh Castle by means of its own invalids, and the recruits and convalescents of the numerous corps and detachments in and about Edinburgh ; and that, as we have more to lose than the brave fellows of the other volunteer regiments who have extended their services, you will allow us to be the first to share the danger, as well as the glory, which we are confident his Majesty's troops will acquire under your command, if opposed to an invading army."

But in the following year Heriot's Green saw the last of these two regiments.

After eight years of military parade, and many a sham fight on Leith Links and at Musselburgh camp, the peace of 1802 came, and they closed their career of service on the 6th of May. Early on the forenoon of that day they mustered reluctantly on Heriot's Green, where they were formed in hollow square, and the Lieutenant-Colonel commanding

where the colours were formally delivered over to the magistrates, who placed them in the Council Chamber, and the corps was dissolved.

When the alarm of invasion was again sounded, in 1803, in few places did the old Scottish spirit

THE NORTH GATEWAY OF HERIOT'S HOSPITAL.

read Lord Hobart's circular letter conveying the thanks of the Crown and also of both Houses. He also read the resolution of the Town Council, conveying in the strongest terms the thanks of the community to all the volunteers of the city, and a very complimentary letter from Lieutenant-General Vyse.

Column was then formed, and the volunteers marched from the Green to the Parliament Square,

blaze up more fiercely than in Edinburgh. A very short time saw Heriot's Green again bristling with arms, and upwards of 4,000 volunteers were enrolled. On the 30th of September in that year the old colours were again unfurled by the Royal Regiment of Edinburgh Volunteers, mustering 1,000 rank and file, clad in scarlet faced with blue; and in 1804, prior to the terrible alarm known as "the Lighting of the Beacons," there were in Edinburgh, and, forming a part of her volunteer forces, six battalions of infantry, two of artillery, and a corps of cavalry.

On the night of the *False Alarm*, on the evening of the 31st January, 1804, Scotland was studded with beacons—something on the system ordered by the twelfth Parliament of James II. By mistake, that on Hume Castle was lighted; other beacons blazed up in all directions; the cry was everywhere that *the French had landed!* All Scotland rushed to arms, and before dawn the volunteers were all on the march, pouring forward to their several rendezvous; in some instances the Scottish Border men rode fifty miles to be there, without drawing bridle, says Scott; and those of Liddesdale, fearing to be late at their post, seized every horse they could find, for a forced march, and then turned them loose to make their way home.

When, in 1806, new regulations were issued, limiting the allowance to volunteers, the First Edinburgh Regiment remained unaffected by them. "I wish to remind you," said the spirited Lieutenant-Colonel Hope, one day while on parade, "that we did not take up arms to please any minister, or set of ministers, but to defend our native land from foreign and domestic enemies."

In 1820, when disturbances occurred in the West Country, the volunteers garrisoned the Castle, and offered, if necessary, to co-operate with the forces in the field, and for that purpose remained a whole night under arms. Soon after the corps was disbanded, without thanks or ceremony.

Northward of the hospital, but entering from the Grassmarket, we find the Heriot brewery, which we must mention before quitting this quarter, as being one of those establishments which have long been famous in Edinburgh, and have made the ancient trade of a "brewster" one of the most important branches of its local manufacturing industry.

The old Heriot brewery has been in operation for considerably over one hundred years, and for upwards of forty has been worked by one firm, the Messrs. J. Jeffrey and Co., whose establishment gives the visitor an adequate idea of the mode in which a great business of that kind is conducted, though it is not laid out according to the more recent idea of brewing, the buildings and works having been added to and increased from time to time, like all institutions that have old and small beginnings; but notwithstanding all the numerous mechanical appliances which exist in the different departments of the Heriot brewery, the manual services of more than 250 men are required there daily.

In Gordon's map of 1647, the old, or last, Greyfriars Church is shown with great distinctness, the body of the edifice not as we see it now on the south side, but with a square tower of four storeys at its western end. The burying ground is of its present form and extent, surrounded by pleasant rows of trees; and north-westward of the church is a species of large circular and ornamental garden seat.

Three gates are shown—one to the Candlemaker Row, where it still is; another on the south to the large open field in the south-east angle of the city wall; and a third—that at the foot of the Row, lofty, arched, and ornate, with a flight of steps *ascending* to it, precisely where, by the vast accumulation of human clay, a flight of steps goes downward now.

Over one of these two last entrances, but which he does not tell us, Monteith, writing in the year 1704, says there used to be the following inscription :—

> "Remember, man, as thou goes by :
> As thou art now, so once was I.
> As I am now, so shalt thou be ;
> Remember, man, that thou must die (*dee*)."

The trees referred to were very probably relics of the days when the burial-place had been the gardens of the Greyfriary in the Grassmarket, at the foot of the slope, especially as two double rows of them would seem distinctly to indicate that they had shaded walks which ran south and north.

Writing of the Greyfriary, Wilson says, we think correctly :—"That a church would form a prominent feature of this royal foundation can hardly be doubted, and we are inclined to infer that the existence both of *it*, and of a churchyard attached to it, long before Queen Mary's grant of the gardens of the monastery for the latter purpose, is implied in such allusions as the following, in the 'Diurnal of Occurrents,' July 7th, 1571. 'The haill merchandis, craftismen, and personis renowned within Edinburgh, made thair moustaris in the Grey Frear *Kirk Yaird*;' and again, when Birrel, in his diary, April 26th, 1598, refers to the 'work at the *Greyfriar Kirke*,' although the date of the erection of the more modern church is only 1613."

In further proof of this idea Scottish history tells that when, in 1474, the prince royal of Scotland, (afterwards James IV.) was betrothed, in the second year of his age, to Cecilia of England, and when on this basis a treaty of peace between the nations was concluded, the ratification thereof, and the betrothal, took place in the church of the Greyfriars, at Edinburgh, when the Earl of Lindesay and Lord Scrope represented their respective monarchs.

The number of the inhabitants having greatly increased, and the churches of the city being insufficient for their accommodation, the magistrates, in 1612, says Arnot, ordered a new one to be built on the ground formerly belonging to the Grey-friars, and bestowed on them by Queen Mary for a public cemetery; but he makes no mention of any preceding church, on which the present edifice might have been engrafted.

The eastern entrance from the Candlemaker Row was formed at some time subsequent to the erection or opening of this church.

On the 28th of February 1638, the National Covenant was first subscribed at the Greyfriars Church, when the aggressive measures of Charles I. roused in arms the whole of Scotland, which then, happily for herself, was not, by the desertion of her nobles and the abolition of her officers of state, unable to resist lawless encroachment; and her sons seemed to come forth as one man in defence of the Church, which had then no more vigorous upholder than the future Marquis of Montrose. "In the old church of the Greyfriars," to quote his memoirs (London, 1858), "which stands upon an eminence south of the ancient capital, and within the wall of 1513, amid quaint and smoke-encrusted tombs, and many headstones sunk deep in the long, rank grass—where now the furious Covenanter, Henderson, and Rosehaugh, 'that persecutor of the saints of God,' as the Whigs named him, are lying side by side in peace among the dead of ages, the *Covenant*, written on a sheet of parchment one ell square, and so named because it resembled those which God is said to have made with the children of Israel, was laid before the representatives of the nation, and there it was signed by a mighty concourse, who, with uplifted hands, with weeping eyes, and drawn swords, animated by the same glorious enthusiasm which fired the crusaders at the voice of Peter the Hermit, vowed, with the assistance of the supreme God, to dedicate life and fortune to the cause of Scotland's Church and the maintenance of their solemn engagement, which professed the reformed faith and bitterly abjured the doctrines and dogmas of the Church of Rome —for with such they classed the canons and the liturgy of Laud."

It was first subscribed by the congregation of the Greyfriars; but the first name really appended to it was that of the venerable and irreproachable Earl of Sutherland. Montrose and other peers followed his example, and it afterwards was sent round the churches of the city; thus it speedily became so crowded with names on both sides, says Maitland, that not the smallest space was left for more.

It appears that when there was so little room left to sign on, the subscriptions were shortened by inserting only the initials of the Covenanters' names, of which the margins and other parts were so full that it was a difficult task to number them. By a cursory view Maitland estimated them at about 5,000. By order of the General Committee every fourth man in Scotland was numbered as a soldier.

In 1650 the church was desecrated, and all its wood-work wasted and destroyed by the soldiers of Cromwell. Nine years afterwards, when Monk was in Edinburgh with his own regiment (now the Coldstream Guards) and Colonel Morgan's, on the 19th of October, he mustered them in the High Street, in all the bravery of their steeple-crowned hats, falling bands, calfskin boots, with matchlocks and bandoleers, some time prior to his march southward to achieve the Restoration. From that street he marched them (doubtless by the West Bow) to the Greyfriars Church, where he told his officers that he "was resolved to make the military power subordinate to the civil, and that since they had protection and entertainment from the Parliament, it was their duty to serve it and obey it against all opposition." The officers and soldiers unanimously declared that they would live and die with him.

In the year 1679 the Greyfriars Church and its burying-ground witnessed a pitiful sight, when that city of the dead was crowded, almost to excess, by those unhappy Covenanters whom the prisons could not contain, after the rising at Bothwell had been quenched in blood. These unhappy people had been collected, principally in the vicinity of Bath-gate, by the cavalry, then employed in "dragooning," or riding down the country, and after being driven like herds of cattle, to the number of 1,200, tied two and two, to the capital, they were penned up in the Greyfriars Churchyard, among the graves and gloomy old tombs of all kinds, and there they were watched and guarded day and night, openly in sight of the citizens.

Since Heselrig destroyed the Scottish prisoners after Dunbar (for which he was arraigned by the House of Commons) no such piteous sight had been witnessed on British ground. They were of both sexes and of all ages, and there they lay five long months, 1,200 souls, exposed to the sun by day and the dew by night—the rain, the wind, and the storm—with no other roof than the changing sky, and no other bed than the rank grass that grew in its hideous luxuriance from the graves beneath them. All were brutally treated by their

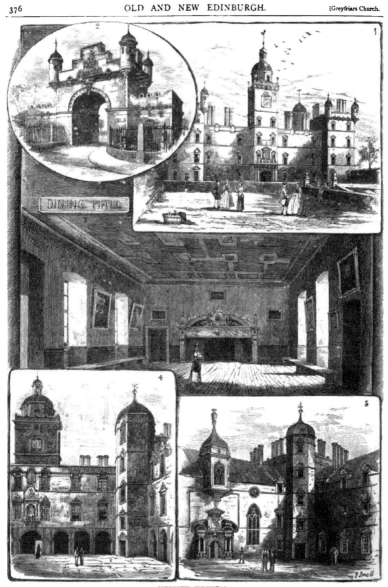

HERIOT'S HOSPITAL.

1, The Hospital, 1779 (*After an Engraving in Arnot's "History of Edinburgh*); 2, Porter's Lodge ; 3, Dining Hall;
4, Quadrangle, looking north ; 5, Quadrangle, looking south.

guards, and a few, driven almost mad, achieved their escape, but many died. All this, at the hands of their own countrymen, these poor people had to endure— the stubborn Scottish peasant, with his pride and rectitude of heart, his tender, it might be weak and ailing wife, with his infants and his aged parents.

to administer to the wants of the prisoners there was one lady who was wont to come attended by a young daughter possessed of considerable personal attractions. Periodically they came to the iron gate with food and raiment, collected among the charitable, and between the young lady and one of the

A ROYAL EDINBURGH VOLUNTEER. (*From a Print of the Period.*)

Some who signed a bond never to take up arms against the Government were released; others found rest amid the graves on which they lay; the remainder, to the number of two hundred and fifty-seven, were sent to be sold as slaves in Barbadoes, Jamaica, and New Jersey, but many were drowned at sea.

"From the gloom of this sad story there is shed one ray of romance," says Chambers, in his "Traditions." Among the sympathising people who dared

younger captives an attachment sprang up. Doubtless she loved him for the dangers he had dared, and he loved her because she pitied them. In happier days, long after, when their constancy had been well tried by an exile which he suffered in the plantations, this pair were married and settled in Edinburgh, where they had sons and daughters. A respectable elderly citizen," adds Chambers, "tells me he is descended from them."

After the Duke of Albany and York came, as

King's Commissioner, the severity of these vile persecutions was greatly lessened; but in the north-east corner of the burying-ground, the portion of it long accorded as the place for the interment of criminals, stands that grim memorial of suffering, tears, and blood, known as the Martyrs' Monument—a tall, pillared tablet, rising on a pedestal surmounted by an entablature and pediment, and bearing the following inscription : —

"Halt, passenger ! take heed what you do see—
This tomb doth show for what some men did die ;
Here lies interred the dust of those who stood
'Gainst perjury, resisting unto blood ;
Adhering to the covenants and laws,
Establishing the same ; which was the cause
Their lives were sacrificed unto the lust
Of prelatists abjured ; though here their dust
Lies mix't with murderers, and other crew,
Whom justice justly did to death pursue.
But, as for them no cause was to be found
Worthy of death ; but only they were found
Constant and stedfast, zealous, witnessing
For the prerogatives of Christ, their King ;
Which truths were sealed by famous Guthrie's head,
And all along to Mr. Renwick's blood.
They did endure the wrath of enemies :
Reproaches, torments, death, and injuries.
But yet they're those who from such troubles came,
And now triumph in glory with the Lamb !"

"From May 27, 1661, that the most noble Marquis of Argyle was beheaded, to the 17th February, 1688, that Mr. James Renwick suffered, were one way or other murdered and destroyed for the same cause about eighteen thousand, of whom were executed at Edinburgh about a hundred of noblemen and gentlemen, ministers, and others—noble martyrs for Jesus Christ. The most of them lie here."

According to the *Edinburgh Courant* of 1728 this tomb was repaired in that year, and there was added to it "a compartment, on which is cut a head and a hand on pikes, as emblems of their (the martyrs) sufferings, betwixt which is to be engraved a motto alluding to both."

The old church had been without a bell till 1681, when the Town Council ordered one which had been formerly used in the Tron church to be hung in its steeple, or tower, at the west end. The latter was blown up on the 17th May, 1718, by a quantity of gunpowder belonging to the city, which was deposited there and exploded by accident.

As the expense of its repair was estimated at £600 sterling, the Town Council resolved to add instead, a new church at the west end of the old, and in the same plain, ungainly, and heavy style of architecture, with an octagonal porch projecting under the great window, all of which was accordingly done, and the edifice, since denominated the New Greyfriars, was finished in 1721, at the expense of £3,045 sterling.

In this process the older church was shortened by a partition wall being erected at the second pillar from the west, that both buildings should be of equal length. Many men of eminence have been incumbents here; among them, Robert Rollock, the first Principal of the University of Edinburgh, and Principal Carstares, the friend of William of Orange.

In 1733, Robert Wallace, D.D., author of "A Dissertation on the Numbers of Mankind," and many other works, and one of the first projectors of the Scottish Ministers' Widows' Fund, was appointed one of the ministers of the Greyfriars, in consequence of a sermon which he preached before the Synod of Moffat, the tenor of which so pleased Queen Caroline, when she read it, that she recommended him to the patronage of the Earl of Islay, then chief manager of Scottish affairs.

In 1736, however, he forfeited the favour of Government by being one of the many clergymen who refused to read from the pulpit the act relative to the Porteous mob; but on the overthrow of Walpole's ministry, in 1742, he was entrusted with the conduct of ecclesiastical affairs, so far as related to crown presentations in Scotland —a delicate duty, in which he continued to give satisfaction to all. In 1744 Dr. Wallace was commissioned as one of the royal chaplains in Scotland, and in 1753 he published his "Dissertation"—a work that is remarkable for the curious mass of statistical information it contains, and for its many ingenious speculations on the subject of population, to one of which the peculiar theories of the Rev. Mr. Malthus owed their origin.

Among many other philosophical publications, he brought forth "Various Prospects of Mankind, Nature, and Providence," in 1761, and died the year after, on the 10th of July, leaving a son, who is not unknown in Scottish literature.

But the most distinguished of the incumbents was William Robertson, D.D., the eminent historian, who was appointed to the Greyfriars in 1761, the same year in which, on the death of Principal Goldie, he was elected Principal of the University of Edinburgh, and whose father, the Rev. William Robertson (a cadet of the Struan family) was minister of the Old Greyfriars in 1733.

Principal Robertson is so well known by the published memoirs of him, and by his many brilliant literary works, that he requires little more than mention here. "Scott, who from youth to manhood was a sitter in the Old Greyfriars, and his parents, Mr. and Mrs. Scott," says an old tutor of Sir Walter, writing to Lockhart, " every Sabbath, when well and at home, attended with their fine young family of children and their domestic servants—a sight so amicable and exemplary as often to excite in my breast a glow of heart-felt satisfaction."

In "Guy Mannering," Scott introduces this old church—now, with St. Giles's, the most interesting place of worship in the city—and its two most distinguished incumbents. When Colonel Mannering came to Edinburgh (where, as we have already said, Romance and History march curiously side by side) to consult Counsellor Pleydell, on the Sunday morning after his arrival at the George Inn, Bristo Port, the latter conducts him "to the Greyfriars, to hear our historian of Scotland, of the Continent, and of America, preach."

Scott next with an able hand sketches one of the most distinguished clergymen of the time, Dr. John Erskine (son of Erskine of Carnock, Professor of Law in the University of Edinburgh), who in July 1767 became the colleague of Principal Robertson in the Old Greyfriars. "His external appearance was not prepossessing. A remarkably fair complexion, strangely contrasted with a black wig, without a grain of powder ; a narrow chest and stooping posture ; hands which, placed like props on each side of the pulpit, seemed necessary rather to support the person than to assist the gesticulation of the preacher ; a gown (not even that of Geneva), a tumbled band, and a gesture which seemed scarcely voluntary, were the first circumstances which struck a stranger."

Dr. Erskine, previously minister of the New Greyfriars, was the author of voluminous theological works, which are known, perhaps, in Scotland only. After ministering at the Greyfriars for forty-five years, he died in January, 1803, and was buried in the churchyard.

Principal Robertson pre-deceased him. He died in June, 1793, in the seventy-first year of his age, and was interred in the same burying-ground.

The Old Greyfriars was suddenly destroyed on the morning of Sunday, 19th January, 1845, by a fire, and presented to the startled people, assembling from all quarters for the first service, a mass of blackened ruins. It has since been repaired at considerable expense, adorned with several beautiful memorial windows, the triplet one in the south aisle being to the Scottish historian, George Buchanan.

Among the ancient tombs within the church were those of Sir William Oliphant, King's Advocate, who died in 1628 ; and of Sir David Falconer, of Newton, Lord President of the Court of Session, who spent the last day of his life seated on the bench in court.

The antiquity of our Scottish churchyards, and the care taken of them, greatly impressed Dr. Southey as being so singularly at variance with the absence of ceremony in the funeral rites of the people. " In Scotland," he ignorantly observes, " where the common rites of sepulture are performed with less decency than in any other Christian country, the care with which family burying-grounds in the remoter parts of the country are preserved may be referred as much to national feeling as to hereditary pride."

In solemn, grand, and melancholy interest no other burial-ground, from its associations, can equal that of the Greyfriars Churchyard ; for crowded within its narrow limits lie the mingling ashes of so many of Scotland's greatest, grandest, and most renowned, who have lived during a period of three hundred years.

THE REPENTANCE STOOL FROM OLD
GREYFRIARS CHURCH.
(*Now in the Scottish Antiquarian Museum.*)

In the year 1562 the Town Council made an application to Queen Mary to grant them the site and yards of the Greyfriars Monastery, to form a new burial-place, as " being somewhat *distant* from the town." Mary, in reply, granted their request at once, and appointed the Greyfriars yard, or garden, to be devoted in future to the use specified, and as St. Giles's Churchyard soon after began to be abandoned, no doubt internments here would proceed rapidly ; all the more so that the other burial-places of the city had become desecrated. " Before the Reformation," says Wilson, " there were the Blackfriars Kirkyard, where the Surgical Hospital or old High School now stands ; the Kirk-of-Field—now occupied by the college, Trinity College, Holyrood Abbey, St. Roque's and St. Leonard's Kirkyards. In all these places human bones are still found on digging to any depth."

During the great plague of 1568 a huge pit, wherein to bury the victims, was ordered to be dug in the "Greyfriars *Kirkyaird*," as Maitland records, thus again indicating the existence of a church here long anterior to the erection of the present one.

Here, about eight in the evening of the 2nd June, 1581, was brought from the scaffold, whereon it had lain for four hours, covered by an old cloak, the headless body of James Douglas, Earl of Morton, who

In this city of the dead have been interred so vast a number of men of eminence that the mere enumeration of their names would make a volume, and we can but select a few. Here lie thirty-seven chief magistrates of the city; twenty-three principals and professors of the university, many of them of more than European celebrity; thirty-three of the most distinguished lawyers of their day—one a Vice Chancellor of England and Master of the

GREYFRIARS CHURCH.

had been Regent of Scotland, and was executed for the murder of King Henry. It was borne by common porters, and interred in the place there set apart for criminals, most probably where now the Martyrs' Monument stands. None of his friends dared follow it to the grave, or show their affection or respect to the deceased Earl by any sign of outward grief.

In 1587 the king having ordered a general weapon-shawing, the Council, on the 15th July, ordained by proclamation a muster of the citizens in the Greyfriars Kirkyard, "boddin in feir of weir, and arrayet in their best armour, to witt, either pike or speer, and the armour effeirand thairto, or with hakbuts and the armour effeirand thairto, and nocht with halbarts or Jedburgh staffes."

Rolls, and another who was Accountant-General of the Court of Chancery; six Lords President of the Supreme Court of Scotland; twenty-two senators of the College of Justice, and a host of men distinguished for the splendour of their genius, piety, and worth.

Here too lie, in unrecorded thousands, citizens of more humble position, dust piled over dust, till the soil of the burial-place is now high above the level of the adjacent Candlemaker Row—the dust of those who lived and breathed, and walked our streets in days gone by, when as yet Edinburgh was confined in the narrower limits of the Old Town.

"The graves are so crowded on each other," says Arnot, writing in 1779, "that the sextons frequently cannot avoid in opening a ripe grave

TOMBS IN GREYFRIARS CHURCHYARD.

1, The Martyrs' Monument : 2, Monument of Sir G. McKenzie, commonly called "Bloody McKenzie," 1692; 3, William Carstares, Reformer, and Principal of the University of Edinburgh, 1715; 4, Entrance to the South Ground, known as the Covenanters' Prison ; 5, John Laying, Keeper of the Signet, 1614; 6, Chiesly of Dalry, 1633; 7, William Adam, Architect, 1748, and William Robertson, D.D., 1793.

encroaching on one not fit to be touched! The whole presents a scene equally nauseous and unwholesome. How soon this spot will be so surcharged with animal juices and oils, that, becoming one mass of corruption, its noxious steams will burst forth with the prey of a pestilence, we shall not pretend to determine; but we will venture to say, the effects of this burying-ground would ere now have been severely felt, were it not that, besides the coldness of the climate, they have been checked by the acidity of the coal smoke and the height of the winds, which in the neighbourhood of Edinburgh blow with extraordinary violence."

Arnot wrote fully a hundred years ago, but since his time the interments in the Greyfriars went on till within a recent period.

George Buchanan was buried here in 1582, under a through-stone, which gradually sank into the earth and disappeared. The site, distinctly known in 1701, is now barely remembered by tradition as being on the north slope of the churchyard; but a monument in the ground, to the great Latin scholar and Scottish historian, was erected by the late great bibliopole, David Laing, so many years Librarian of the Signet Library, at his own expense. An essential feature in the memorial is a head of Buchanan in bronze, from the best likeness of him extant. The design was furnished by D. W. Stevenson, A.R.S.A.

Taking some of the interments at random, here is the grave of George Heriot (father of the founder of the adjacent hospital), who died in 1610; of George Jameson, the Scottish Vandyke, who died in 1644; and of Alexander Henderson, 1646, the great covenanting divine, and leading delegate from Scotland to the Westminster Assembly, and the principal author of the Assembly's Catechism. His ashes lie under a square pedestal tomb, erected by his nephew, and surmounted by a carved urn. There are long inscriptions on the four sides.

John Milne's tomb, 1667, Royal Master Mason (by sixth descent), erected by his nephew, Robert Milne, also Royal Master Mason, and builder of the modern portions of Holyrood House, records in rhyme how—

> "John Milne, who maketh the fourth John,
> And, by descent from father unto son,
> Sixth Master Mason to a royal race
> Of seven successive kings, sleeps in this place."

It is a handsome tomb, with columns and a pediment, and immediately adjoins the eastern or Candlemaker Row entrance, in the formation of which some old mural tombs were removed; among them that of Alexander Millar, Master

Tailor to James VI., dated 1616—*obiit Principis et Civium luctu decoratus,* as it bore.

A flat stone which, by 1816, was much sunk in the earth, dated 1613, covered the grave of Dr. John Nasmyth, of the family of Posso, surgeon of the king of France's troop of Scottish Guards, who died in London, but whose remains had been sent to the Greyfriars by order of James VI.

The tomb of Sir George Mackenzie of Rosehaugh—the celebrated lawyer, and founder of the Advocates' Library, and who, as a persecutor, was so abhorred by the people that his spirit was supposed to haunt the place where he lies—is a handsome and ornate octagon temple, with eight pillars, a cornice, and a dome, on the southern side of the ground, and its traditional terrors we have already referred to. But other interments than his have taken place here. One notably in 1814, when the widow of Lieutenant Roderick Mackenzie of Linessie was, at her own desire, laid there, "in the tomb of the celebrated Sir George Mackenzie, who was at the head of the Lochslin family, and to whom, by the mother's side, she was nearly related." (*Gentleman's Mag.,* 1814.)

Near it is the somewhat remarkable tomb of William Little, whilom Provost of Edinburgh in 1591. He was Laird of Over Liberton, and the tomb was erected by his great-grandchild in 1683. His kinsman, Clement Little, Advocate and Commissary of Edinburgh, whose meagre library formed the nucleus of that of the university, is also buried here. It is a mausoleum, composed of a recumbent female figure, with a pillar-supported canopy above her, on which stand four female figures at the several corners. The popular story is that the lady was poisoned by her four daughters, whose statues were placed over her in eternal remembrance of their wickedness; but the effigies are in reality those of Justice, Charity, Faith, &c., favourite emblematical characters in that age when the monument was erected; and the object in placing them there was merely ornamental.

Here are interred Archibald Pitcairn, the poet, 1713, under a rectangular slab on four pillars, with an inscription by his friend Ruddiman, near the north entry of the ground; Colin MacLaurin, the mathematician, 1746; and William Ged, the inventor of stereotype printing.

Here was worthy and gentle Allan Ramsay committed to the grave in 1758, and the just and upright Lord President Duncan Forbes of Culloden, eleven years before that time. Another famous Lord President, Robert Blair of Avontoun, was laid here in 1811.

Here, too, lie the two famous Monros, father and

son, buried respectively 1767 and 1817, Alexander Monro *primus*, the great anatomist, and Alexander Monro *secundus*, who in 1756 was admitted joint Professor of Anatomy and Surgery with his distinguished father.

In the same ground, in 1799, were laid Professor Joseph Black, the great chemist; Dr. Hugh Blair, in 1800; Henry Mackenzie, "the Man of Feeling," in 1831; Alexander Tytler, another distinguished *littérateur*; John Kay, the caricaturist, in 1826; and Dr. McCrie, the well-known biographer of John Knox.

The monument to Dr. Hugh Blair was erected in 1817, and is placed on the south side of the church, in the same compartment with that of Professor MacLaurin. Thus, one of the most eminent philosophers and one of the most distinguished preachers that Scotland has produced are commemorated side by side.

On the eastern gable of the Old Greyfriars Church, a grim, repellent, and remarkable monument catches the eye. In the centre is sculptured a skeleton, festooned around with surgical implements, but the inscription is nearly obliterated by time and the fire of the church, yet it is always an object of much curiosity.

It marks the grave of James Borthwick, whose portrait is the oldest now hanging in the Hall of the Royal College of Surgeons, the incorporation of which he entered in 1645; he was a cadet of the House of Crookston, and nearly related to Lord Borthwick, who defended his castle of that name against Oliver Cromwell after the battle of Dunbar. He acquired the estate of Stow, in which he was succeeded by his son James, who erected this hideously grotesque memorial to his memory.

Another monument of a different kind, in the form of a brass plate inserted into a stone, on the western wall of the church, bore some fine elegiac verses to the memory of Francisca, daughter of "Alexander Swinton, advocate; who died . . . . aged 7 years."

But these verses were quite obliterated by 1816. They ran thus :—

"The sweetest children, like these transient flowers,
Which please the fancy for a few short hours,—
Lovely at morning, see them burst in birth,
At evening withered—scattered on the earth,
Their stay, their place, shall never more be known,
Save traits engraven on those hearts alone
That fostered these frail buds while here beneath ;
Yes, these shall triumph o'er the powers of death,
Shall spring eternal in the parent's mind
Till hence transplanted to a realm refined."

Northward of the two churches stands the tomb and grave of Duncan Ban MacIntyre, commonly known in the Highlands as *Donnachan ban nan Oran*, who died in the year 1812, and who, though he fought at Falkirk, outlived all the bards and nearly all the warriors associated in the Highland heart with the last chivalrous struggle for the House of Stuart.

A handsome monument marks the place where his ashes lie. Though little known in the Lowlands, Duncan is deemed one of the sweetest of the Gaelic poets, and was so humble in his wants that he had no higher ambition than to become a soldier in the old City Guard.

The burial place of Sir Walter Scott's family lies on the west side of the ground. "Our family," he wrote, "heretofore (Dec., 1819) buried close by the entrance to Heriot's Hospital, on the southern or left-hand side as you pass from the churchyard." Here the father, Walter Scott, W.S., and several of his children who died in the old house in the College Wynd, are interred. Mrs. Scott, her sisters, and her brother, Dr. Rutherford, are interred in the burial-ground attached to St. John's Church, at the west end of Princes Street. Sir Walter purchased a piece of ground there, "moved by its extreme seclusion, privacy, and security; for," as he wrote to brother Thomas, who was paymaster of the 70th Foot, conveying an account of their mother's death, "when poor Jack (their brother) was buried in the Greyfriars Churchyard, where my father and Anne (their sister) lie, I thought their graves more encroached upon than I liked to witness."

The Greyfriars Churchyard is, curiously enough, noted as being the scene of Scott's first love affair with a handsome young woman. Lockhart tells us that their acquaintance began in that place of dreary associations, "when the rain was beginning to fall one Sunday, as the congregation were dispersing. Scott happened to offer his umbrella, the tender being accepted, so escorted her to her residence, which proved to be at no great distance from his own. I have neither the power nor the wish," adds his biographer, "to give in detail the sequel to this story. It is sufficient to say that after he had through several long years nourished the dream of an ultimate union with this lady— Margaret, daughter of Sir John and Lady Jane Stewart Belshes of Invermay—his hopes terminated in her being married to the late Sir William Forbes, Bart., of Pitsligo."

In December, 1879, there were interred in the Greyfriars Churchyard, under the direction of the city authorities, the great quantity of human bones which had been gathered from under the floor of St. Giles's Church. The whole were contained in twenty large boxes, and amounted to several tons in weight. Dr. William Chambers having been exceedingly anxious to discover, if possible, the mutilated remains of the Marquis of Montrose, which had been interred in St. Giles's in 1661, caused the whole of these bones to be examined for this purpose prior to their removal to the Greyfriars. This examination was most carefully carried out under the direction of Professors Maclagan and Turner, of the Edinburgh University, but no trace of those lost and interesting remains could be discovered.

MONOGRAM OF GEORGE HERIOT'S NAME.
(*Made on a Chimney-piece in the Hospital.*)

CASSELL, PETTER, GALPIN & CO., BELLE SAUVAGE WORKS, LONDON, E.C.

Milton Keynes UK
Ingram Content Group UK Ltd.
UKHW050009060124
435443UK00004BA/79